AN ONI PRESS PUBLICATION

WEEA

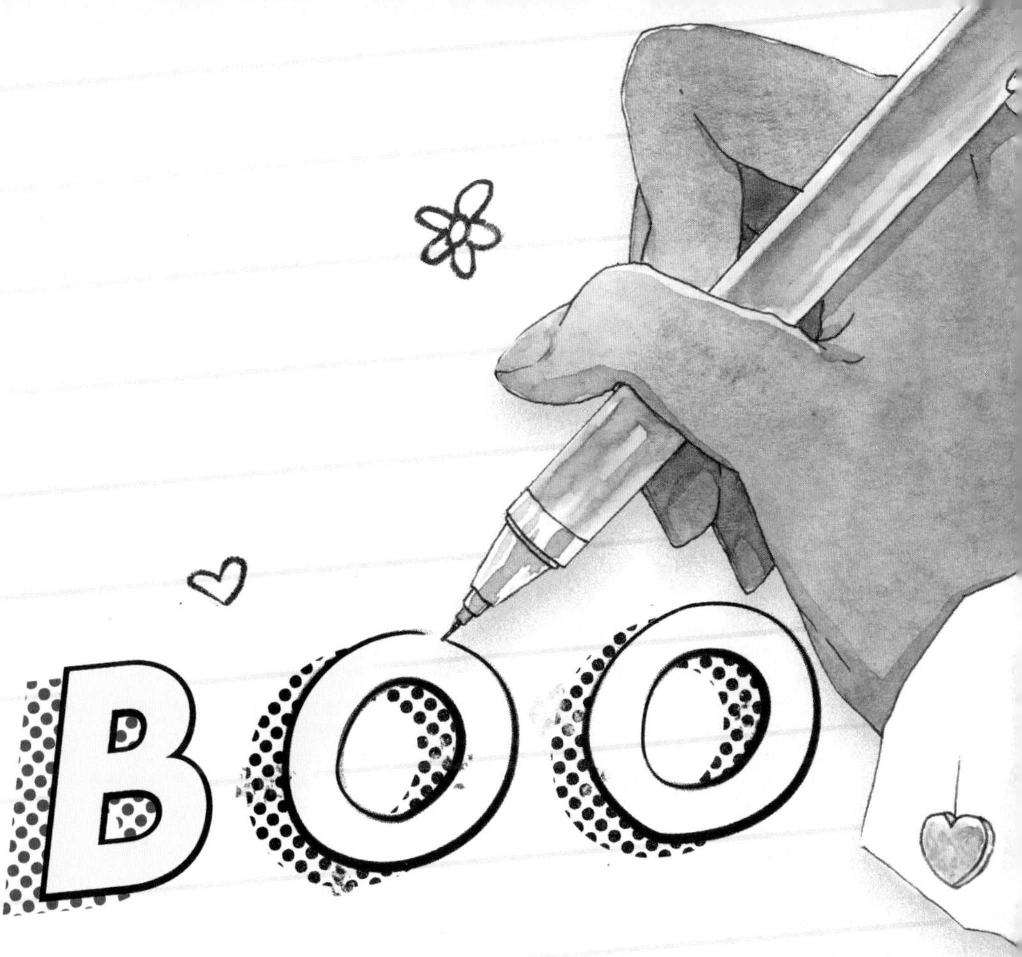
BOO

By Alissa Sallah

Lettered by Susie Lee

Designed by Angie Knowles

Edited by Sarah Gaydos and Shawna Gore

Sensitivity Read by Shenwei Chang

PUBLISHED BY ONI-LION FORGE PUBLISHING GROUP, LLC

James Lucas Jones, president & publisher · Charlie Chu, e.v.p. of creative & business development
Alex Segura, s.v.p of marketing & sales · Michelle Nguyen, associate publisher · Brad Rooks,
director of operations · Amber O'Neill, special projects manager · Margot Wood, director of
marketing & sales · Katie Sainz, marketing manager · Tara Lehmann, publicist · Holly Aitchison,
consumer marketing manager · Troy Look, director of design & production · Angie Knowles,
production manager · Kate Z. Stone, senior graphic designer · Carey Hall, graphic designer
Hilary Thompson, graphic designer · Sarah Rockwell, graphic designer · Vincent Kukua, digital
prepress technician · Chris Cerasi, managing editor · Jasmine Amiri, senior editor · Shawna Gore,
senior editor · Amanda Meadows, senior editor · Robert Meyers, senior editor, licensing · Desiree
Rodriguez, editor · Grace Scheipeter, editor · Zack Soto, editor · Steve Ellis, vice president of games
Ben Eisner, game developer · Jung Lee, logistics coordinator · Kuian Kellum, warehouse assistant

Joe Nozemack, publisher emeritus

1319 SE Martin Luther King Jr. Blvd.
Suite 240
Portland, OR 97214

ONIPRESS.COM 🅕 🅧 🅘 **LIONFORGE.COM**

First edition: November 2021

ISBN 978-1-62010-939-7
eISBN 978-1-62010-952-6

PRINTED IN CHINA.

Library of Congress Control Number: 2021936091

1 2 3 4 5 6 7 8 9 10

For Dominique, Shari, Marissa,
and the rest of my weebs
whom this book celebrates.
With your wind, my wings can fly.

"Today is my farewell party.
    To love?
        N-O.
Inside am I a man? A woman?
    I strike a pose as one
        and the other grows bored.
Well,
    when the next page is turned
        another me."

- *Mine izu main* (Mine is mine), 1986
    Mine Saori

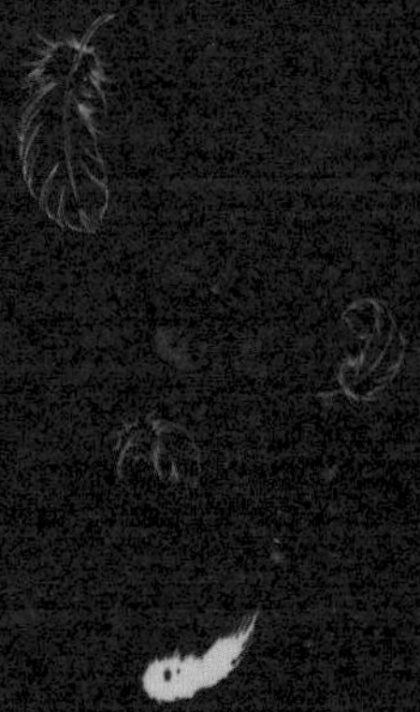

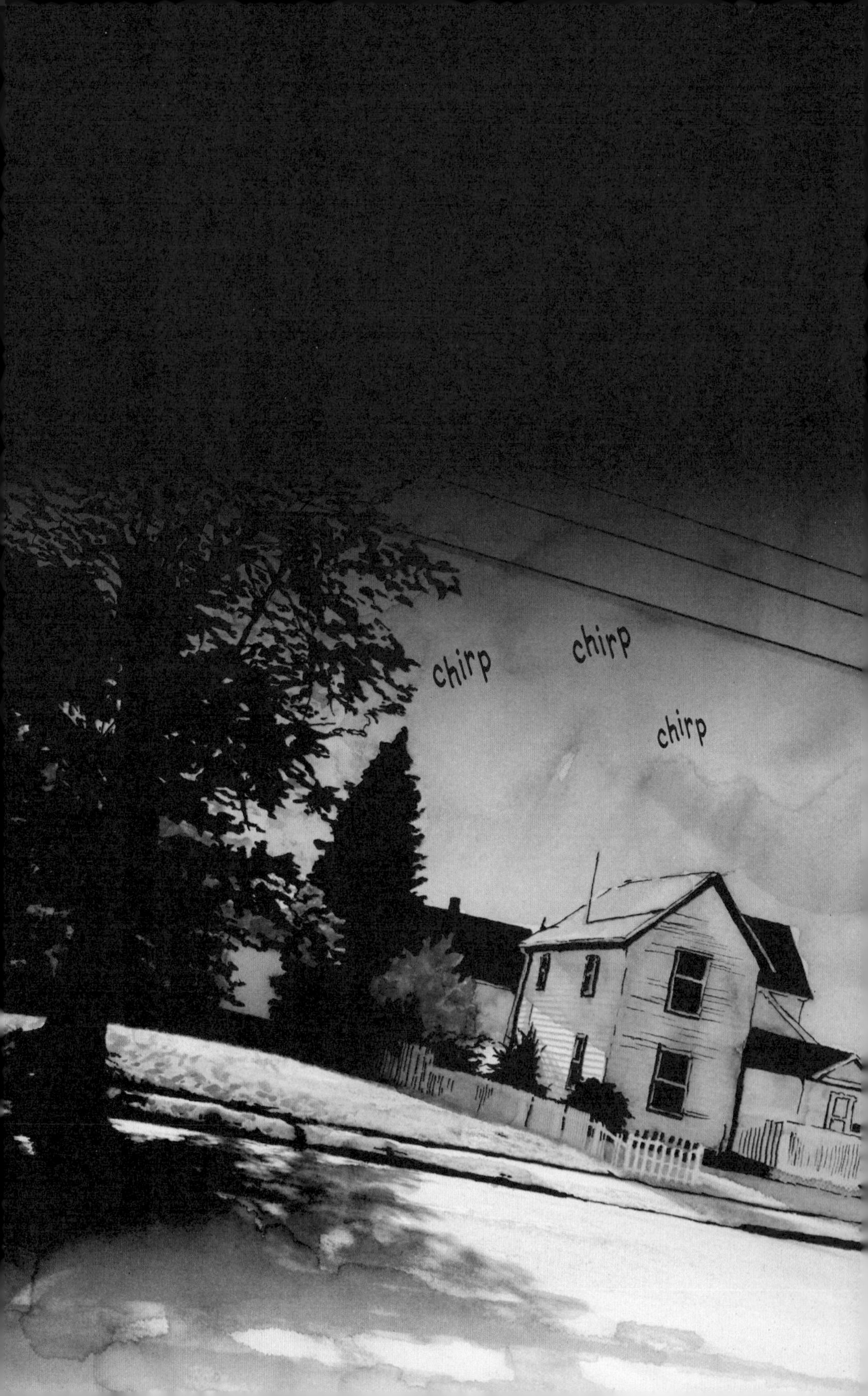
chirp
chirp
chirp

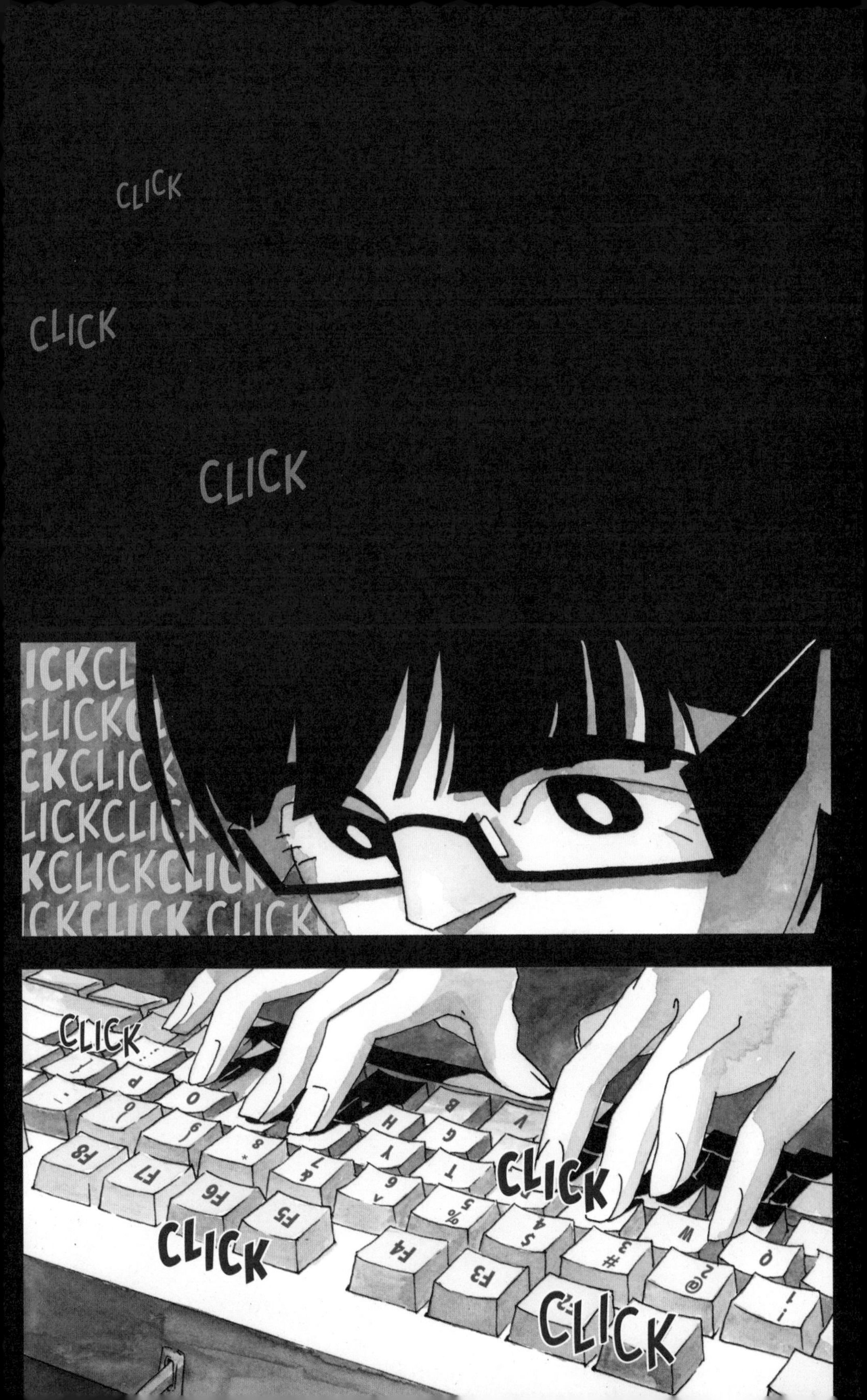
CLICK
CLICK
CLICK
ICKCL
CLICKC
CKCLIC
LICKCLIC
KCLICKCLIC
ICKCLICK CLICK
CLICK
CLICK
CLICK
CLICK

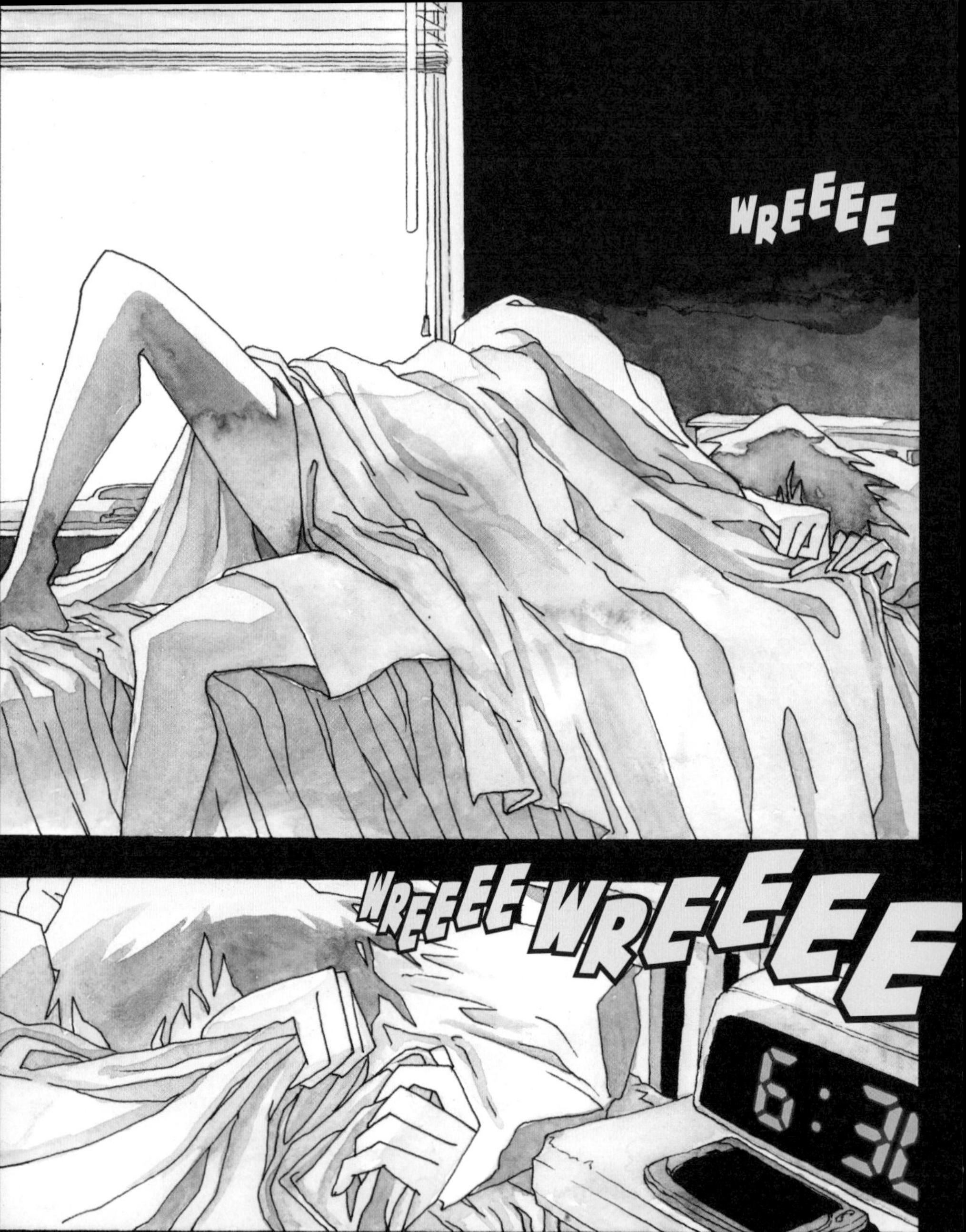
WREEEE
WREEEE WREEEE

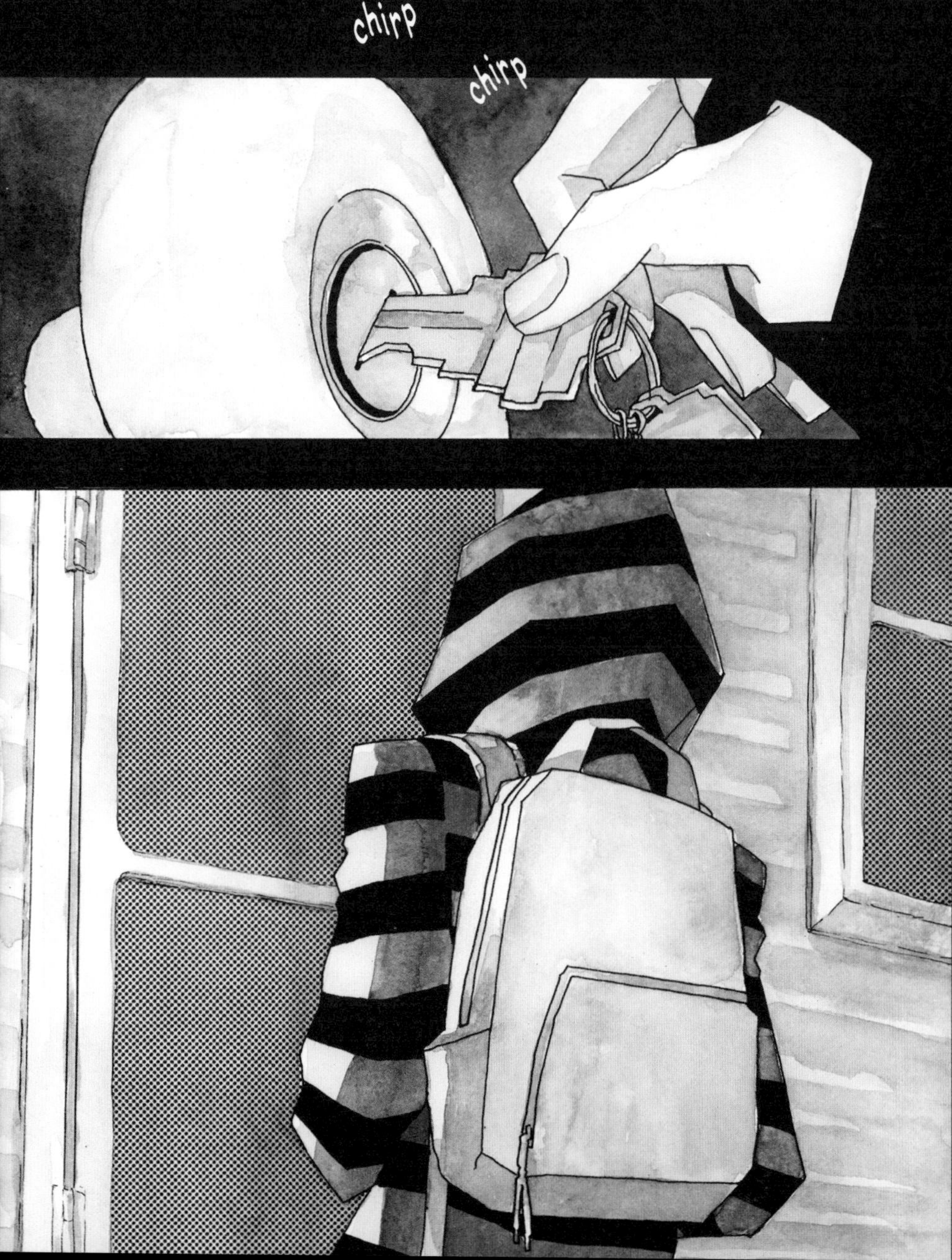
chirp
chirp

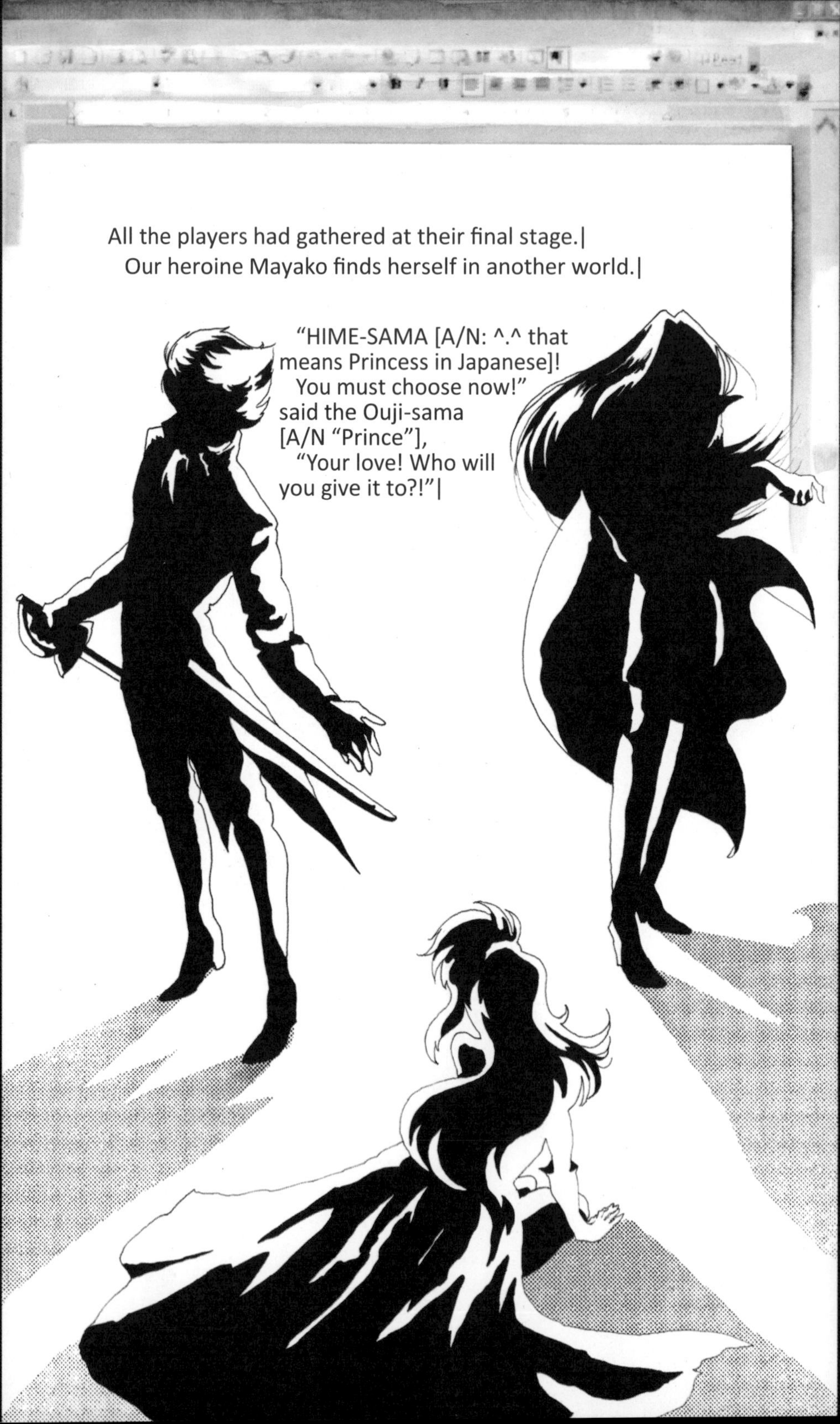
All the players had gathered at their final stage.|
Our heroine Mayako finds herself in another world.|
"HIME-SAMA [A/N: ^.^ that means Princess in Japanese]! You must choose now!" said the Ouji-sama [A/N "Prince"], "Your love! Who will you give it to?!"|

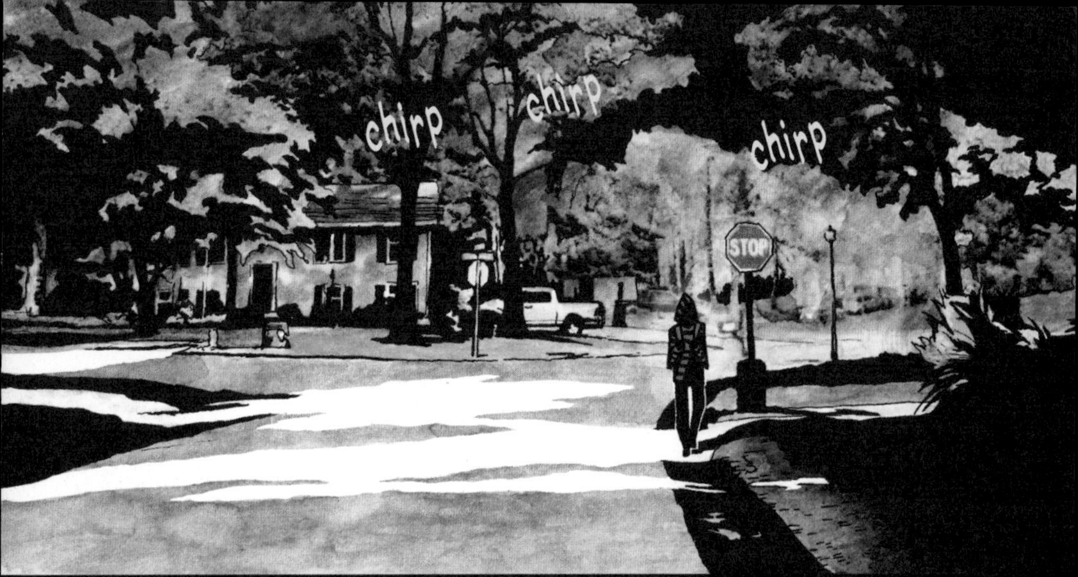
chirp
chirp
chirp
STOP

Mayako blushes, "Ouji-sama! I-" |

But then!!!

"Choose me Mayako!" said the Maho*, [*Maho = :3 mage in Japanese]
"Think of all the POWER we could have together!" |

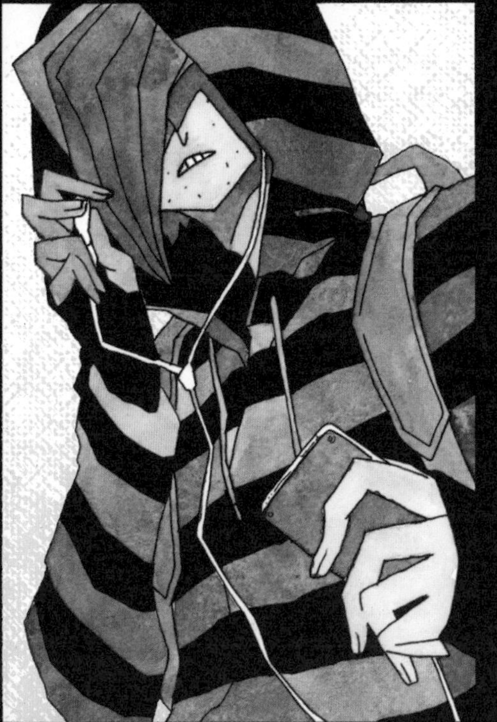

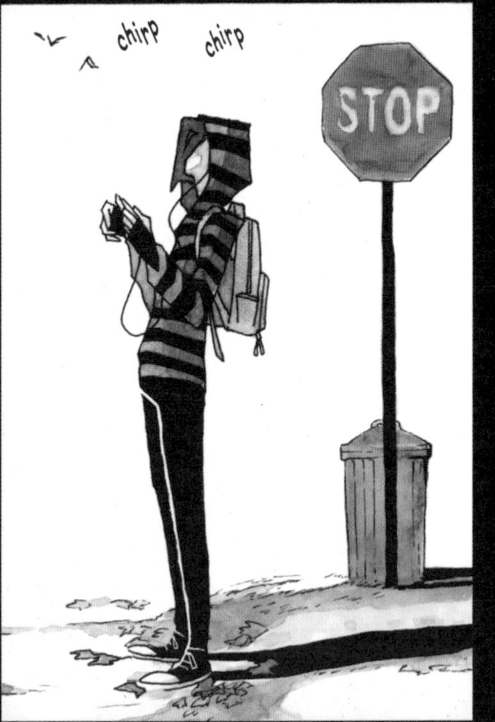
chirp
chirp
STOP

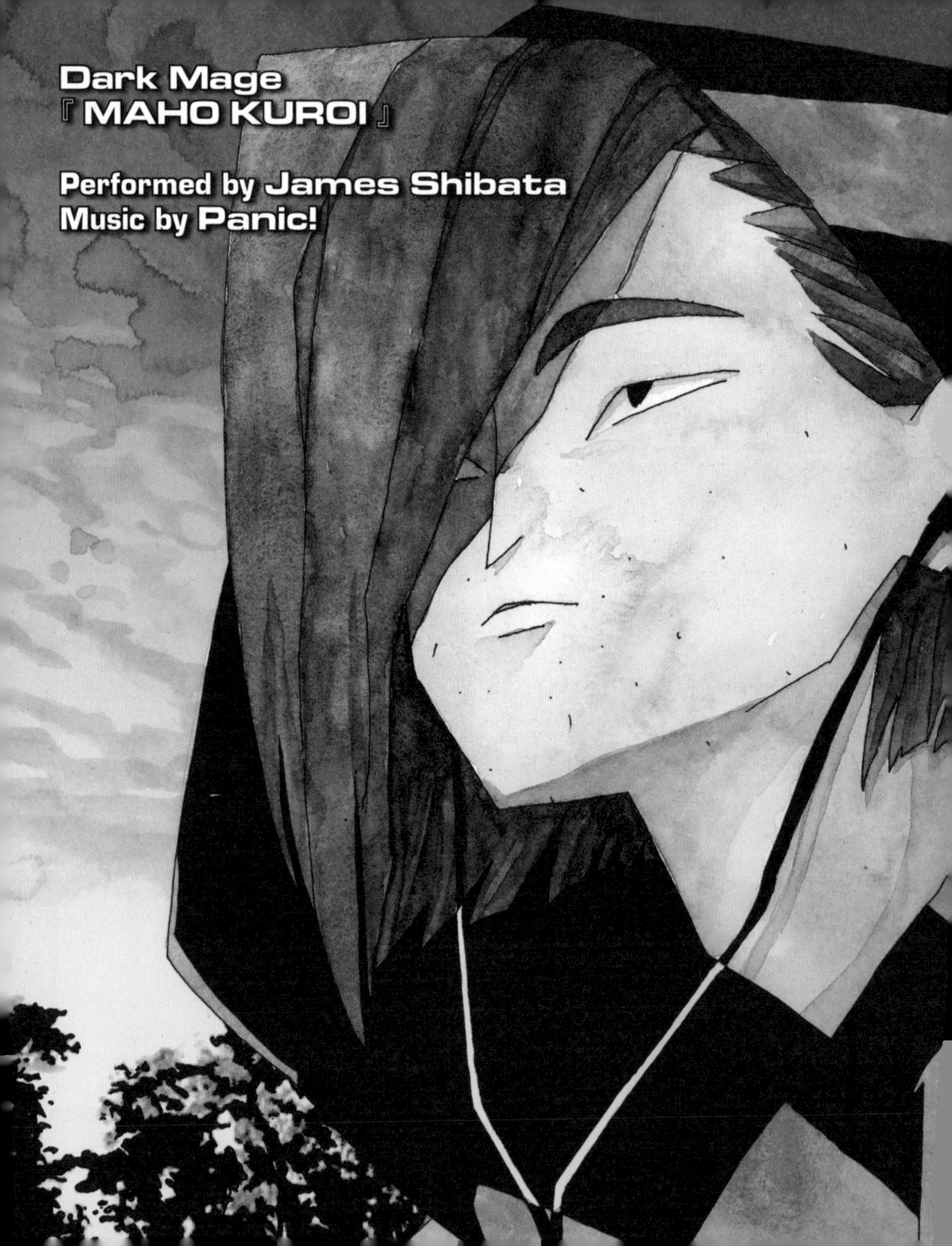
Dark Mage
『 MAHO KUROI 』
Performed by James Shibata
Music by Panic!

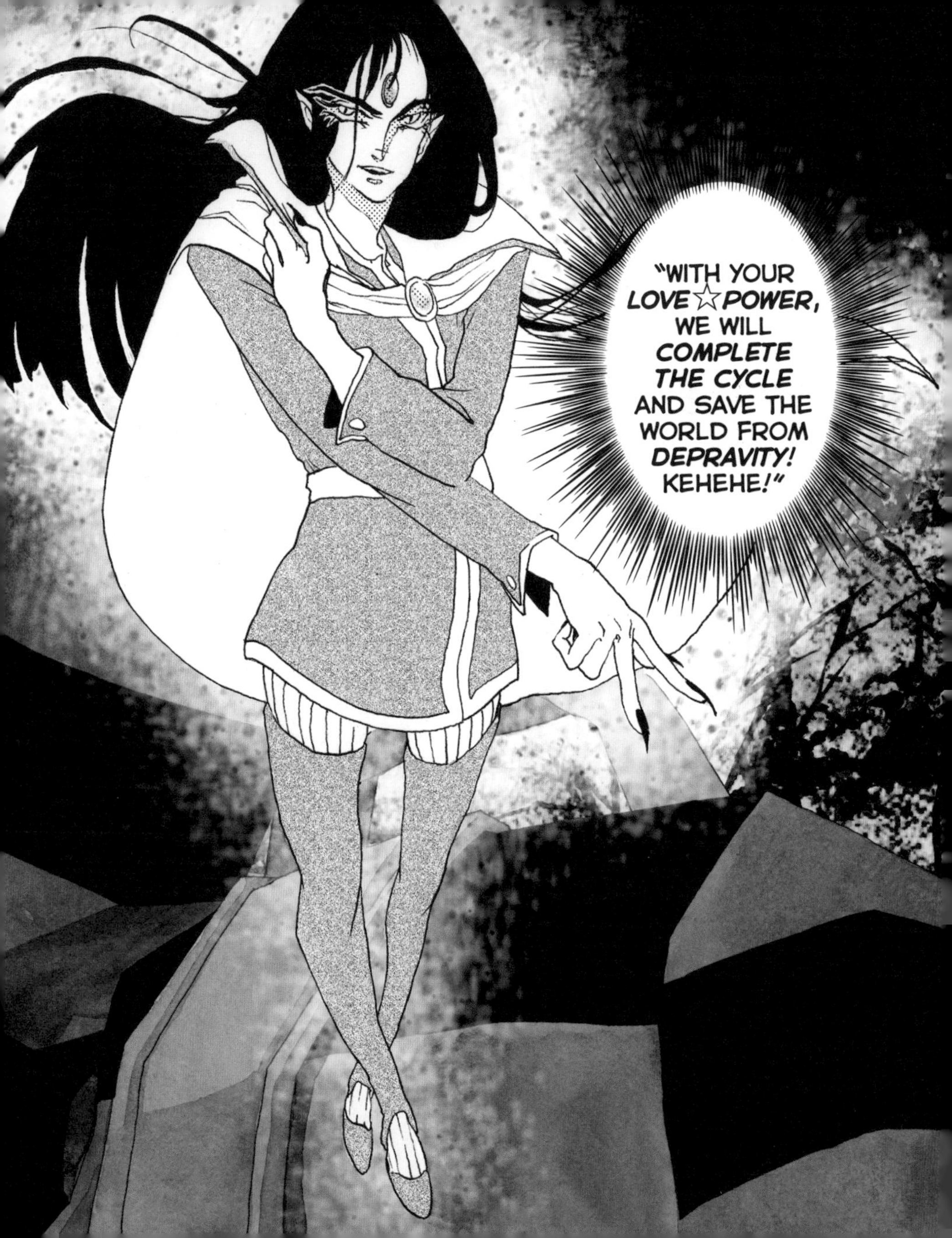
"WITH YOUR LOVE☆POWER, WE WILL COMPLETE THE CYCLE AND SAVE THE WORLD FROM DEPRAVITY! KEHEHE!"

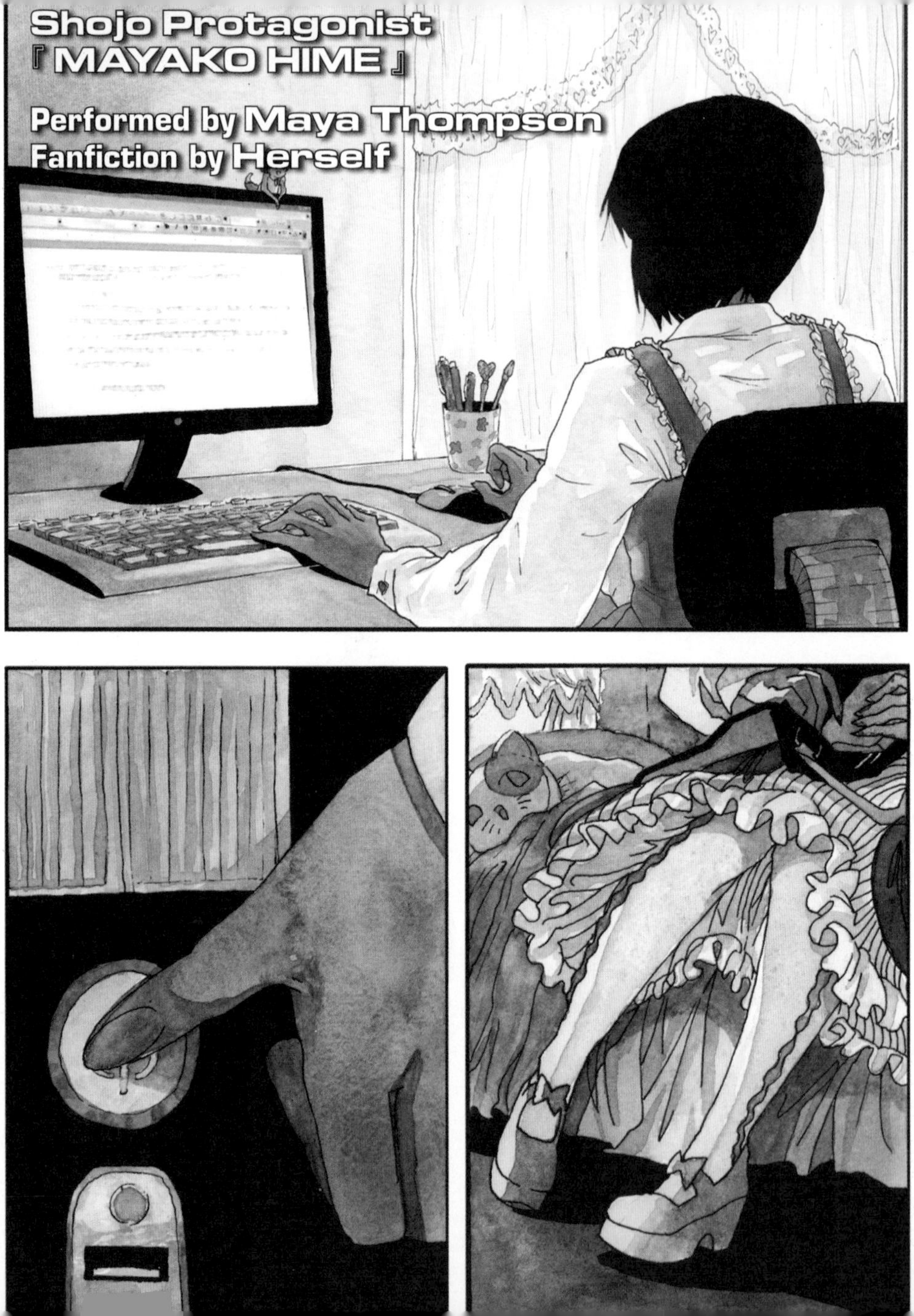
Shojo Protagonist
『MAYAKO HIME』
Performed by Maya Thompson
Fanfiction by Herself

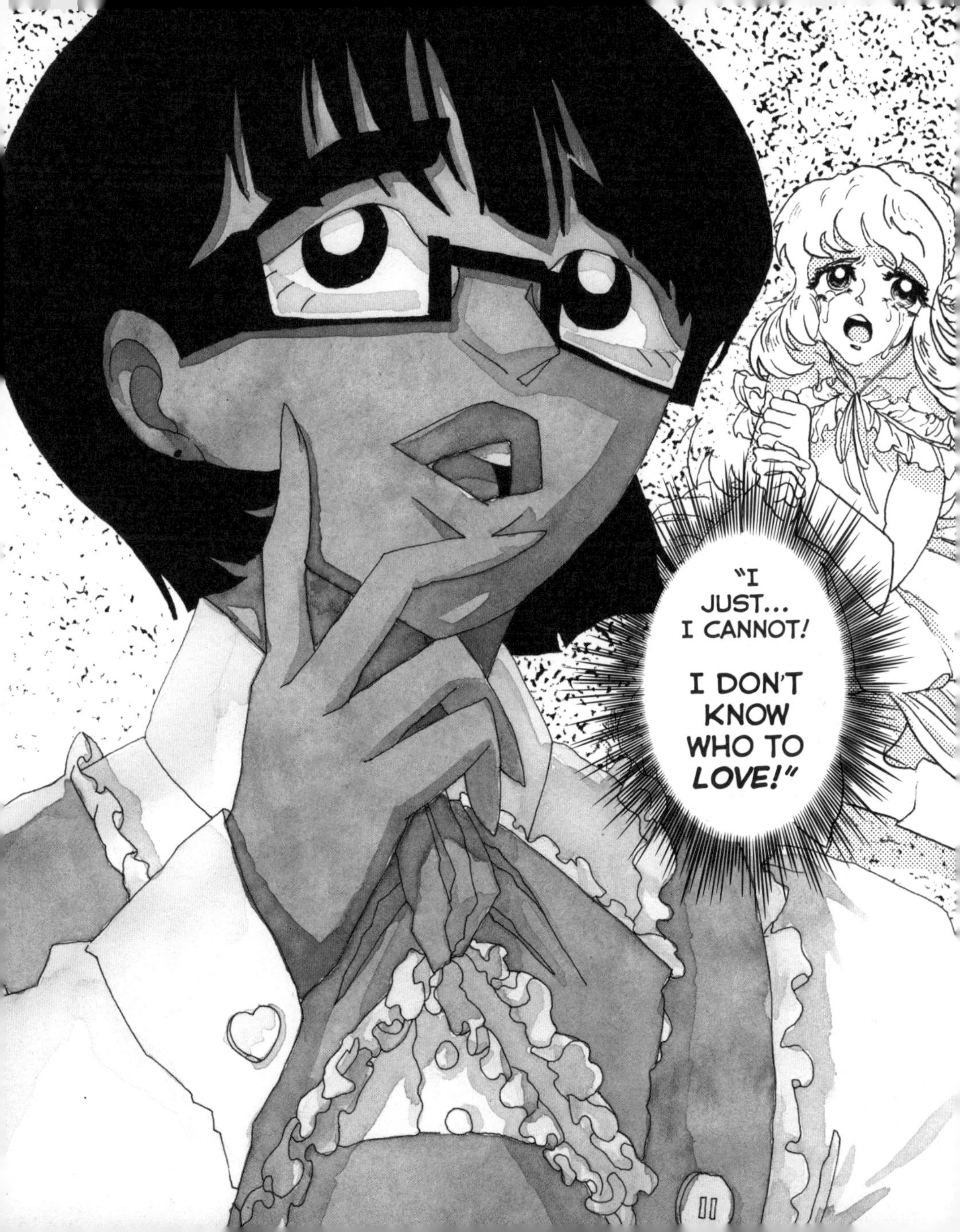
"I JUST... I CANNOT!
I DON'T KNOW WHO TO *LOVE!*"

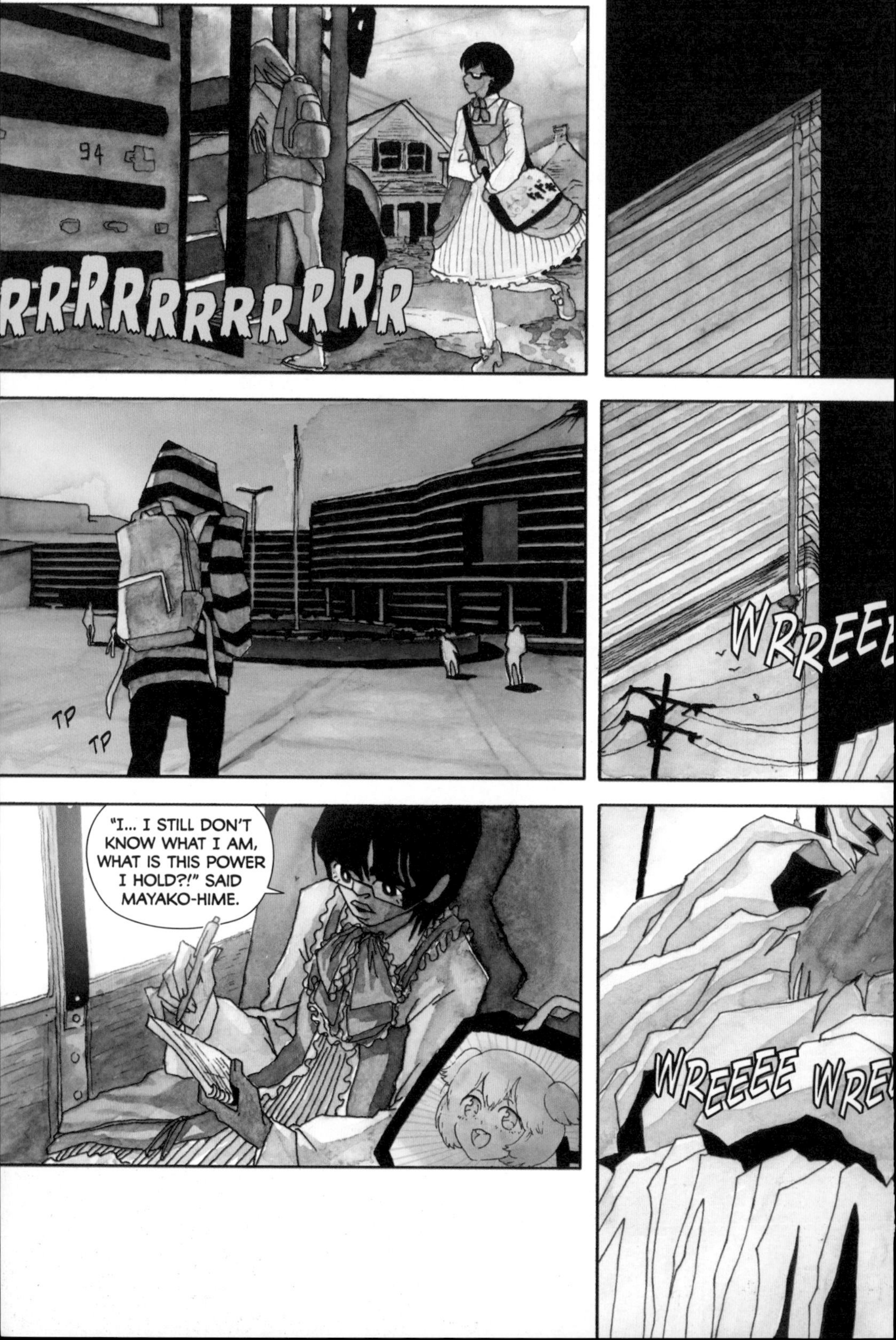
RRRRRRRRRRR
TP
TP
WRREEE
"I... I STILL DON'T KNOW WHAT I AM, WHAT IS THIS POWER I HOLD?!" SAID MAYAKO-HIME.
WREEEE WRE

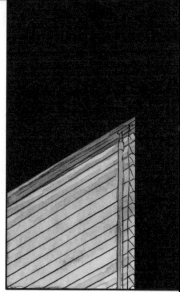

Then the Prince ran toward Mayako, grabbing her into his arms!

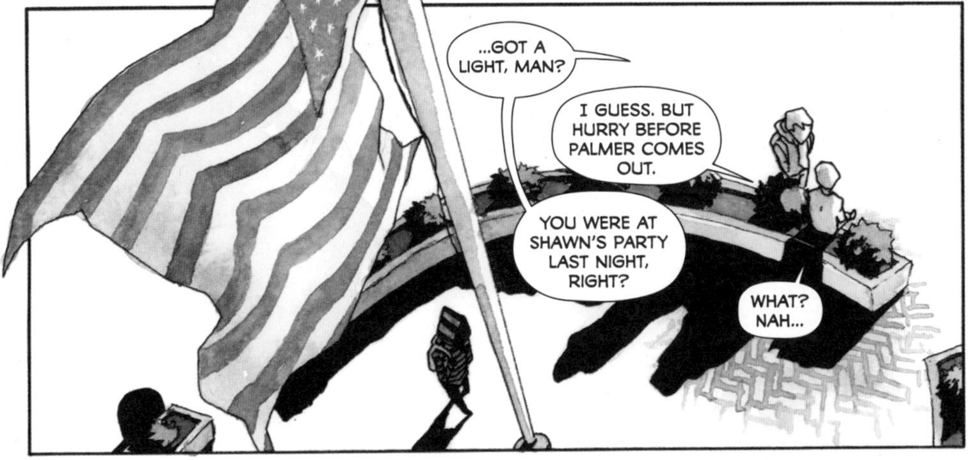
...GOT A LIGHT, MAN?
I GUESS. BUT HURRY BEFORE PALMER COMES OUT.
YOU WERE AT SHAWN'S PARTY LAST NIGHT, RIGHT?
WHAT? NAH...

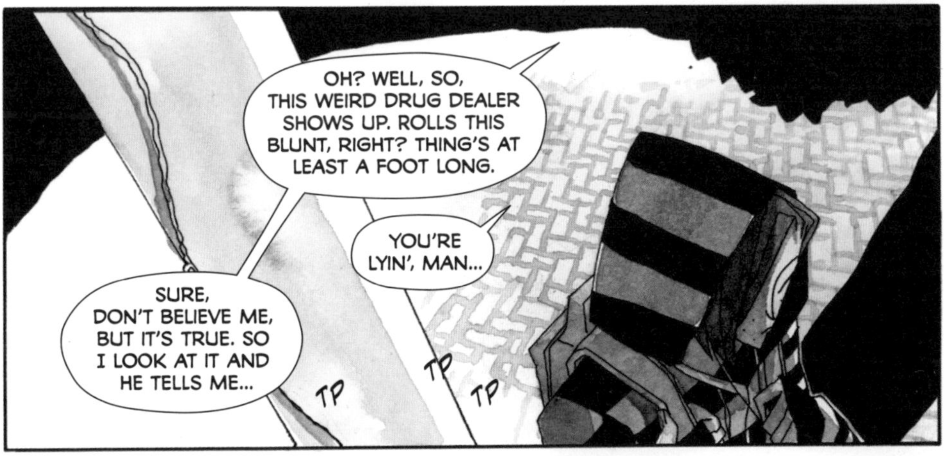
OH? WELL, SO, THIS WEIRD DRUG DEALER SHOWS UP. ROLLS THIS BLUNT, RIGHT? THING'S AT LEAST A FOOT LONG.
YOU'RE LYIN', MAN...
SURE, DON'T BELIEVE ME, BUT IT'S TRUE. SO I LOOK AT IT AND HE TELLS ME...
TP
TP
TP

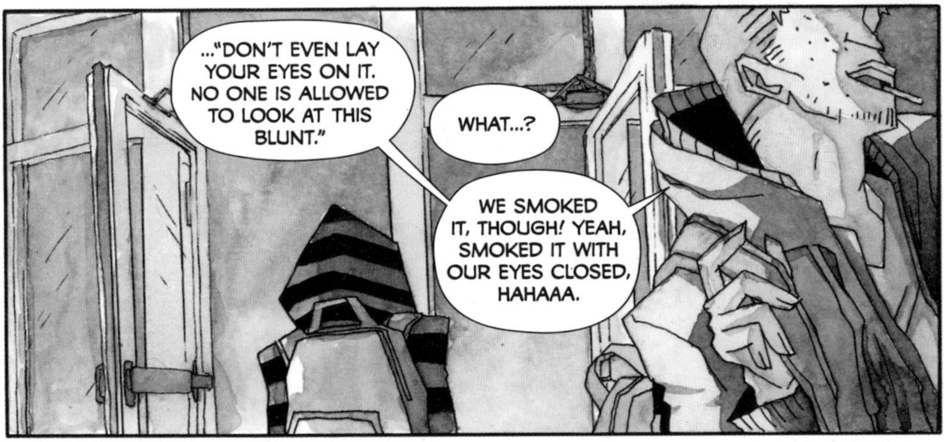
..."DON'T EVEN LAY YOUR EYES ON IT. NO ONE IS ALLOWED TO LOOK AT THIS BLUNT."
WHAT...?
WE SMOKED IT, THOUGH! YEAH, SMOKED IT WITH OUR EYES CLOSED, HAHAAA.

"I know what you are!" he says.

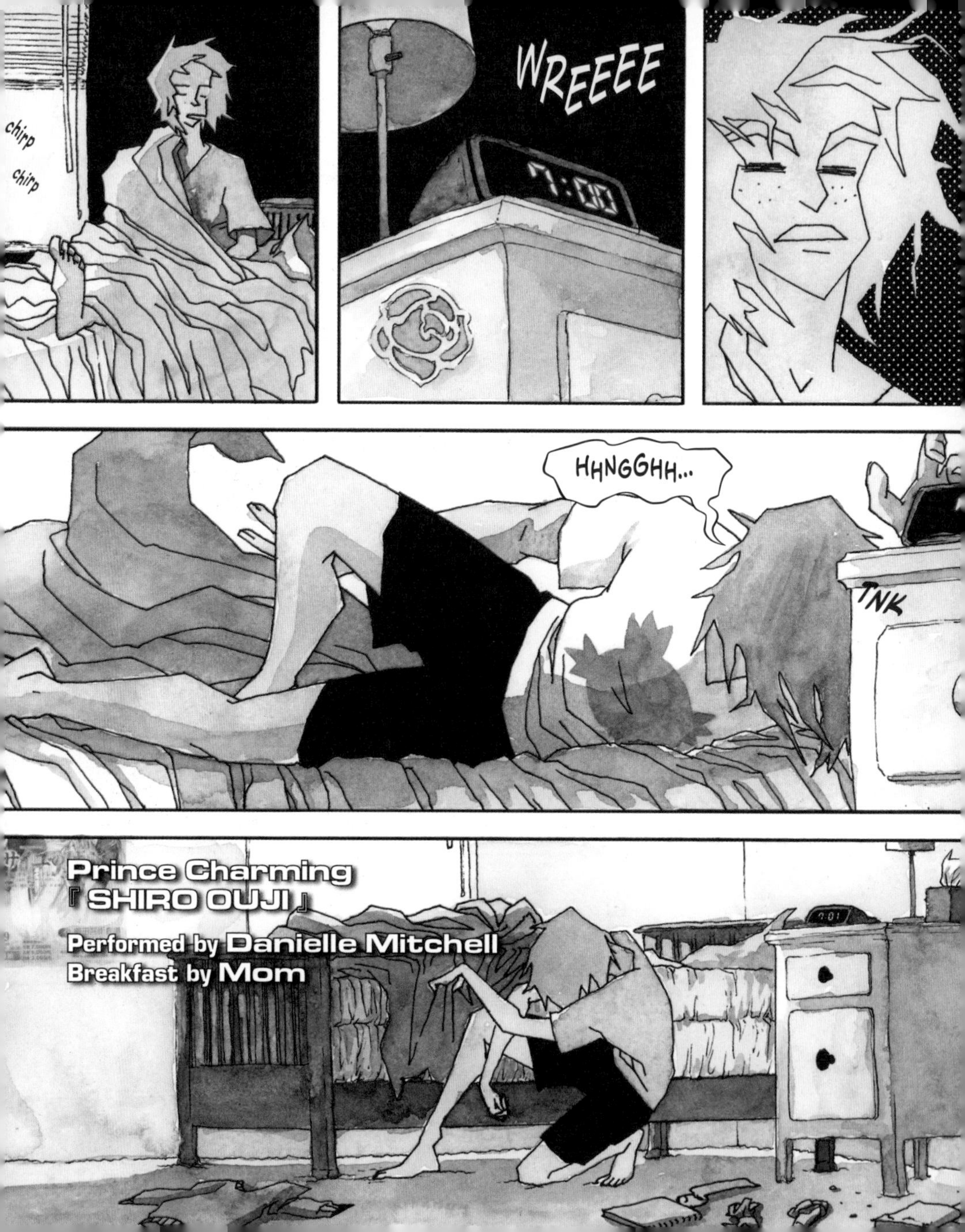
chirp
chirp
WREEEE
7:00
HHNGGHH...
TNK
Prince Charming
『SHIRO OUJI』
Performed by Danielle Mitchell
Breakfast by Mom

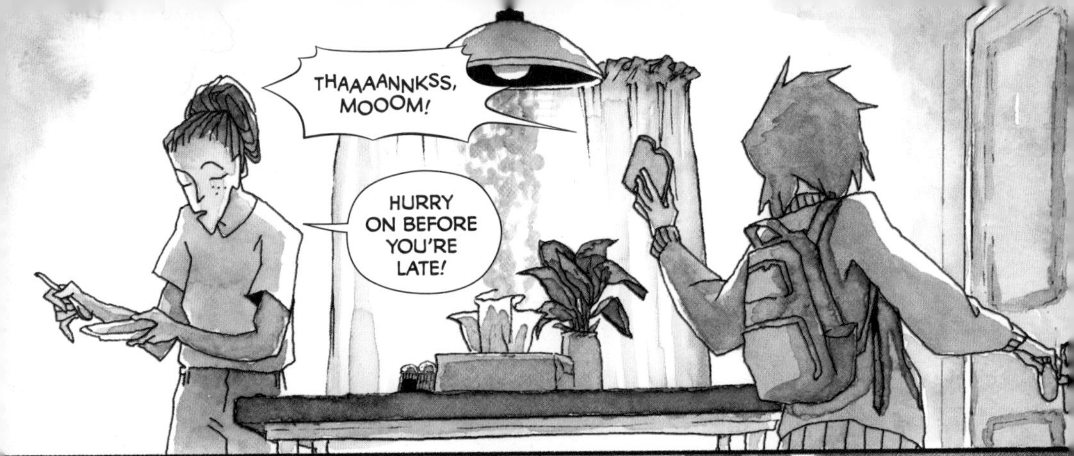
THAAAANNKSS, MOOOM!
HURRY ON BEFORE YOU'RE LATE!

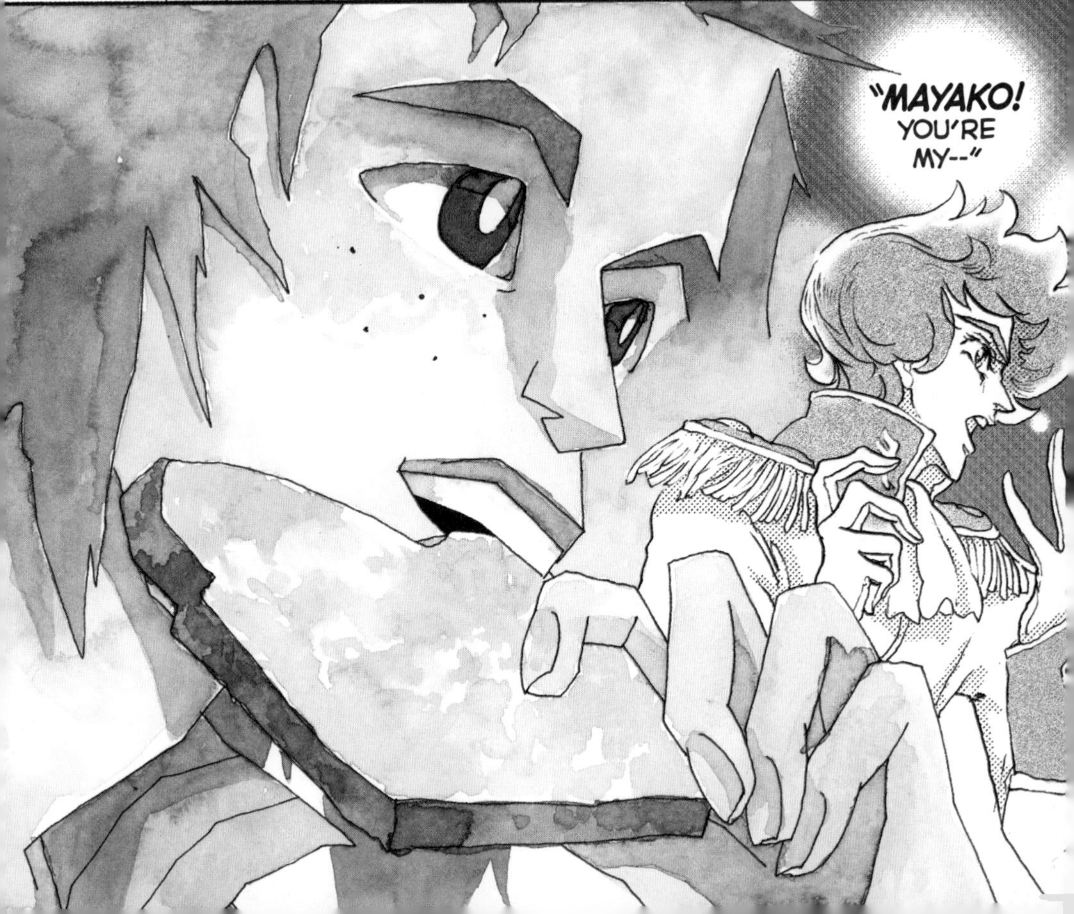
"MAYAKO! YOU'RE MY--"

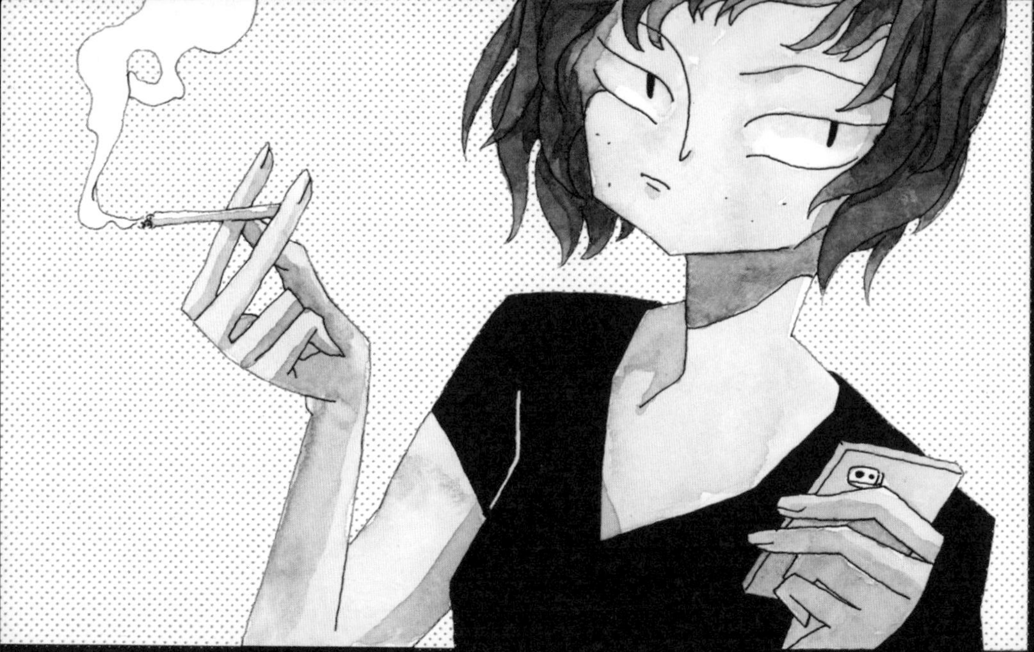

Big Sister **Hana Shibata**

Nice Guy **André Butler**

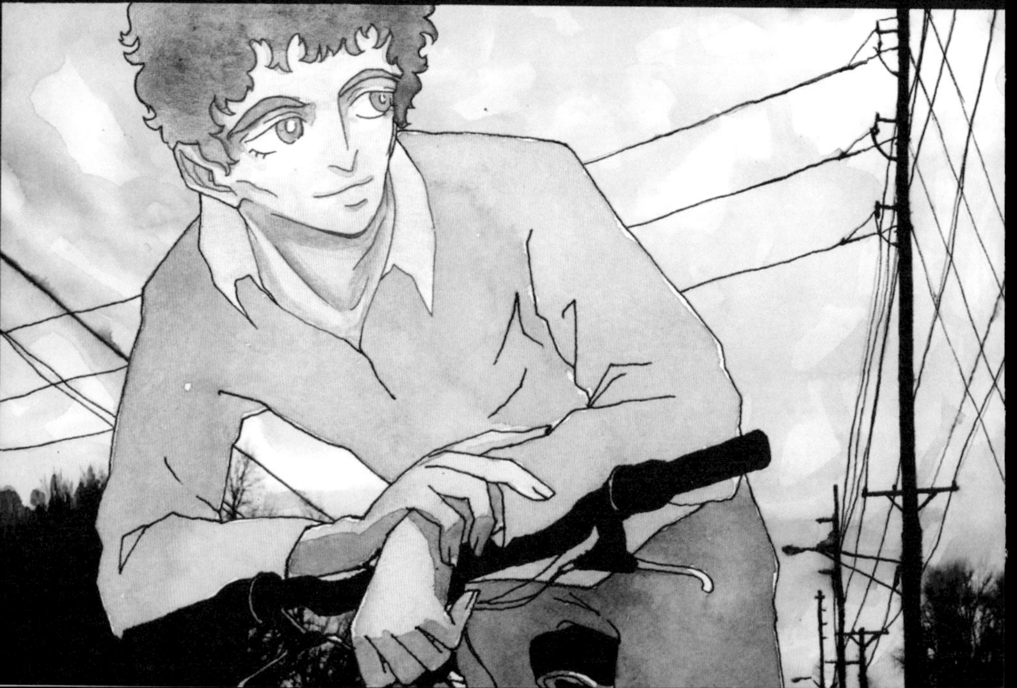

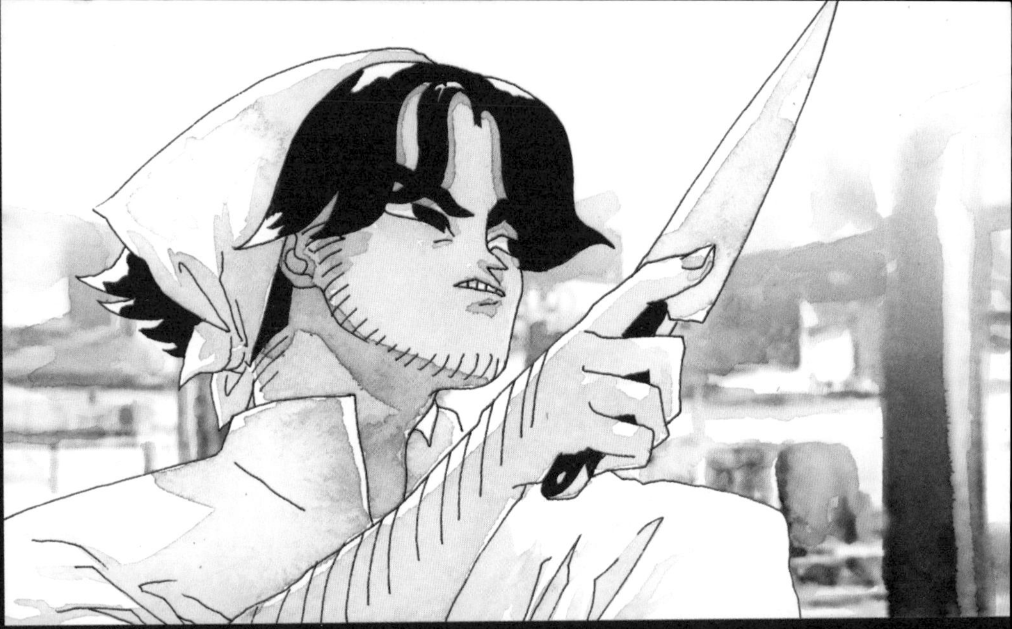

Sushi Chefs
Jun & Tyler

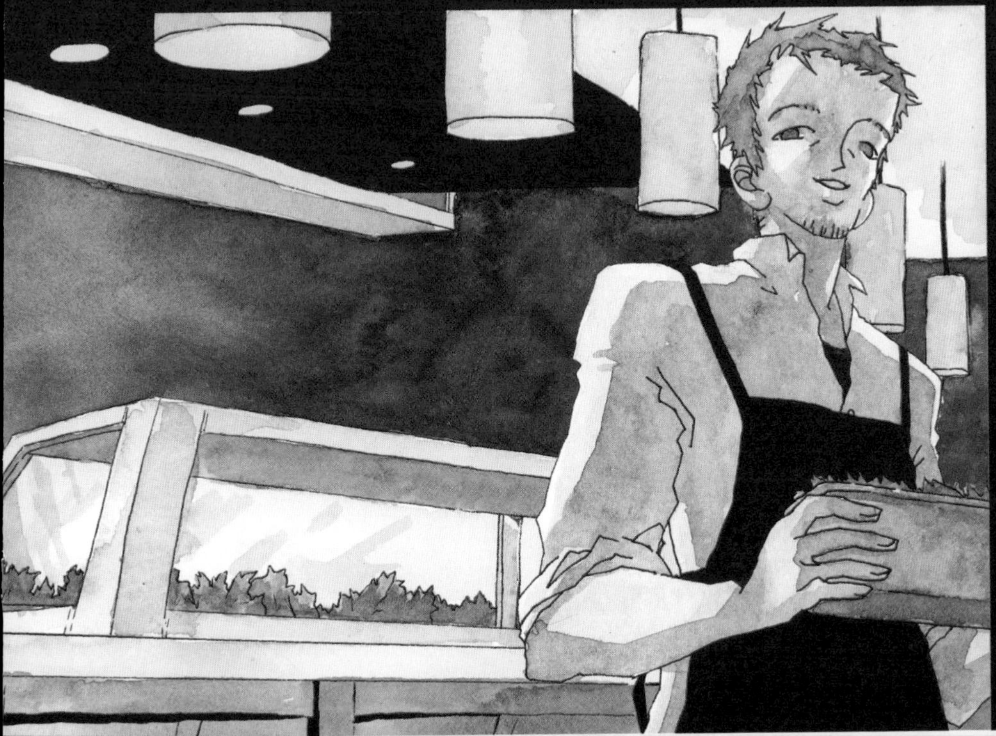

WEEABOO

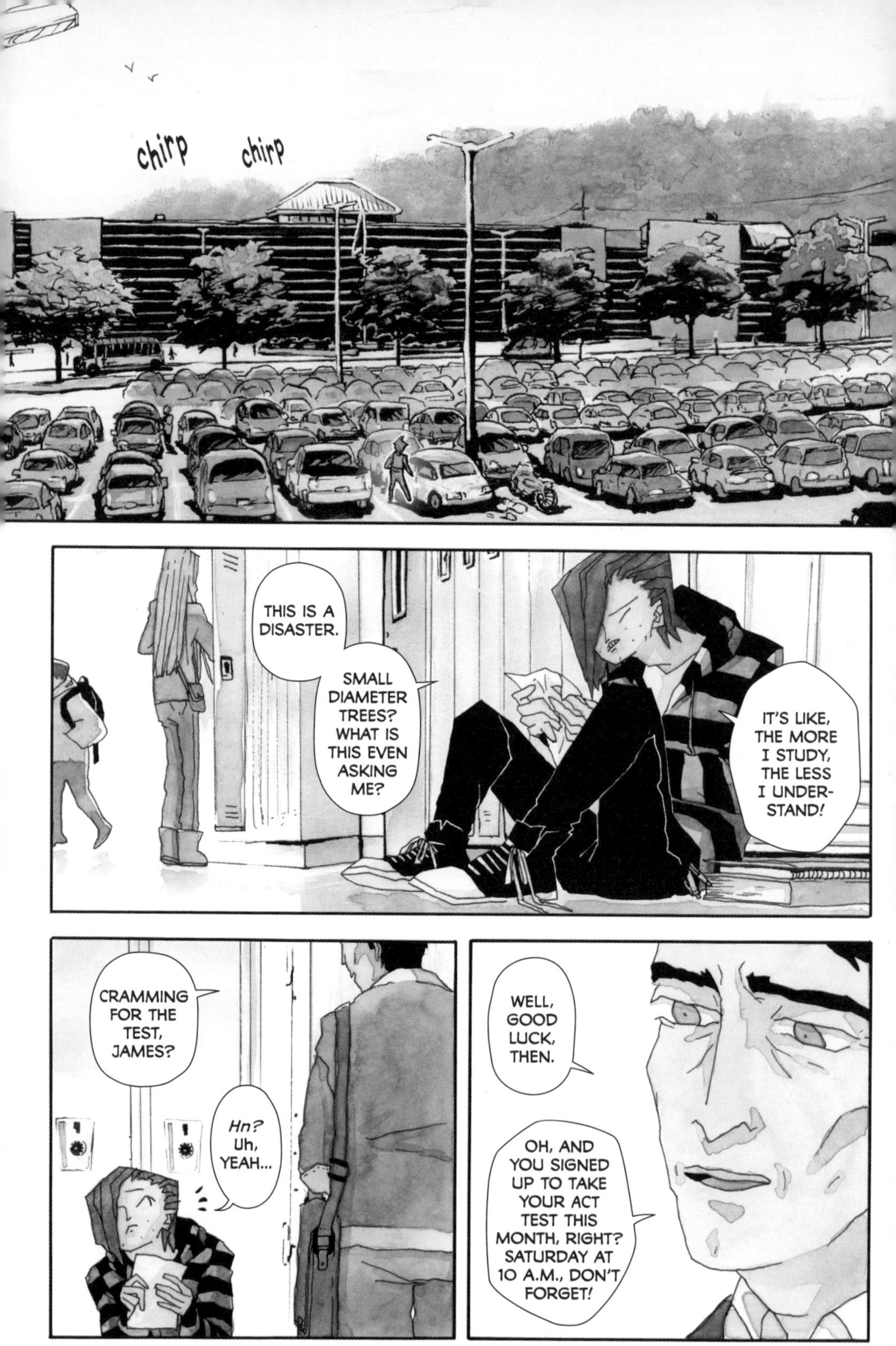
chirp chirp
THIS IS A DISASTER.
SMALL DIAMETER TREES? WHAT IS THIS EVEN ASKING ME?
IT'S LIKE, THE MORE I STUDY, THE LESS I UNDER-STAND!
CRAMMING FOR THE TEST, JAMES?
Hn? Uh, YEAH...
WELL, GOOD LUCK, THEN.
OH, AND YOU SIGNED UP TO TAKE YOUR ACT TEST THIS MONTH, RIGHT? SATURDAY AT 10 A.M., DON'T FORGET!

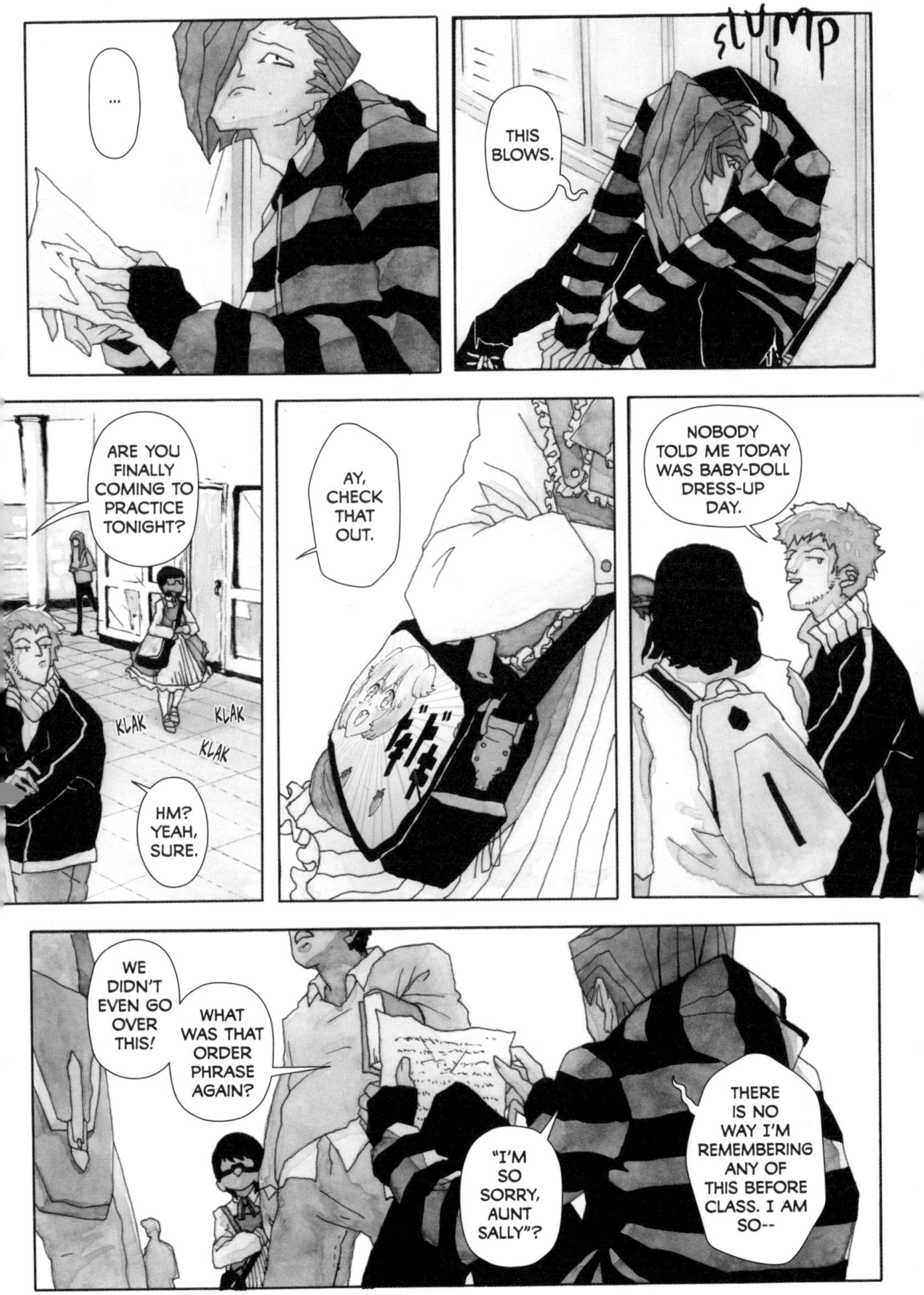
...
slump
THIS BLOWS.
ARE YOU FINALLY COMING TO PRACTICE TONIGHT?
KLAK
KLAK
KLAK
HM? YEAH, SURE.
AY, CHECK THAT OUT.
NOBODY TOLD ME TODAY WAS BABY-DOLL DRESS-UP DAY.
WE DIDN'T EVEN GO OVER THIS!
WHAT WAS THAT ORDER PHRASE AGAIN?
"I'M SO SORRY, AUNT SALLY"?
THERE IS NO WAY I'M REMEMBERING ANY OF THIS BEFORE CLASS. I AM SO--

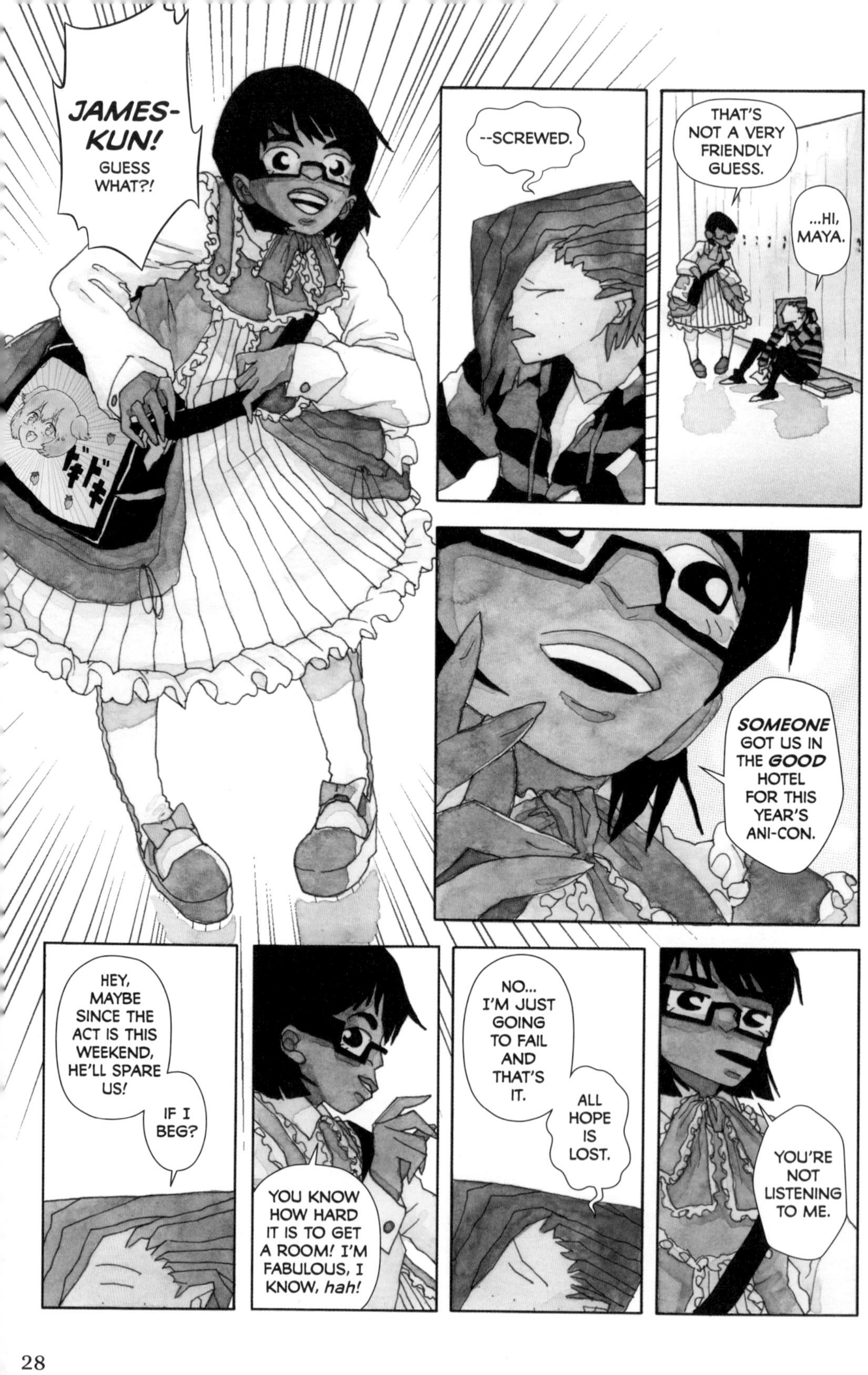
JAMES-KUN! GUESS WHAT?!
--SCREWED.
THAT'S NOT A VERY FRIENDLY GUESS.
...HI, MAYA.
SOMEONE GOT US IN THE GOOD HOTEL FOR THIS YEAR'S ANI-CON.
HEY, MAYBE SINCE THE ACT IS THIS WEEKEND, HE'LL SPARE US!
IF I BEG?
YOU KNOW HOW HARD IT IS TO GET A ROOM! I'M FABULOUS, I KNOW, hah!
NO... I'M JUST GOING TO FAIL AND THAT'S IT.
ALL HOPE IS LOST.
YOU'RE NOT LISTENING TO ME.

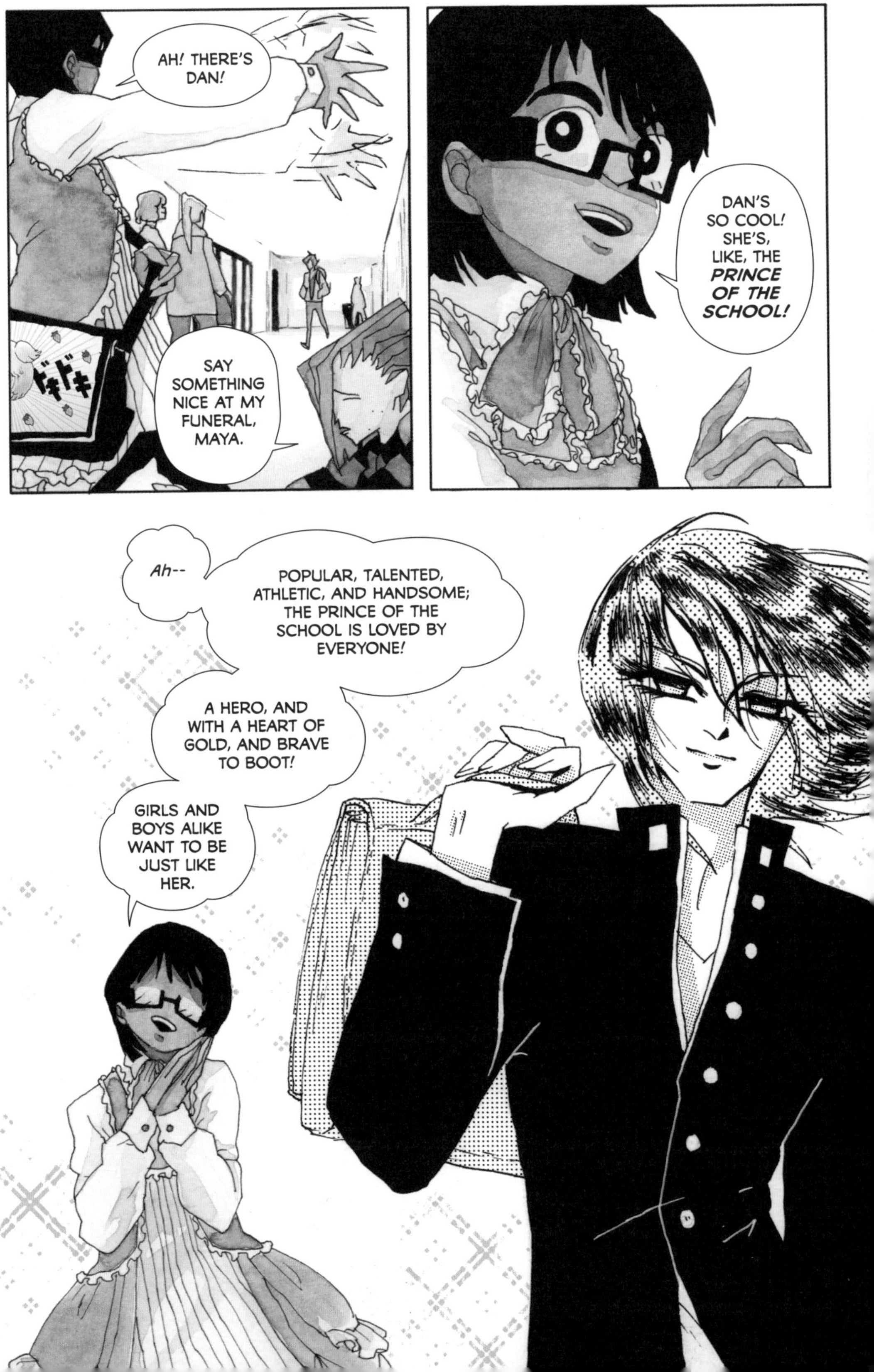
AH! THERE'S DAN!
ドキドキ
SAY SOMETHING NICE AT MY FUNERAL, MAYA.
DAN'S SO COOL! SHE'S, LIKE, THE PRINCE OF THE SCHOOL!
Ah--
POPULAR, TALENTED, ATHLETIC, AND HANDSOME; THE PRINCE OF THE SCHOOL IS LOVED BY EVERYONE!
A HERO, AND WITH A HEART OF GOLD, AND BRAVE TO BOOT!
GIRLS AND BOYS ALIKE WANT TO BE JUST LIKE HER.

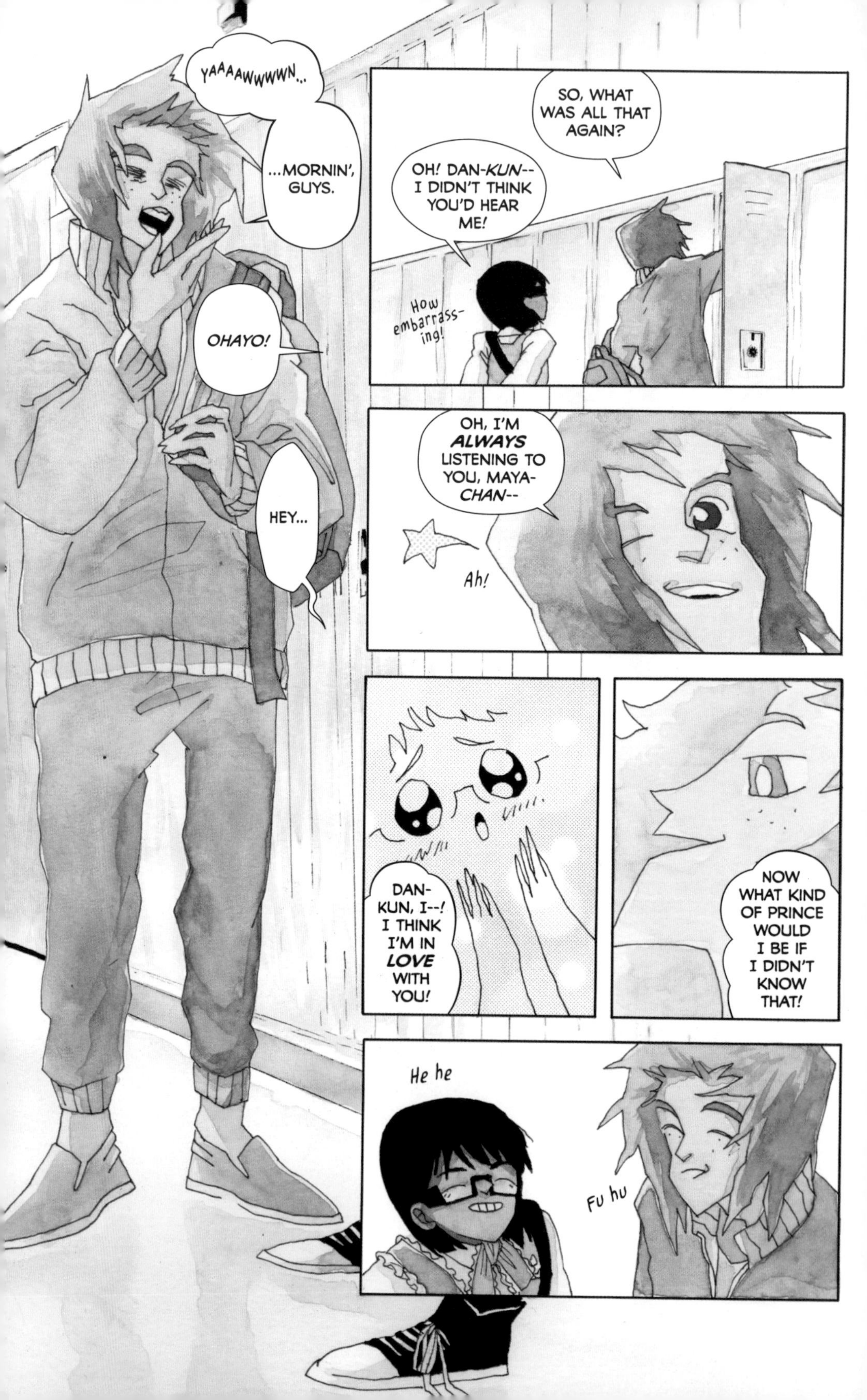
YAAAAWWWWN...
...MORNIN', GUYS.
OHAYO!
HEY...
SO, WHAT WAS ALL THAT AGAIN?
OH! DAN-KUN-- I DIDN'T THINK YOU'D HEAR ME!
How embarrass-ing!
OH, I'M ALWAYS LISTENING TO YOU, MAYA-CHAN--
Ah!
DAN-KUN, I--! I THINK I'M IN LOVE WITH YOU!
NOW WHAT KIND OF PRINCE WOULD I BE IF I DIDN'T KNOW THAT!
He he
Fu hu

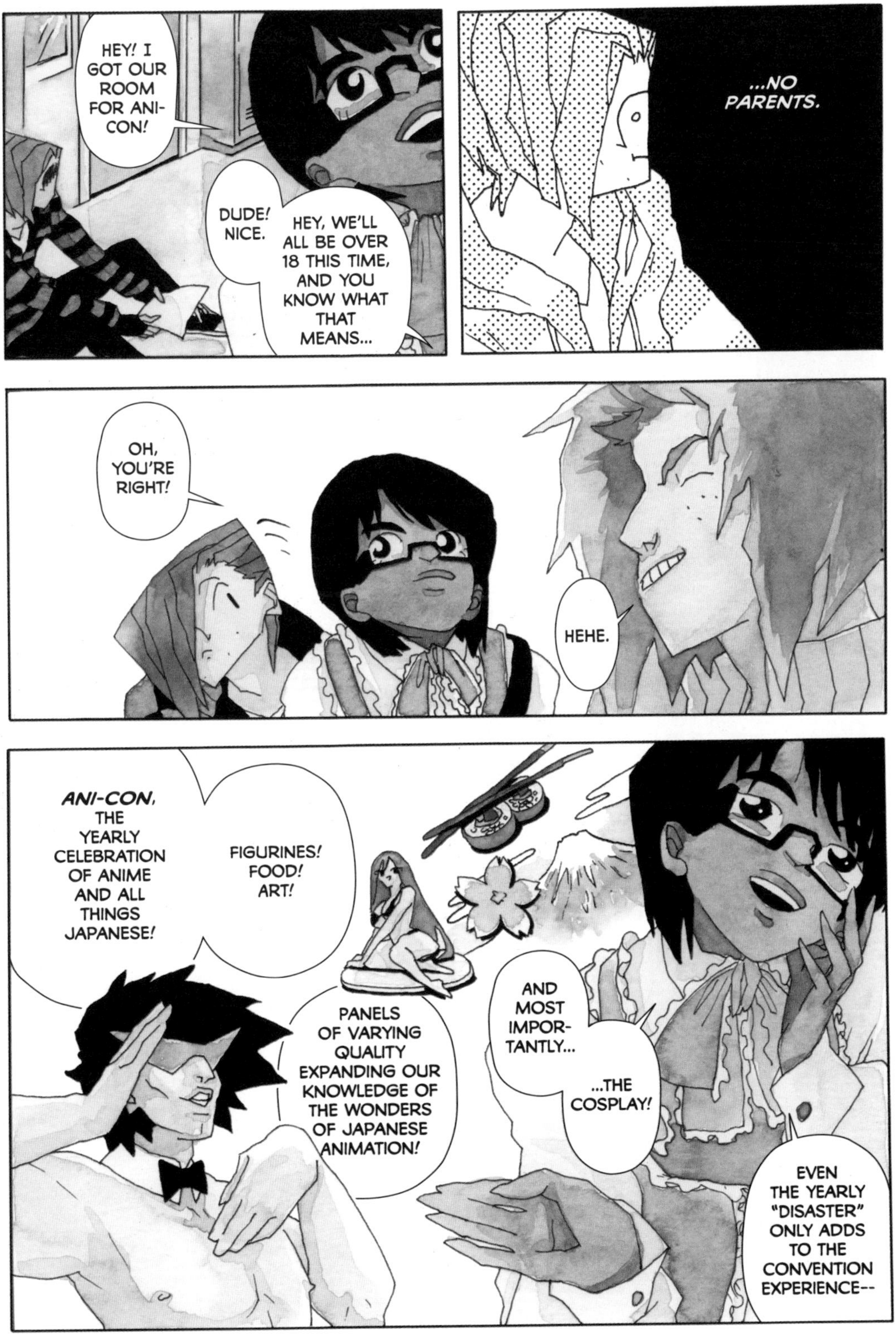
HEY! I GOT OUR ROOM FOR ANI-CON!
DUDE! NICE.
HEY, WE'LL ALL BE OVER 18 THIS TIME, AND YOU KNOW WHAT THAT MEANS...
...NO PARENTS.
OH, YOU'RE RIGHT!
HEHE.
ANI-CON, THE YEARLY CELEBRATION OF ANIME AND ALL THINGS JAPANESE!
FIGURINES! FOOD! ART!
PANELS OF VARYING QUALITY EXPANDING OUR KNOWLEDGE OF THE WONDERS OF JAPANESE ANIMATION!
AND MOST IMPORTANTLY...
...THE COSPLAY!
EVEN THE YEARLY "DISASTER" ONLY ADDS TO THE CONVENTION EXPERIENCE--

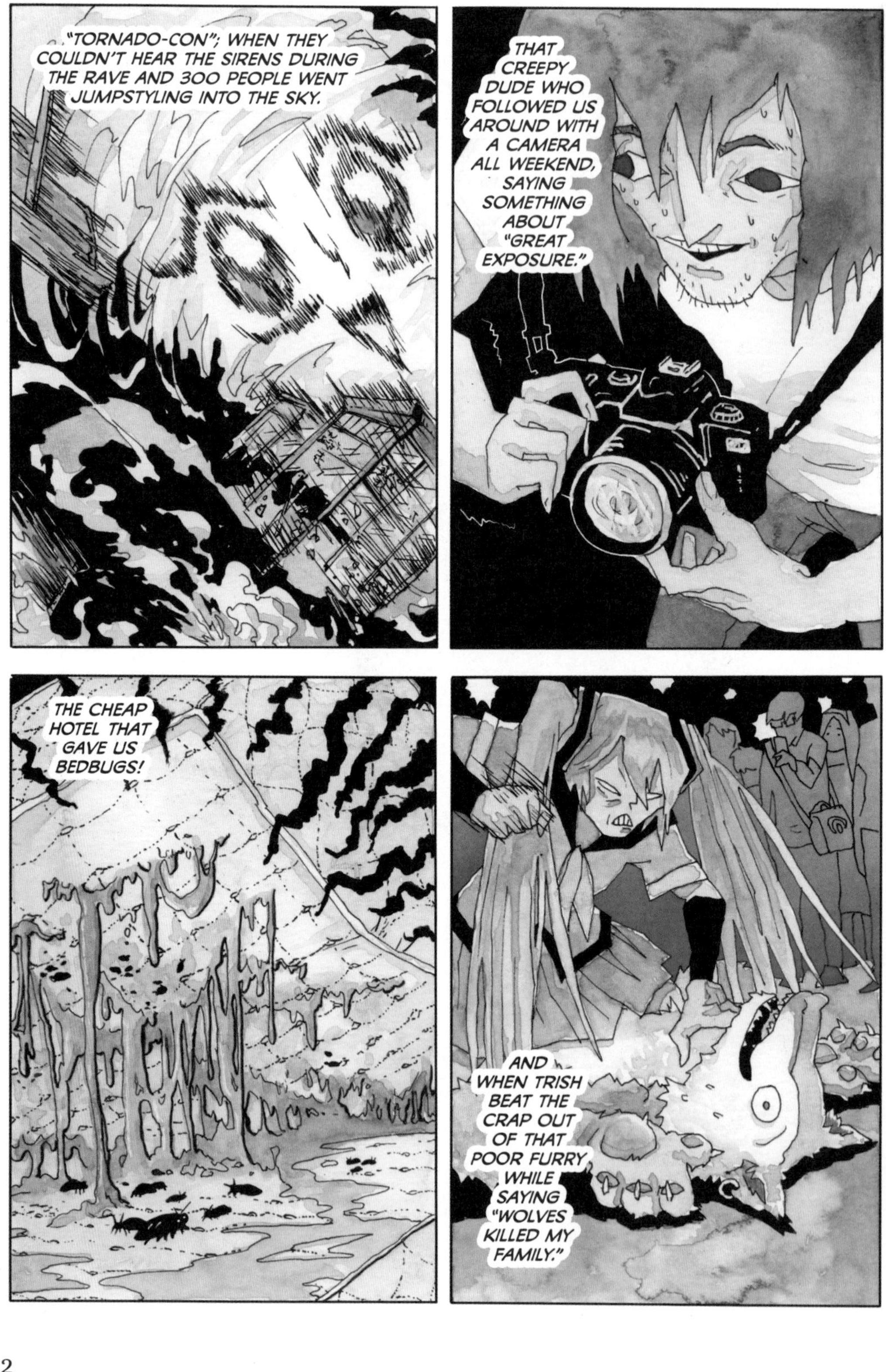
"TORNADO-CON"; WHEN THEY COULDN'T HEAR THE SIRENS DURING THE RAVE AND 300 PEOPLE WENT JUMPSTYLING INTO THE SKY.
THAT CREEPY DUDE WHO FOLLOWED US AROUND WITH A CAMERA ALL WEEKEND, SAYING SOMETHING ABOUT "GREAT EXPOSURE."
THE CHEAP HOTEL THAT GAVE US BEDBUGS!
AND WHEN TRISH BEAT THE CRAP OUT OF THAT POOR FURRY WHILE SAYING "WOLVES KILLED MY FAMILY."

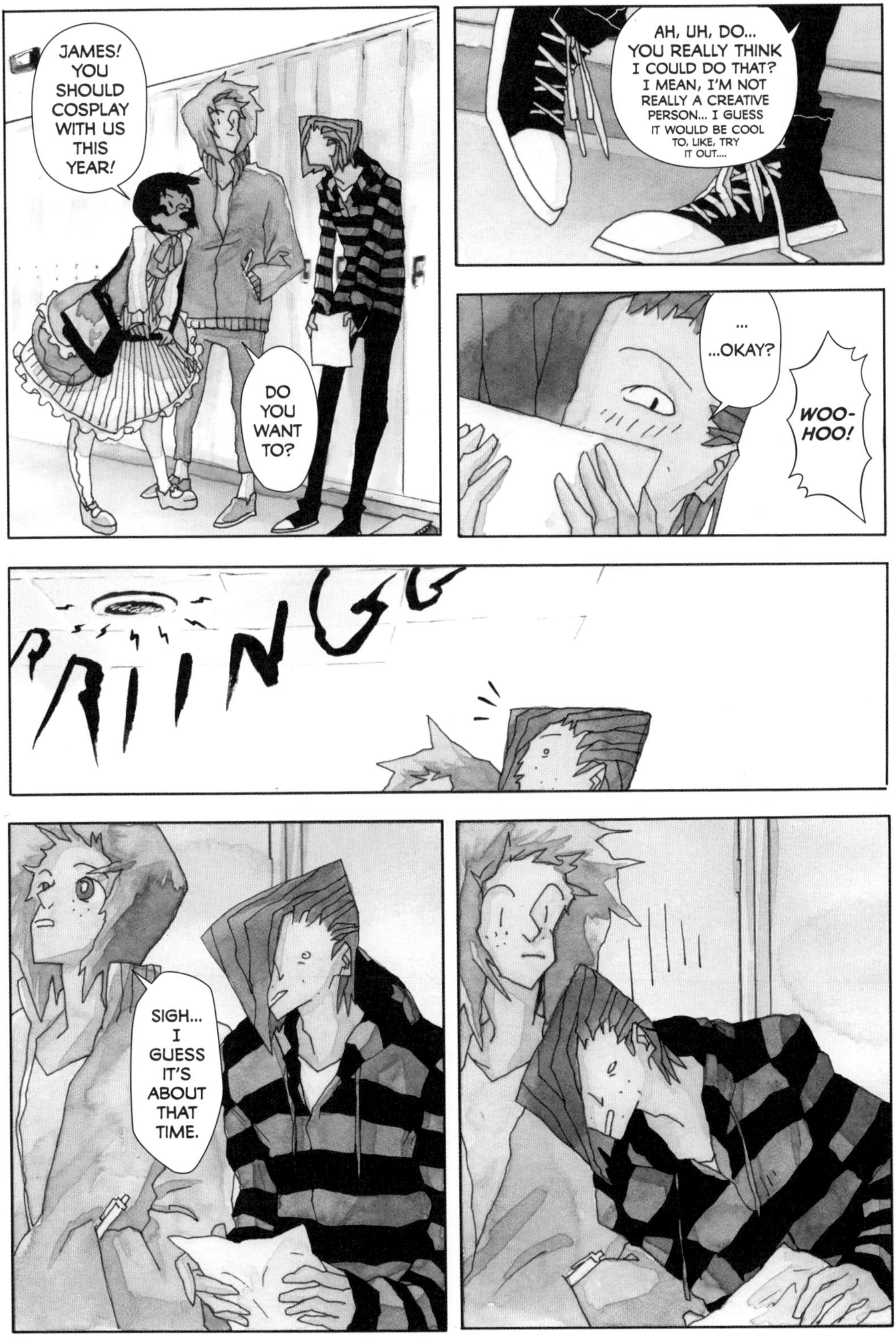
JAMES! YOU SHOULD COSPLAY WITH US THIS YEAR!
DO YOU WANT TO?
AH, UH, DO... YOU REALLY THINK I COULD DO THAT? I MEAN, I'M NOT REALLY A CREATIVE PERSON... I GUESS IT WOULD BE COOL TO, LIKE, TRY IT OUT....
... ...OKAY?
WOO-HOO!
BRIINGG
SIGH... I GUESS IT'S ABOUT THAT TIME.

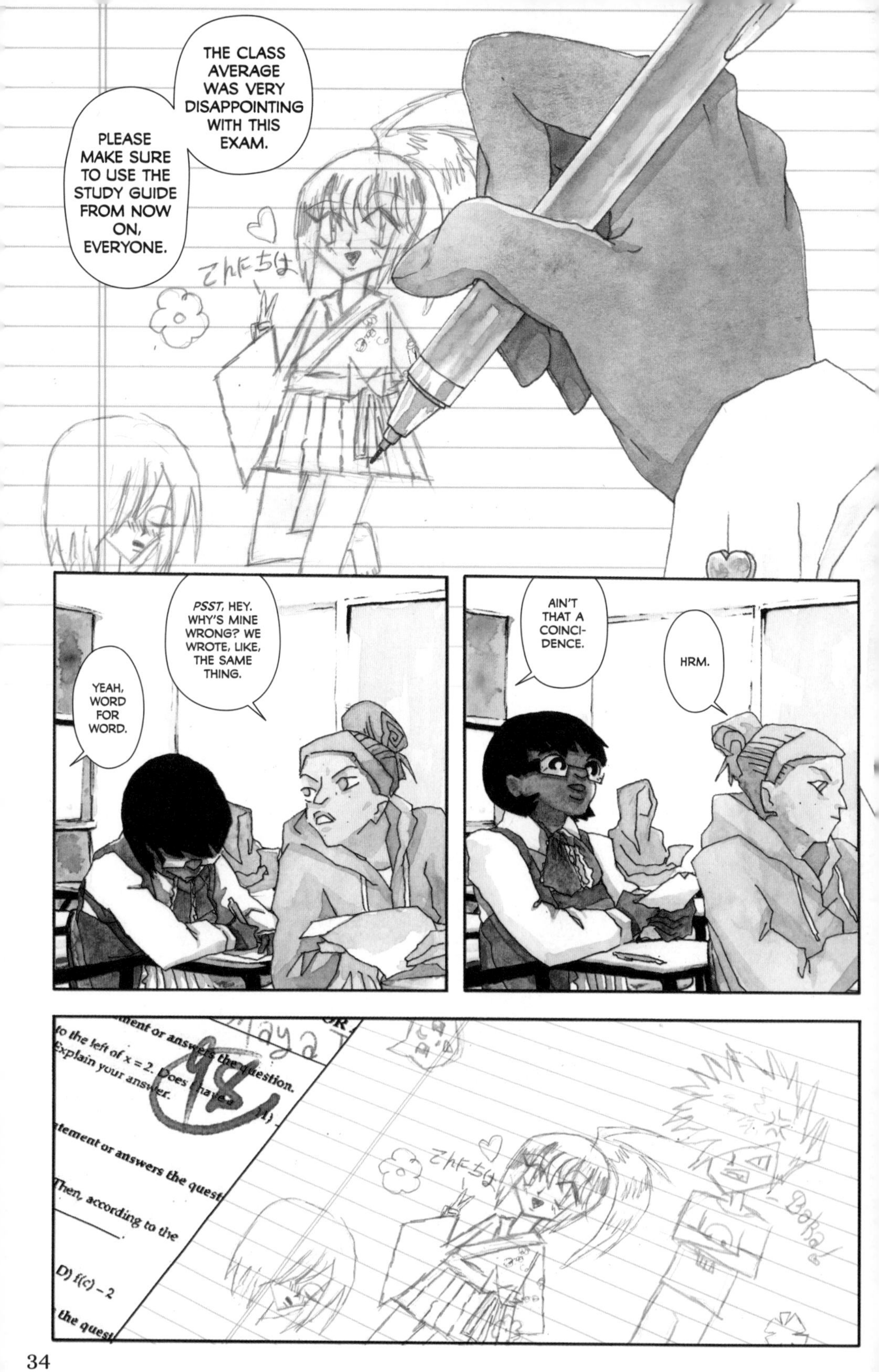
THE CLASS AVERAGE WAS VERY DISAPPOINTING WITH THIS EXAM.
PLEASE MAKE SURE TO USE THE STUDY GUIDE FROM NOW ON, EVERYONE.
こんにちは
PSST, HEY. WHY'S MINE WRONG? WE WROTE, LIKE, THE SAME THING.
YEAH, WORD FOR WORD.
AIN'T THAT A COINCIDENCE.
HRM.
98
ement or answers the question.
to the left of x = 2. Does
Explain your answer.
tement or answers the quest
Then, according to the
D) f(c) – 2
the quest
こんにちは
Baka!

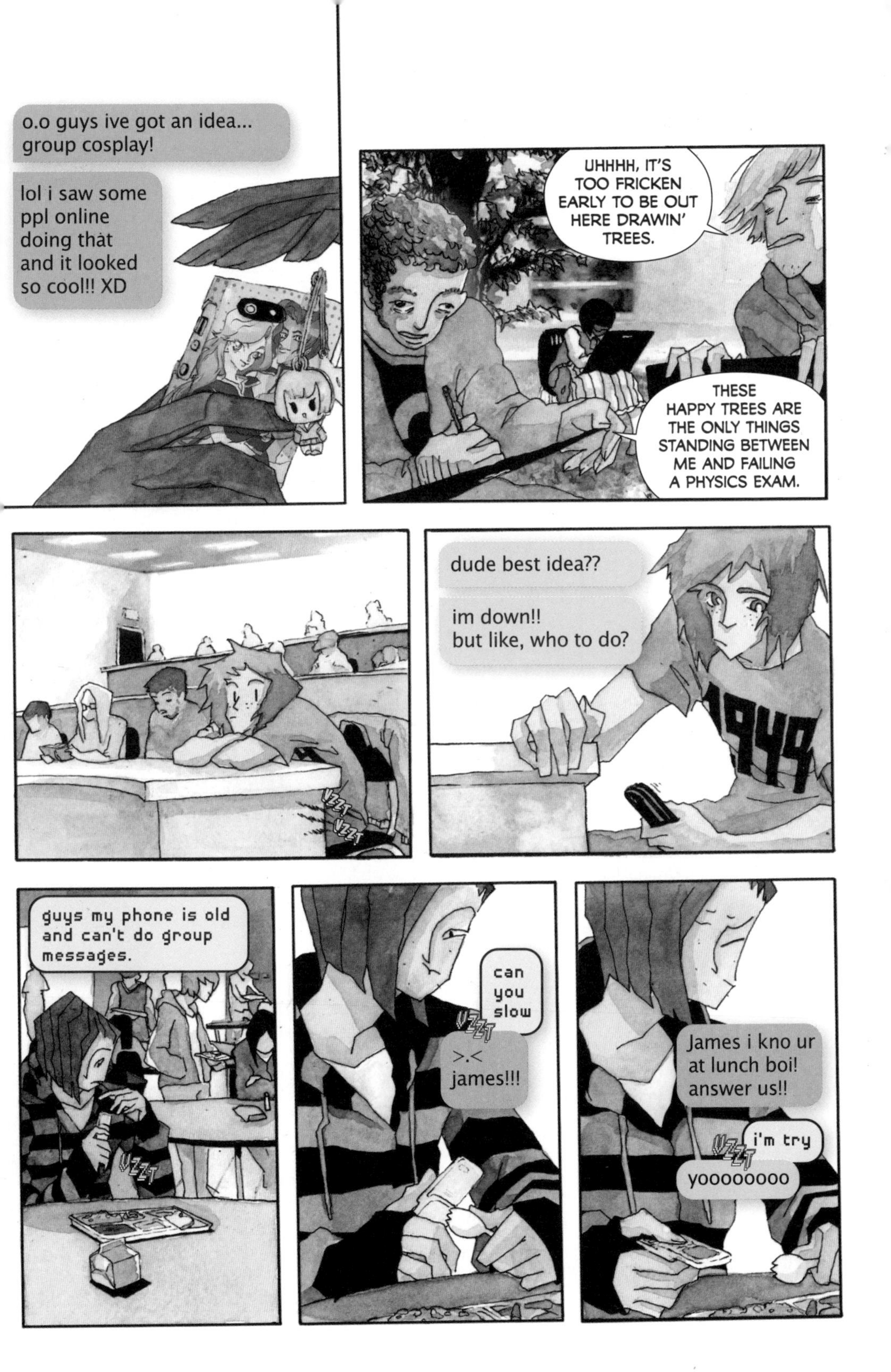
o.o guys ive got an idea...
group cosplay!
lol i saw some ppl online doing that and it looked so cool!! XD
UHHHH, IT'S TOO FRICKEN EARLY TO BE OUT HERE DRAWIN' TREES.
THESE HAPPY TREES ARE THE ONLY THINGS STANDING BETWEEN ME AND FAILING A PHYSICS EXAM.
VZZT VZZT
dude best idea??
im down!!
but like, who to do?
guys my phone is old and can't do group messages.
VZZT
can you slow
VZZT
>.<
james!!!
James i kno ur at lunch boi! answer us!!
i'm try
VZZT
yoooooooo

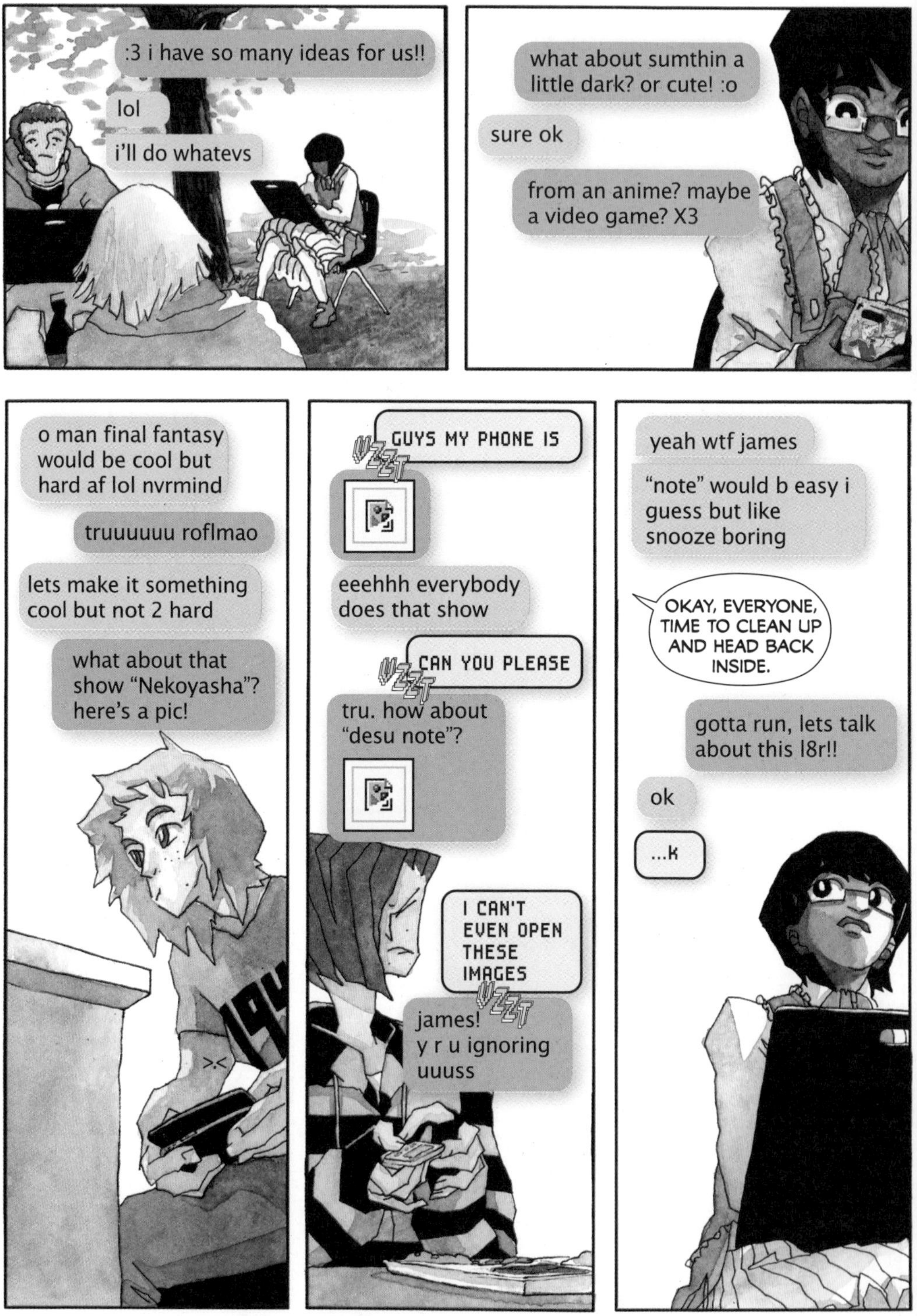
:3 i have so many ideas for us!!
lol
i'll do whatevs
what about sumthin a little dark? or cute! :o
sure ok
from an anime? maybe a video game? X3
o man final fantasy would be cool but hard af lol nvrmind
truuuuuu roflmao
lets make it something cool but not 2 hard
what about that show "Nekoyasha"? here's a pic!
GUYS MY PHONE IS
VZZT
eeehhh everybody does that show
CAN YOU PLEASE
VZZT
tru. how about "desu note"?
I CAN'T EVEN OPEN THESE IMAGES
VZZT
james! y r u ignoring uuuss
yeah wtf james
"note" would b easy i guess but like snooze boring
OKAY, EVERYONE, TIME TO CLEAN UP AND HEAD BACK INSIDE.
gotta run, lets talk about this l8r!!
ok
...k

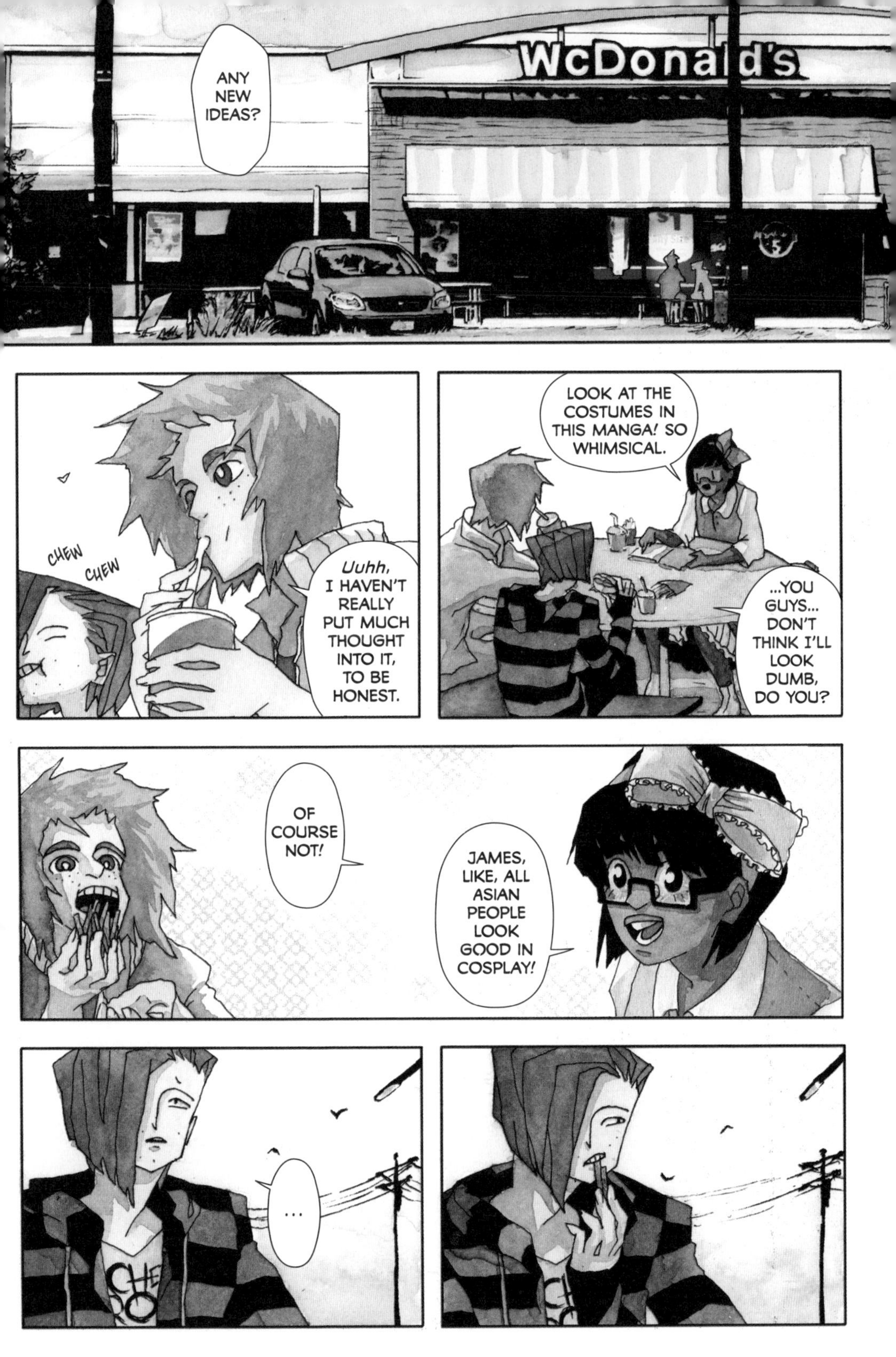
WcDonald's
ANY NEW IDEAS?
CHEW CHEW
Uuhh, I HAVEN'T REALLY PUT MUCH THOUGHT INTO IT, TO BE HONEST.
LOOK AT THE COSTUMES IN THIS MANGA! SO WHIMSICAL.
...YOU GUYS... DON'T THINK I'LL LOOK DUMB, DO YOU?
OF COURSE NOT!
JAMES, LIKE, ALL ASIAN PEOPLE LOOK GOOD IN COSPLAY!
...

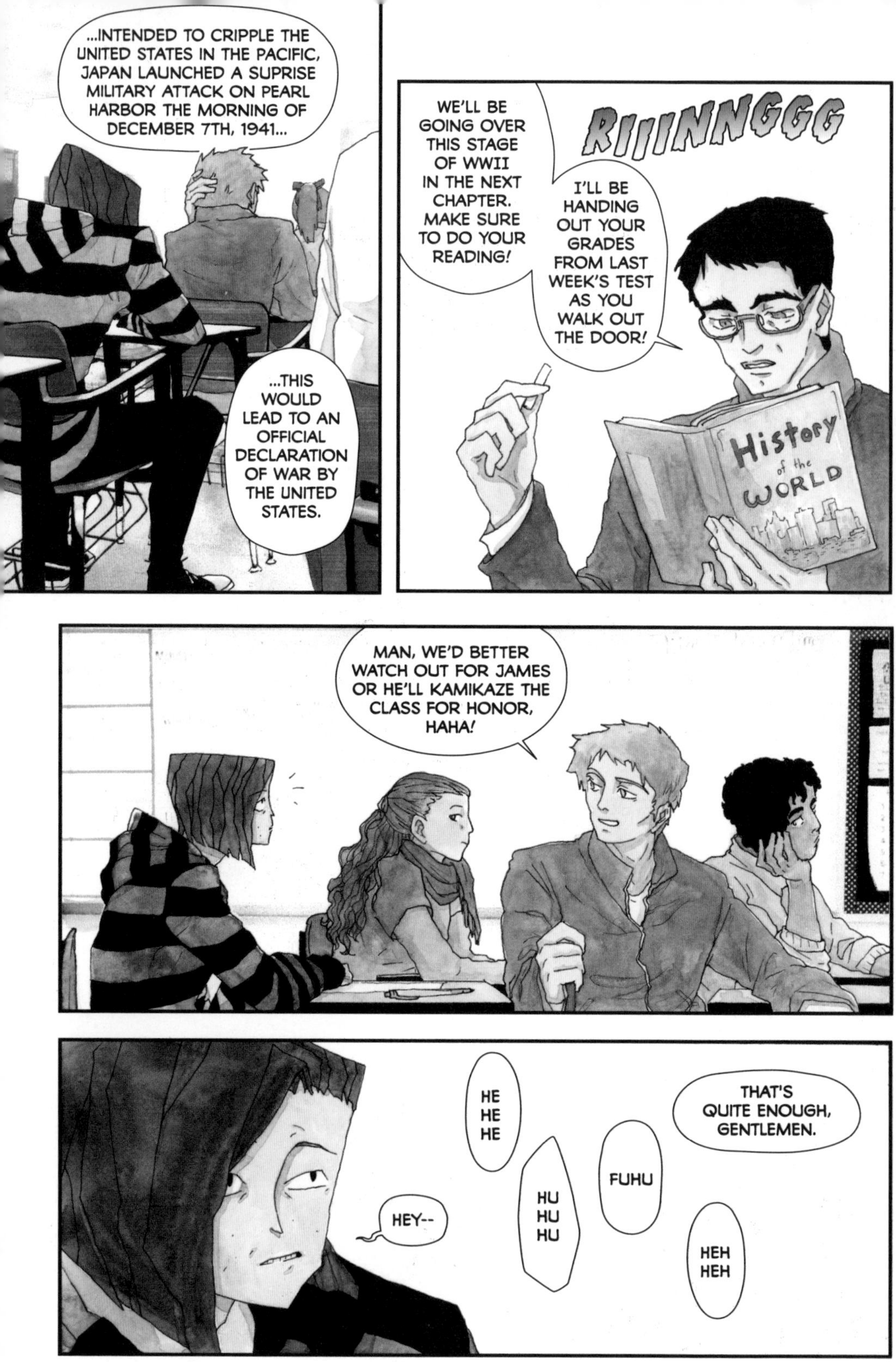
...INTENDED TO CRIPPLE THE UNITED STATES IN THE PACIFIC, JAPAN LAUNCHED A SUPRISE MILITARY ATTACK ON PEARL HARBOR THE MORNING OF DECEMBER 7TH, 1941...
...THIS WOULD LEAD TO AN OFFICIAL DECLARATION OF WAR BY THE UNITED STATES.
RIIINNGGG
WE'LL BE GOING OVER THIS STAGE OF WWII IN THE NEXT CHAPTER. MAKE SURE TO DO YOUR READING!
I'LL BE HANDING OUT YOUR GRADES FROM LAST WEEK'S TEST AS YOU WALK OUT THE DOOR!
History of the WORLD
MAN, WE'D BETTER WATCH OUT FOR JAMES OR HE'LL KAMIKAZE THE CLASS FOR HONOR, HAHA!
HEY--
HE HE HE
HU HU HU
FUHU
HEH HEH
THAT'S QUITE ENOUGH, GENTLEMEN.

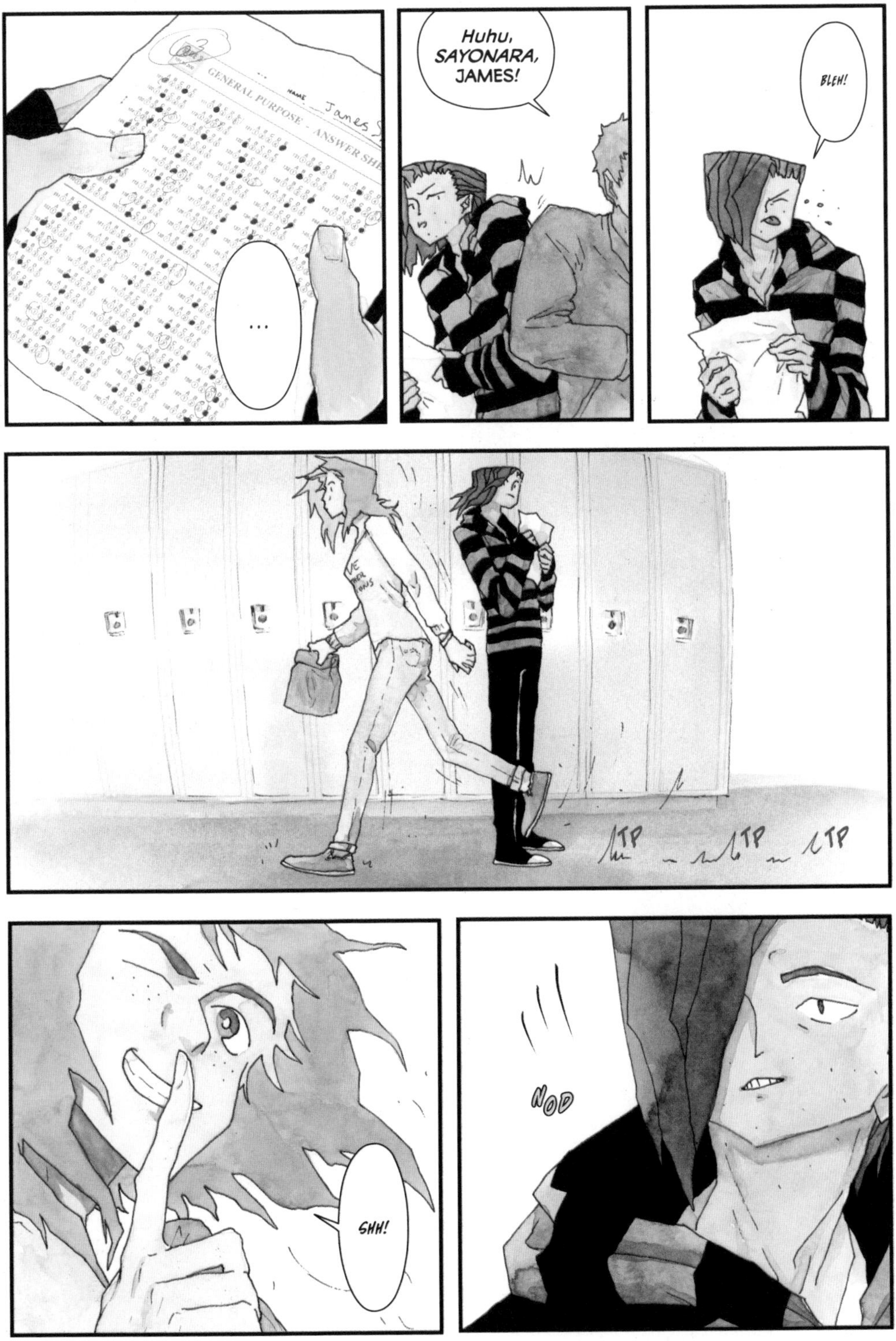
GENERAL PURPOSE - ANSWER SHE
NAME James
...
Huhu, SAYONARA, JAMES!
BLEH!
TP
TP
TP
SHH!
NOD

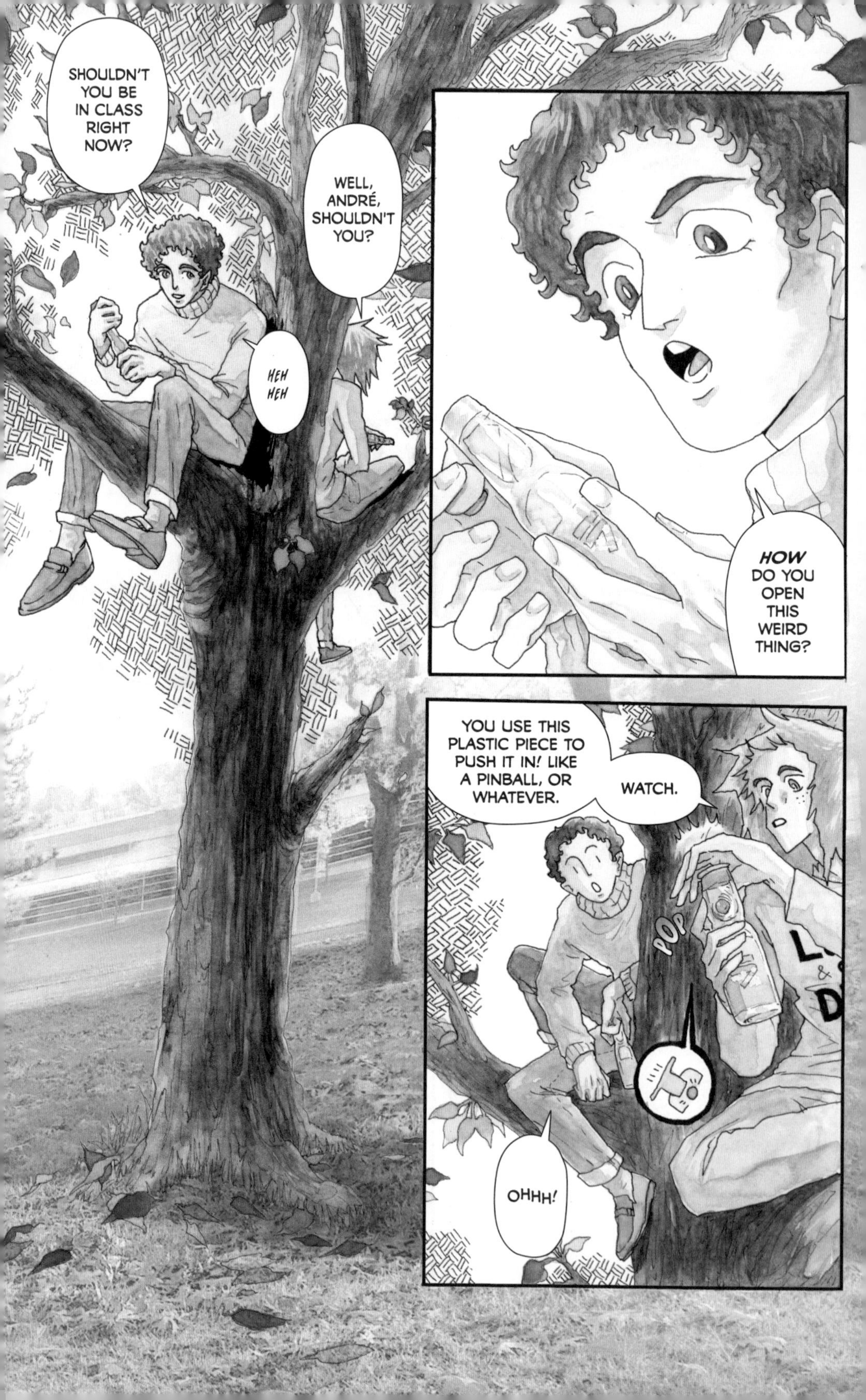

SHOULDN'T YOU BE IN CLASS RIGHT NOW?
WELL, ANDRÉ, SHOULDN'T YOU?
HEH HEH
HOW DO YOU OPEN THIS WEIRD THING?
YOU USE THIS PLASTIC PIECE TO PUSH IT IN! LIKE A PINBALL, OR WHATEVER.
WATCH.
POP
OHHH!

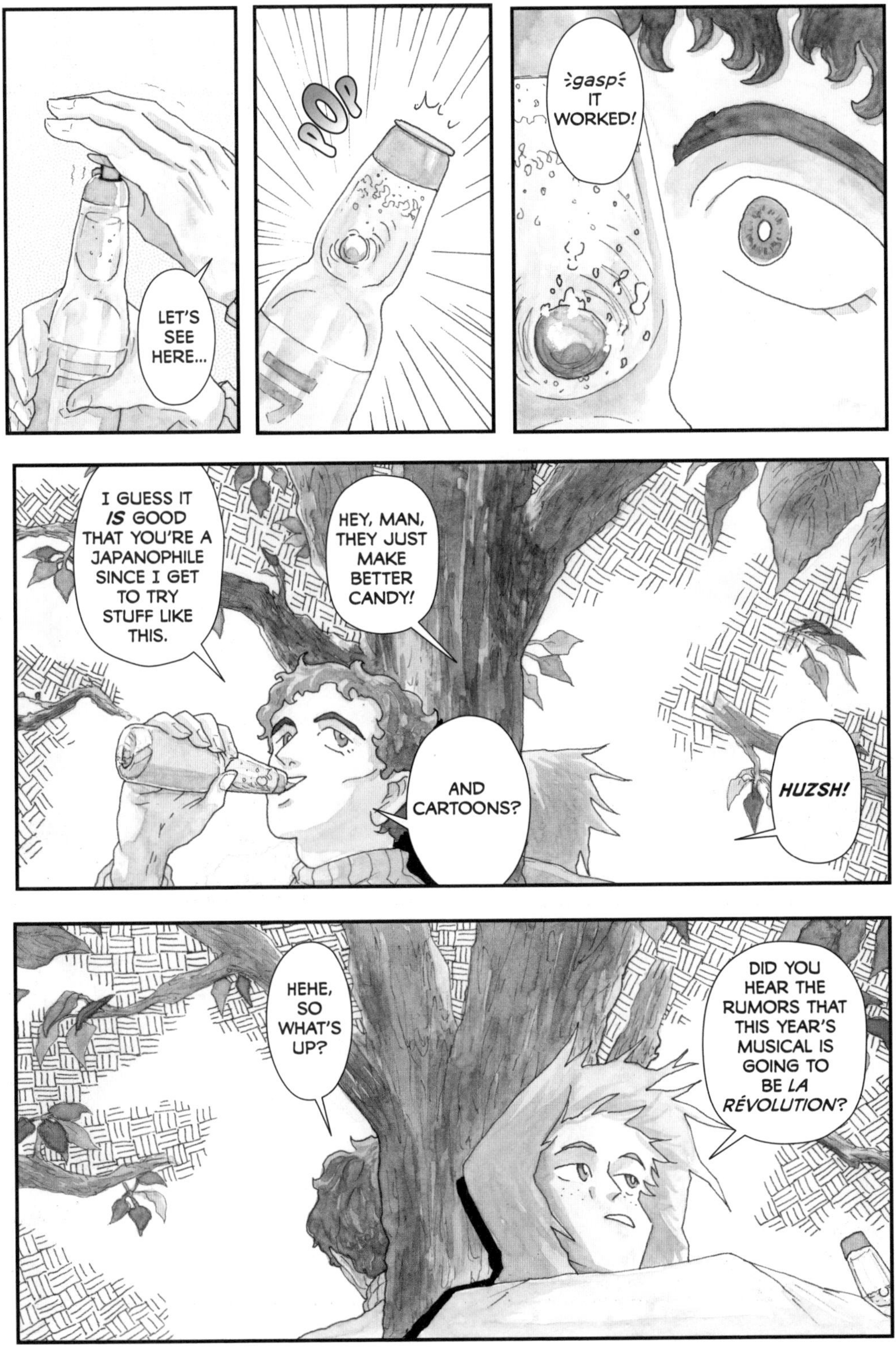
LET'S SEE HERE...
POP
gasp IT WORKED!
I GUESS IT *IS* GOOD THAT YOU'RE A JAPANOPHILE SINCE I GET TO TRY STUFF LIKE THIS.
HEY, MAN, THEY JUST MAKE BETTER CANDY!
AND CARTOONS?
HUZSH!
HEHE, SO WHAT'S UP?
DID YOU HEAR THE RUMORS THAT THIS YEAR'S MUSICAL IS GOING TO BE *LA RÉVOLUTION*?

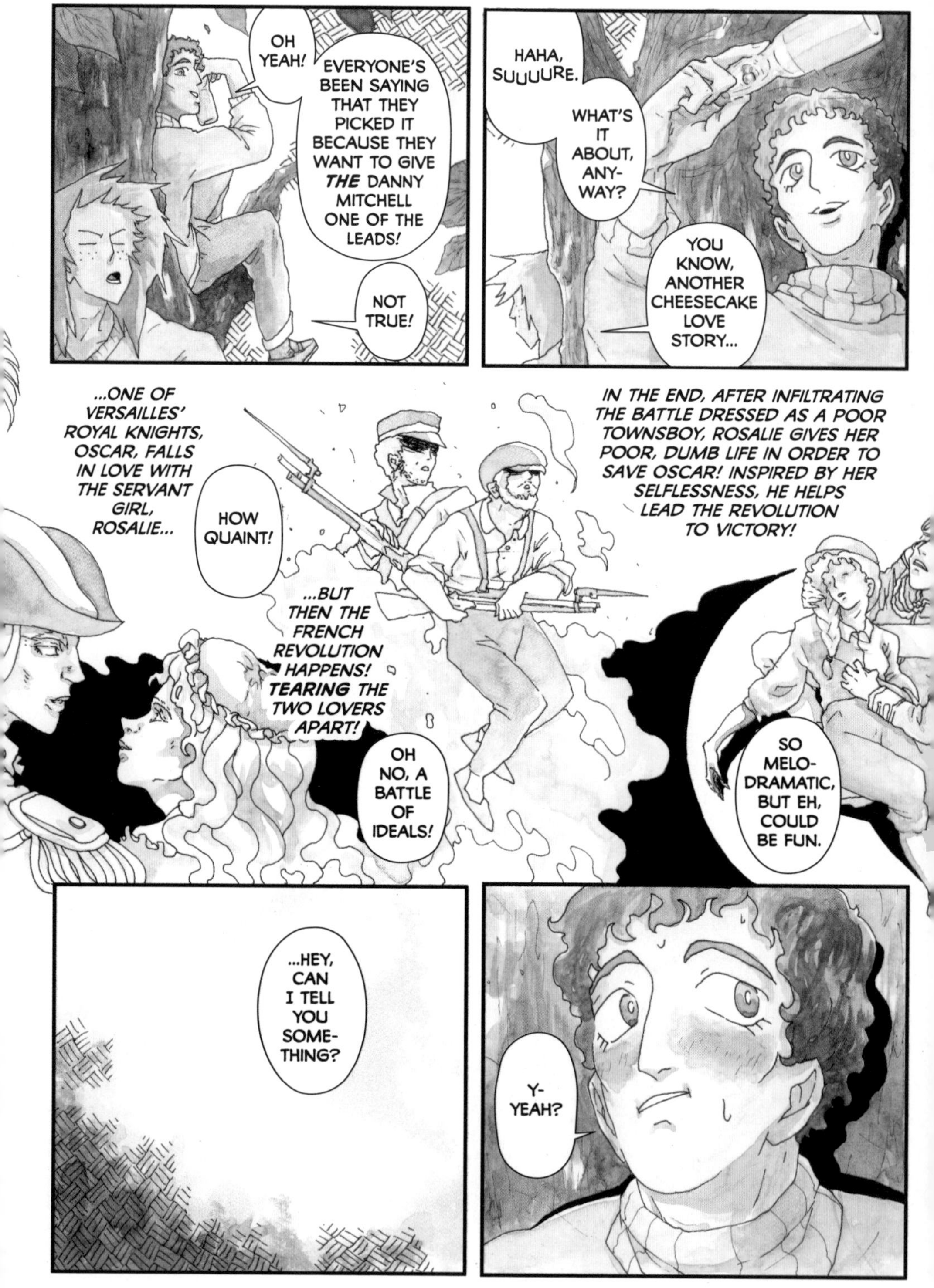
OH YEAH!
EVERYONE'S BEEN SAYING THAT THEY PICKED IT BECAUSE THEY WANT TO GIVE THE DANNY MITCHELL ONE OF THE LEADS!
NOT TRUE!
HAHA, SUUUURE.
WHAT'S IT ABOUT, ANYWAY?
YOU KNOW, ANOTHER CHEESECAKE LOVE STORY...
...ONE OF VERSAILLES' ROYAL KNIGHTS, OSCAR, FALLS IN LOVE WITH THE SERVANT GIRL, ROSALIE...
HOW QUAINT!
...BUT THEN THE FRENCH REVOLUTION HAPPENS! TEARING THE TWO LOVERS APART!
OH NO, A BATTLE OF IDEALS!
IN THE END, AFTER INFILTRATING THE BATTLE DRESSED AS A POOR TOWNSBOY, ROSALIE GIVES HER POOR, DUMB LIFE IN ORDER TO SAVE OSCAR! INSPIRED BY HER SELFLESSNESS, HE HELPS LEAD THE REVOLUTION TO VICTORY!
SO MELODRAMATIC, BUT EH, COULD BE FUN.
...HEY, CAN I TELL YOU SOMETHING?
Y-YEAH?

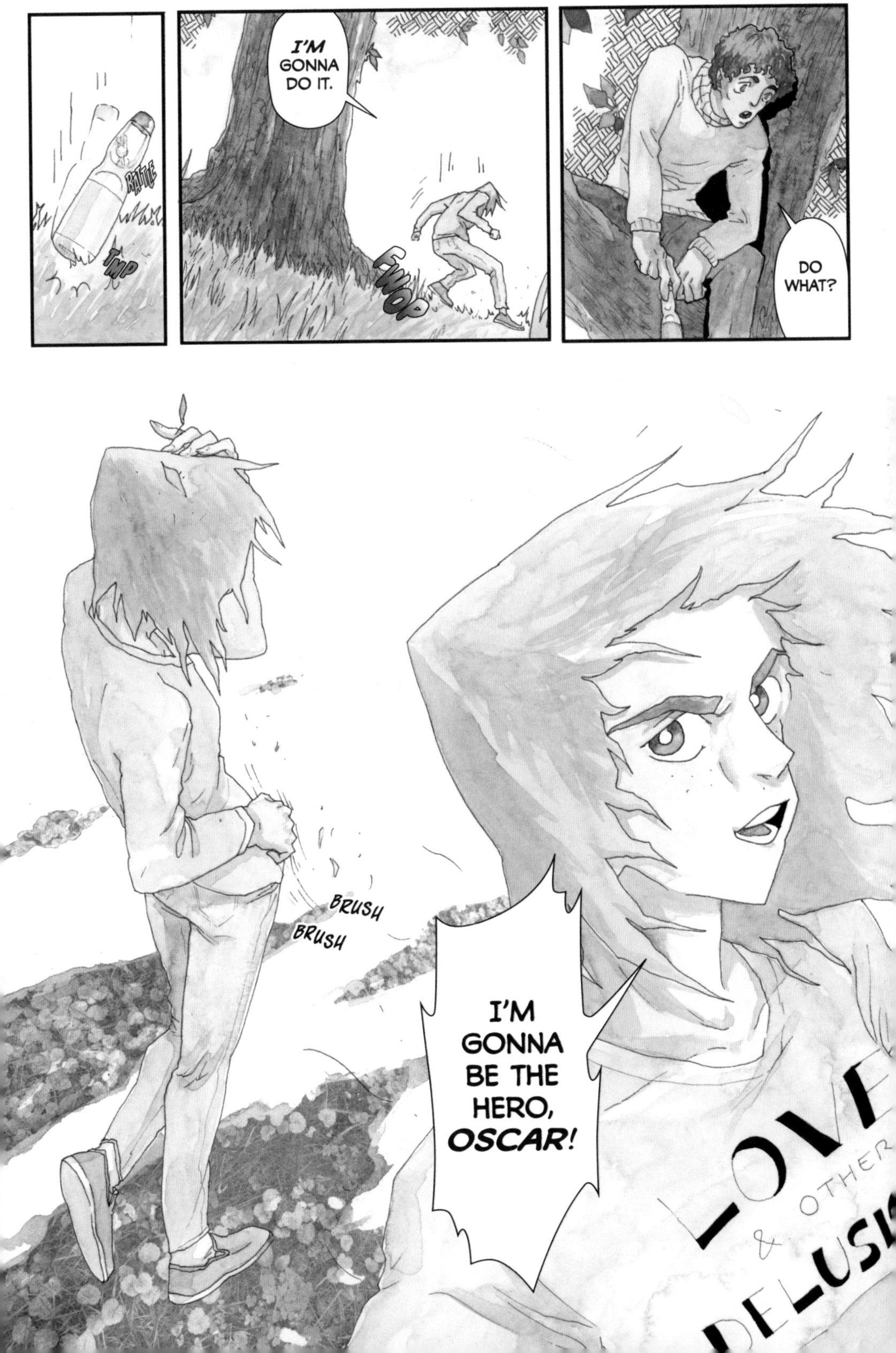
RATTLE
TMP
I'M GONNA DO IT.
FWOP
DO WHAT?
BRUSH
BRUSH
I'M GONNA BE THE HERO, *OSCAR*!
& OTHER

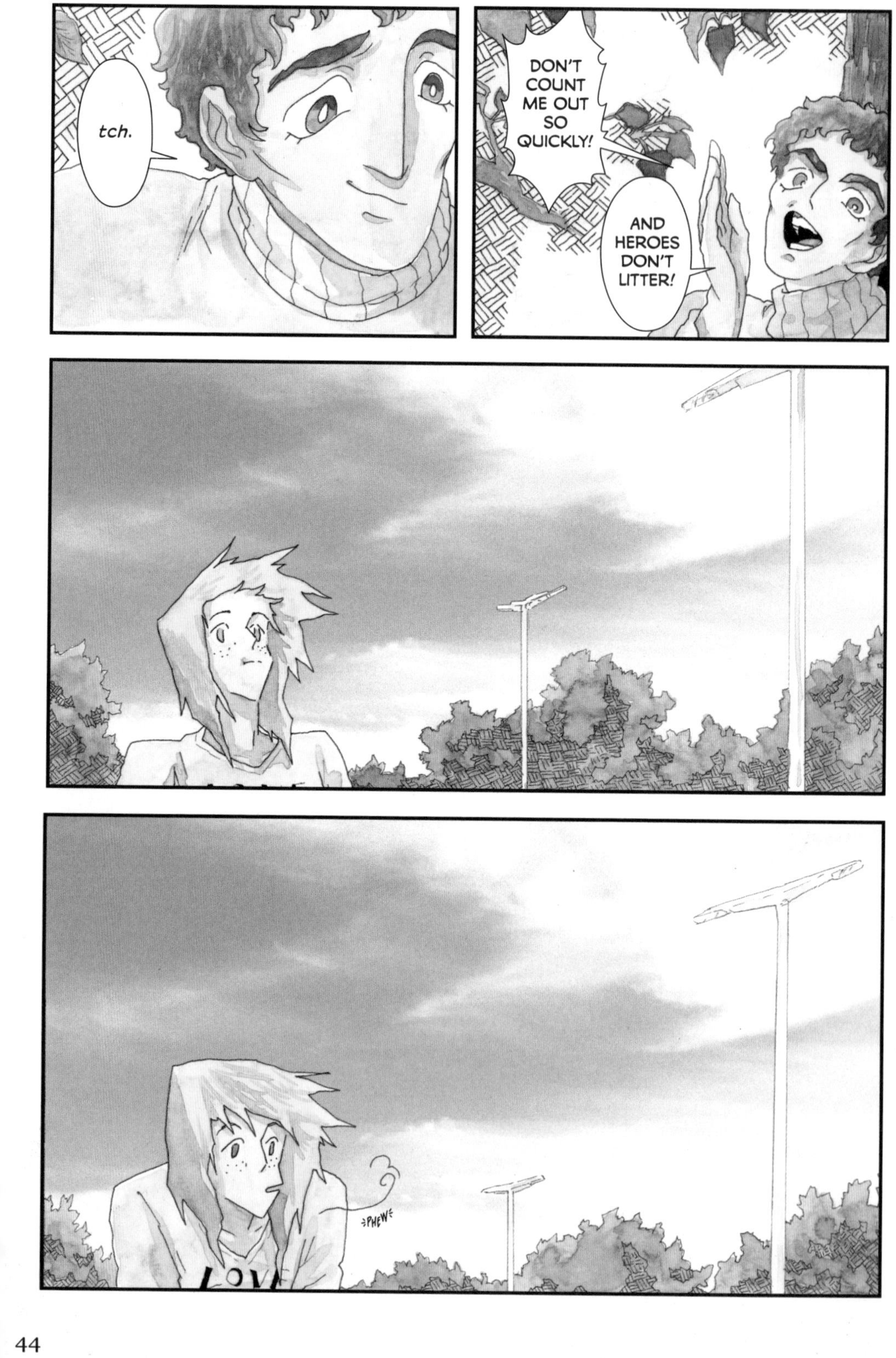
tch.
DON'T COUNT ME OUT SO QUICKLY!
AND HEROES DON'T LITTER!
PHEW

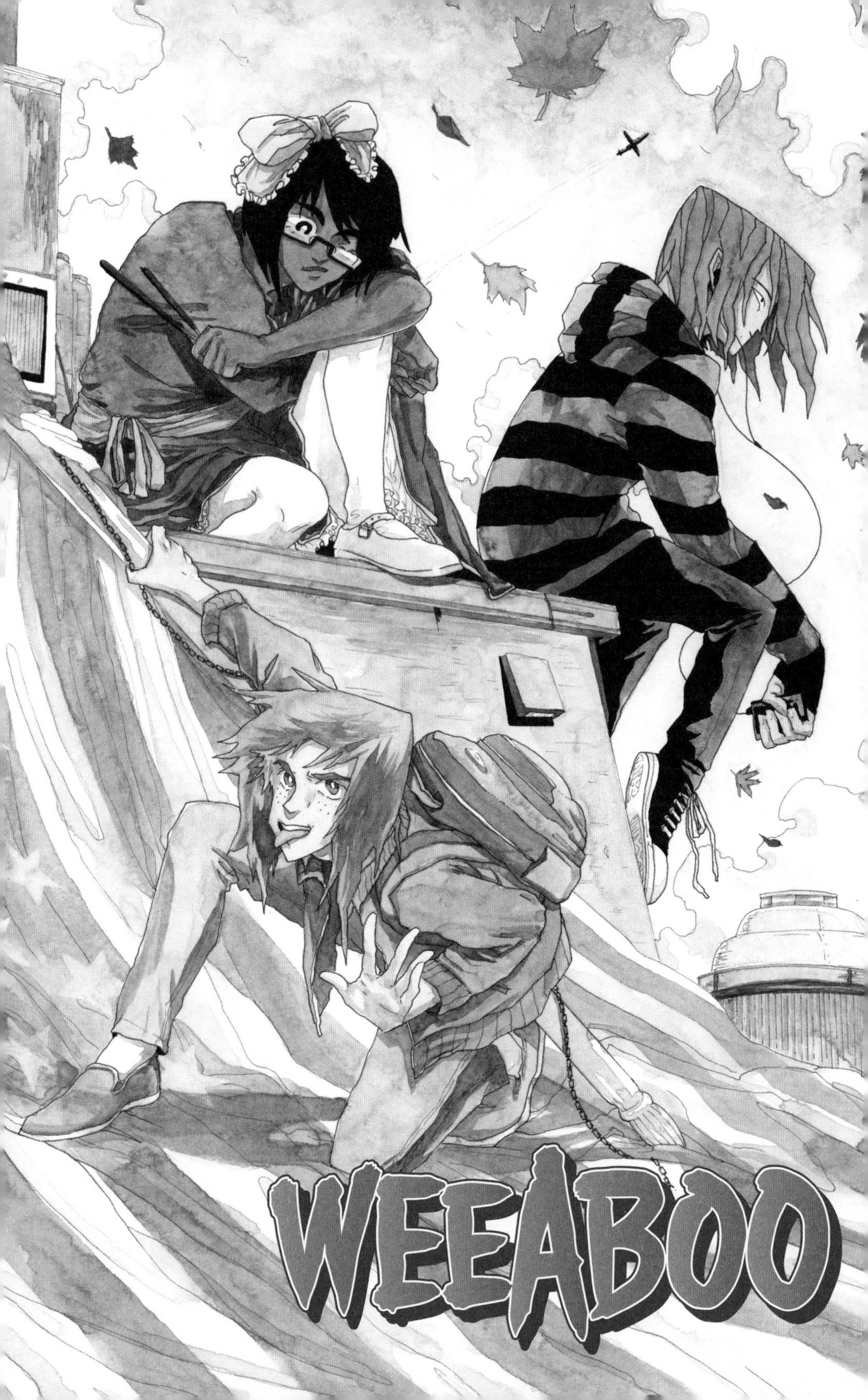
WEEABOO

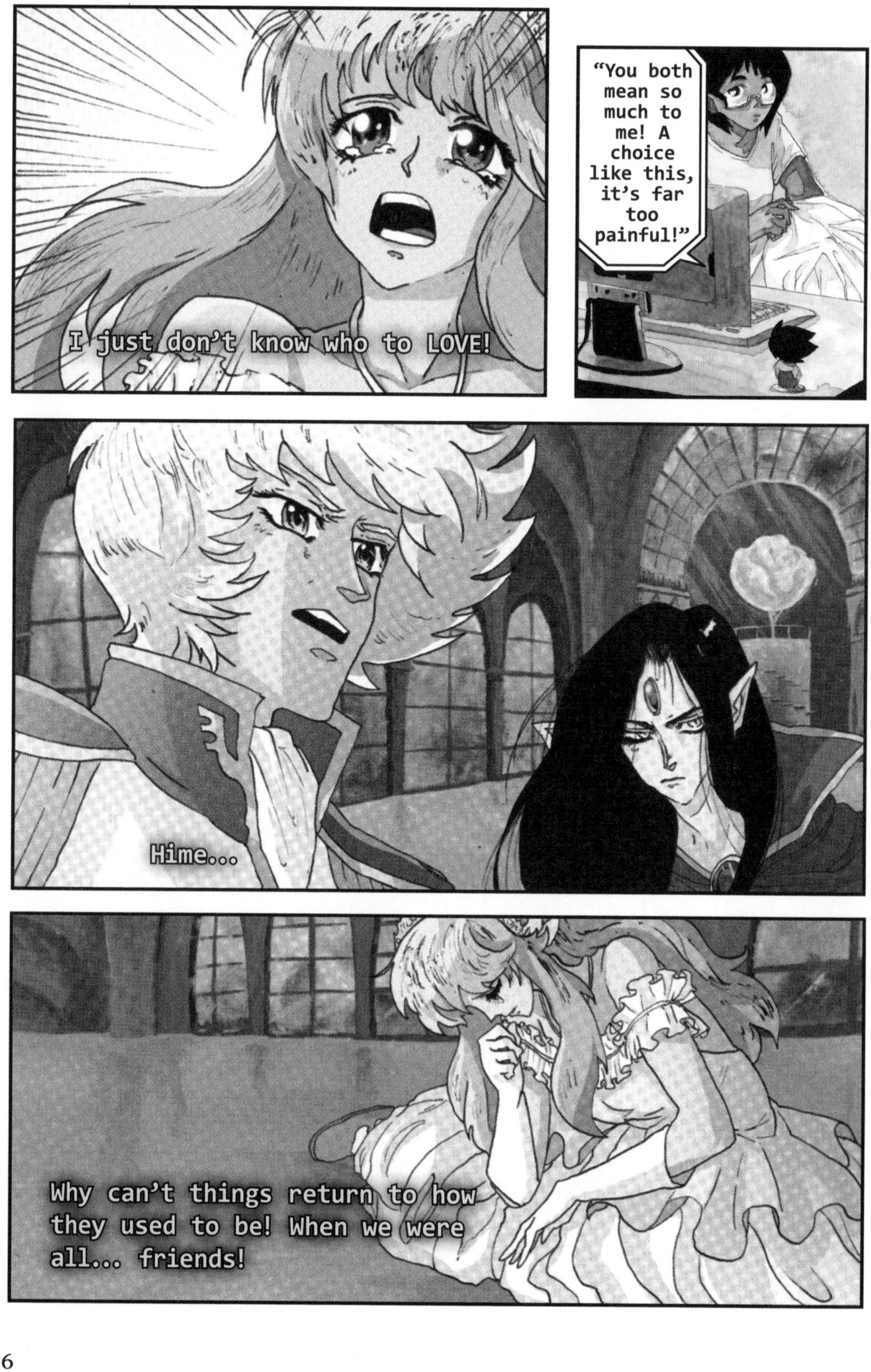
I just don't know who to LOVE!
"You both mean so much to me! A choice like this, it's far too painful!"
Hime...
Why can't things return to how they used to be! When we were all... friends!

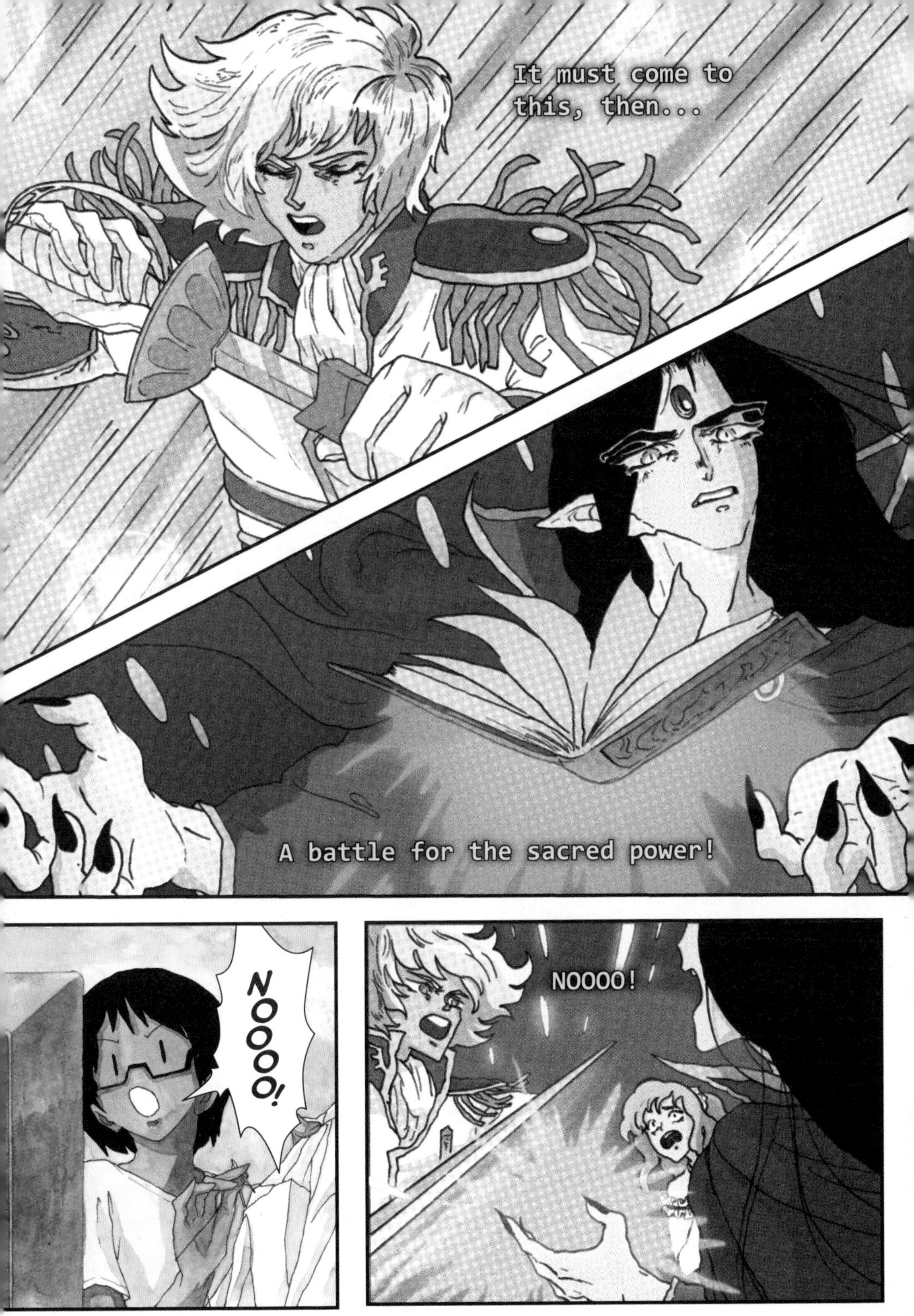
It must come to this, then...
A battle for the sacred power!
NOOOO!
NOOOO!

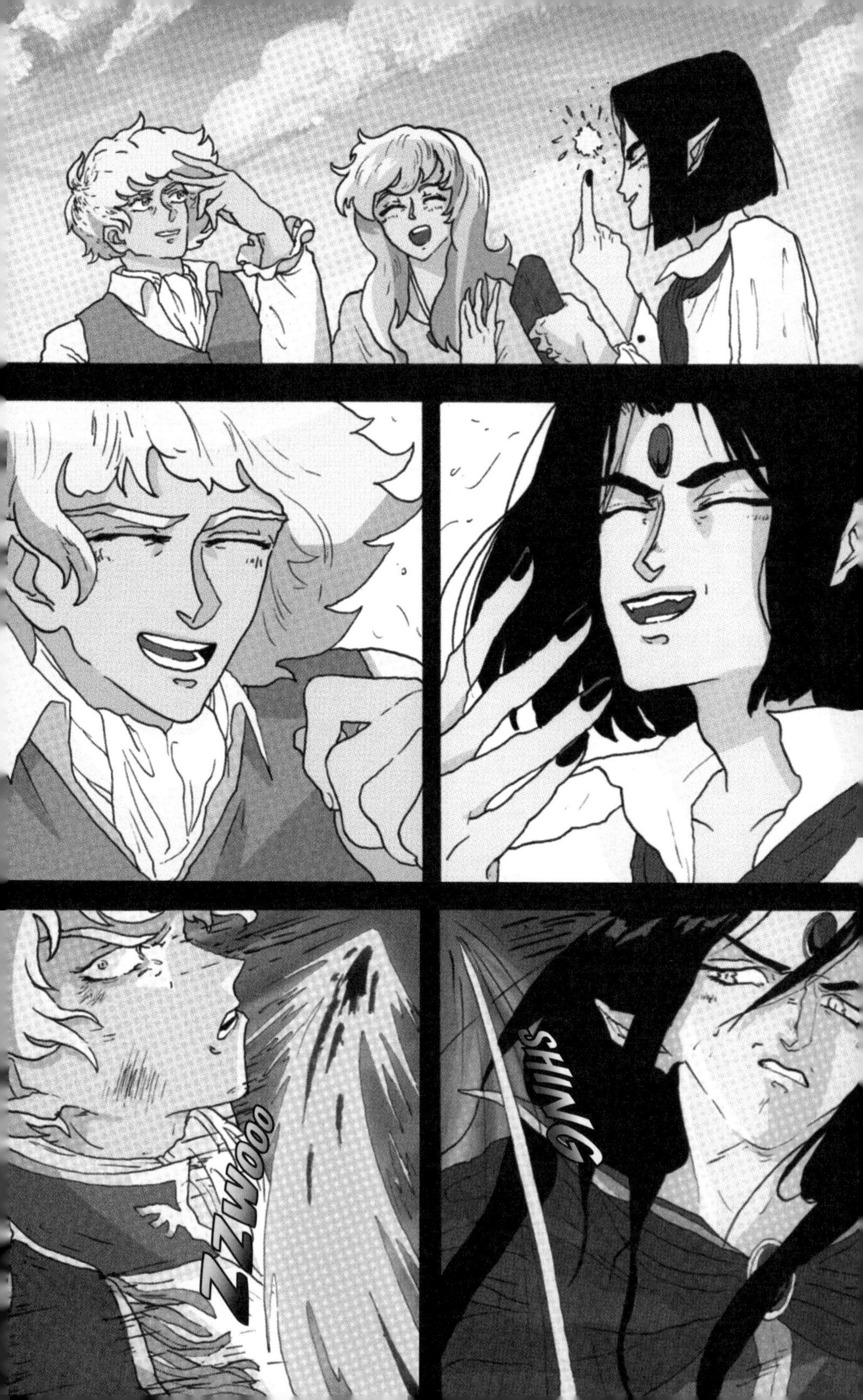
ZZWOOO
SHING

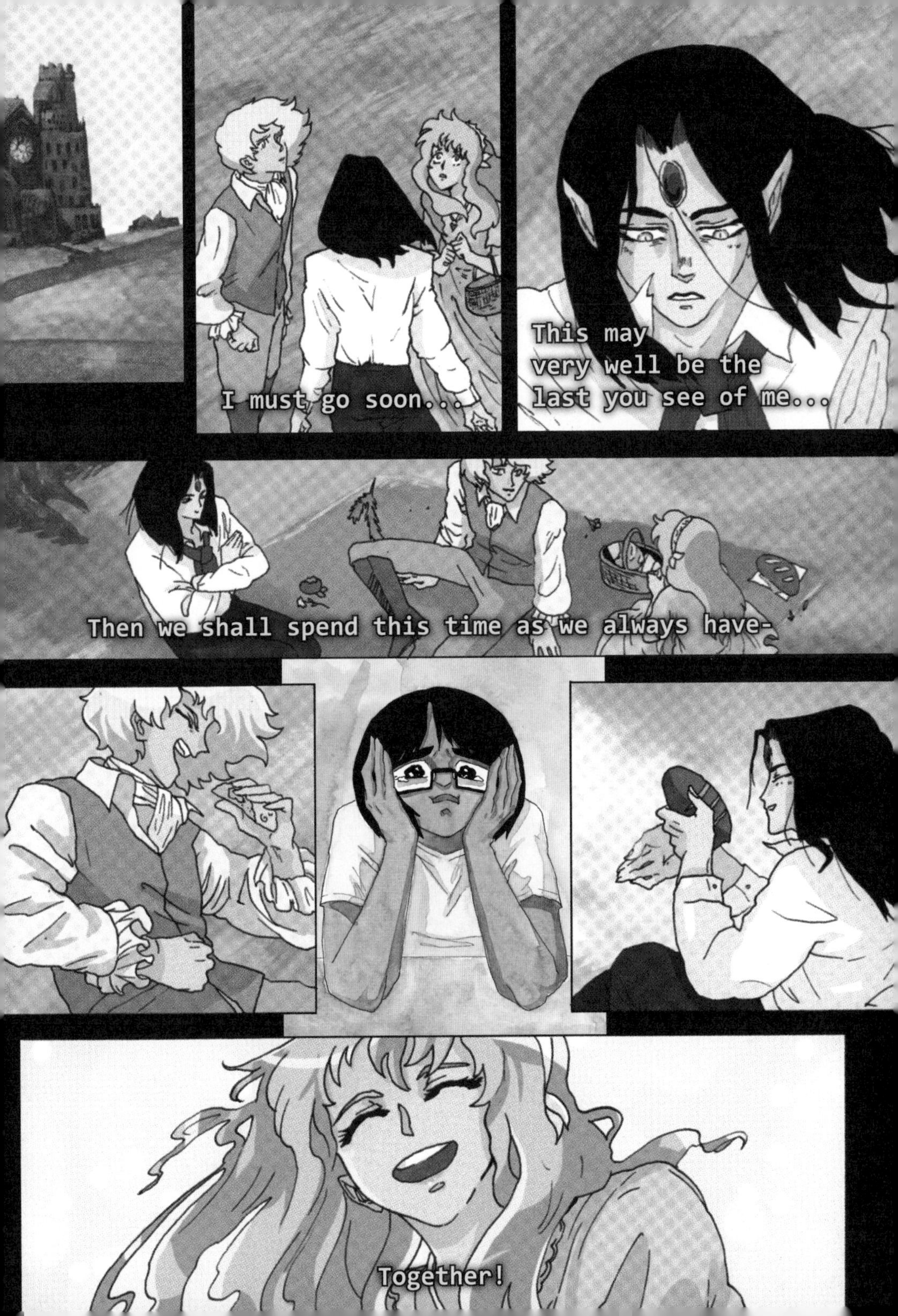
I must go soon...
This may very well be the last you see of me...
Then we shall spend this time as we always have-
Together!

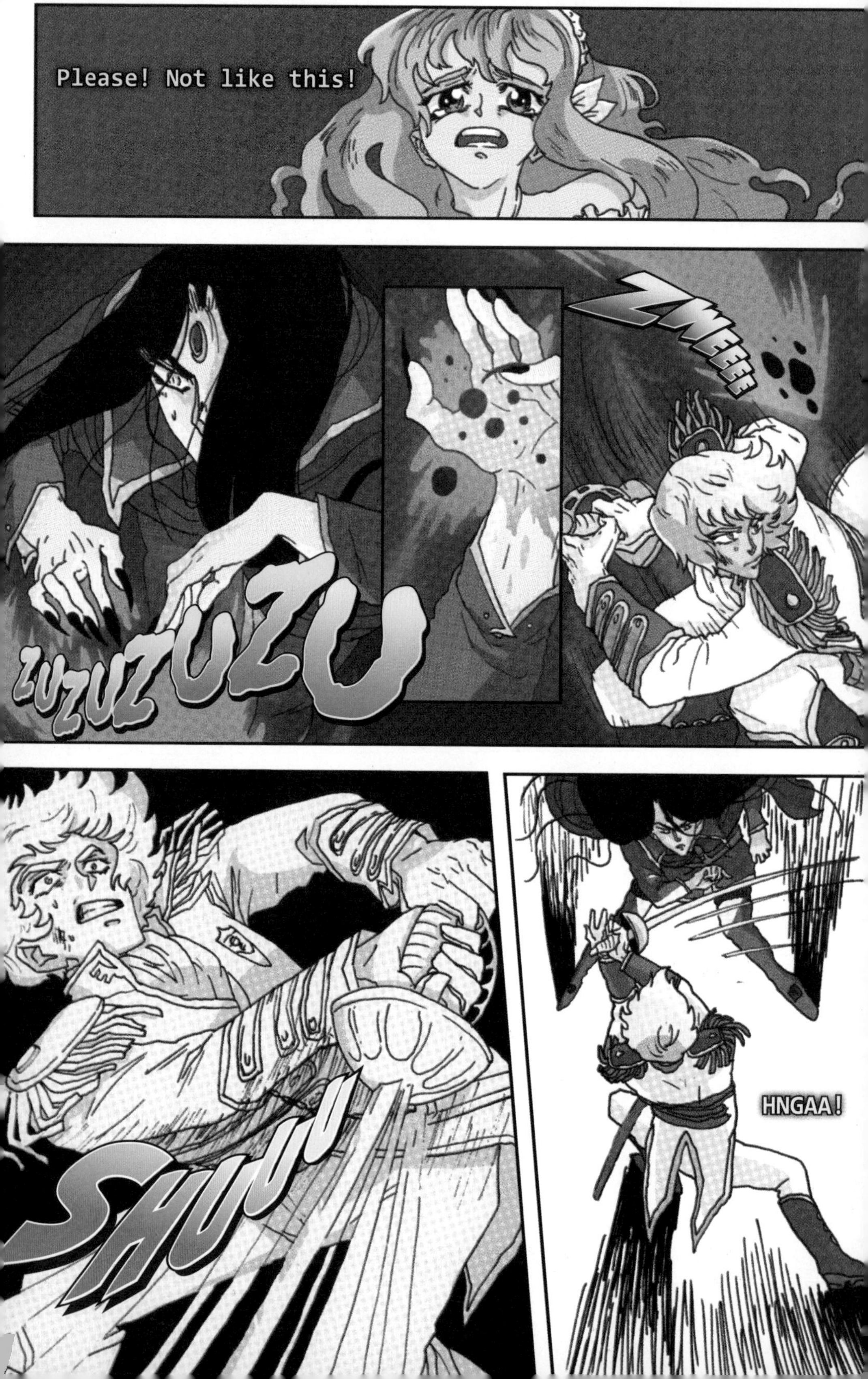

Please! Not like this!
ZWEEEE
ZUZUZUZUZU
SHUUU
HNGAA!

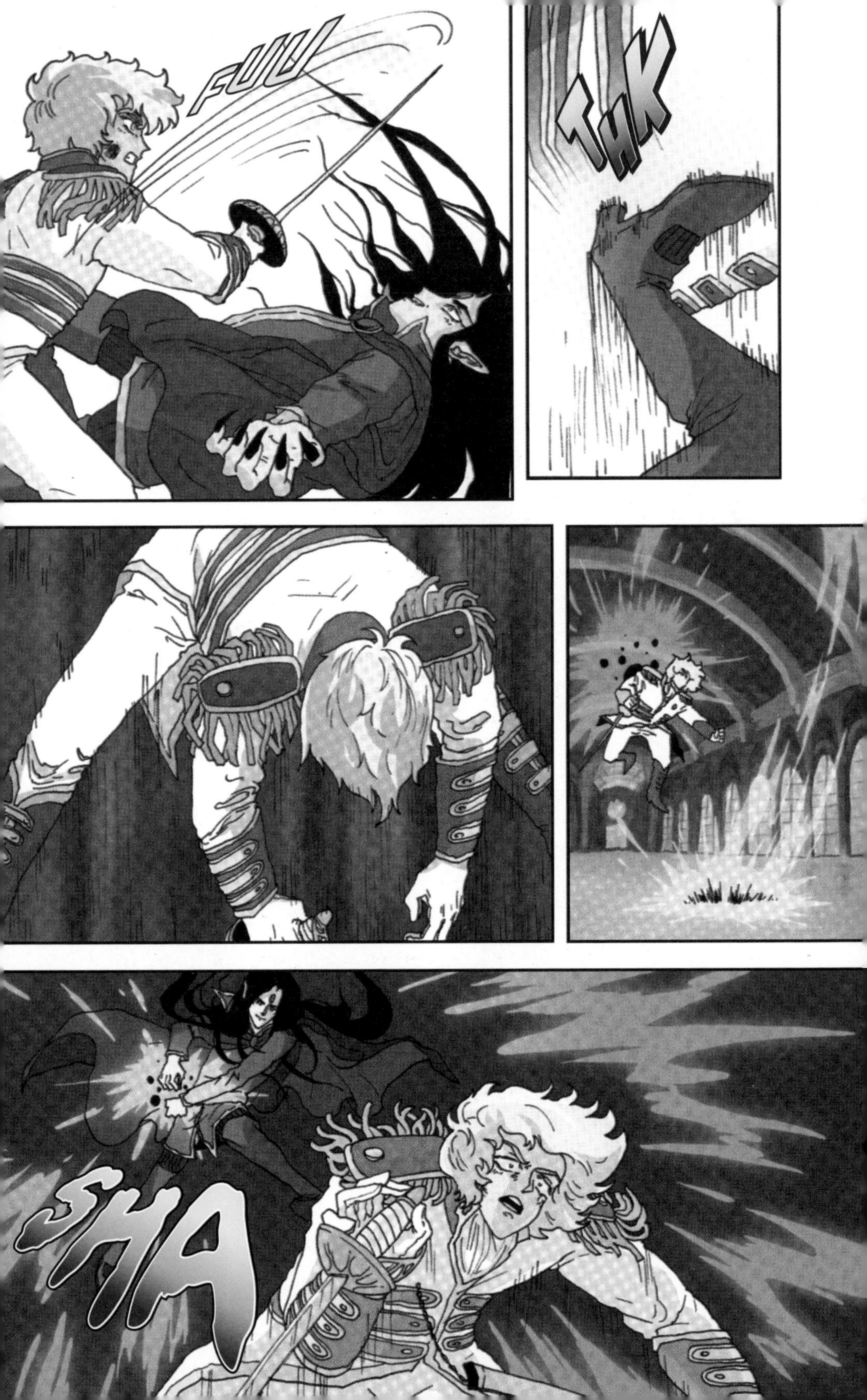
FUU
TAK
SHA

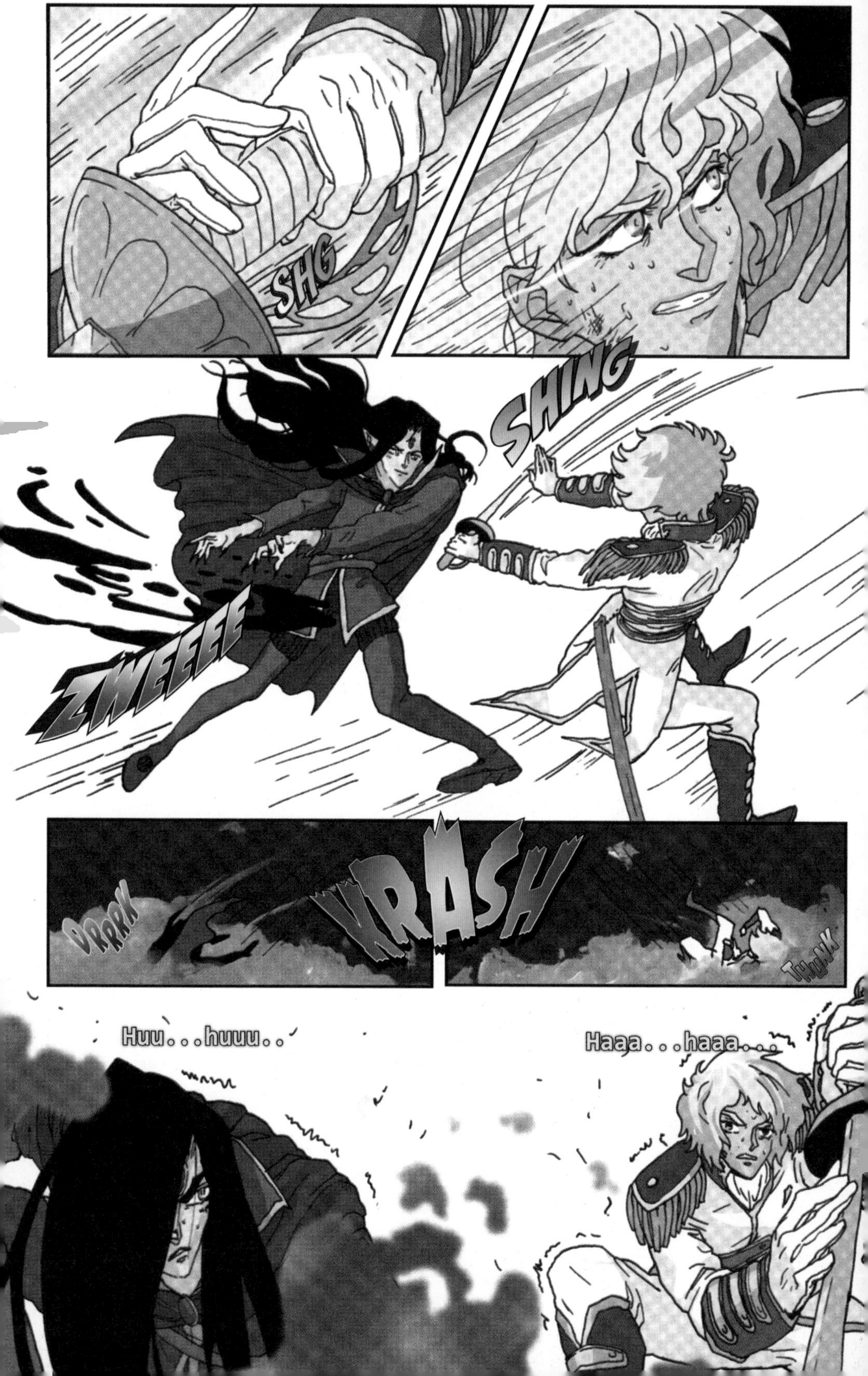
SHG
SHING
ZWEEEEE
DRRRK
KRASH
THUNK
Huu...huuu..
Haaa...haaa...

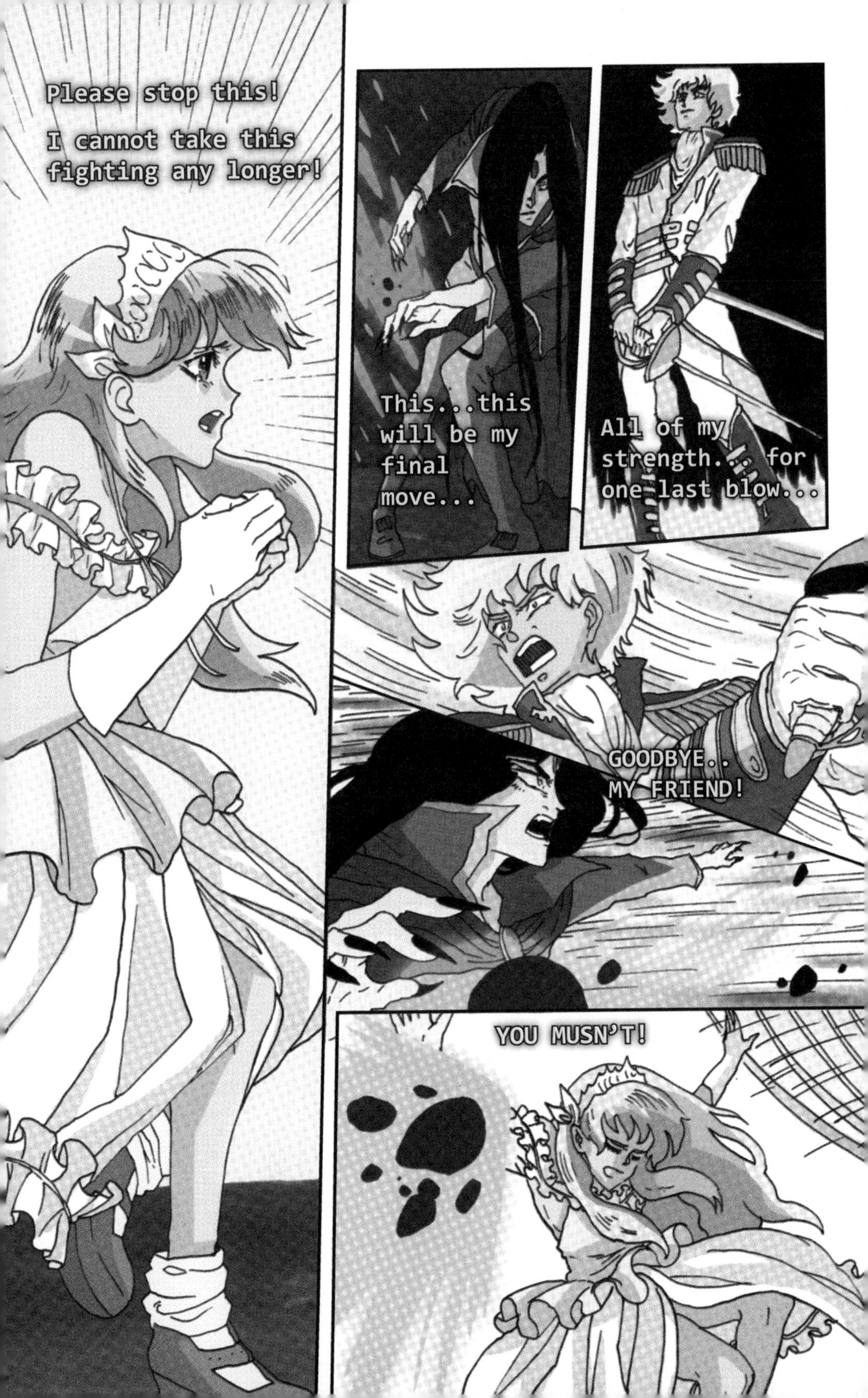

Please stop this!
I cannot take this fighting any longer!
This...this will be my final move...
All of my strength... for one last blow...
GOODBYE.. MY FRIEND!
YOU MUSN'T!

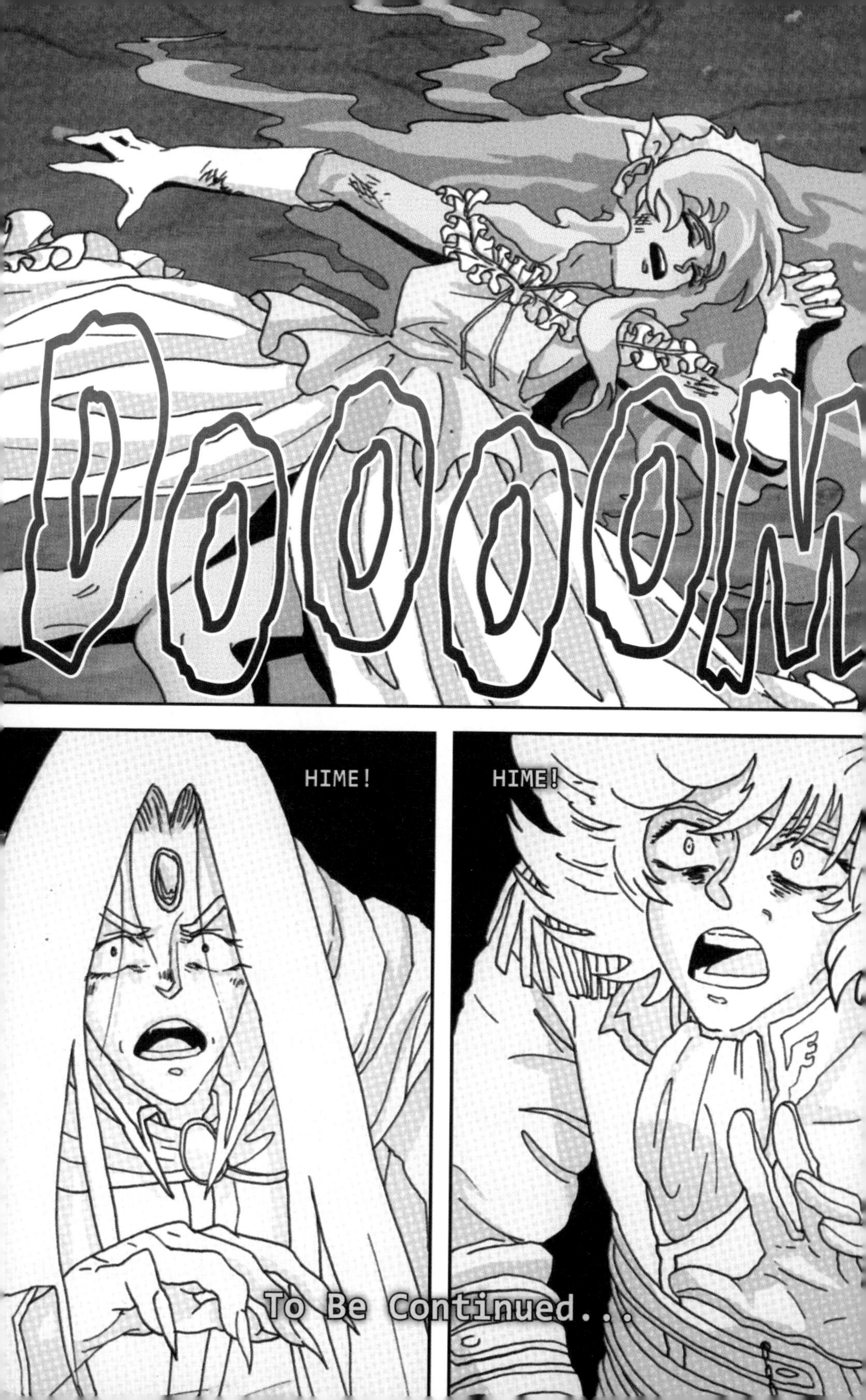
DOOOOOM
HIME!
HIME!
To Be Continued...

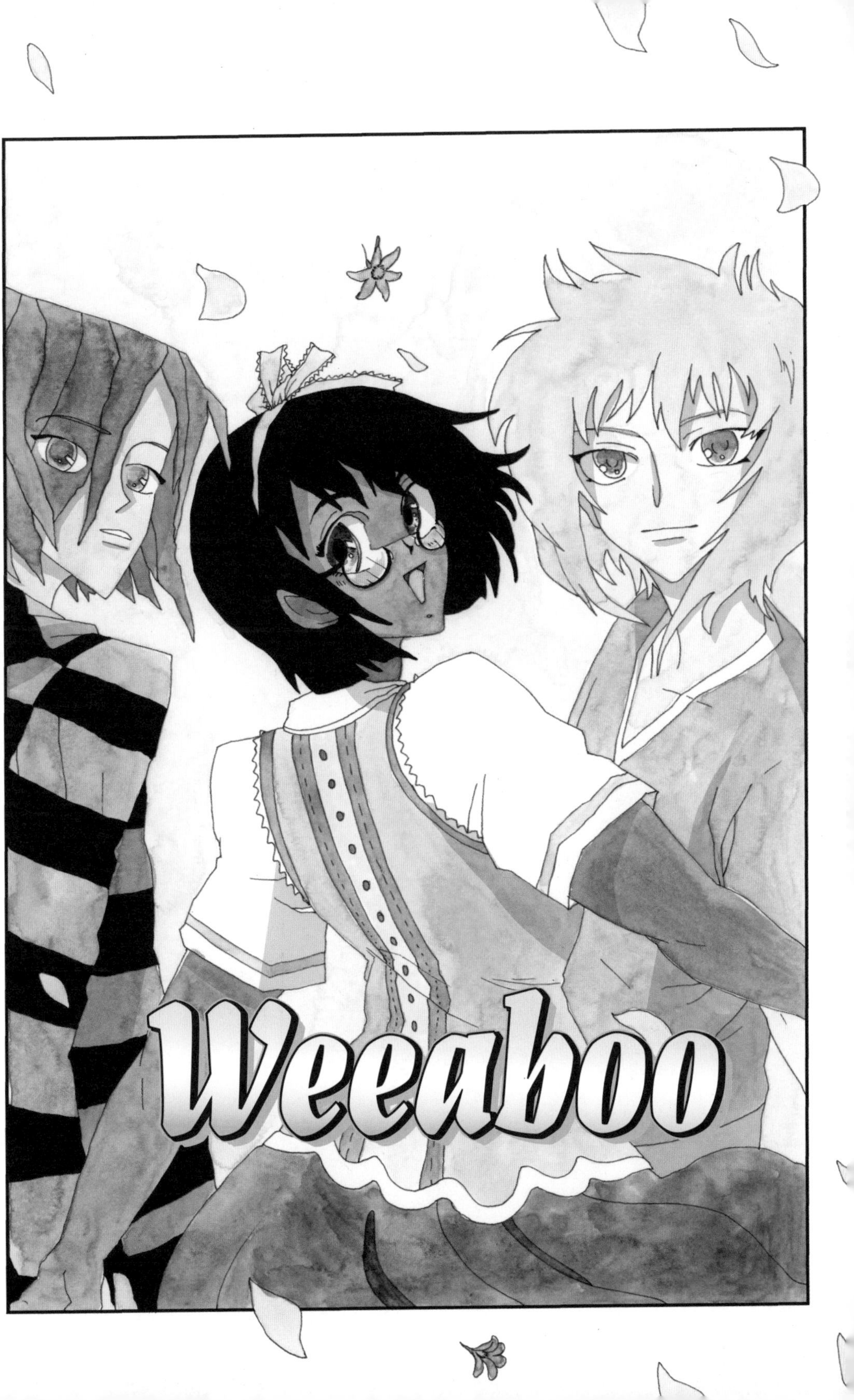
Weeaboo

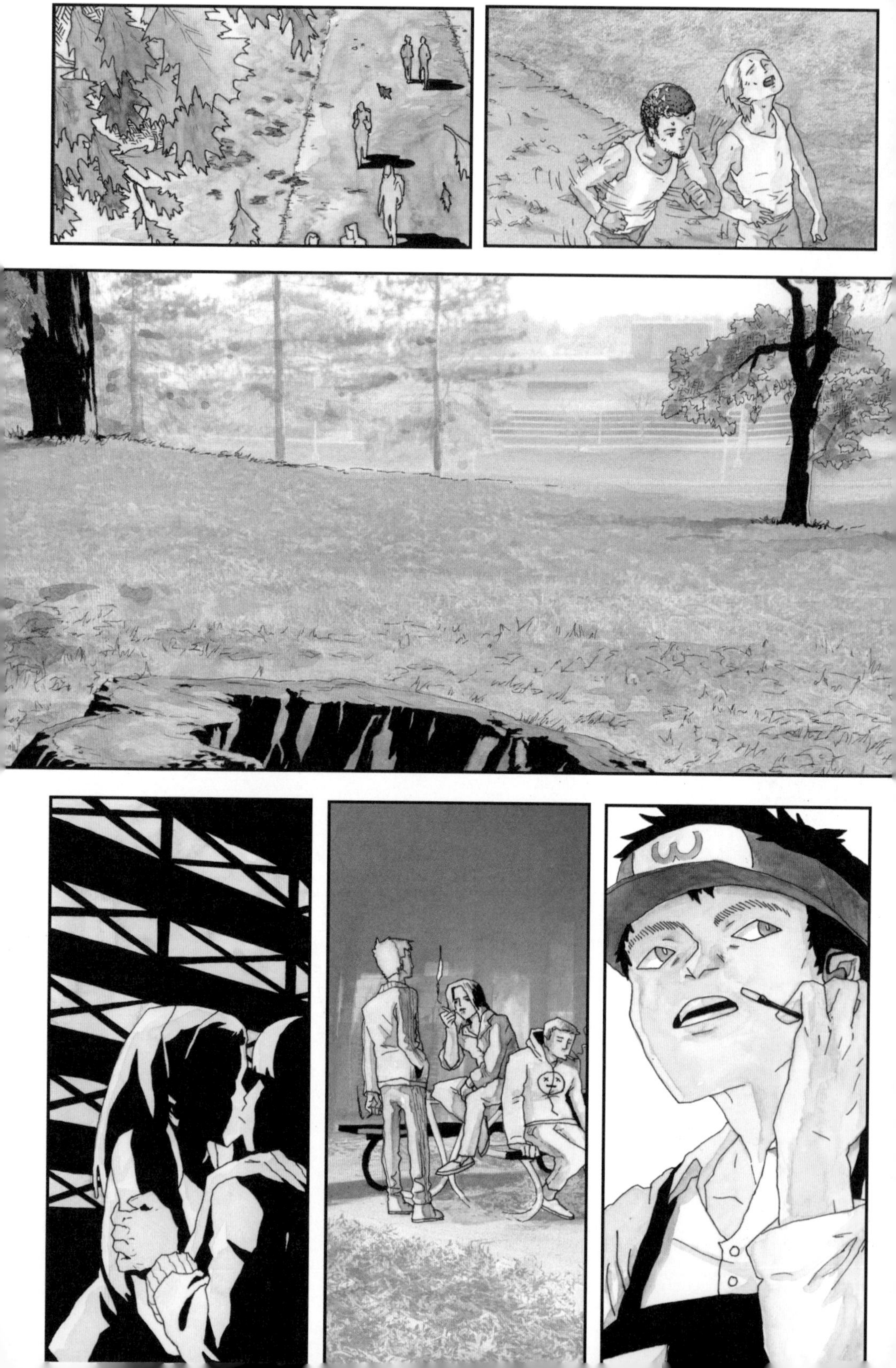

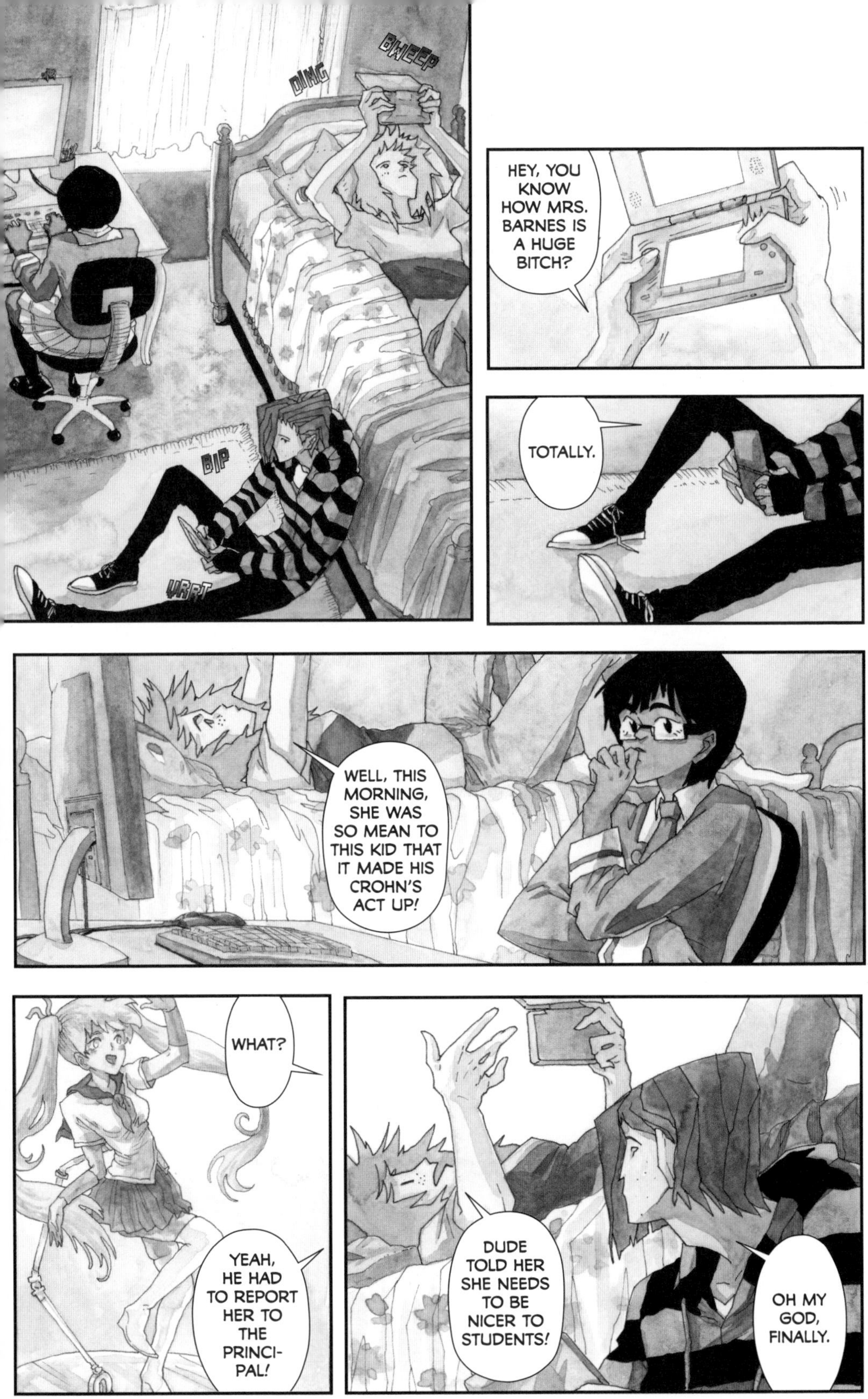
DING
BWEEP
BIP
VRRT
HEY, YOU KNOW HOW MRS. BARNES IS A HUGE BITCH?
TOTALLY.
WELL, THIS MORNING, SHE WAS SO MEAN TO THIS KID THAT IT MADE HIS CROHN'S ACT UP!
WHAT?
YEAH, HE HAD TO REPORT HER TO THE PRINCI-PAL!
DUDE TOLD HER SHE NEEDS TO BE NICER TO STUDENTS!
OH MY GOD, FINALLY.

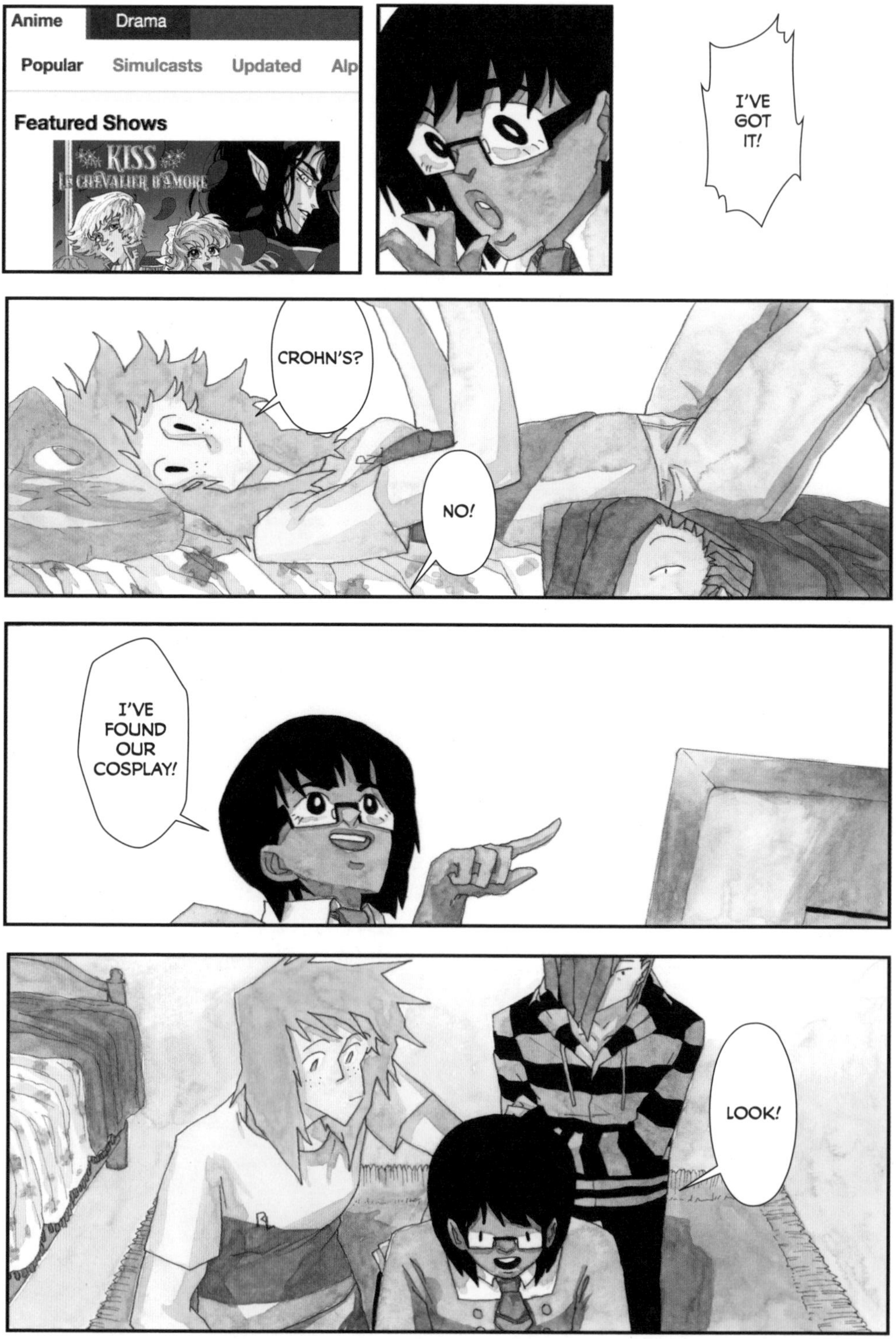
Anime
Drama
Popular
Simulcasts
Updated
Featured Shows
KISS
LE CHEVALIER D'AMORE
I'VE GOT IT!
CROHN'S?
NO!
I'VE FOUND OUR COSPLAY!
LOOK!

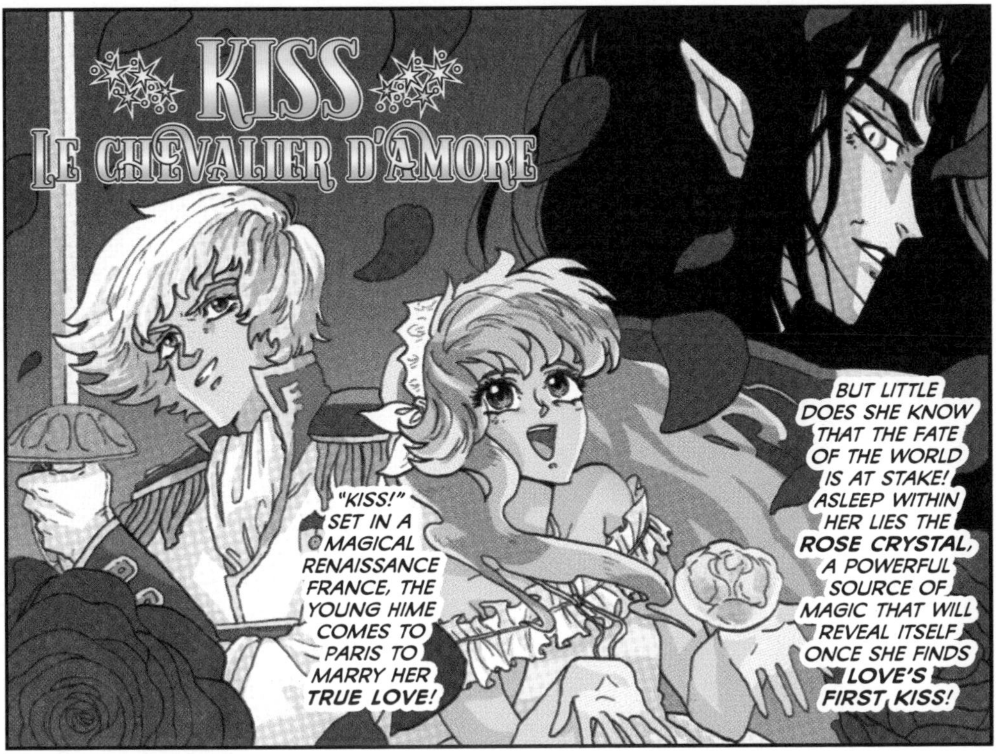
KISS
LE CHEVALIER D'AMORE
"KISS!" SET IN A MAGICAL RENAISSANCE FRANCE, THE YOUNG HIME COMES TO PARIS TO MARRY HER TRUE LOVE!
BUT LITTLE DOES SHE KNOW THAT THE FATE OF THE WORLD IS AT STAKE! ASLEEP WITHIN HER LIES THE ROSE CRYSTAL, A POWERFUL SOURCE OF MAGIC THAT WILL REVEAL ITSELF ONCE SHE FINDS LOVE'S FIRST KISS!

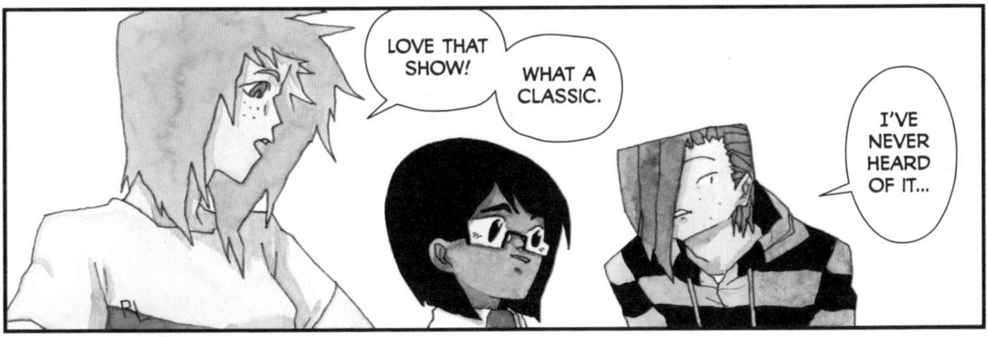
LOVE THAT SHOW!
WHAT A CLASSIC.
I'VE NEVER HEARD OF IT...

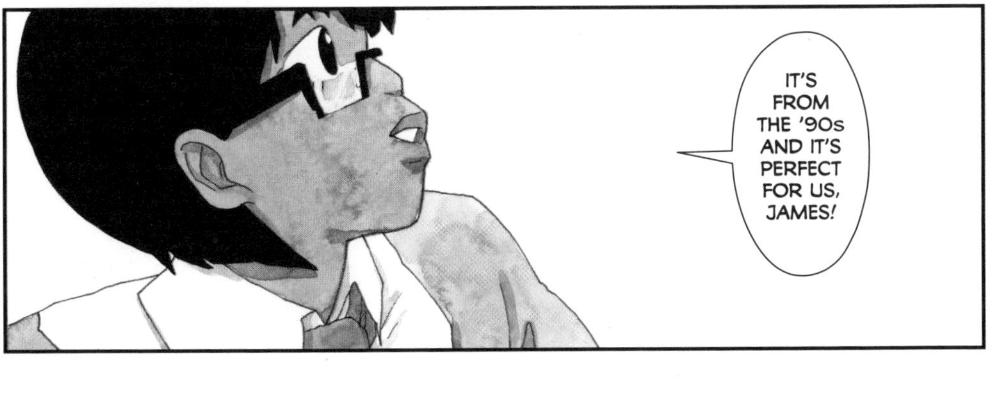
IT'S FROM THE '90s AND IT'S PERFECT FOR US, JAMES!

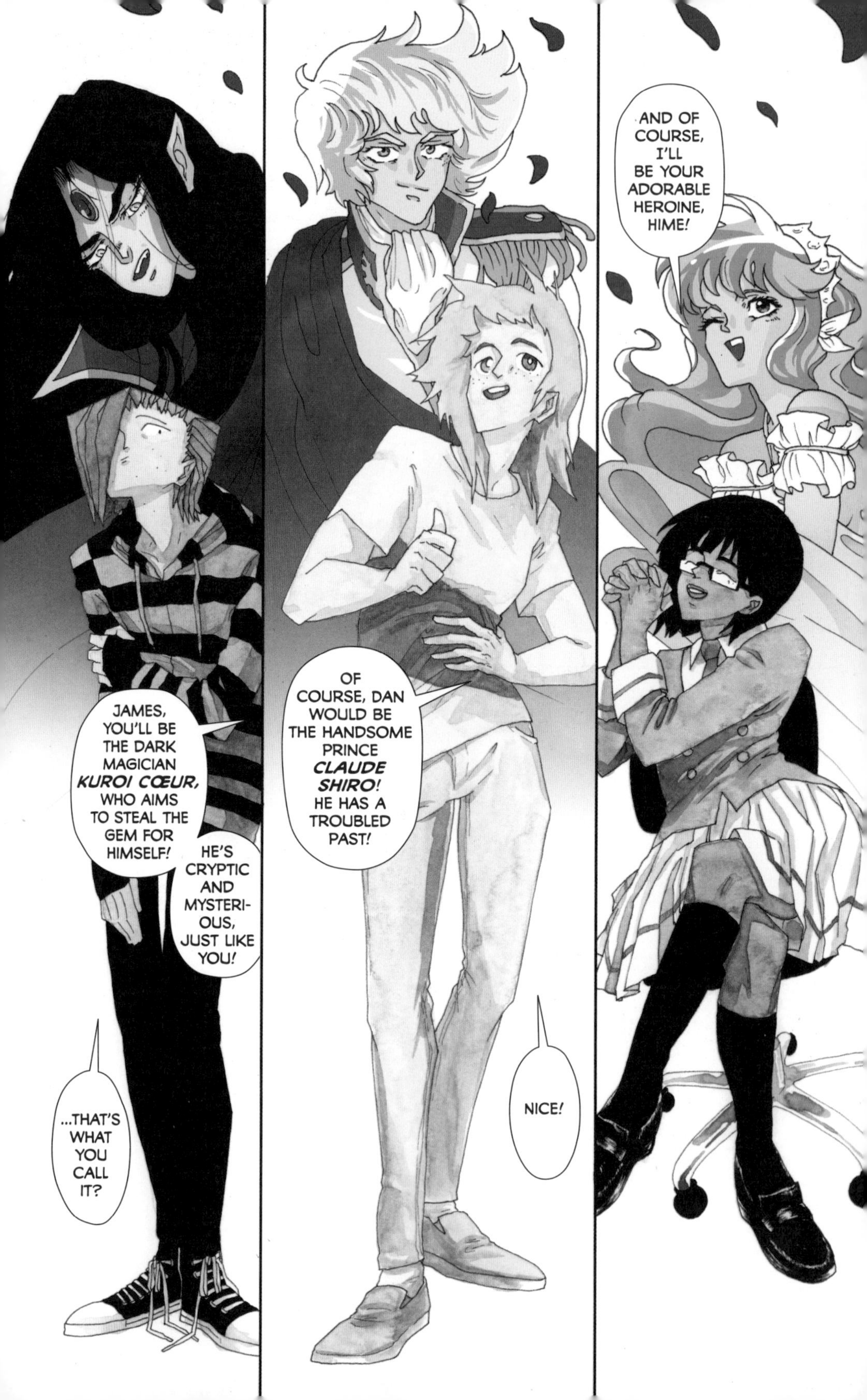
JAMES, YOU'LL BE THE DARK MAGICIAN ***KUROI CŒUR,*** WHO AIMS TO STEAL THE GEM FOR HIMSELF!
HE'S CRYPTIC AND MYSTERI-OUS, JUST LIKE YOU!
...THAT'S WHAT YOU CALL IT?
OF COURSE, DAN WOULD BE THE HANDSOME PRINCE ***CLAUDE SHIRO!*** HE HAS A TROUBLED PAST!
NICE!
AND OF COURSE, I'LL BE YOUR ADORABLE HEROINE, HIME!

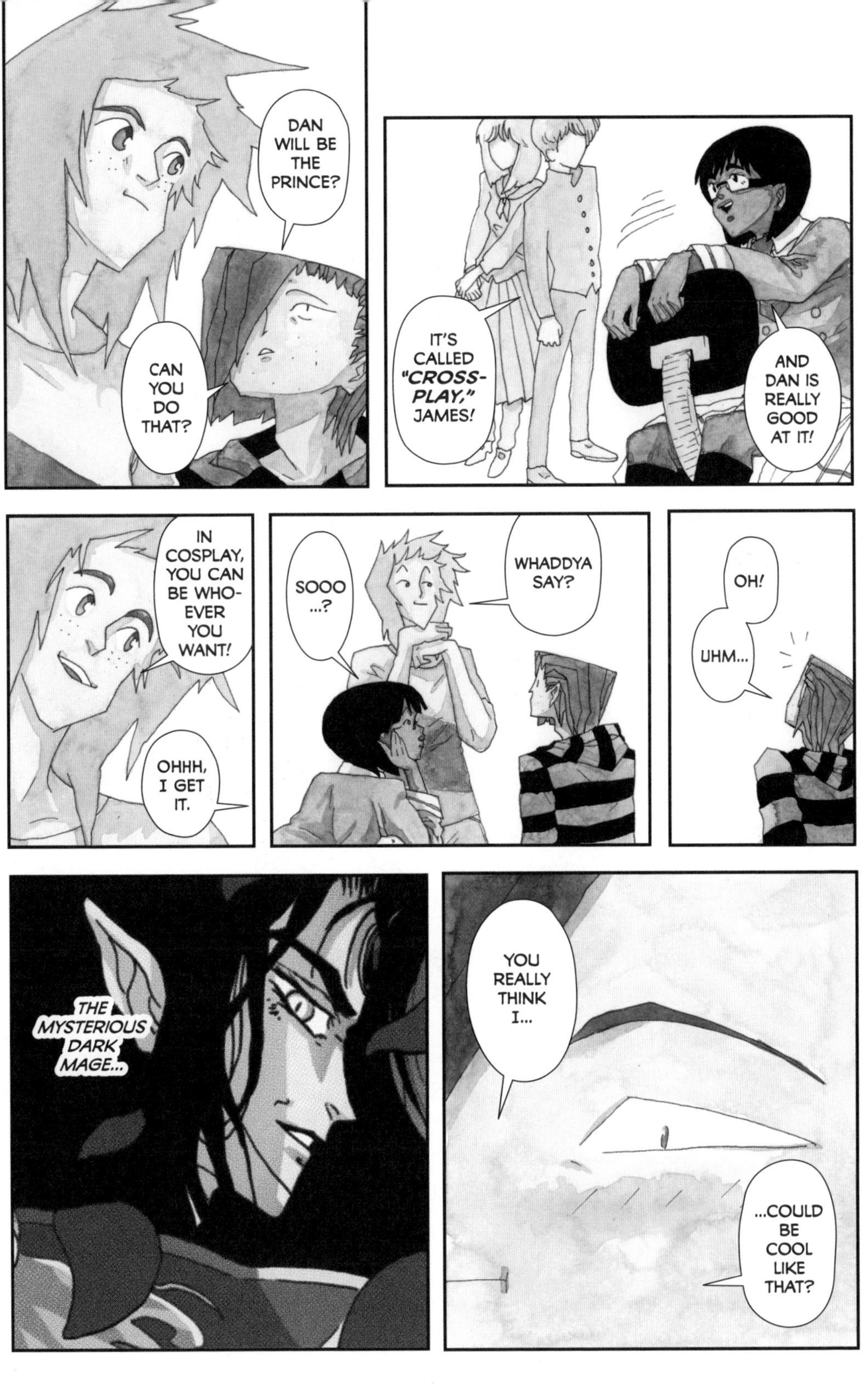
DAN WILL BE THE PRINCE?
CAN YOU DO THAT?
IT'S CALLED "CROSS-PLAY," JAMES!
AND DAN IS REALLY GOOD AT IT!
IN COSPLAY, YOU CAN BE WHO-EVER YOU WANT!
OHHH, I GET IT.
SOOO ...?
WHADDYA SAY?
OH!
UHM...
THE MYSTERIOUS DARK MAGE...
YOU REALLY THINK I...
...COULD BE COOL LIKE THAT?

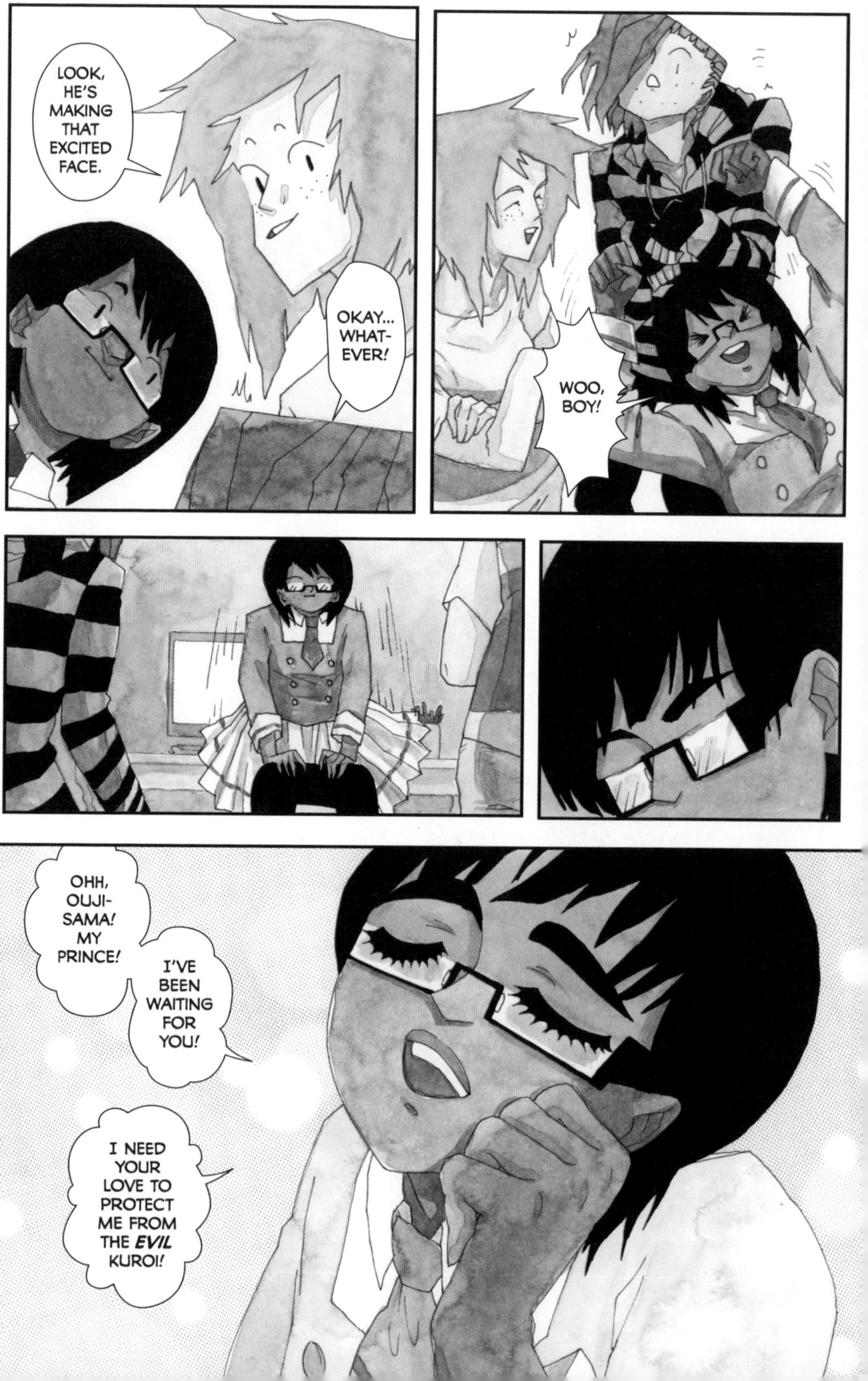
LOOK, HE'S MAKING THAT EXCITED FACE.
OKAY... WHATEVER!
WOO, BOY!
OHH, OUJI-SAMA! MY PRINCE!
I'VE BEEN WAITING FOR YOU!
I NEED YOUR LOVE TO PROTECT ME FROM THE *EVIL* KUROI!

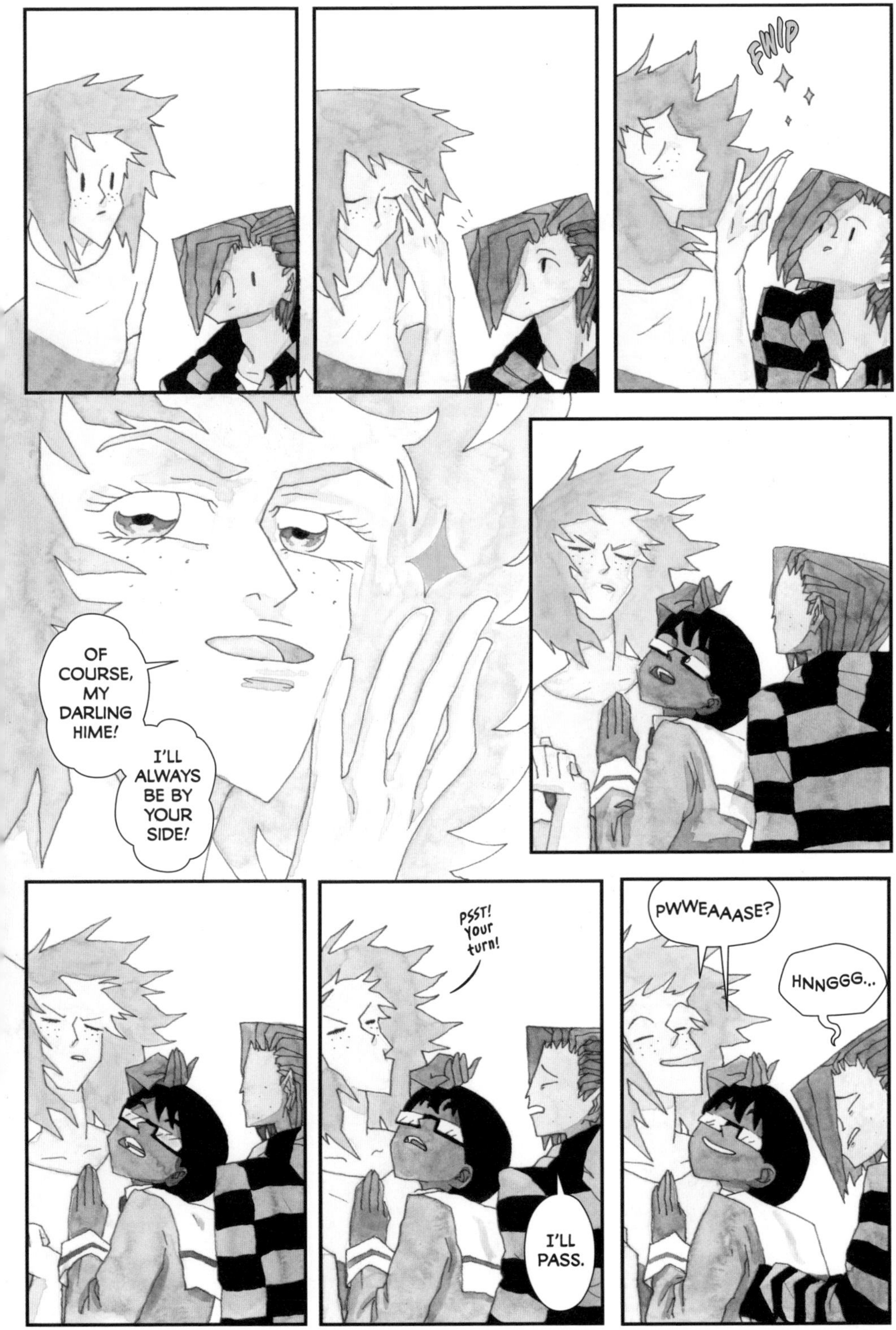
FWIP
OF COURSE, MY DARLING HIME!
I'LL ALWAYS BE BY YOUR SIDE!
PSST! Your turn!
I'LL PASS.
PWWEAAASE?
HNNGGG...

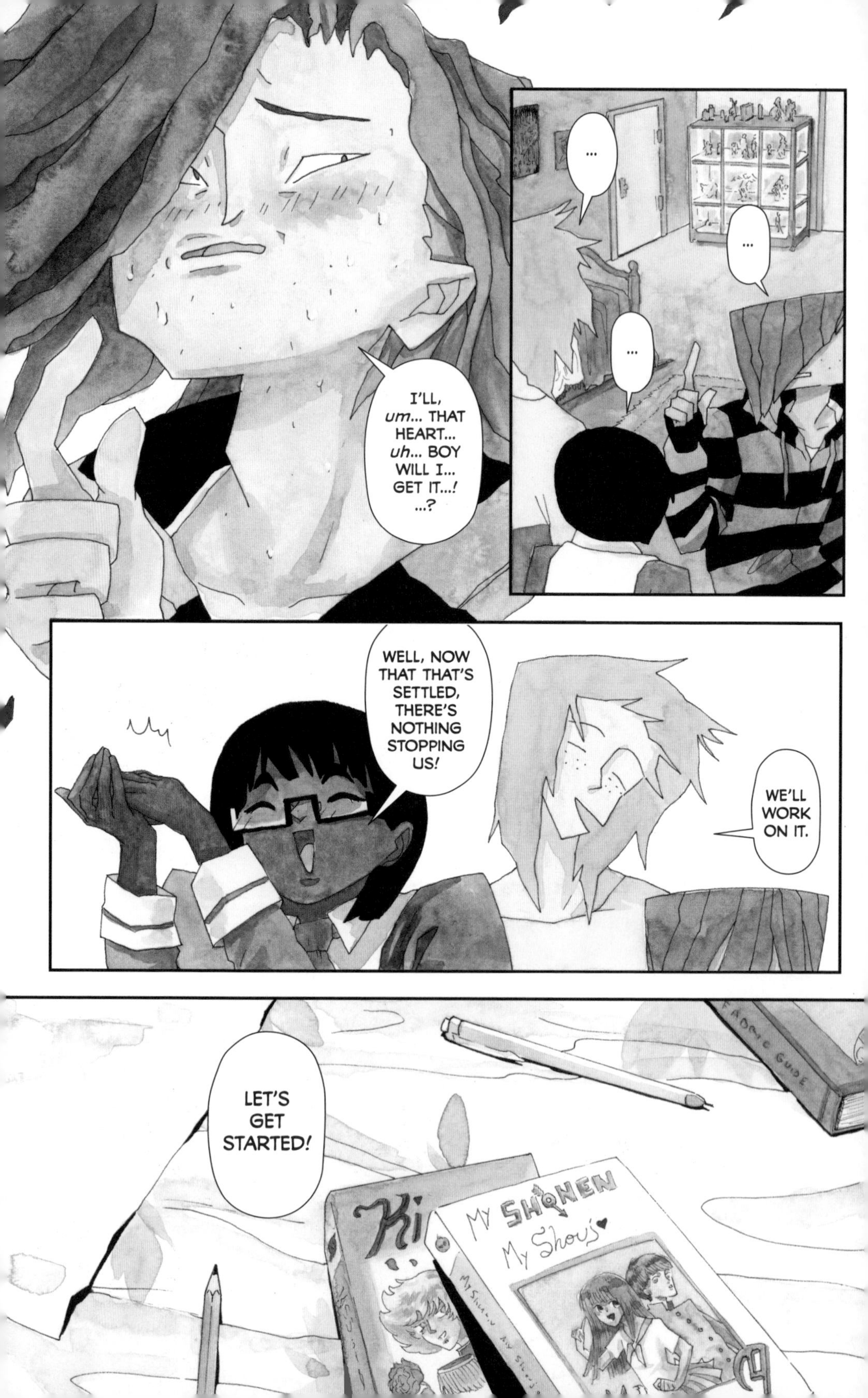

I'LL, *um*... THAT HEART... *uh*... BOY WILL I... GET IT...! ...?
...
...
...
WELL, NOW THAT THAT'S SETTLED, THERE'S NOTHING STOPPING US!
WE'LL WORK ON IT.
LET'S GET STARTED!

WEEABOO

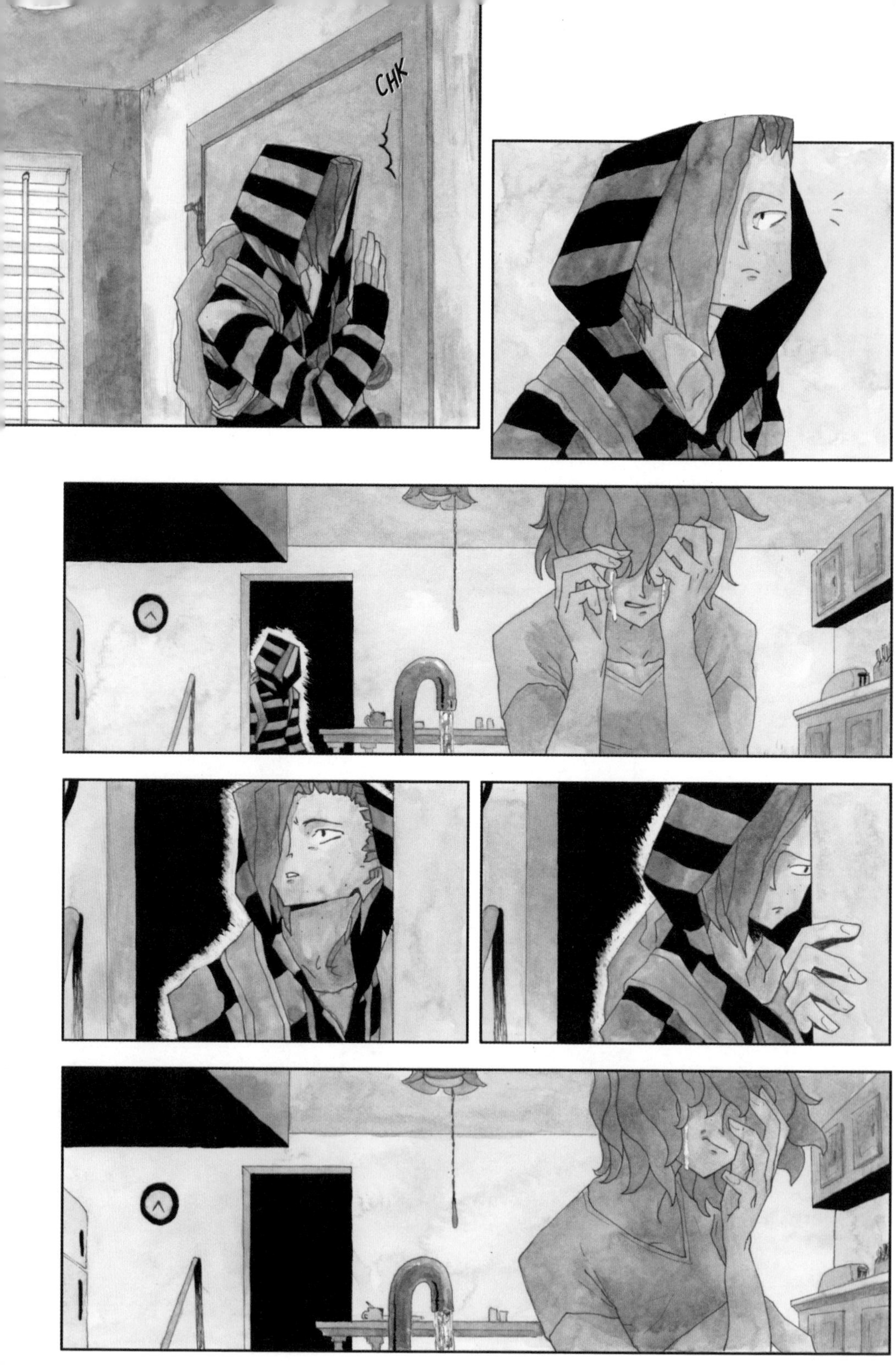
CHK

LOTUS BLOSSOM

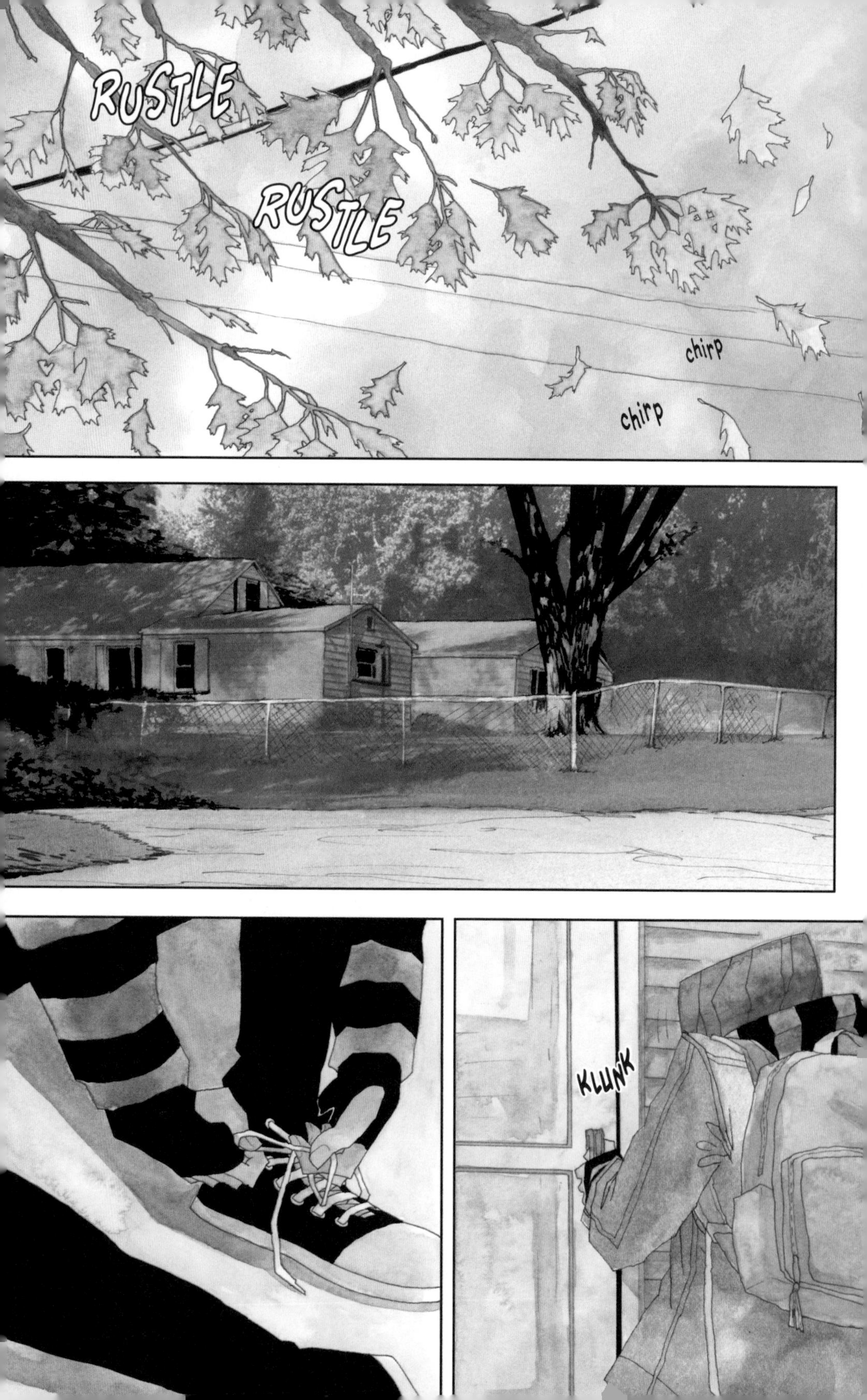
RUSTLE
RUSTLE
chirp
chirp
KLUNK

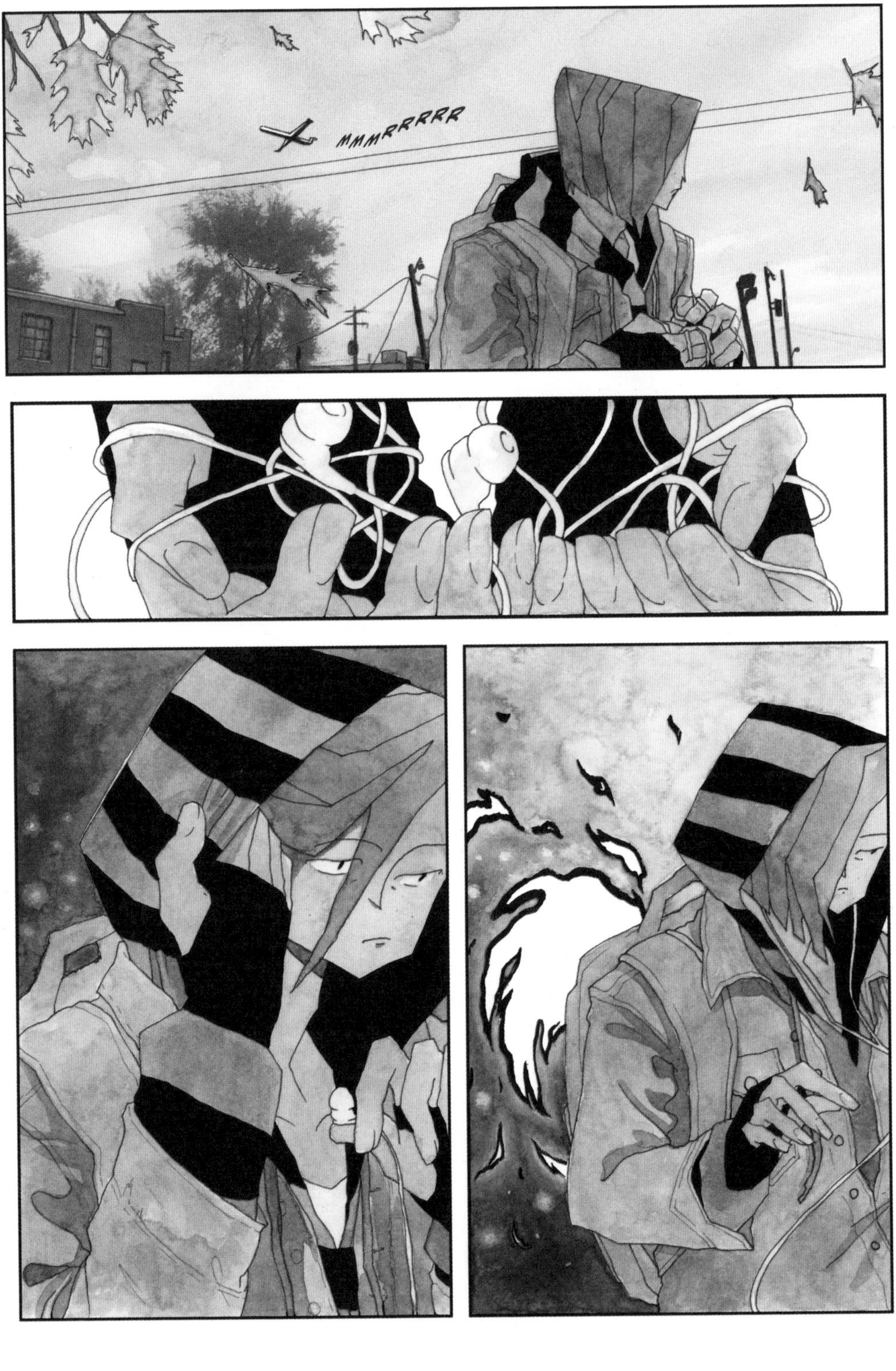
MMMRRRRRR

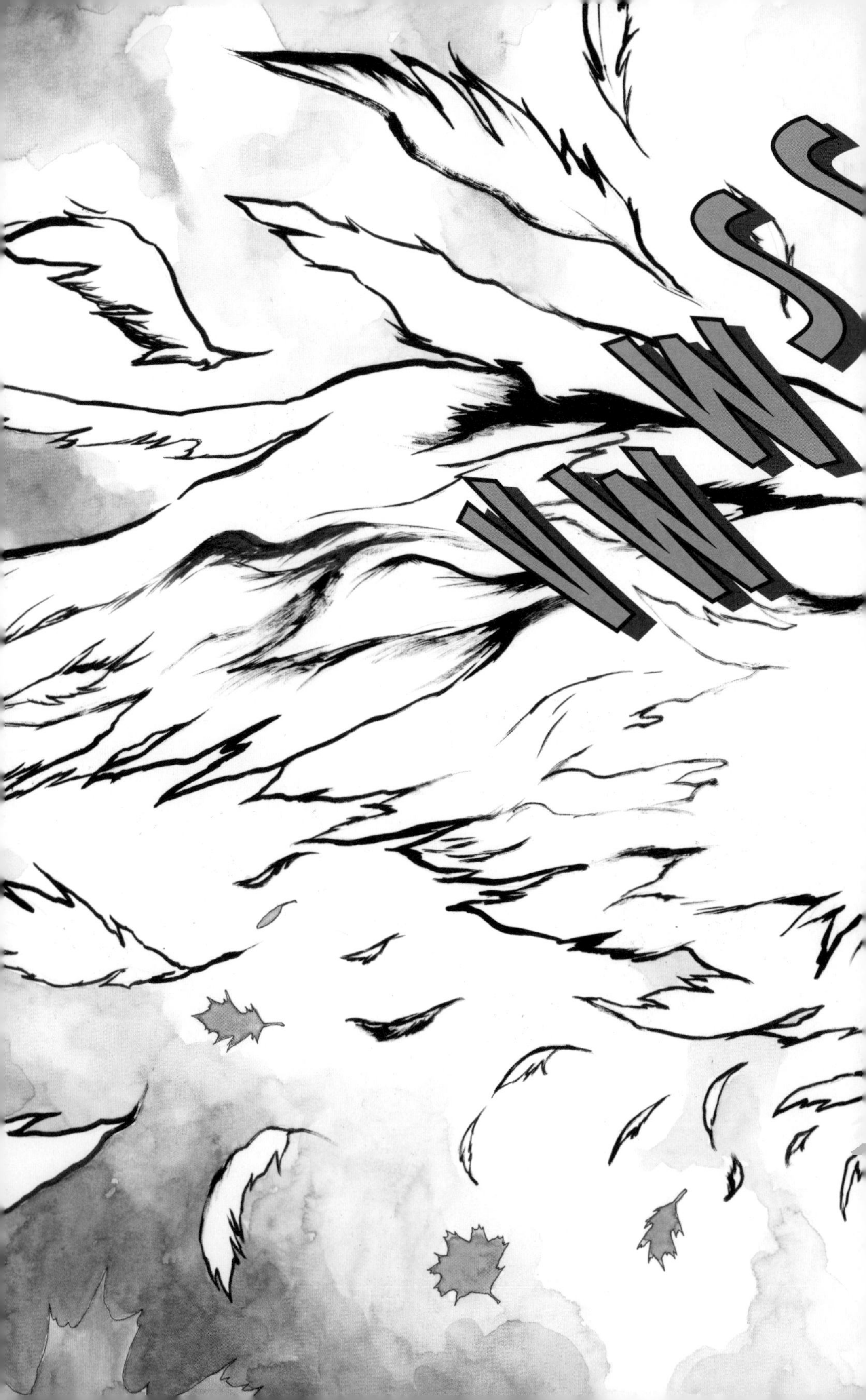
VWWSS

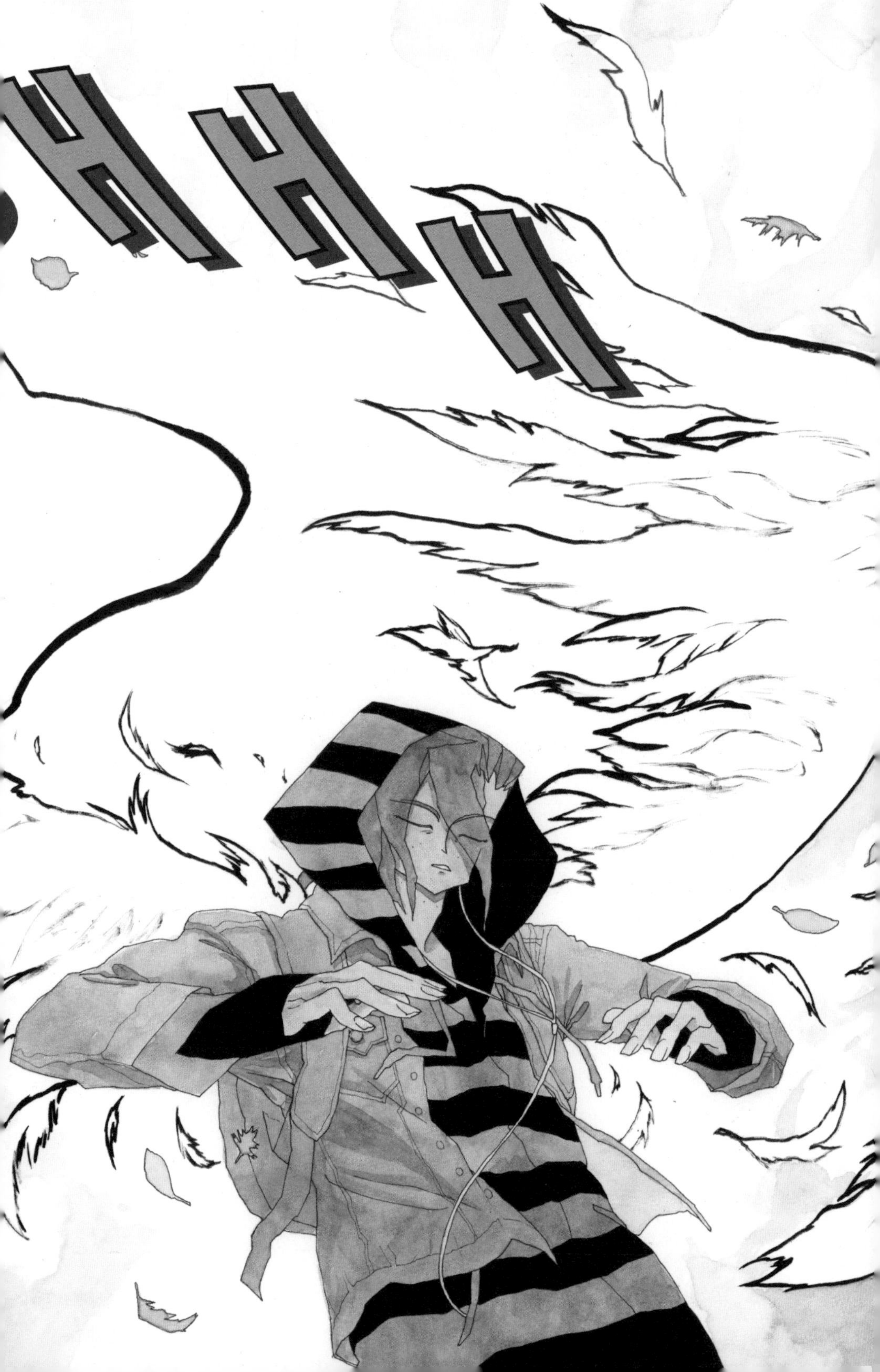
HHH

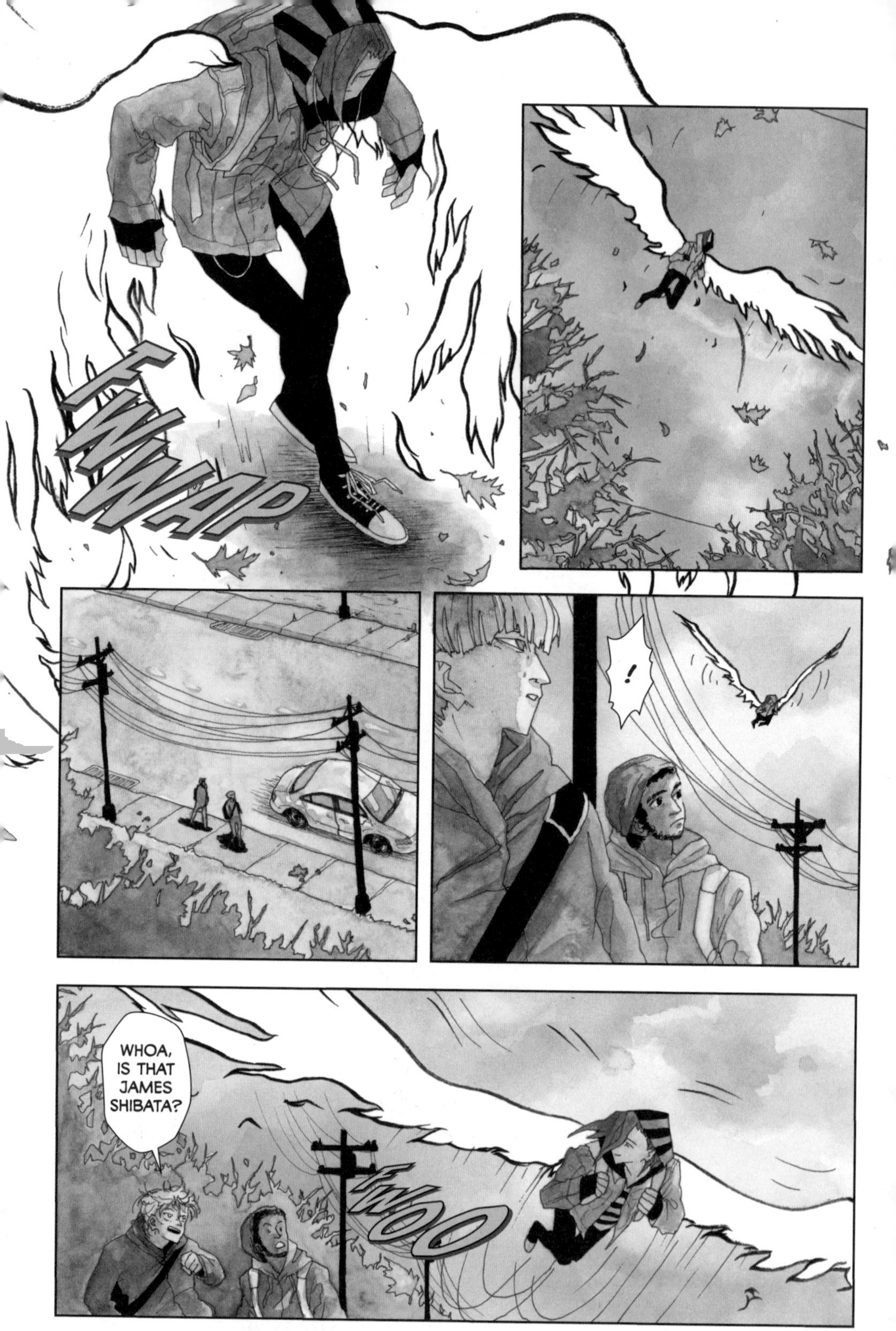
FWWAP
!
WHOA, IS THAT JAMES SHIBATA?
FWOO

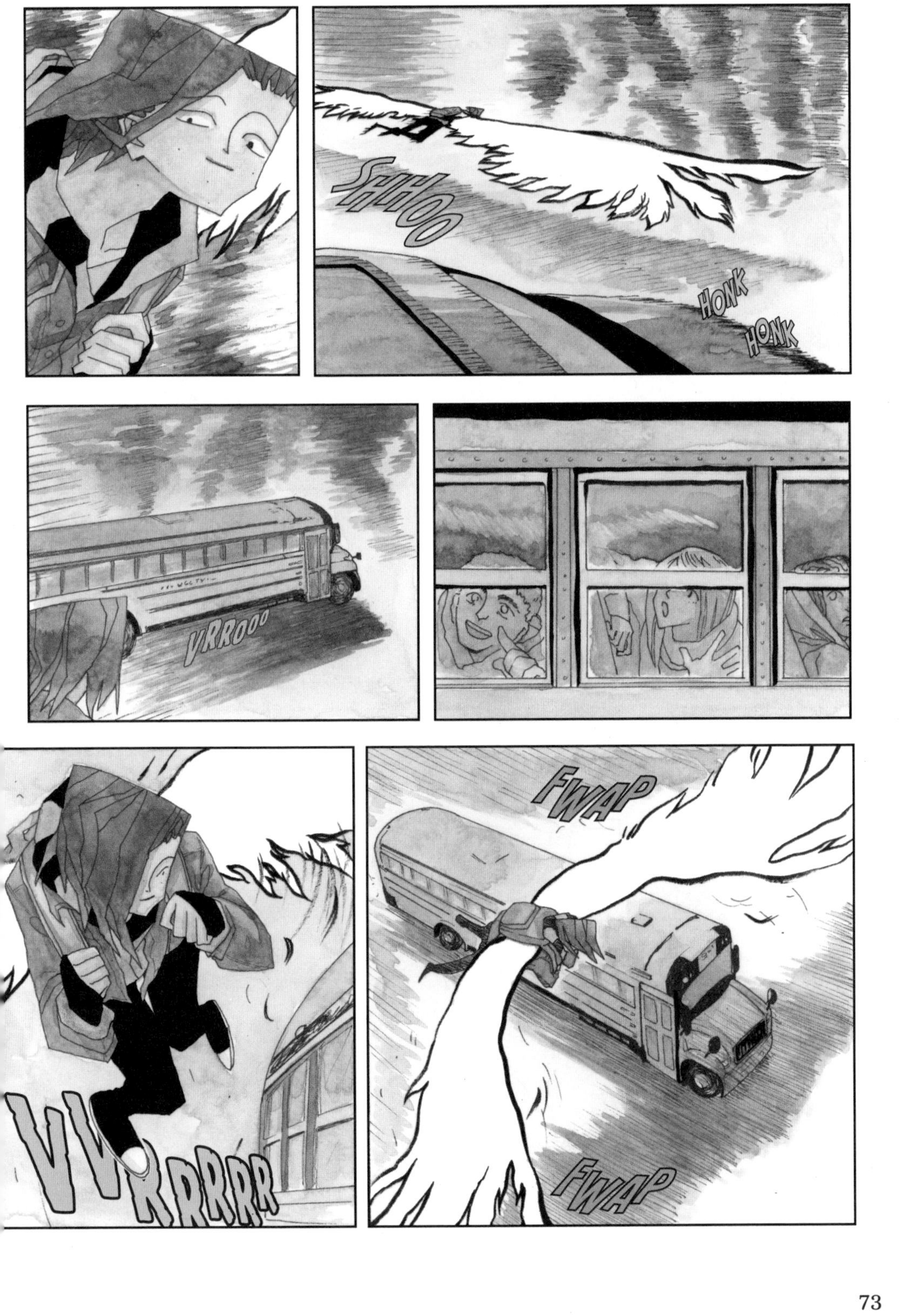
SHHOO
HONK
HONK
VRROOO
VVRRRRR
FWAP
FWAP

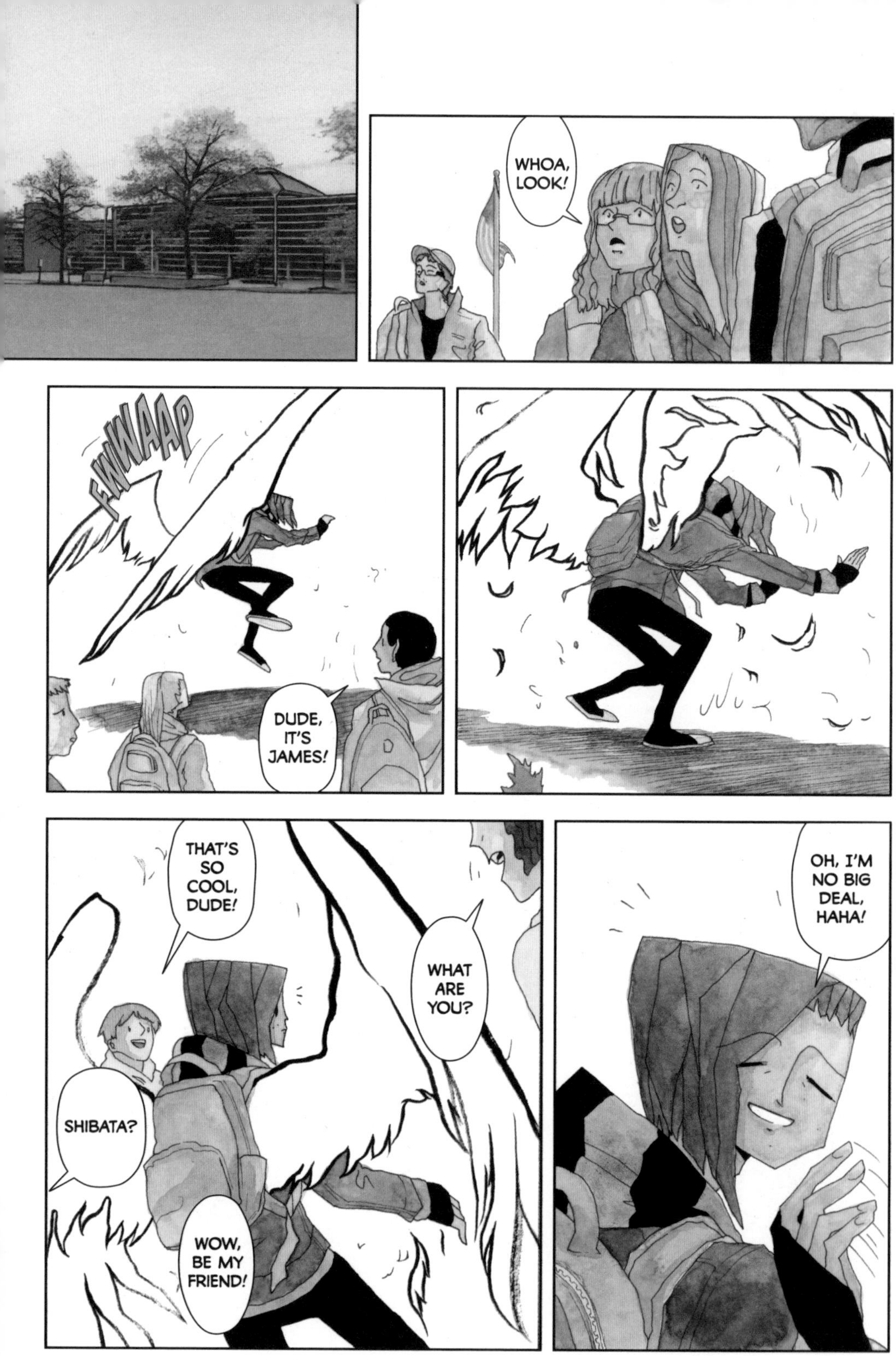
WHOA, LOOK!
FWWAAP
DUDE, IT'S JAMES!
THAT'S SO COOL, DUDE!
WHAT ARE YOU?
SHIBATA?
WOW, BE MY FRIEND!
OH, I'M NO BIG DEAL, HAHA!

...THEN I SHOWED UP TWO DAYS LATER COVERED IN BLOOD, SHARPIE PENTAGRAMS, AND PEANUT BUTTER.

WHAT DID YOU TELL YOUR PARENTS?

LOST A BET.

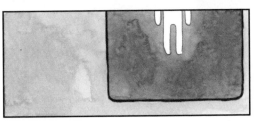

RUSTLE

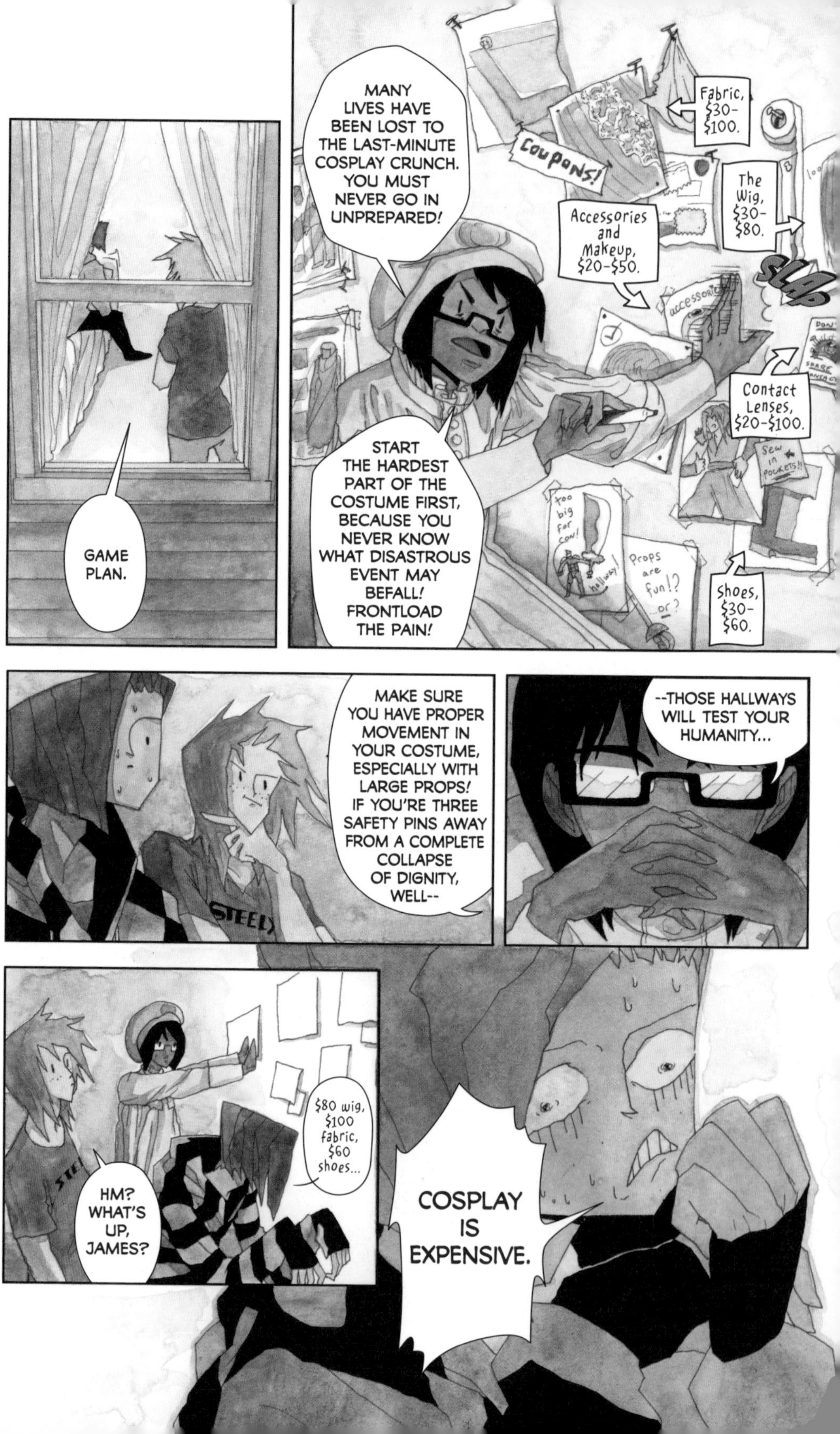

GAME PLAN.
MANY LIVES HAVE BEEN LOST TO THE LAST-MINUTE COSPLAY CRUNCH. YOU MUST NEVER GO IN UNPREPARED!
COUPONS!
Fabric, $30-$100.
The Wig, $30-$80.
Accessories and Makeup, $20-$50.
SLAP
accessories
Contact Lenses, $20-$100.
START THE HARDEST PART OF THE COSTUME FIRST, BECAUSE YOU NEVER KNOW WHAT DISASTROUS EVENT MAY BEFALL! FRONTLOAD THE PAIN!
too big for con!
hallway!
Props are fun!? ...or?
Sew in pockets!!
Shoes, $30-$60.
MAKE SURE YOU HAVE PROPER MOVEMENT IN YOUR COSTUME, ESPECIALLY WITH LARGE PROPS! IF YOU'RE THREE SAFETY PINS AWAY FROM A COMPLETE COLLAPSE OF DIGNITY, WELL--
STEEL
--THOSE HALLWAYS WILL TEST YOUR HUMANITY...
$80 wig, $100 fabric, $60 shoes...
HM? WHAT'S UP, JAMES?
COSPLAY IS EXPENSIVE.

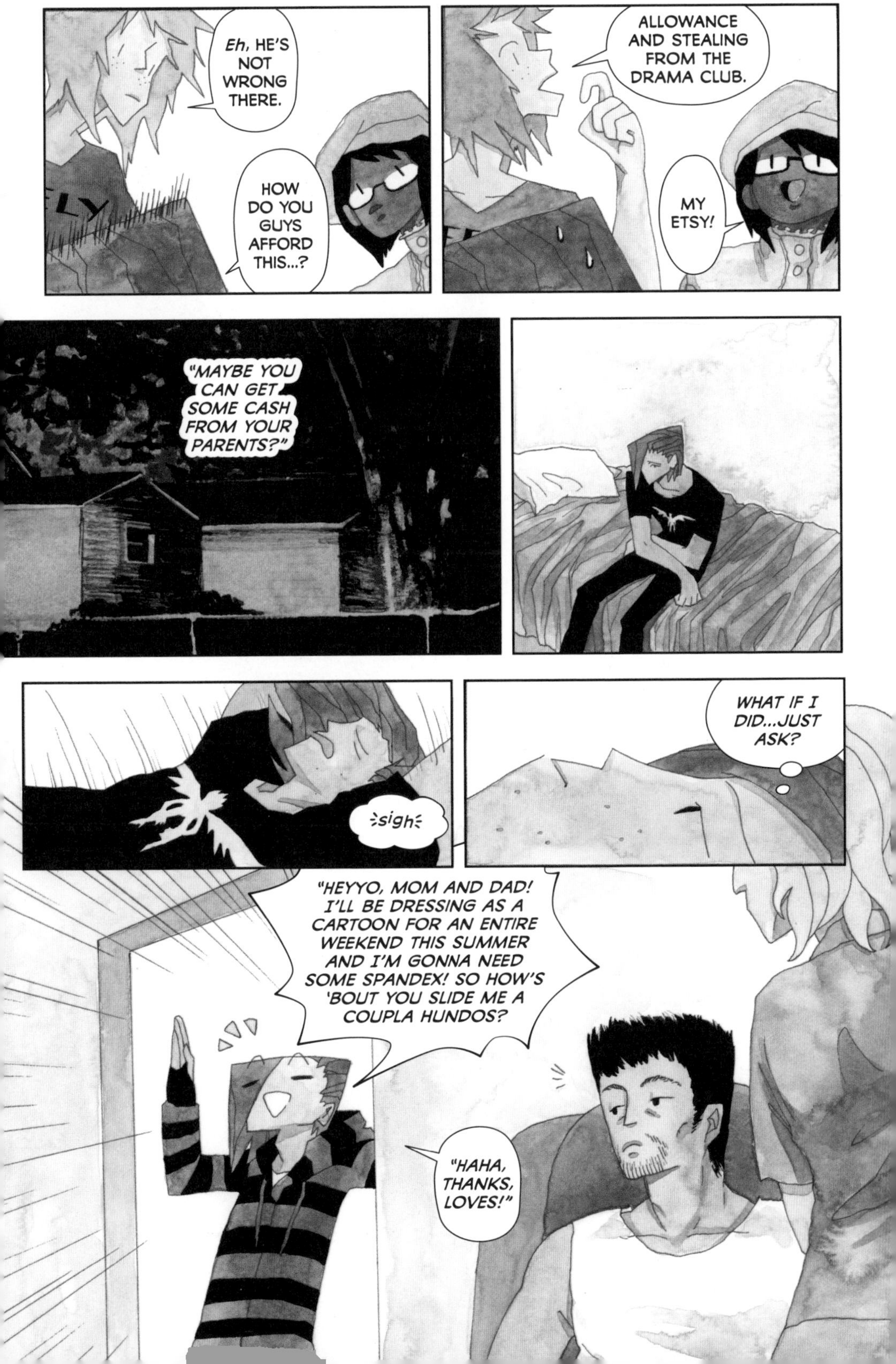
Eh, HE'S NOT WRONG THERE.
HOW DO YOU GUYS AFFORD THIS...?
ALLOWANCE AND STEALING FROM THE DRAMA CLUB.
MY ETSY!
"MAYBE YOU CAN GET SOME CASH FROM YOUR PARENTS?"
sigh
WHAT IF I DID...JUST ASK?
"HEYYO, MOM AND DAD! I'LL BE DRESSING AS A CARTOON FOR AN ENTIRE WEEKEND THIS SUMMER AND I'M GONNA NEED SOME SPANDEX! SO HOW'S 'BOUT YOU SLIDE ME A COUPLA HUNDOS?
"HAHA, THANKS, LOVES!"

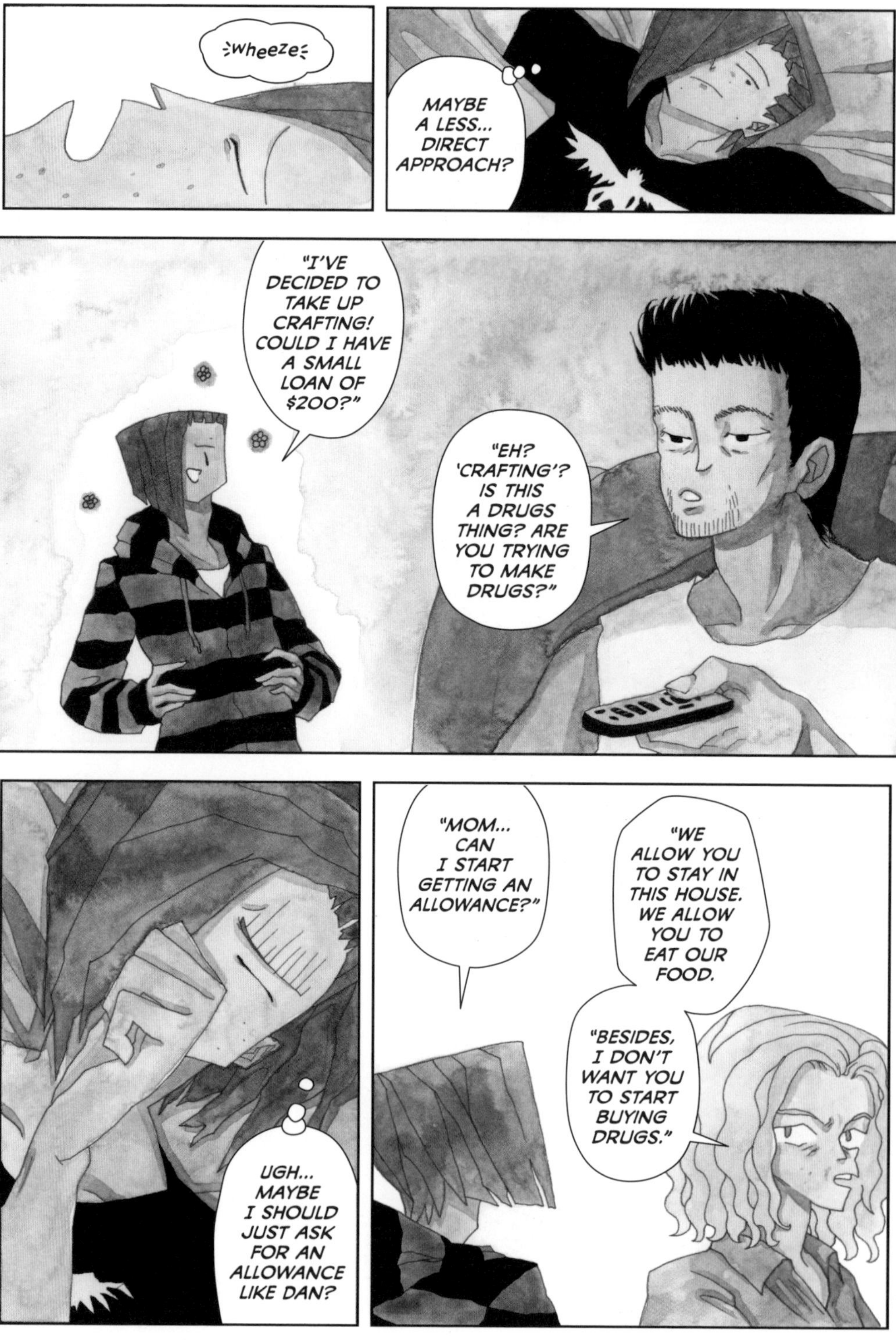
Wheeze
MAYBE A LESS... DIRECT APPROACH?
"I'VE DECIDED TO TAKE UP CRAFTING! COULD I HAVE A SMALL LOAN OF $200?"
"EH? 'CRAFTING'? IS THIS A DRUGS THING? ARE YOU TRYING TO MAKE DRUGS?"
UGH... MAYBE I SHOULD JUST ASK FOR AN ALLOWANCE LIKE DAN?
"MOM... CAN I START GETTING AN ALLOWANCE?"
"WE ALLOW YOU TO STAY IN THIS HOUSE. WE ALLOW YOU TO EAT OUR FOOD.
"BESIDES, I DON'T WANT YOU TO START BUYING DRUGS."

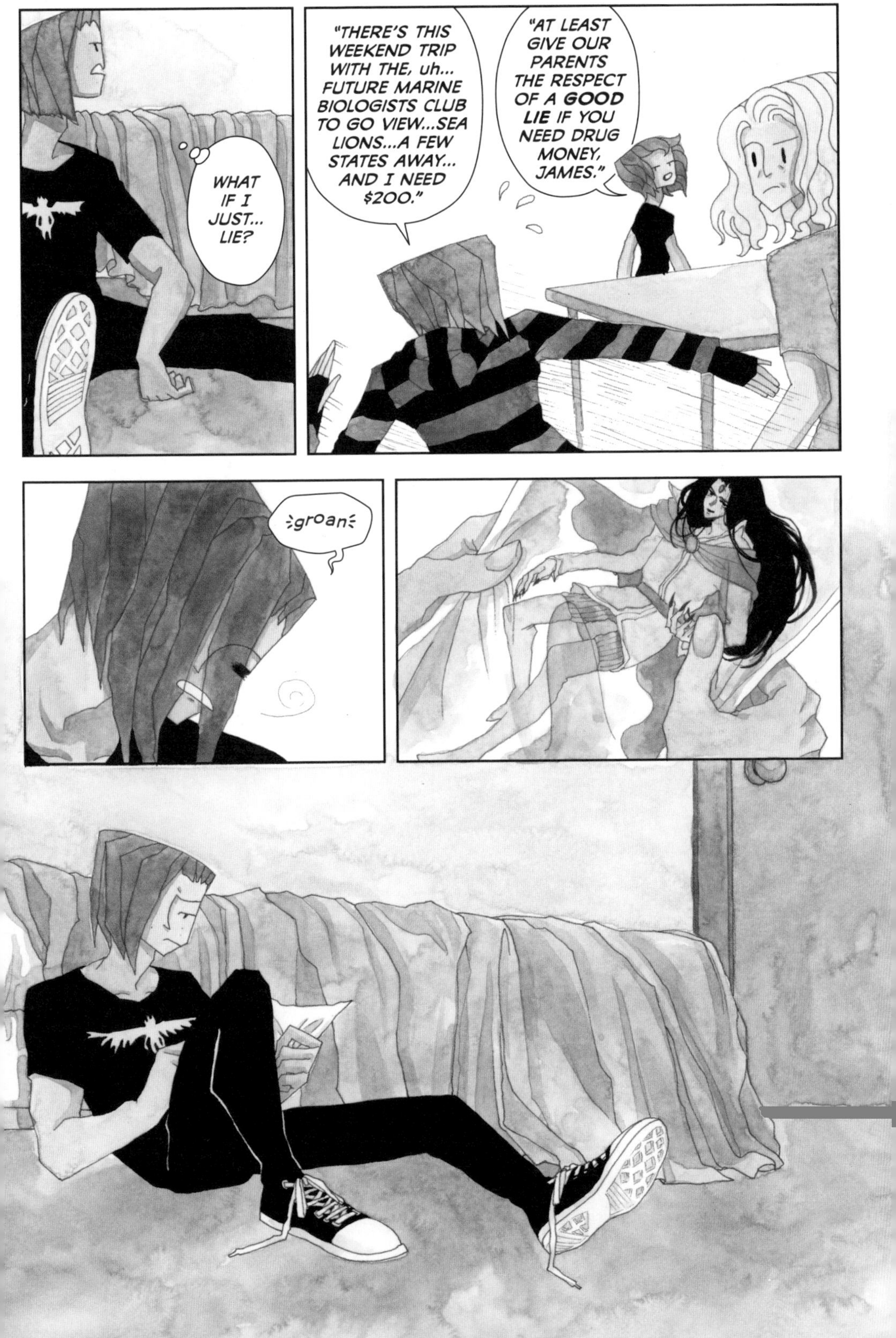
WHAT IF I JUST... LIE?
"THERE'S THIS WEEKEND TRIP WITH THE, uh... FUTURE MARINE BIOLOGISTS CLUB TO GO VIEW...SEA LIONS...A FEW STATES AWAY... AND I NEED $200."
"AT LEAST GIVE OUR PARENTS THE RESPECT OF A **GOOD LIE** IF YOU NEED DRUG MONEY, JAMES."
groan

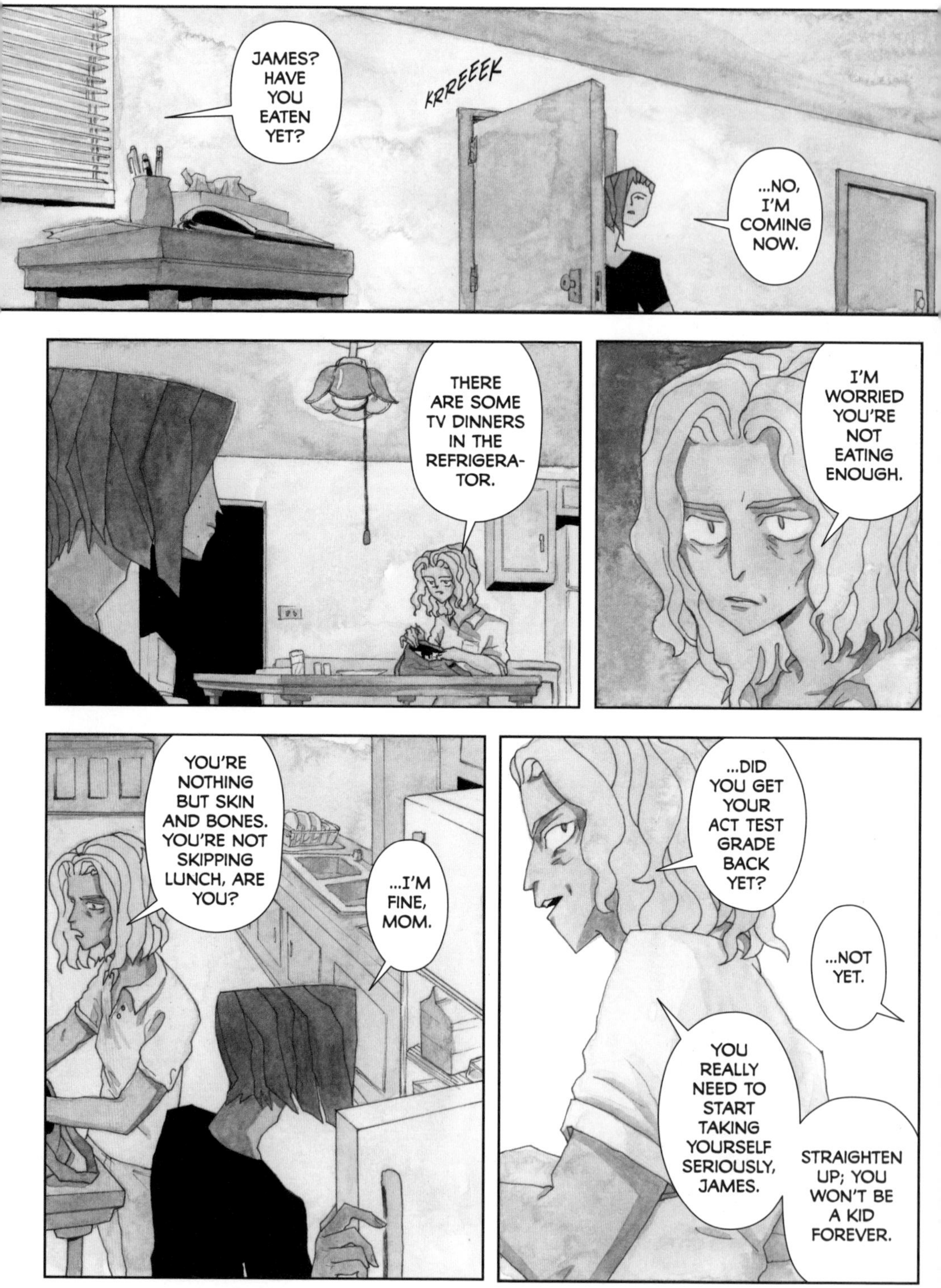
JAMES? HAVE YOU EATEN YET?
KRREEEK
...NO, I'M COMING NOW.
THERE ARE SOME TV DINNERS IN THE REFRIGERA-TOR.
I'M WORRIED YOU'RE NOT EATING ENOUGH.
YOU'RE NOTHING BUT SKIN AND BONES. YOU'RE NOT SKIPPING LUNCH, ARE YOU?
...I'M FINE, MOM.
...DID YOU GET YOUR ACT TEST GRADE BACK YET?
...NOT YET.
YOU REALLY NEED TO START TAKING YOURSELF SERIOUSLY, JAMES.
STRAIGHTEN UP; YOU WON'T BE A KID FOREVER.

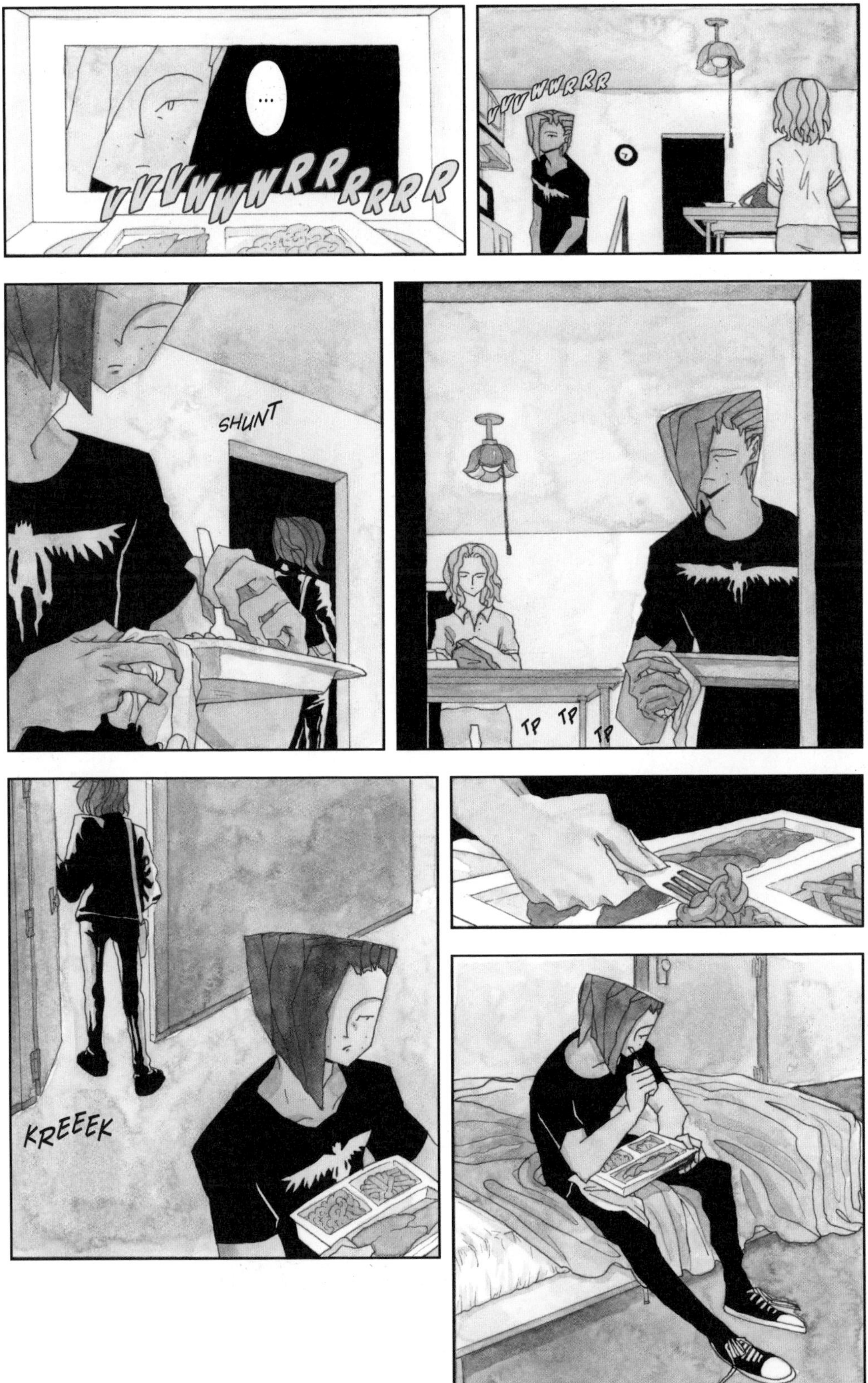
...
VVVWWWRRRRRR
VVVWWWRRR
SHUNT
TP TP TP
KREEEK

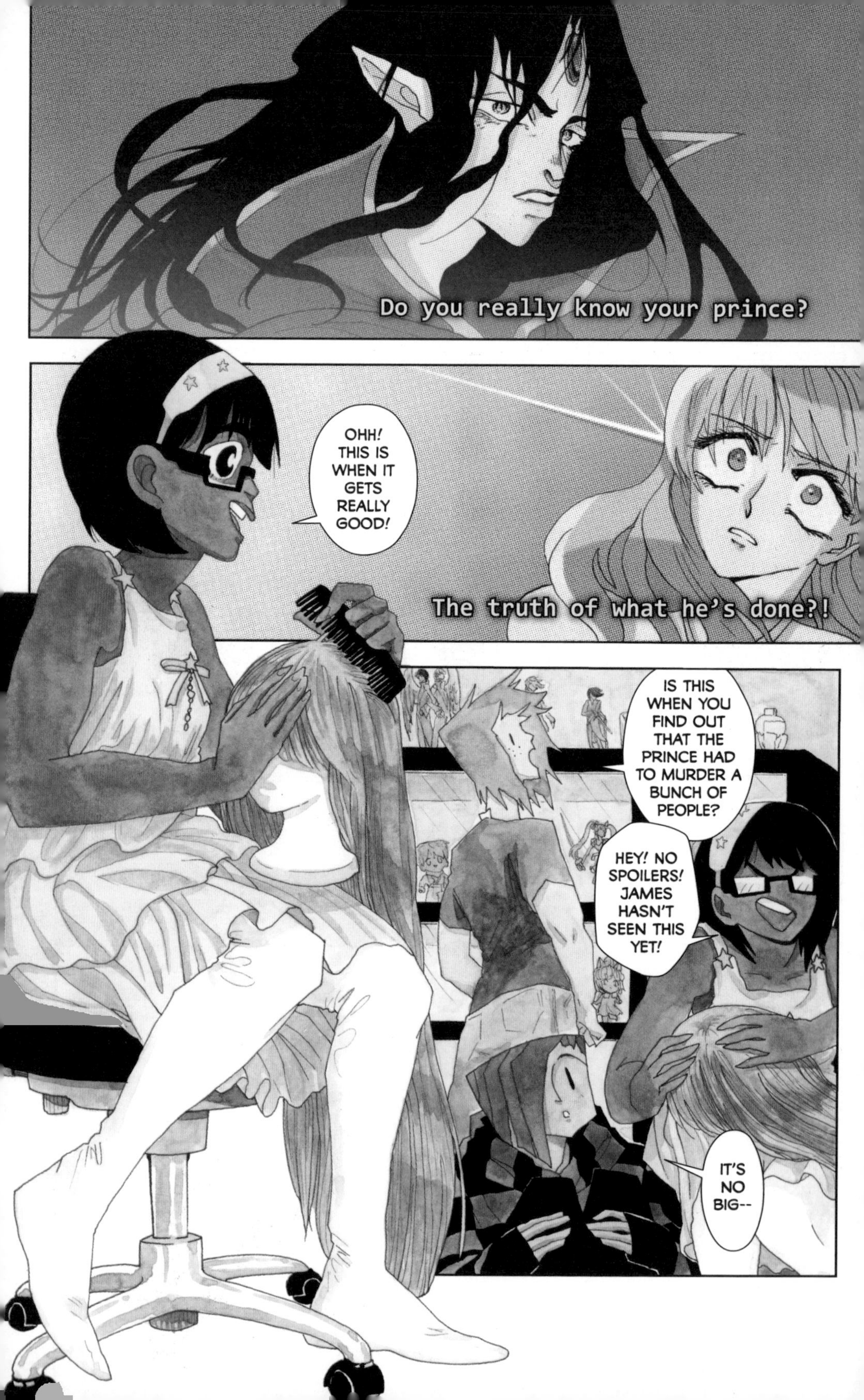
Do you really know your prince?
OHH! THIS IS WHEN IT GETS REALLY GOOD!
The truth of what he's done?!
IS THIS WHEN YOU FIND OUT THAT THE PRINCE HAD TO MURDER A BUNCH OF PEOPLE?
HEY! NO SPOILERS! JAMES HASN'T SEEN THIS YET!
IT'S NO BIG--

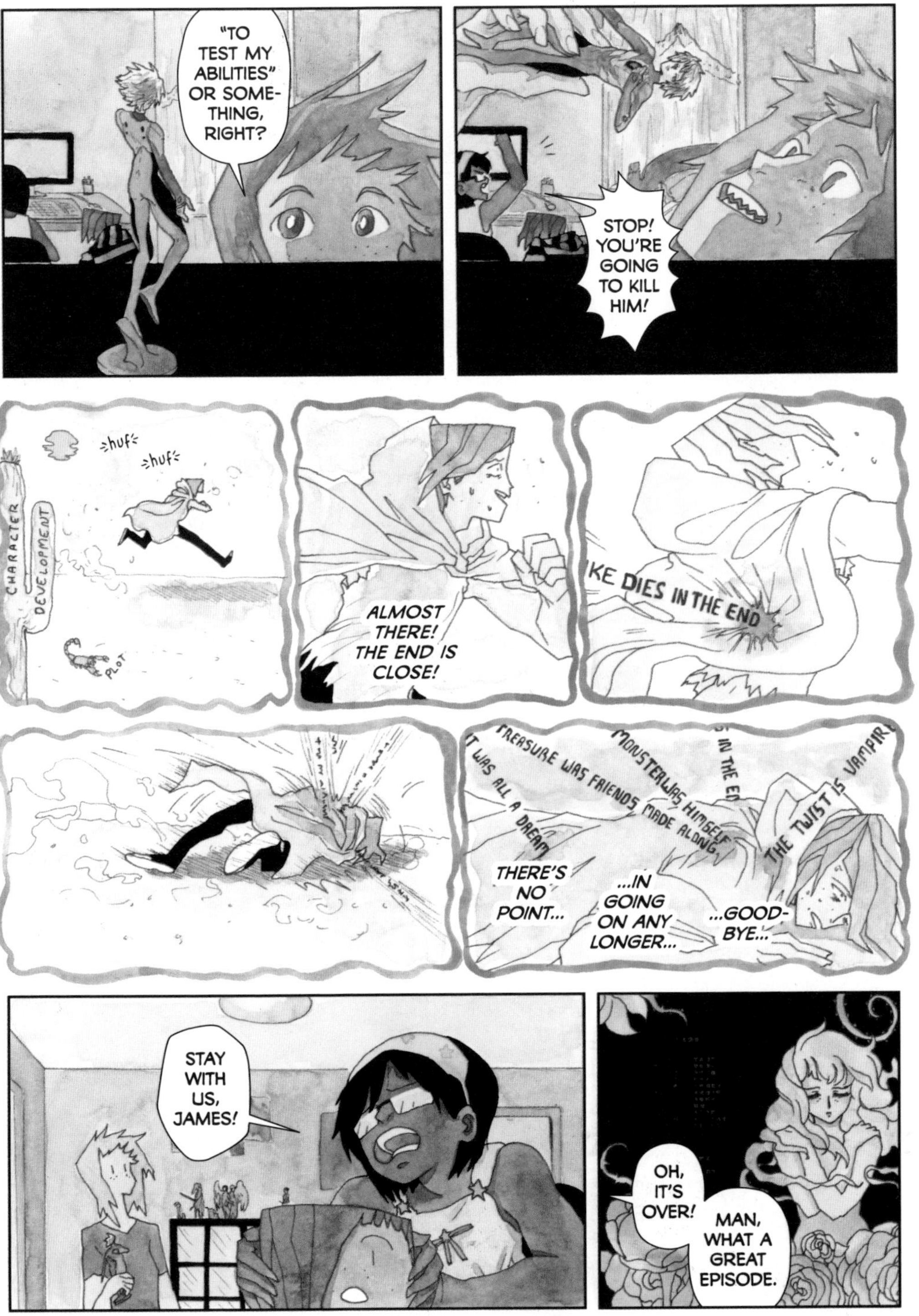
"TO TEST MY ABILITIES" OR SOMETHING, RIGHT?
STOP! YOU'RE GOING TO KILL HIM!
huf
huf
CHARACTER DEVELOPMENT
PLOT
ALMOST THERE! THE END IS CLOSE!
KE DIES IN THE END
T WAS ALL A DREAM
TREASURE WAS FRIENDS MADE ALONG
MONSTER WAS HIMSELF
IN THE EN
THE TWIST IS VAMPIRE
THERE'S NO POINT...
...IN GOING ON ANY LONGER...
...GOODBYE...
STAY WITH US, JAMES!
OH, IT'S OVER!
MAN, WHAT A GREAT EPISODE.

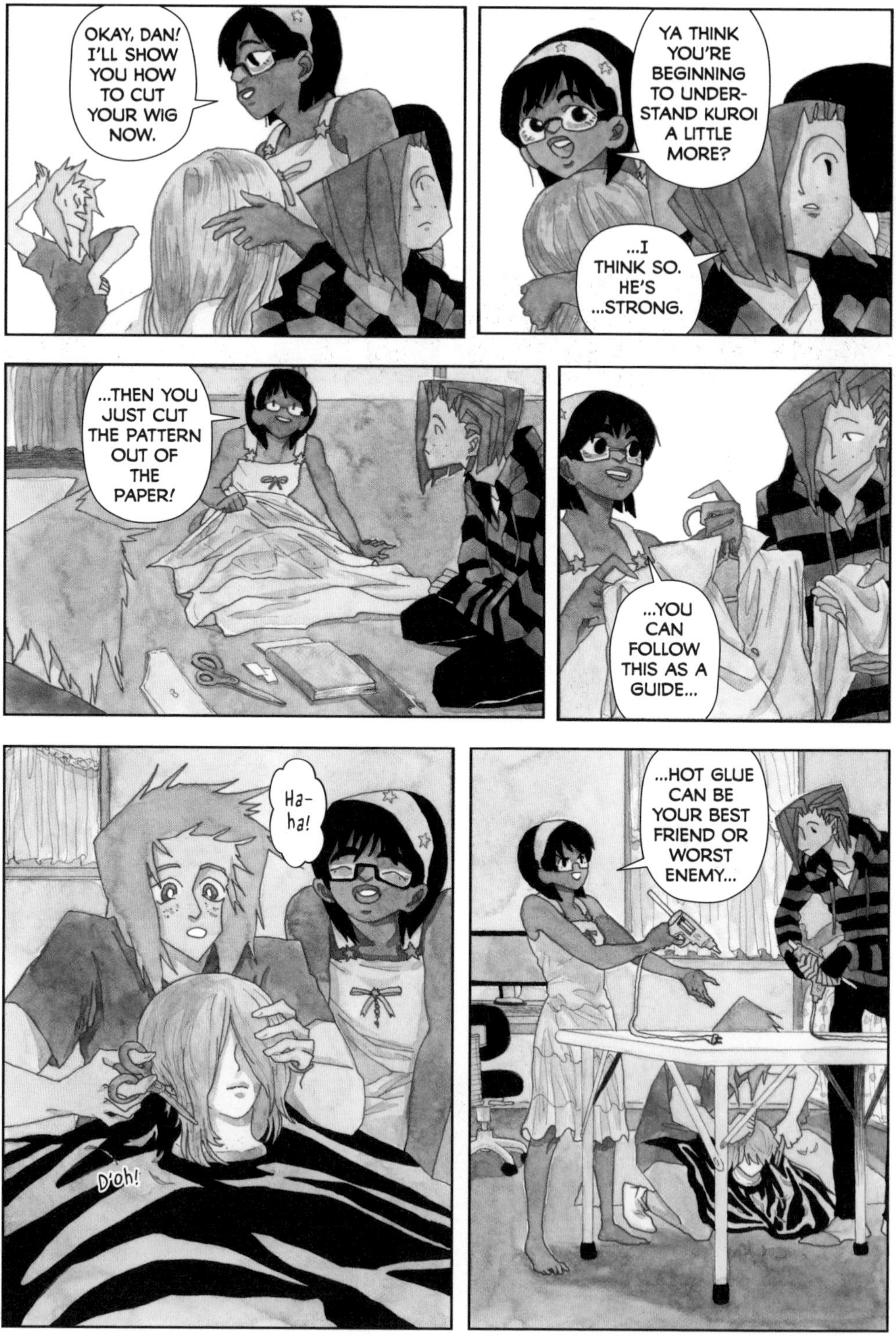
OKAY, DAN! I'LL SHOW YOU HOW TO CUT YOUR WIG NOW.
YA THINK YOU'RE BEGINNING TO UNDER-STAND KUROI A LITTLE MORE?
...I THINK SO. HE'S ...STRONG.
...THEN YOU JUST CUT THE PATTERN OUT OF THE PAPER!
...YOU CAN FOLLOW THIS AS A GUIDE...
Ha-ha!
D'oh!
...HOT GLUE CAN BE YOUR BEST FRIEND OR WORST ENEMY...

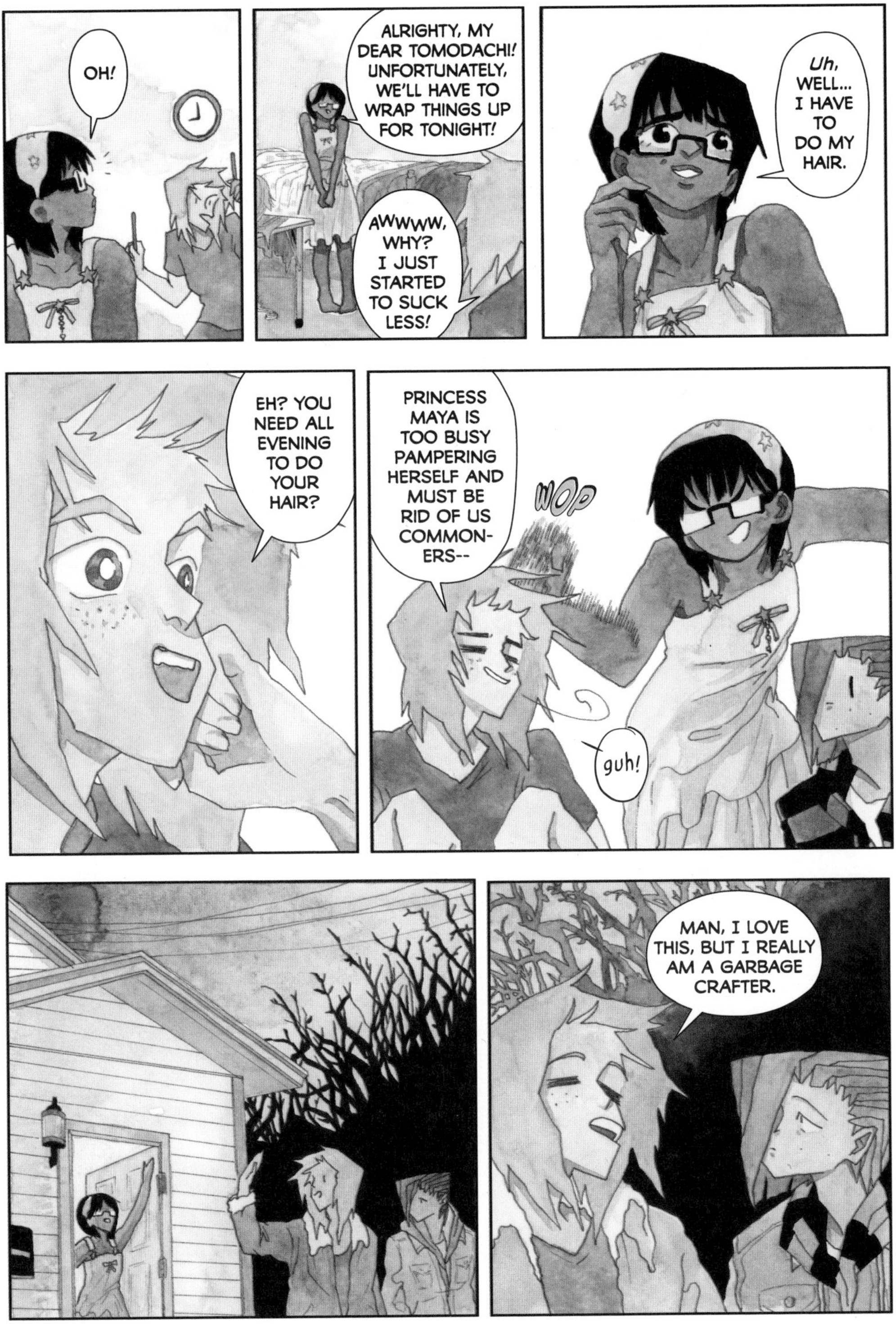
OH!
ALRIGHTY, MY DEAR TOMODACHI! UNFORTUNATELY, WE'LL HAVE TO WRAP THINGS UP FOR TONIGHT!
AWWWW, WHY? I JUST STARTED TO SUCK LESS!
Uh, WELL... I HAVE TO DO MY HAIR.
EH? YOU NEED ALL EVENING TO DO YOUR HAIR?
PRINCESS MAYA IS TOO BUSY PAMPERING HERSELF AND MUST BE RID OF US COMMONERS--
WOP
guh!
MAN, I LOVE THIS, BUT I REALLY AM A GARBAGE CRAFTER.

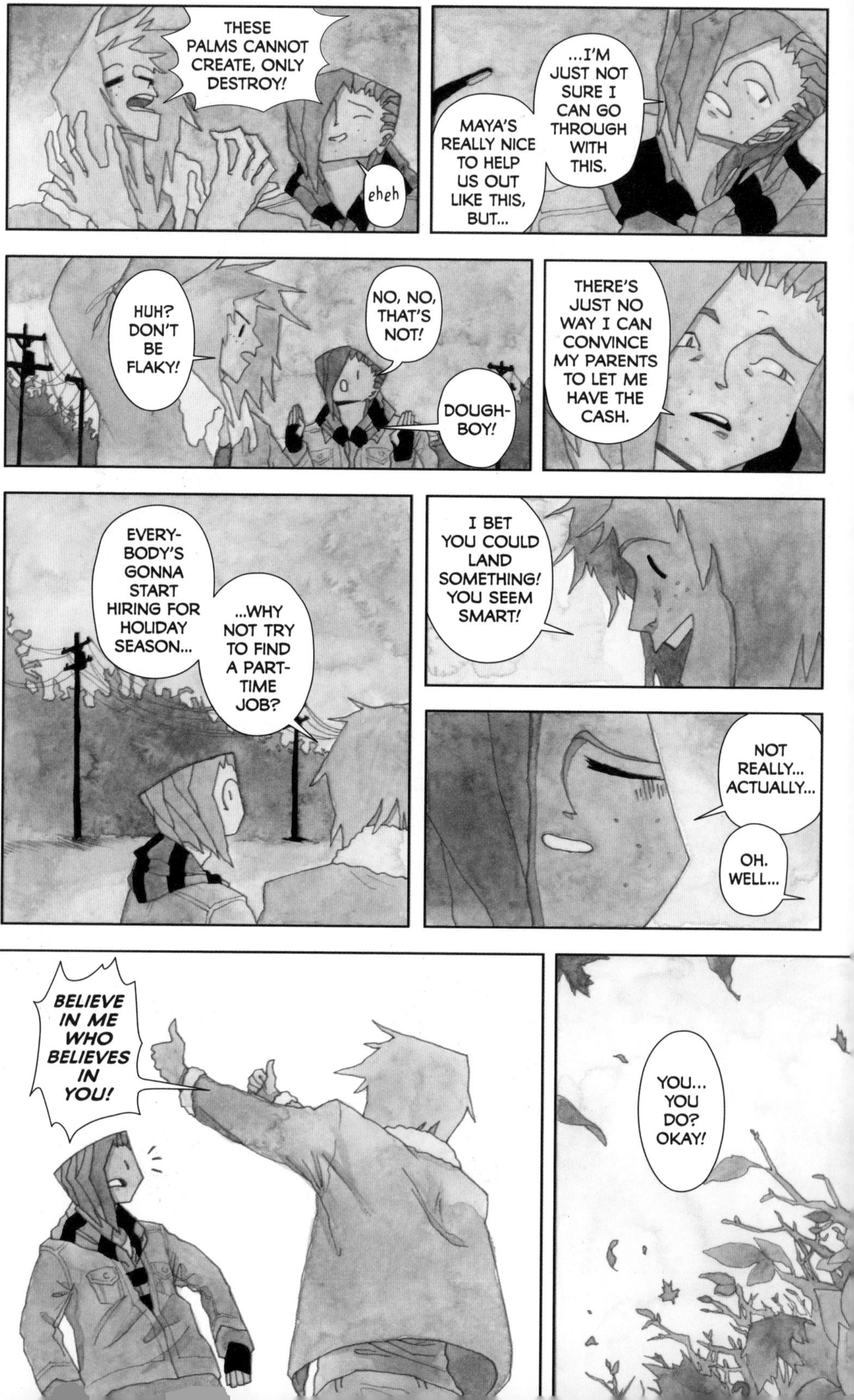
THESE PALMS CANNOT CREATE, ONLY DESTROY!
eheh
...I'M JUST NOT SURE I CAN GO THROUGH WITH THIS.
MAYA'S REALLY NICE TO HELP US OUT LIKE THIS, BUT...
HUH? DON'T BE FLAKY!
NO, NO, THAT'S NOT!
DOUGH-BOY!
THERE'S JUST NO WAY I CAN CONVINCE MY PARENTS TO LET ME HAVE THE CASH.
EVERY-BODY'S GONNA START HIRING FOR HOLIDAY SEASON...
...WHY NOT TRY TO FIND A PART-TIME JOB?
I BET YOU COULD LAND SOMETHING! YOU SEEM SMART!
NOT REALLY... ACTUALLY...
OH. WELL...
BELIEVE IN ME WHO BELIEVES IN YOU!
YOU... YOU DO? OKAY!

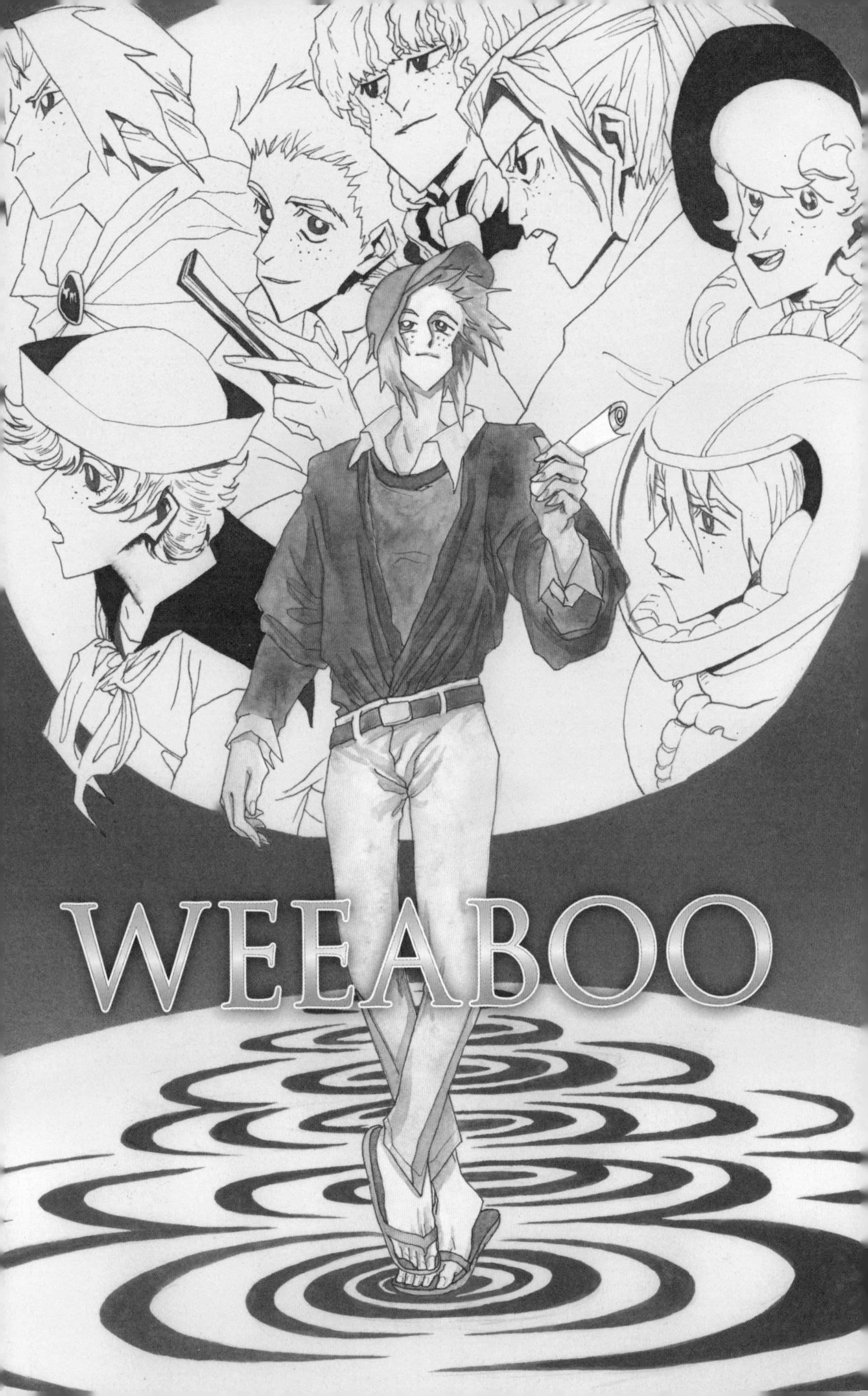
WEEABOO

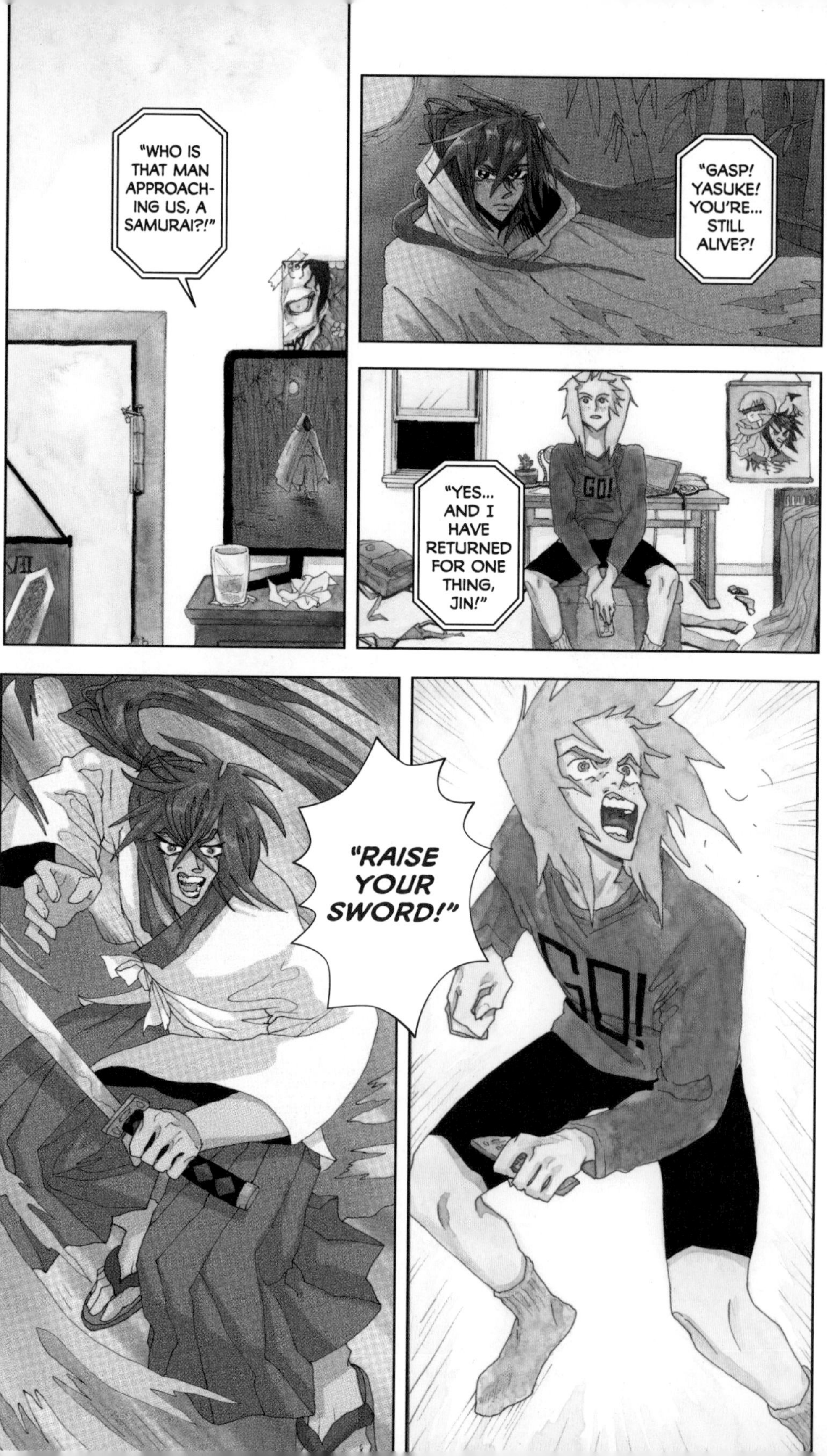
"WHO IS THAT MAN APPROACHING US, A SAMURAI?!"
"GASP! YASUKE! YOU'RE... STILL ALIVE?!
"YES... AND I HAVE RETURNED FOR ONE THING, JIN!"
GO!
"RAISE YOUR SWORD!"
GO!

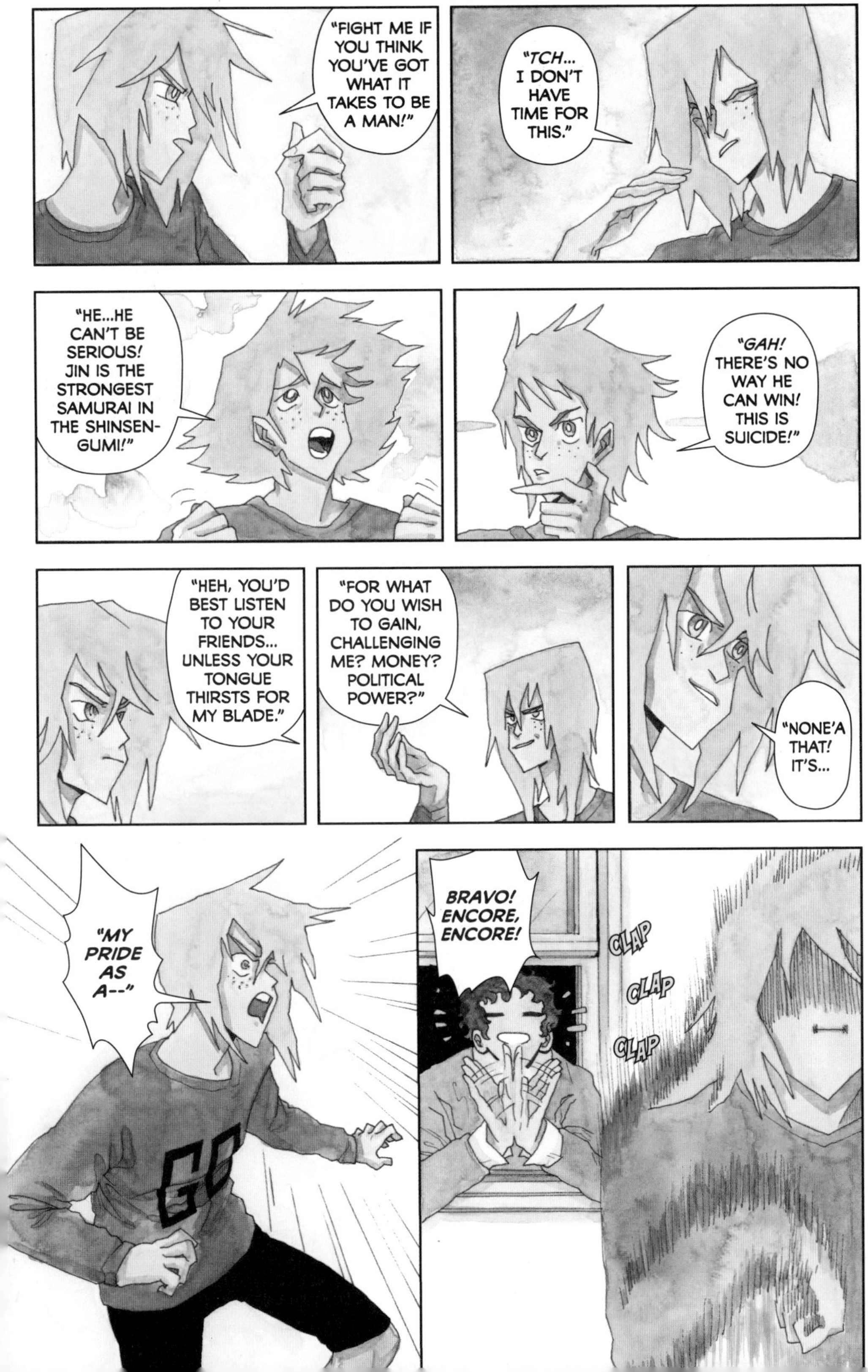
"FIGHT ME IF YOU THINK YOU'VE GOT WHAT IT TAKES TO BE A MAN!"
"TCH... I DON'T HAVE TIME FOR THIS."
"HE...HE CAN'T BE SERIOUS! JIN IS THE STRONGEST SAMURAI IN THE SHINSEN-GUMI!"
"GAH! THERE'S NO WAY HE CAN WIN! THIS IS SUICIDE!"
"HEH, YOU'D BEST LISTEN TO YOUR FRIENDS... UNLESS YOUR TONGUE THIRSTS FOR MY BLADE."
"FOR WHAT DO YOU WISH TO GAIN, CHALLENGING ME? MONEY? POLITICAL POWER?"
"NONE'A THAT! IT'S...
"MY PRIDE AS A--"
BRAVO! ENCORE, ENCORE!
CLAP
CLAP
CLAP

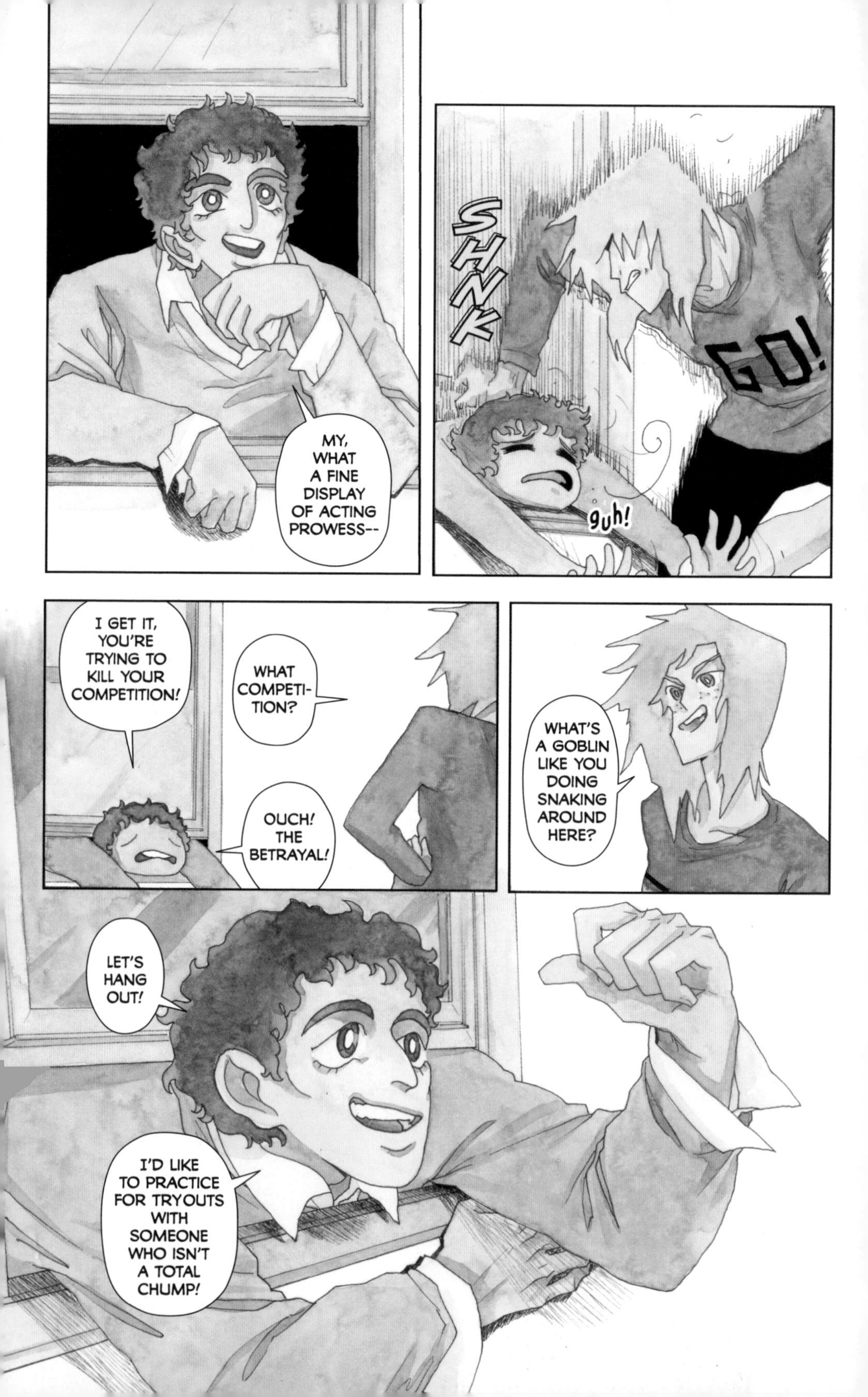
MY, WHAT A FINE DISPLAY OF ACTING PROWESS--
SHNK
GO!
guh!
I GET IT, YOU'RE TRYING TO KILL YOUR COMPETITION!
WHAT COMPETITION?
OUCH! THE BETRAYAL!
WHAT'S A GOBLIN LIKE YOU DOING SNAKING AROUND HERE?
LET'S HANG OUT!
I'D LIKE TO PRACTICE FOR TRYOUTS WITH SOMEONE WHO ISN'T A TOTAL CHUMP!

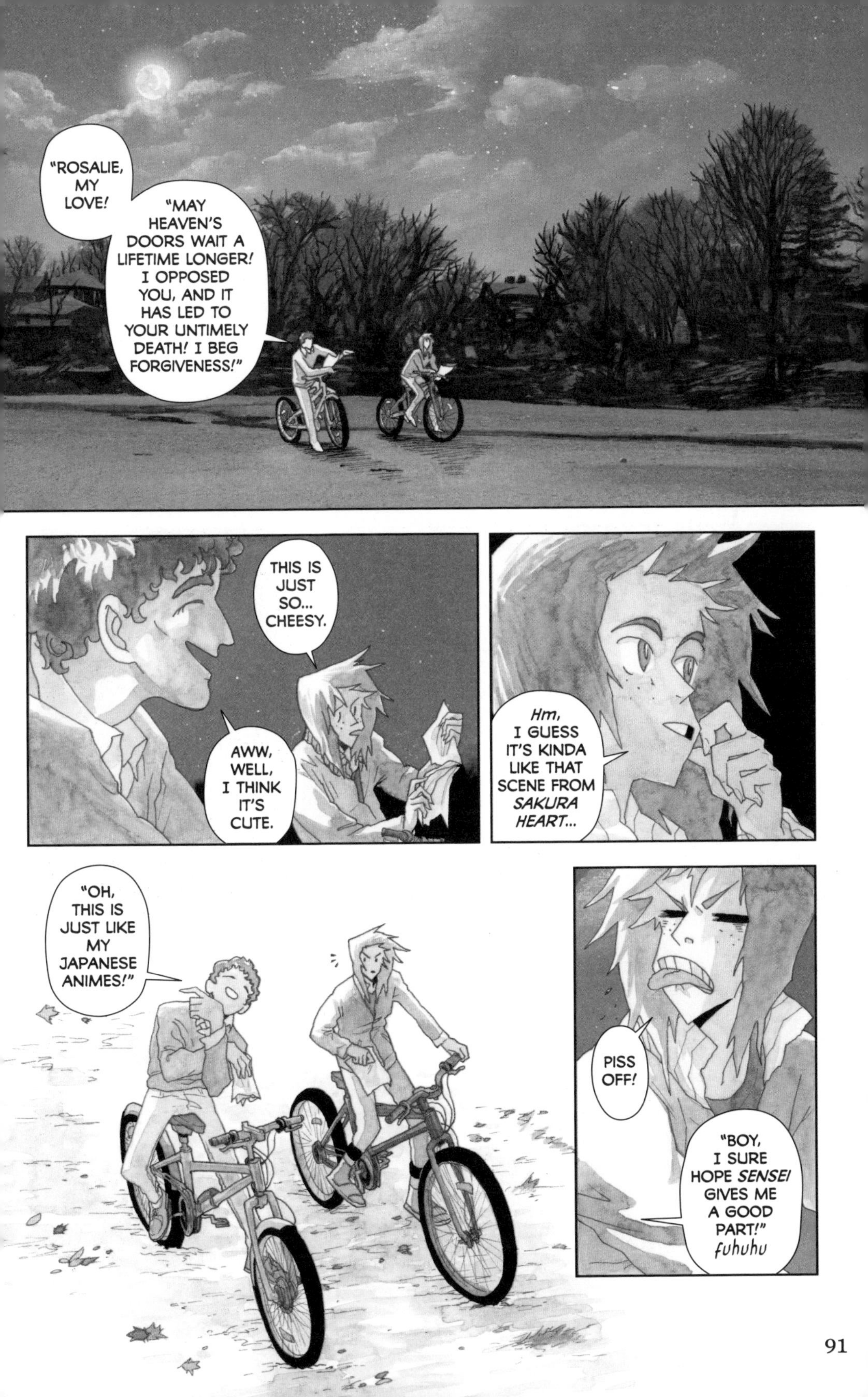
"ROSALIE, MY LOVE!
"MAY HEAVEN'S DOORS WAIT A LIFETIME LONGER! I OPPOSED YOU, AND IT HAS LED TO YOUR UNTIMELY DEATH! I BEG FORGIVENESS!"
THIS IS JUST SO... CHEESY.
AWW, WELL, I THINK IT'S CUTE.
Hm, I GUESS IT'S KINDA LIKE THAT SCENE FROM *SAKURA HEART*...
"OH, THIS IS JUST LIKE MY JAPANESE ANIMES!"
PISS OFF!
"BOY, I SURE HOPE *SENSEI* GIVES ME A GOOD PART!" *fuhuhu*

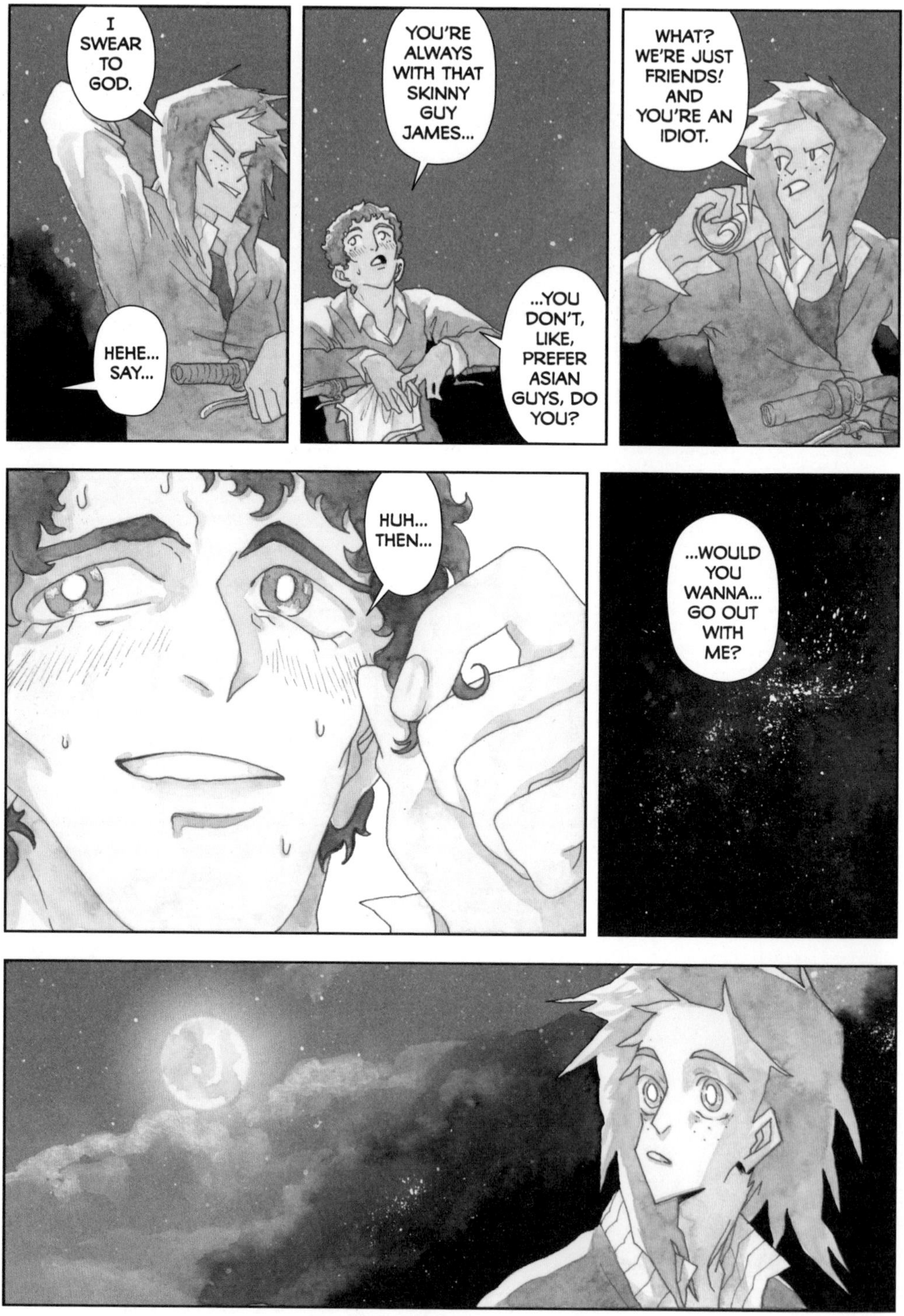
I SWEAR TO GOD.
HEHE... SAY...
YOU'RE ALWAYS WITH THAT SKINNY GUY JAMES...
...YOU DON'T, LIKE, PREFER ASIAN GUYS, DO YOU?
WHAT? WE'RE JUST FRIENDS! AND YOU'RE AN IDIOT.
HUH... THEN...
...WOULD YOU WANNA... GO OUT WITH ME?

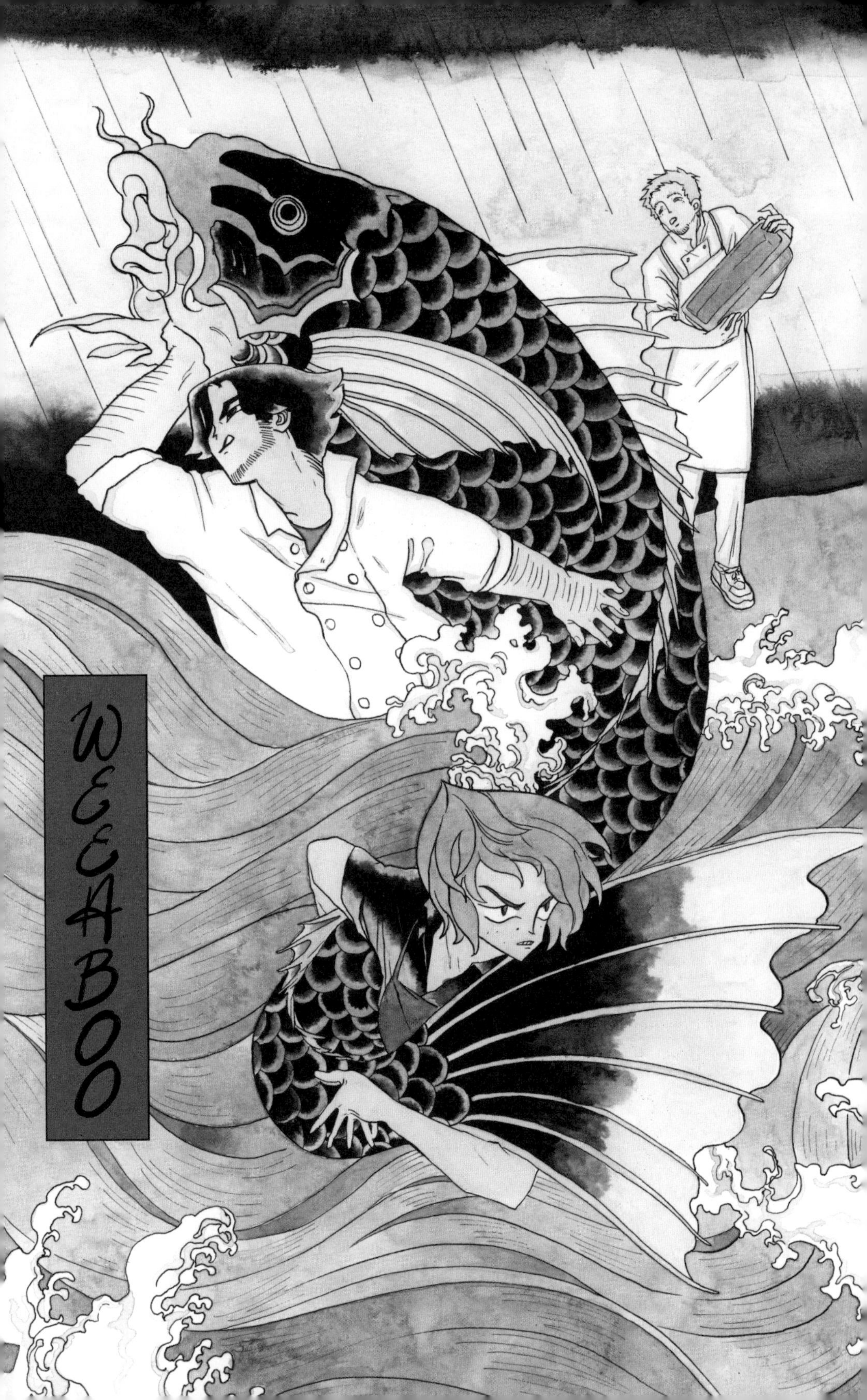
WEEABOO

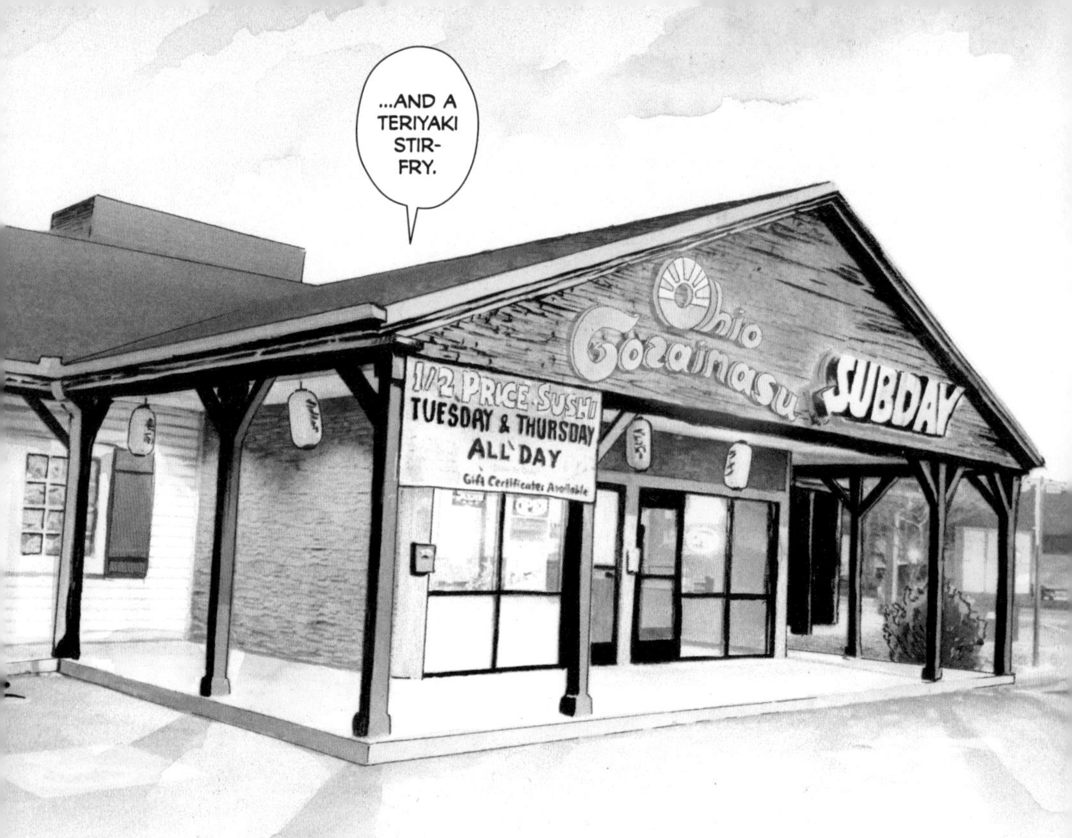
...AND A TERIYAKI STIR-FRY.
Ohio Gozainasu
SUBDAY
1/2 PRICE SUSHI
TUESDAY & THURSDAY
ALL DAY
Gift Certificates Available

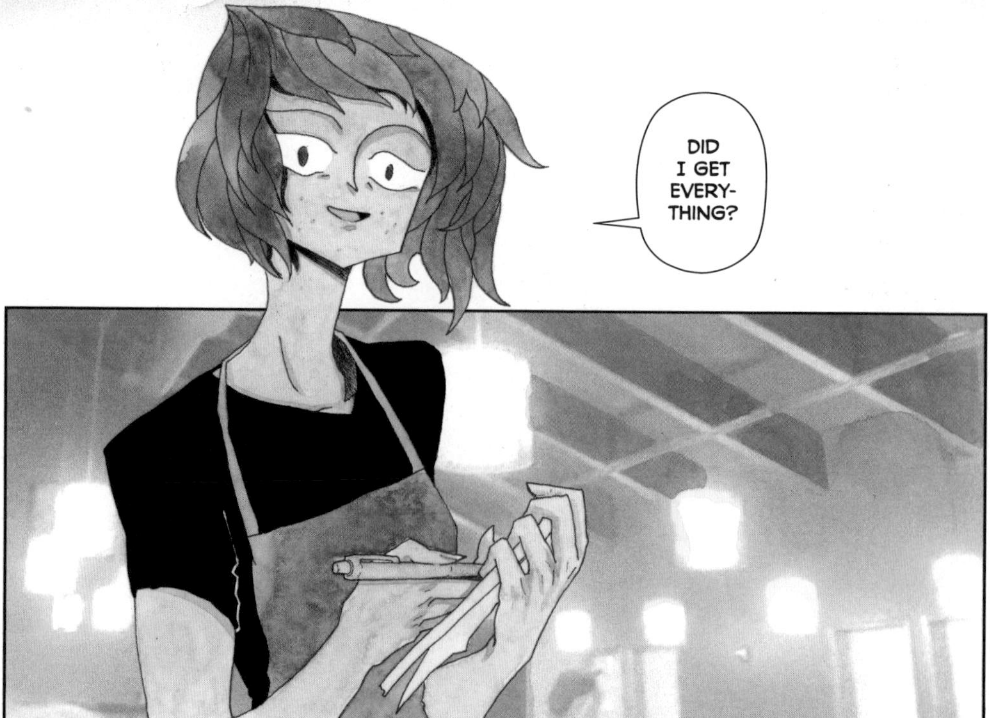
DID I GET EVERY-THING?

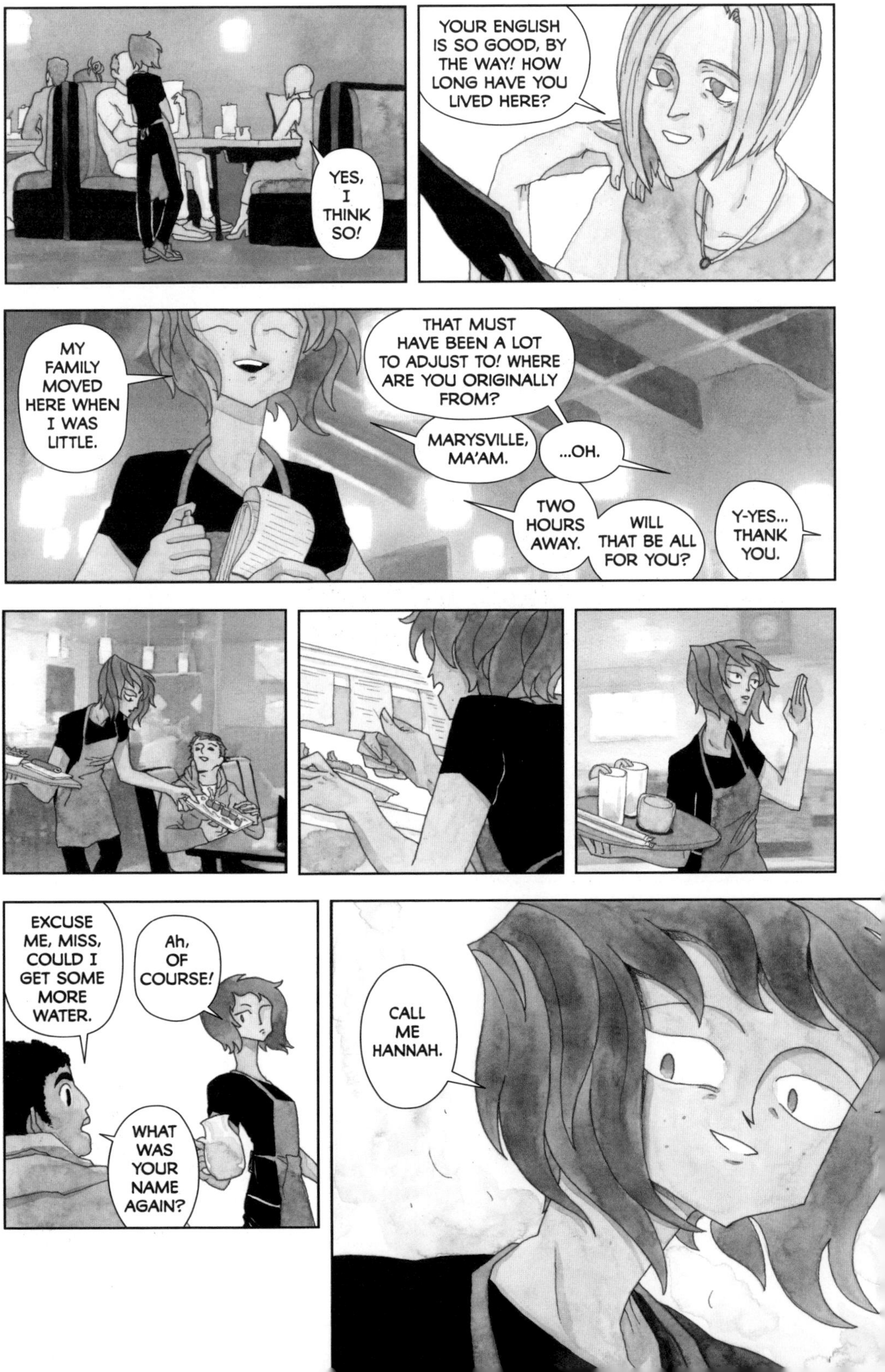
YES, I THINK SO!
YOUR ENGLISH IS SO GOOD, BY THE WAY! HOW LONG HAVE YOU LIVED HERE?
MY FAMILY MOVED HERE WHEN I WAS LITTLE.
THAT MUST HAVE BEEN A LOT TO ADJUST TO! WHERE ARE YOU ORIGINALLY FROM?
MARYSVILLE, MA'AM.
...OH.
TWO HOURS AWAY.
WILL THAT BE ALL FOR YOU?
Y-YES... THANK YOU.
EXCUSE ME, MISS, COULD I GET SOME MORE WATER.
Ah, OF COURSE!
WHAT WAS YOUR NAME AGAIN?
CALL ME HANNAH.

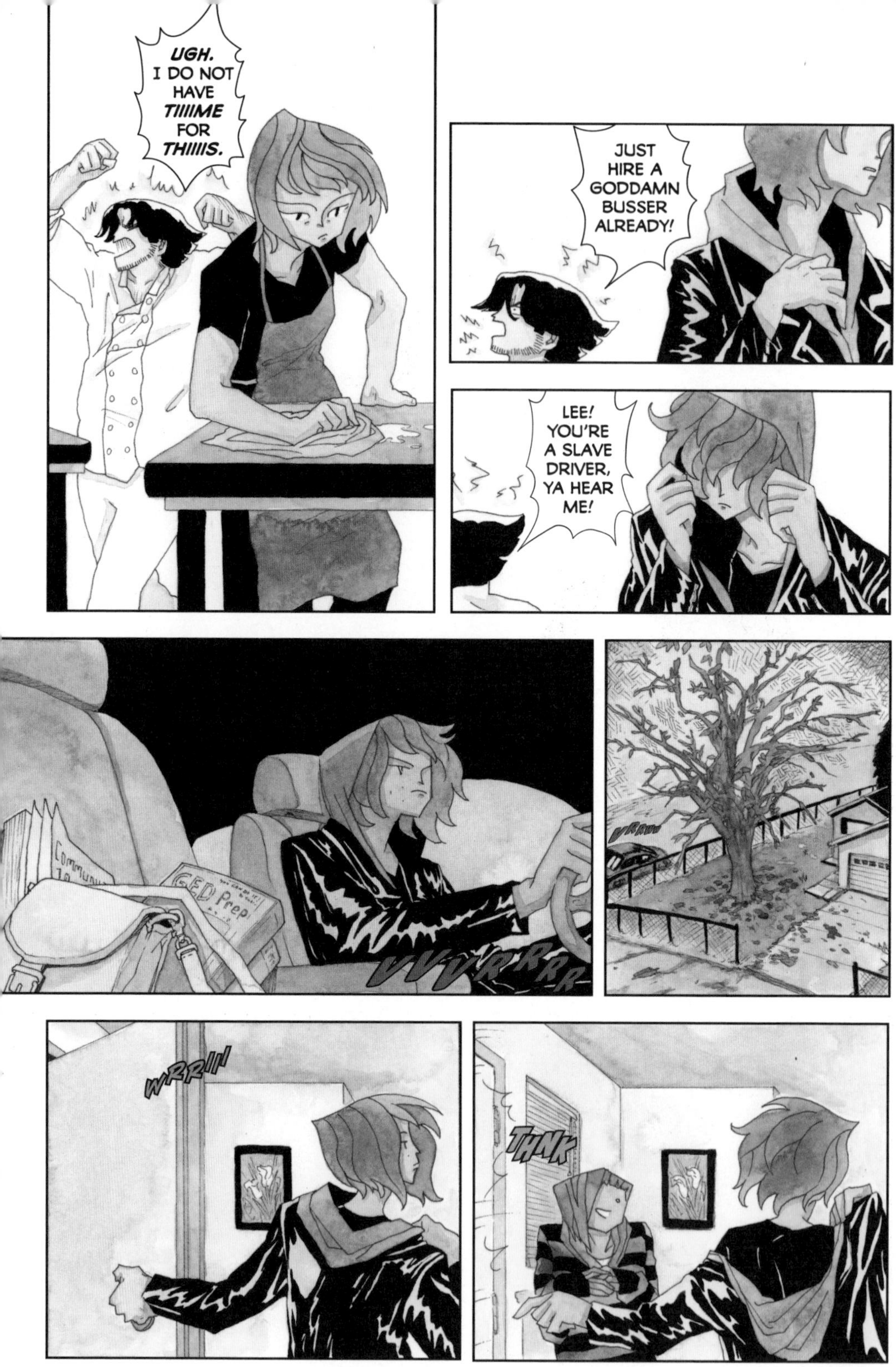
UGH. I DO NOT HAVE TIIIIME FOR THIIIIS.
JUST HIRE A GODDAMN BUSSER ALREADY!
LEE! YOU'RE A SLAVE DRIVER, YA HEAR ME!
GED Prep
VVVRRRR
VRRRR
WRRIII
THNK

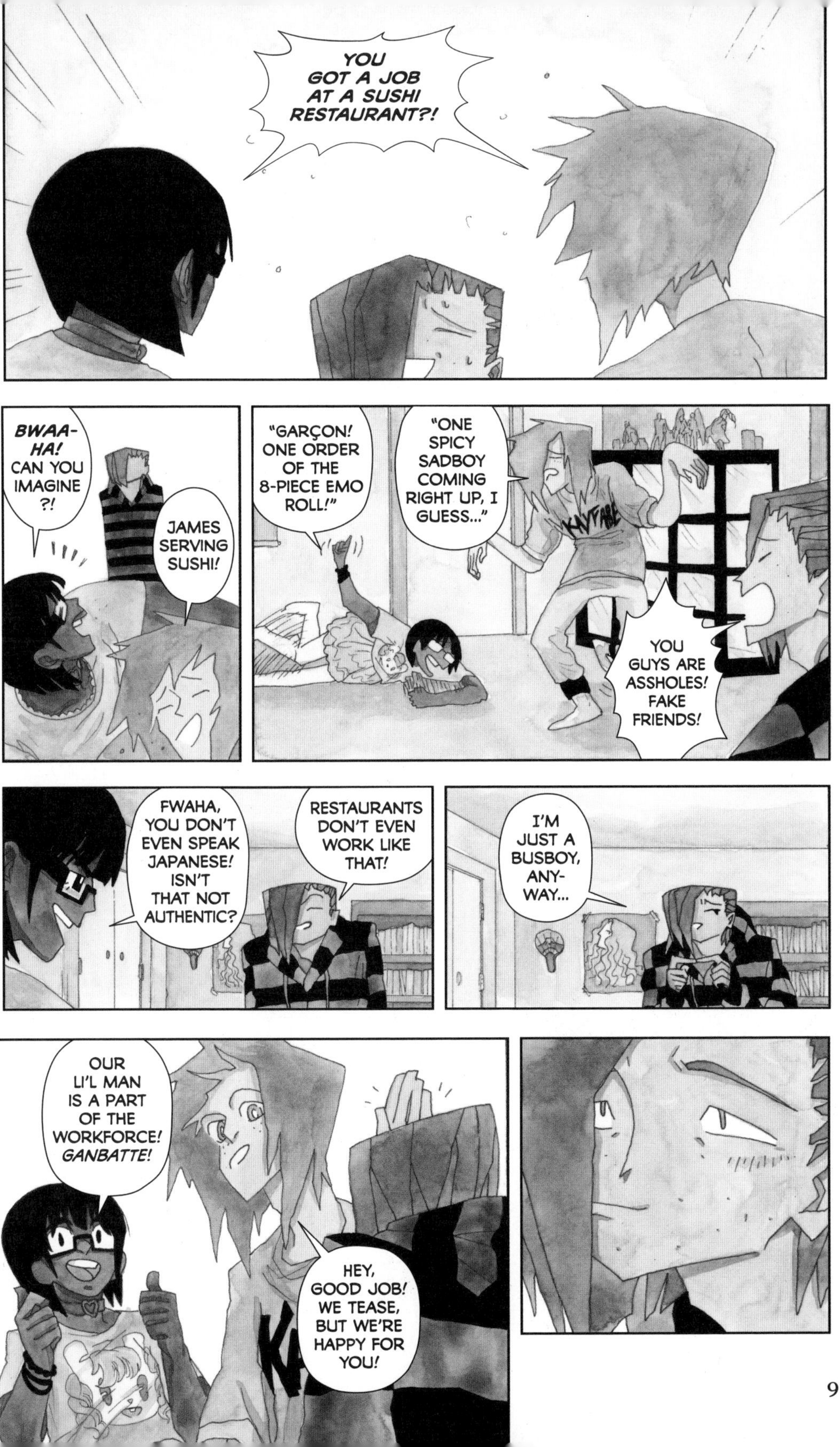
YOU GOT A JOB AT A SUSHI RESTAURANT?!
BWAA-HA! CAN YOU IMAGINE?!
JAMES SERVING SUSHI!
"GARÇON! ONE ORDER OF THE 8-PIECE EMO ROLL!"
"ONE SPICY SADBOY COMING RIGHT UP, I GUESS..."
KAYFABE
YOU GUYS ARE ASSHOLES! FAKE FRIENDS!
FWAHA, YOU DON'T EVEN SPEAK JAPANESE! ISN'T THAT NOT AUTHENTIC?
RESTAURANTS DON'T EVEN WORK LIKE THAT!
I'M JUST A BUSBOY, ANY-WAY...
OUR LI'L MAN IS A PART OF THE WORKFORCE! *GANBATTE!*
HEY, GOOD JOB! WE TEASE, BUT WE'RE HAPPY FOR YOU!

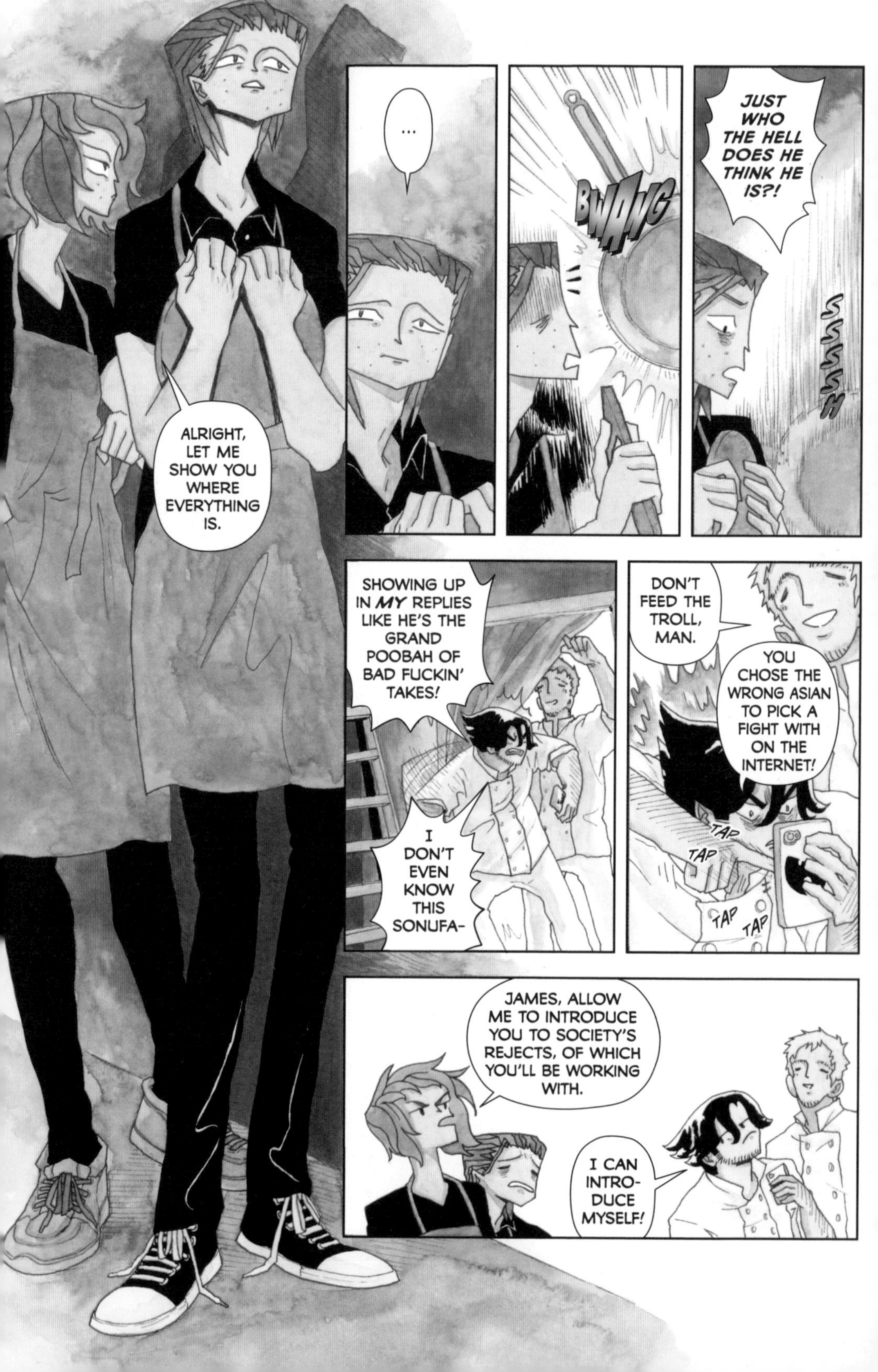
ALRIGHT, LET ME SHOW YOU WHERE EVERYTHING IS.
...
BWANG
JUST WHO THE HELL DOES HE THINK HE IS?!
SSSSSH
SHOWING UP IN MY REPLIES LIKE HE'S THE GRAND POOBAH OF BAD FUCKIN' TAKES!
I DON'T EVEN KNOW THIS SONUFA-
DON'T FEED THE TROLL, MAN.
YOU CHOSE THE WRONG ASIAN TO PICK A FIGHT WITH ON THE INTERNET!
TAP
TAP
TAP
TAP
JAMES, ALLOW ME TO INTRODUCE YOU TO SOCIETY'S REJECTS, OF WHICH YOU'LL BE WORKING WITH.
I CAN INTRODUCE MYSELF!

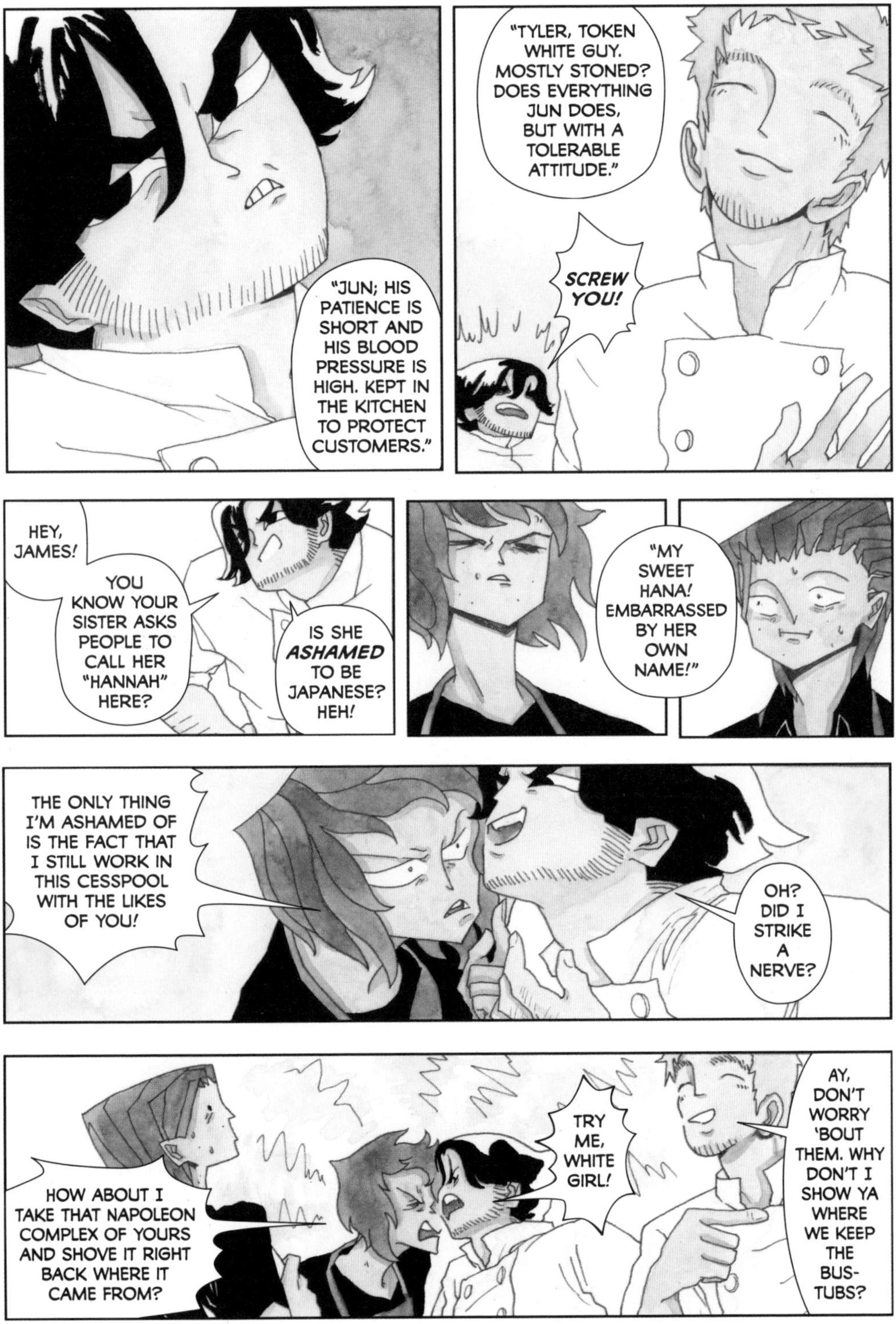
"JUN; HIS PATIENCE IS SHORT AND HIS BLOOD PRESSURE IS HIGH. KEPT IN THE KITCHEN TO PROTECT CUSTOMERS."
"TYLER, TOKEN WHITE GUY. MOSTLY STONED? DOES EVERYTHING JUN DOES, BUT WITH A TOLERABLE ATTITUDE."
SCREW YOU!
HEY, JAMES!
YOU KNOW YOUR SISTER ASKS PEOPLE TO CALL HER "HANNAH" HERE?
IS SHE ASHAMED TO BE JAPANESE? HEH!
"MY SWEET HANA! EMBARRASSED BY HER OWN NAME!"
THE ONLY THING I'M ASHAMED OF IS THE FACT THAT I STILL WORK IN THIS CESSPOOL WITH THE LIKES OF YOU!
OH? DID I STRIKE A NERVE?
HOW ABOUT I TAKE THAT NAPOLEON COMPLEX OF YOURS AND SHOVE IT RIGHT BACK WHERE IT CAME FROM?
TRY ME, WHITE GIRL!
AY, DON'T WORRY 'BOUT THEM. WHY DON'T I SHOW YA WHERE WE KEEP THE BUS-TUBS?

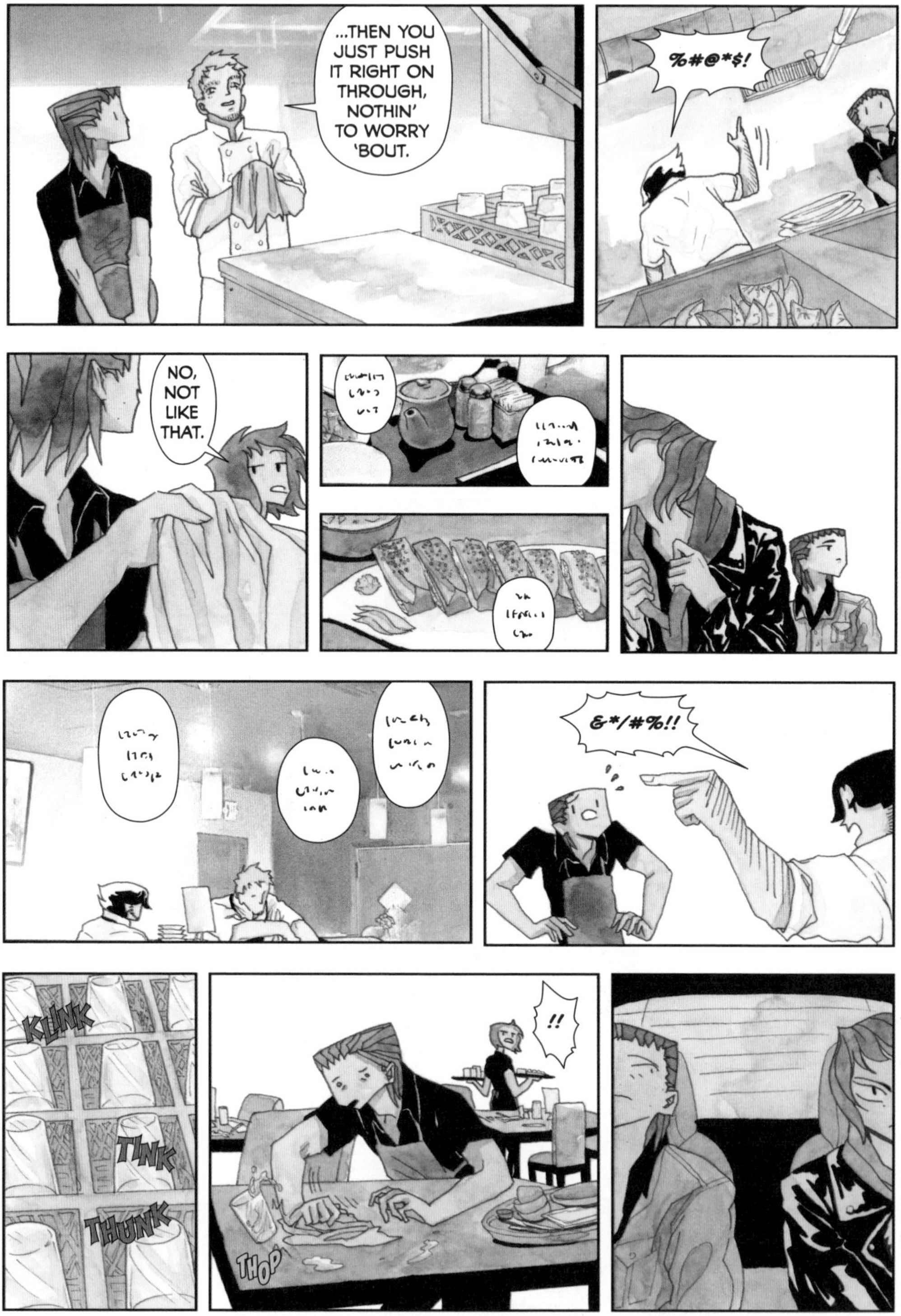
...THEN YOU JUST PUSH IT RIGHT ON THROUGH, NOTHIN' TO WORRY 'BOUT.
%#@*$!
NO, NOT LIKE THAT.
&*/#%!!
KLINK
TINK
THUNK
THOP
!!

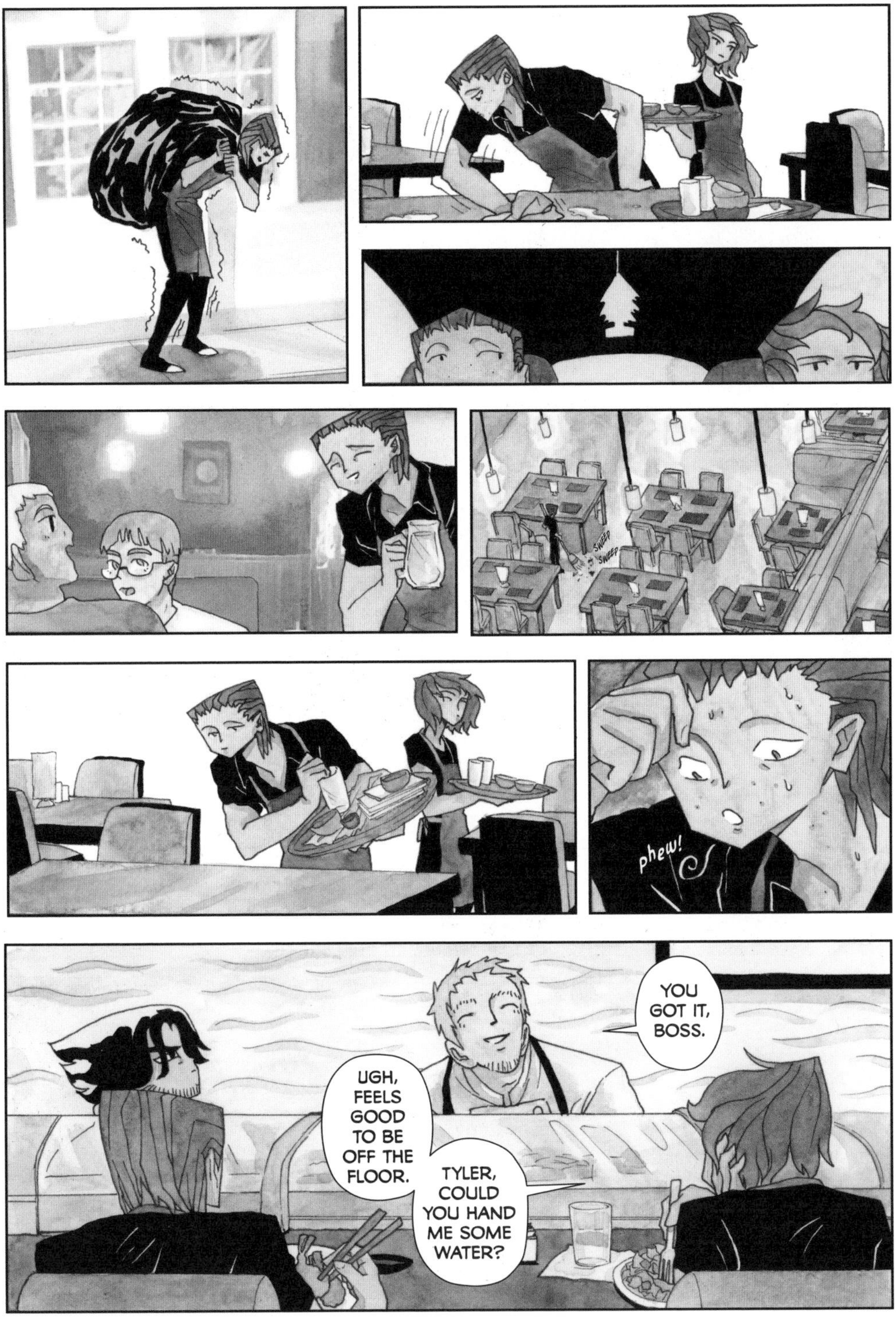
SWEEP
SWEEP
phew!
YOU GOT IT, BOSS.
UGH, FEELS GOOD TO BE OFF THE FLOOR.
TYLER, COULD YOU HAND ME SOME WATER?

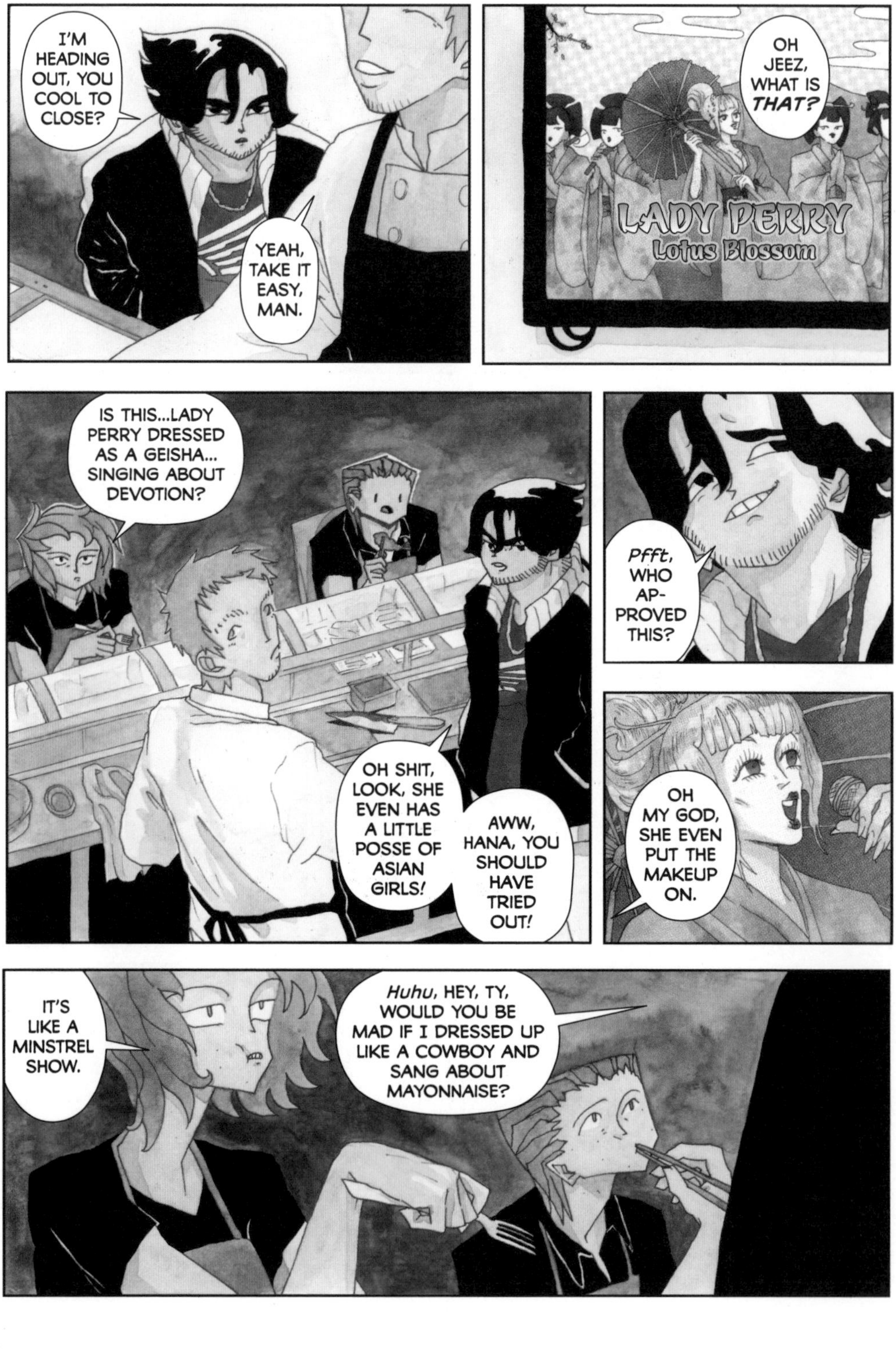
I'M HEADING OUT, YOU COOL TO CLOSE?
YEAH, TAKE IT EASY, MAN.
OH JEEZ, WHAT IS *THAT?*
LADY PERRY
Lotus Blossom
IS THIS...LADY PERRY DRESSED AS A GEISHA... SINGING ABOUT DEVOTION?
Pfft, WHO AP-PROVED THIS?
OH SHIT, LOOK, SHE EVEN HAS A LITTLE POSSE OF ASIAN GIRLS!
AWW, HANA, YOU SHOULD HAVE TRIED OUT!
OH MY GOD, SHE EVEN PUT THE MAKEUP ON.
IT'S LIKE A MINSTREL SHOW.
Huhu, HEY, TY, WOULD YOU BE MAD IF I DRESSED UP LIKE A COWBOY AND SANG ABOUT MAYONNAISE?

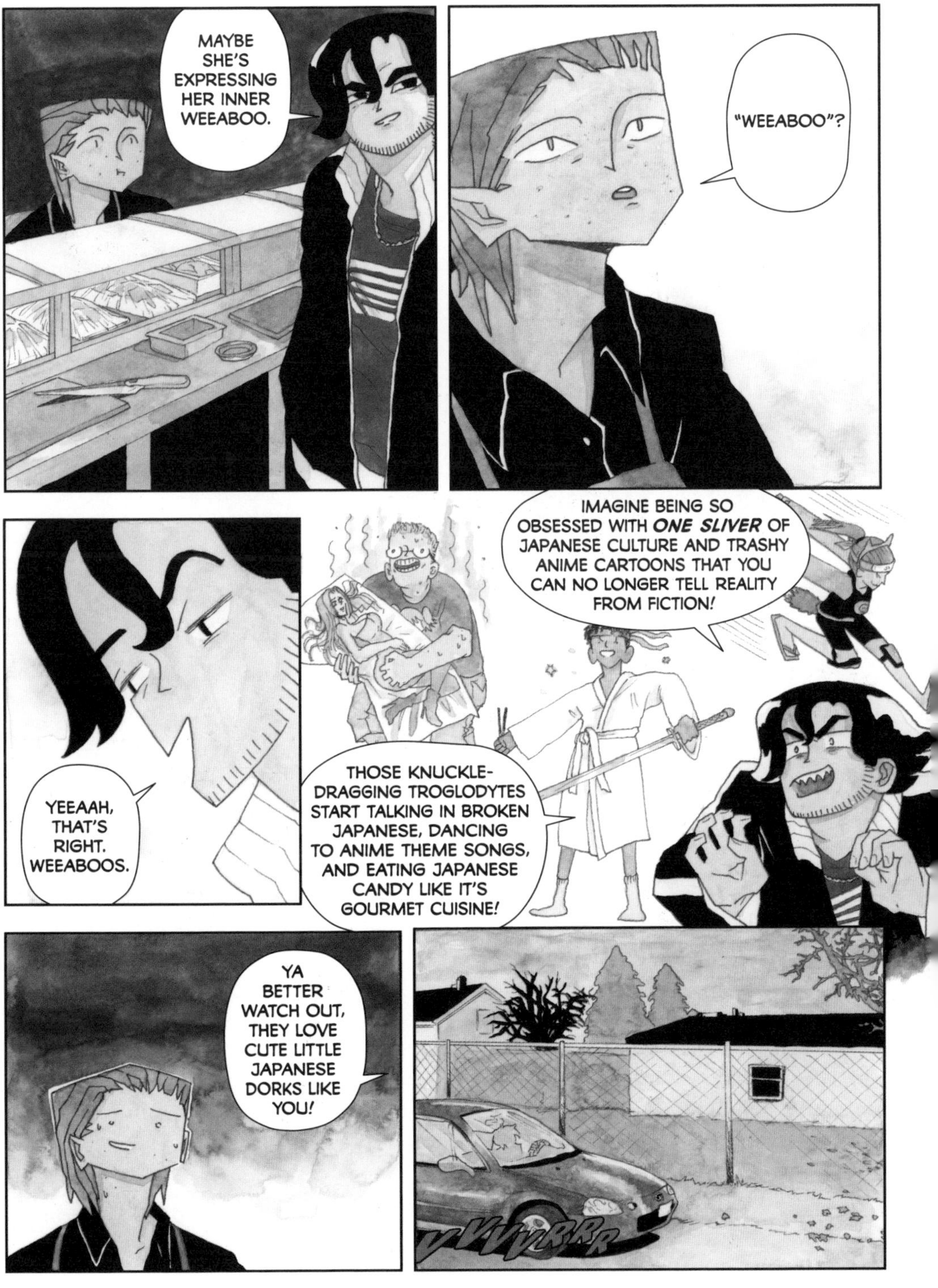
MAYBE SHE'S EXPRESSING HER INNER WEEABOO.
"WEEABOO"?
YEEAAH, THAT'S RIGHT. WEEABOOS.
IMAGINE BEING SO OBSESSED WITH ***ONE SLIVER*** OF JAPANESE CULTURE AND TRASHY ANIME CARTOONS THAT YOU CAN NO LONGER TELL REALITY FROM FICTION!
THOSE KNUCKLE-DRAGGING TROGLODYTES START TALKING IN BROKEN JAPANESE, DANCING TO ANIME THEME SONGS, AND EATING JAPANESE CANDY LIKE IT'S GOURMET CUISINE!
YA BETTER WATCH OUT, THEY LOVE CUTE LITTLE JAPANESE DORKS LIKE YOU!
VVVVVVRRRR

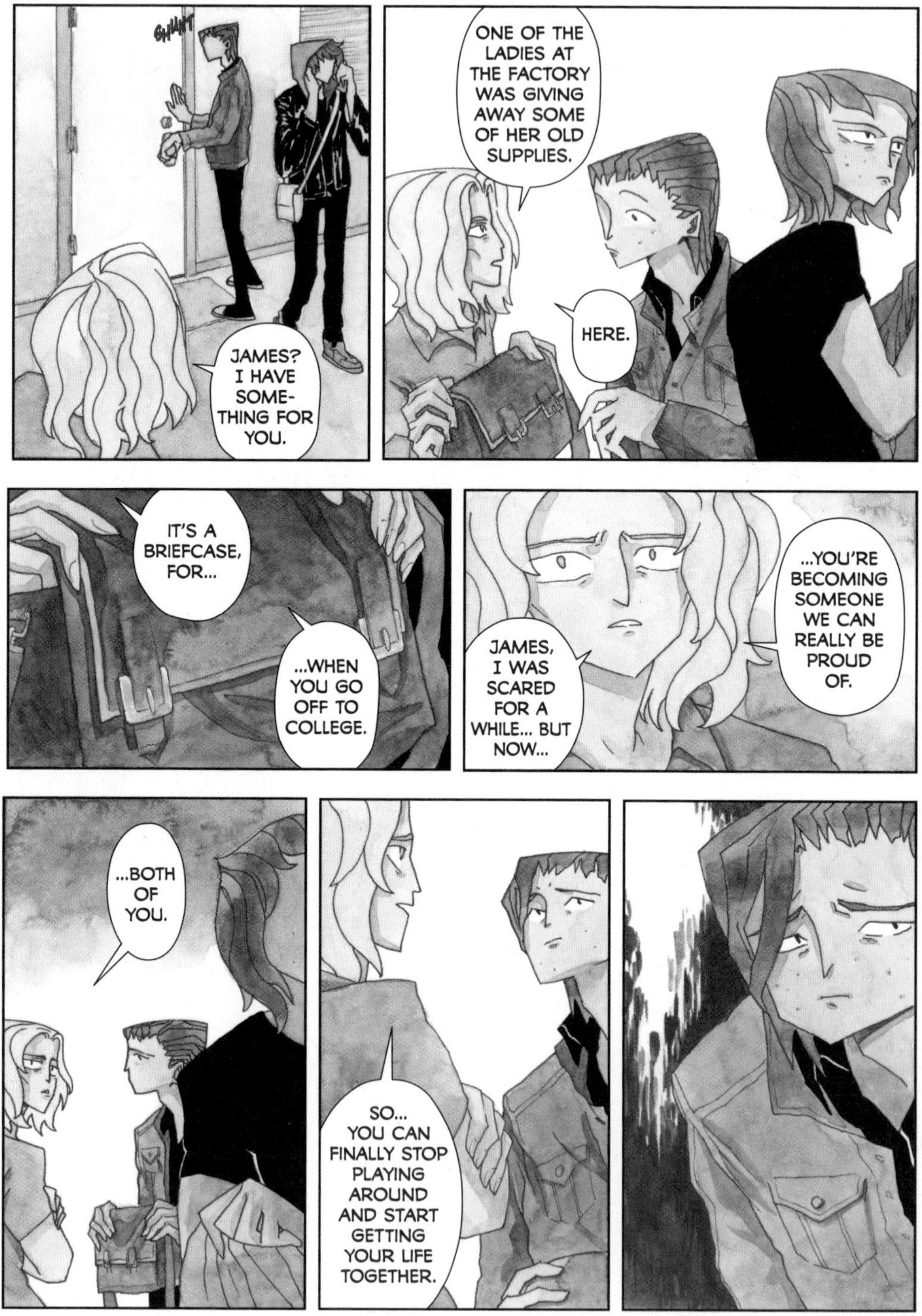
SHUNT
JAMES? I HAVE SOME-THING FOR YOU.
ONE OF THE LADIES AT THE FACTORY WAS GIVING AWAY SOME OF HER OLD SUPPLIES.
HERE.
IT'S A BRIEFCASE, FOR...
...WHEN YOU GO OFF TO COLLEGE.
JAMES, I WAS SCARED FOR A WHILE... BUT NOW...
...YOU'RE BECOMING SOMEONE WE CAN REALLY BE PROUD OF.
...BOTH OF YOU.
SO... YOU CAN FINALLY STOP PLAYING AROUND AND START GETTING YOUR LIFE TOGETHER.

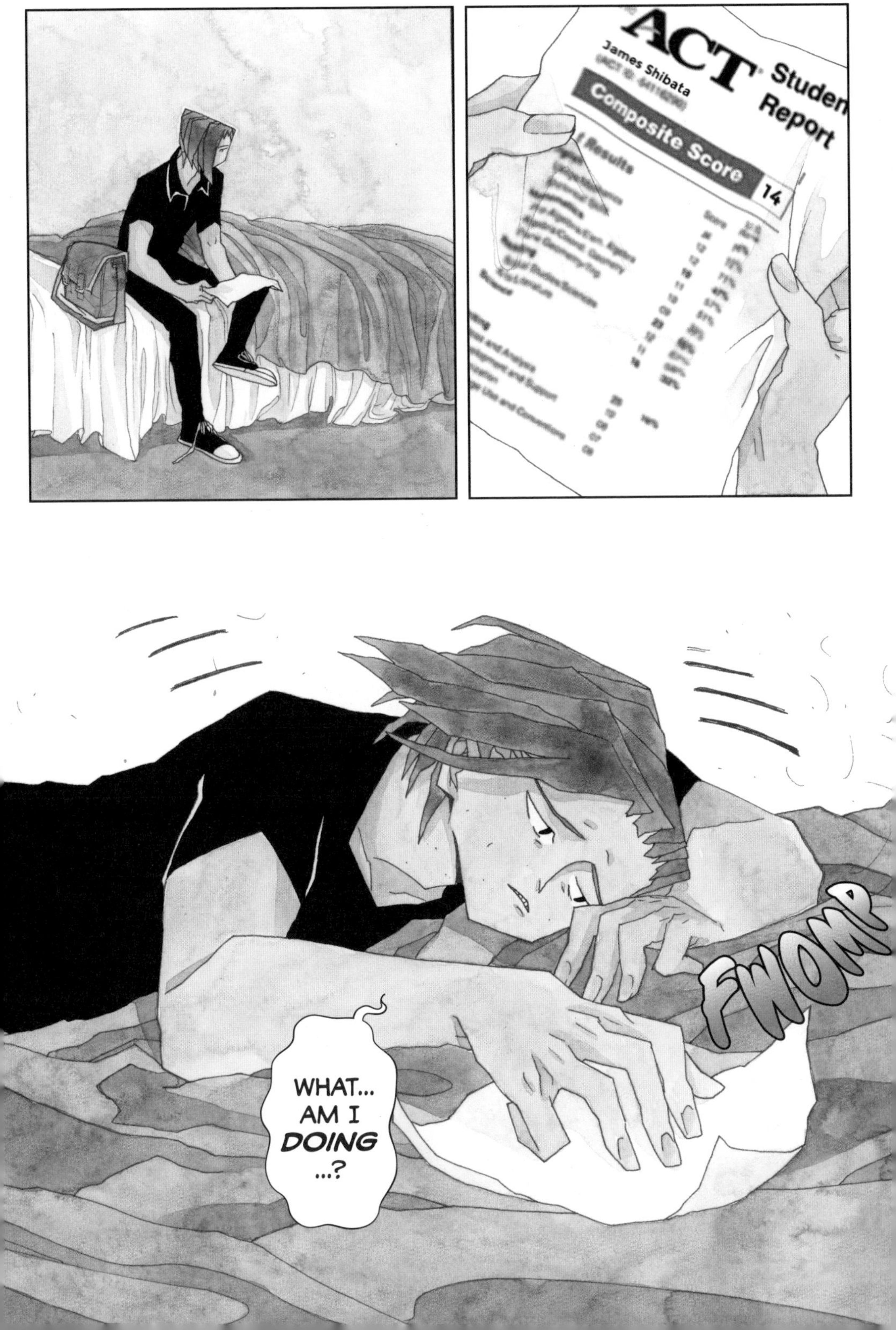
ACT Studen
Report
James Shibata
Composite Score
14
FWOMP
WHAT... AM I DOING ...?

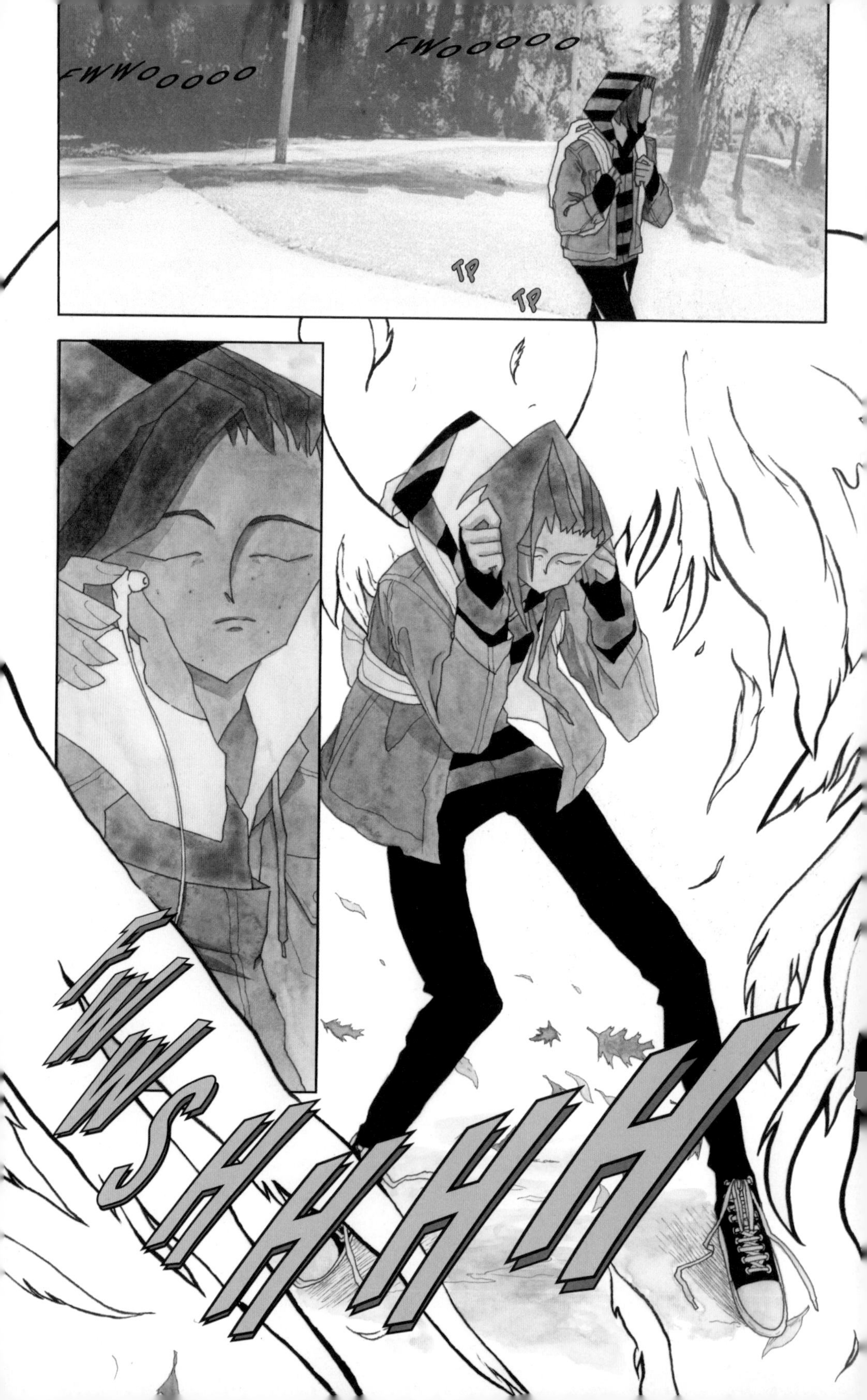
FWWOOOOO
FWOOOOOO
TP
TP
FWWSHHHHH

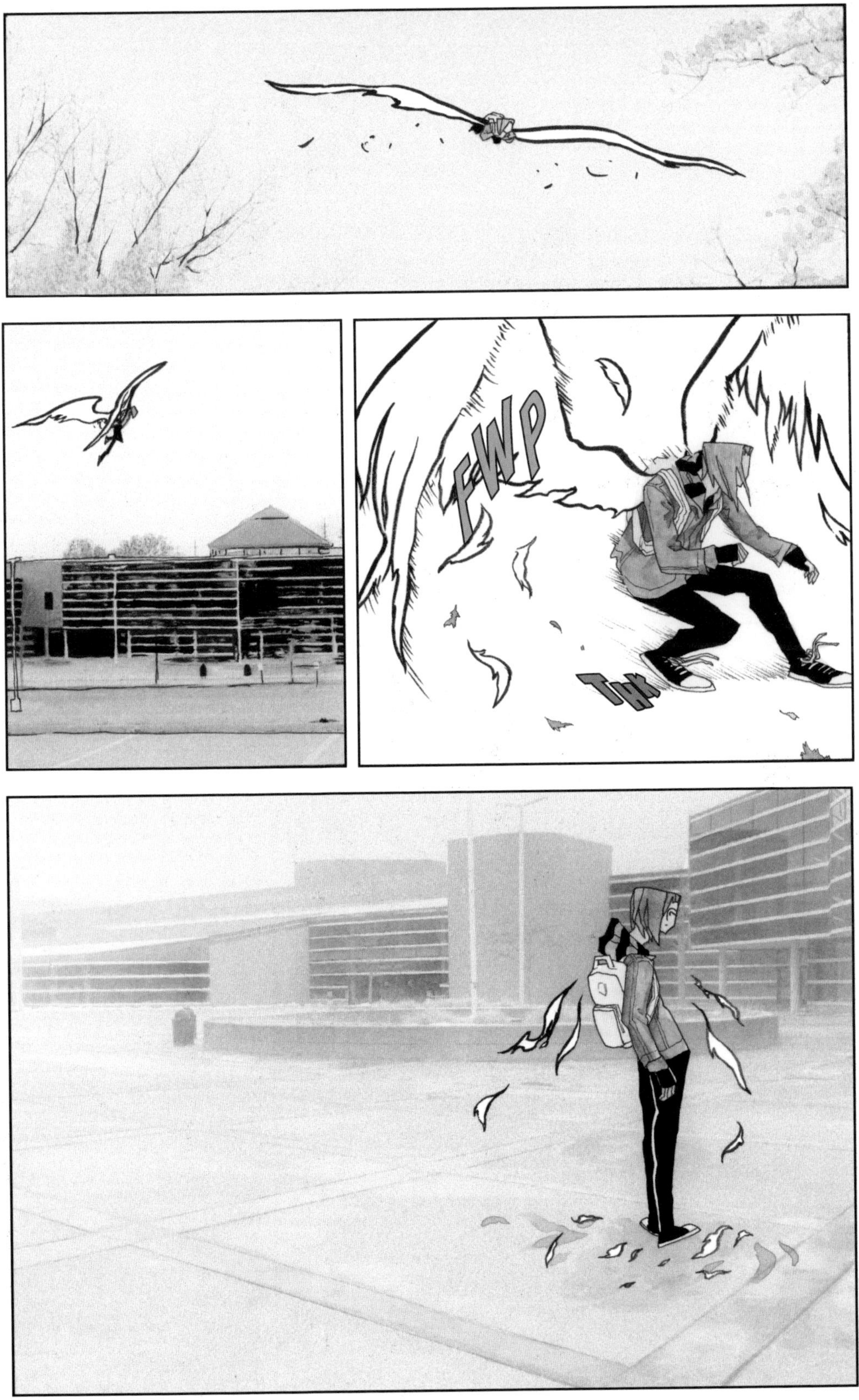
FWP
THK

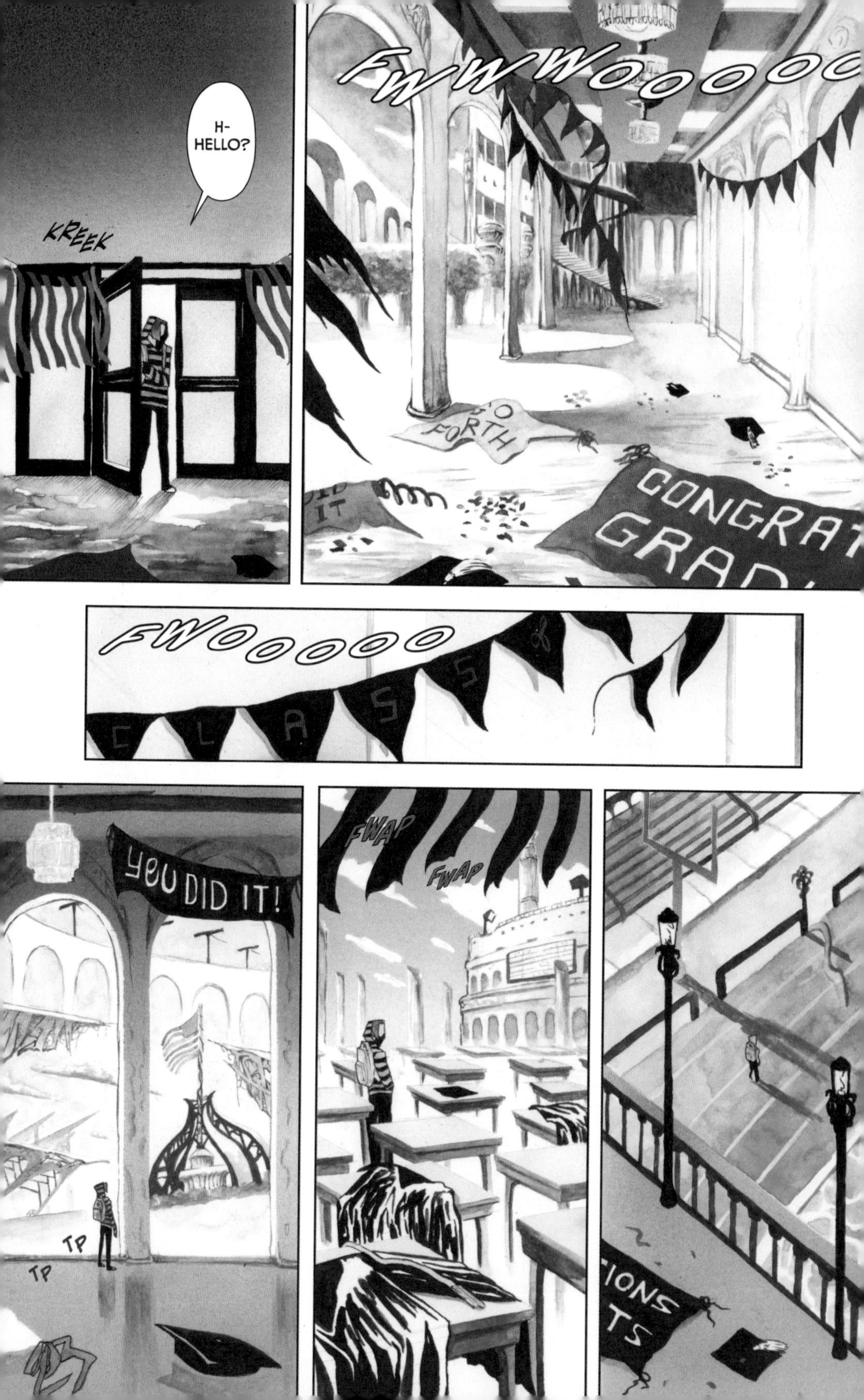
KREEK
H-
HELLO?
FWWWOOOOO
SO
FORTH
ID
IT
CONGRAT
GRAD
FWOOOOOO
CLASS
YOU DID IT!
TP
TP
FWAP
FWAP
IONS
TS

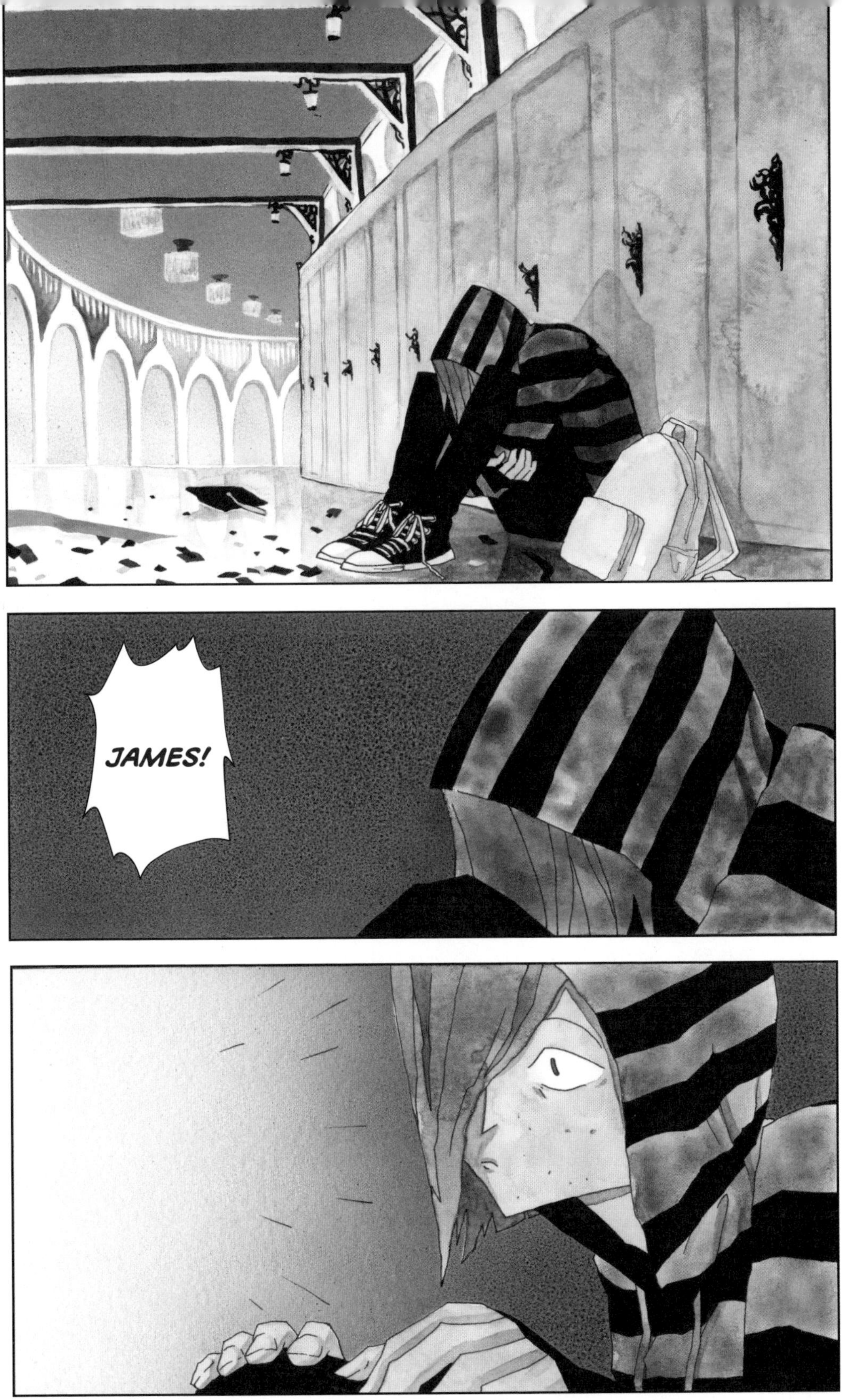
JAMES!

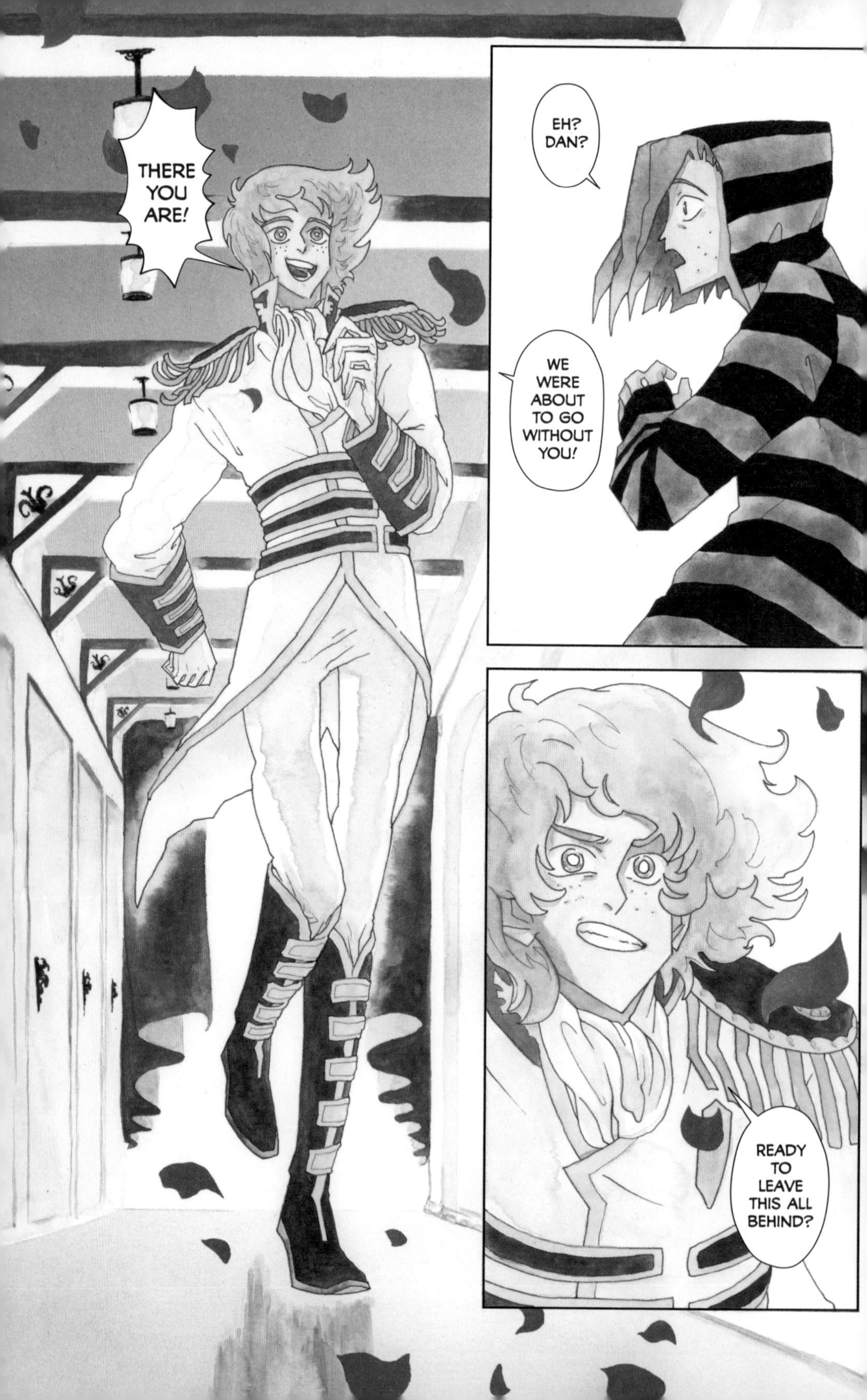
THERE YOU ARE!
EH? DAN?
WE WERE ABOUT TO GO WITHOUT YOU!
READY TO LEAVE THIS ALL BEHIND?

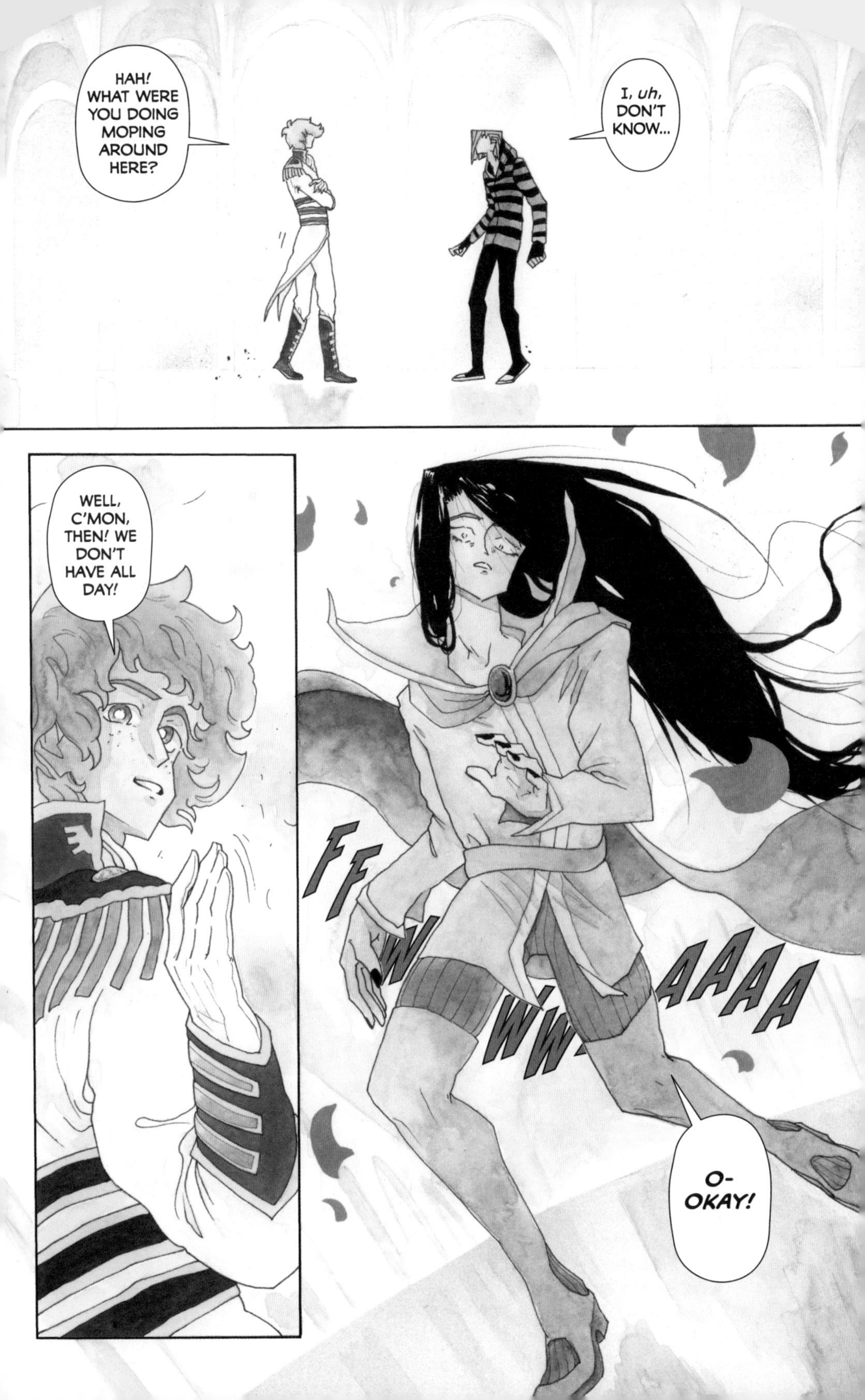
HAH! WHAT WERE YOU DOING MOPING AROUND HERE?
I, *uh*, DON'T KNOW...
WELL, C'MON, THEN! WE DON'T HAVE ALL DAY!
FFWWWAAAAA
O-OKAY!

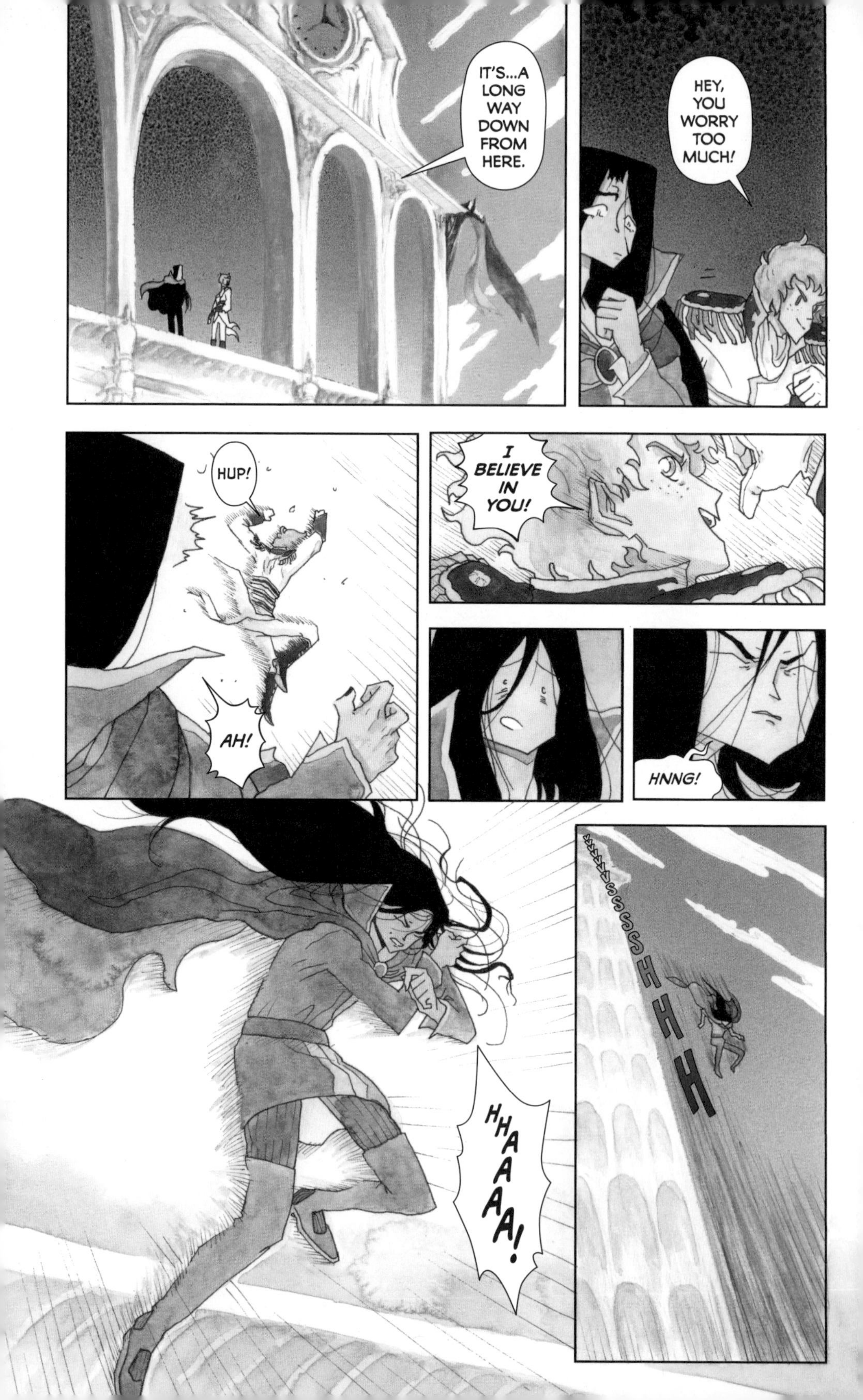
IT'S...A LONG WAY DOWN FROM HERE.
HEY, YOU WORRY TOO MUCH!
HUP!
AH!
I BELIEVE IN YOU!
HNNG!
HHAAAAAA!
VVVVVSSSSSHHHHH

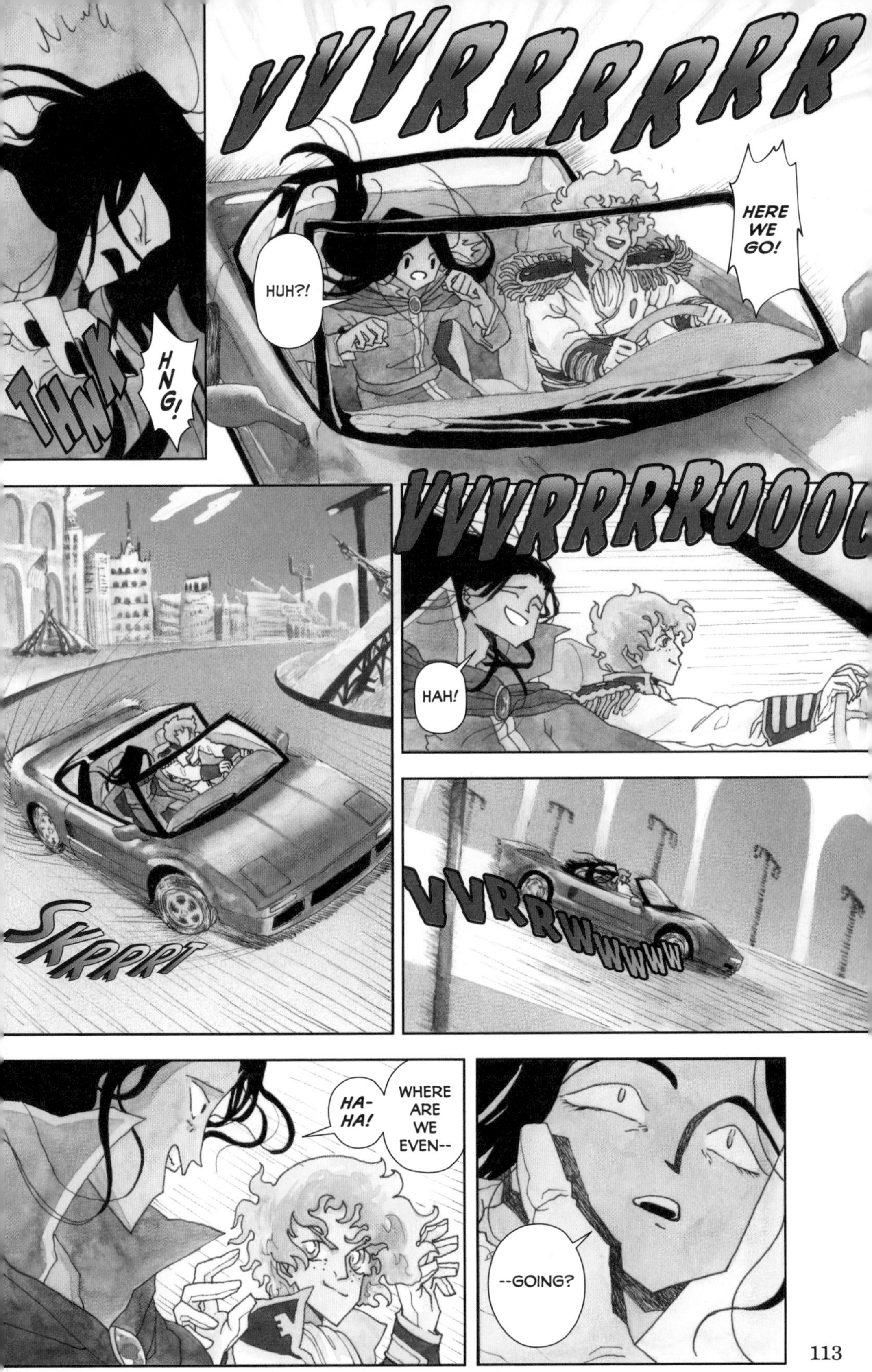
THNK
HNG!
VVVRRRRRRR
HUH?!
HERE WE GO!
SKRRRT
VVVRRRROOOO
HAH!
VVRRWWWWWW
HA-HA!
WHERE ARE WE EVEN--
--GOING?

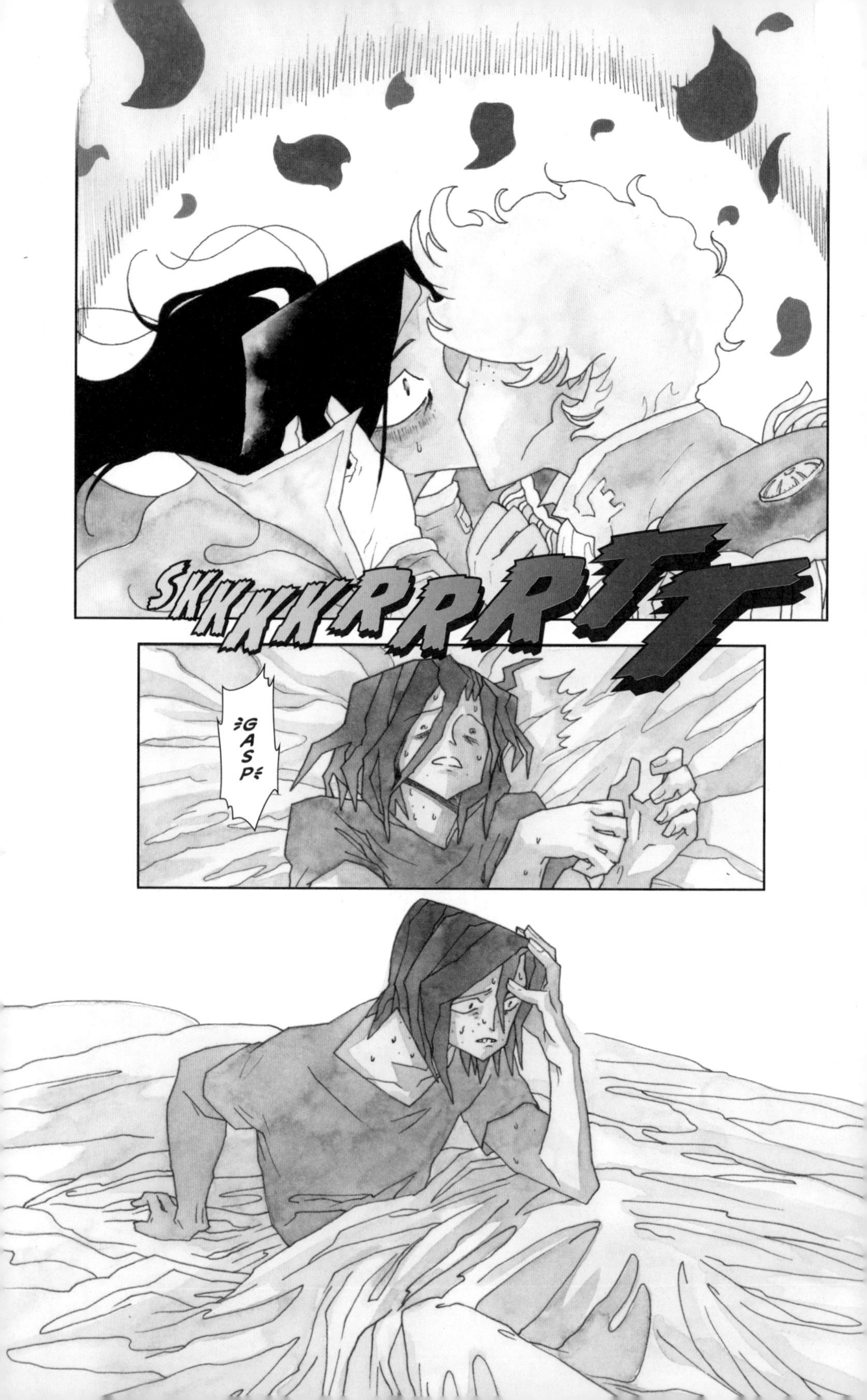
SKKKKKRRRRTT
GASP

WEEABOO

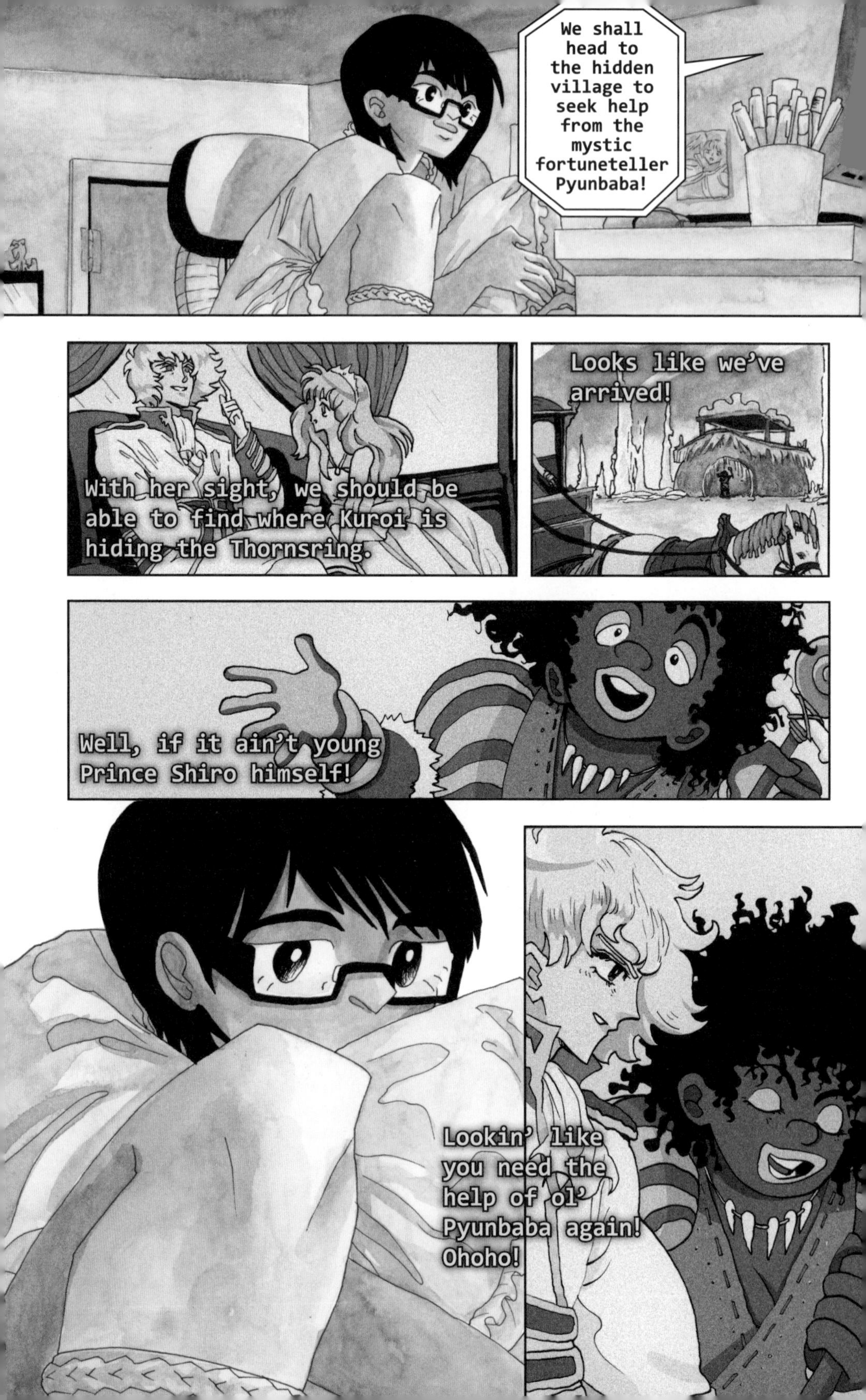

We shall head to the hidden village to seek help from the mystic fortuneteller Pyunbaba!
With her sight, we should be able to find where Kuroi is hiding the Thornsring.
Looks like we've arrived!
Well, if it ain't young Prince Shiro himself!
Lookin' like you need the help of ol' Pyunbaba again! Ohoho!

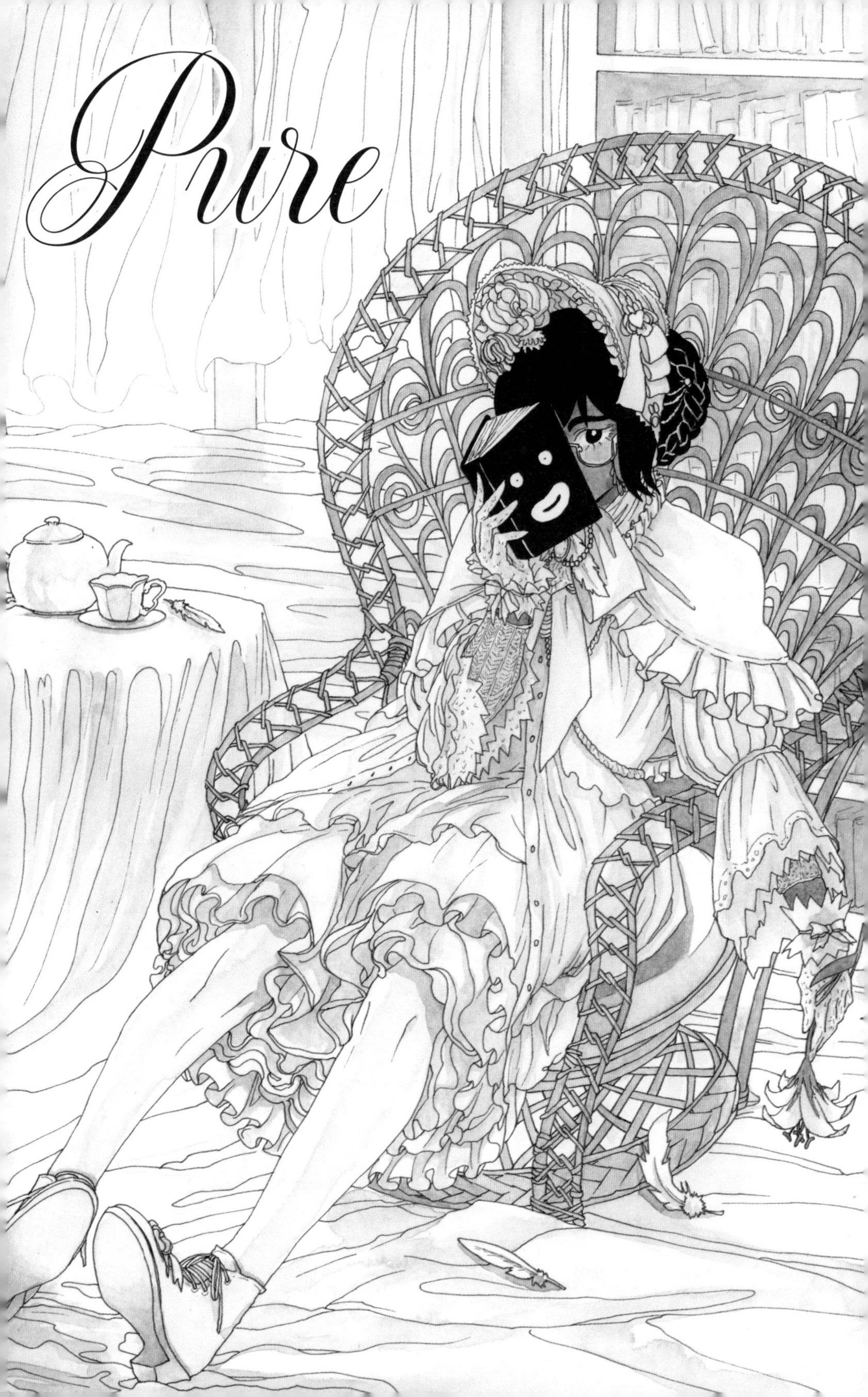
Pure

Mayako's Room

Home
Blog
Fashion
Shop
Gallery

Tumble down
~Mayako's Wonderland~

New Shop Update!

Latest Post: 12/18

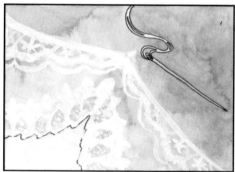

Post 12/5

The tribute to my lady Hime has begun! ♥
I'm fitting a lovely body frame, this dress
shall be my best yet~

lovely_angelic2: Wow! can't wait to see this

soprettyveryrotten: will there be a tutorial??

kam1neko: can't wait to see you in it ~.^

Post 12/9

A lady is nothing without her fine lace!
I'll be practicing hand weaving lace this
time, I hope you'll join me through this
journey~

xXxLostAlicexXx: Don't prick yourself,
princess~

BebasPapa: i CANNOT wait to put this in
my eyes

BabyTheKidsAreAlright: Impressive! owo

soprettyveryrotten: tutorial?

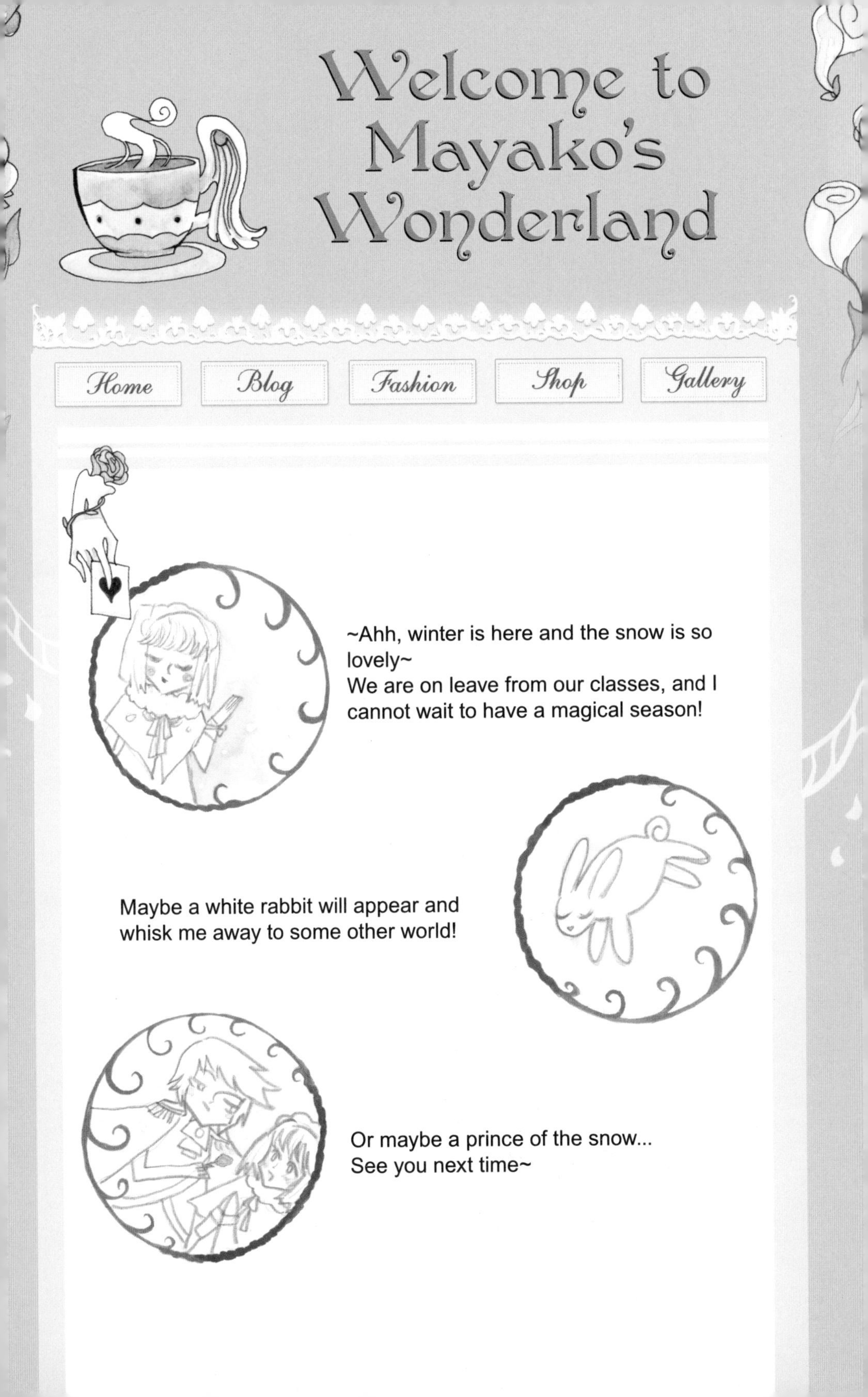
Welcome to Mayako's Wonderland
Home
Blog
Fashion
Shop
Gallery
~Ahh, winter is here and the snow is so lovely~
We are on leave from our classes, and I cannot wait to have a magical season!
Maybe a white rabbit will appear and whisk me away to some other world!
Or maybe a prince of the snow...
See you next time~

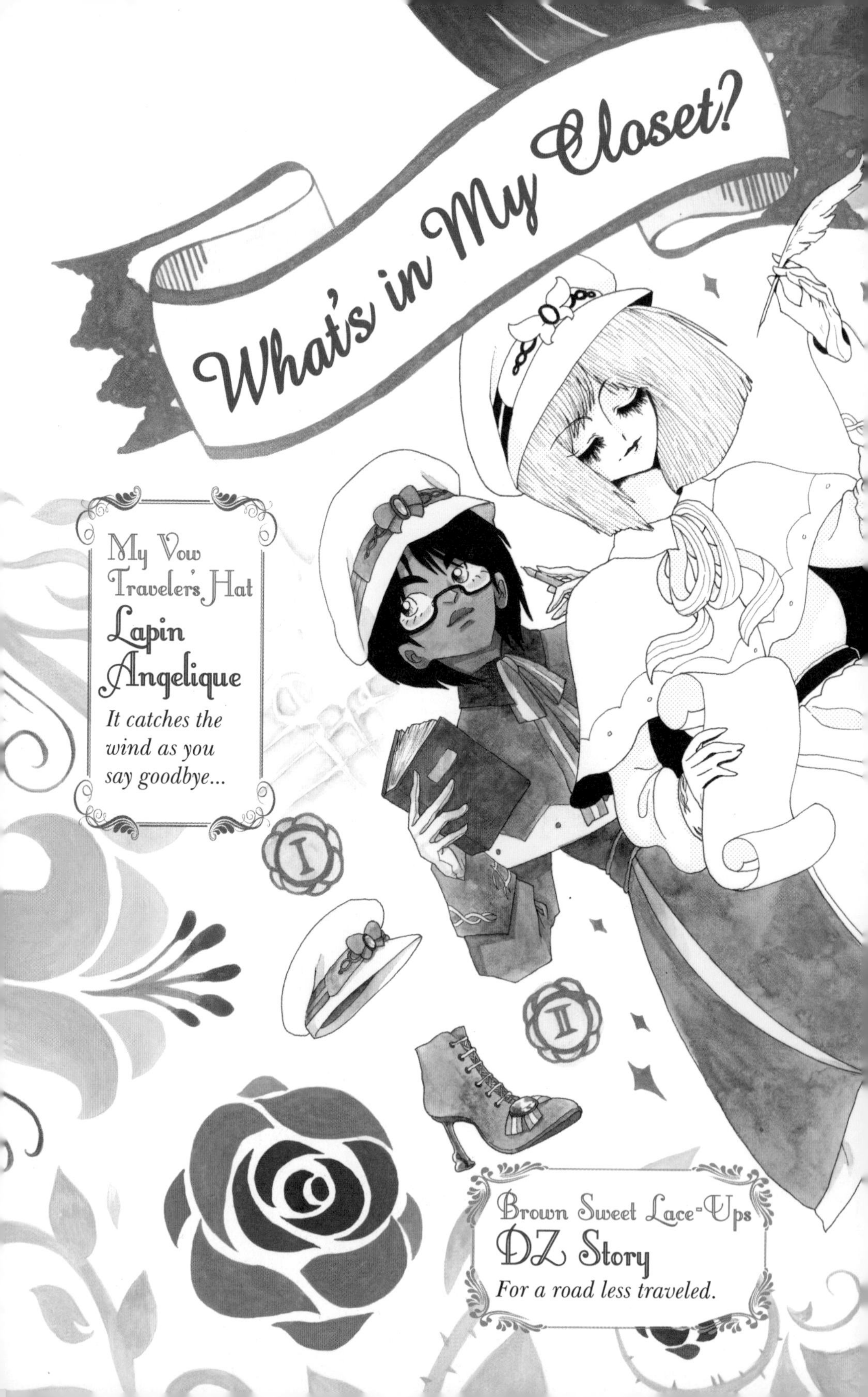

What's in My Closet?
My Vow Traveler's Hat
Lapin Angelique
It catches the wind as you say goodbye...
I
II
Brown Sweet Lace-Ups
DZ Story
For a road less traveled.

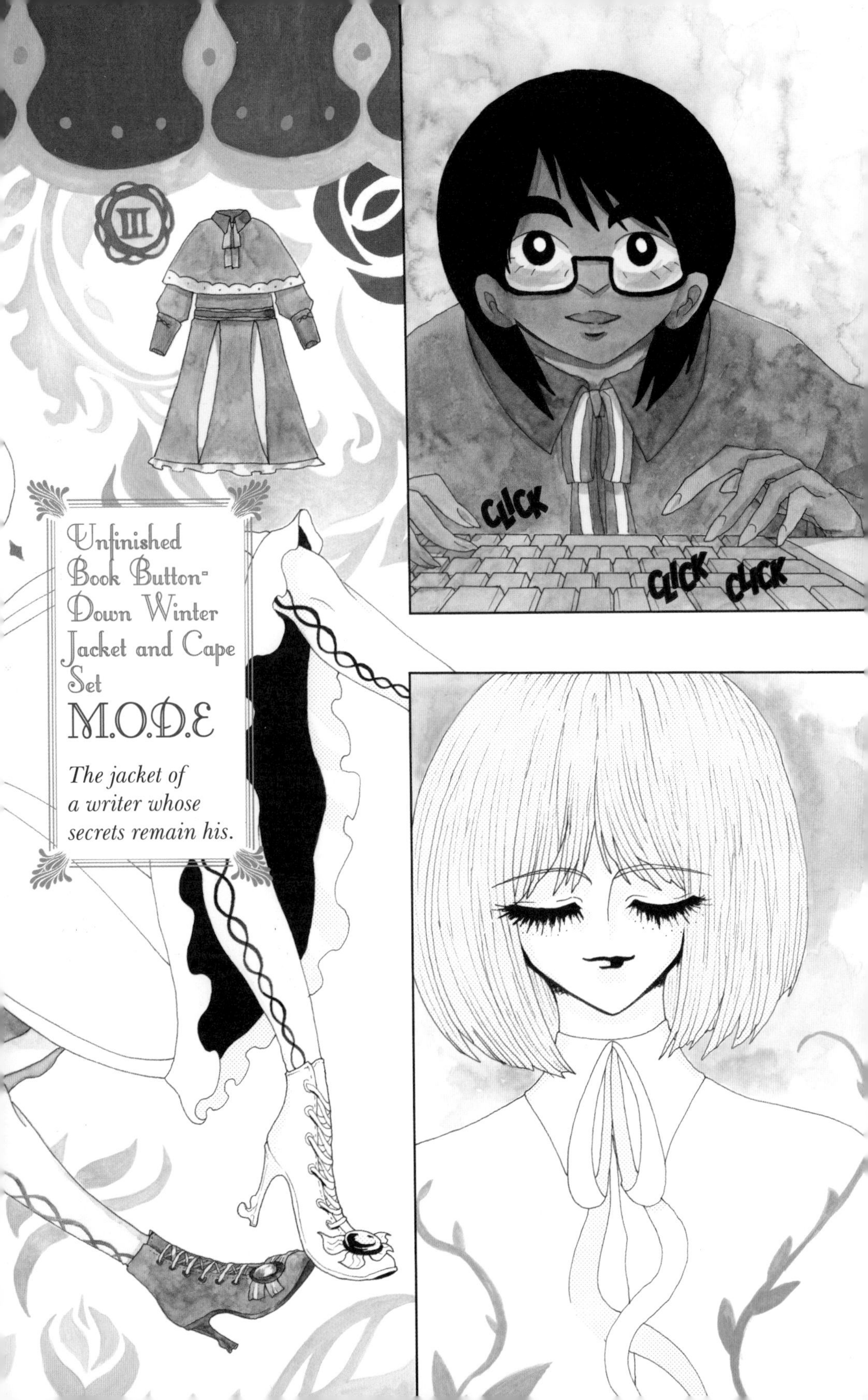
Unfinished Book Button-Down Winter Jacket and Cape Set
M.O.D.E
The jacket of a writer whose secrets remain his.
CLICK
CLICK CLICK

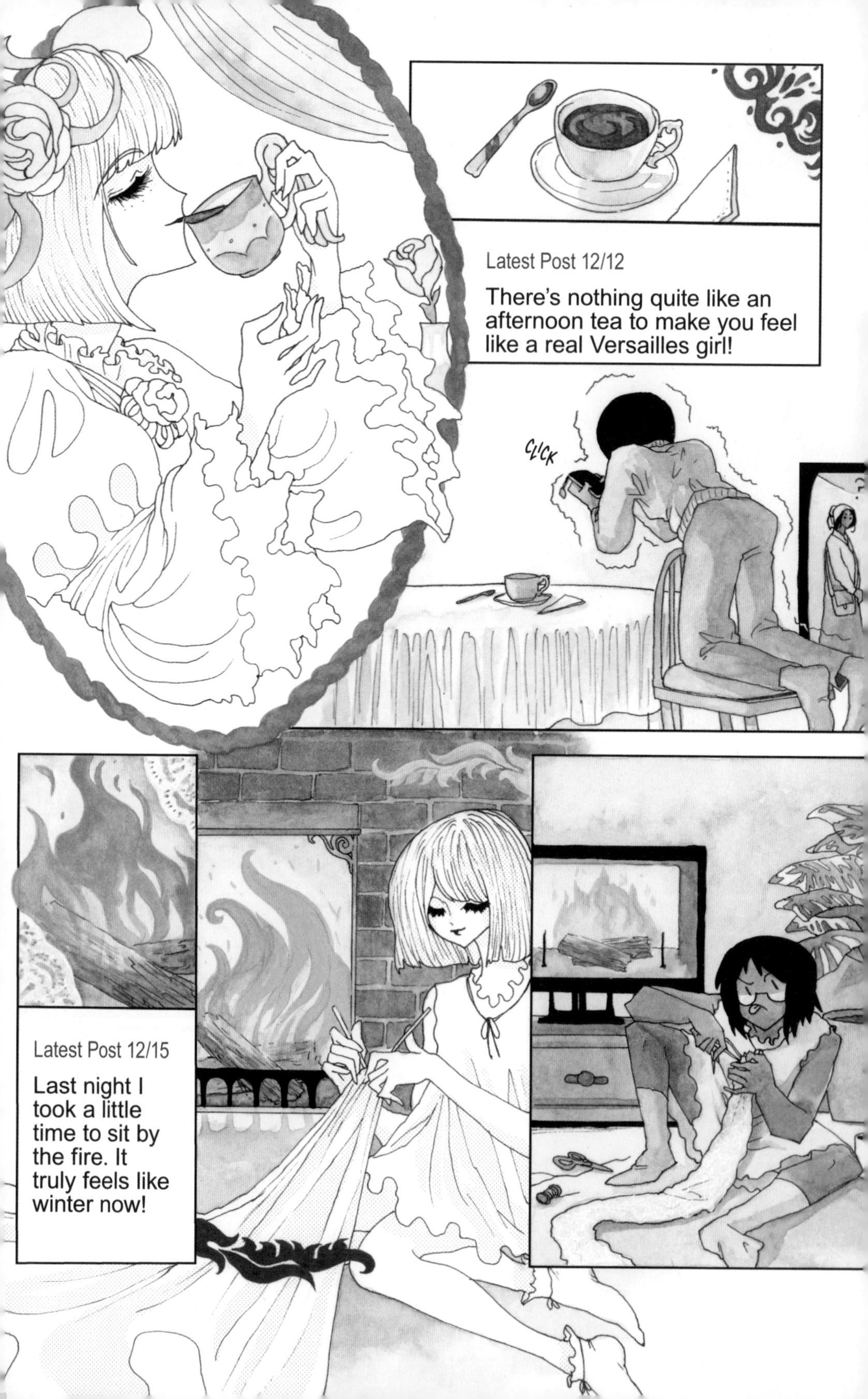
Latest Post 12/12
There's nothing quite like an afternoon tea to make you feel like a real Versailles girl!
CLICK
Latest Post 12/15
Last night I took a little time to sit by the fire. It truly feels like winter now!

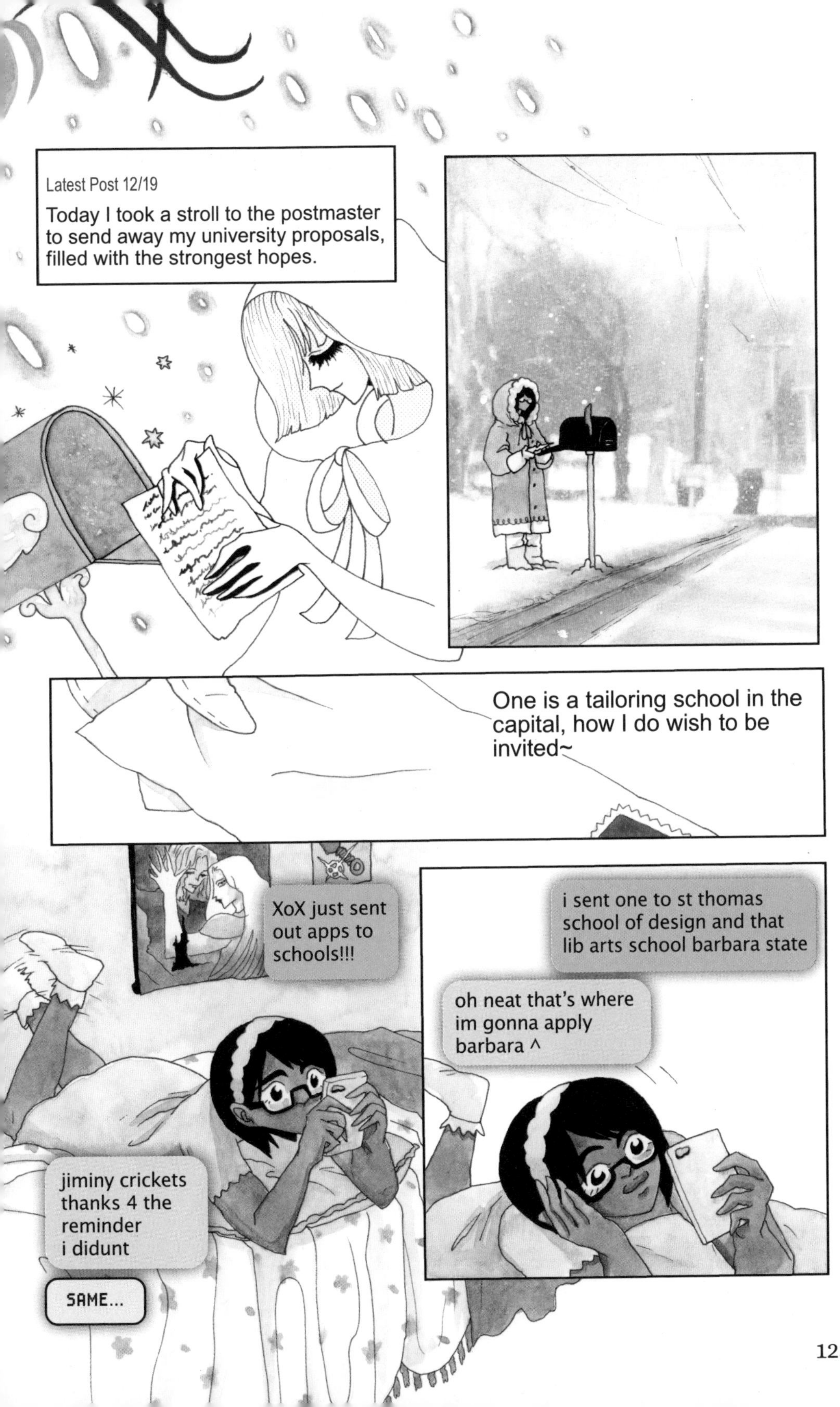
Latest Post 12/19
Today I took a stroll to the postmaster to send away my university proposals, filled with the strongest hopes.
One is a tailoring school in the capital, how I do wish to be invited~
XoX just sent out apps to schools!!!
jiminy crickets thanks 4 the reminder i didunt
SAME...
i sent one to st thomas school of design and that lib arts school barbara state
oh neat that's where im gonna apply barbara ^

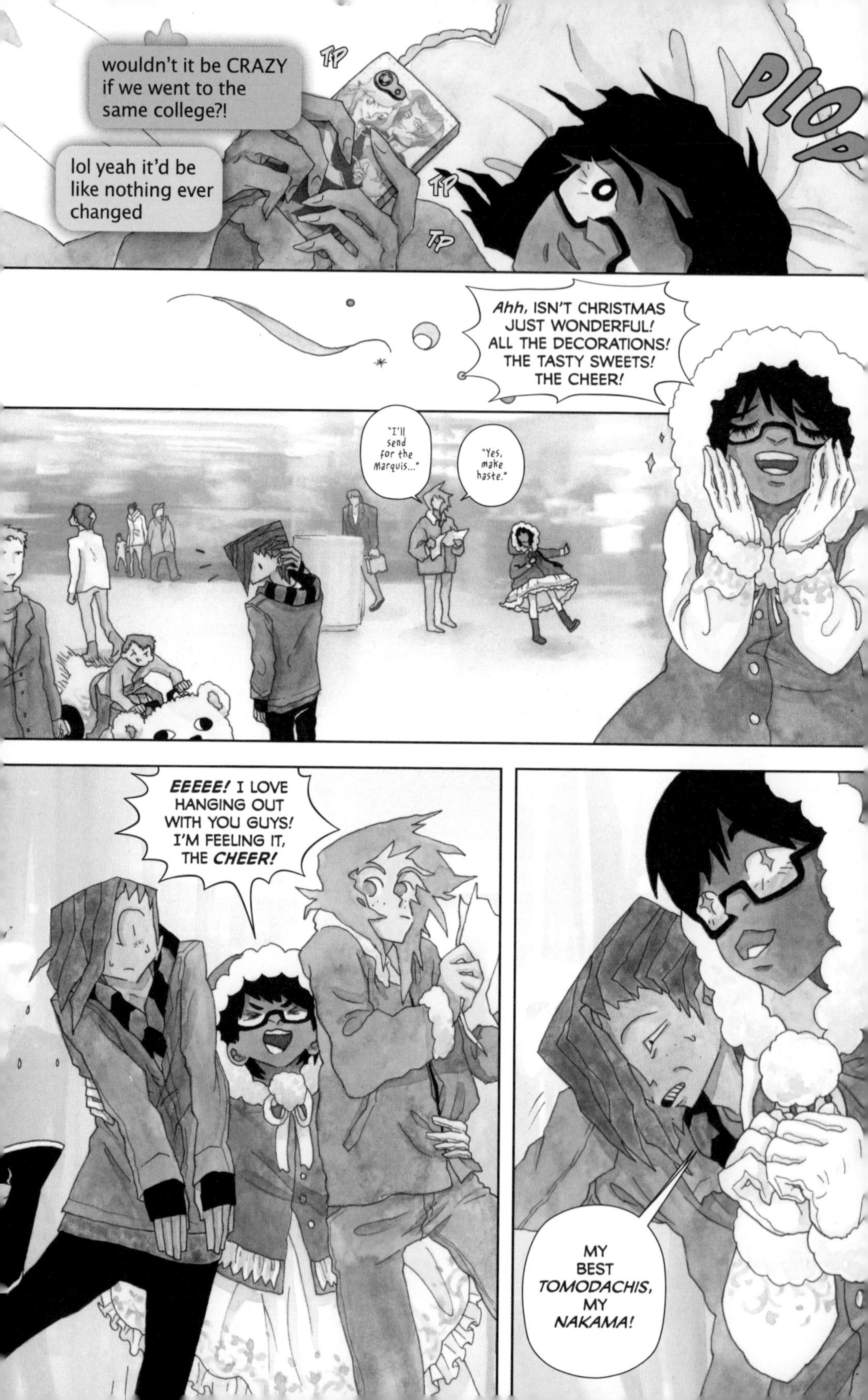
wouldn't it be CRAZY if we went to the same college?!
lol yeah it'd be like nothing ever changed
TP
TP
TP
PLOP
Ahh, ISN'T CHRISTMAS JUST WONDERFUL! ALL THE DECORATIONS! THE TASTY SWEETS! THE CHEER!
"I'll send for the Marquis..."
"Yes, make haste."
EEEEE! I LOVE HANGING OUT WITH YOU GUYS! I'M FEELING IT, THE CHEER!
MY BEST TOMODACHIS, MY NAKAMA!

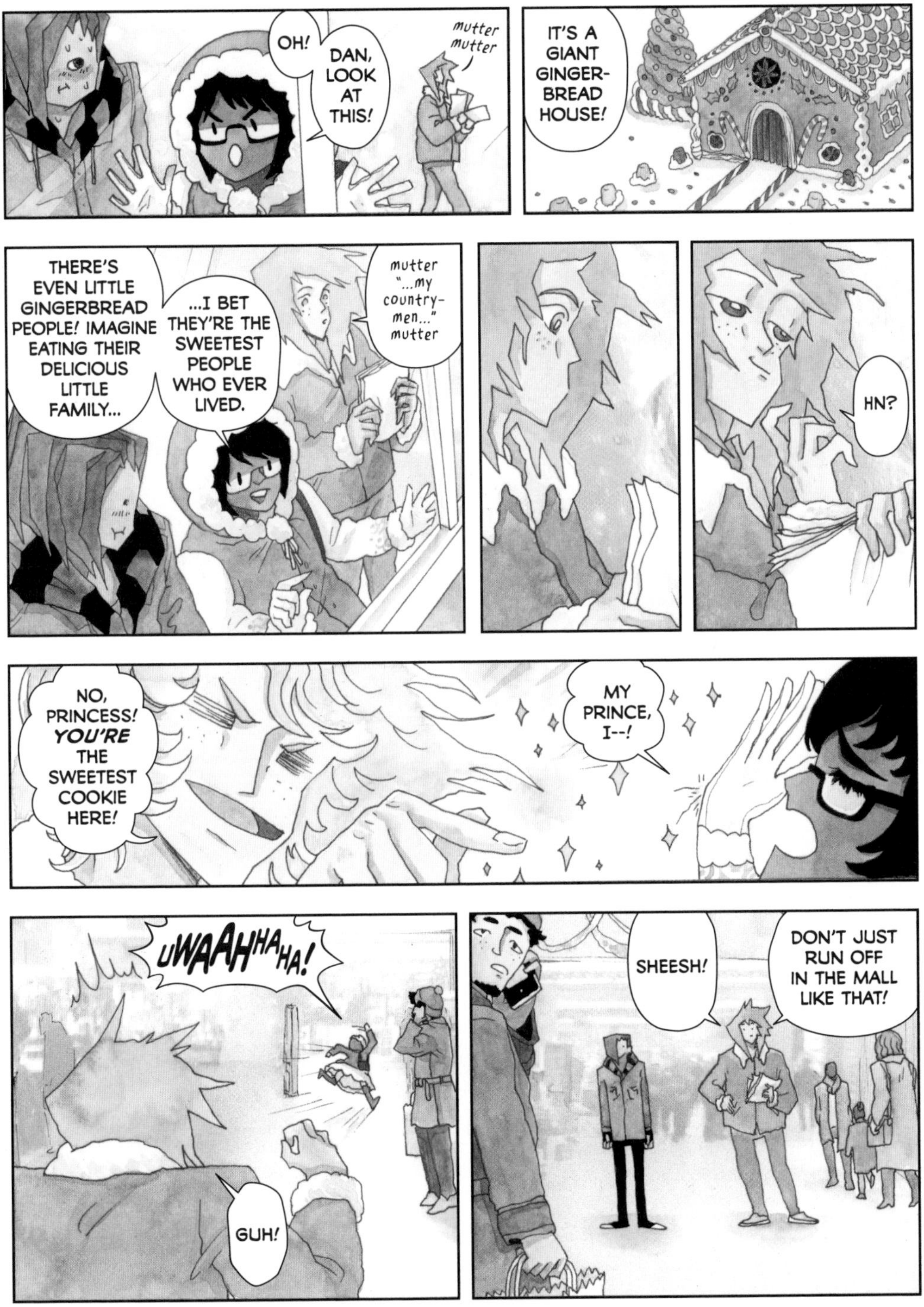
OH!
DAN, LOOK AT THIS!
mutter mutter
IT'S A GIANT GINGER-BREAD HOUSE!
THERE'S EVEN LITTLE GINGERBREAD PEOPLE! IMAGINE EATING THEIR DELICIOUS LITTLE FAMILY...
...I BET THEY'RE THE SWEETEST PEOPLE WHO EVER LIVED.
mutter "...my country-men..." mutter
HN?
NO, PRINCESS! *YOU'RE* THE SWEETEST COOKIE HERE!
MY PRINCE, I--!
UWAAHHAHA!
GUH!
SHEESH!
DON'T JUST RUN OFF IN THE MALL LIKE THAT!

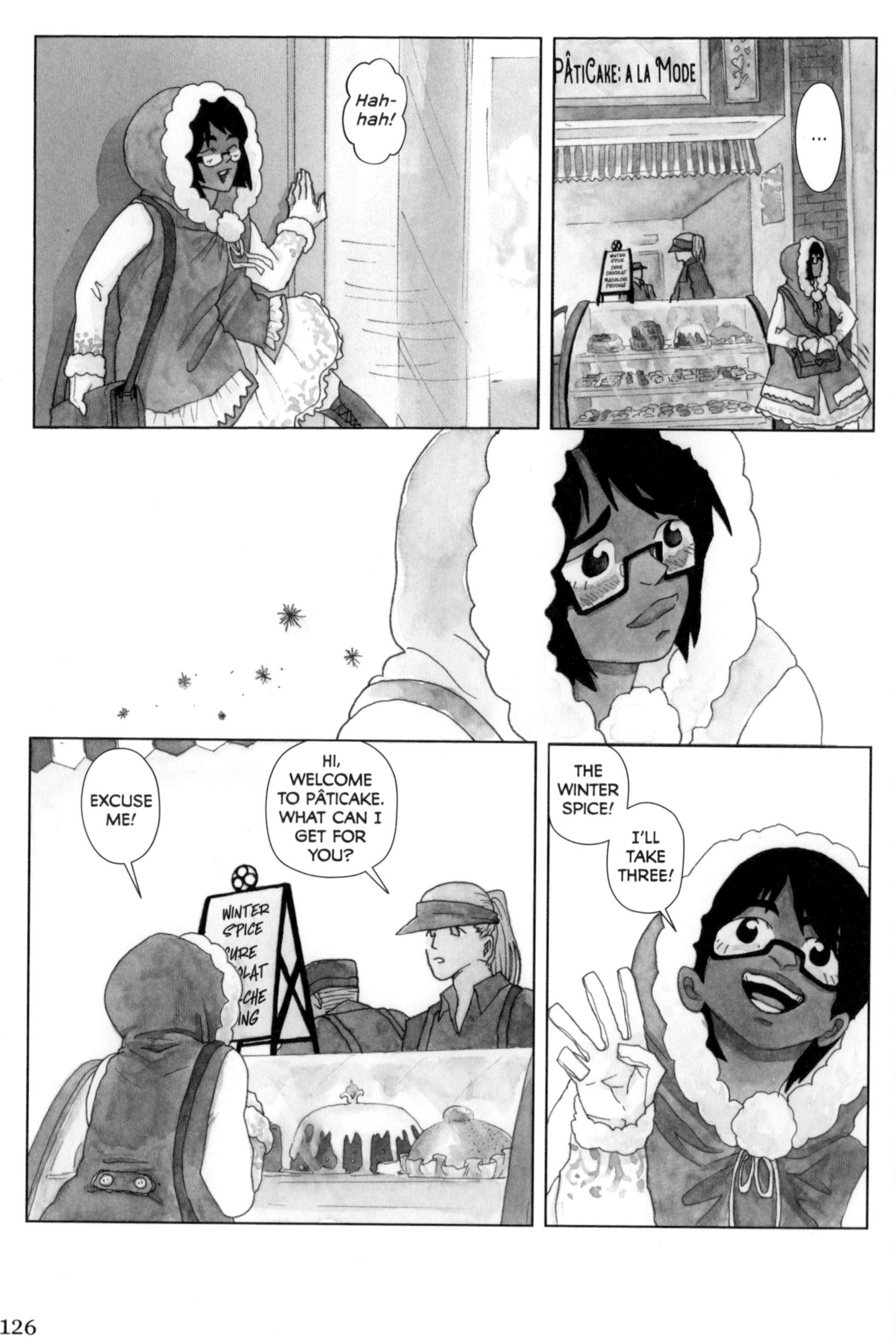

Hah-hah!
PÂTICAKE: A LA MODE
...
EXCUSE ME!
HI, WELCOME TO PÂTICAKE. WHAT CAN I GET FOR YOU?
WINTER SPICE
THE WINTER SPICE!
I'LL TAKE THREE!

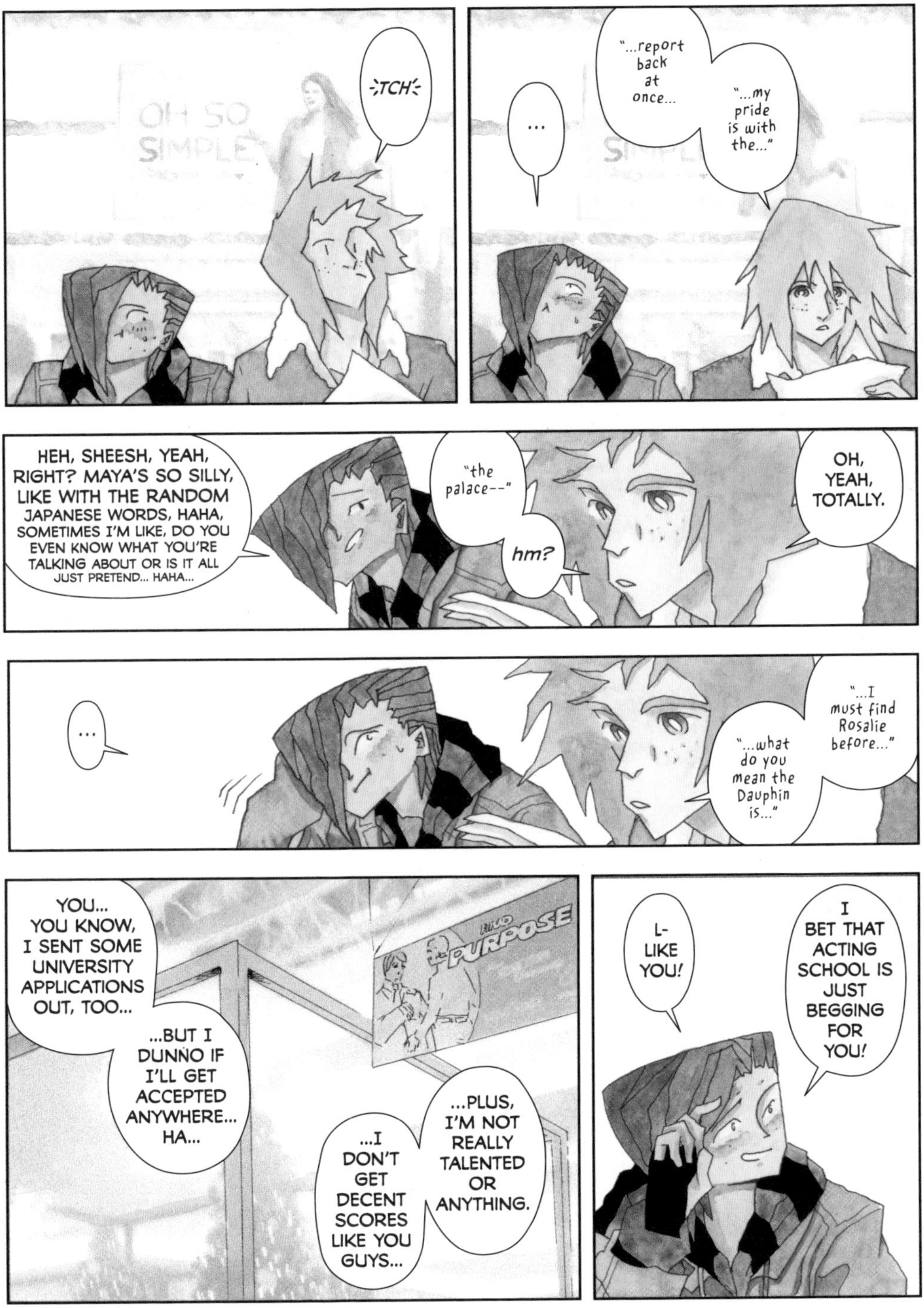
OH SO SIMPLE
;TCH;
...
"...report back at once..."
"...my pride is with the..."
HEH, SHEESH, YEAH, RIGHT? MAYA'S SO SILLY, LIKE WITH THE RANDOM JAPANESE WORDS, HAHA, SOMETIMES I'M LIKE, DO YOU EVEN KNOW WHAT YOU'RE TALKING ABOUT OR IS IT ALL JUST PRETEND... HAHA...
"the palace--"
hm?
OH, YEAH, TOTALLY.
...
"...what do you mean the Dauphin is..."
"...I must find Rosalie before..."
YOU... YOU KNOW, I SENT SOME UNIVERSITY APPLICATIONS OUT, TOO...
...BUT I DUNNO IF I'LL GET ACCEPTED ANYWHERE... HA...
PURPOSE
...PLUS, I'M NOT REALLY TALENTED OR ANYTHING.
...I DON'T GET DECENT SCORES LIKE YOU GUYS...
I BET THAT ACTING SCHOOL IS JUST BEGGING FOR YOU!
L-LIKE YOU!

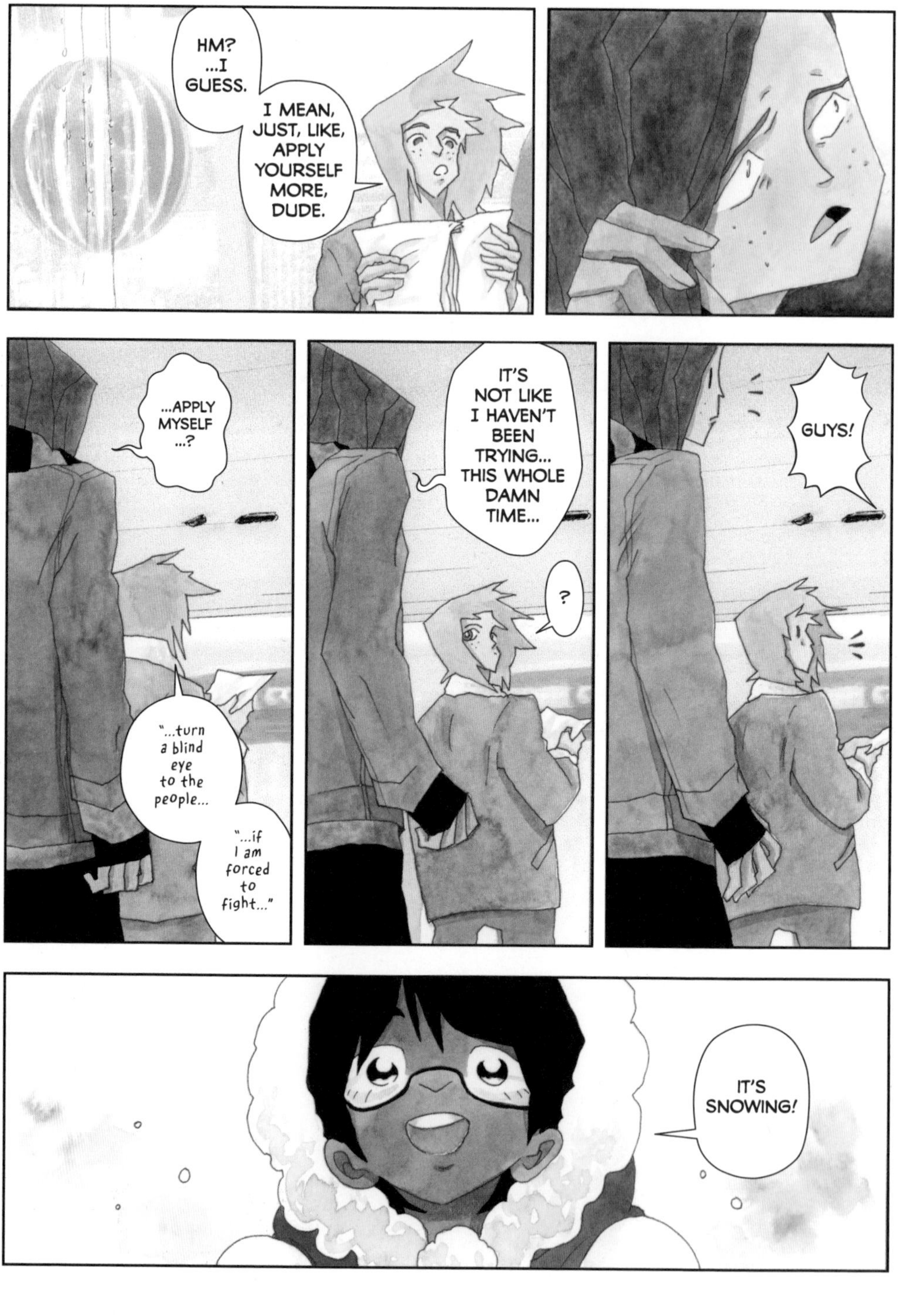
HM? ...I GUESS.
I MEAN, JUST, LIKE, APPLY YOURSELF MORE, DUDE.
...APPLY MYSELF ...?
"...turn a blind eye to the people...
"...if I am forced to fight..."
IT'S NOT LIKE I HAVEN'T BEEN TRYING... THIS WHOLE DAMN TIME...
?
GUYS!
IT'S SNOWING!

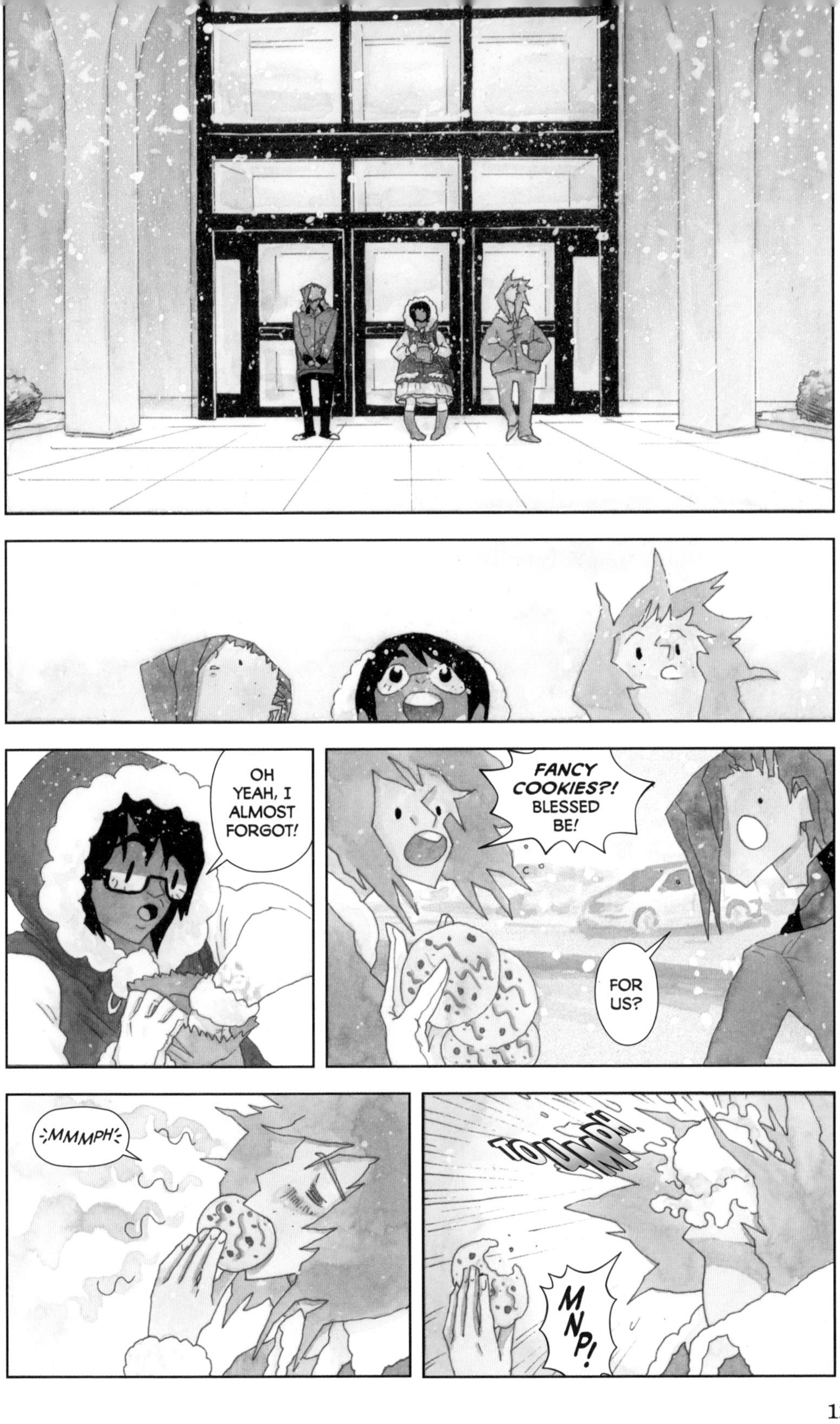
OH YEAH, I ALMOST FORGOT!
FANCY COOKIES?! BLESSED BE!
FOR US?
MMMPH
THUMP!
MNP!

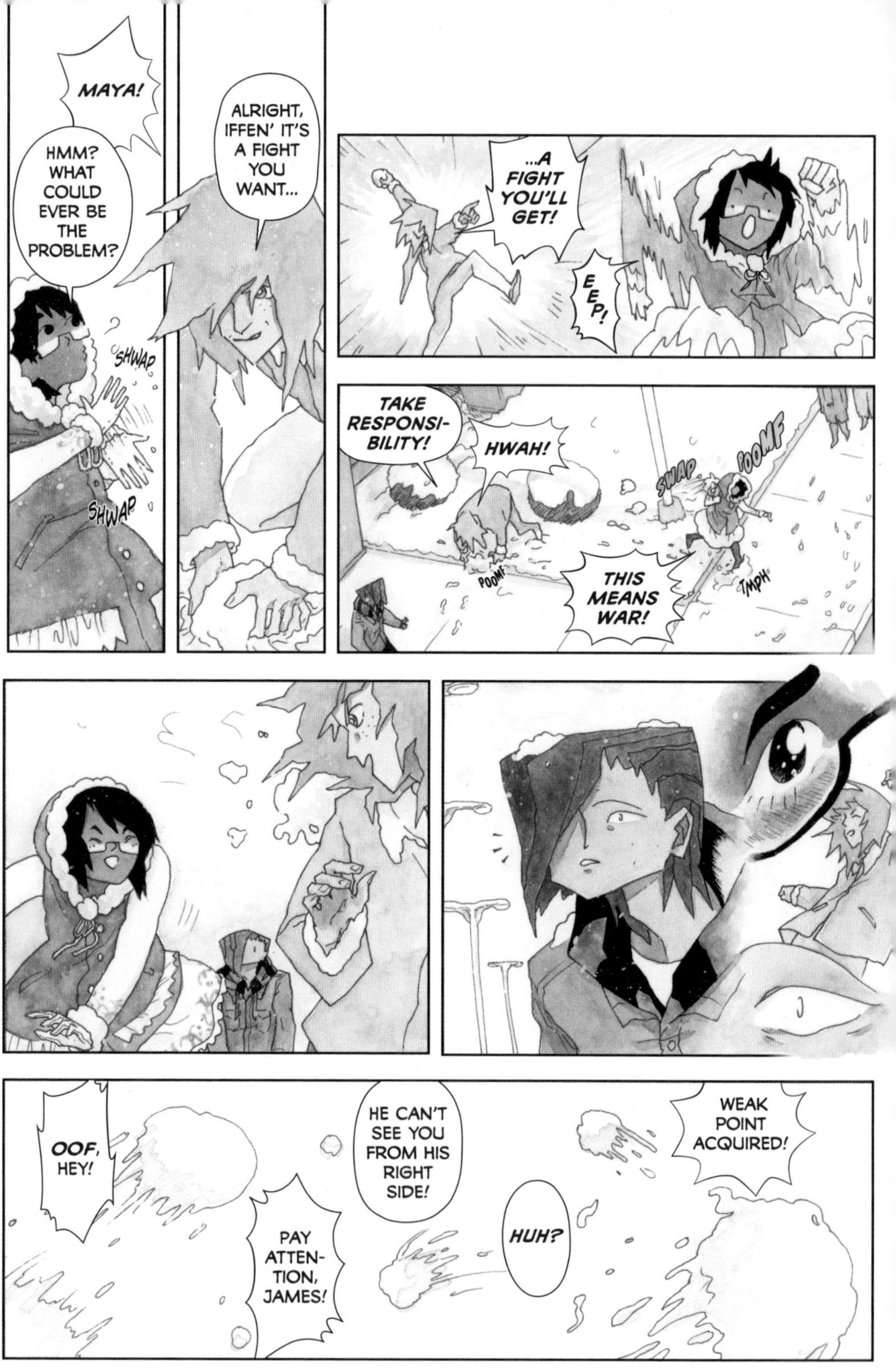
MAYA!
HMM? WHAT COULD EVER BE THE PROBLEM?
SHWAP
SHWAP
ALRIGHT, IFFEN' IT'S A FIGHT YOU WANT...
...A FIGHT YOU'LL GET!
EEP!
TAKE RESPONSI-BILITY!
HWAH!
SWAP
POOMF
POOMF
THIS MEANS WAR!
TMPH
OOF, HEY!
HE CAN'T SEE YOU FROM HIS RIGHT SIDE!
PAY ATTEN-TION, JAMES!
HUH?
WEAK POINT ACQUIRED!

KREEK

Haha ha!

YOU'RE ALL WET! YOU'D BETTER NOT TRACK MUD ALL UP THE STAIRS!

He-hehe!

POMF

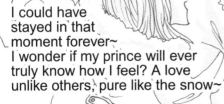

CLICK

CLICK

CLICK

Latest Post 12/22

Hello dears, today was such a special day~
The grandest snowfall of the season! My prince joined me and we frolicked in the snow for what seemed like a lifetime!

I could have stayed in that moment forever~
I wonder if my prince will ever truly know how I feel? A love unlike others, pure like the snow~

Thank you, my darlings, for your continued support!

♥ Mayako

chirp

chirp

chirp

MNCH
MNCH

Sakura_Valentine: lovely!

godchildcain98: <3 the winter cape where's it from??

kam1neko: lolitas arent supposed 2b black...

- xXxLostAlicexXx: can you not

- lovely_angelic2: yeah dude wtf thats racist

- kam1neko: shes just some weeaboo pretending to b lolita lol

- kam1neko: not pretty

- xXxLostAlicexXx: ur just a bigoted idiot and

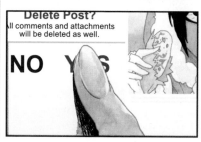

Delete Post?
All comments and attachments will be deleted as well.

NO   **YES**

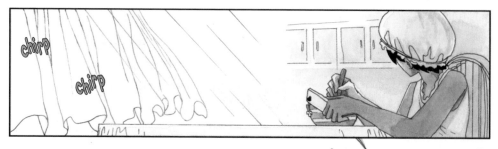

chirp

chirp

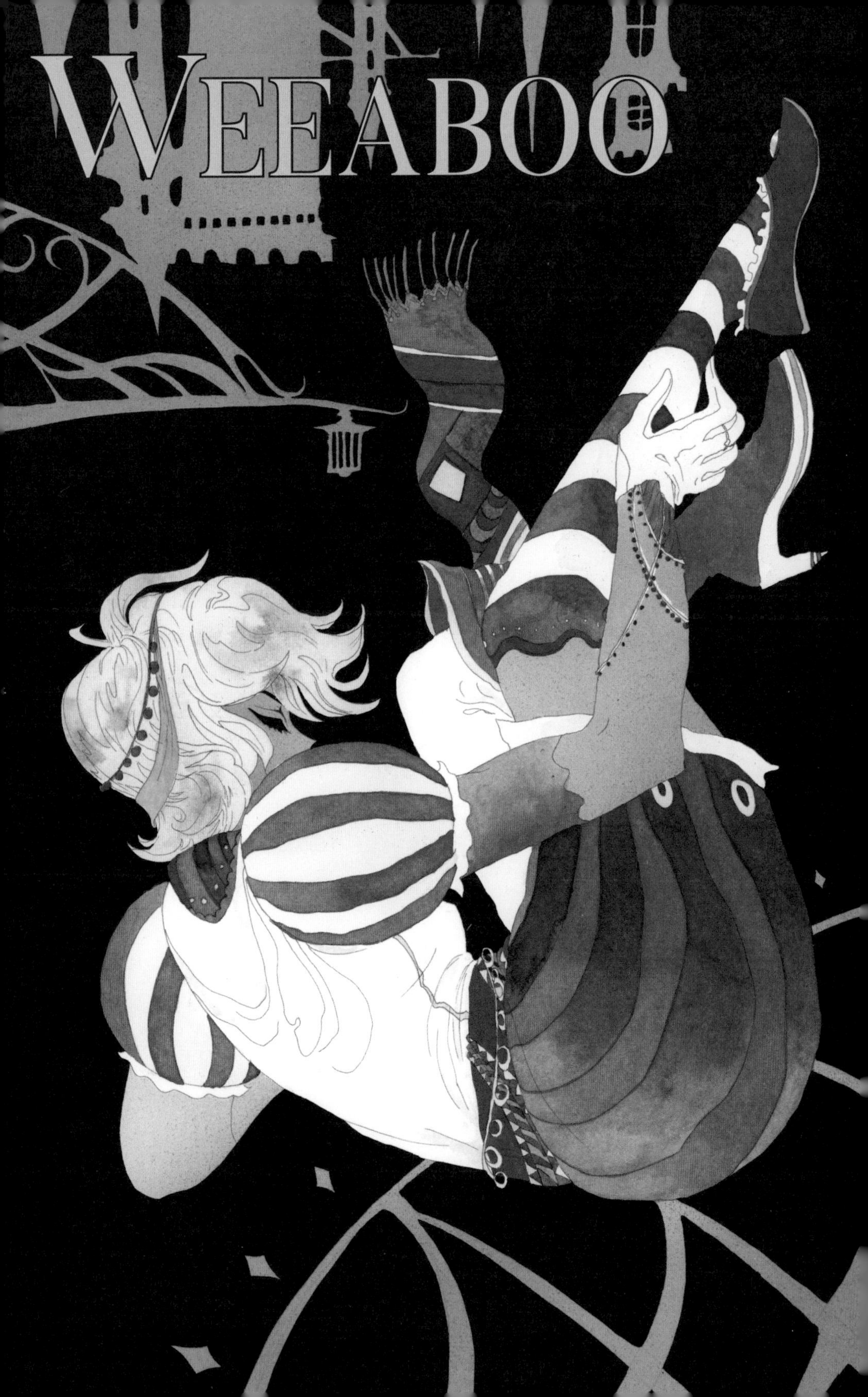
WEEABOO

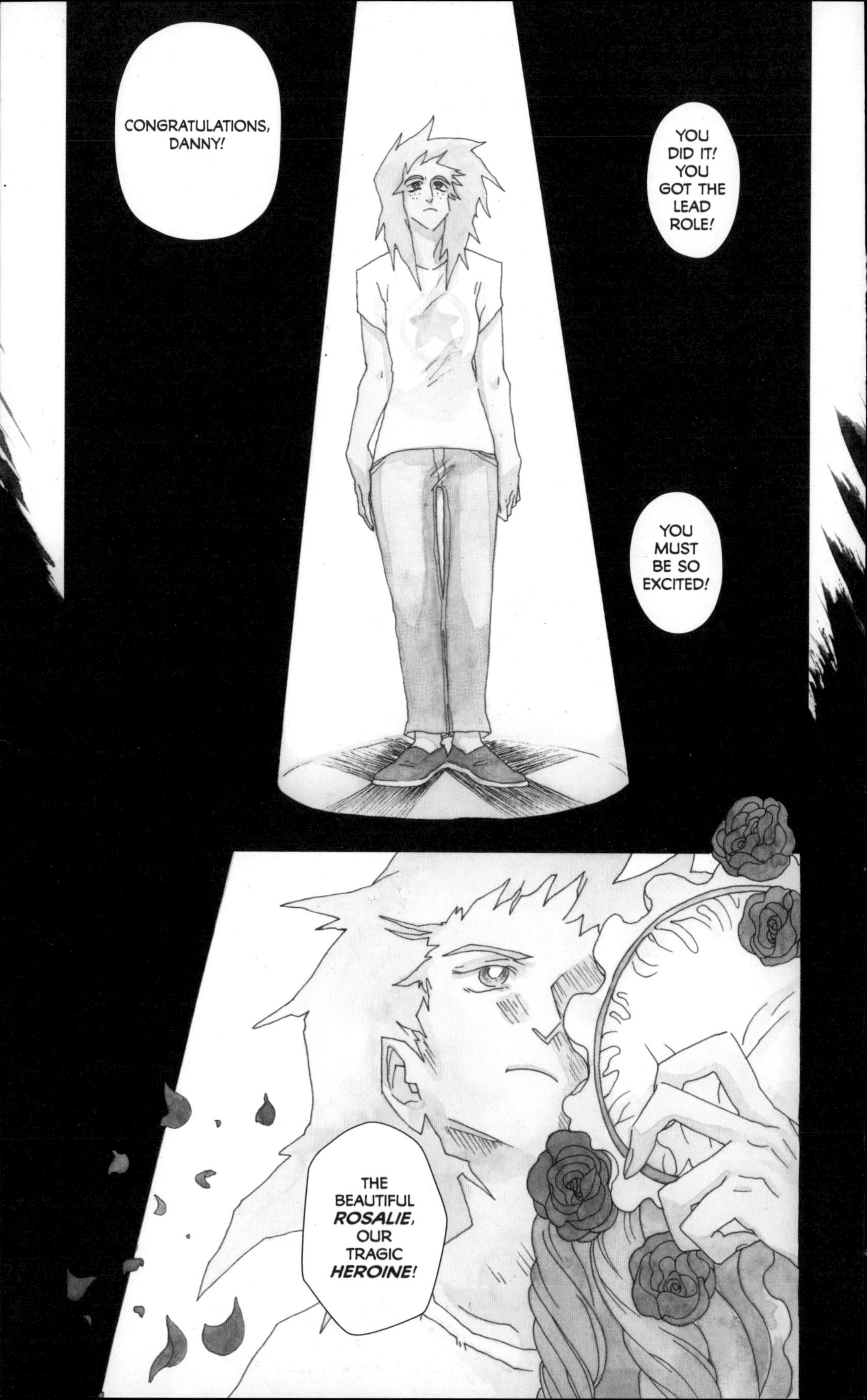
CONGRATULATIONS, DANNY!
YOU DID IT! YOU GOT THE LEAD ROLE!
YOU MUST BE SO EXCITED!
THE BEAUTIFUL ***ROSALIE***, OUR TRAGIC ***HEROINE***!

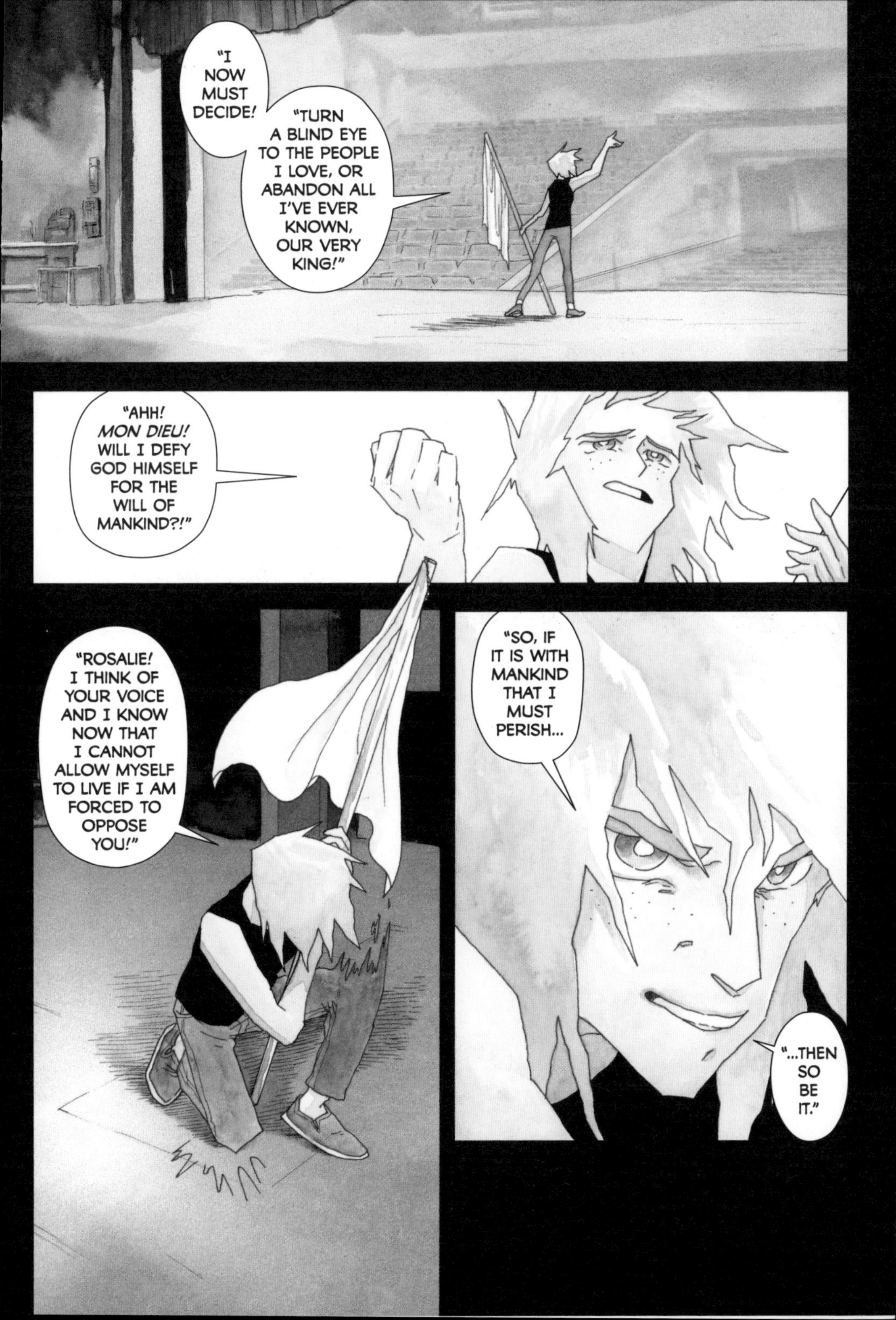
"I NOW MUST DECIDE!
"TURN A BLIND EYE TO THE PEOPLE I LOVE, OR ABANDON ALL I'VE EVER KNOWN, OUR VERY KING!"
"AHH! *MON DIEU!* WILL I DEFY GOD HIMSELF FOR THE WILL OF MANKIND?!"
"ROSALIE! I THINK OF YOUR VOICE AND I KNOW NOW THAT I CANNOT ALLOW MYSELF TO LIVE IF I AM FORCED TO OPPOSE YOU!"
"SO, IF IT IS WITH MANKIND THAT I MUST PERISH...
"...THEN SO BE IT."

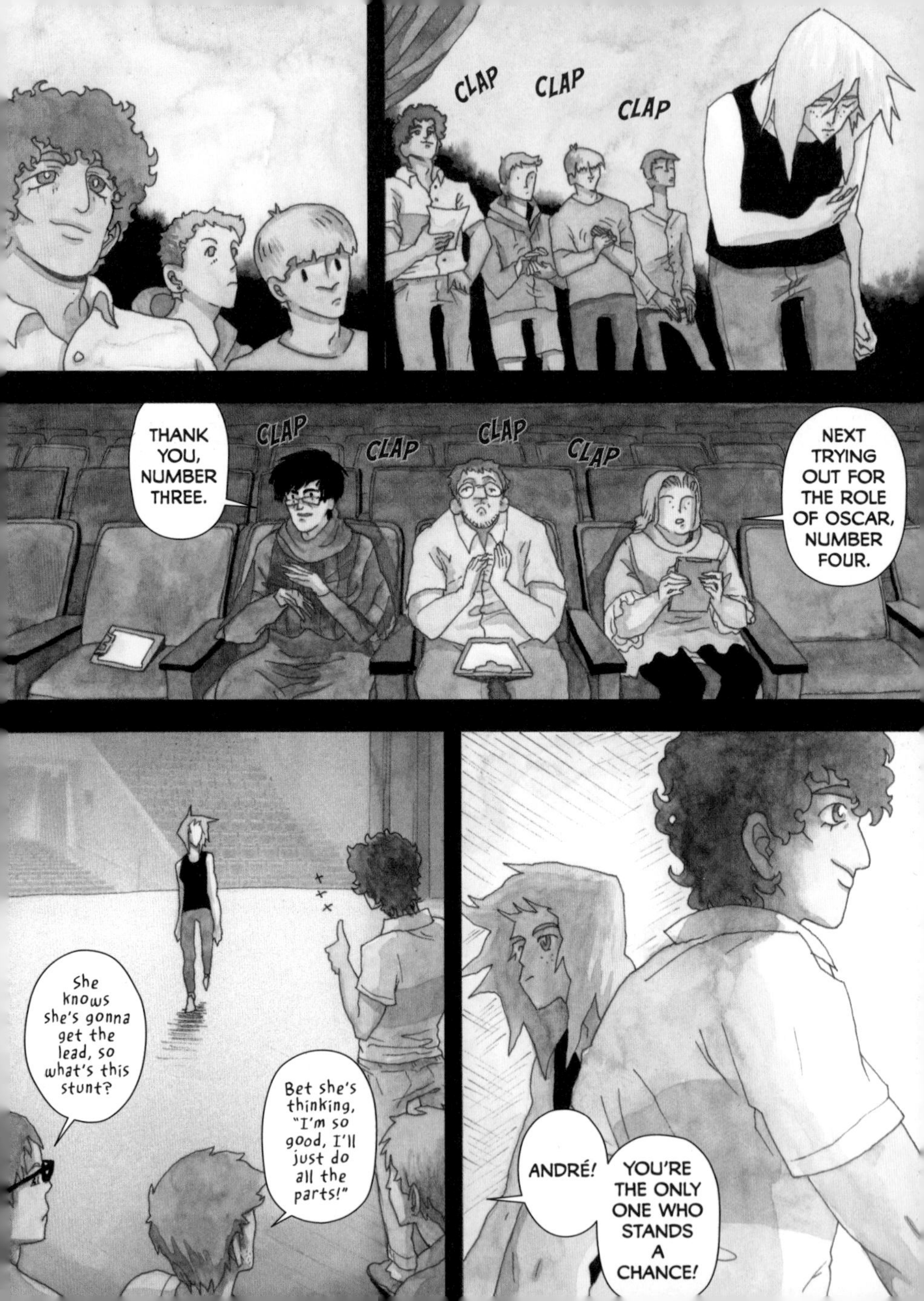
CLAP
CLAP
CLAP
THANK YOU, NUMBER THREE.
CLAP
CLAP
CLAP
CLAP
NEXT TRYING OUT FOR THE ROLE OF OSCAR, NUMBER FOUR.
She knows she's gonna get the lead, so what's this stunt?
Bet she's thinking, "I'm so good, I'll just do all the parts!"
ANDRÉ!
YOU'RE THE ONLY ONE WHO STANDS A CHANCE!

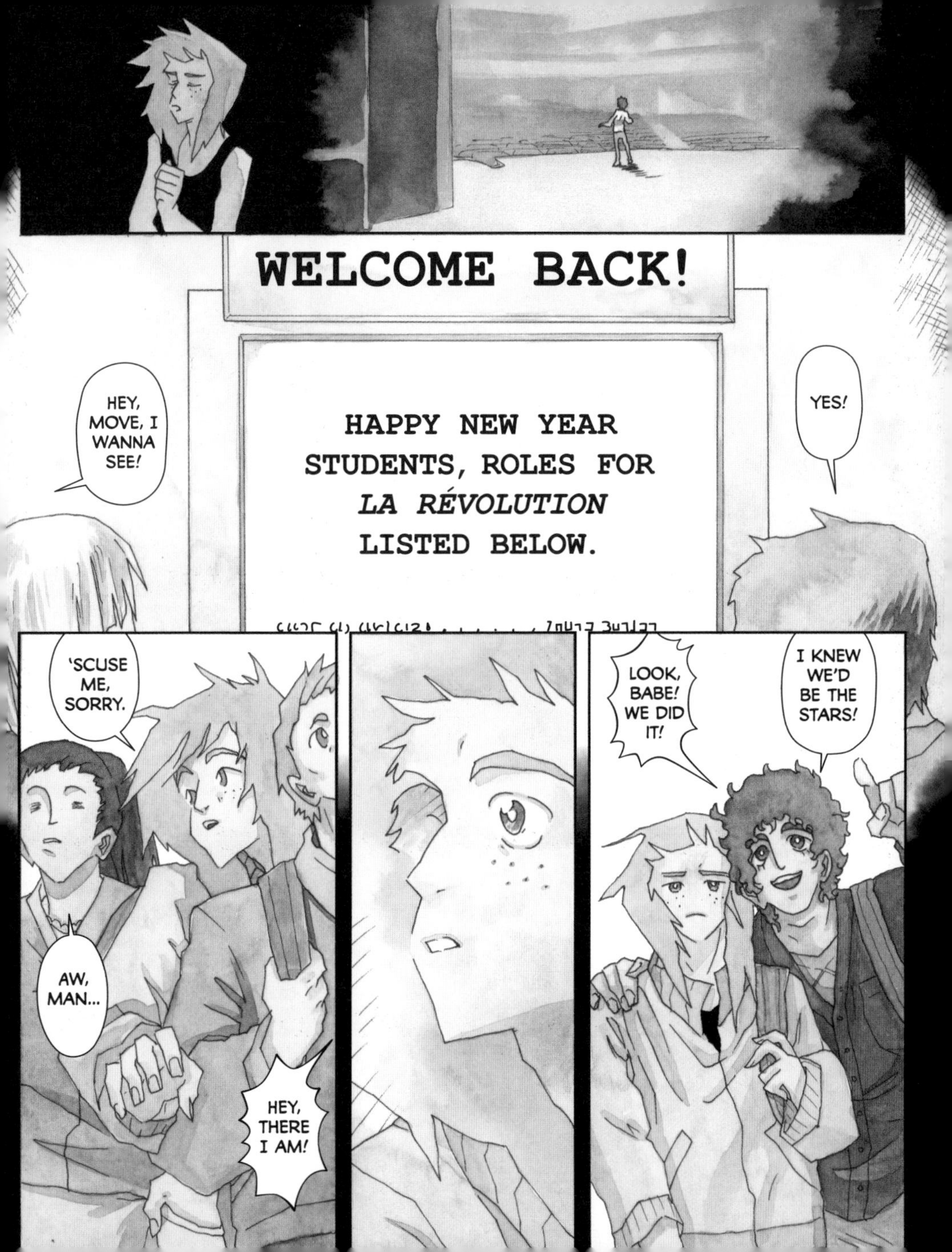
WELCOME BACK!
HEY, MOVE, I WANNA SEE!
HAPPY NEW YEAR STUDENTS, ROLES FOR *LA RÉVOLUTION* LISTED BELOW.
YES!
'SCUSE ME, SORRY.
AW, MAN...
HEY, THERE I AM!
LOOK, BABE! WE DID IT!
I KNEW WE'D BE THE STARS!

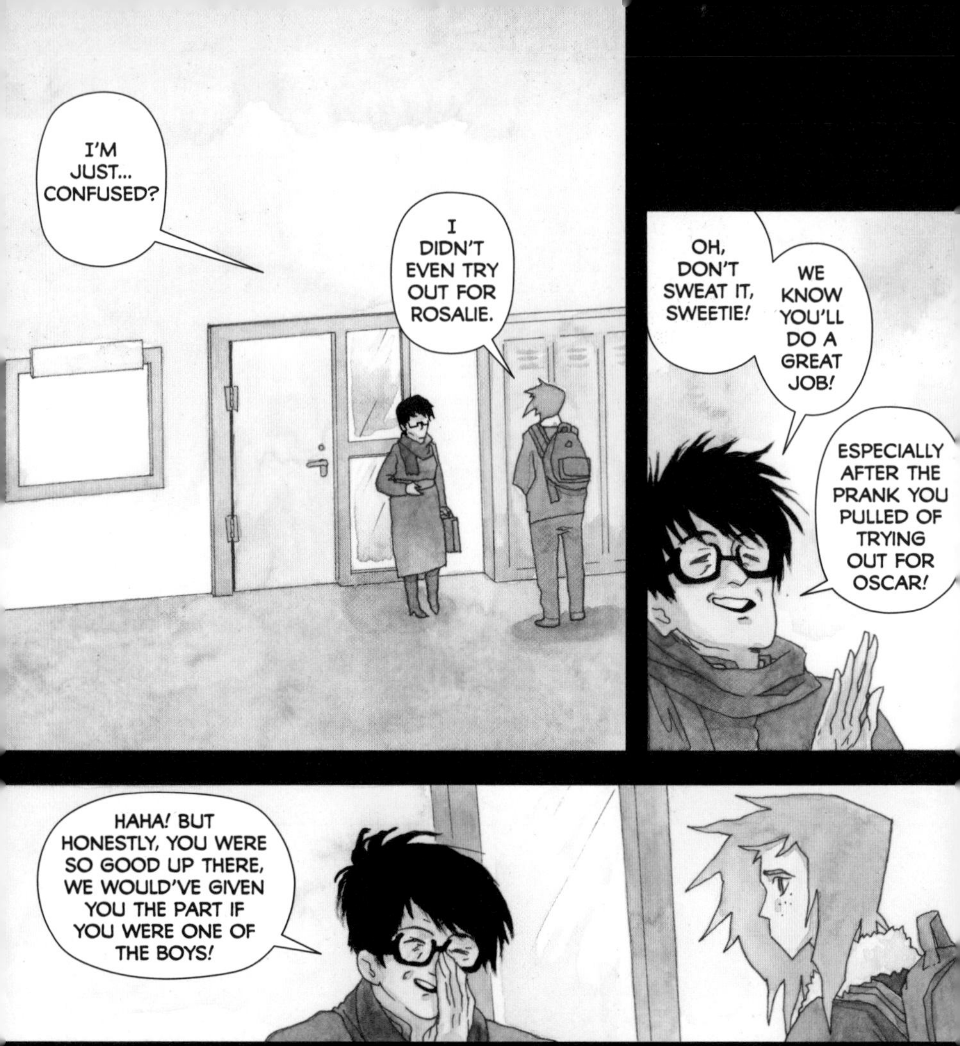
I'M JUST... CONFUSED?
I DIDN'T EVEN TRY OUT FOR ROSALIE.
OH, DON'T SWEAT IT, SWEETIE!
WE KNOW YOU'LL DO A GREAT JOB!
ESPECIALLY AFTER THE PRANK YOU PULLED OF TRYING OUT FOR OSCAR!
HAHA! BUT HONESTLY, YOU WERE SO GOOD UP THERE, WE WOULD'VE GIVEN YOU THE PART IF YOU WERE ONE OF THE BOYS!

Oscar de Montesse . . . . . . André Butler

Rosalie Gabrielle . . . . . . Danielle Mitchell

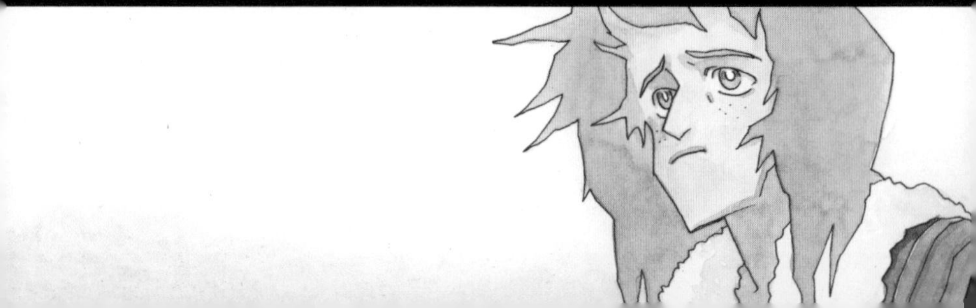

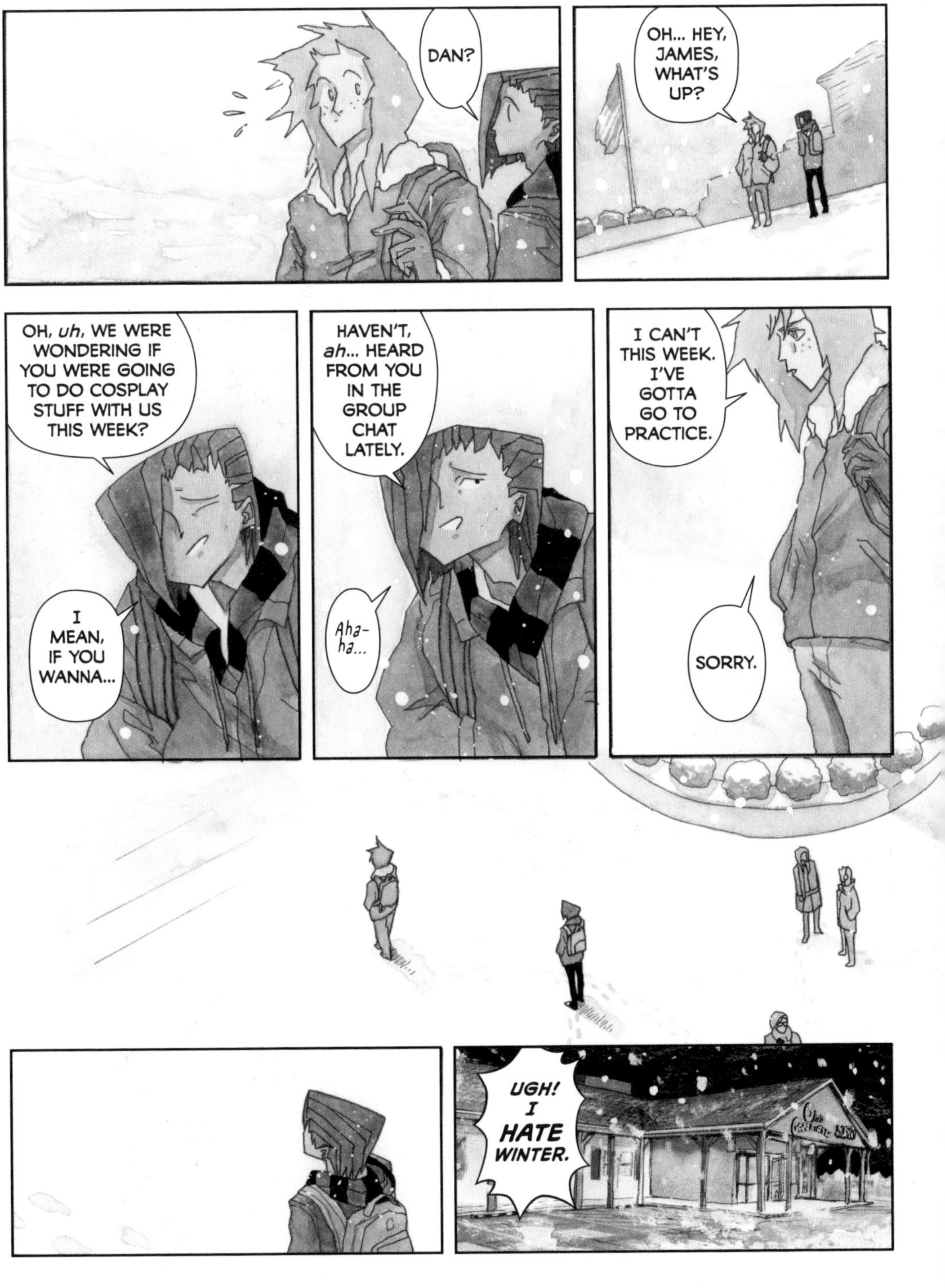
DAN?
OH... HEY, JAMES, WHAT'S UP?
OH, *uh*, WE WERE WONDERING IF YOU WERE GOING TO DO COSPLAY STUFF WITH US THIS WEEK?
I MEAN, IF YOU WANNA...
HAVEN'T, *ah*... HEARD FROM YOU IN THE GROUP CHAT LATELY.
Aha-ha...
I CAN'T THIS WEEK. I'VE GOTTA GO TO PRACTICE.
SORRY.
UGH! I **HATE** WINTER.

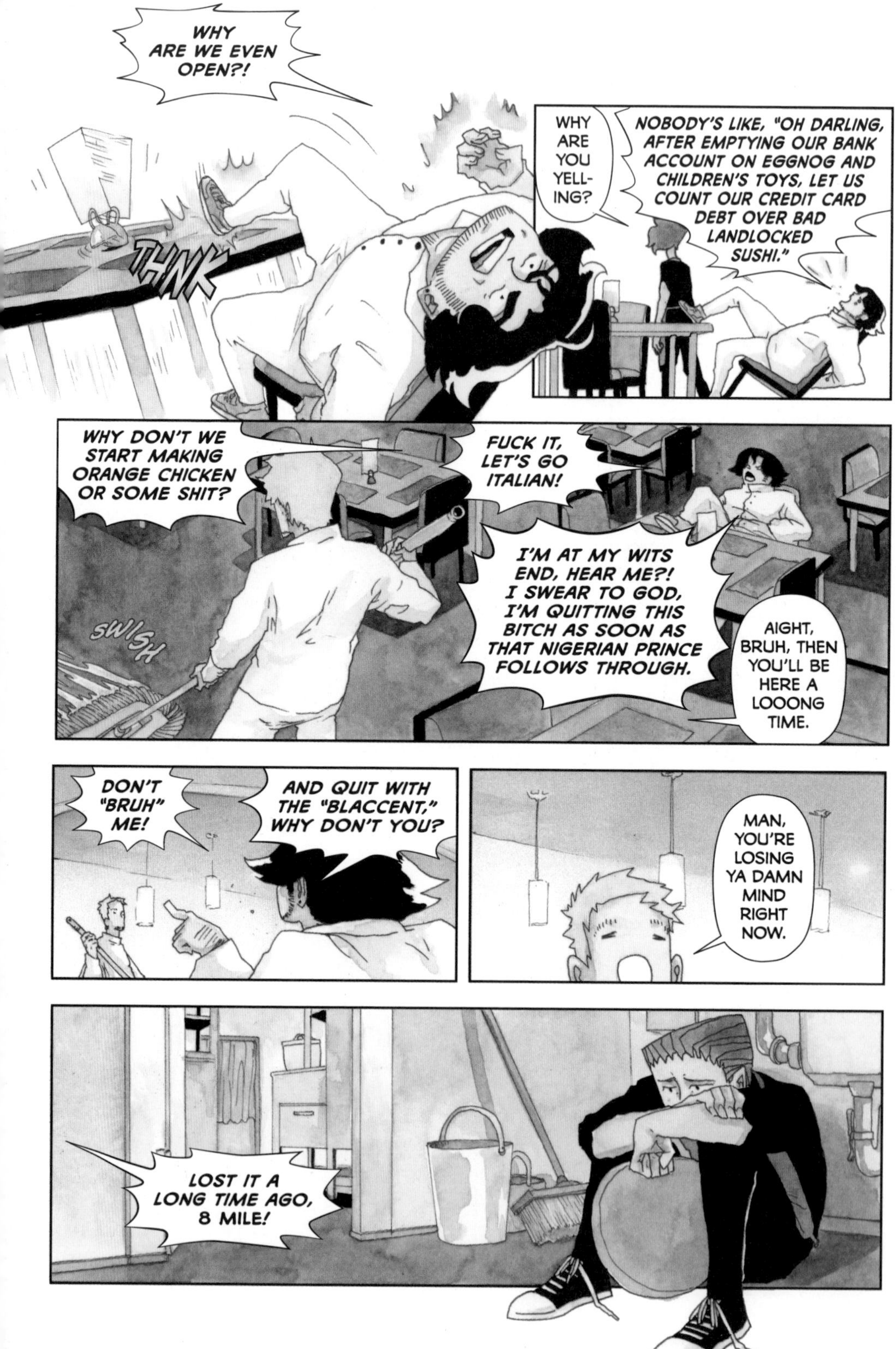
WHY ARE WE EVEN OPEN?!
THNK
WHY ARE YOU YELL-ING?
NOBODY'S LIKE, "OH DARLING, AFTER EMPTYING OUR BANK ACCOUNT ON EGGNOG AND CHILDREN'S TOYS, LET US COUNT OUR CREDIT CARD DEBT OVER BAD LANDLOCKED SUSHI."
WHY DON'T WE START MAKING ORANGE CHICKEN OR SOME SHIT?
FUCK IT, LET'S GO ITALIAN!
I'M AT MY WITS END, HEAR ME?! I SWEAR TO GOD, I'M QUITTING THIS BITCH AS SOON AS THAT NIGERIAN PRINCE FOLLOWS THROUGH.
SWISH
AIGHT, BRUH, THEN YOU'LL BE HERE A LOOONG TIME.
DON'T "BRUH" ME!
AND QUIT WITH THE "BLACCENT," WHY DON'T YOU?
MAN, YOU'RE LOSING YA DAMN MIND RIGHT NOW.
LOST IT A LONG TIME AGO, 8 MILE!

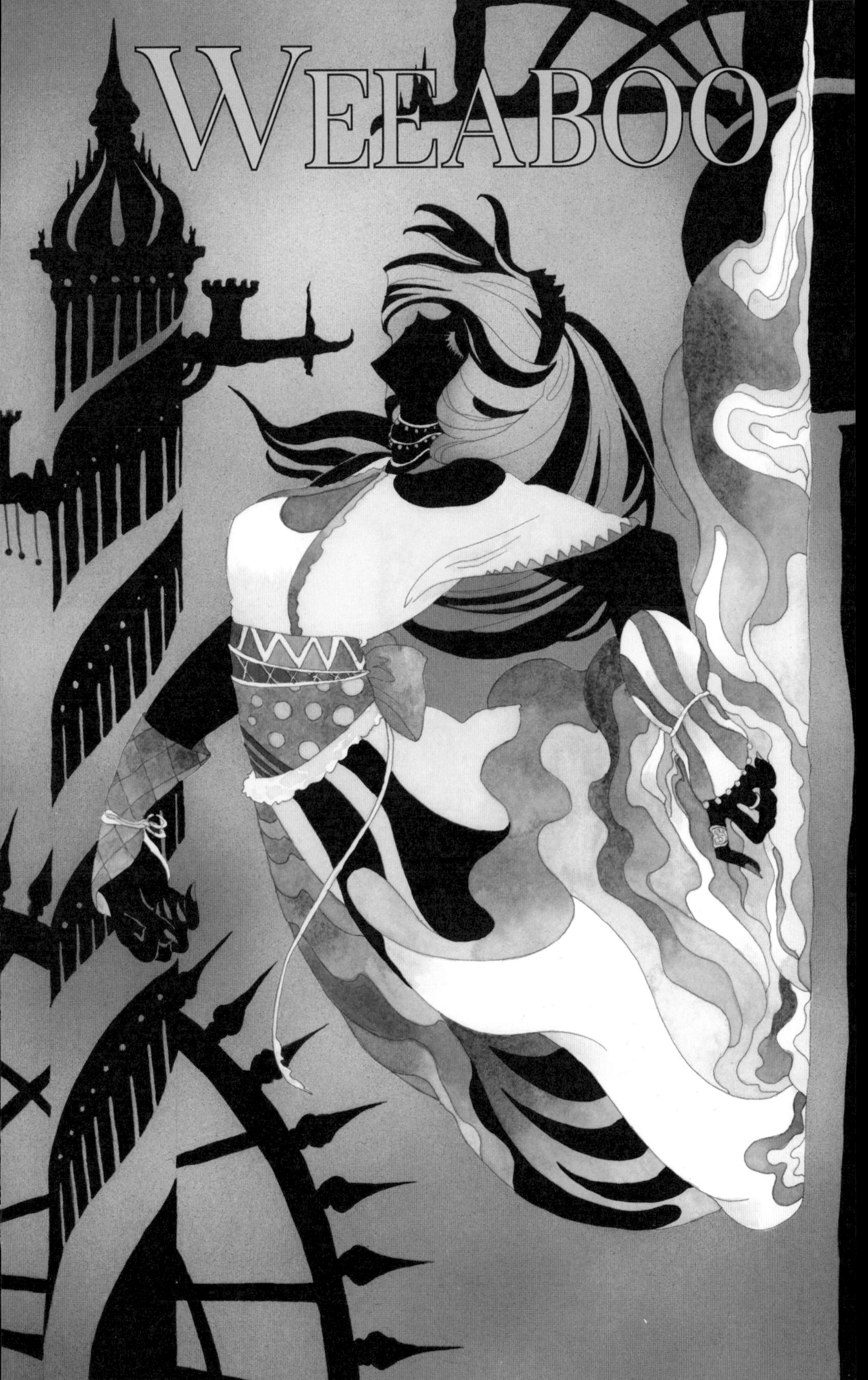
WEEABOO

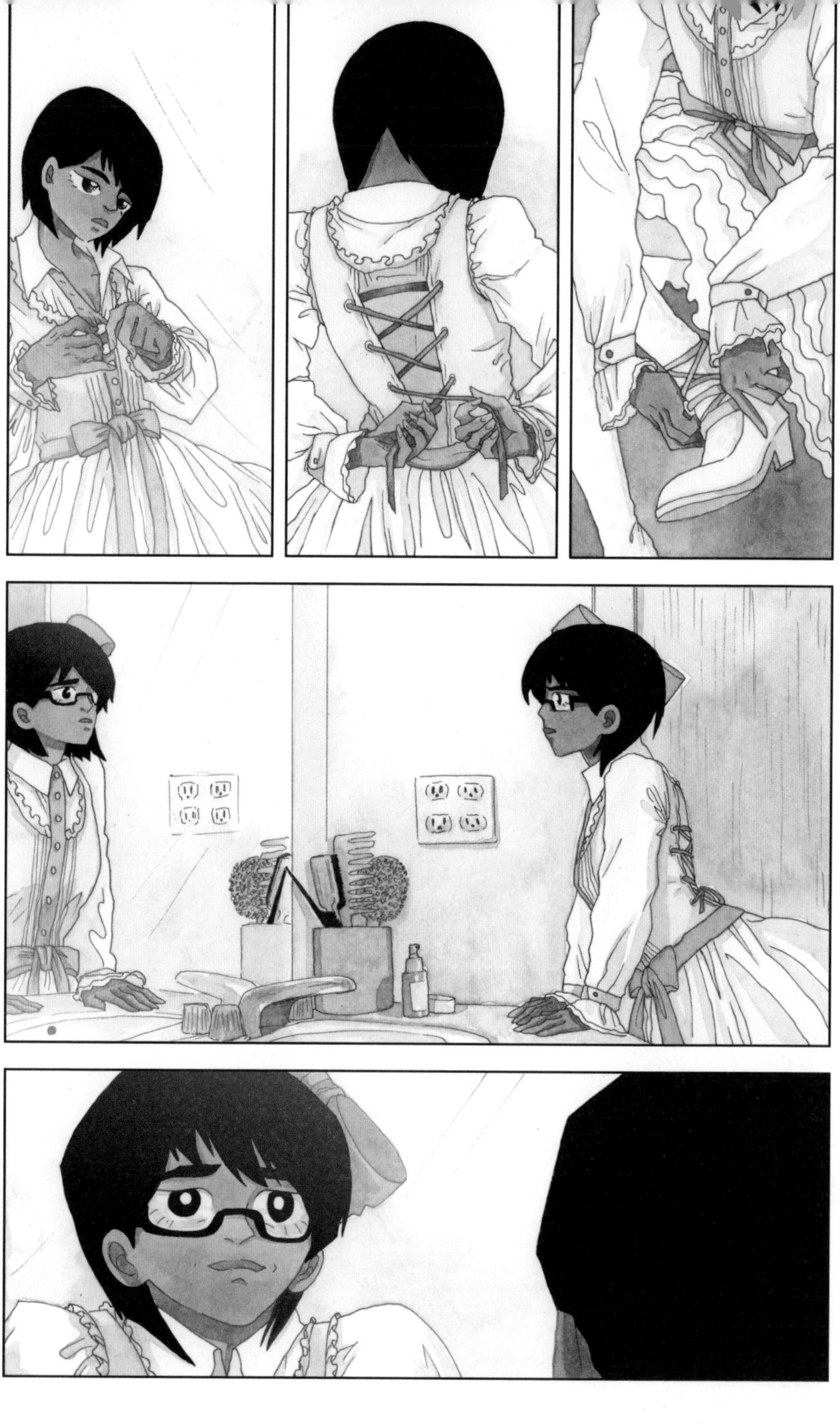

...EVERYTHING ON THIS QUIZ WILL BE IN THE TEST NEXT WEEK, SO MAKE SURE TO CHECK YOUR MISTAKES.

IF YOU HAVE QUESTIONS ABOUT YOUR GRADE, COME TALK TO ME AFTER CLASS.

SKRTCH

SKRTCH

Really?! Ahh, I studied so long for this, too.

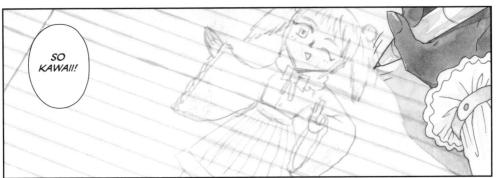

SO KAWAII!

Psst! James, help me out with my drawing!

I really thought I did okay this time...

PSST...

...Jaaammeesss-kuuuuhhn!

I don't even get what I did wrong here!

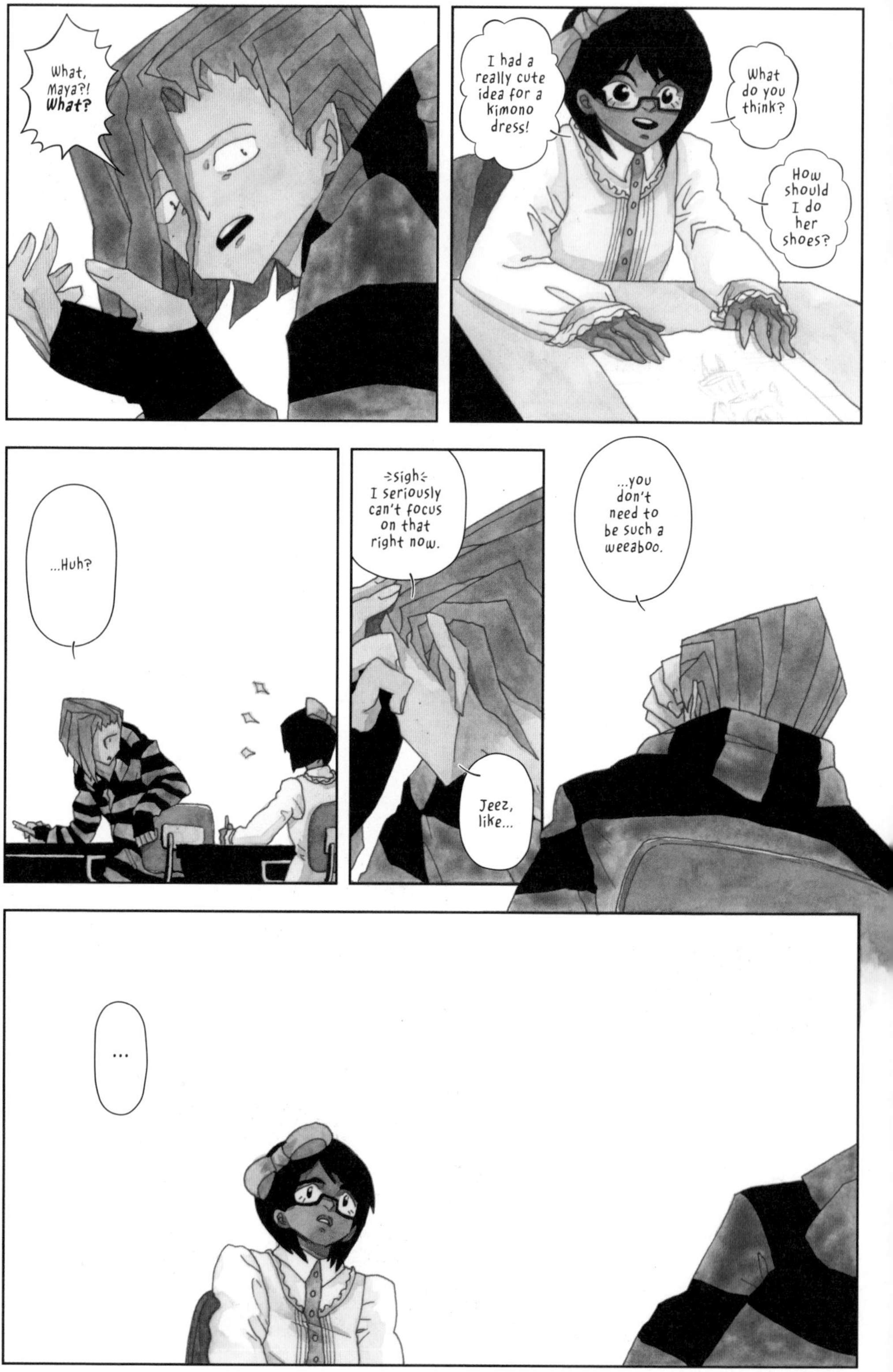
What, Maya?! **What?**
I had a really cute idea for a kimono dress!
What do you think?
How should I do her shoes?
...Huh?
=sigh= I seriously can't focus on that right now.
Jeez, like...
...you don't need to be such a weeaboo.
...

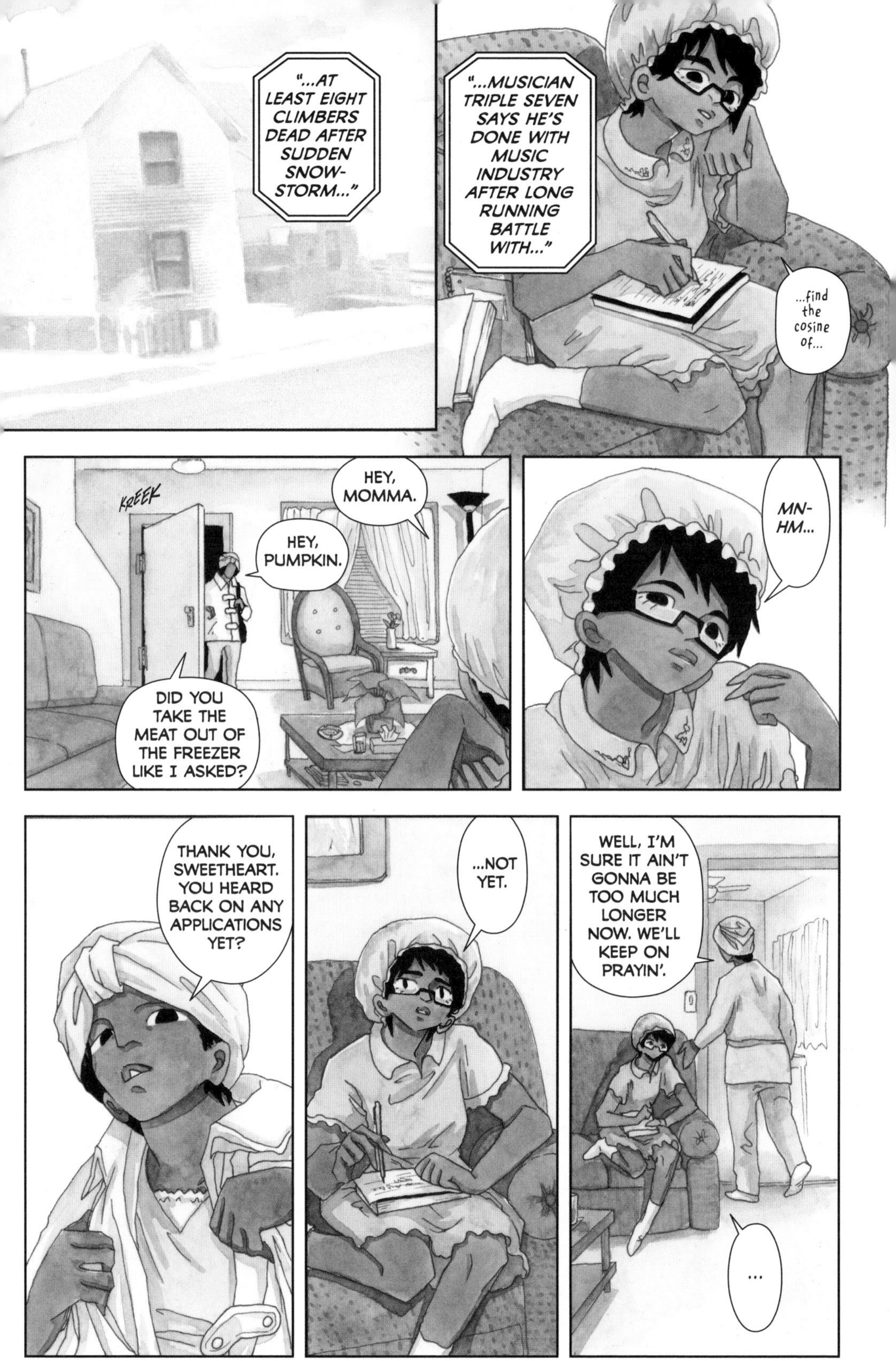
"...AT LEAST EIGHT CLIMBERS DEAD AFTER SUDDEN SNOW-STORM..."
"...MUSICIAN TRIPLE SEVEN SAYS HE'S DONE WITH MUSIC INDUSTRY AFTER LONG RUNNING BATTLE WITH..."
...find the cosine of...
KREEK
HEY, PUMPKIN.
HEY, MOMMA.
DID YOU TAKE THE MEAT OUT OF THE FREEZER LIKE I ASKED?
MN-HM...
THANK YOU, SWEETHEART. YOU HEARD BACK ON ANY APPLICATIONS YET?
...NOT YET.
WELL, I'M SURE IT AIN'T GONNA BE TOO MUCH LONGER NOW. WE'LL KEEP ON PRAYIN'.
...

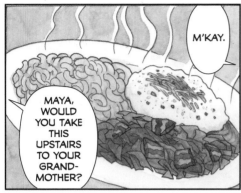

MAYA, WOULD YOU TAKE THIS UPSTAIRS TO YOUR GRAND-MOTHER?

M'KAY.

GRAN? YOU AWAKE?

NOK NOK

AH, MAYA, I'M UP.

BROUGHT YOUR DINNER.

THANK YOU, DARLIN'. GO ON AN' PUT IT OVER HERE.

DID THAT MOTHER OF YOURS PUT CHICKEN GRAVY ON THESE MASHED POTATOES AGAIN?

NOW, SHE KNOWS I HATE WHEN IT WHEN SHE DOES THAT. BOY, SHE JUST DOESN'T LISTEN TO ANYBODY.

MAYA, MAKE SURE YOU LISTEN WHEN FOLKS TELL YOU SOMETHIN'.

YOU GOT IT, GRAN.

146

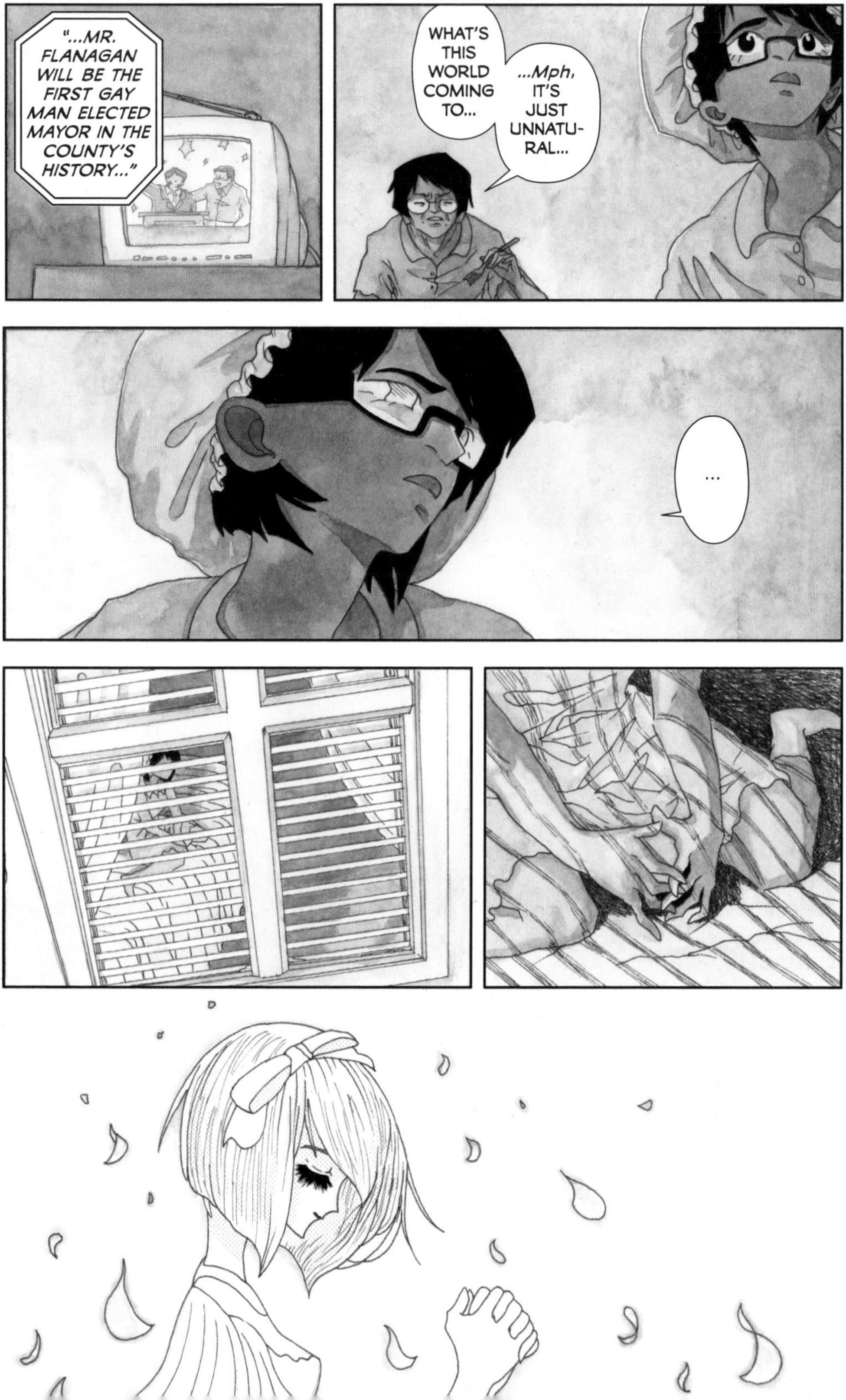
"...MR. FLANAGAN WILL BE THE FIRST GAY MAN ELECTED MAYOR IN THE COUNTY'S HISTORY..."
WHAT'S THIS WORLD COMING TO...
...Mph, IT'S JUST UNNATU-RAL...
...

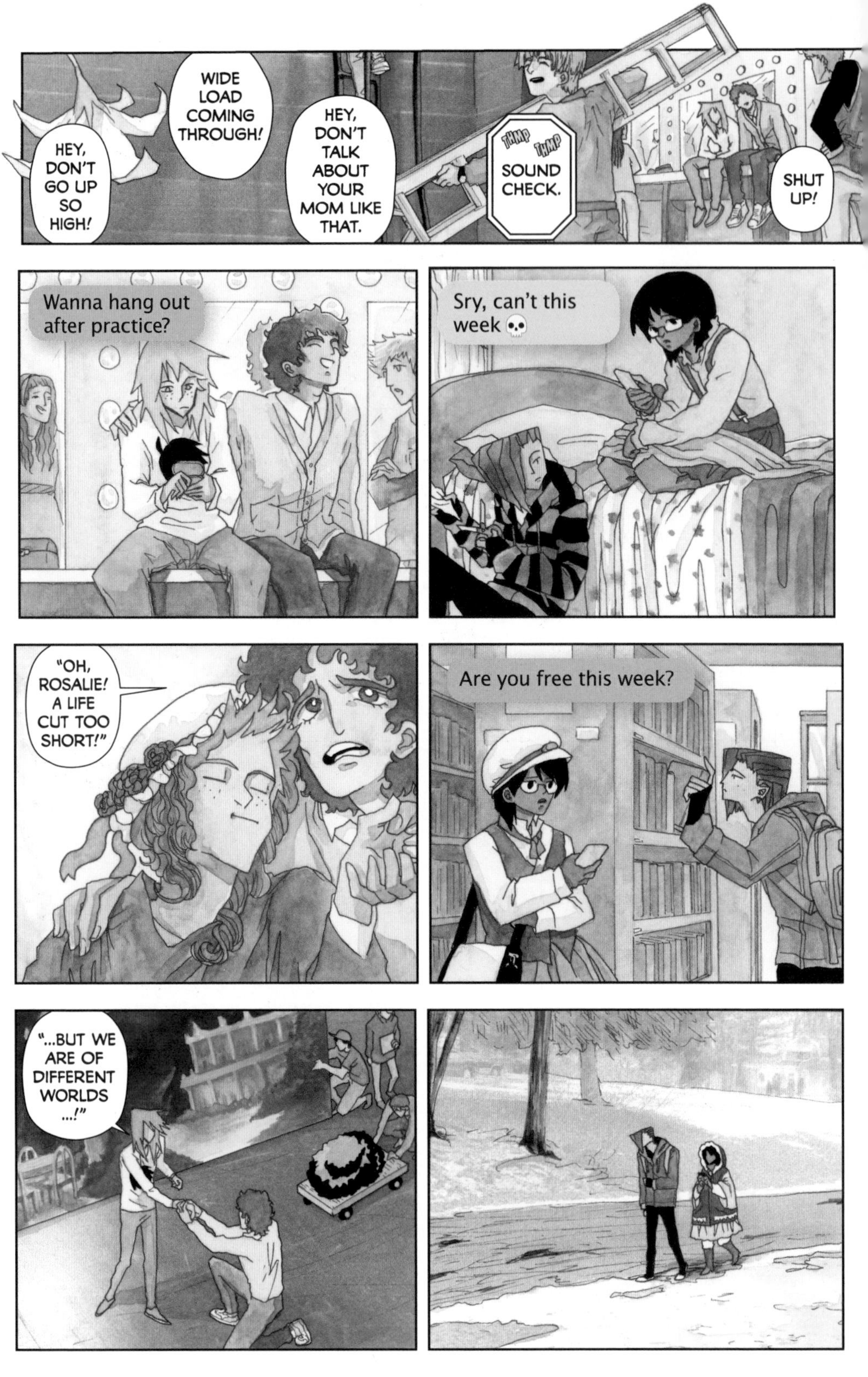
HEY, DON'T GO UP SO HIGH!
WIDE LOAD COMING THROUGH!
HEY, DON'T TALK ABOUT YOUR MOM LIKE THAT.
THMP THMP
SOUND CHECK.
SHUT UP!
Wanna hang out after practice?
Sry, can't this week
"OH, ROSALIE! A LIFE CUT TOO SHORT!"
Are you free this week?
"...BUT WE ARE OF DIFFERENT WORLDS ...!"

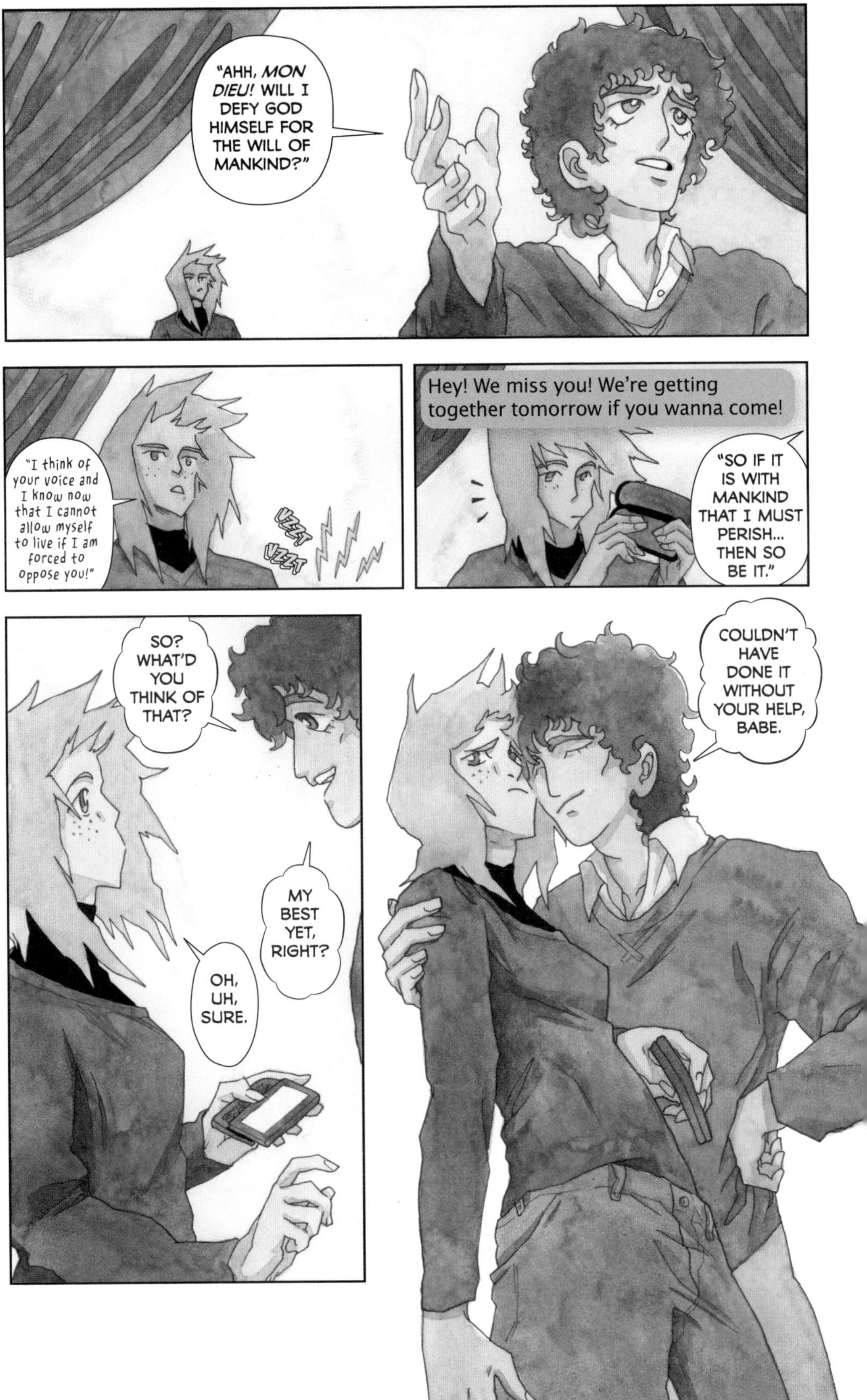
"AHH, *MON DIEU!* WILL I DEFY GOD HIMSELF FOR THE WILL OF MANKIND?"
"I think of your voice and I know now that I cannot allow myself to live if I am forced to oppose you!"
VZZZT VZZZT
Hey! We miss you! We're getting together tomorrow if you wanna come!
"SO IF IT IS WITH MANKIND THAT I MUST PERISH... THEN SO BE IT."
SO? WHAT'D YOU THINK OF THAT?
MY BEST YET, RIGHT?
OH, UH, SURE.
COULDN'T HAVE DONE IT WITHOUT YOUR HELP, BABE.

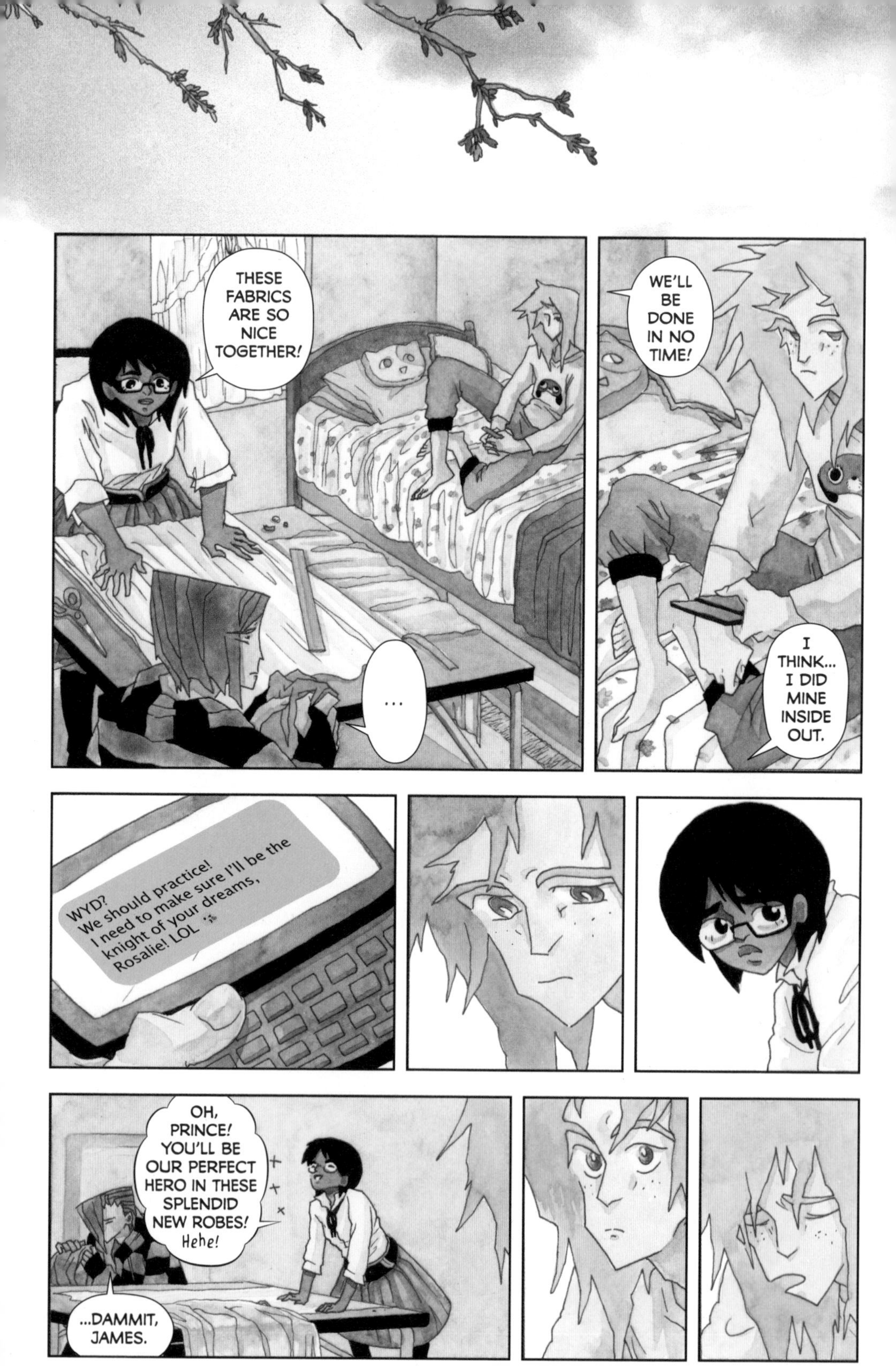
THESE FABRICS ARE SO NICE TOGETHER!
...
WE'LL BE DONE IN NO TIME!
I THINK... I DID MINE INSIDE OUT.
WYD? We should practice! I need to make sure I'll be the knight of your dreams, Rosalie! LOL
OH, PRINCE! YOU'LL BE OUR PERFECT HERO IN THESE SPLENDID NEW ROBES! Hehe!
...DAMMIT, JAMES.

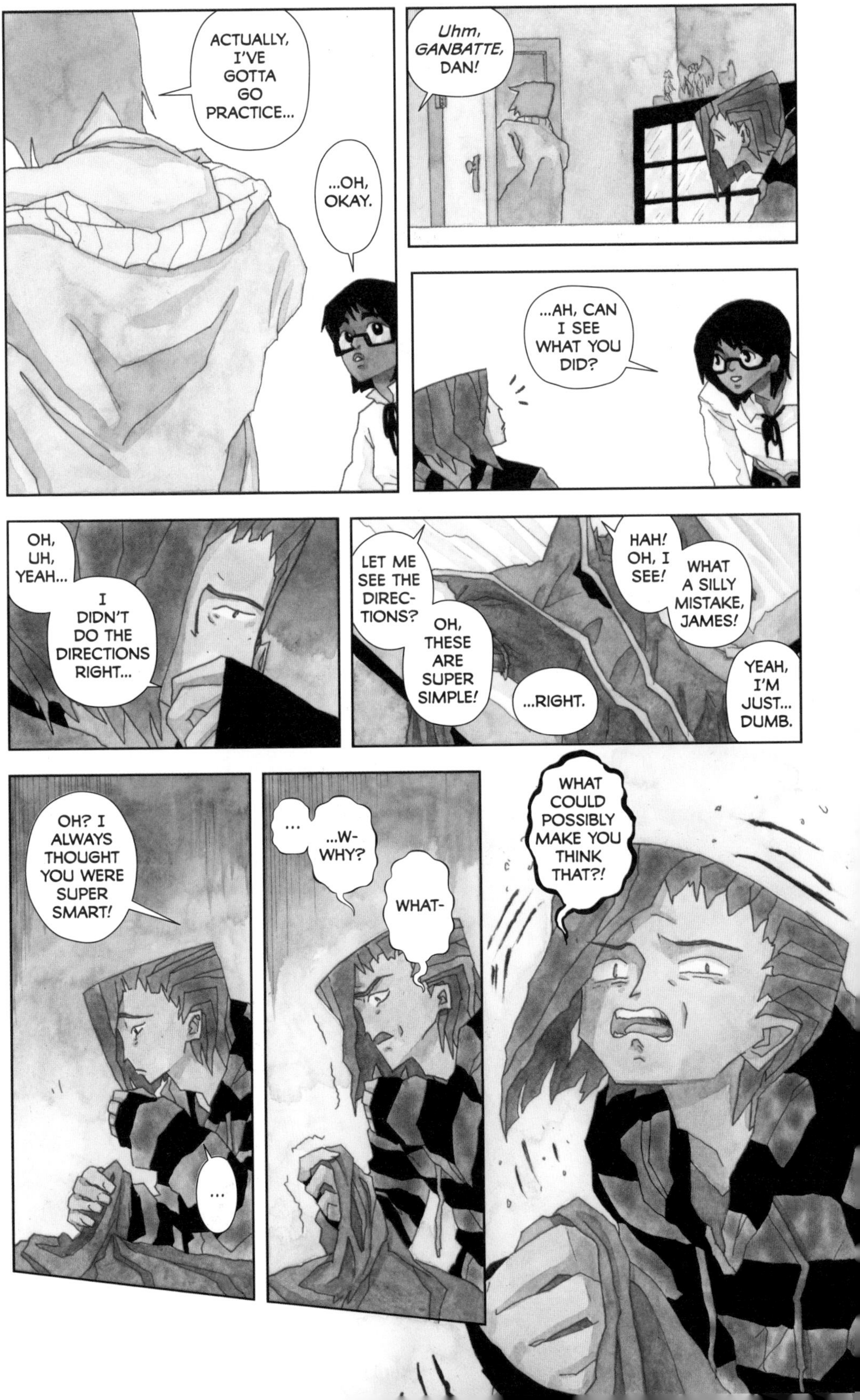
ACTUALLY, I'VE GOTTA GO PRACTICE...
...OH, OKAY.
Uhm, GANBATTE, DAN!
...AH, CAN I SEE WHAT YOU DID?
OH, UH, YEAH...
I DIDN'T DO THE DIRECTIONS RIGHT...
LET ME SEE THE DIREC-TIONS?
OH, THESE ARE SUPER SIMPLE!
...RIGHT.
HAH! OH, I SEE!
WHAT A SILLY MISTAKE, JAMES!
YEAH, I'M JUST... DUMB.
OH? I ALWAYS THOUGHT YOU WERE SUPER SMART!
...
...
...W-WHY?
WHAT-
WHAT COULD POSSIBLY MAKE YOU THINK THAT?!

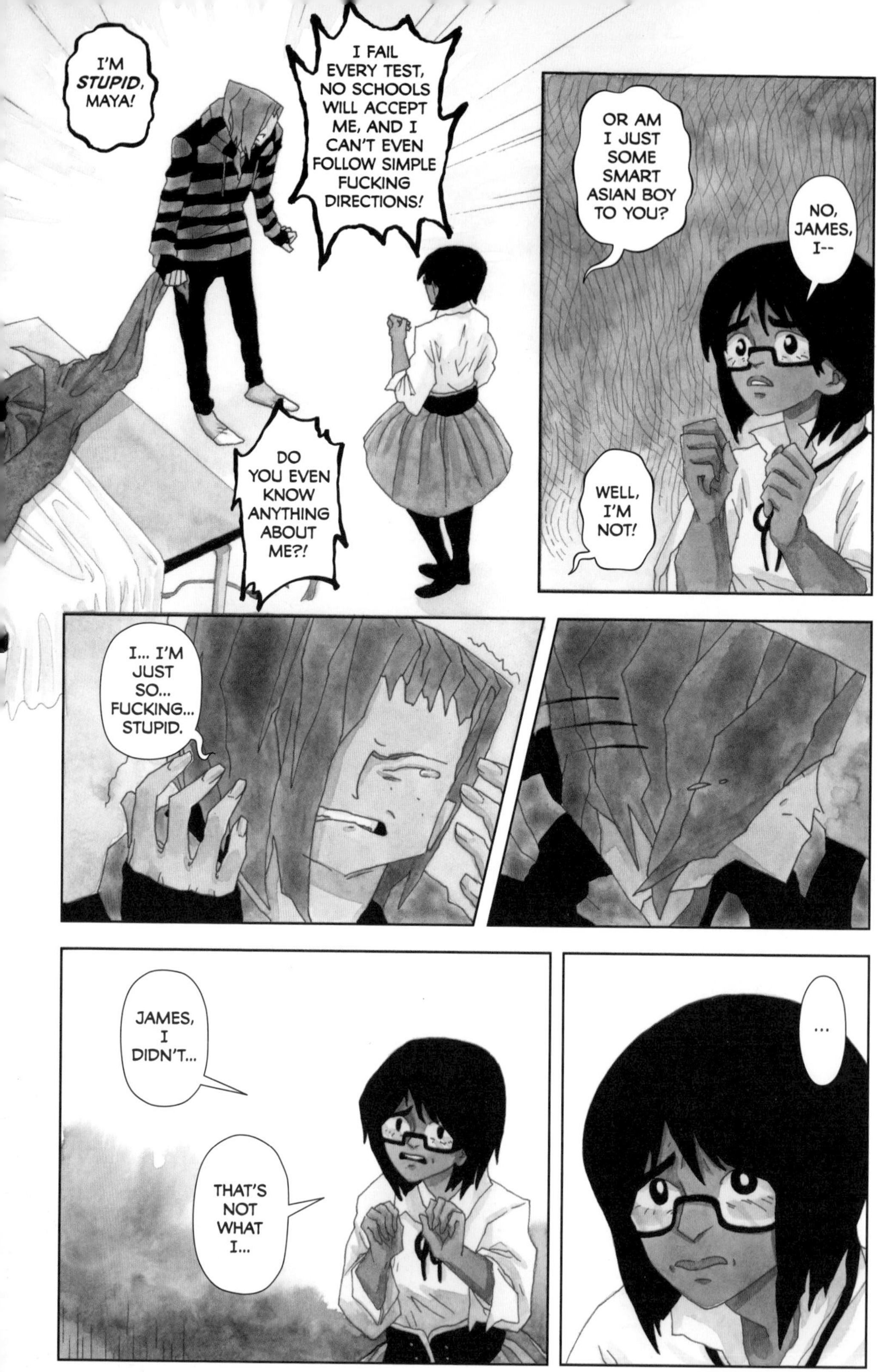
I'M *STUPID*, MAYA!
I FAIL EVERY TEST, NO SCHOOLS WILL ACCEPT ME, AND I CAN'T EVEN FOLLOW SIMPLE FUCKING DIRECTIONS!
DO YOU EVEN KNOW ANYTHING ABOUT ME?!
OR AM I JUST SOME SMART ASIAN BOY TO YOU?
NO, JAMES, I--
WELL, I'M NOT!
I... I'M JUST SO... FUCKING... STUPID.
JAMES, I DIDN'T...
THAT'S NOT WHAT I...
...

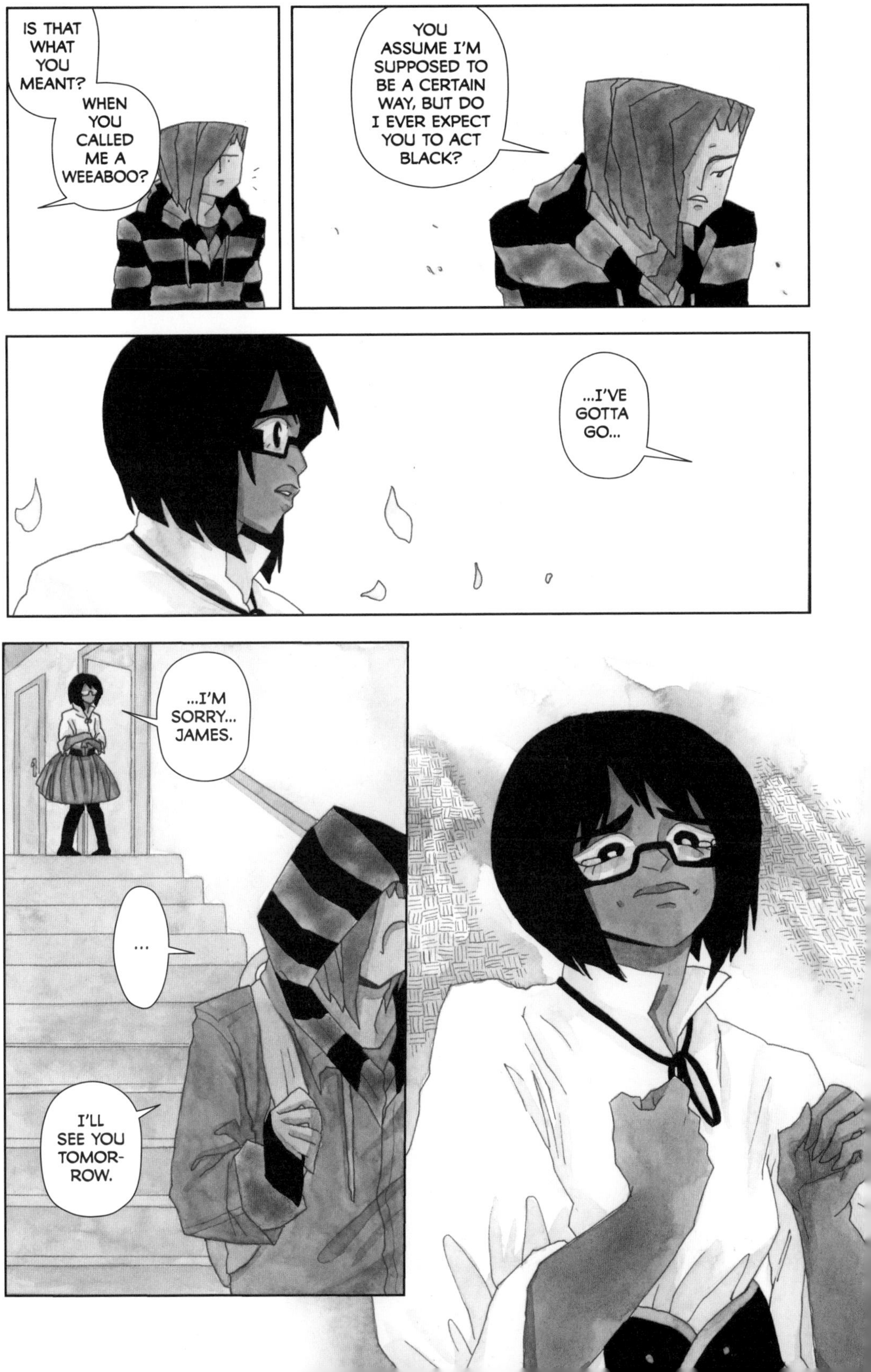
IS THAT WHAT YOU MEANT?
WHEN YOU CALLED ME A WEEABOO?
YOU ASSUME I'M SUPPOSED TO BE A CERTAIN WAY, BUT DO I EVER EXPECT YOU TO ACT BLACK?
...I'VE GOTTA GO...
...I'M SORRY... JAMES.
...
I'LL SEE YOU TOMOR-ROW.

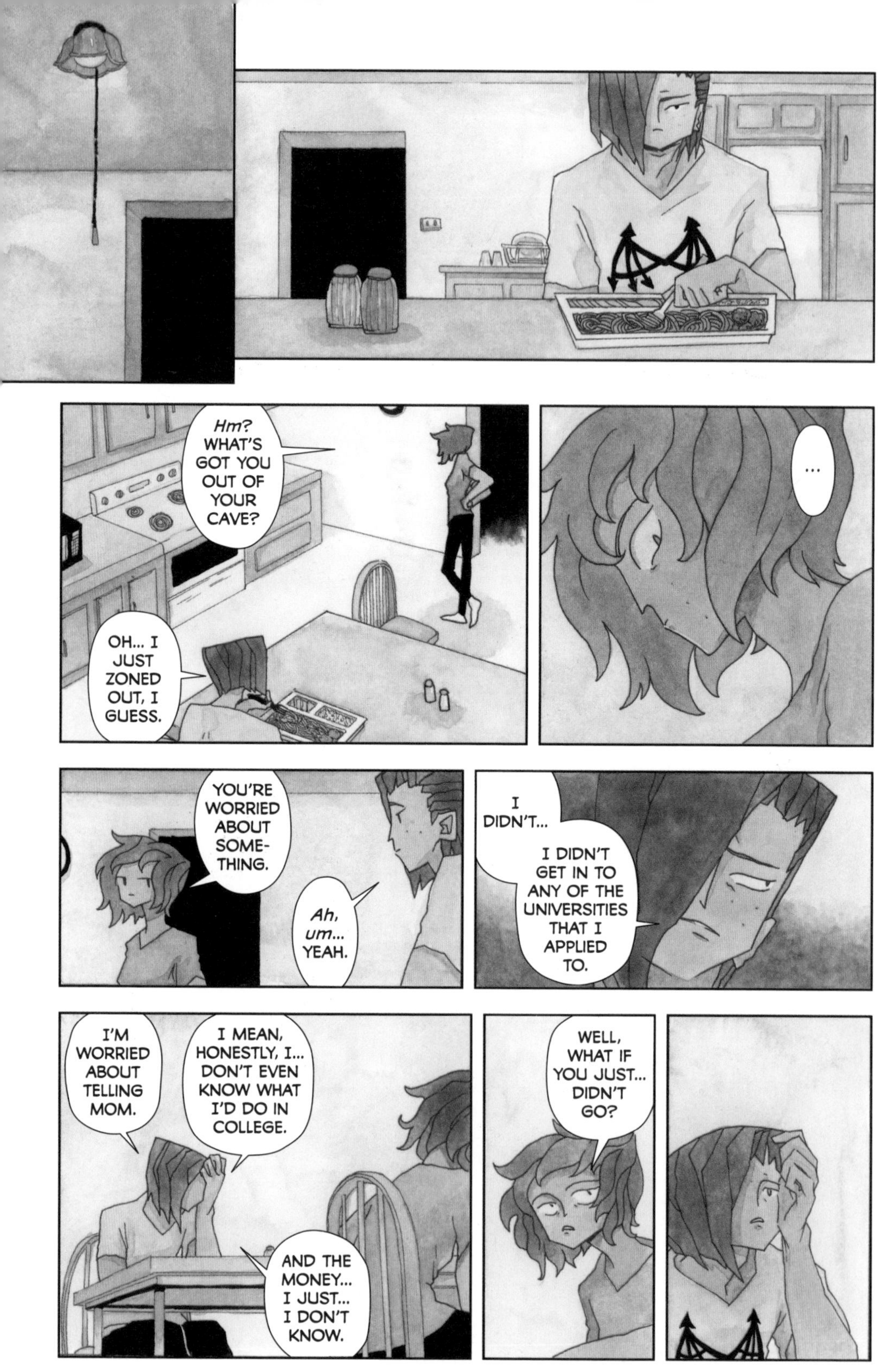
Hm? WHAT'S GOT YOU OUT OF YOUR CAVE?
OH... I JUST ZONED OUT, I GUESS.
...
YOU'RE WORRIED ABOUT SOME-THING.
Ah, um... YEAH.
I DIDN'T...
I DIDN'T GET IN TO ANY OF THE UNIVERSITIES THAT I APPLIED TO.
I'M WORRIED ABOUT TELLING MOM.
I MEAN, HONESTLY, I... DON'T EVEN KNOW WHAT I'D DO IN COLLEGE.
AND THE MONEY... I JUST... I DON'T KNOW.
WELL, WHAT IF YOU JUST... DIDN'T GO?

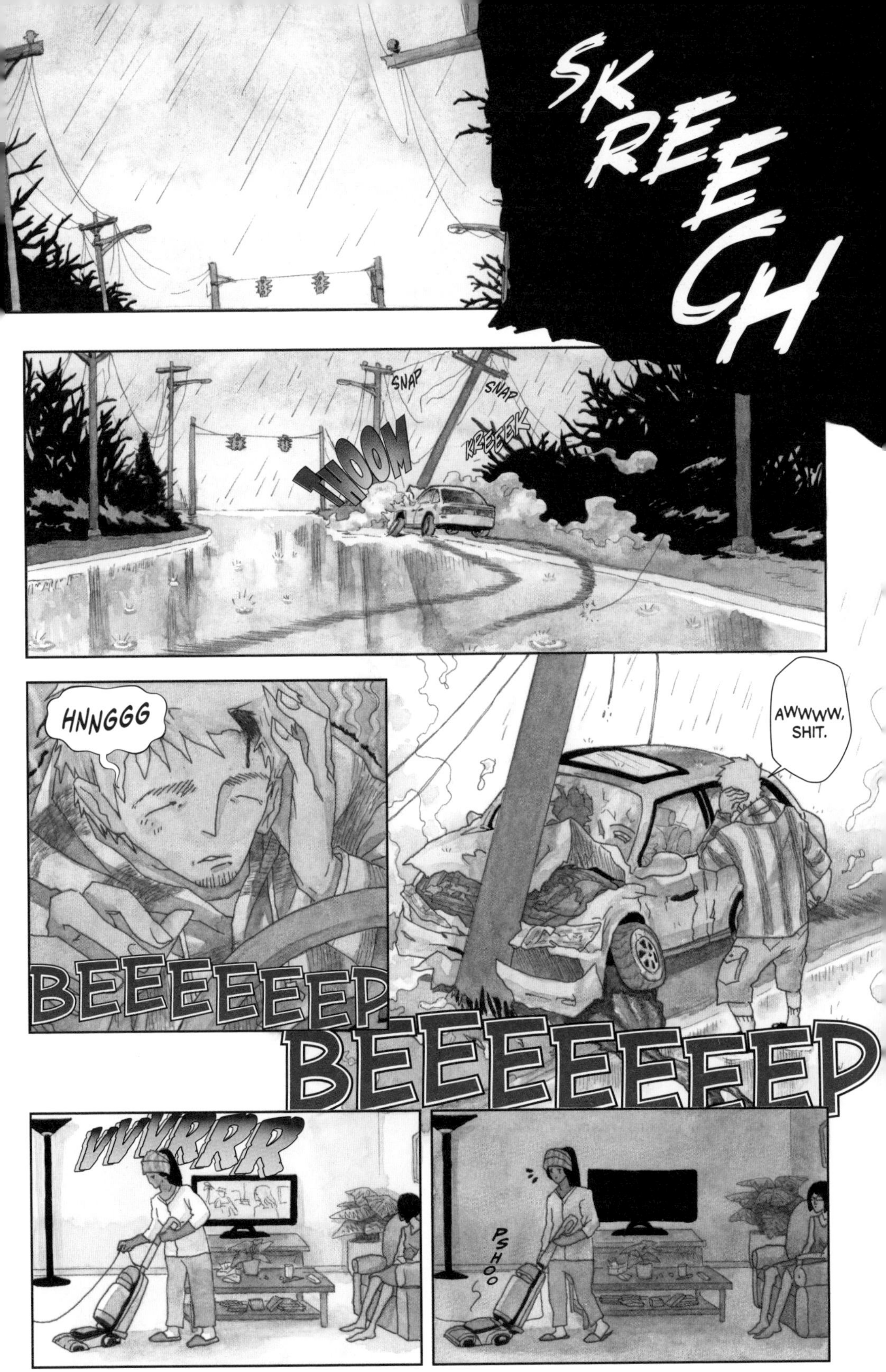
SKREECH
SNAP
SNAP
KREEEK
THOOM
HNNGGG
AWWWW, SHIT.
BEEEEEEEP
BEEEEEEEP
VVVRRR
PSHOO

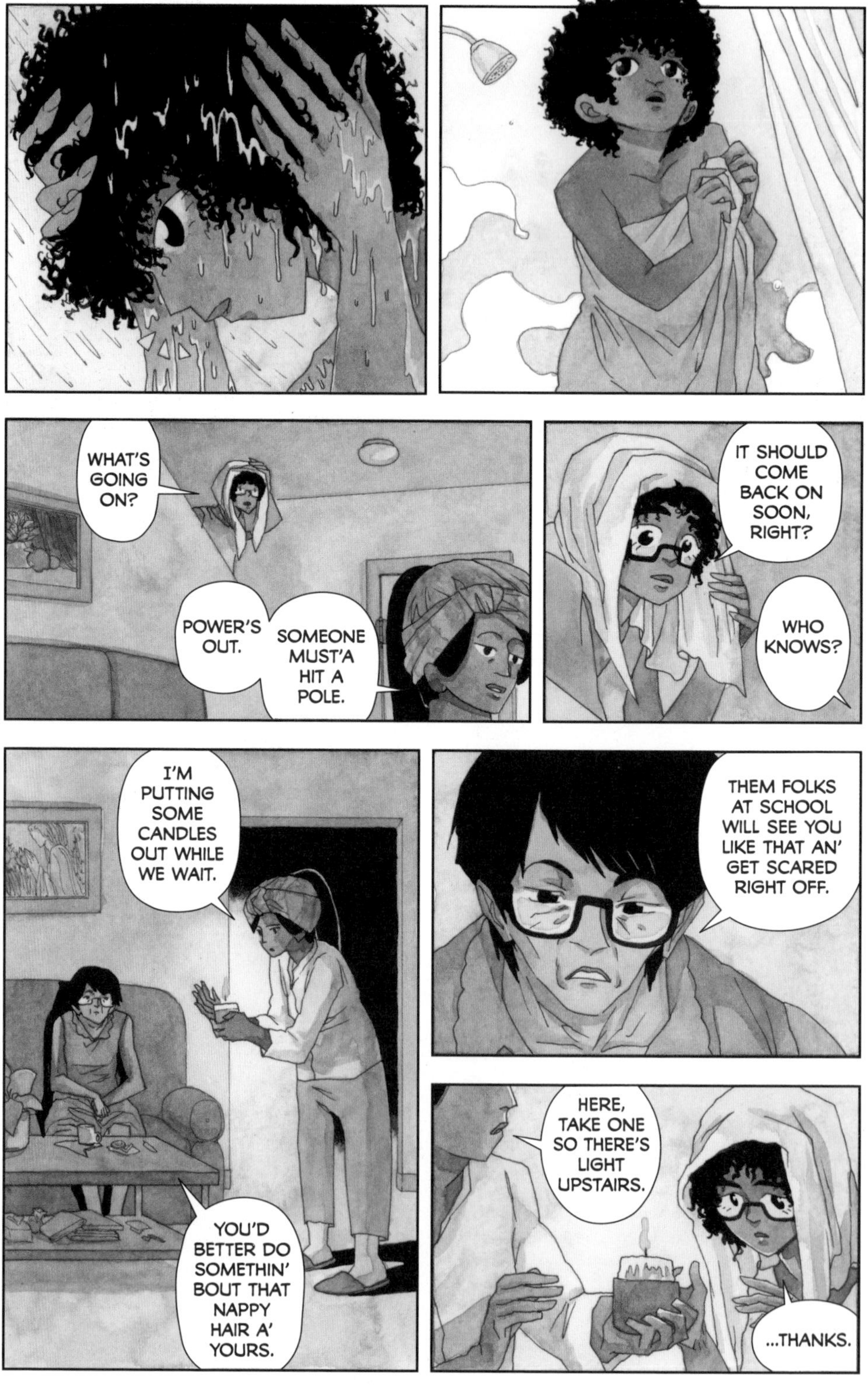
WHAT'S GOING ON?
POWER'S OUT.
SOMEONE MUST'A HIT A POLE.
IT SHOULD COME BACK ON SOON, RIGHT?
WHO KNOWS?
I'M PUTTING SOME CANDLES OUT WHILE WE WAIT.
YOU'D BETTER DO SOMETHIN' BOUT THAT NAPPY HAIR A' YOURS.
THEM FOLKS AT SCHOOL WILL SEE YOU LIKE THAT AN' GET SCARED RIGHT OFF.
HERE, TAKE ONE SO THERE'S LIGHT UPSTAIRS.
...THANKS.

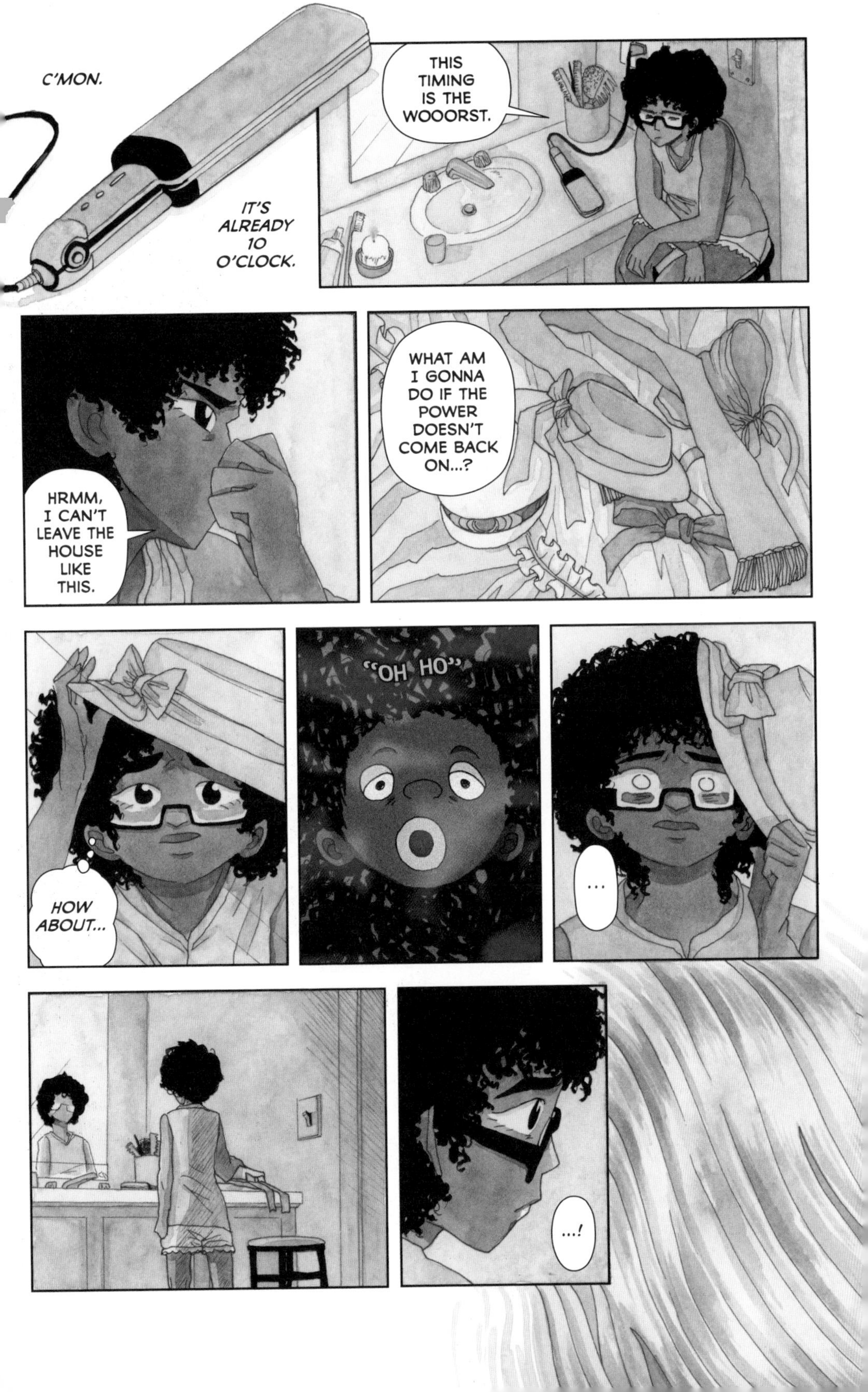
C'MON.
IT'S ALREADY 10 O'CLOCK.
THIS TIMING IS THE WOOORST.
HRMM, I CAN'T LEAVE THE HOUSE LIKE THIS.
WHAT AM I GONNA DO IF THE POWER DOESN'T COME BACK ON...?
HOW ABOUT...
"OH HO"
...
...!

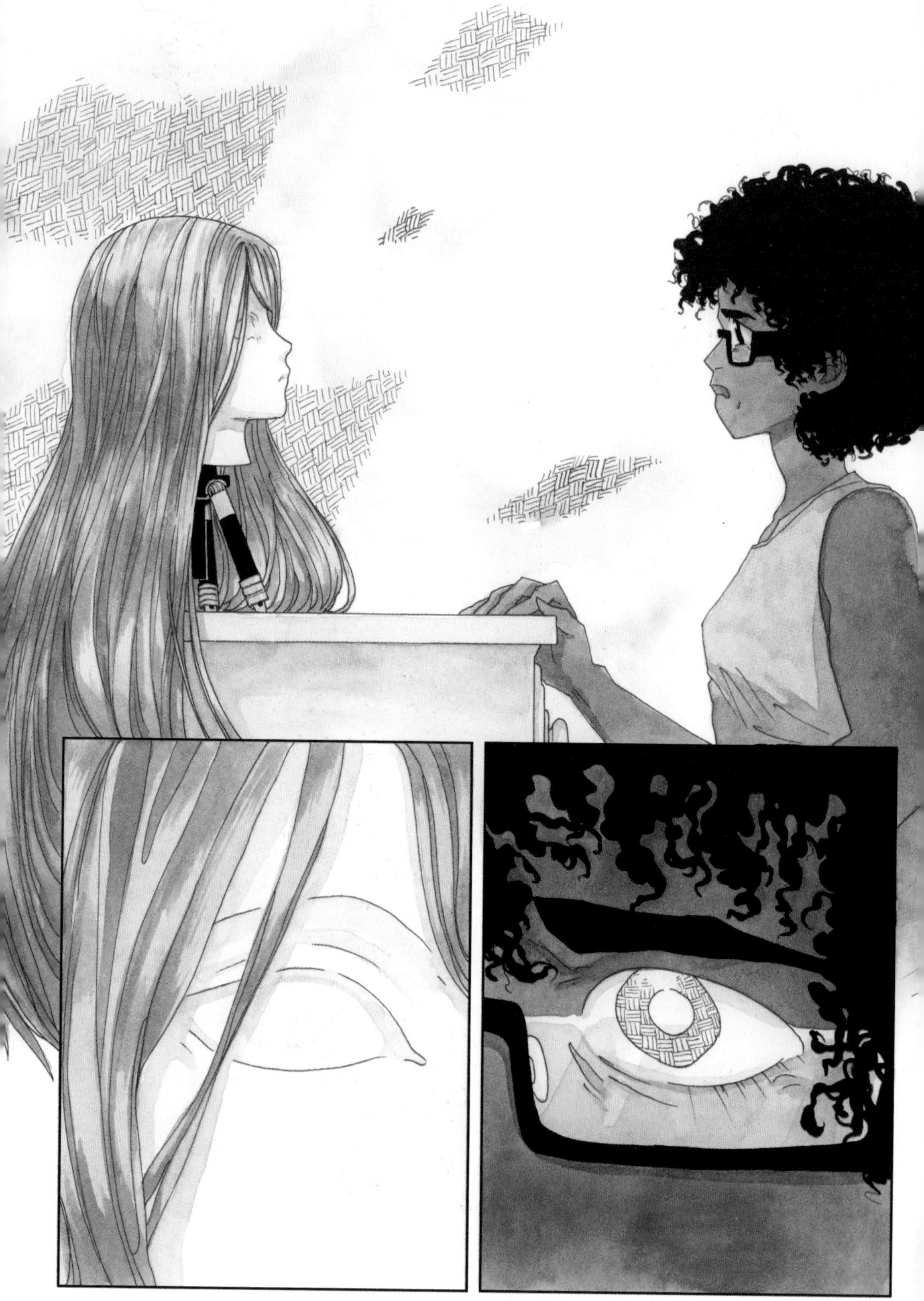

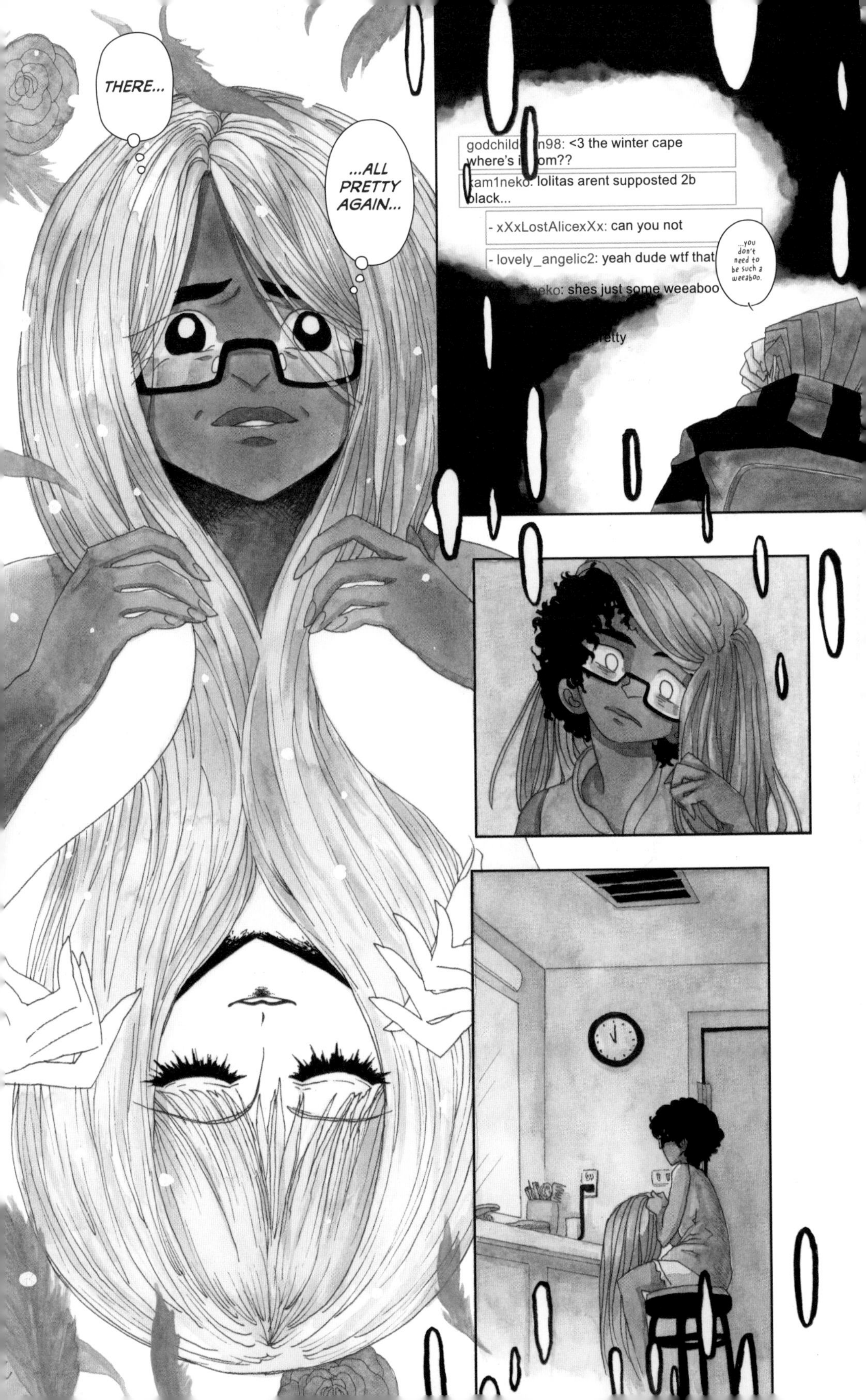
THERE...
...ALL PRETTY AGAIN...
godchild n98: <3 the winter cape where's i om??
am1neko: lolitas arent supposted 2b black...
- xXxLostAlicexXx: can you not
- lovely_angelic2: yeah dude wtf that
...you don't need to be such a weeaboo.
eko: shes just some weeaboo
etty

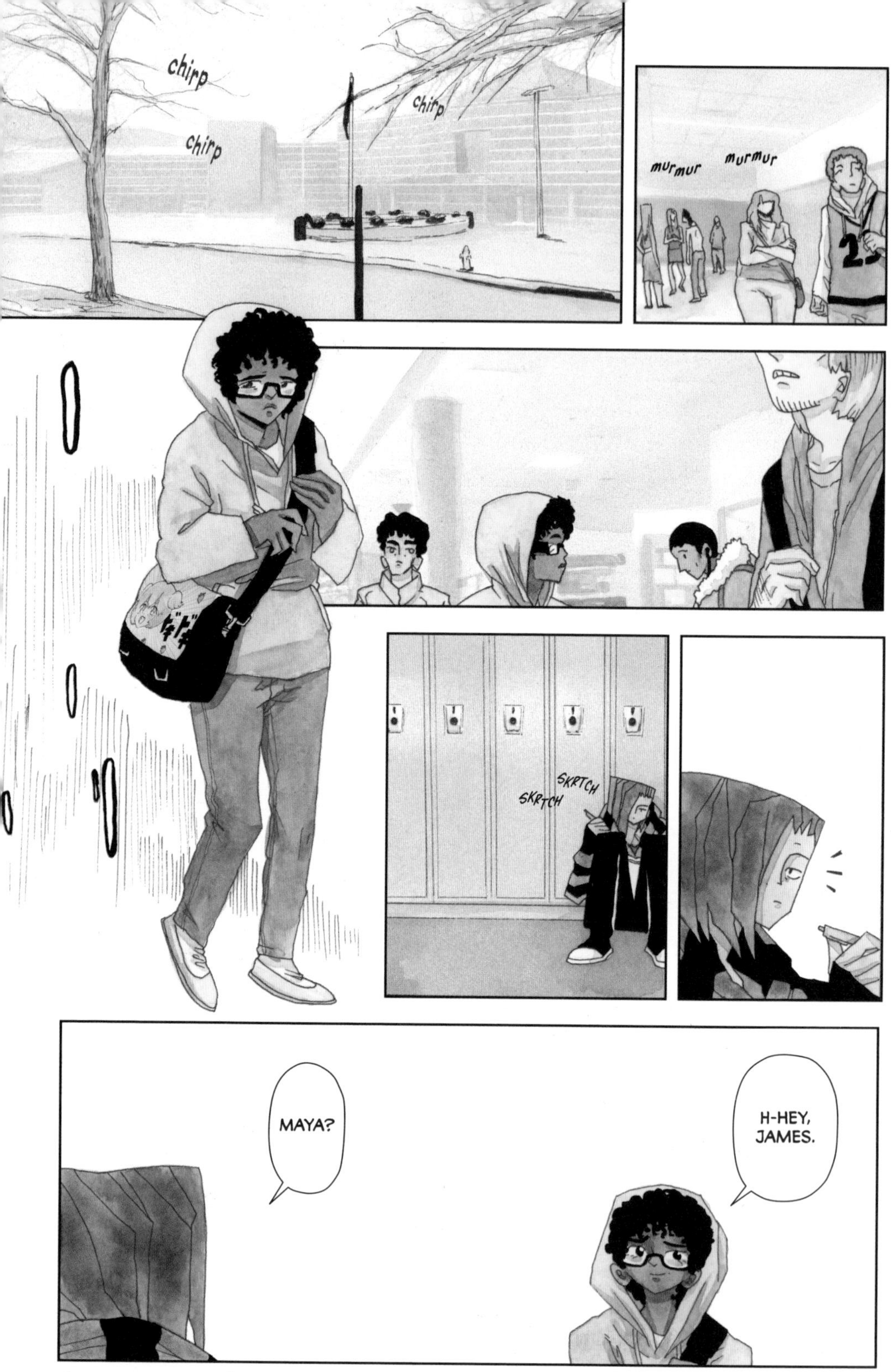
chirp
chirp
chirp
murmur
murmur
SKRTCH
SKRTCH
MAYA?
H-HEY, JAMES.

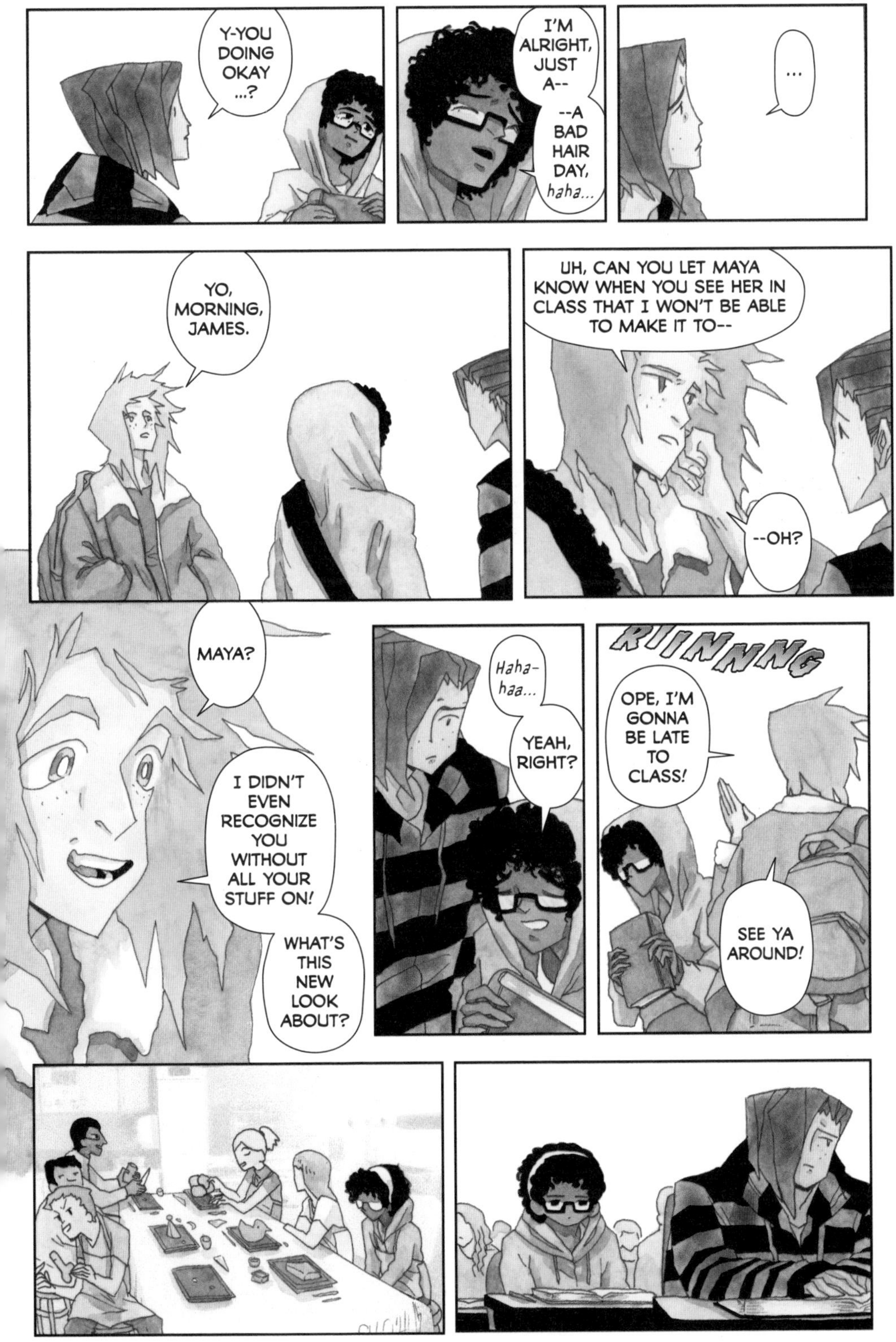
Y-YOU DOING OKAY ...?
I'M ALRIGHT, JUST A--
--A BAD HAIR DAY, haha...
...
YO, MORNING, JAMES.
UH, CAN YOU LET MAYA KNOW WHEN YOU SEE HER IN CLASS THAT I WON'T BE ABLE TO MAKE IT TO--
--OH?
MAYA?
I DIDN'T EVEN RECOGNIZE YOU WITHOUT ALL YOUR STUFF ON!
WHAT'S THIS NEW LOOK ABOUT?
Haha-haa...
YEAH, RIGHT?
RIINNNG
OPE, I'M GONNA BE LATE TO CLASS!
SEE YA AROUND!

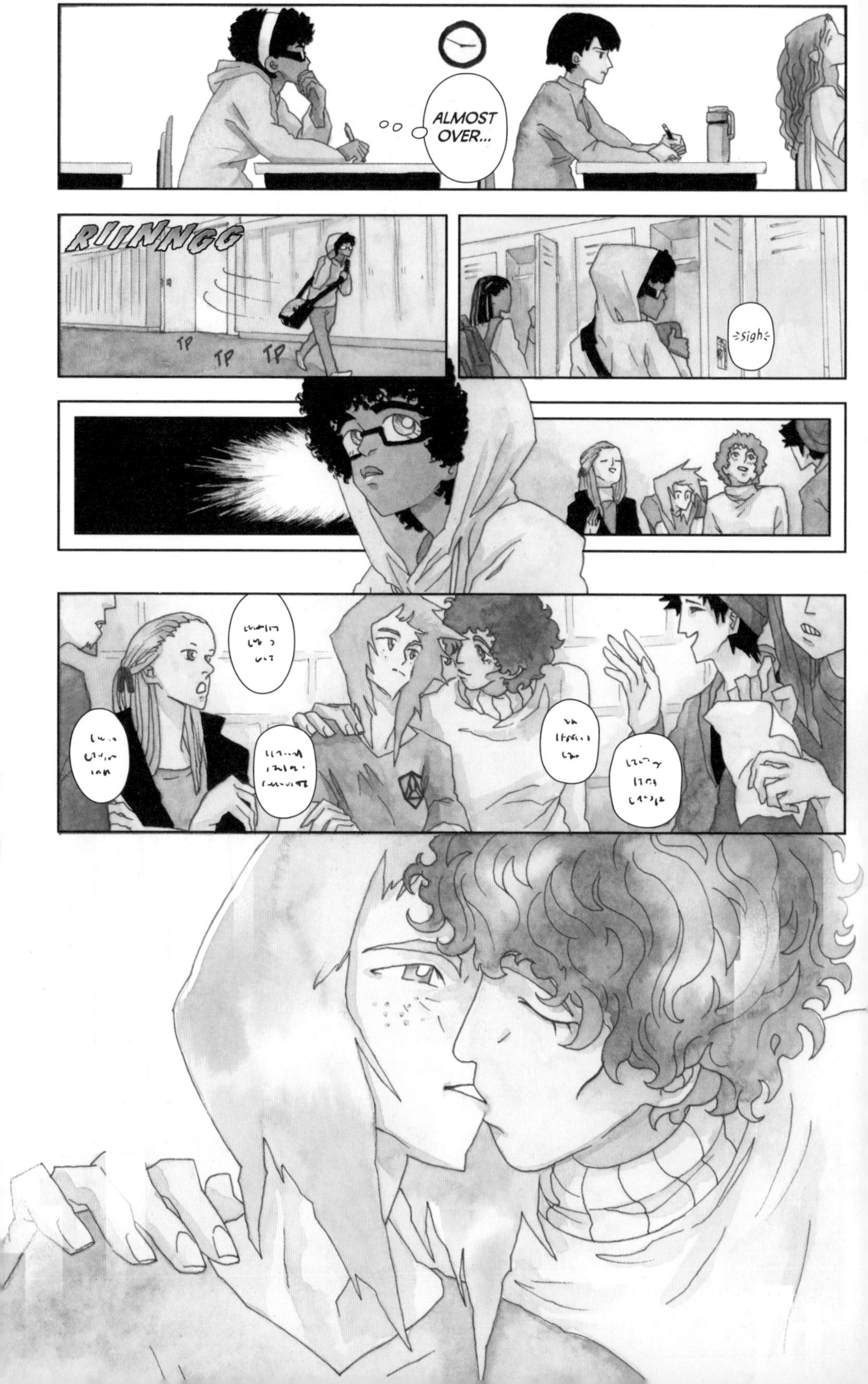
ALMOST OVER...
RIIINNGG
TP TP TP
sigh

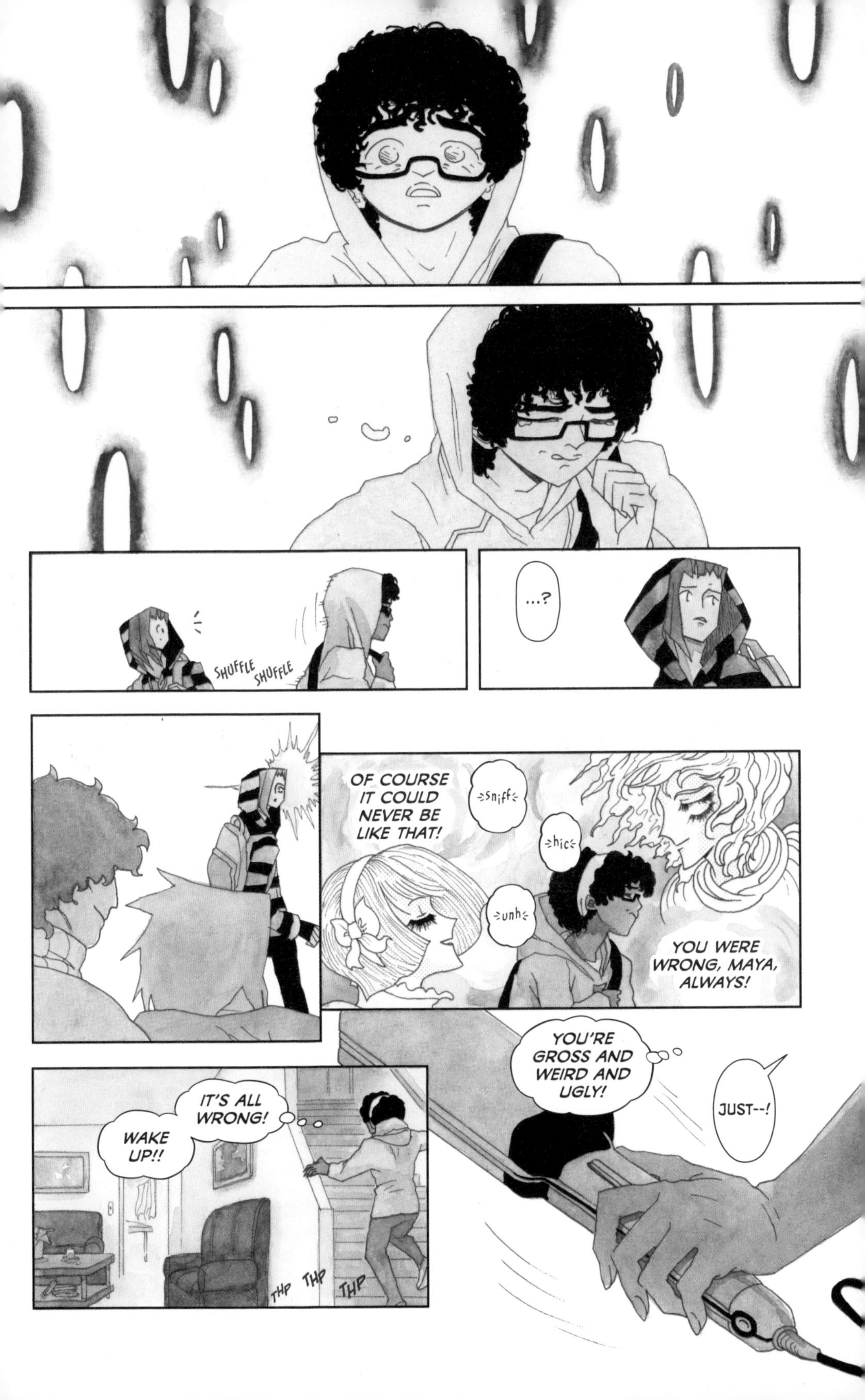
SHUFFLE SHUFFLE
...?
OF COURSE IT COULD NEVER BE LIKE THAT!
sniff
hic
unh
YOU WERE WRONG, MAYA, ALWAYS!
YOU'RE GROSS AND WEIRD AND UGLY!
JUST--!
IT'S ALL WRONG!
WAKE UP!!
THP THP THP

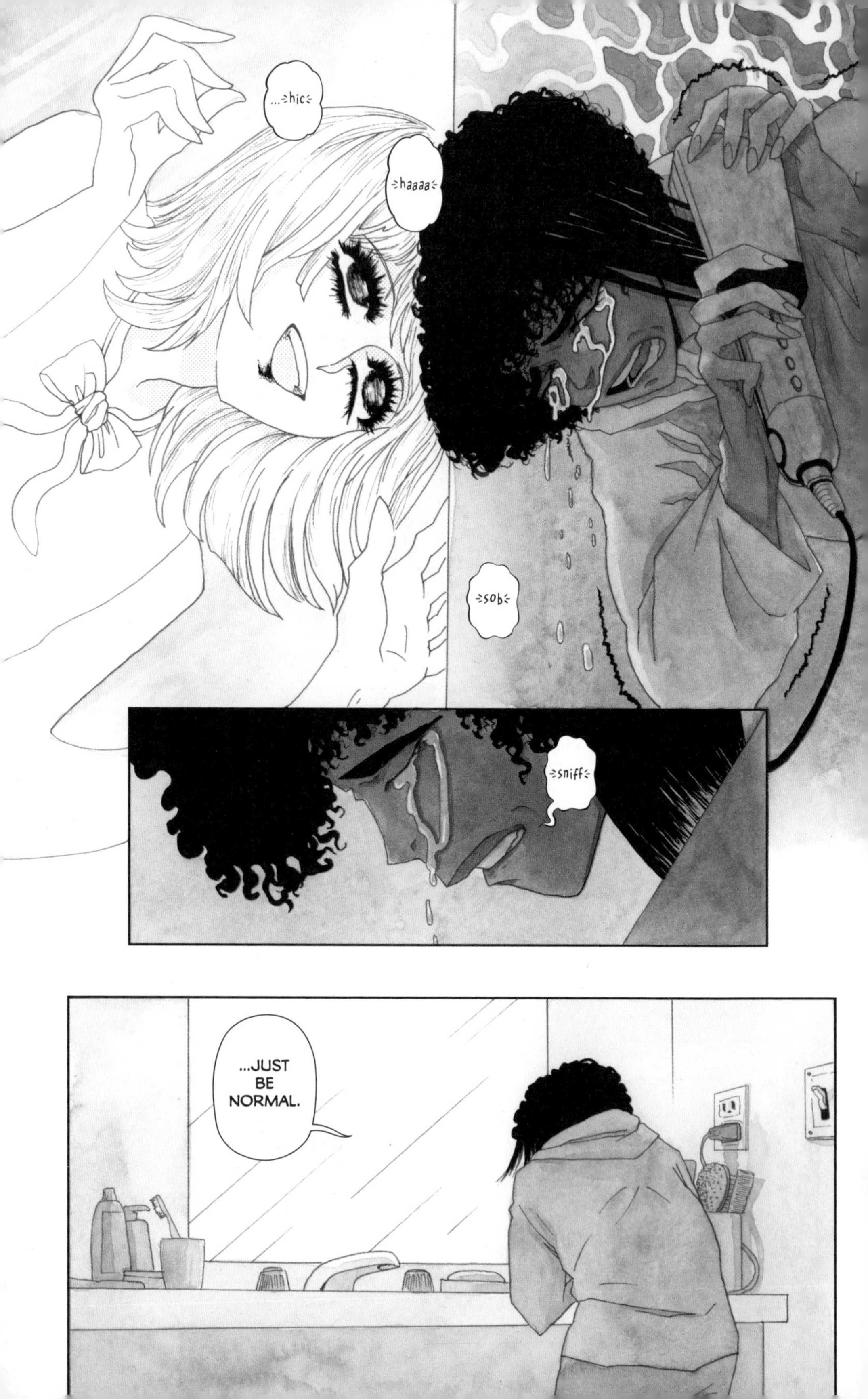

...hic
haaaa
sob
sniff
...JUST BE NORMAL.

WEEABOO

"THIS NEXT ONE IS FOR ALL YOU LOVERS OUT THERE..."

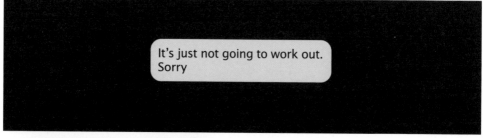

It's just not going to work out. Sorry

"HOPE THIS NIGHT TAKES YOU FARTHER THAN YOU'VE EVER BEEN..."

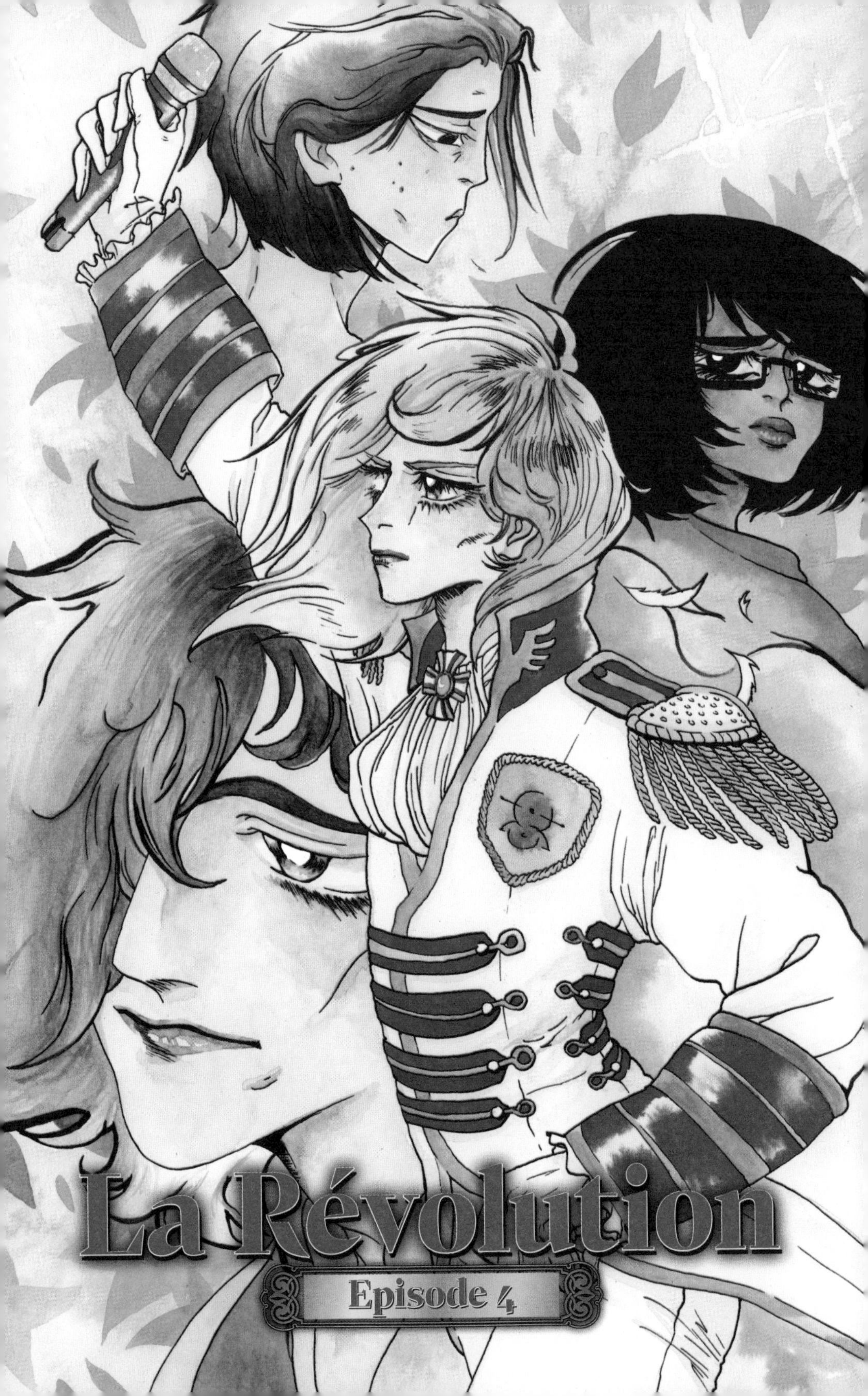
La Révolution
Episode 4

IT'S SO BRIGHT TODAY.

HM?

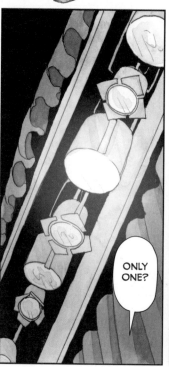

ONLY ONE?

DANNY!

YOUR TURN FOR DRESS REHEARSAL FITTING.

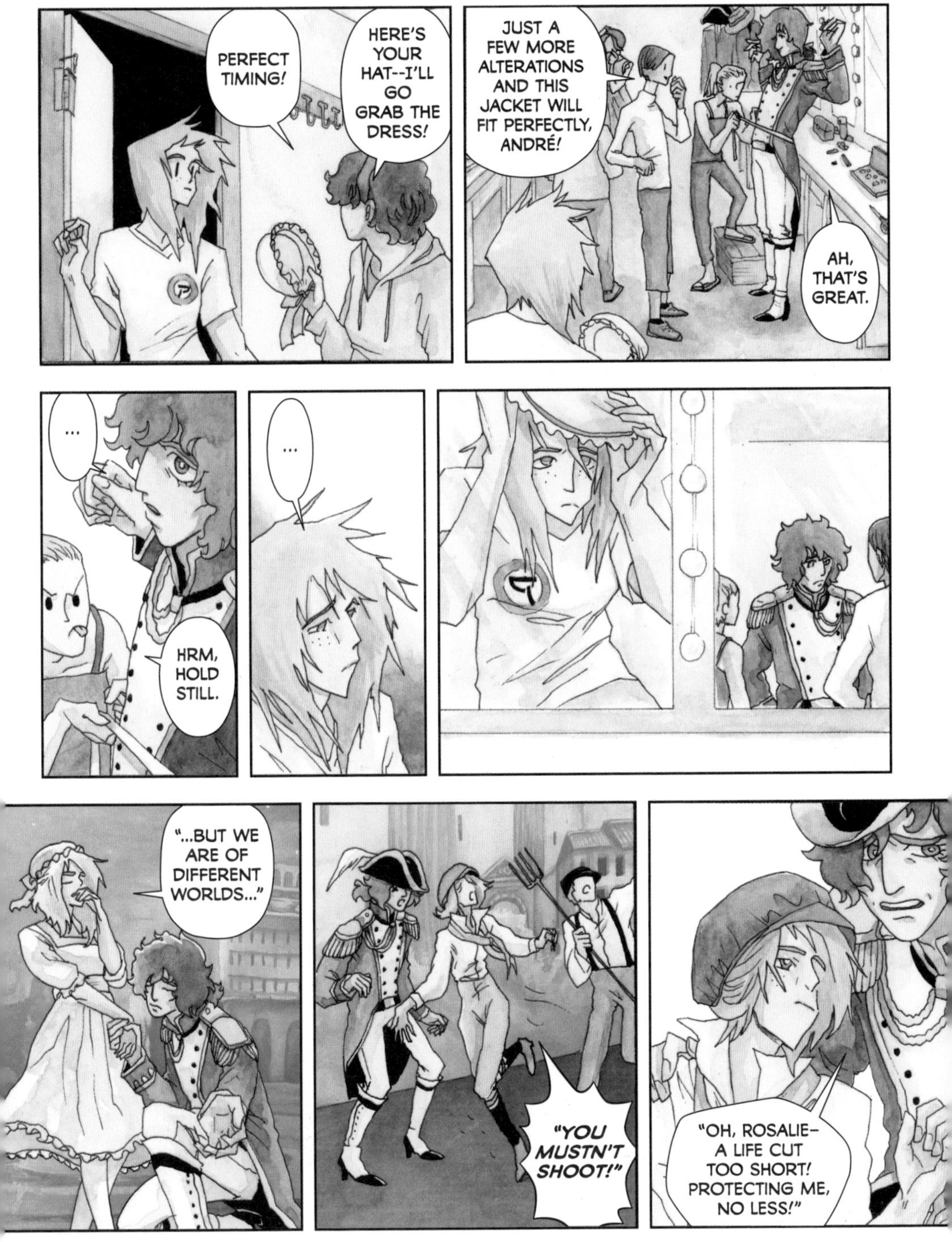
PERFECT TIMING!
HERE'S YOUR HAT--I'LL GO GRAB THE DRESS!
JUST A FEW MORE ALTERATIONS AND THIS JACKET WILL FIT PERFECTLY, ANDRÉ!
AH, THAT'S GREAT.
...
HRM, HOLD STILL.
...
"...BUT WE ARE OF DIFFERENT WORLDS..."
"YOU MUSTN'T SHOOT!"
"OH, ROSALIE– A LIFE CUT TOO SHORT! PROTECTING ME, NO LESS!"

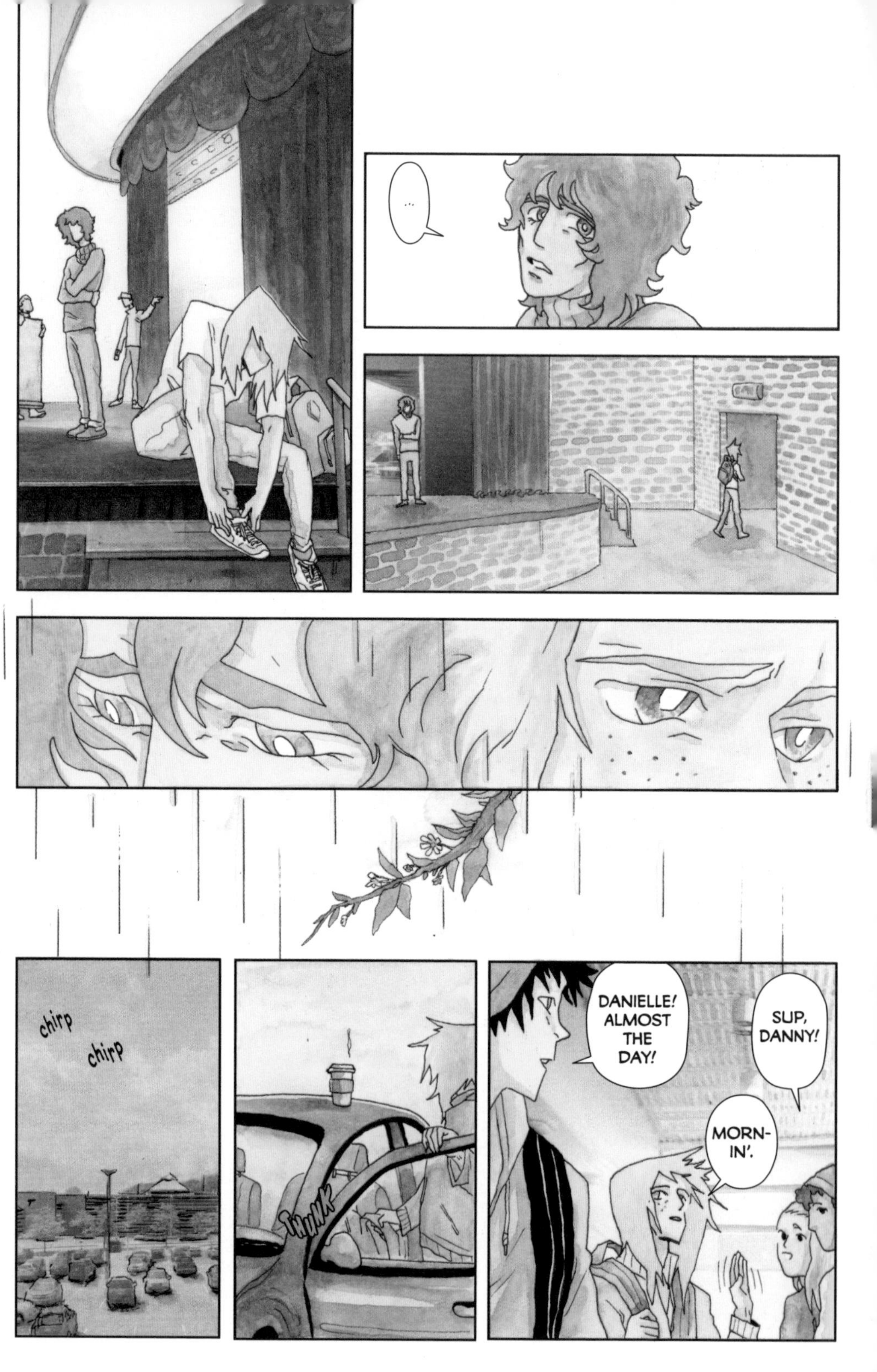
...
chirp
chirp
THUNK
DANIELLE! ALMOST THE DAY!
SUP, DANNY!
MORN-IN'.

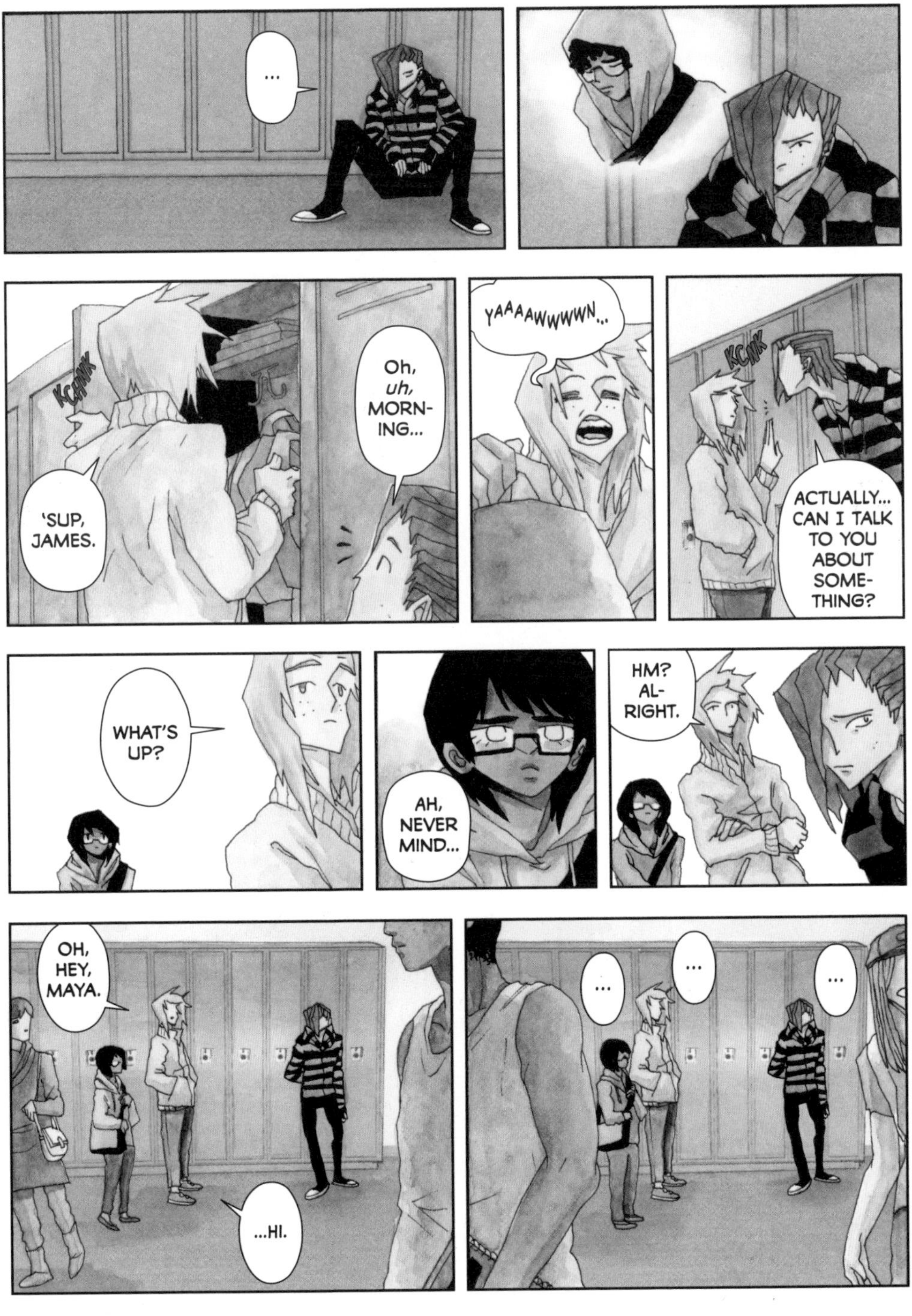
...
'SUP, JAMES.
KCHNK
Oh, *uh,* MORNING...
YAAAAWWWWN...
KCNK
ACTUALLY... CAN I TALK TO YOU ABOUT SOMETHING?
WHAT'S UP?
AH, NEVER MIND...
HM? ALRIGHT.
OH, HEY, MAYA.
...HI.
...
...
...

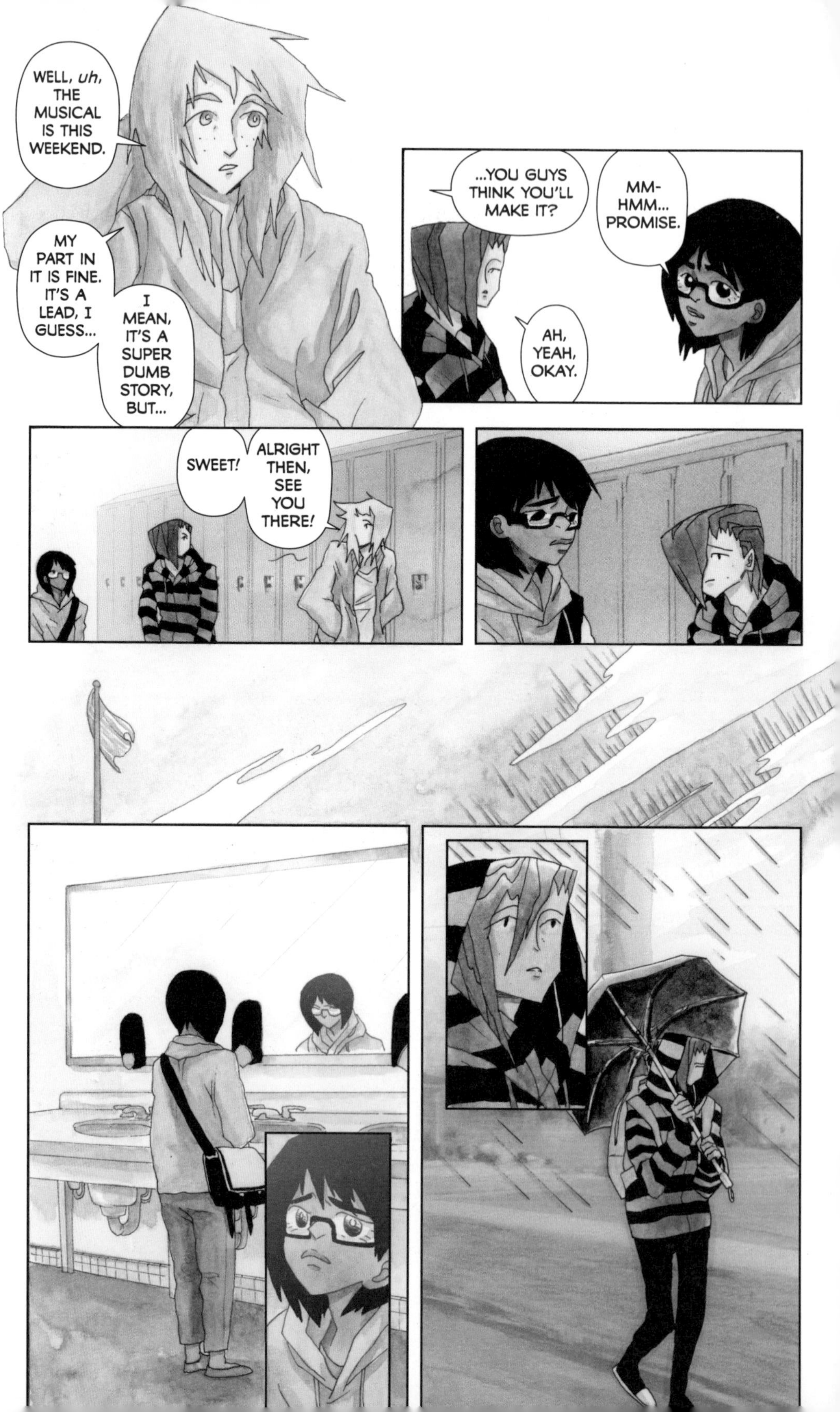
WELL, *uh*, THE MUSICAL IS THIS WEEKEND.
MY PART IN IT IS FINE. IT'S A LEAD, I GUESS...
I MEAN, IT'S A SUPER DUMB STORY, BUT...
...YOU GUYS THINK YOU'LL MAKE IT?
MM-HMM... PROMISE.
AH, YEAH, OKAY.
SWEET!
ALRIGHT THEN, SEE YOU THERE!

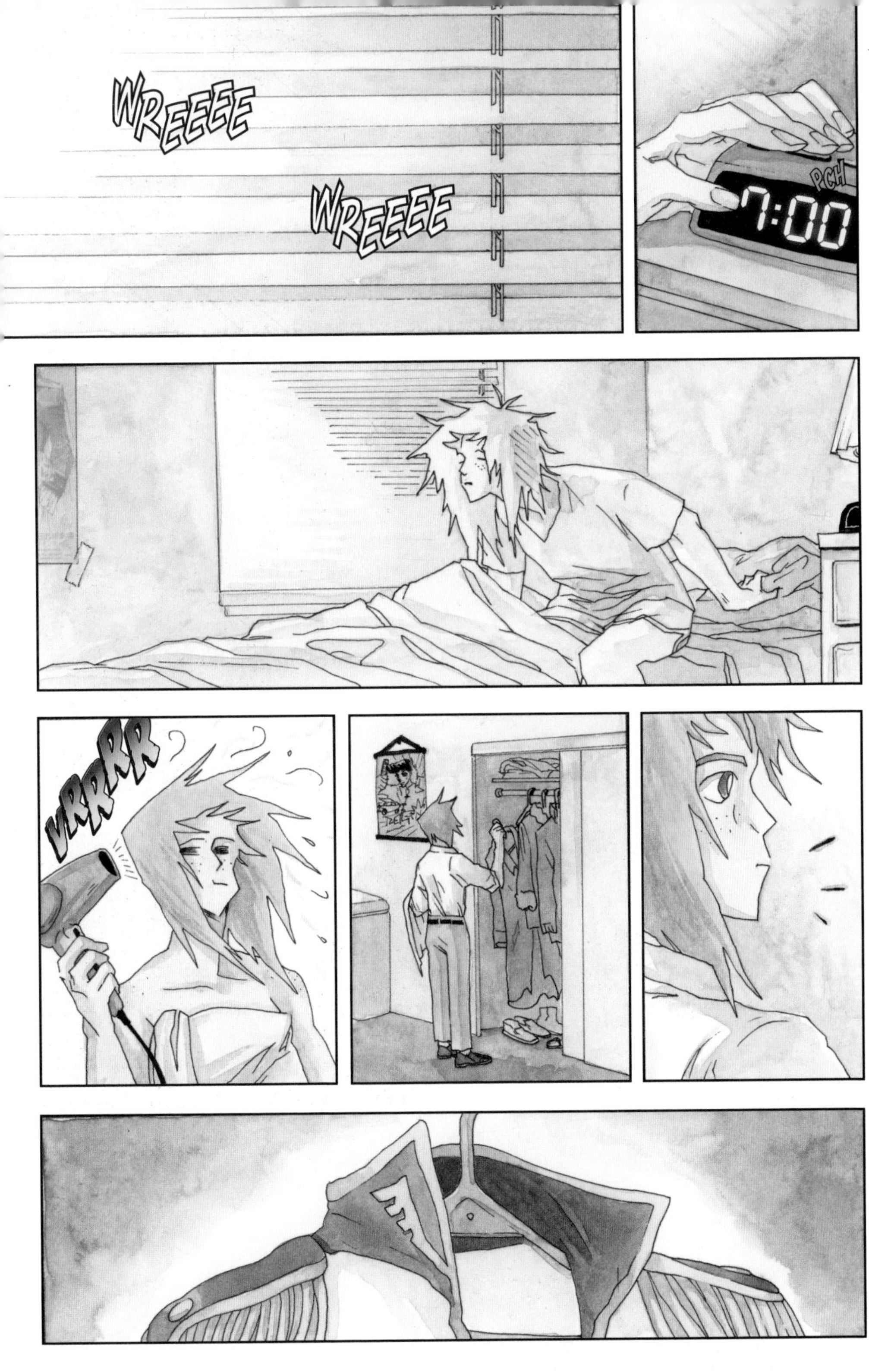
WREEEE
WREEEE
PCH
7:00
vRRRR

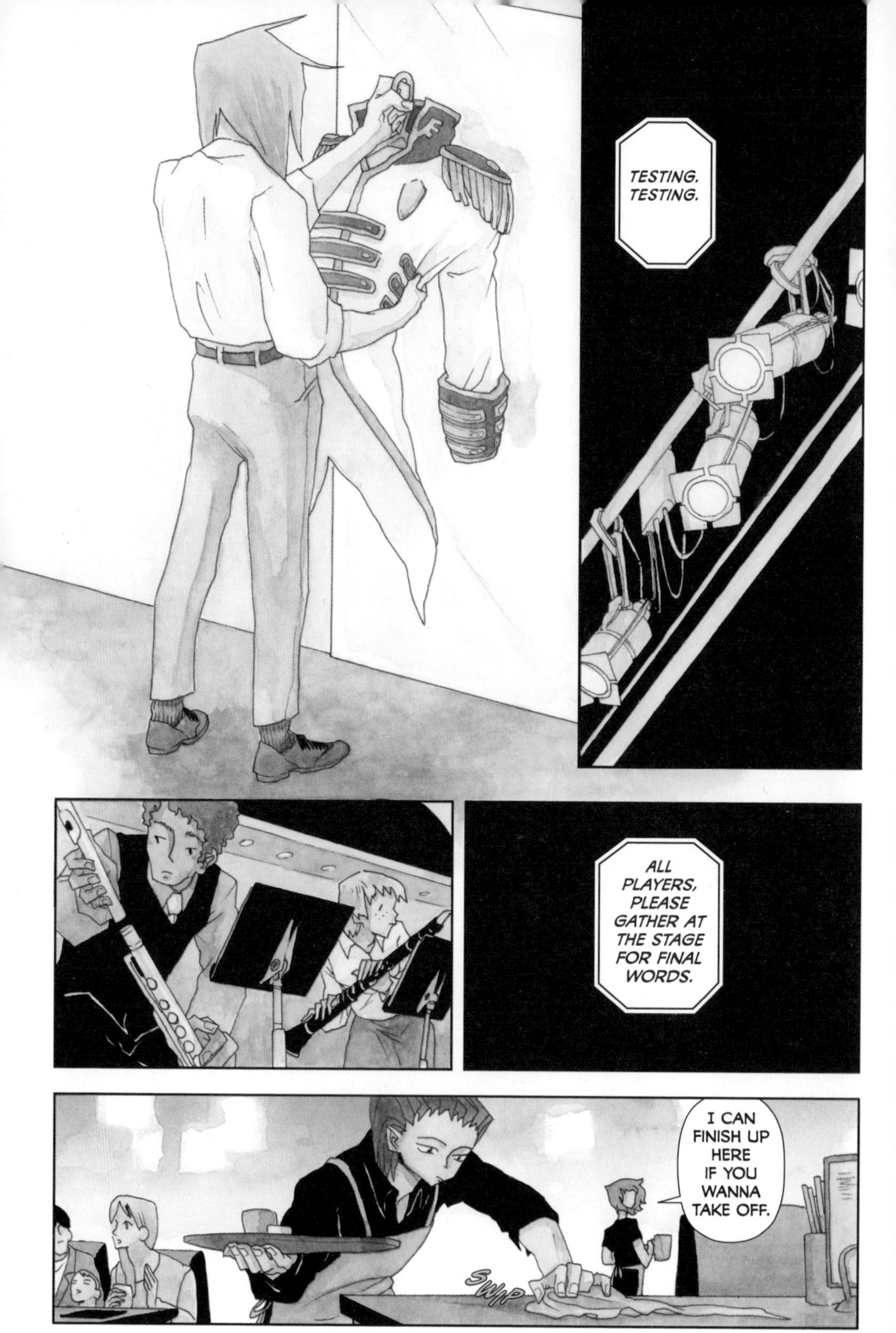
TESTING. TESTING.
ALL PLAYERS, PLEASE GATHER AT THE STAGE FOR FINAL WORDS.
I CAN FINISH UP HERE IF YOU WANNA TAKE OFF.
SWIP

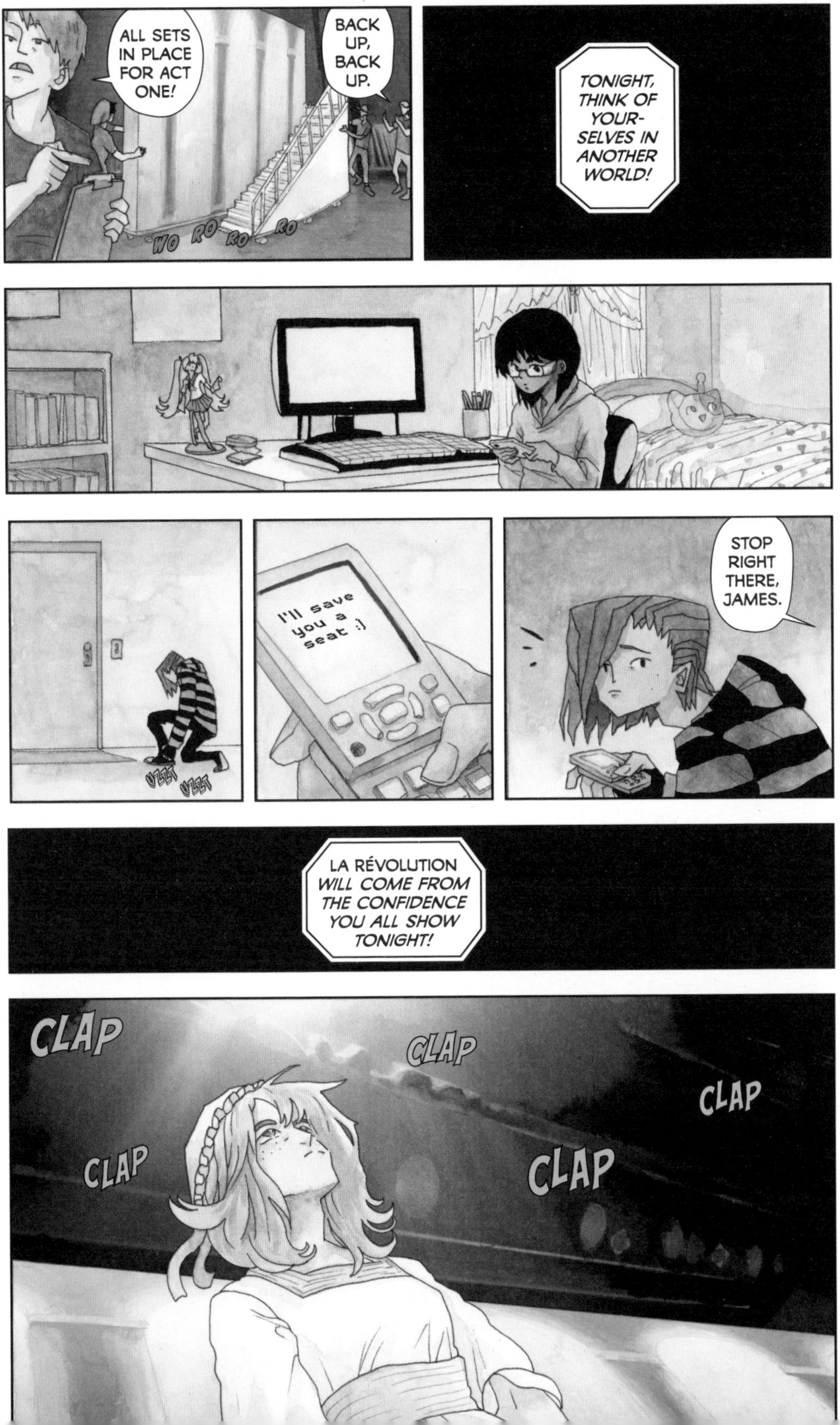
ALL SETS IN PLACE FOR ACT ONE!
BACK UP, BACK UP.
WO RO RO RO
TONIGHT, THINK OF YOUR-SELVES IN ANOTHER WORLD!
I'll save you a seat :)
STOP RIGHT THERE, JAMES.
LA RÉVOLUTION WILL COME FROM THE CONFIDENCE YOU ALL SHOW TONIGHT!
CLAP
CLAP
CLAP
CLAP
CLAP

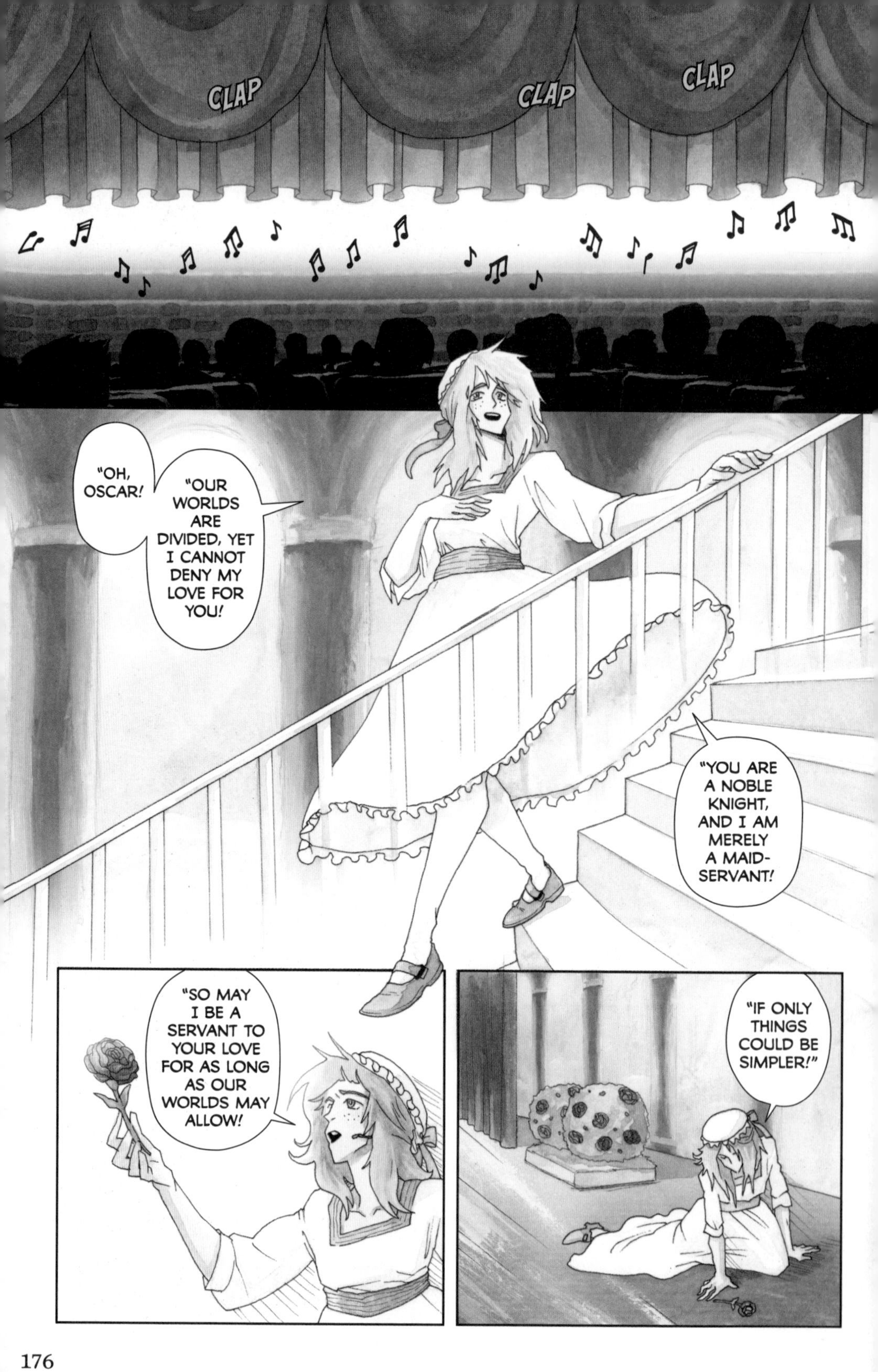
CLAP
CLAP
CLAP
"OH, OSCAR!
"OUR WORLDS ARE DIVIDED, YET I CANNOT DENY MY LOVE FOR YOU!
"YOU ARE A NOBLE KNIGHT, AND I AM MERELY A MAID-SERVANT!
"SO MAY I BE A SERVANT TO YOUR LOVE FOR AS LONG AS OUR WORLDS MAY ALLOW!
"IF ONLY THINGS COULD BE SIMPLER!"

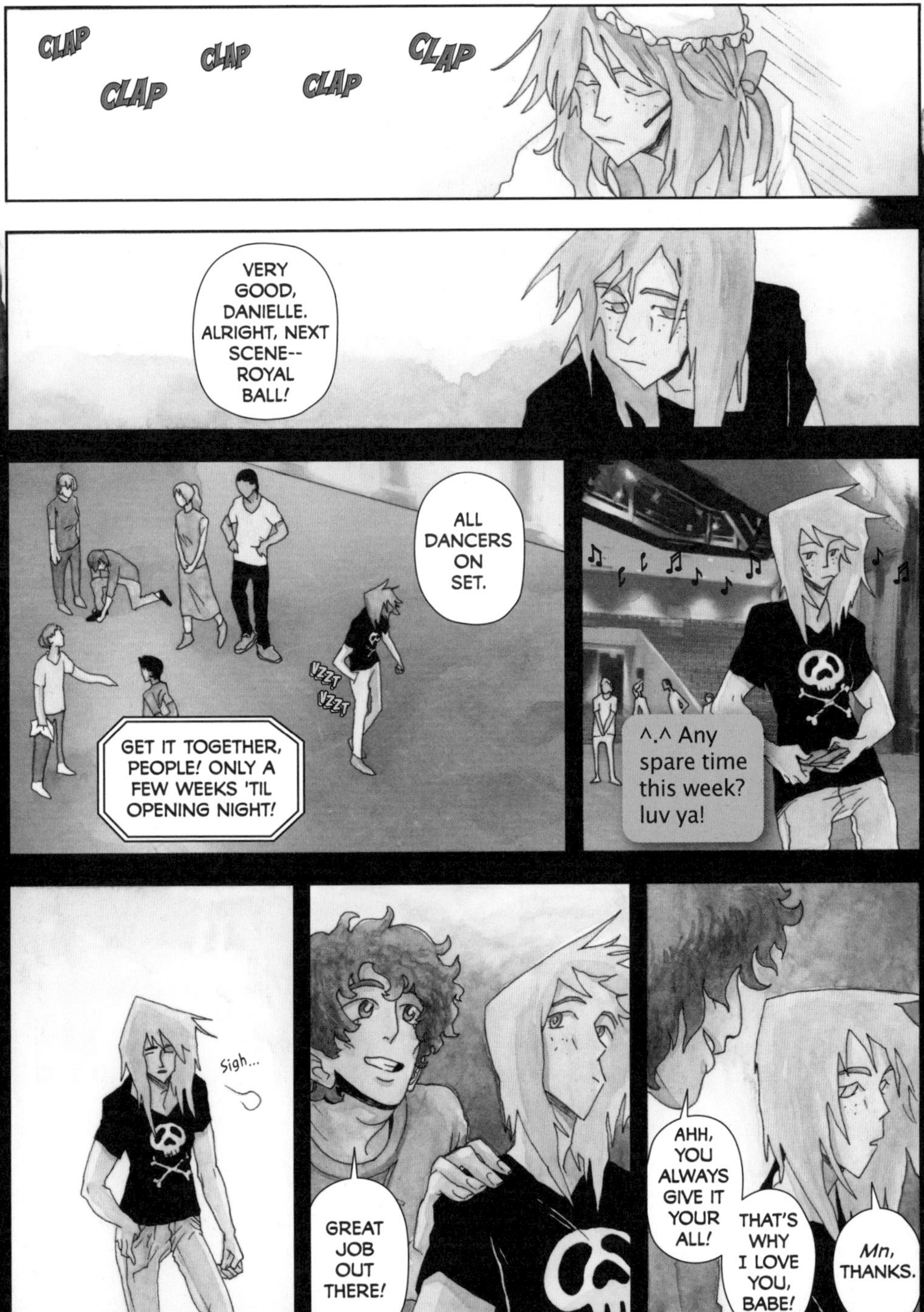
CLAP
CLAP
CLAP
CLAP
CLAP
VERY GOOD, DANIELLE. ALRIGHT, NEXT SCENE-- ROYAL BALL!
ALL DANCERS ON SET.
VZZT
VZZT
GET IT TOGETHER, PEOPLE! ONLY A FEW WEEKS 'TIL OPENING NIGHT!
^.^ Any spare time this week? luv ya!
Sigh...
GREAT JOB OUT THERE!
AHH, YOU ALWAYS GIVE IT YOUR ALL!
THAT'S WHY I LOVE YOU, BABE!
Mn, THANKS.

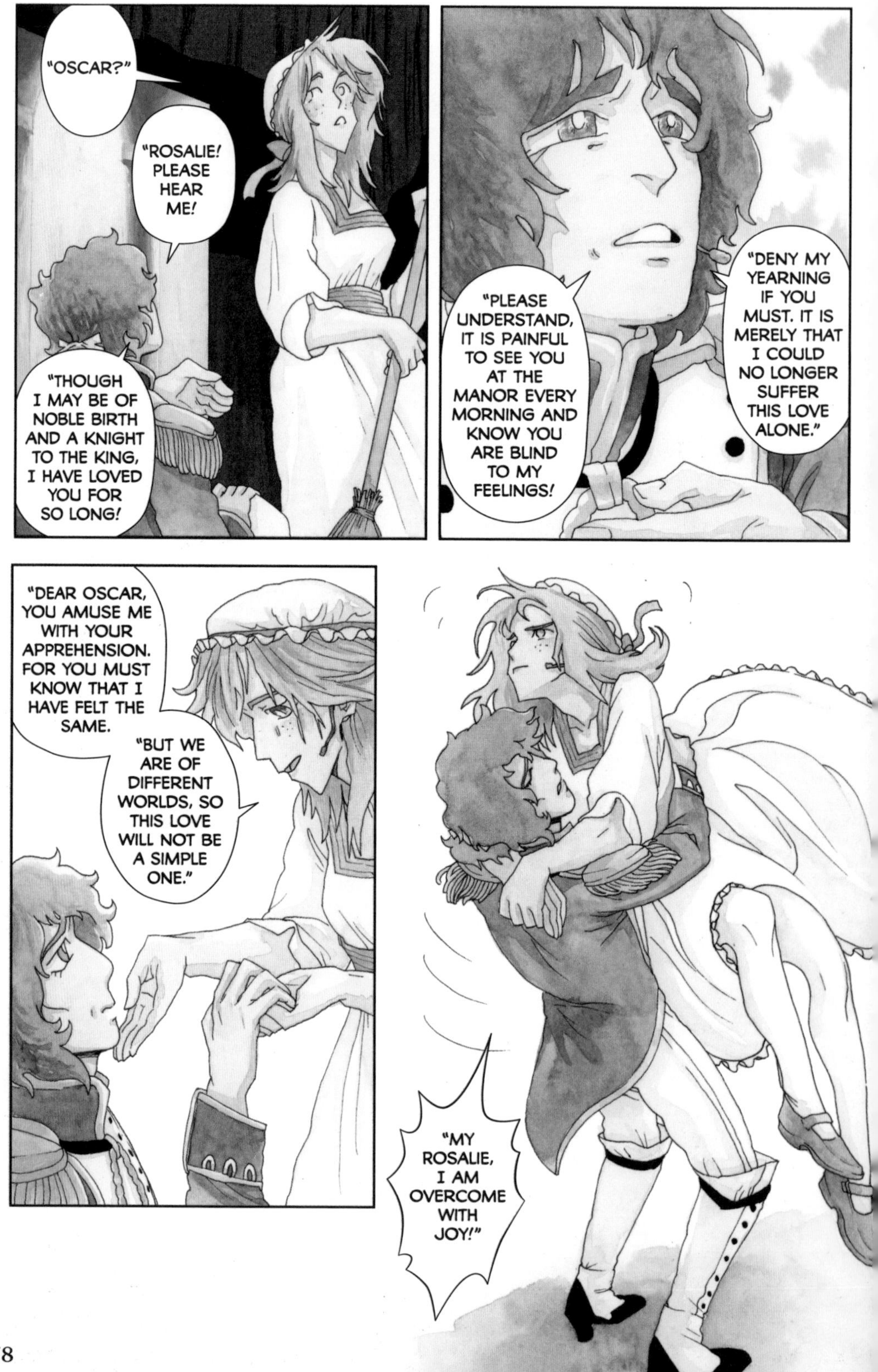
"OSCAR?"
"ROSALIE! PLEASE HEAR ME!
"THOUGH I MAY BE OF NOBLE BIRTH AND A KNIGHT TO THE KING, I HAVE LOVED YOU FOR SO LONG!
"PLEASE UNDERSTAND, IT IS PAINFUL TO SEE YOU AT THE MANOR EVERY MORNING AND KNOW YOU ARE BLIND TO MY FEELINGS!
"DENY MY YEARNING IF YOU MUST. IT IS MERELY THAT I COULD NO LONGER SUFFER THIS LOVE ALONE."
"DEAR OSCAR, YOU AMUSE ME WITH YOUR APPREHENSION. FOR YOU MUST KNOW THAT I HAVE FELT THE SAME.
"BUT WE ARE OF DIFFERENT WORLDS, SO THIS LOVE WILL NOT BE A SIMPLE ONE."
"MY ROSALIE, I AM OVERCOME WITH JOY!"

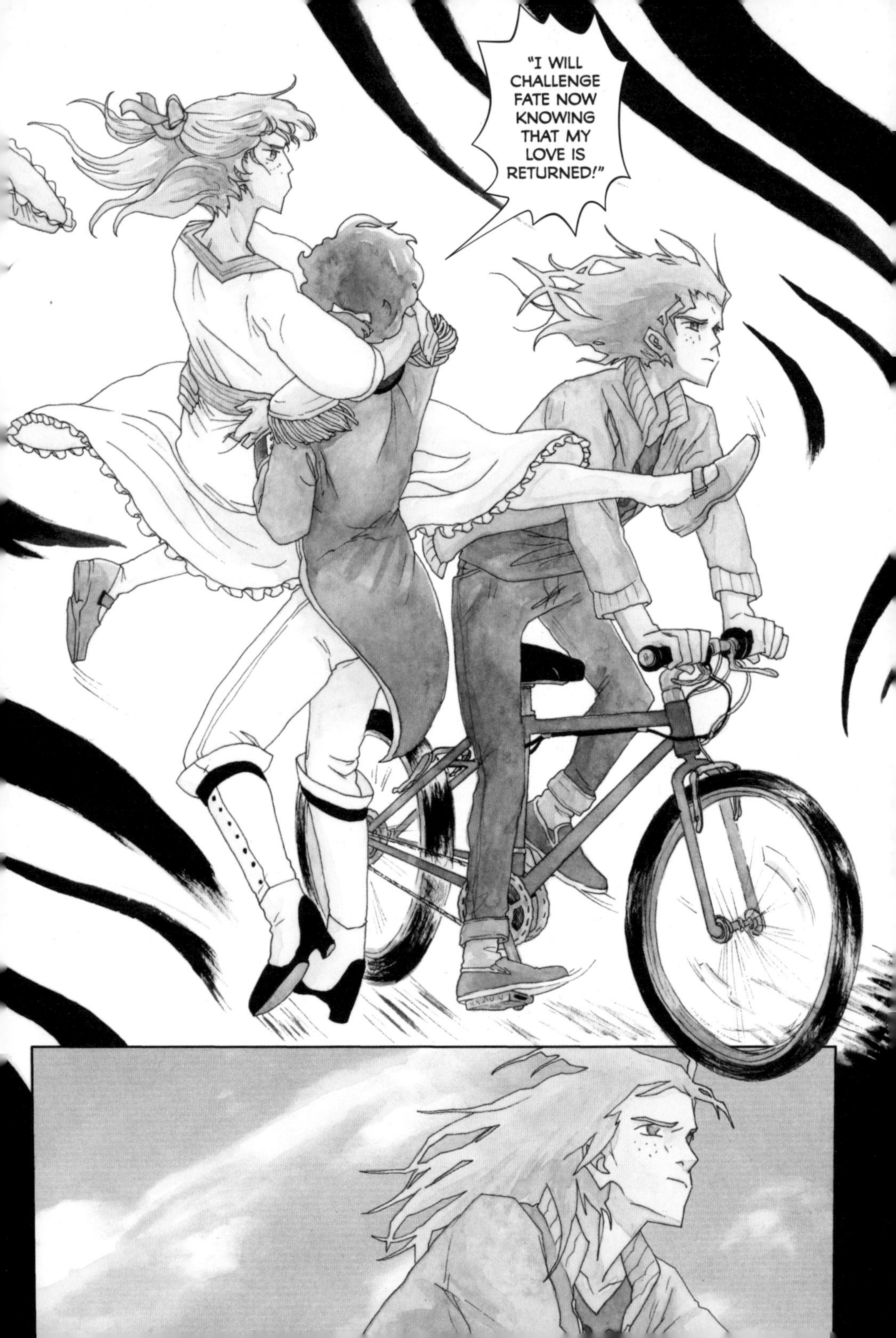
"I WILL CHALLENGE FATE NOW KNOWING THAT MY LOVE IS RETURNED!"

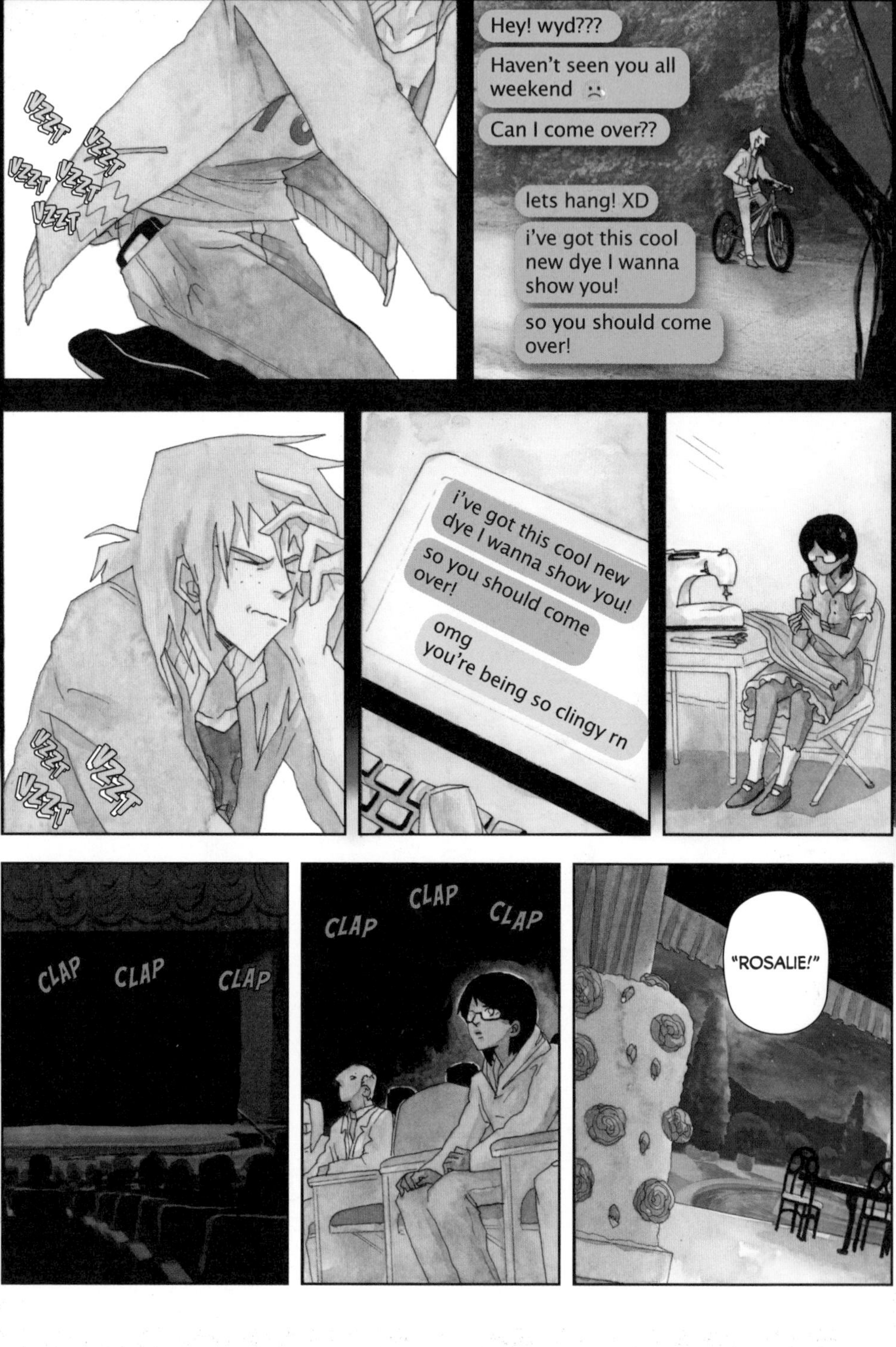
VZZT
VZZT
VZZT
VZZT
VZZT
Hey! wyd???
Haven't seen you all weekend :(
Can I come over??
lets hang! XD
i've got this cool new dye I wanna show you!
so you should come over!
VZZT
VZZT
VZZT
i've got this cool new dye I wanna show you!
so you should come over!
omg
you're being so clingy rn
CLAP
CLAP
CLAP
CLAP
CLAP
CLAP
"ROSALIE!"

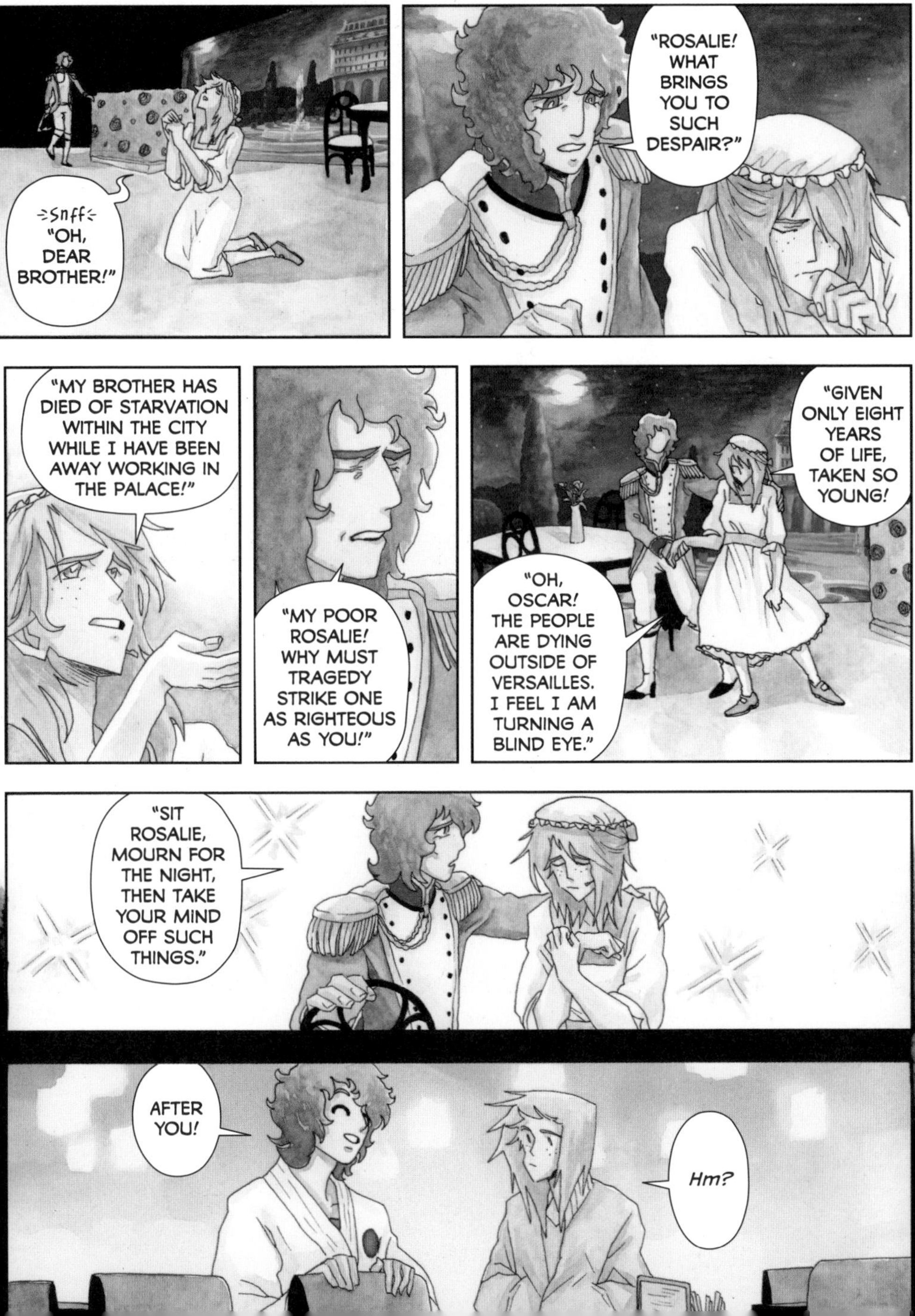

=Snff=
"OH, DEAR BROTHER!"
"ROSALIE! WHAT BRINGS YOU TO SUCH DESPAIR?"
"MY BROTHER HAS DIED OF STARVATION WITHIN THE CITY WHILE I HAVE BEEN AWAY WORKING IN THE PALACE!"
"MY POOR ROSALIE! WHY MUST TRAGEDY STRIKE ONE AS RIGHTEOUS AS YOU!"
"GIVEN ONLY EIGHT YEARS OF LIFE, TAKEN SO YOUNG!
"OH, OSCAR! THE PEOPLE ARE DYING OUTSIDE OF VERSAILLES. I FEEL I AM TURNING A BLIND EYE."
"SIT ROSALIE, MOURN FOR THE NIGHT, THEN TAKE YOUR MIND OFF SUCH THINGS."
AFTER YOU!
Hm?

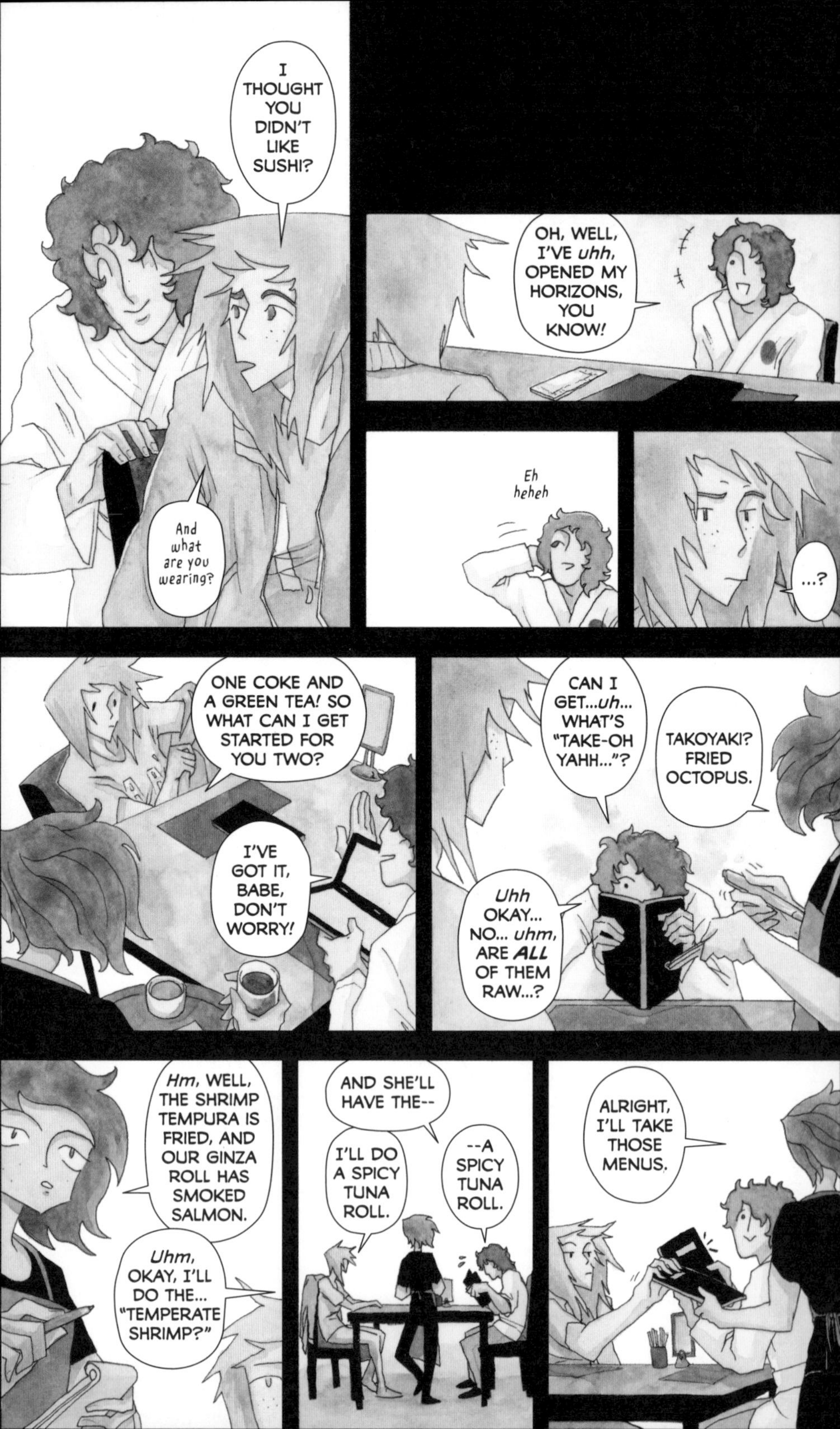
I THOUGHT YOU DIDN'T LIKE SUSHI?
And what are you wearing?
OH, WELL, I'VE *uhh*, OPENED MY HORIZONS, YOU KNOW!
Eh heheh
...?
ONE COKE AND A GREEN TEA! SO WHAT CAN I GET STARTED FOR YOU TWO?
I'VE GOT IT, BABE, DON'T WORRY!
CAN I GET...*uh*... WHAT'S "TAKE-OH YAHH..."?
TAKOYAKI? FRIED OCTOPUS.
Uhh OKAY... NO... *uhm*, ARE ***ALL*** OF THEM RAW...?
Hm, WELL, THE SHRIMP TEMPURA IS FRIED, AND OUR GINZA ROLL HAS SMOKED SALMON.
Uhm, OKAY, I'LL DO THE... "TEMPERATE SHRIMP?"
AND SHE'LL HAVE THE--
I'LL DO A SPICY TUNA ROLL.
--A SPICY TUNA ROLL.
ALRIGHT, I'LL TAKE THOSE MENUS.

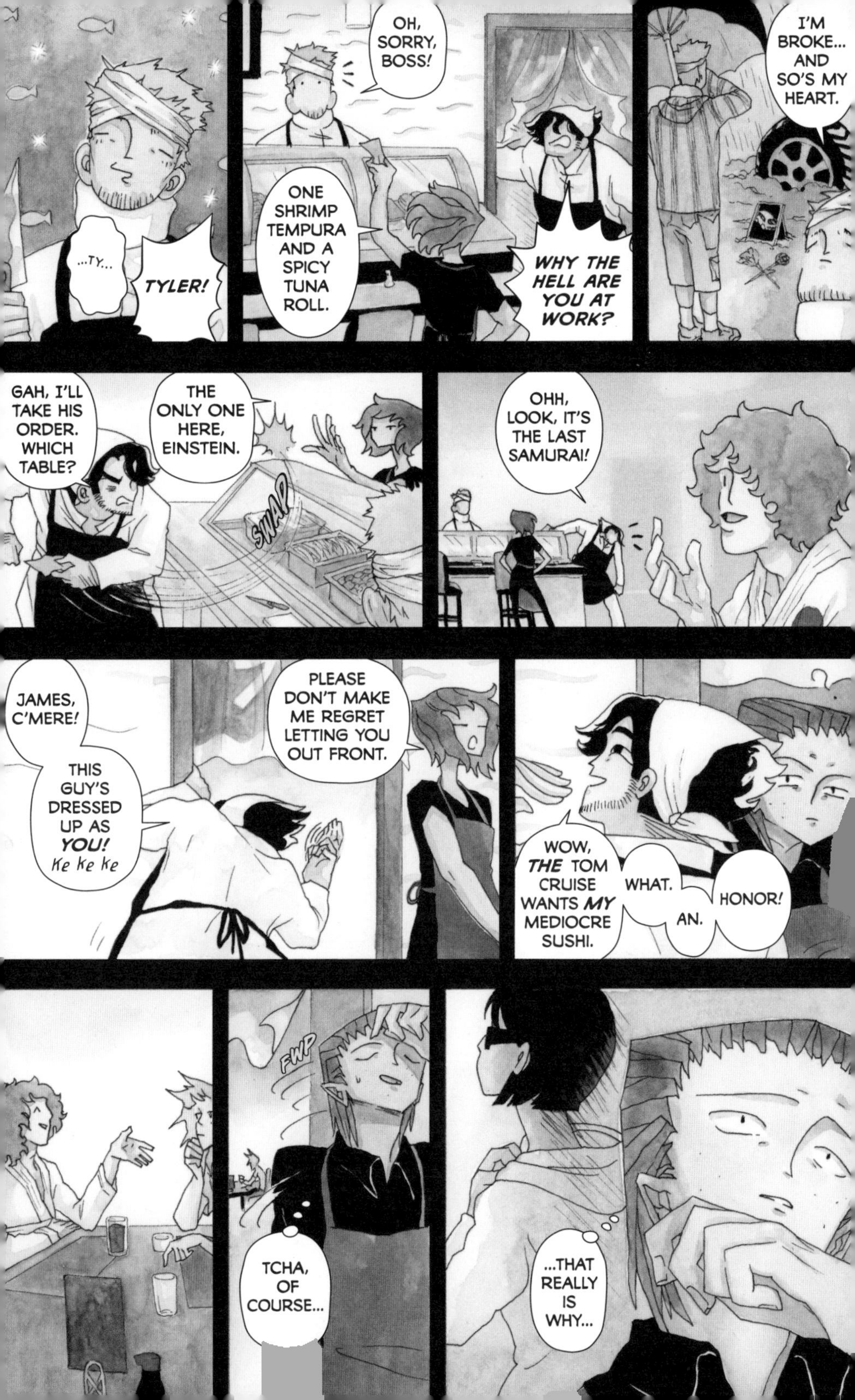
...TY...
TYLER!
OH, SORRY, BOSS!
ONE SHRIMP TEMPURA AND A SPICY TUNA ROLL.
WHY THE HELL ARE YOU AT WORK?
I'M BROKE... AND SO'S MY HEART.
GAH, I'LL TAKE HIS ORDER. WHICH TABLE?
THE ONLY ONE HERE, EINSTEIN.
SWAP
OHH, LOOK, IT'S THE LAST SAMURAI!
JAMES, C'MERE!
THIS GUY'S DRESSED UP AS YOU! Ke ke ke
PLEASE DON'T MAKE ME REGRET LETTING YOU OUT FRONT.
WOW, THE TOM CRUISE WANTS MY MEDIOCRE SUSHI.
WHAT.
AN.
HONOR!
FWP
TCHA, OF COURSE...
...THAT REALLY IS WHY...

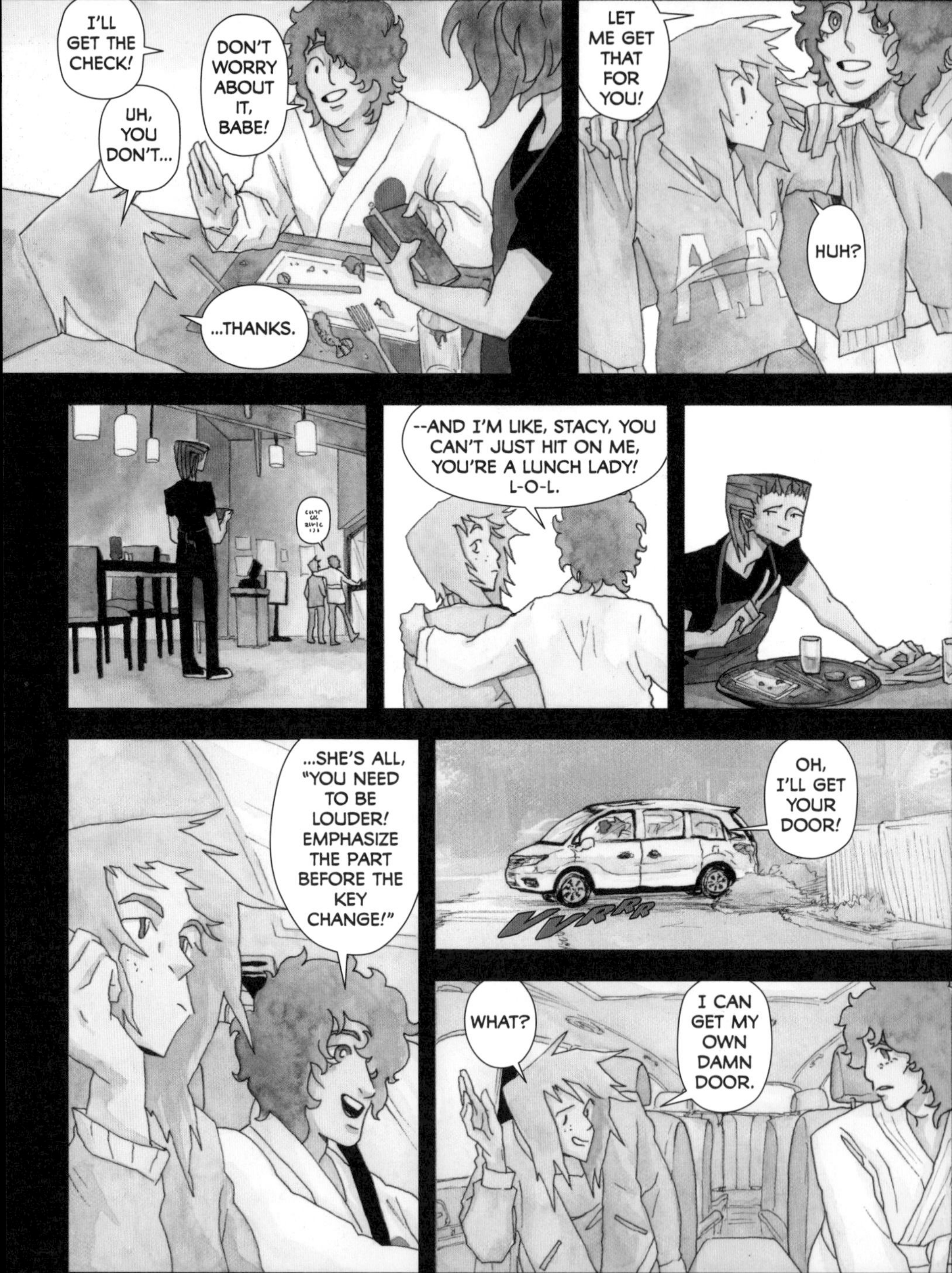

I'LL GET THE CHECK!
DON'T WORRY ABOUT IT, BABE!
UH, YOU DON'T...
...THANKS.
LET ME GET THAT FOR YOU!
HUH?
--AND I'M LIKE, STACY, YOU CAN'T JUST HIT ON ME, YOU'RE A LUNCH LADY! L-O-L.
...SHE'S ALL, "YOU NEED TO BE LOUDER! EMPHASIZE THE PART BEFORE THE KEY CHANGE!"
OH, I'LL GET YOUR DOOR!
VVRRRR
WHAT?
I CAN GET MY OWN DAMN DOOR.

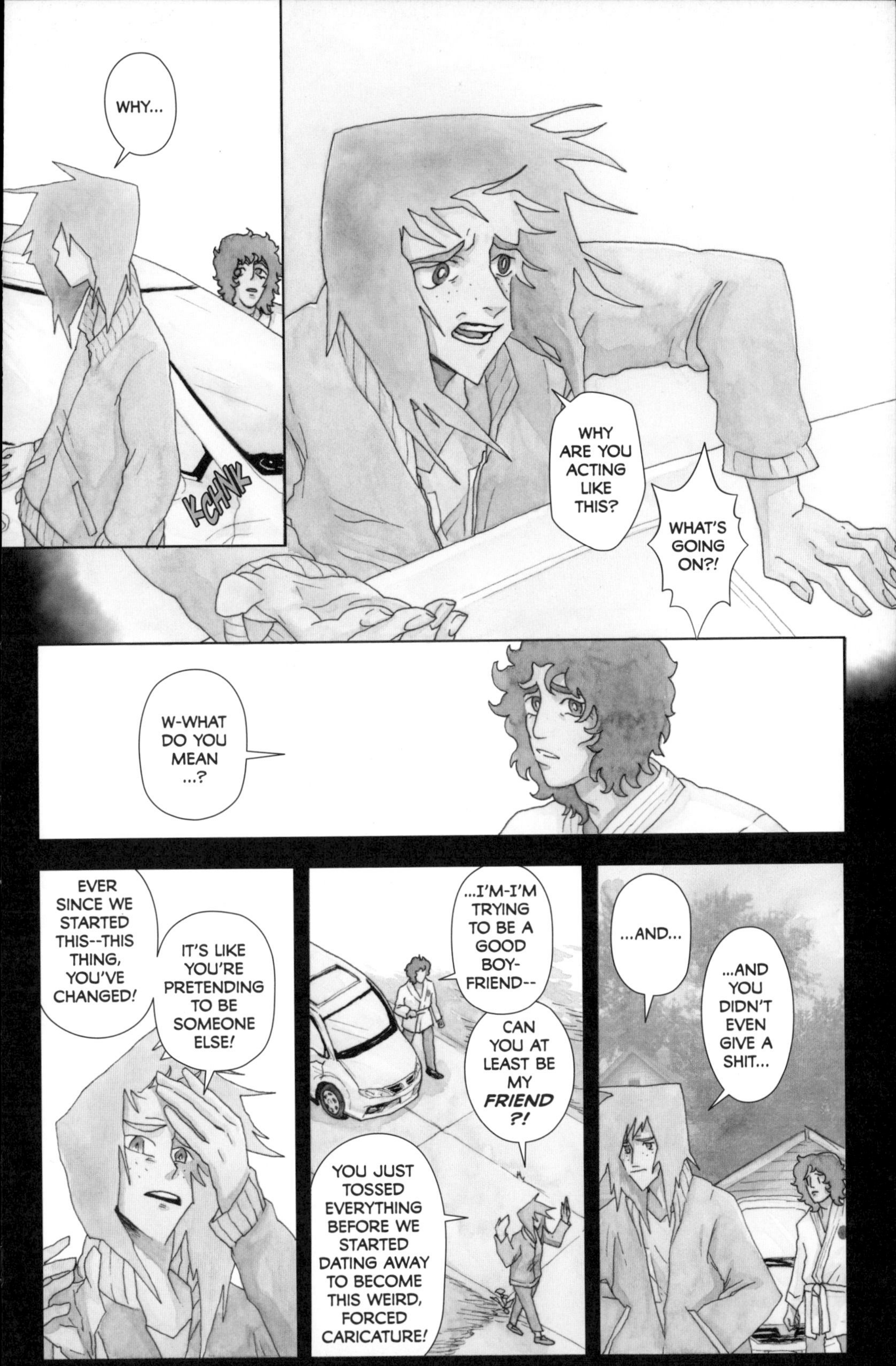
WHY...
K-CHNK
WHY ARE YOU ACTING LIKE THIS?
WHAT'S GOING ON?!
W-WHAT DO YOU MEAN ...?
EVER SINCE WE STARTED THIS--THIS THING, YOU'VE CHANGED!
IT'S LIKE YOU'RE PRETENDING TO BE SOMEONE ELSE!
...I'M-I'M TRYING TO BE A GOOD BOY-FRIEND--
CAN YOU AT LEAST BE MY *FRIEND* ?!
YOU JUST TOSSED EVERYTHING BEFORE WE STARTED DATING AWAY TO BECOME THIS WEIRD, FORCED CARICATURE!
...AND...
...AND YOU DIDN'T EVEN GIVE A SHIT...

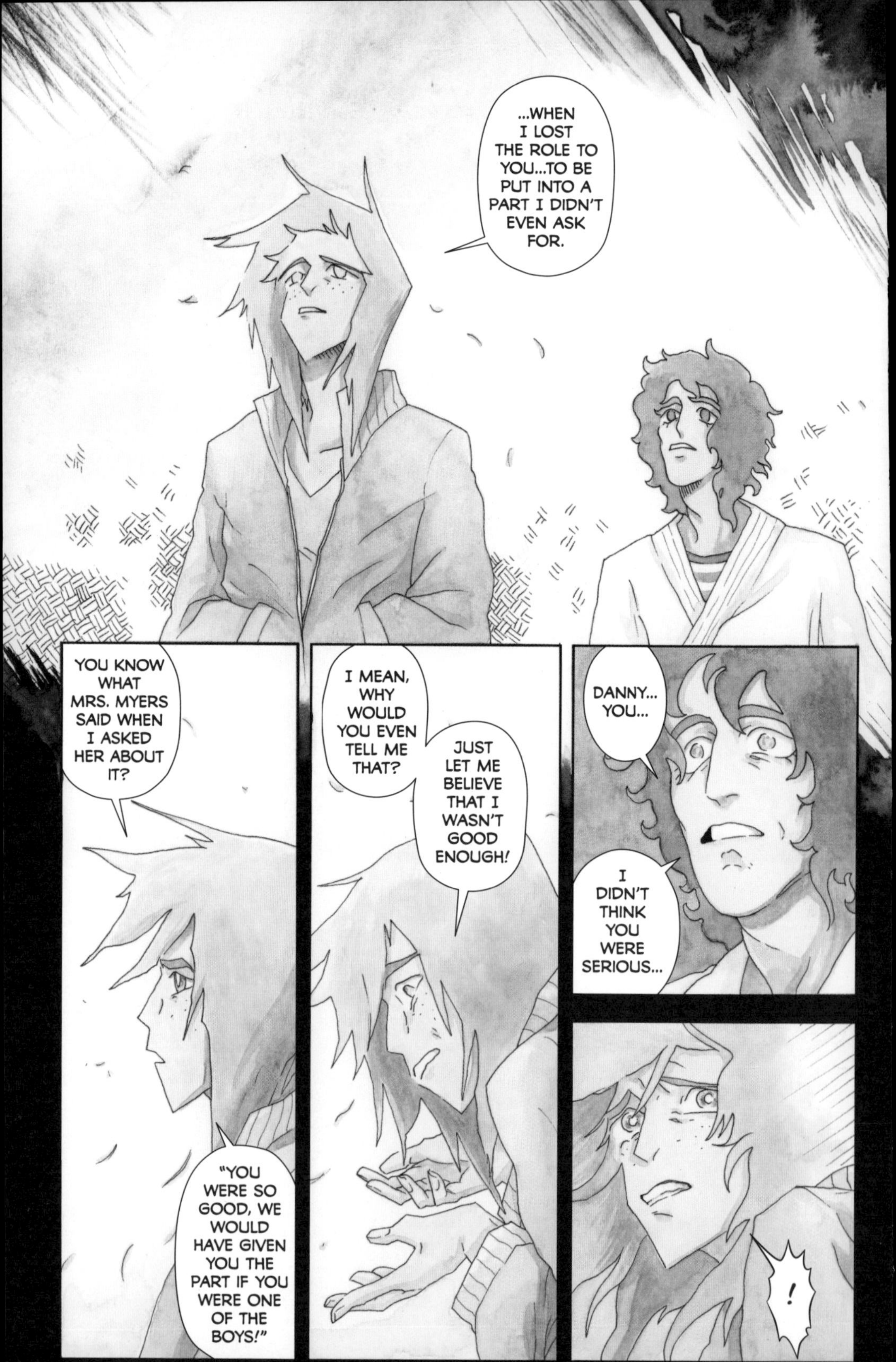
...WHEN I LOST THE ROLE TO YOU...TO BE PUT INTO A PART I DIDN'T EVEN ASK FOR.
YOU KNOW WHAT MRS. MYERS SAID WHEN I ASKED HER ABOUT IT?
"YOU WERE SO GOOD, WE WOULD HAVE GIVEN YOU THE PART IF YOU WERE ONE OF THE BOYS!"
I MEAN, WHY WOULD YOU EVEN TELL ME THAT?
JUST LET ME BELIEVE THAT I WASN'T GOOD ENOUGH!
DANNY... YOU...
I DIDN'T THINK YOU WERE SERIOUS...
!

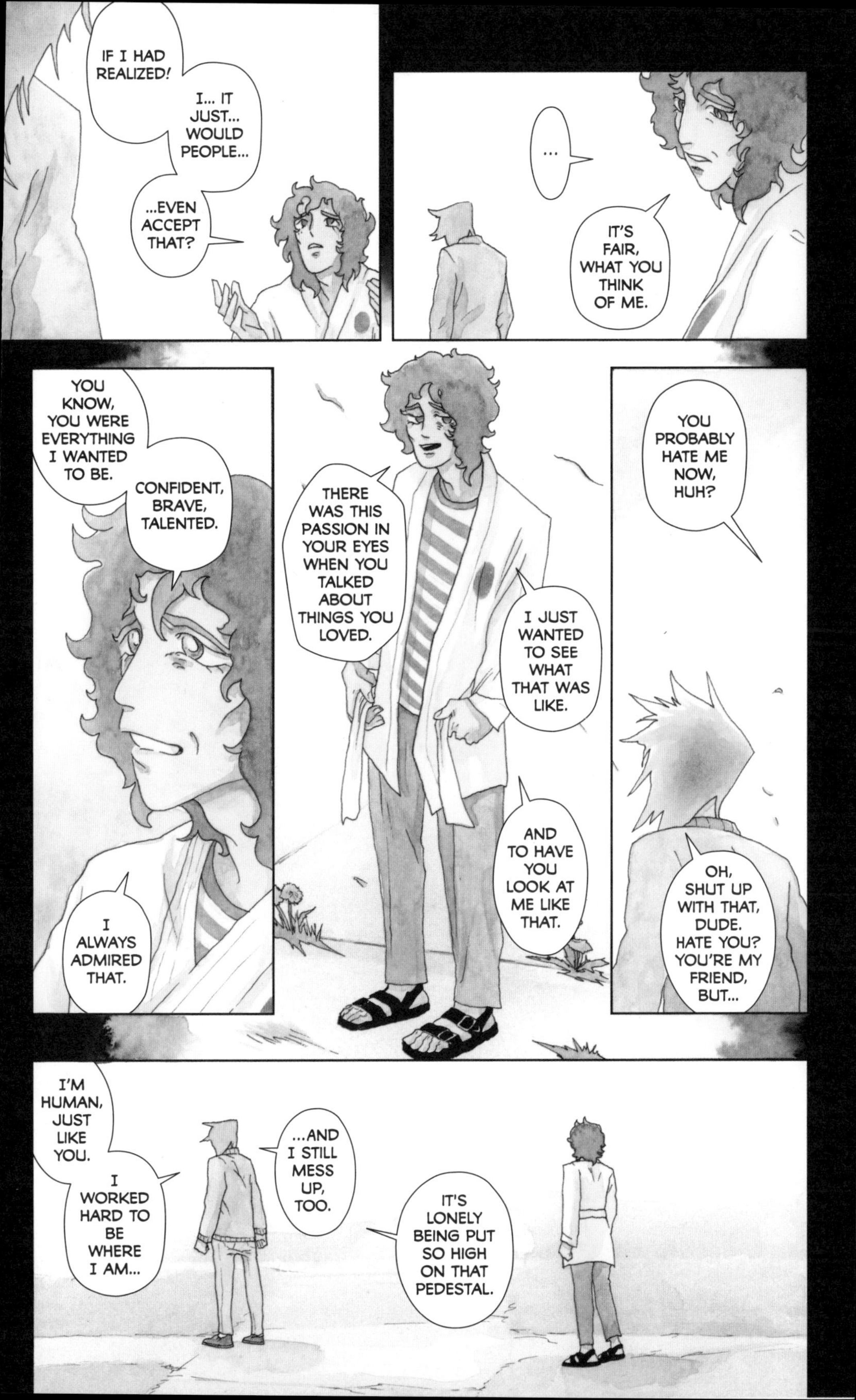
IF I HAD REALIZED!
I... IT JUST... WOULD PEOPLE...
...EVEN ACCEPT THAT?
...
IT'S FAIR, WHAT YOU THINK OF ME.
YOU KNOW, YOU WERE EVERYTHING I WANTED TO BE.
CONFIDENT, BRAVE, TALENTED.
I ALWAYS ADMIRED THAT.
THERE WAS THIS PASSION IN YOUR EYES WHEN YOU TALKED ABOUT THINGS YOU LOVED.
I JUST WANTED TO SEE WHAT THAT WAS LIKE.
AND TO HAVE YOU LOOK AT ME LIKE THAT.
YOU PROBABLY HATE ME NOW, HUH?
OH, SHUT UP WITH THAT, DUDE. HATE YOU? YOU'RE MY FRIEND, BUT...
I'M HUMAN, JUST LIKE YOU.
I WORKED HARD TO BE WHERE I AM...
...AND I STILL MESS UP, TOO.
IT'S LONELY BEING PUT SO HIGH ON THAT PEDESTAL.

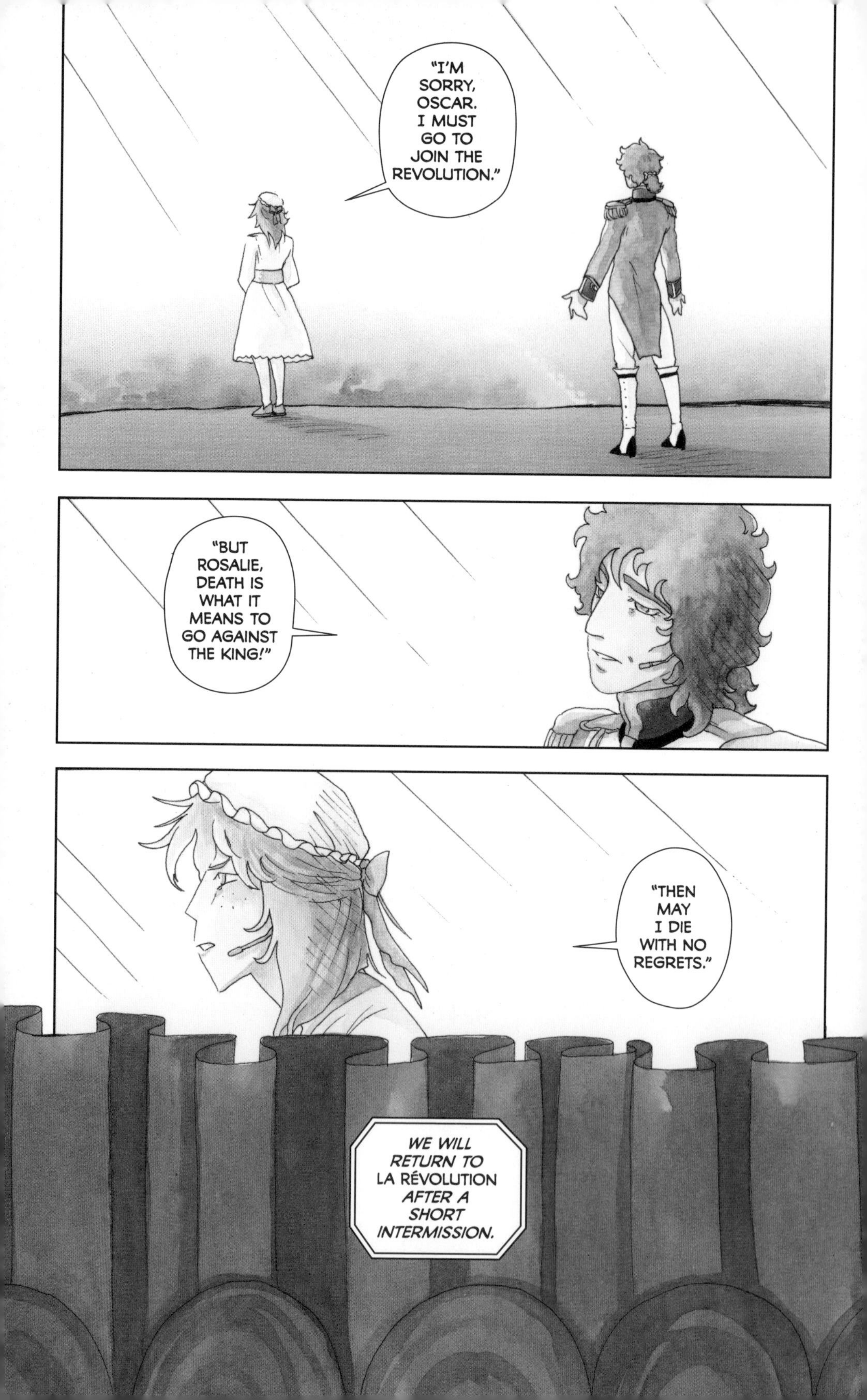
"I'M SORRY, OSCAR. I MUST GO TO JOIN THE REVOLUTION."
"BUT ROSALIE, DEATH IS WHAT IT MEANS TO GO AGAINST THE KING!"
"THEN MAY I DIE WITH NO REGRETS."
WE WILL RETURN TO LA RÉVOLUTION *AFTER A SHORT INTERMISSION.*

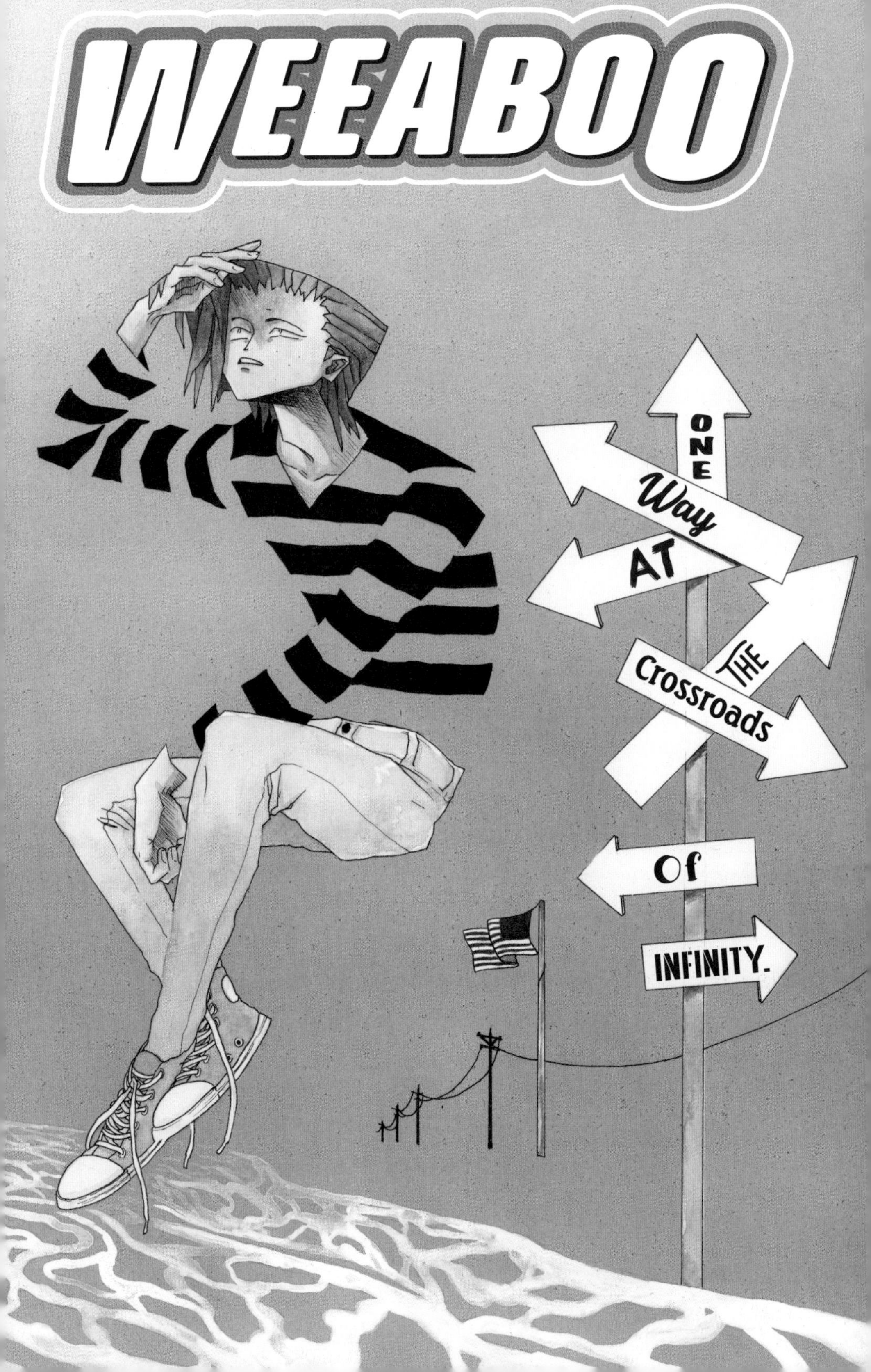
WEEABOO
ONE
Way
AT
THE
Crossroads
Of
INFINITY.

YOU'RE NOT GOING ANY-WHERE.

YOU'RE GOING TO TALK TO US ABOUT THESE SECRETS YOU'VE BEEN KEEPING.

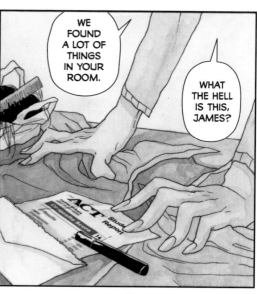

WE FOUND A LOT OF THINGS IN YOUR ROOM.

WHAT THE HELL IS THIS, JAMES?

!

YOU WEREN'T GOING TO TELL US ABOUT HOW YOU'VE BEEN FLUNKING TESTS AND BARELY PASSING YOUR CLASSES?

ABOUT THESE REJECTION LETTERS?

HUH?

190

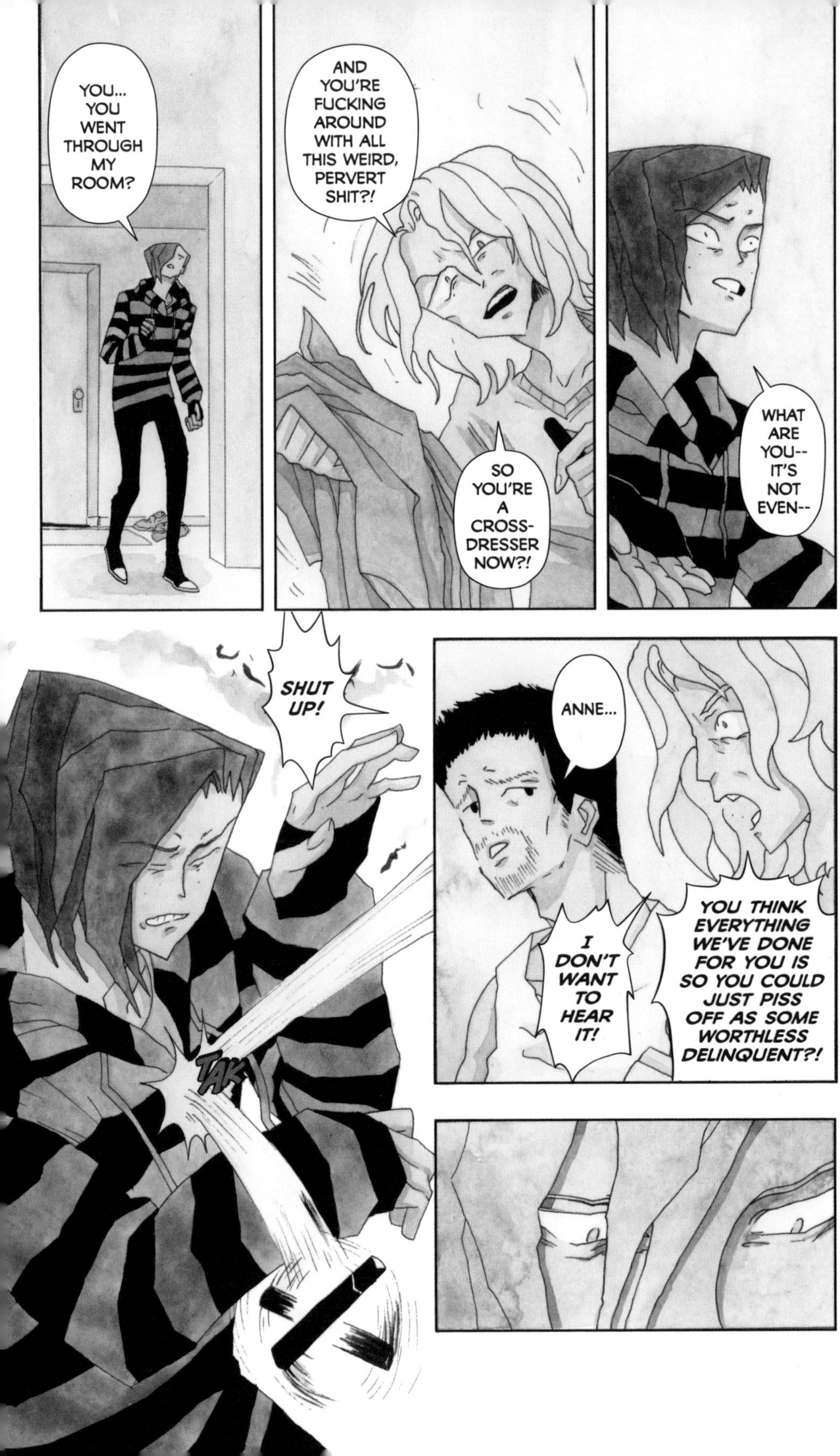
YOU... YOU WENT THROUGH MY ROOM?
AND YOU'RE FUCKING AROUND WITH ALL THIS WEIRD, PERVERT SHIT?!
SO YOU'RE A CROSS-DRESSER NOW?!
WHAT ARE YOU-- IT'S NOT EVEN--
ANNE...
YOU THINK EVERYTHING WE'VE DONE FOR YOU IS SO YOU COULD JUST PISS OFF AS SOME WORTHLESS DELINQUENT?!
I DON'T WANT TO HEAR IT!
SHUT UP!
TAK

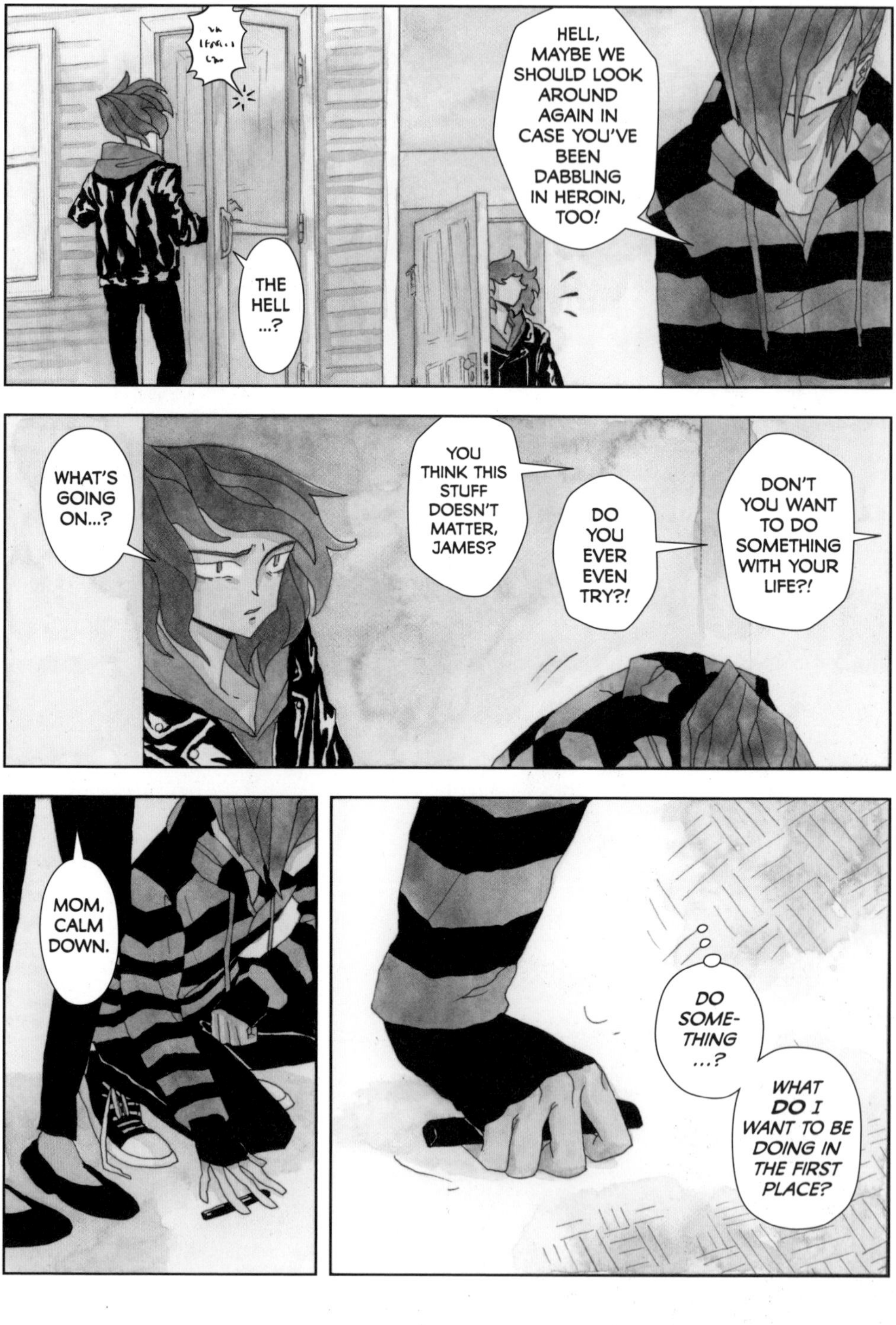
THE HELL ...?
HELL, MAYBE WE SHOULD LOOK AROUND AGAIN IN CASE YOU'VE BEEN DABBLING IN HEROIN, TOO!
WHAT'S GOING ON...?
YOU THINK THIS STUFF DOESN'T MATTER, JAMES?
DO YOU EVER EVEN TRY?!
DON'T YOU WANT TO DO SOMETHING WITH YOUR LIFE?!
MOM, CALM DOWN.
DO SOME-THING ...?
WHAT ***DO*** *I WANT TO BE DOING IN THE FIRST PLACE?*

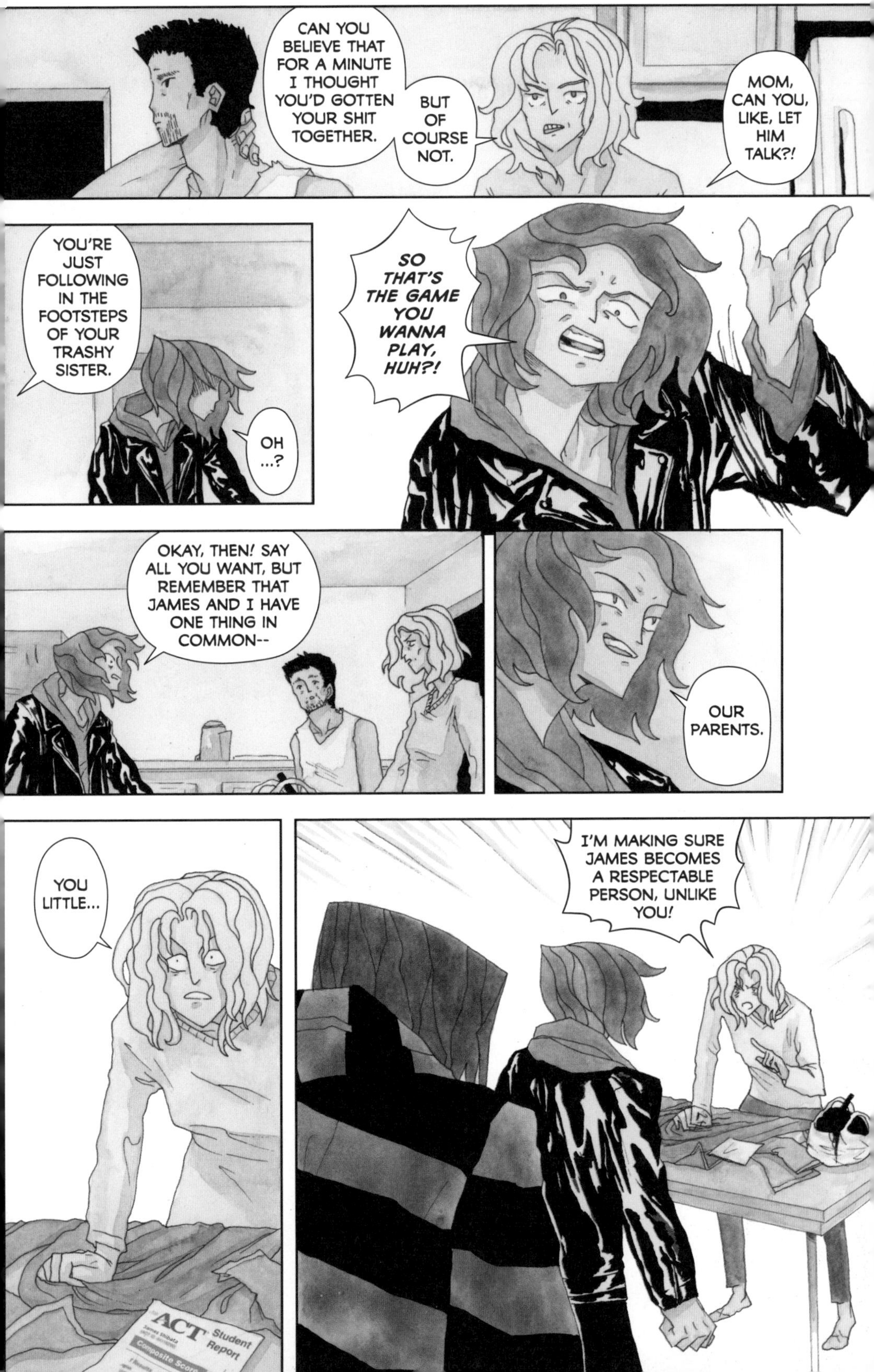
CAN YOU BELIEVE THAT FOR A MINUTE I THOUGHT YOU'D GOTTEN YOUR SHIT TOGETHER.
BUT OF COURSE NOT.
MOM, CAN YOU, LIKE, LET HIM TALK?!
YOU'RE JUST FOLLOWING IN THE FOOTSTEPS OF YOUR TRASHY SISTER.
OH ...?
SO THAT'S THE GAME YOU WANNA PLAY, HUH?!
OKAY, THEN! SAY ALL YOU WANT, BUT REMEMBER THAT JAMES AND I HAVE ONE THING IN COMMON--
OUR PARENTS.
YOU LITTLE...
ACT Student Report
Composite Score
I'M MAKING SURE JAMES BECOMES A RESPECTABLE PERSON, UNLIKE YOU!

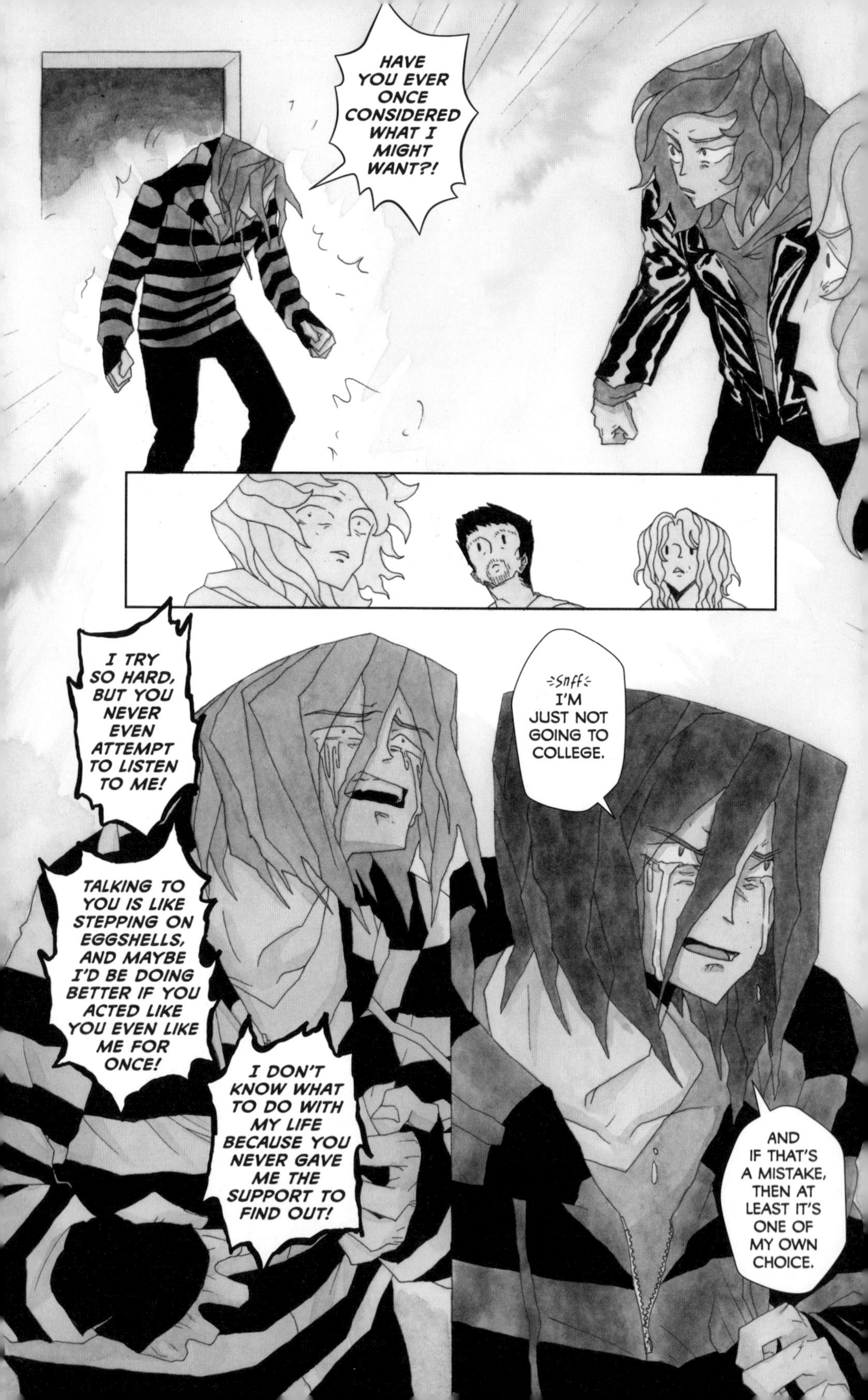
HAVE YOU EVER ONCE CONSIDERED WHAT I MIGHT WANT?!
I TRY SO HARD, BUT YOU NEVER EVEN ATTEMPT TO LISTEN TO ME!
TALKING TO YOU IS LIKE STEPPING ON EGGSHELLS, AND MAYBE I'D BE DOING BETTER IF YOU ACTED LIKE YOU EVEN LIKE ME FOR ONCE!
I DON'T KNOW WHAT TO DO WITH MY LIFE BECAUSE YOU NEVER GAVE ME THE SUPPORT TO FIND OUT!
Snff
I'M JUST NOT GOING TO COLLEGE.
AND IF THAT'S A MISTAKE, THEN AT LEAST IT'S ONE OF MY OWN CHOICE.

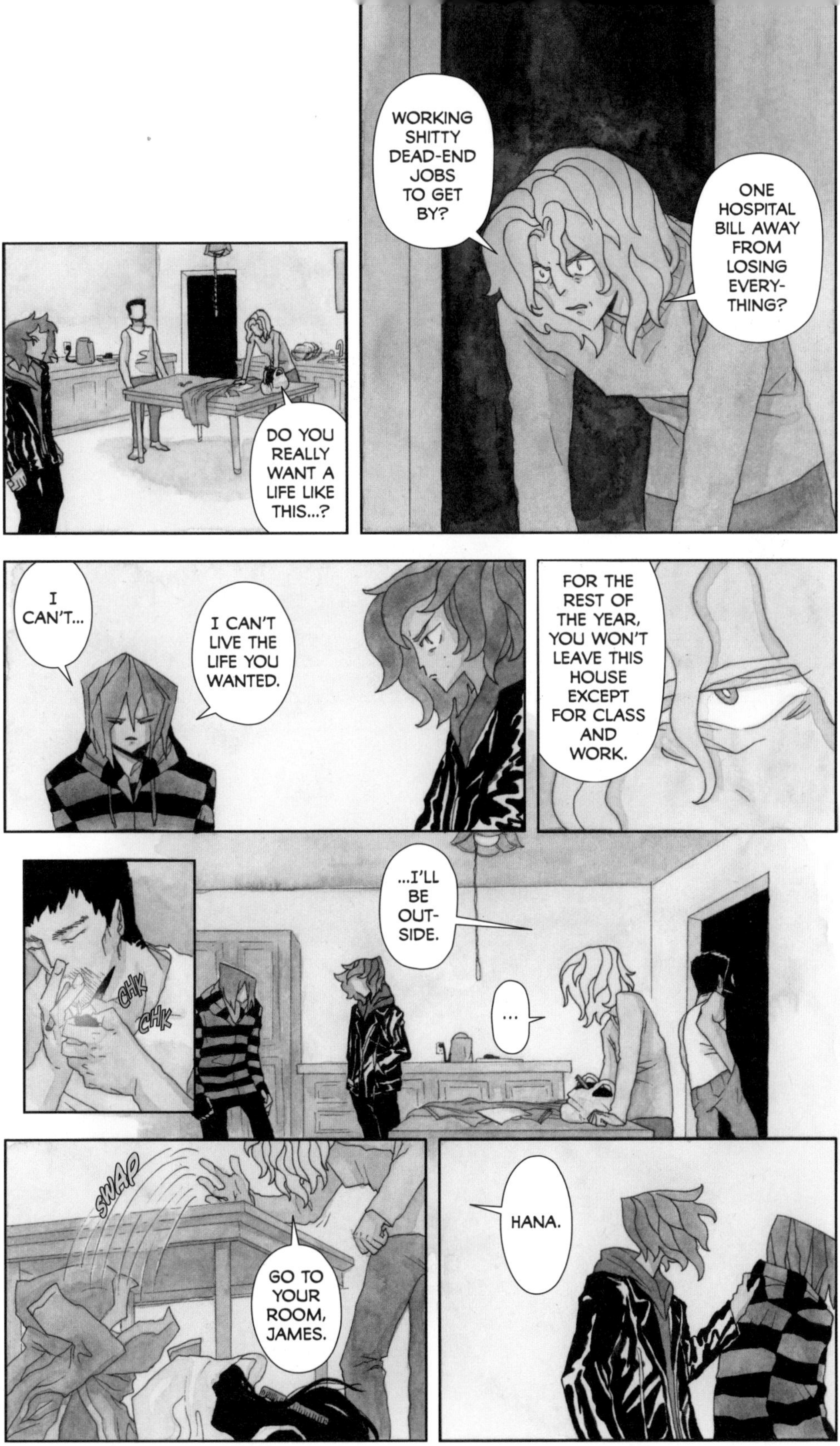
WORKING SHITTY DEAD-END JOBS TO GET BY?
ONE HOSPITAL BILL AWAY FROM LOSING EVERY-THING?
DO YOU REALLY WANT A LIFE LIKE THIS...?
I CAN'T...
I CAN'T LIVE THE LIFE YOU WANTED.
FOR THE REST OF THE YEAR, YOU WON'T LEAVE THIS HOUSE EXCEPT FOR CLASS AND WORK.
CHK
CHK
...I'LL BE OUT-SIDE.
...
SWAP
GO TO YOUR ROOM, JAMES.
HANA.

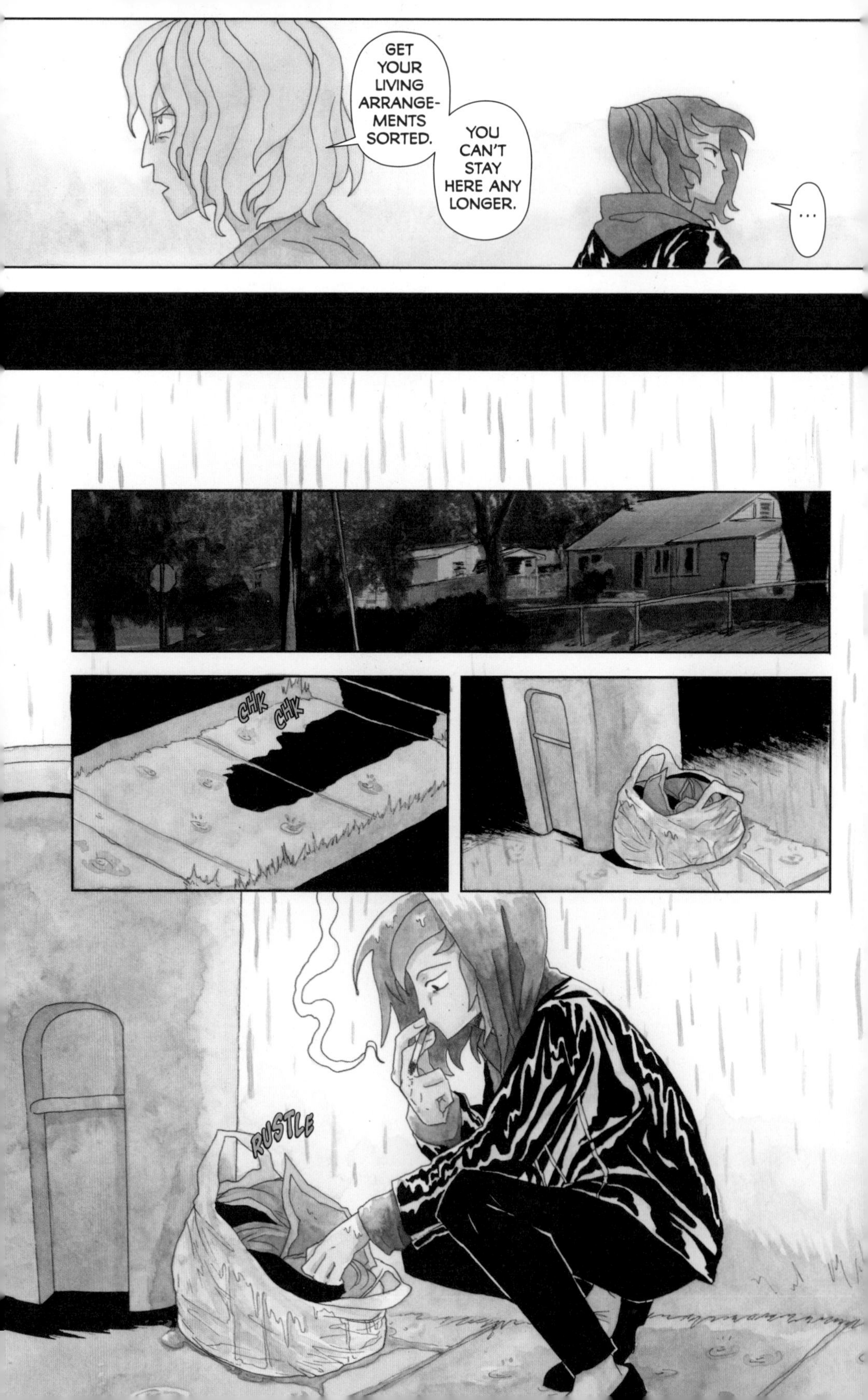
GET YOUR LIVING ARRANGE-MENTS SORTED.
YOU CAN'T STAY HERE ANY LONGER.
...
CHK CHK
RUSTLE

Weeaboo

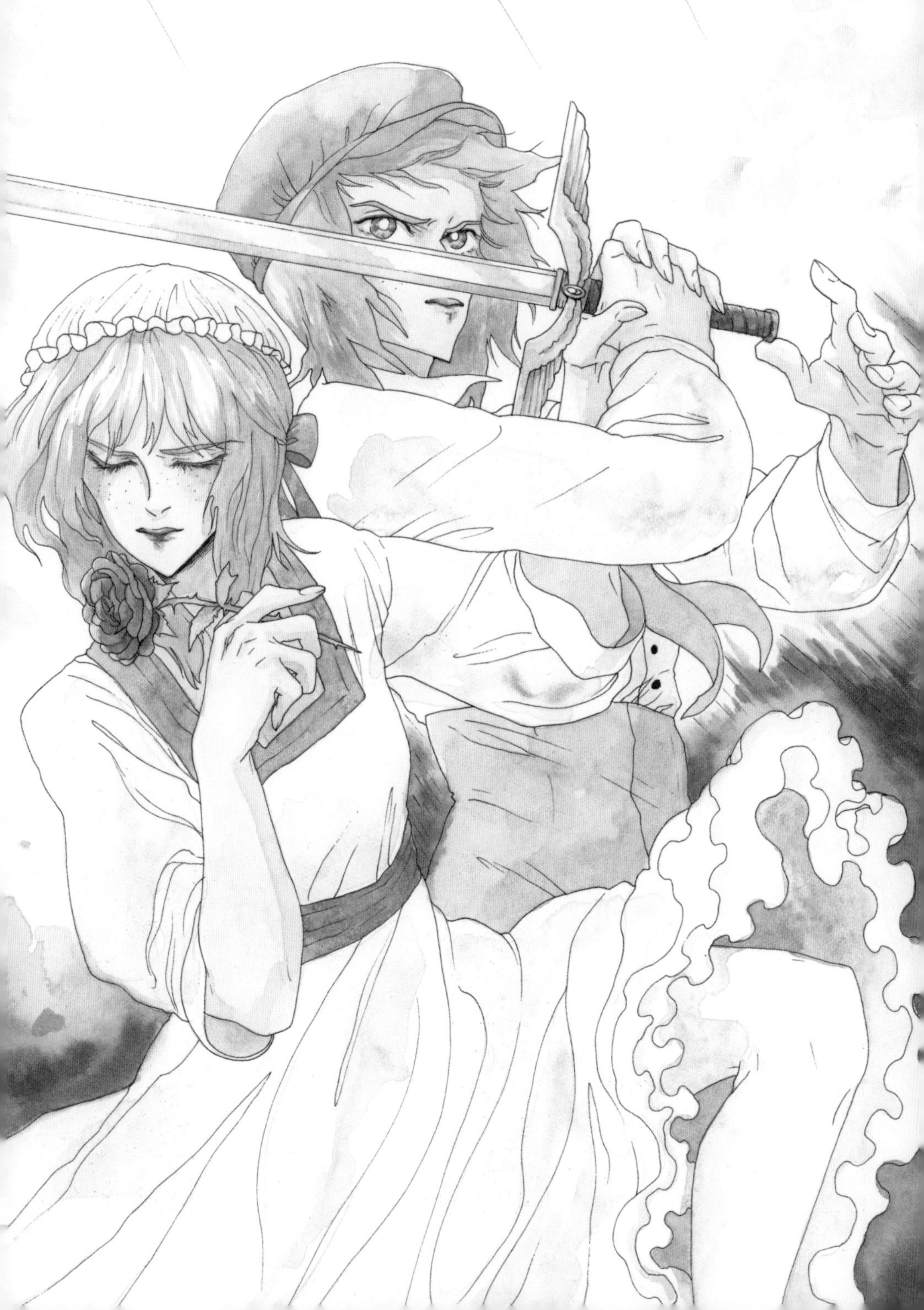

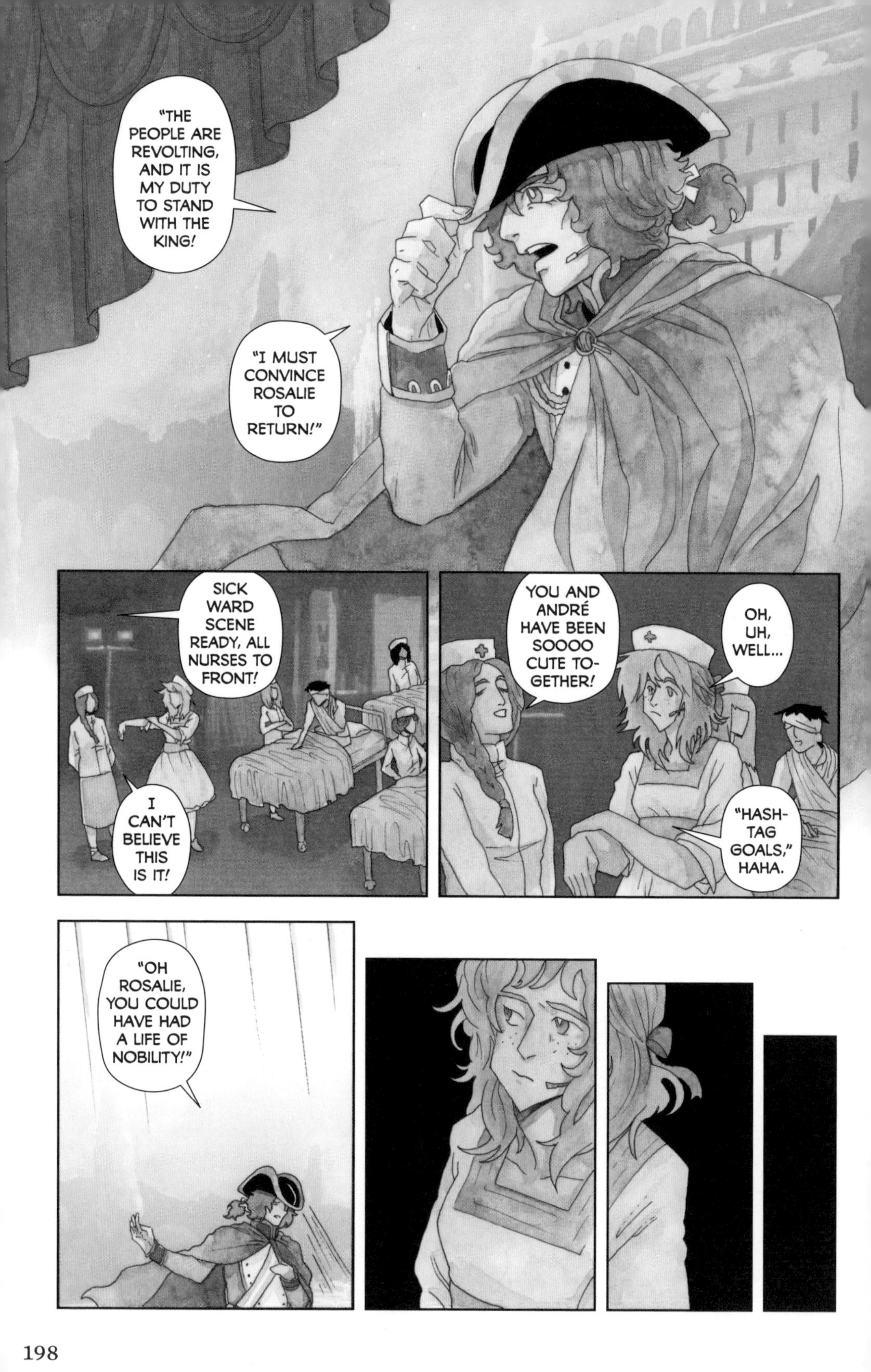
"THE PEOPLE ARE REVOLTING, AND IT IS MY DUTY TO STAND WITH THE KING!
"I MUST CONVINCE ROSALIE TO RETURN!"
SICK WARD SCENE READY, ALL NURSES TO FRONT!
I CAN'T BELIEVE THIS IS IT!
YOU AND ANDRÉ HAVE BEEN SOOOO CUTE TO-GETHER!
OH, UH, WELL...
"HASH-TAG GOALS," HAHA.
"OH ROSALIE, YOU COULD HAVE HAD A LIFE OF NOBILITY!"

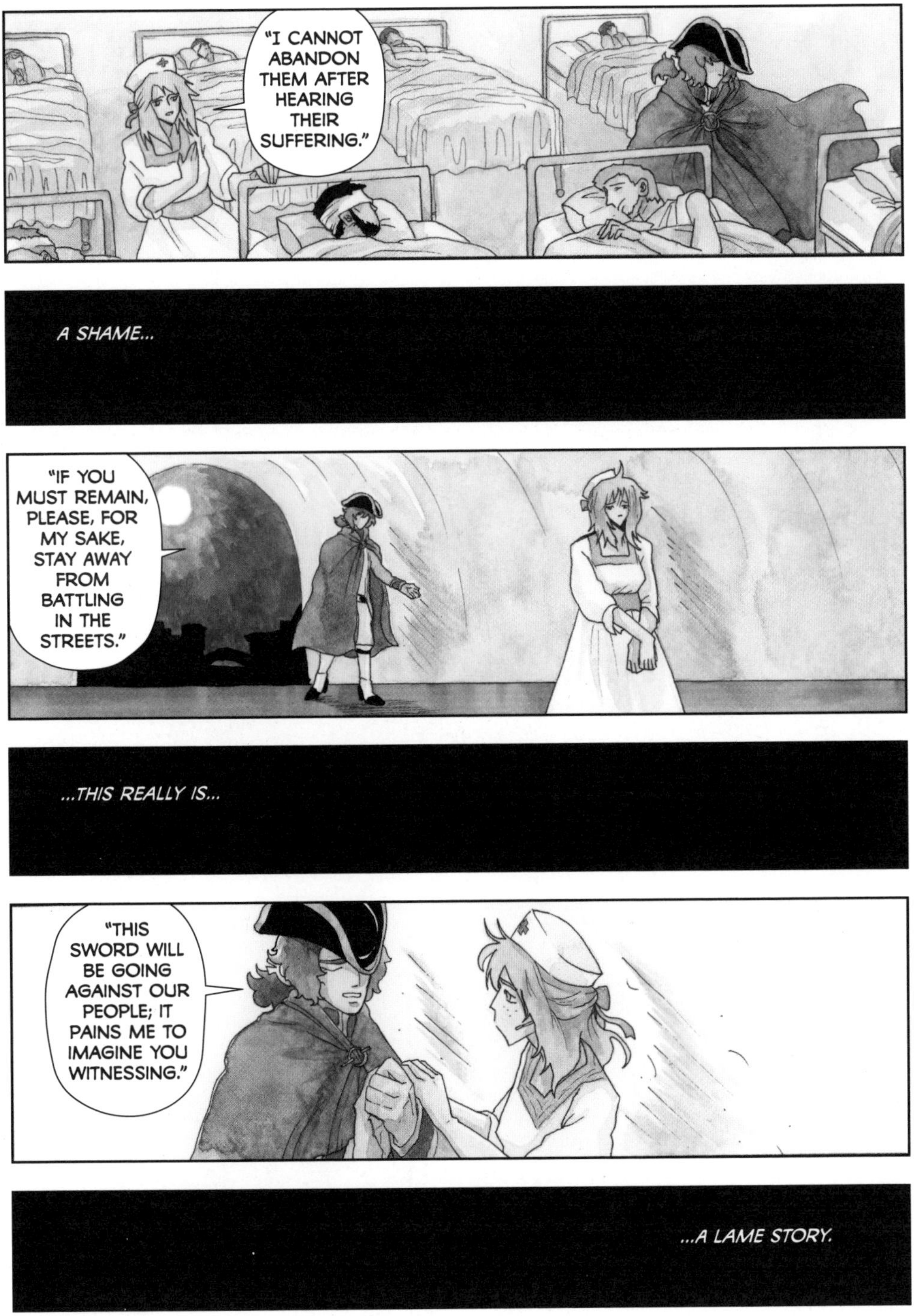
"I CANNOT ABANDON THEM AFTER HEARING THEIR SUFFERING."
A SHAME...
"IF YOU MUST REMAIN, PLEASE, FOR MY SAKE, STAY AWAY FROM BATTLING IN THE STREETS."
...THIS REALLY IS...
"THIS SWORD WILL BE GOING AGAINST OUR PEOPLE; IT PAINS ME TO IMAGINE YOU WITNESSING."
...A LAME STORY.

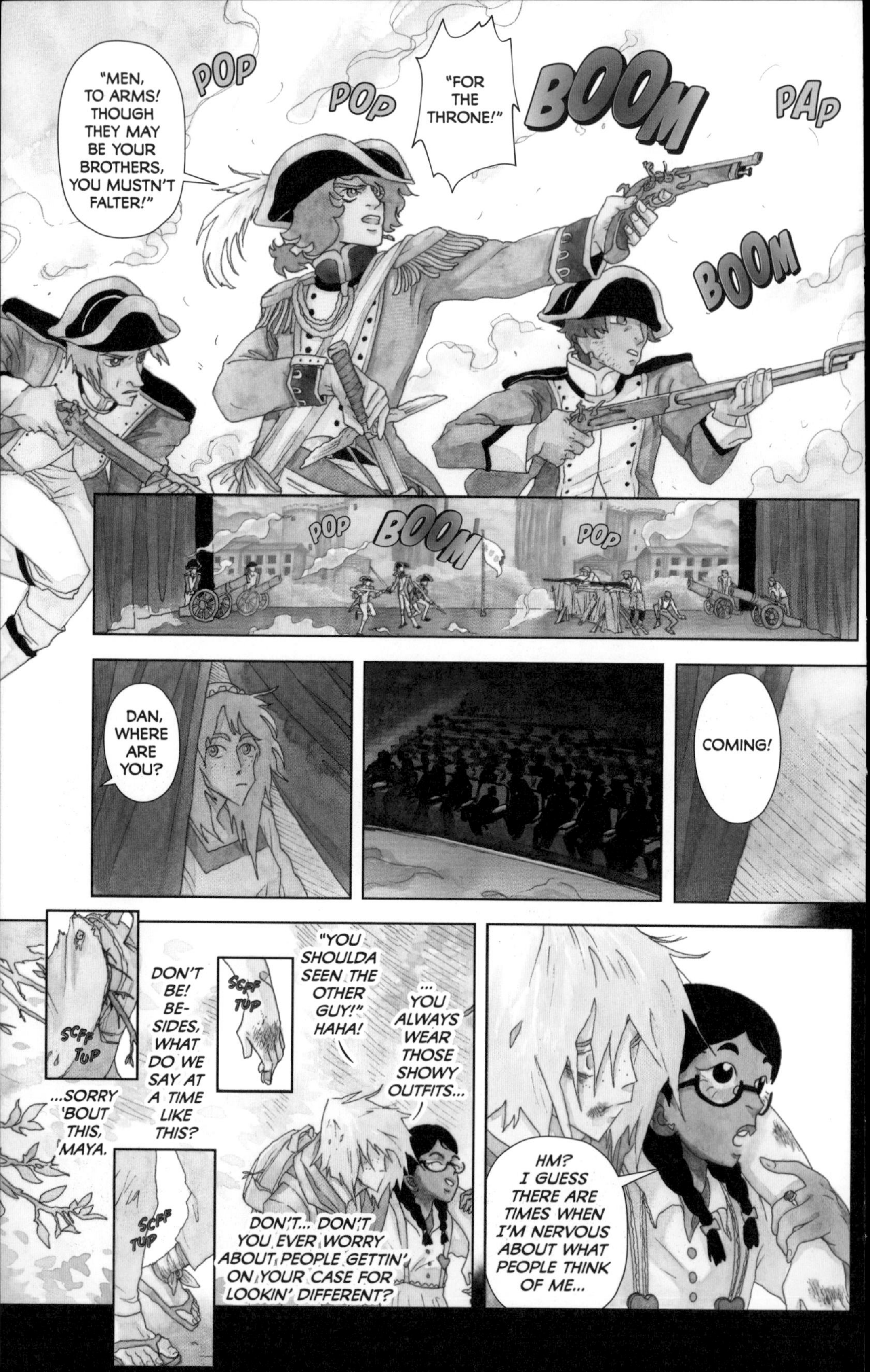
"MEN, TO ARMS! THOUGH THEY MAY BE YOUR BROTHERS, YOU MUSTN'T FALTER!"
POP
POP
"FOR THE THRONE!"
BOOM
PAP
BOOM
POP
BOOM
POP
DAN, WHERE ARE YOU?
COMING!
SCFF
TUP
...SORRY 'BOUT THIS, MAYA.
DON'T BE! BE-SIDES, WHAT DO WE SAY AT A TIME LIKE THIS?
SCFF
TUP
"YOU SHOULDA SEEN THE OTHER GUY!" HAHA!
... YOU ALWAYS WEAR THOSE SHOWY OUTFITS...
SCFF
TUP
DON'T... DON'T YOU EVER WORRY ABOUT PEOPLE GETTIN' ON YOUR CASE FOR LOOKIN' DIFFERENT?
HM? I GUESS THERE ARE TIMES WHEN I'M NERVOUS ABOUT WHAT PEOPLE THINK OF ME...

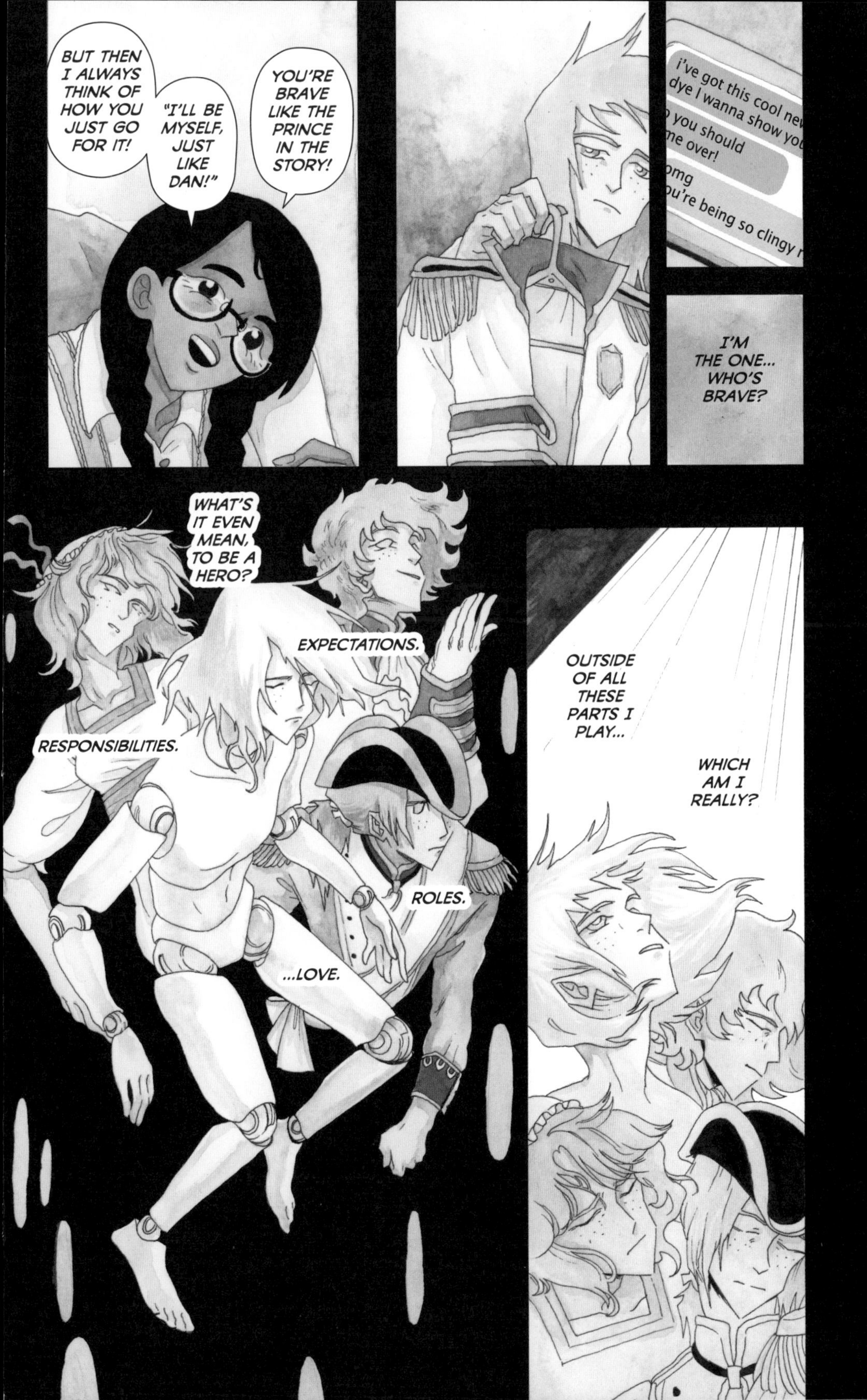
BUT THEN I ALWAYS THINK OF HOW YOU JUST GO FOR IT!
"I'LL BE MYSELF, JUST LIKE DAN!"
YOU'RE BRAVE LIKE THE PRINCE IN THE STORY!
i've got this cool new dye I wanna show you
you should me over!
omg you're being so clingy
I'M THE ONE... WHO'S BRAVE?
WHAT'S IT EVEN MEAN, TO BE A HERO?
EXPECTATIONS.
RESPONSIBILITIES.
ROLES.
...LOVE.
OUTSIDE OF ALL THESE PARTS I PLAY...
WHICH AM I REALLY?

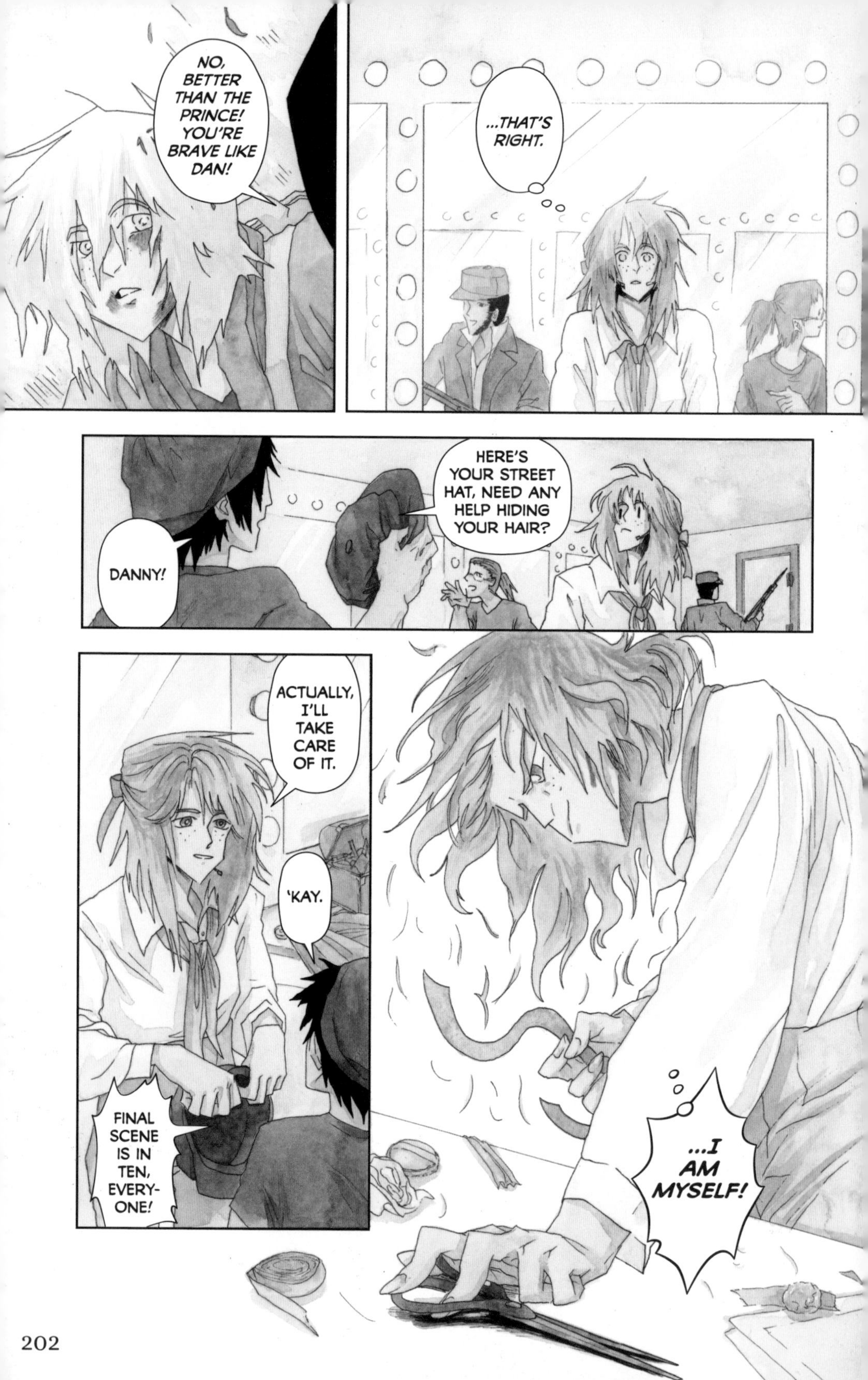
NO, BETTER THAN THE PRINCE! YOU'RE BRAVE LIKE DAN!
...THAT'S RIGHT.
HERE'S YOUR STREET HAT, NEED ANY HELP HIDING YOUR HAIR?
DANNY!
ACTUALLY, I'LL TAKE CARE OF IT.
'KAY.
FINAL SCENE IS IN TEN, EVERY-ONE!
...I AM MYSELF!

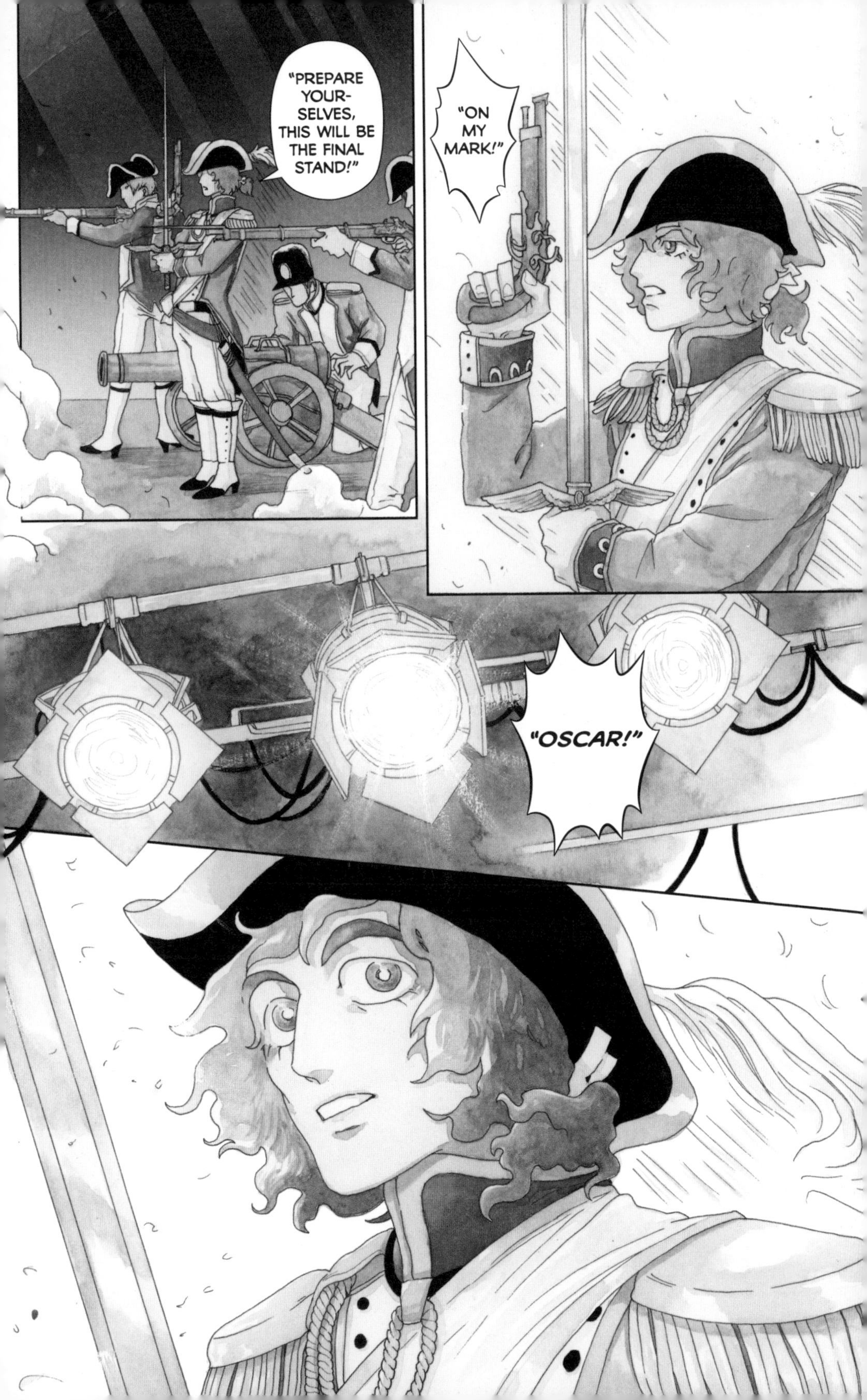
"PREPARE YOUR-SELVES, THIS WILL BE THE FINAL STAND!"
"ON MY MARK!"
"OSCAR!"

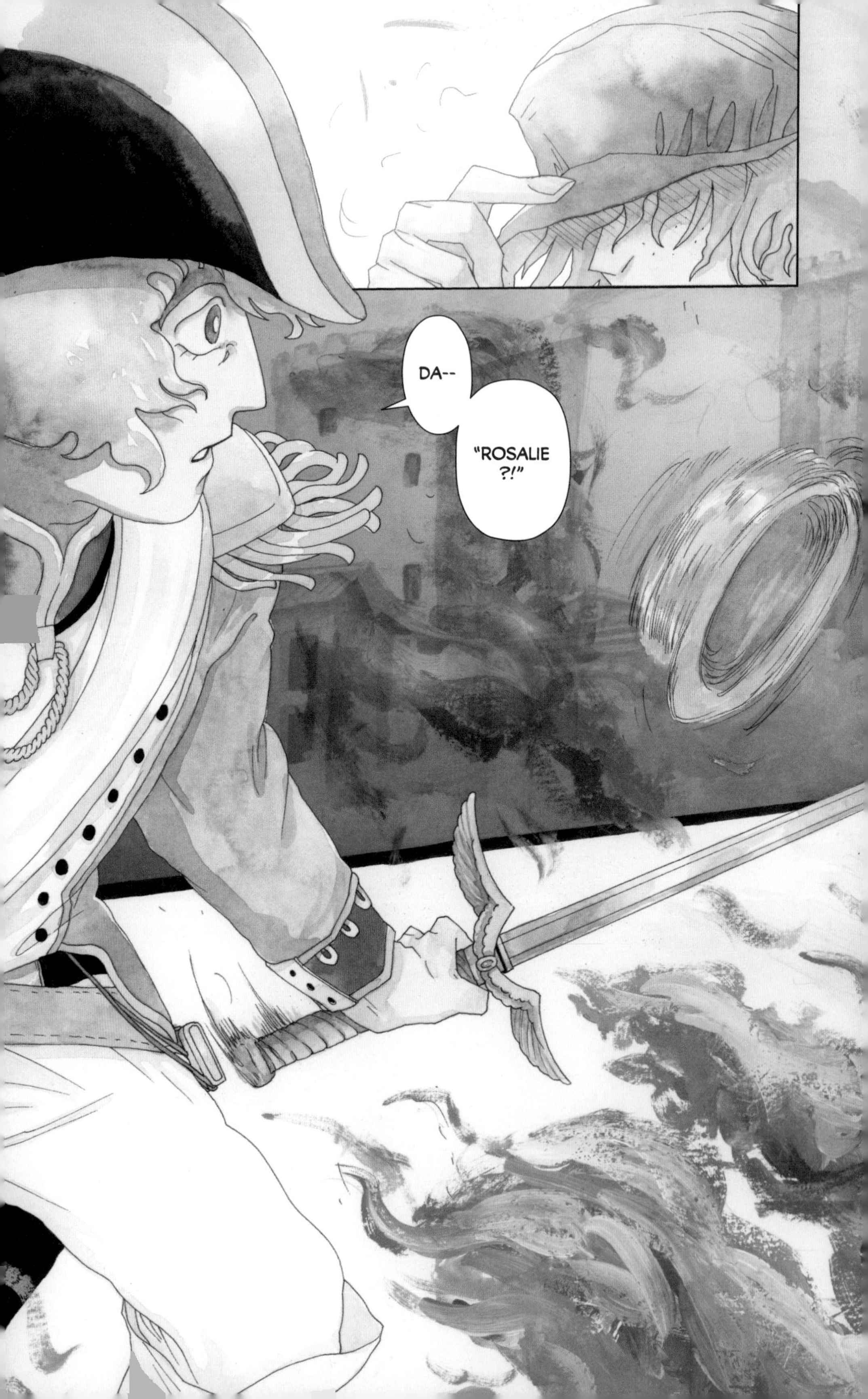
DA--
"ROSALIE ?!"

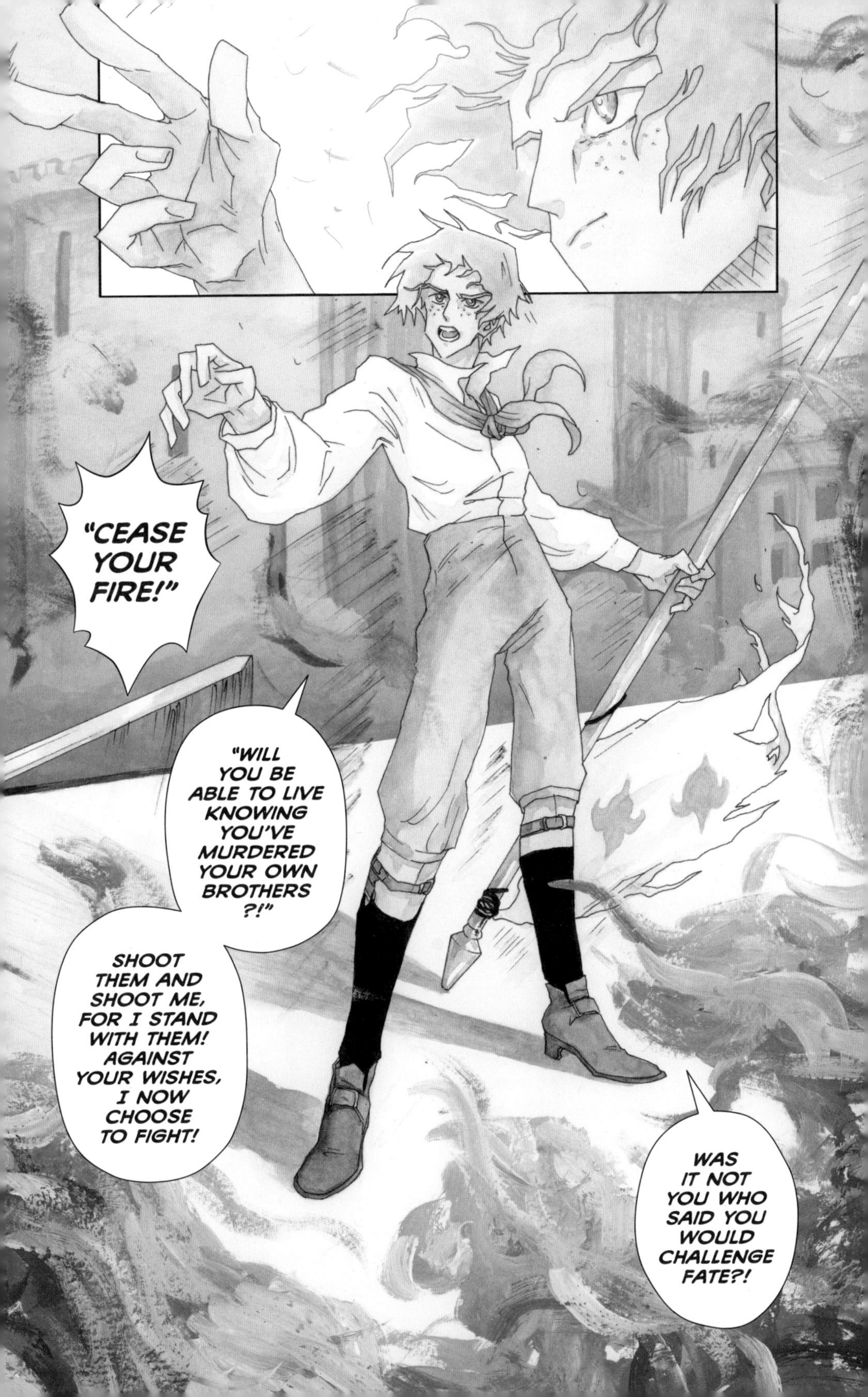
"CEASE YOUR FIRE!"
"WILL YOU BE ABLE TO LIVE KNOWING YOU'VE MURDERED YOUR OWN BROTHERS ?!"
SHOOT THEM AND SHOOT ME, FOR I STAND WITH THEM! AGAINST YOUR WISHES, I NOW CHOOSE TO FIGHT!
WAS IT NOT YOU WHO SAID YOU WOULD CHALLENGE FATE?!

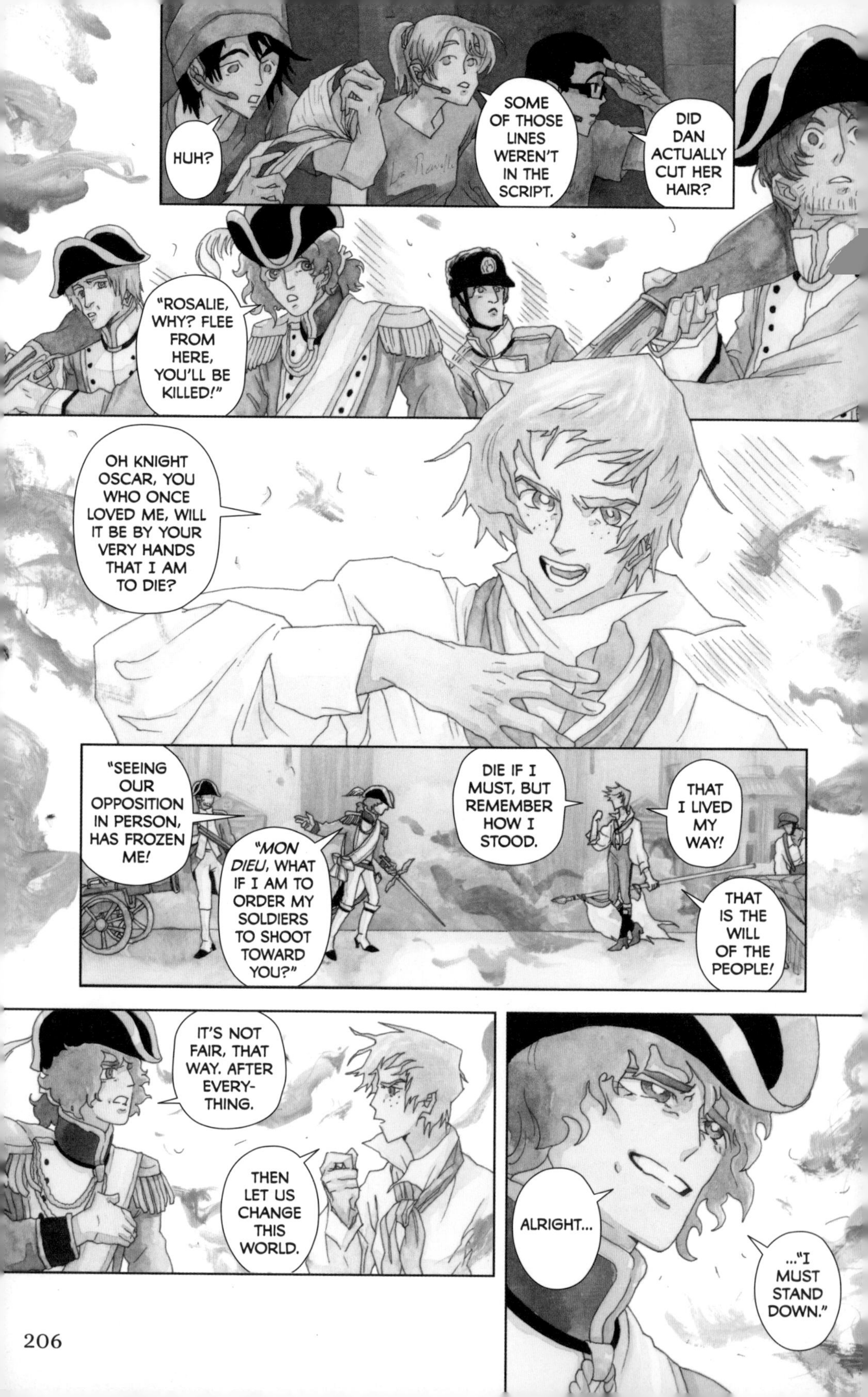
HUH?
SOME OF THOSE LINES WEREN'T IN THE SCRIPT.
DID DAN ACTUALLY CUT HER HAIR?
"ROSALIE, WHY? FLEE FROM HERE, YOU'LL BE KILLED!"
OH KNIGHT OSCAR, YOU WHO ONCE LOVED ME, WILL IT BE BY YOUR VERY HANDS THAT I AM TO DIE?
"SEEING OUR OPPOSITION IN PERSON, HAS FROZEN ME!
"*MON DIEU*, WHAT IF I AM TO ORDER MY SOLDIERS TO SHOOT TOWARD YOU?"
DIE IF I MUST, BUT REMEMBER HOW I STOOD.
THAT I LIVED MY WAY!
THAT IS THE WILL OF THE PEOPLE!
IT'S NOT FAIR, THAT WAY. AFTER EVERY-THING.
THEN LET US CHANGE THIS WORLD.
ALRIGHT...
..."I MUST STAND DOWN."

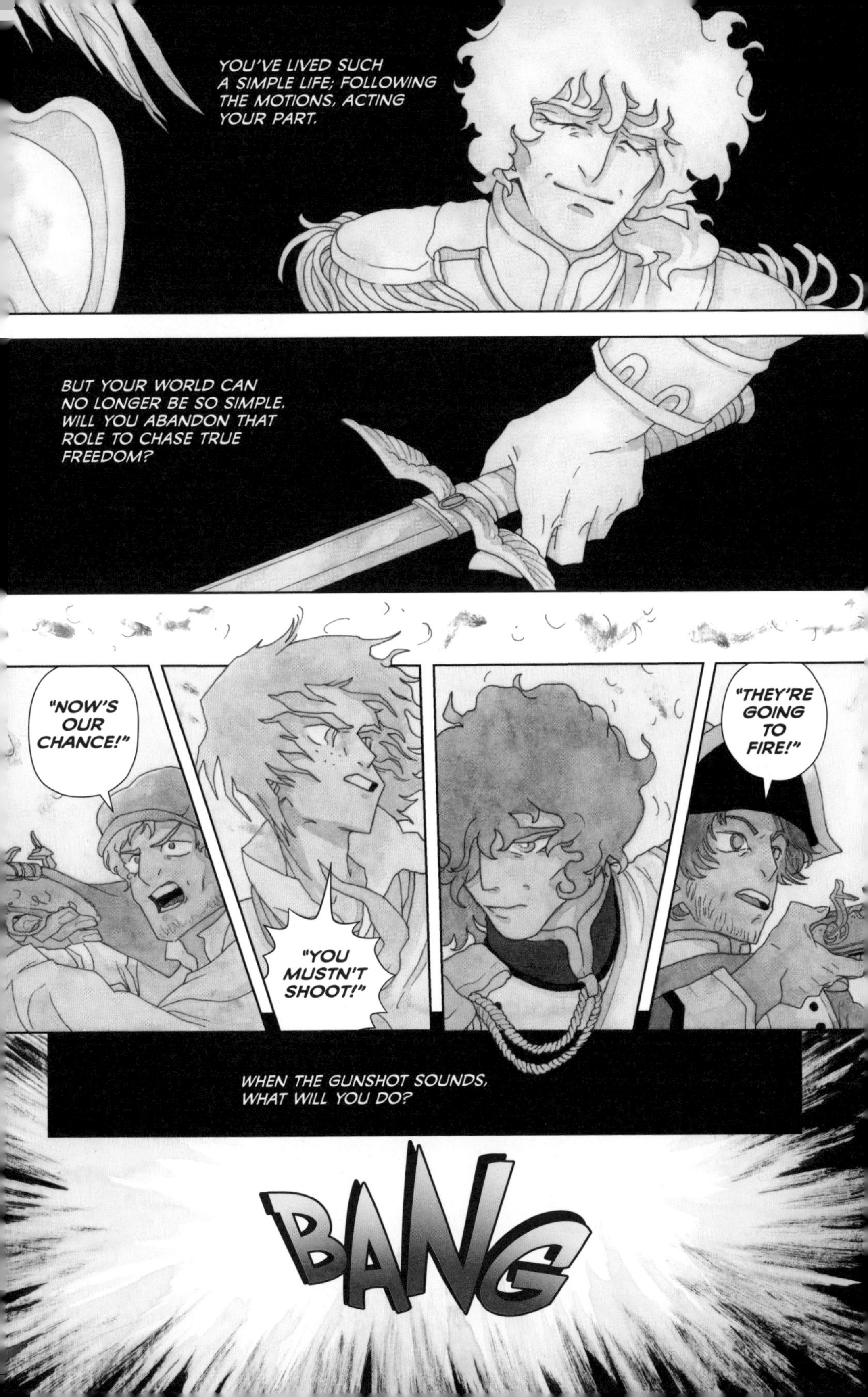
YOU'VE LIVED SUCH A SIMPLE LIFE; FOLLOWING THE MOTIONS, ACTING YOUR PART.
BUT YOUR WORLD CAN NO LONGER BE SO SIMPLE. WILL YOU ABANDON THAT ROLE TO CHASE TRUE FREEDOM?
"NOW'S OUR CHANCE!"
"YOU MUSTN'T SHOOT!"
"THEY'RE GOING TO FIRE!"
WHEN THE GUNSHOT SOUNDS, WHAT WILL YOU DO?
BANG

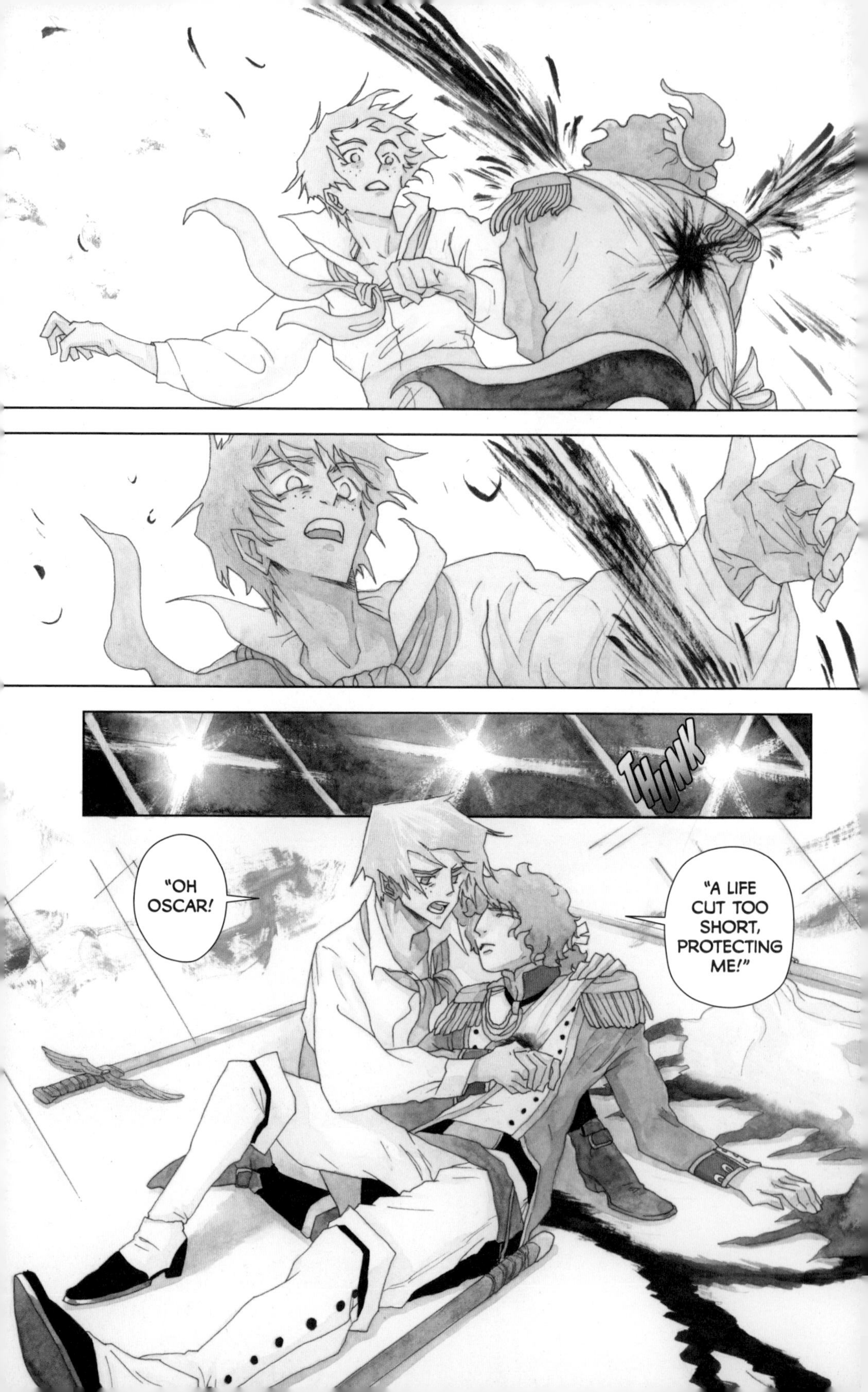
THUNK
"OH OSCAR!
"A LIFE CUT TOO SHORT, PROTECTING ME!"

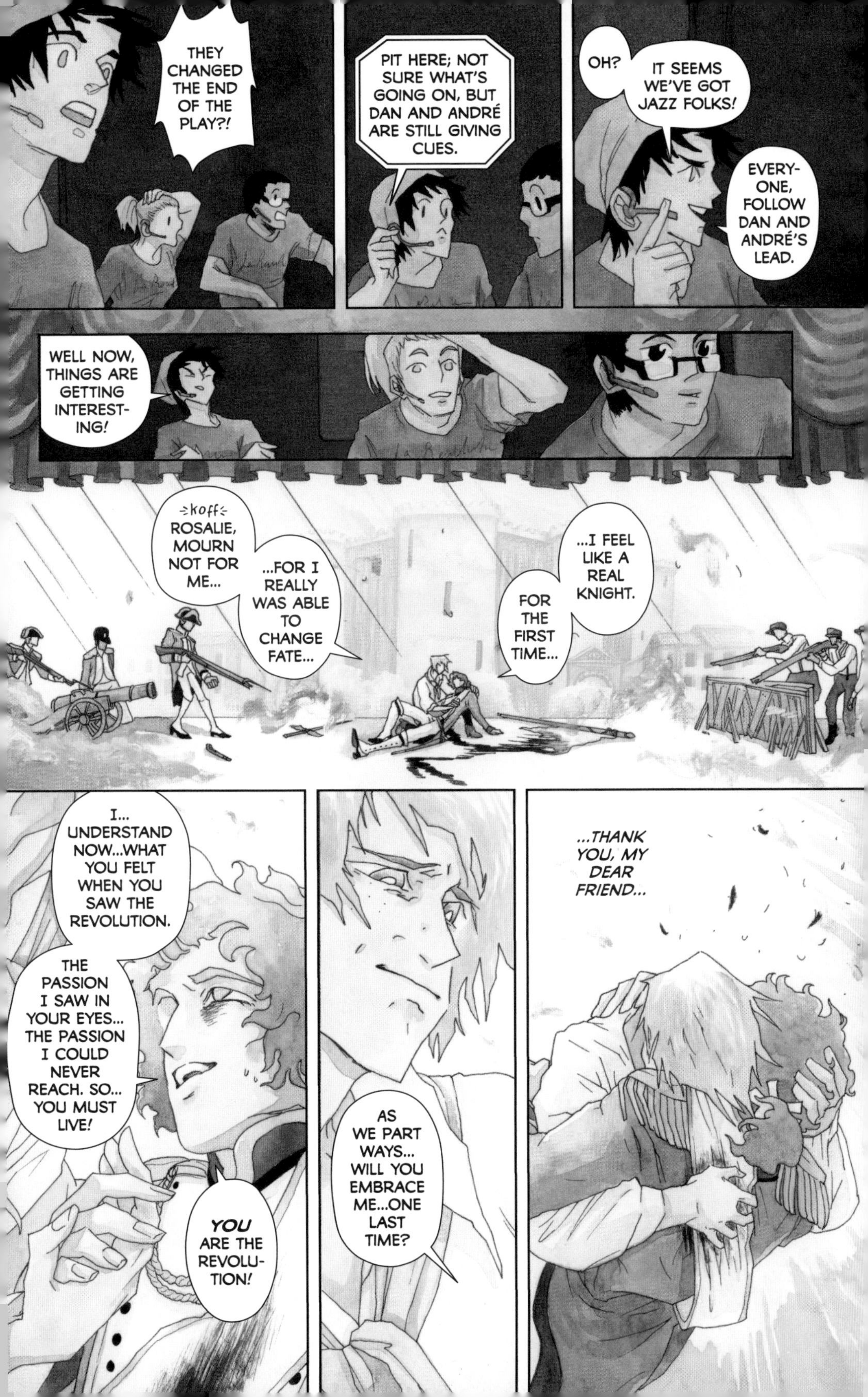
THEY CHANGED THE END OF THE PLAY?!
PIT HERE; NOT SURE WHAT'S GOING ON, BUT DAN AND ANDRÉ ARE STILL GIVING CUES.
OH?
IT SEEMS WE'VE GOT JAZZ FOLKS!
EVERY-ONE, FOLLOW DAN AND ANDRÉ'S LEAD.
WELL NOW, THINGS ARE GETTING INTEREST-ING!
koff
ROSALIE, MOURN NOT FOR ME...
...FOR I REALLY WAS ABLE TO CHANGE FATE...
...I FEEL LIKE A REAL KNIGHT.
FOR THE FIRST TIME...
I... UNDERSTAND NOW...WHAT YOU FELT WHEN YOU SAW THE REVOLUTION.
THE PASSION I SAW IN YOUR EYES... THE PASSION I COULD NEVER REACH. SO... YOU MUST LIVE!
YOU ARE THE REVOLU-TION!
AS WE PART WAYS... WILL YOU EMBRACE ME...ONE LAST TIME?
...THANK YOU, MY DEAR FRIEND...

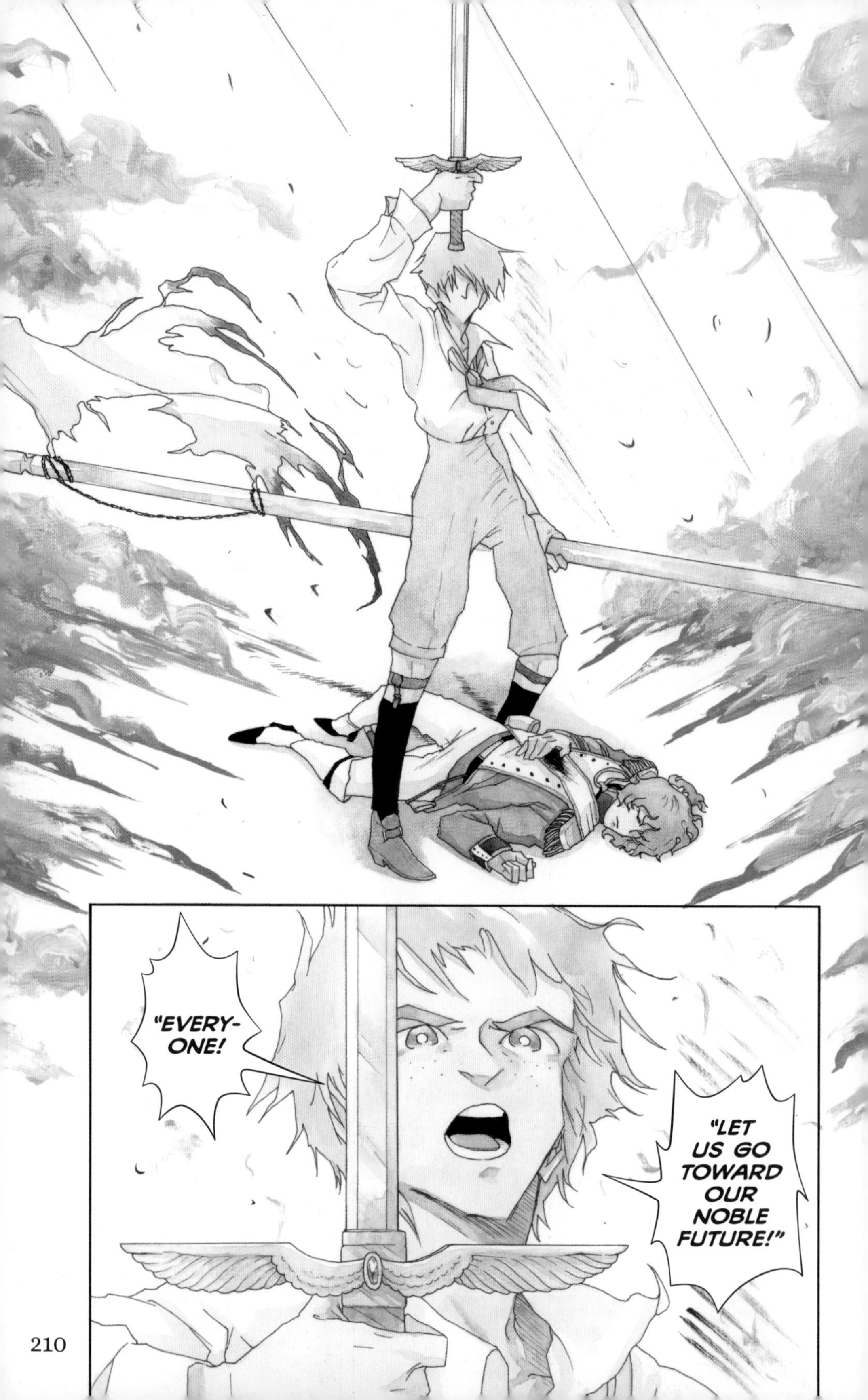
"EVERY-
ONE!
"LET US GO TOWARD OUR NOBLE FUTURE!"

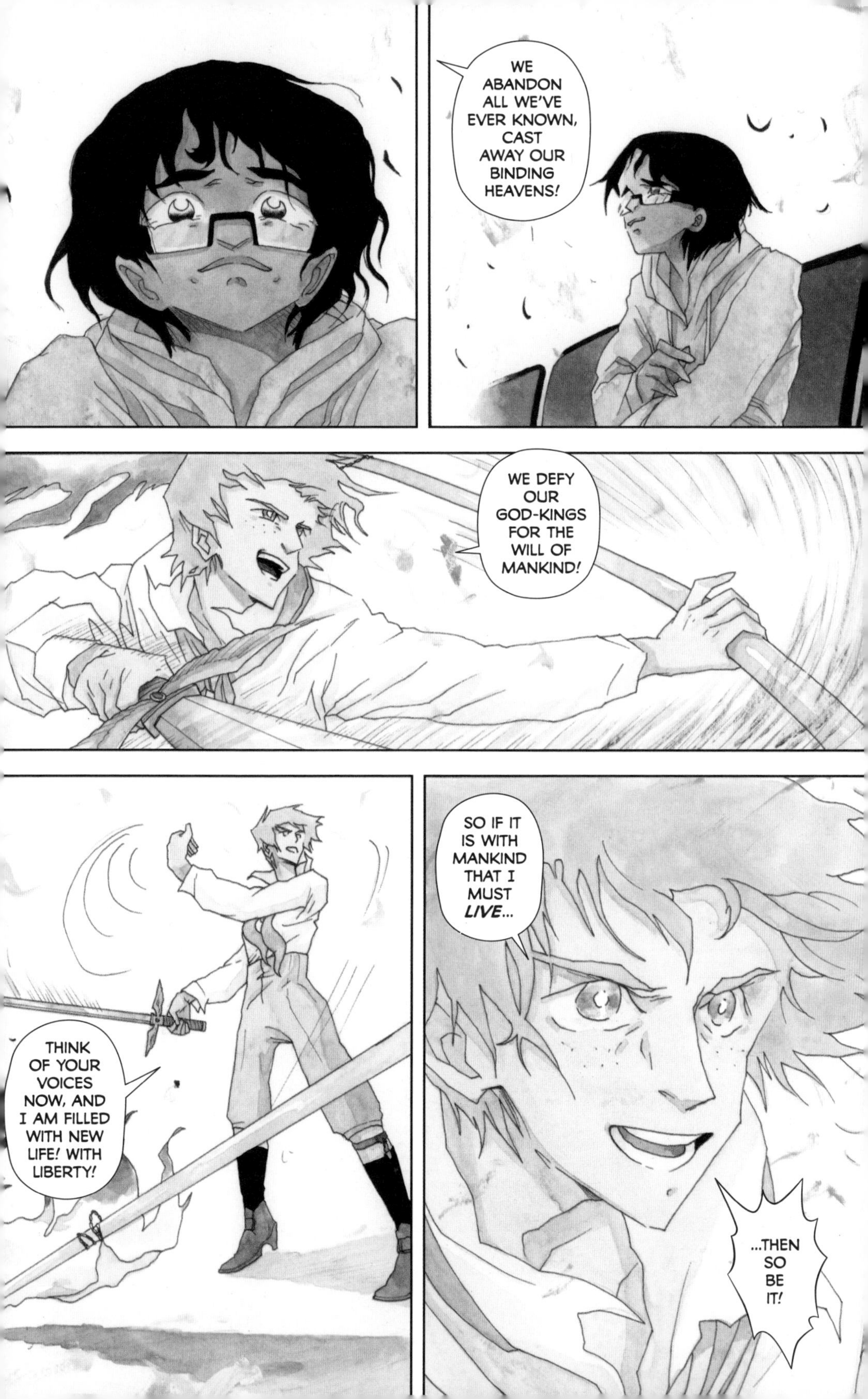
WE ABANDON ALL WE'VE EVER KNOWN, CAST AWAY OUR BINDING HEAVENS!
WE DEFY OUR GOD-KINGS FOR THE WILL OF MANKIND!
THINK OF YOUR VOICES NOW, AND I AM FILLED WITH NEW LIFE! WITH LIBERTY!
SO IF IT IS WITH MANKIND THAT I MUST *LIVE*...
...THEN SO BE IT!

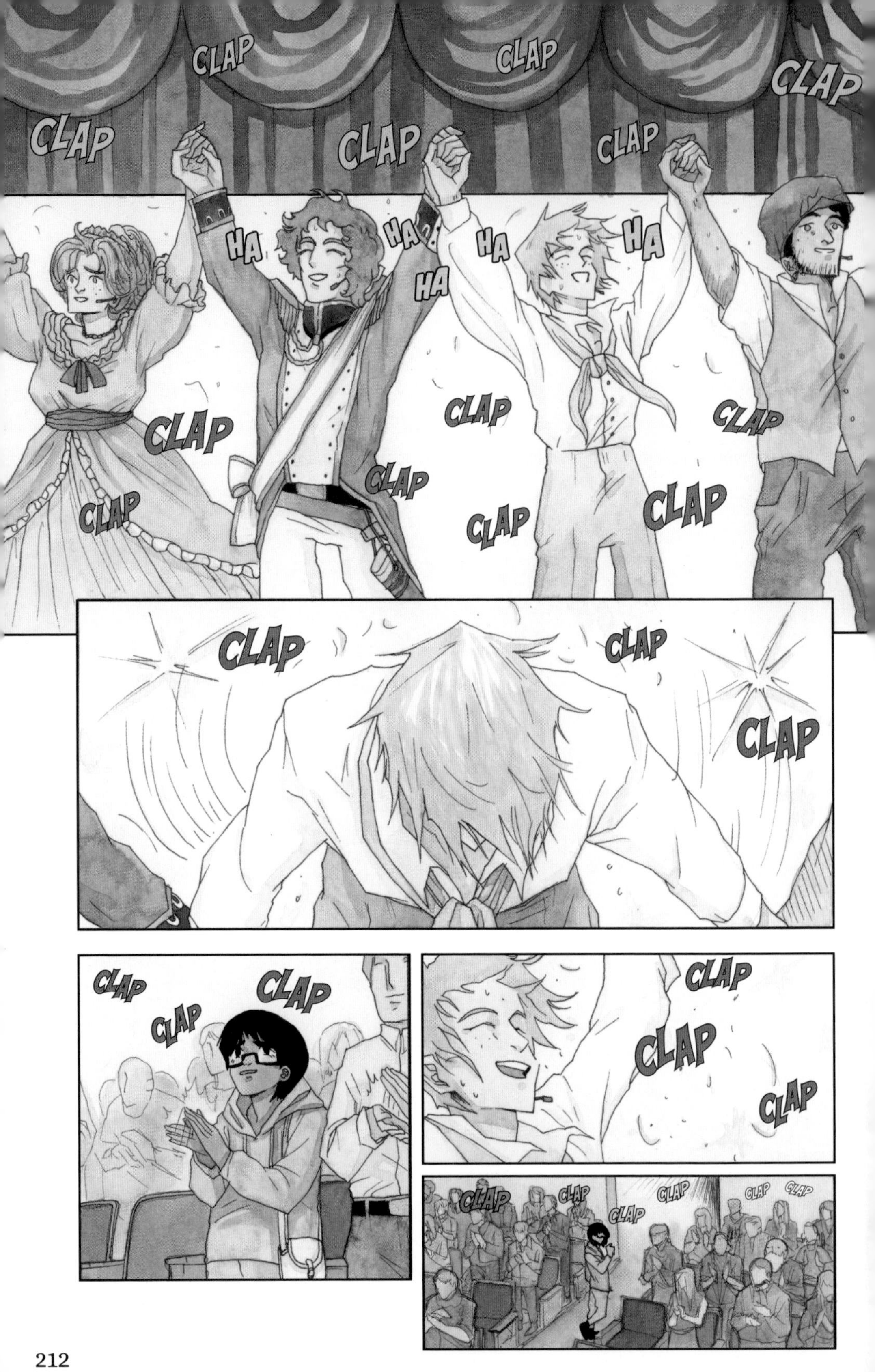
CLAP
CLAP
CLAP
CLAP
CLAP
CLAP
HA
HA
HA
HA
HA
CLAP
CLAP
CLAP
CLAP
CLAP
CLAP
CLAP
CLAP
CLAP
CLAP
CLAP
CLAP
CLAP
CLAP
CLAP
CLAP
CLAP
CLAP
CLAP
CLAP
CLAP
CLAP

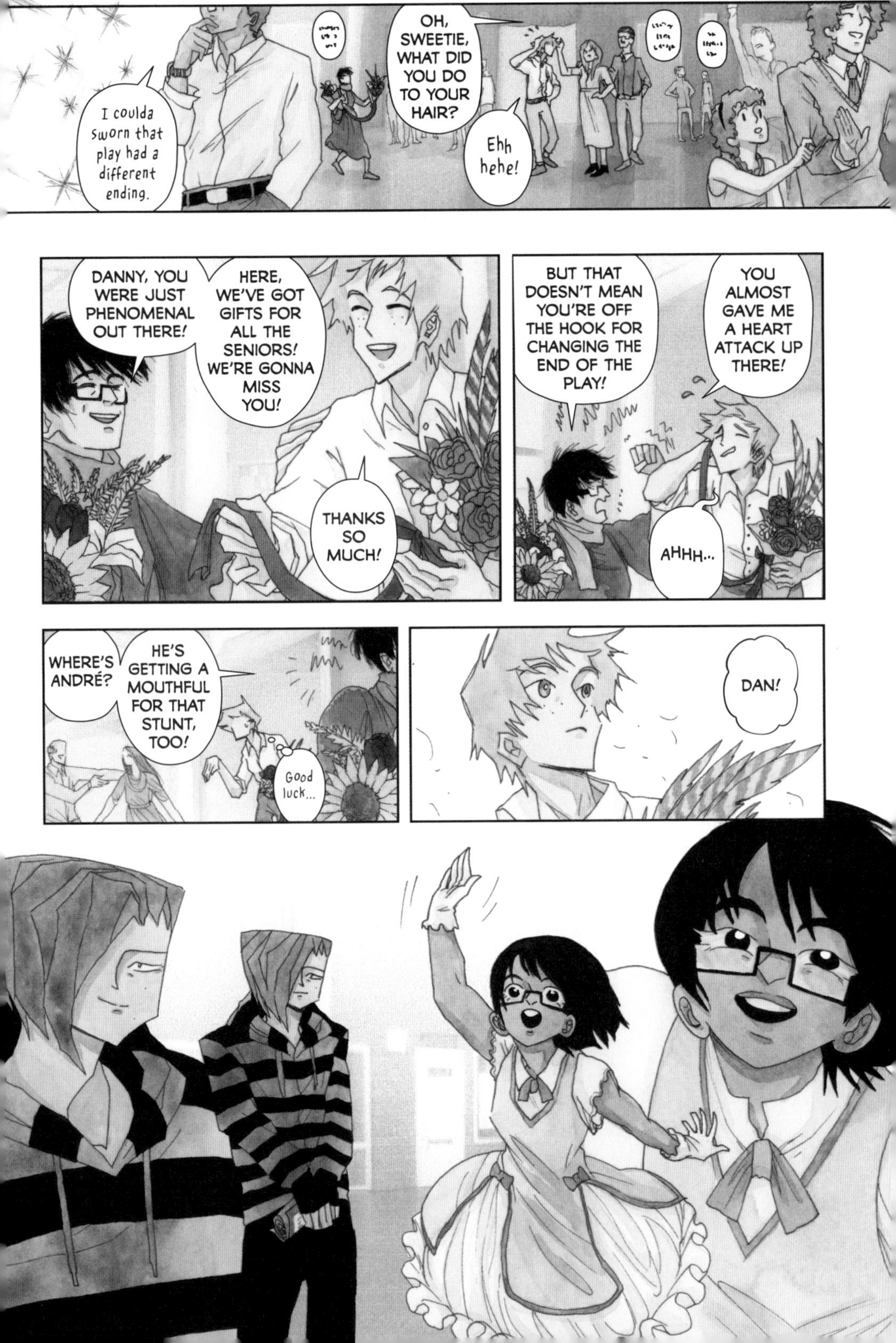
I coulda sworn that play had a different ending.
OH, SWEETIE, WHAT DID YOU DO TO YOUR HAIR?
Ehh hehe!
DANNY, YOU WERE JUST PHENOMENAL OUT THERE!
HERE, WE'VE GOT GIFTS FOR ALL THE SENIORS! WE'RE GONNA MISS YOU!
THANKS SO MUCH!
BUT THAT DOESN'T MEAN YOU'RE OFF THE HOOK FOR CHANGING THE END OF THE PLAY!
YOU ALMOST GAVE ME A HEART ATTACK UP THERE!
AHHH...
WHERE'S ANDRÉ?
HE'S GETTING A MOUTHFUL FOR THAT STUNT, TOO!
Good luck...
DAN!

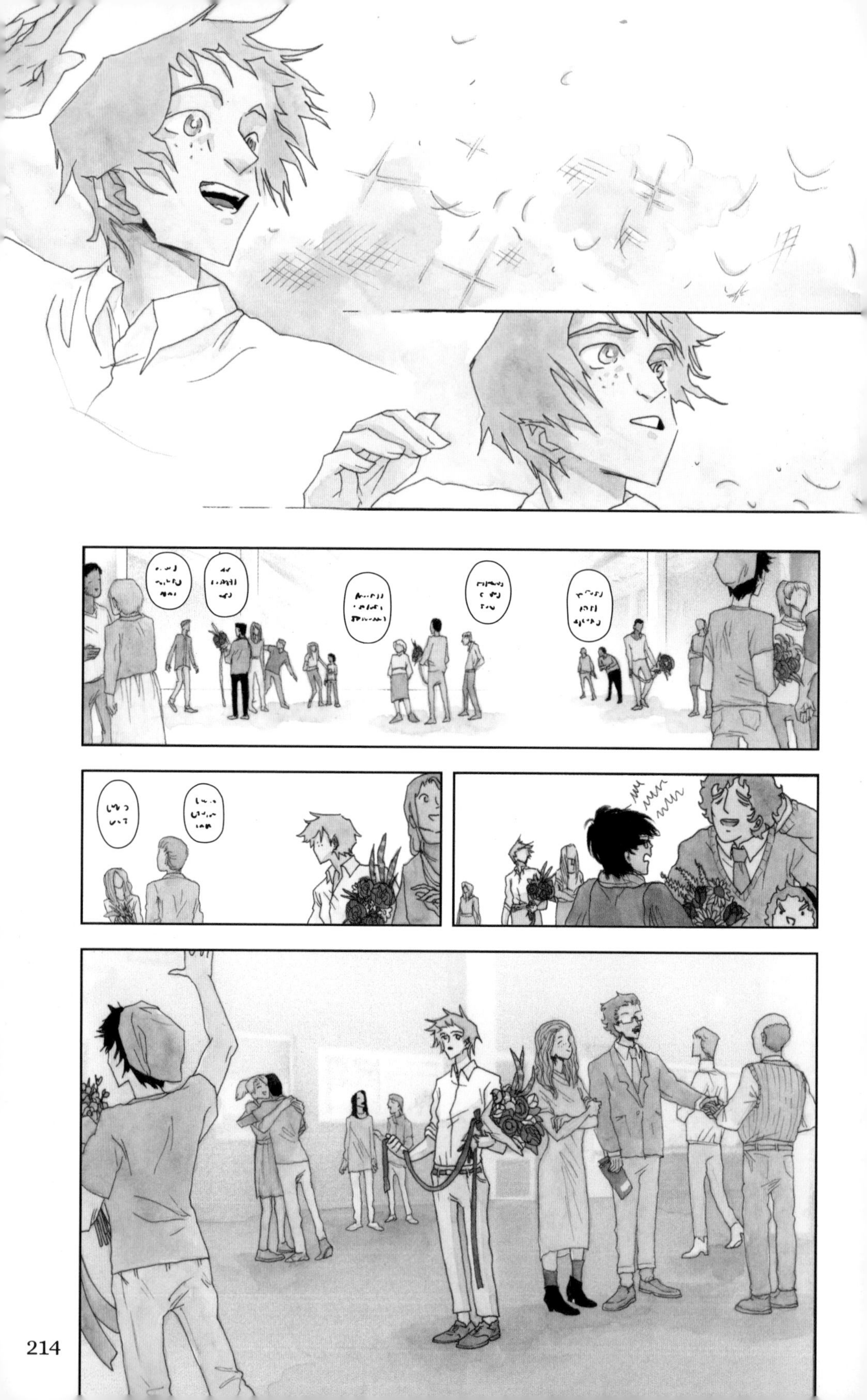

WEEABOO

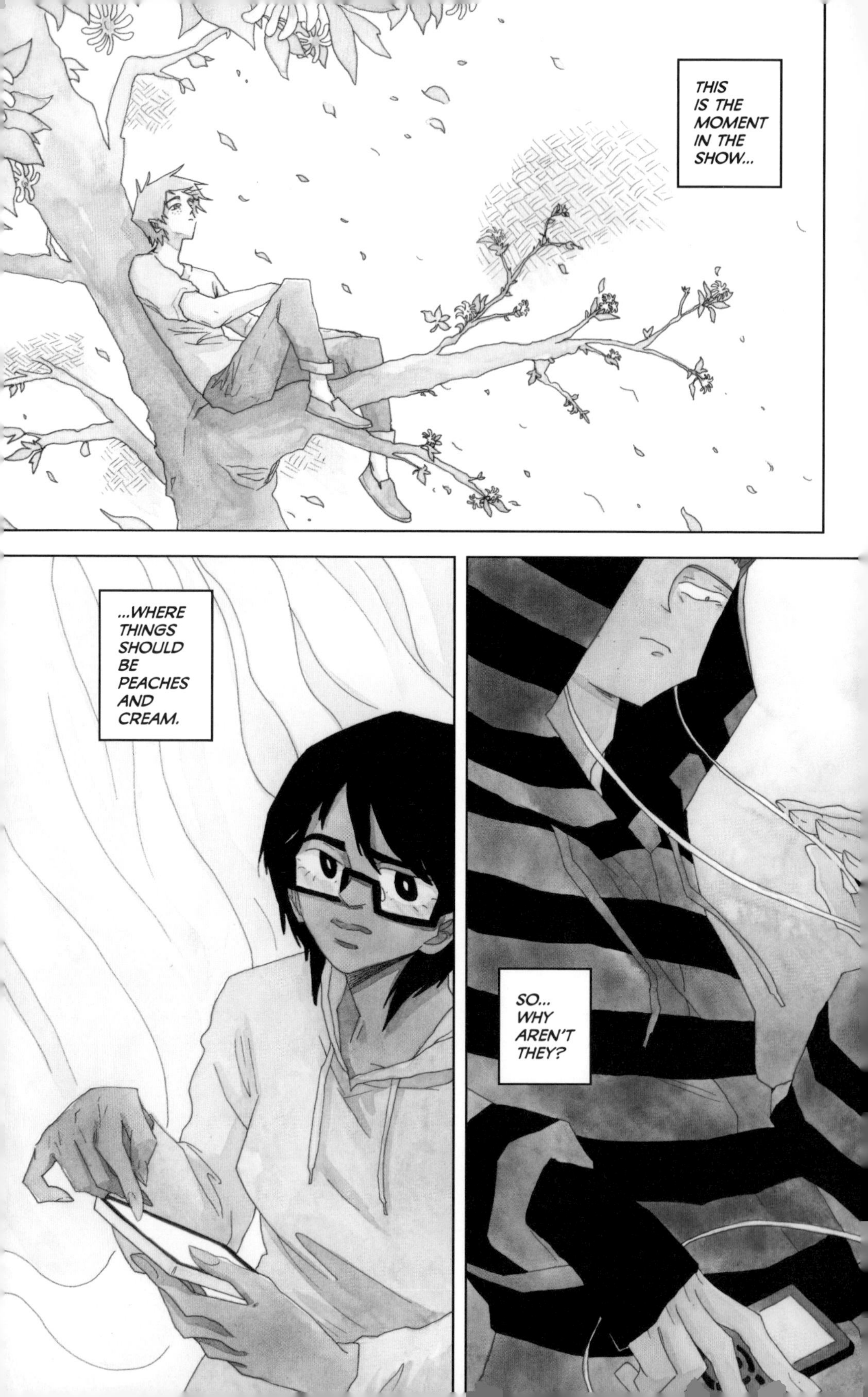
THIS IS THE MOMENT IN THE SHOW...
...WHERE THINGS SHOULD BE PEACHES AND CREAM.
SO... WHY AREN'T THEY?

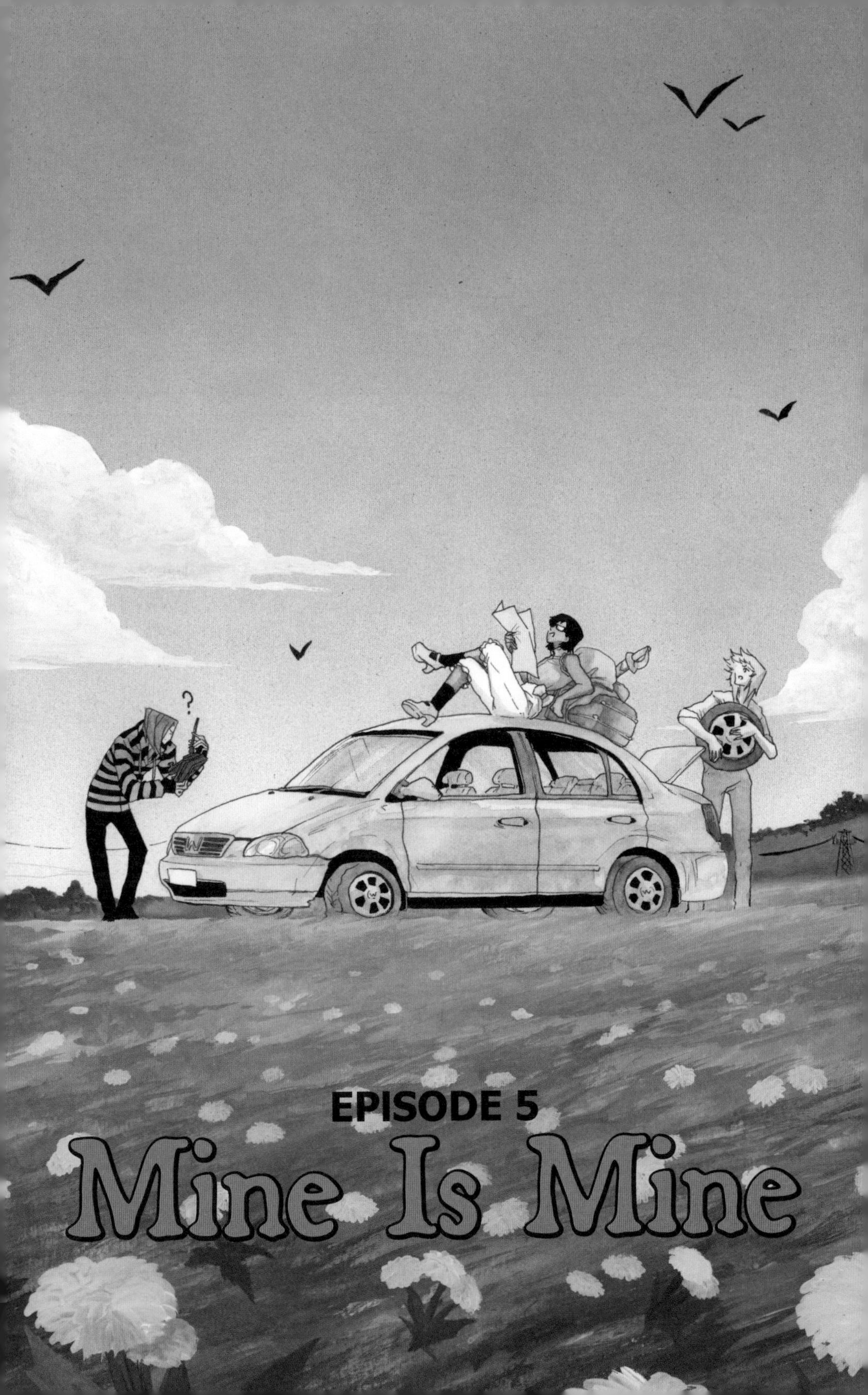
?

EPISODE 5

Mine Is Mine

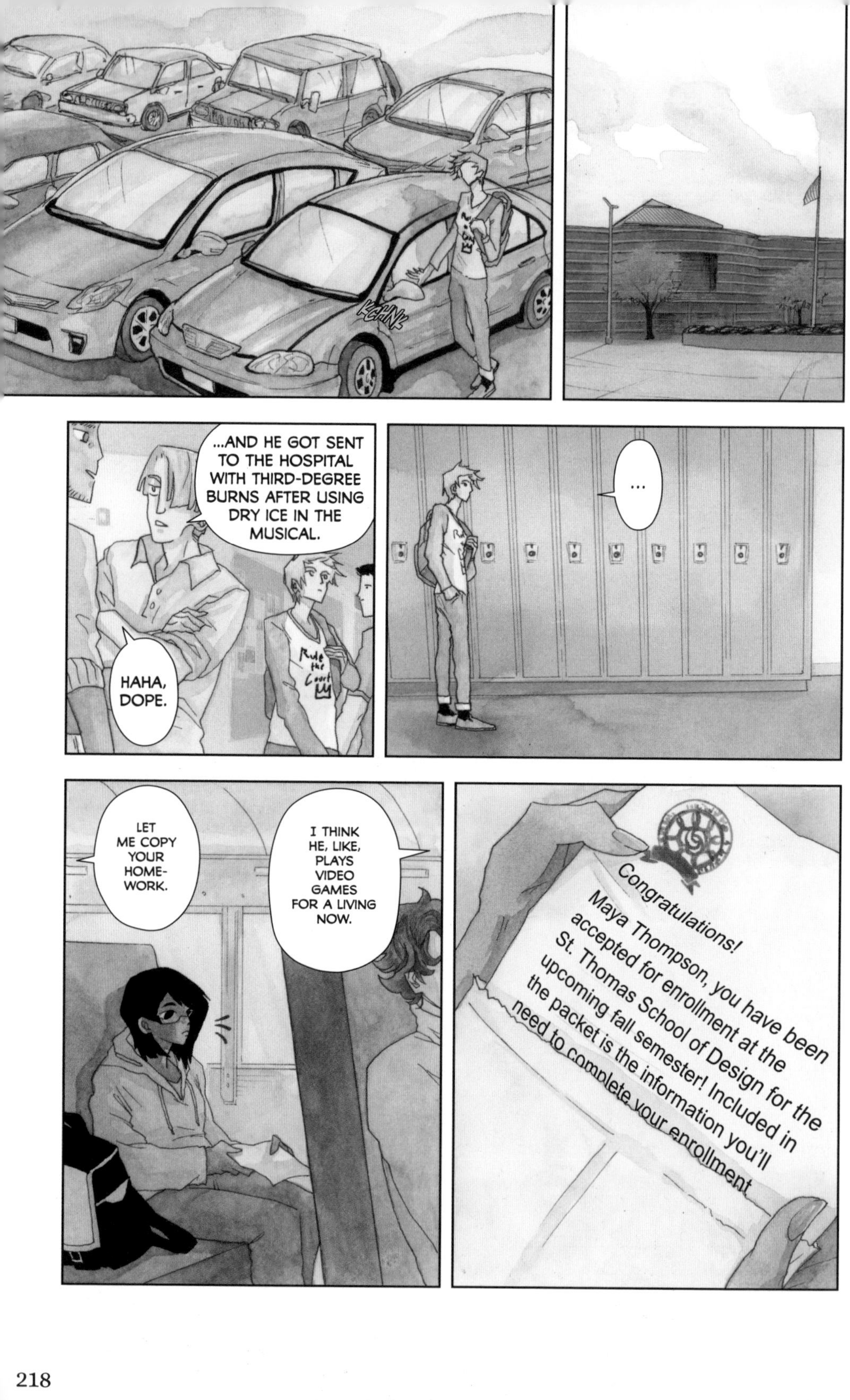
KCHNK
...AND HE GOT SENT TO THE HOSPITAL WITH THIRD-DEGREE BURNS AFTER USING DRY ICE IN THE MUSICAL.
HAHA, DOPE.
...
LET ME COPY YOUR HOME-WORK.
I THINK HE, LIKE, PLAYS VIDEO GAMES FOR A LIVING NOW.
Congratulations!
Maya Thompson, you have been accepted for enrollment at the St. Thomas School of Design for the upcoming fall semester! Included in the packet is the information you'll need to complete your enrollment

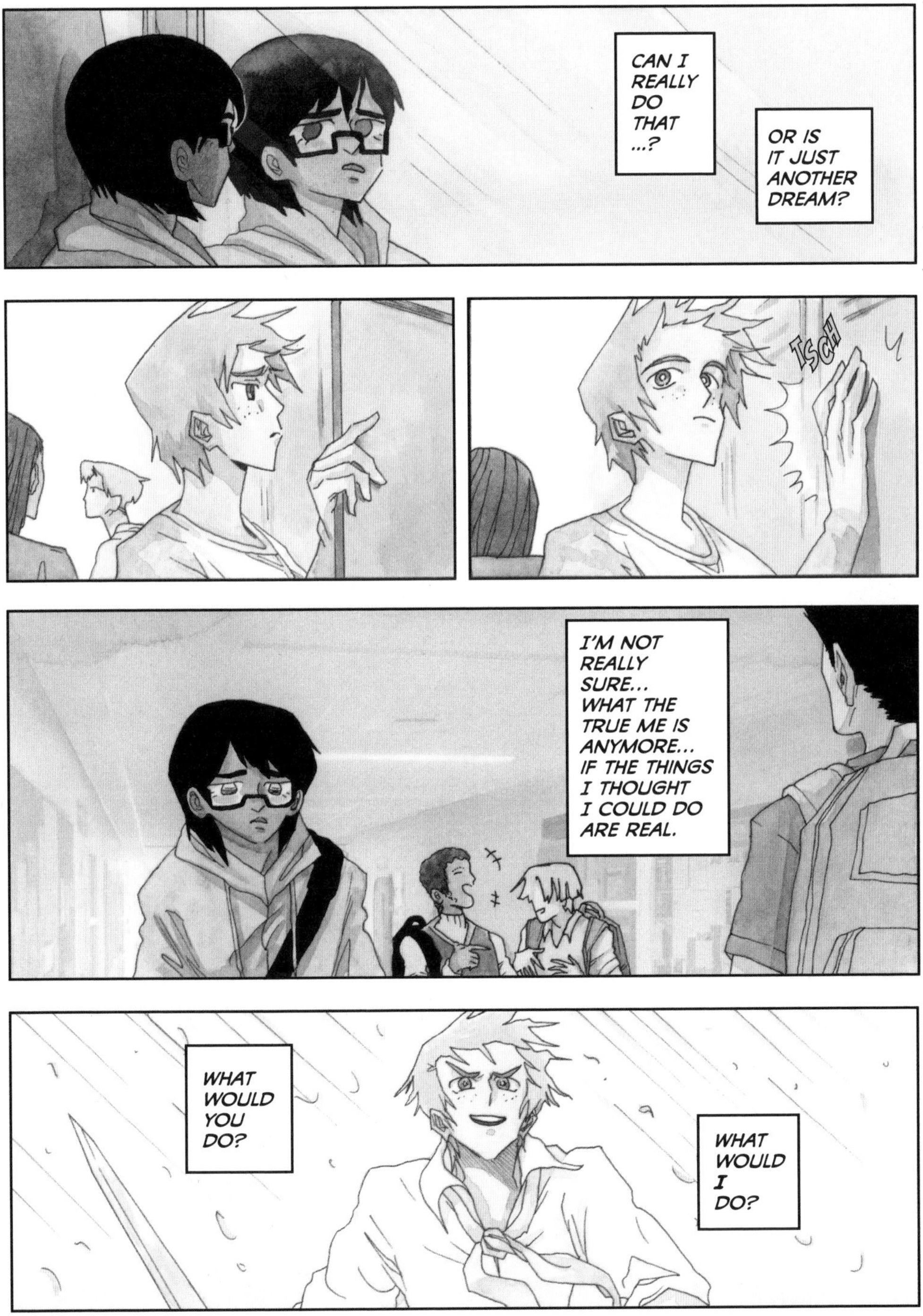
CAN I REALLY DO THAT ...?
OR IS IT JUST ANOTHER DREAM?
TSCH
I'M NOT REALLY SURE... WHAT THE TRUE ME IS ANYMORE... IF THE THINGS I THOUGHT I COULD DO ARE REAL.
WHAT WOULD YOU DO?
WHAT WOULD I DO?

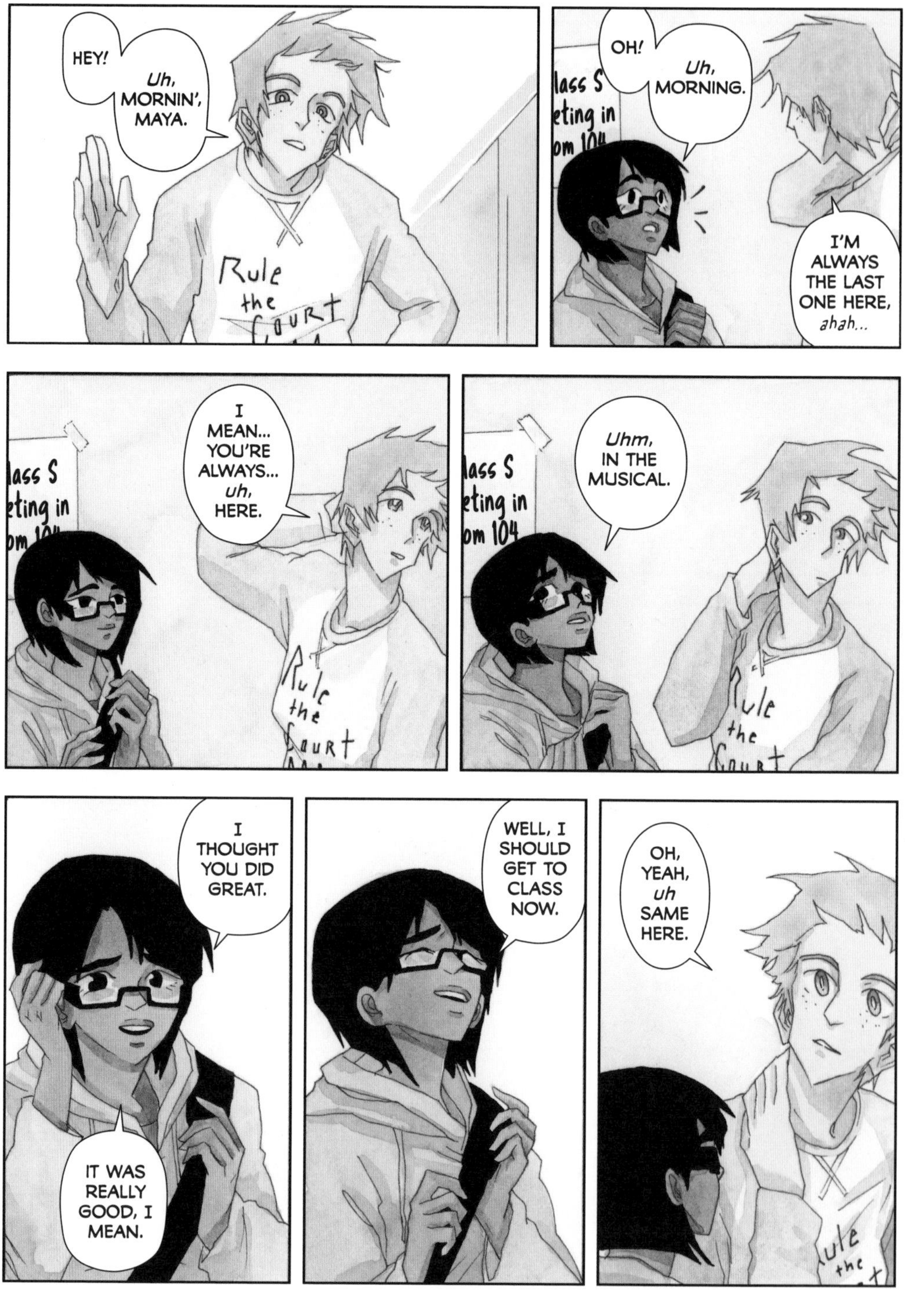
HEY!
Uh, MORNIN', MAYA.
OH!
Uh, MORNING.
I'M ALWAYS THE LAST ONE HERE, *ahah...*
I MEAN... YOU'RE ALWAYS... *uh,* HERE.
Uhm, IN THE MUSICAL.
I THOUGHT YOU DID GREAT.
IT WAS REALLY GOOD, I MEAN.
WELL, I SHOULD GET TO CLASS NOW.
OH, YEAH, *uh* SAME HERE.

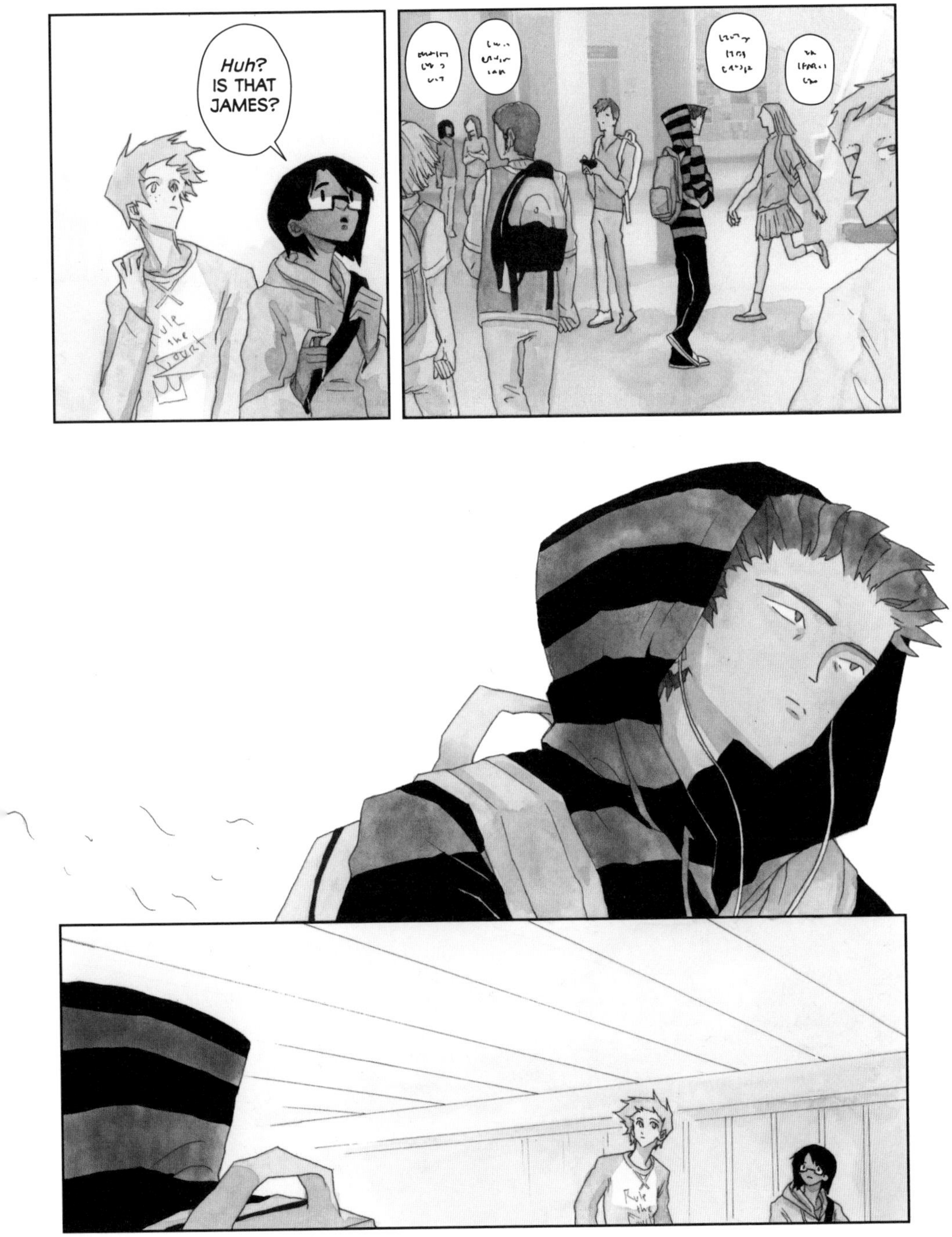
Huh? IS THAT JAMES?

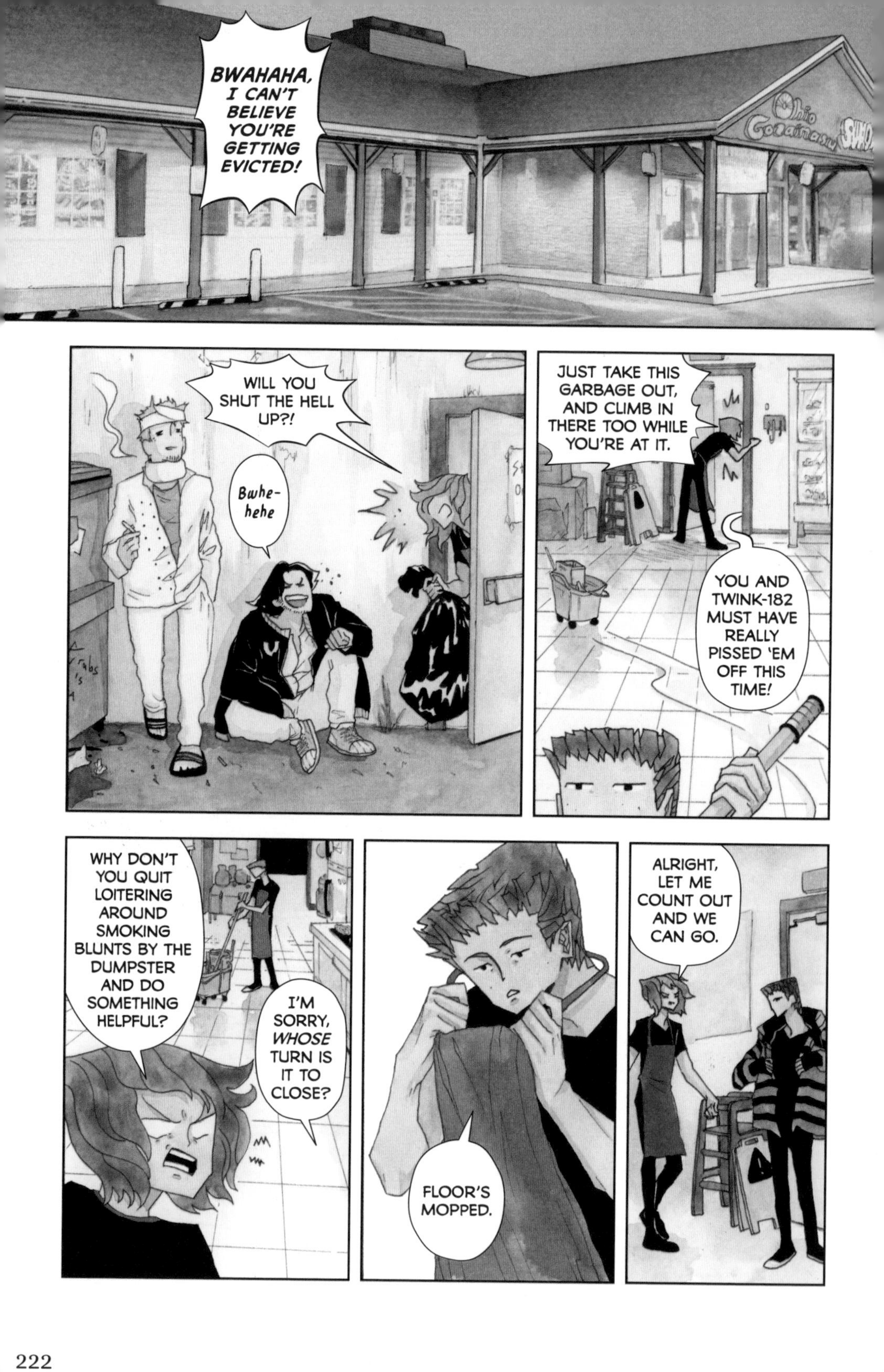
BWAHAHA, I CAN'T BELIEVE YOU'RE GETTING EVICTED!
WILL YOU SHUT THE HELL UP?!
Bwhe-hehe
JUST TAKE THIS GARBAGE OUT, AND CLIMB IN THERE TOO WHILE YOU'RE AT IT.
YOU AND TWINK-182 MUST HAVE REALLY PISSED 'EM OFF THIS TIME!
WHY DON'T YOU QUIT LOITERING AROUND SMOKING BLUNTS BY THE DUMPSTER AND DO SOMETHING HELPFUL?
I'M SORRY, *WHOSE* TURN IS IT TO CLOSE?
FLOOR'S MOPPED.
ALRIGHT, LET ME COUNT OUT AND WE CAN GO.

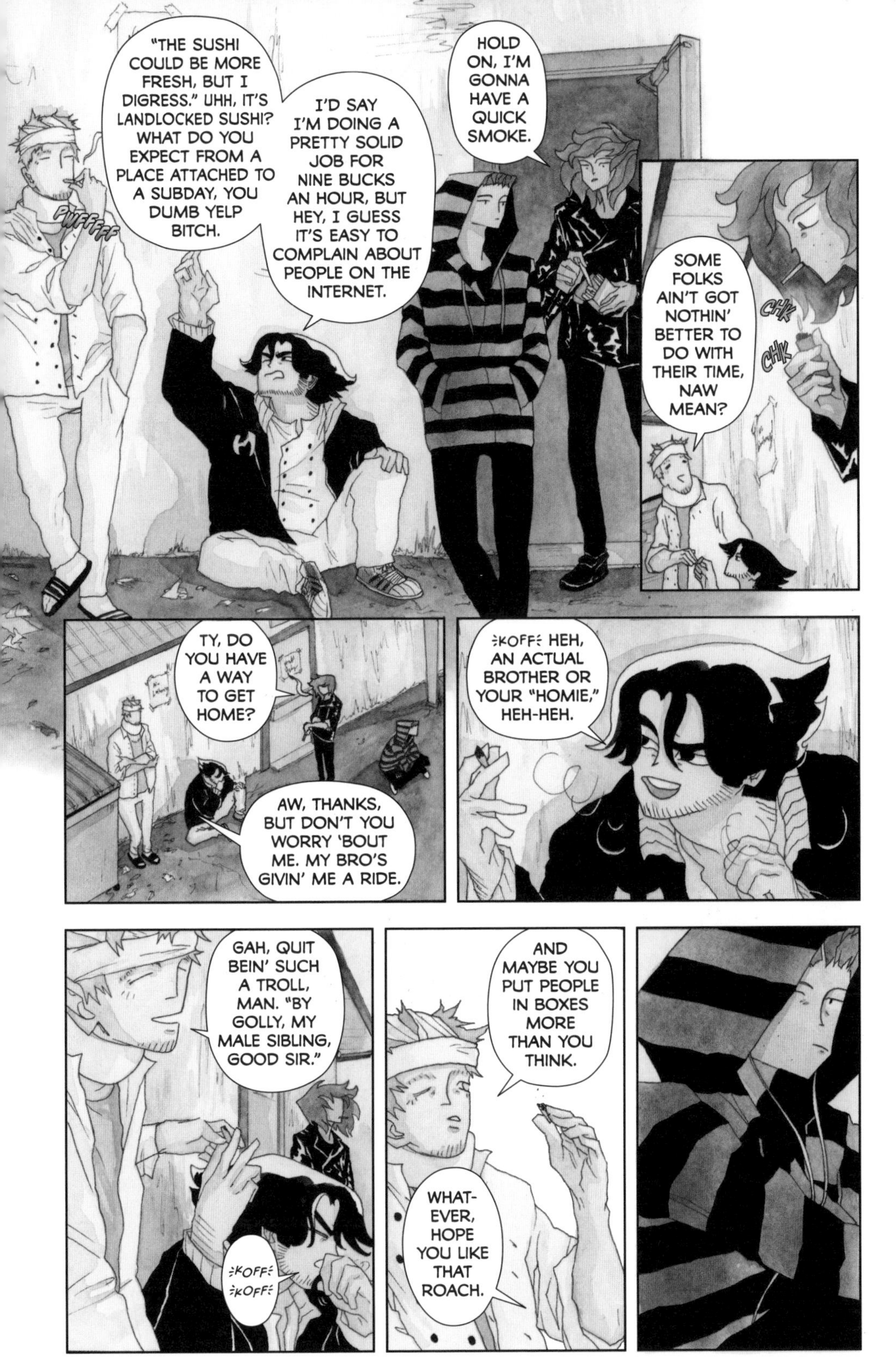
"THE SUSHI COULD BE MORE FRESH, BUT I DIGRESS." UHH, IT'S LANDLOCKED SUSHI? WHAT DO YOU EXPECT FROM A PLACE ATTACHED TO A SUBDAY, YOU DUMB YELP BITCH.
PWFFFFF
I'D SAY I'M DOING A PRETTY SOLID JOB FOR NINE BUCKS AN HOUR, BUT HEY, I GUESS IT'S EASY TO COMPLAIN ABOUT PEOPLE ON THE INTERNET.
HOLD ON, I'M GONNA HAVE A QUICK SMOKE.
SOME FOLKS AIN'T GOT NOTHIN' BETTER TO DO WITH THEIR TIME, NAW MEAN?
CHK
CHK
TY, DO YOU HAVE A WAY TO GET HOME?
AW, THANKS, BUT DON'T YOU WORRY 'BOUT ME. MY BRO'S GIVIN' ME A RIDE.
KOFF HEH, AN ACTUAL BROTHER OR YOUR "HOMIE," HEH-HEH.
GAH, QUIT BEIN' SUCH A TROLL, MAN. "BY GOLLY, MY MALE SIBLING, GOOD SIR."
KOFF
KOFF
AND MAYBE YOU PUT PEOPLE IN BOXES MORE THAN YOU THINK.
WHAT-EVER, HOPE YOU LIKE THAT ROACH.

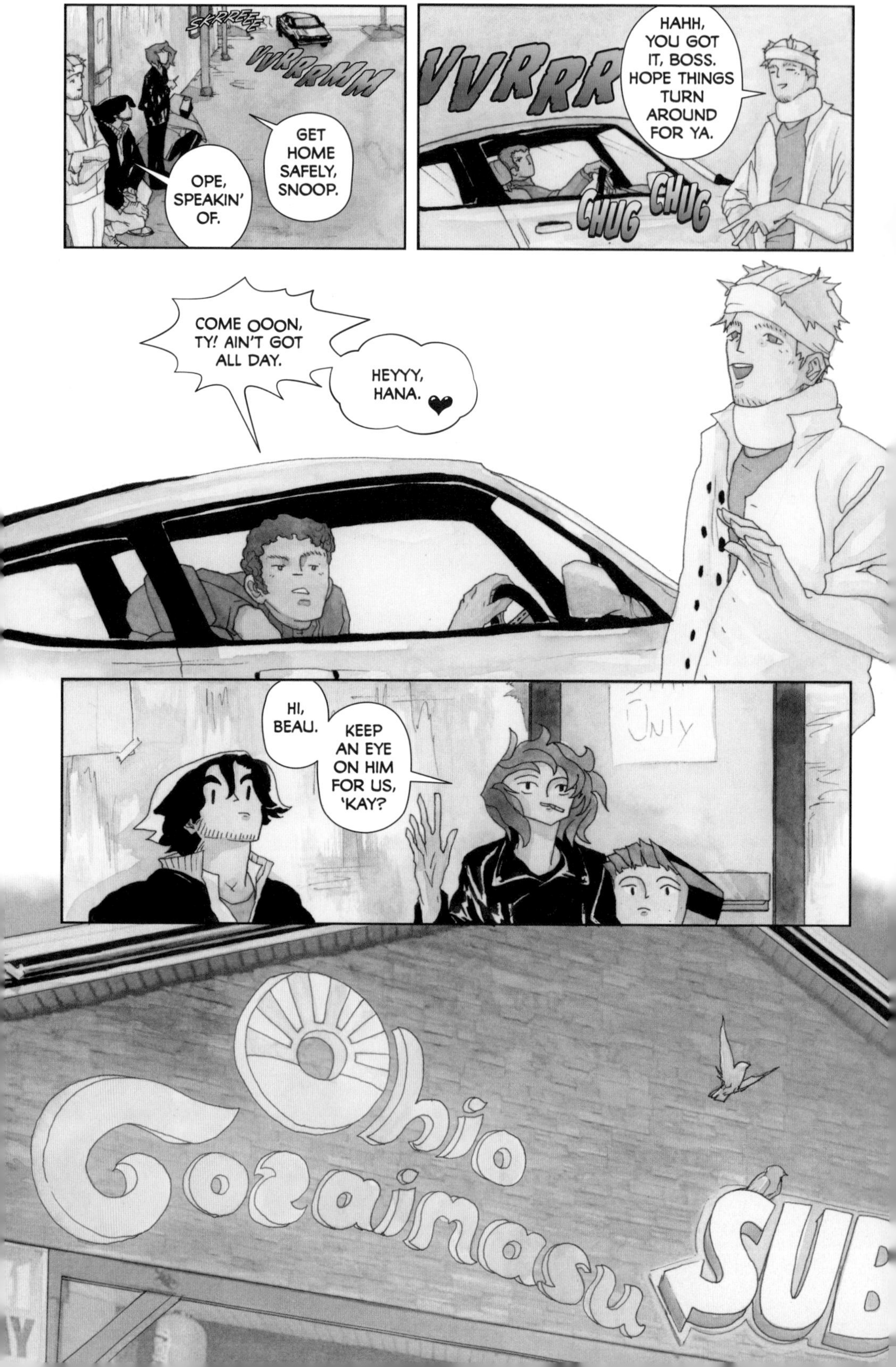
SKRREEE
VVRRRMM
GET HOME SAFELY, SNOOP.
OPE, SPEAKIN' OF.
VVRRR
HAHH, YOU GOT IT, BOSS. HOPE THINGS TURN AROUND FOR YA.
CHUG CHUG
COME OOON, TY! AIN'T GOT ALL DAY.
HEYYY, HANA. ♥
HI, BEAU.
KEEP AN EYE ON HIM FOR US, 'KAY?
Only
Ohio Gozaimasu SUB

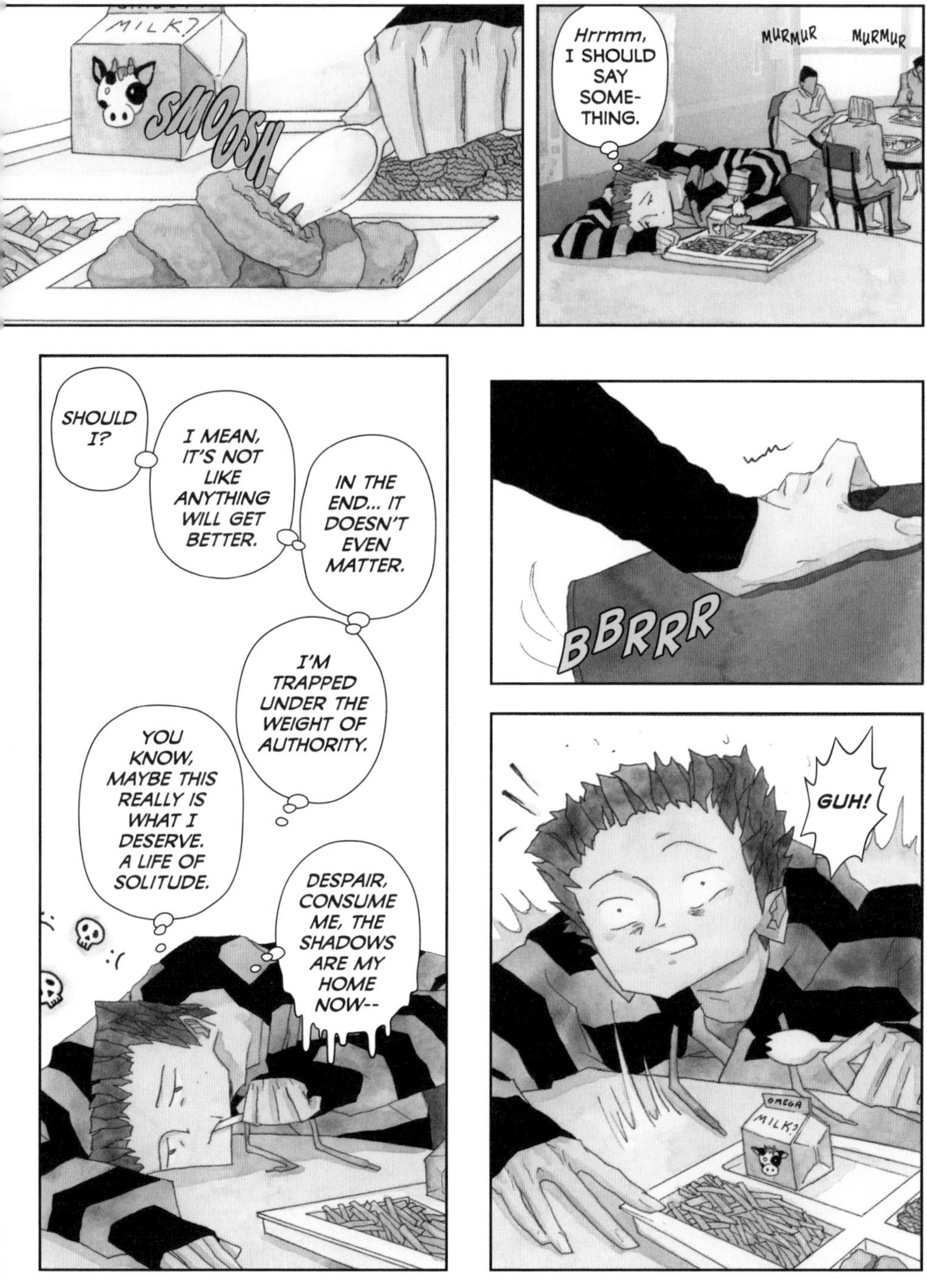
MILK?
SMOOSH
Hrrmm, I SHOULD SAY SOME-THING.
MURMUR
MURMUR
SHOULD I?
I MEAN, IT'S NOT LIKE ANYTHING WILL GET BETTER.
IN THE END... IT DOESN'T EVEN MATTER.
I'M TRAPPED UNDER THE WEIGHT OF AUTHORITY.
YOU KNOW, MAYBE THIS REALLY IS WHAT I DESERVE. A LIFE OF SOLITUDE.
DESPAIR, CONSUME ME, THE SHADOWS ARE MY HOME NOW--
BBRRR
GUH!
OMEGA
MILK?

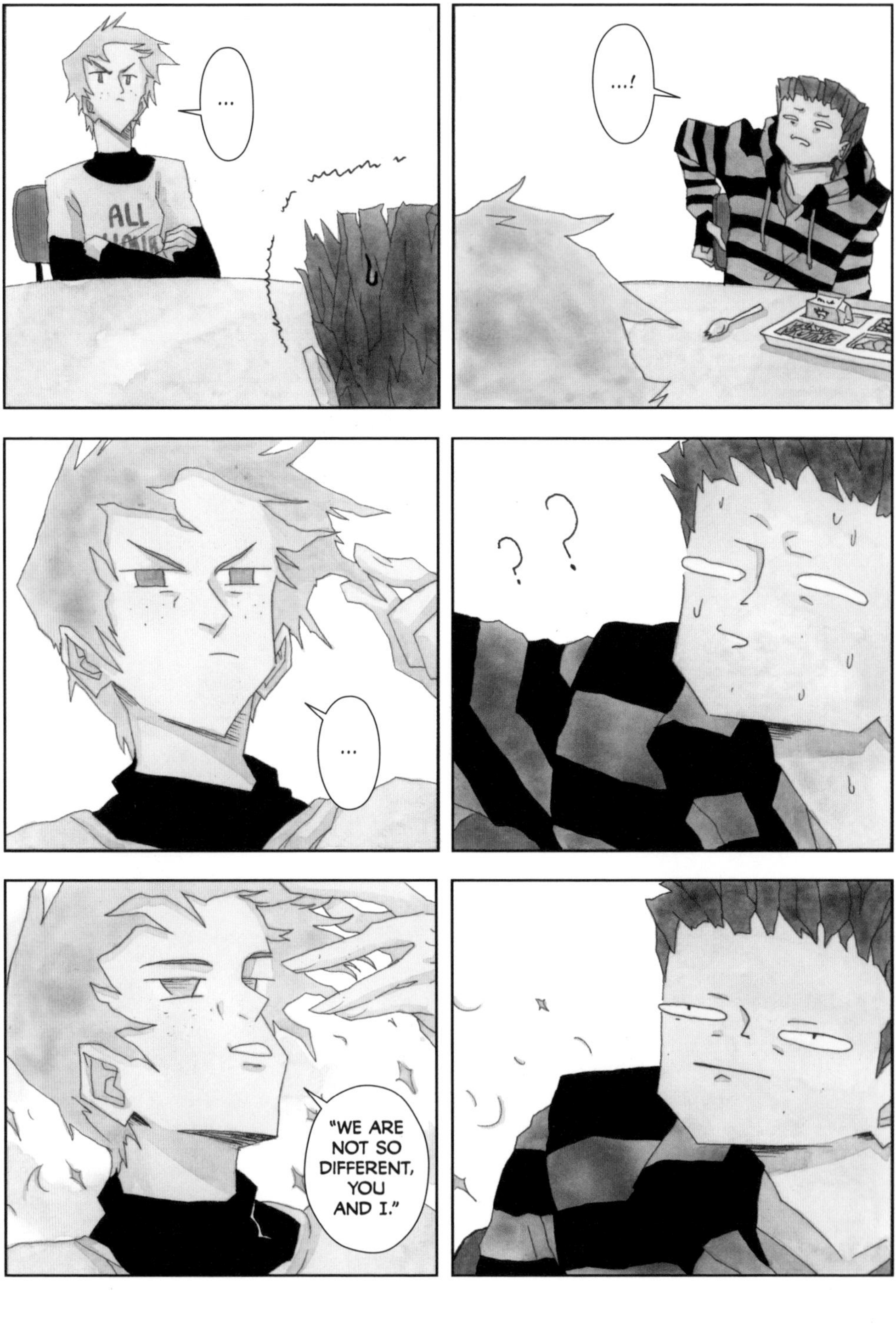
...
...!
...
"WE ARE NOT SO DIFFERENT, YOU AND I."

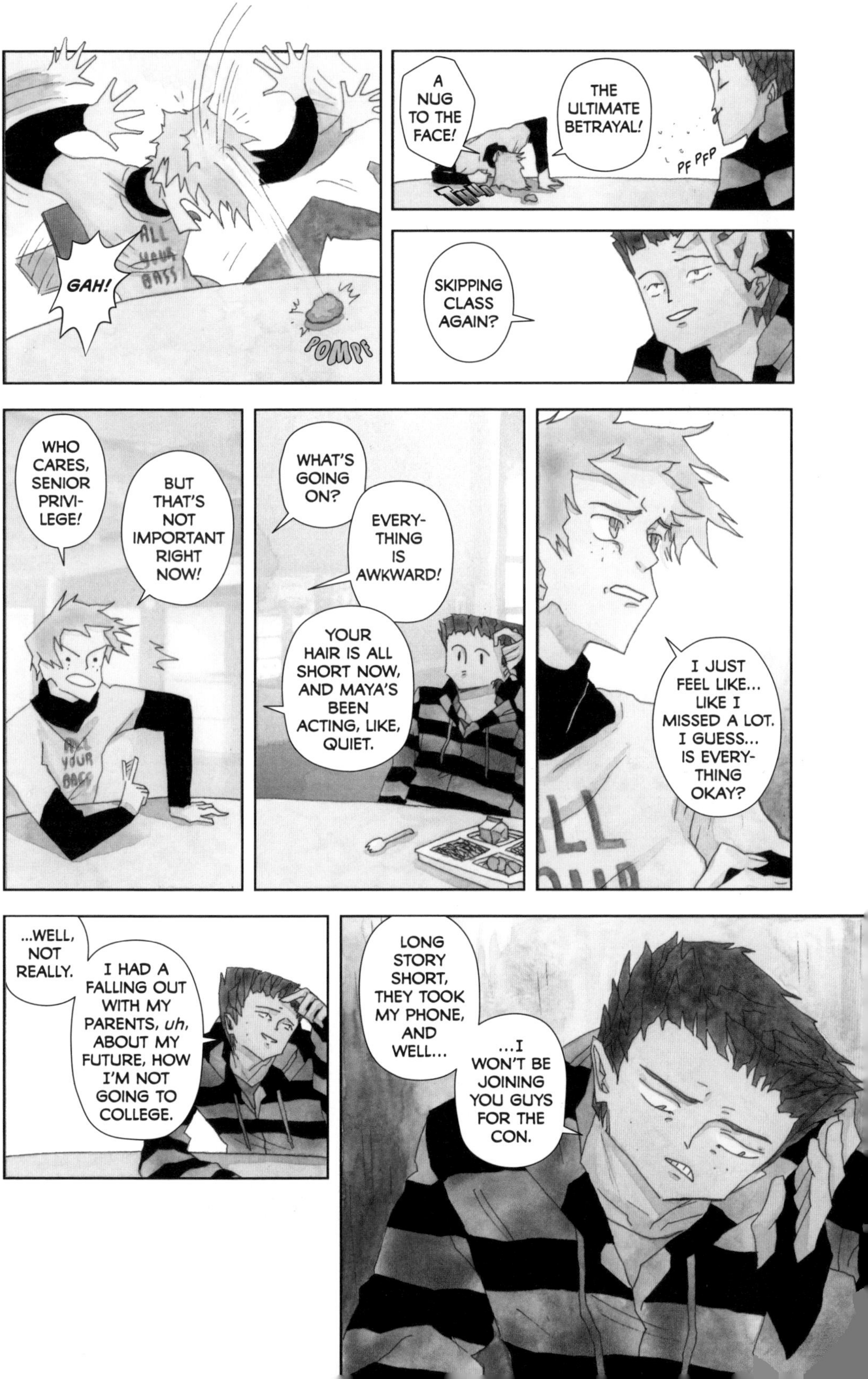
GAH!
POMPF
A NUG TO THE FACE!
THE ULTIMATE BETRAYAL!
PF PFP
SKIPPING CLASS AGAIN?
WHO CARES, SENIOR PRIVI-LEGE!
BUT THAT'S NOT IMPORTANT RIGHT NOW!
WHAT'S GOING ON?
EVERY-THING IS AWKWARD!
YOUR HAIR IS ALL SHORT NOW, AND MAYA'S BEEN ACTING, LIKE, QUIET.
I JUST FEEL LIKE... LIKE I MISSED A LOT. I GUESS... IS EVERY-THING OKAY?
...WELL, NOT REALLY.
I HAD A FALLING OUT WITH MY PARENTS, *uh*, ABOUT MY FUTURE, HOW I'M NOT GOING TO COLLEGE.
LONG STORY SHORT, THEY TOOK MY PHONE, AND WELL...
...I WON'T BE JOINING YOU GUYS FOR THE CON.

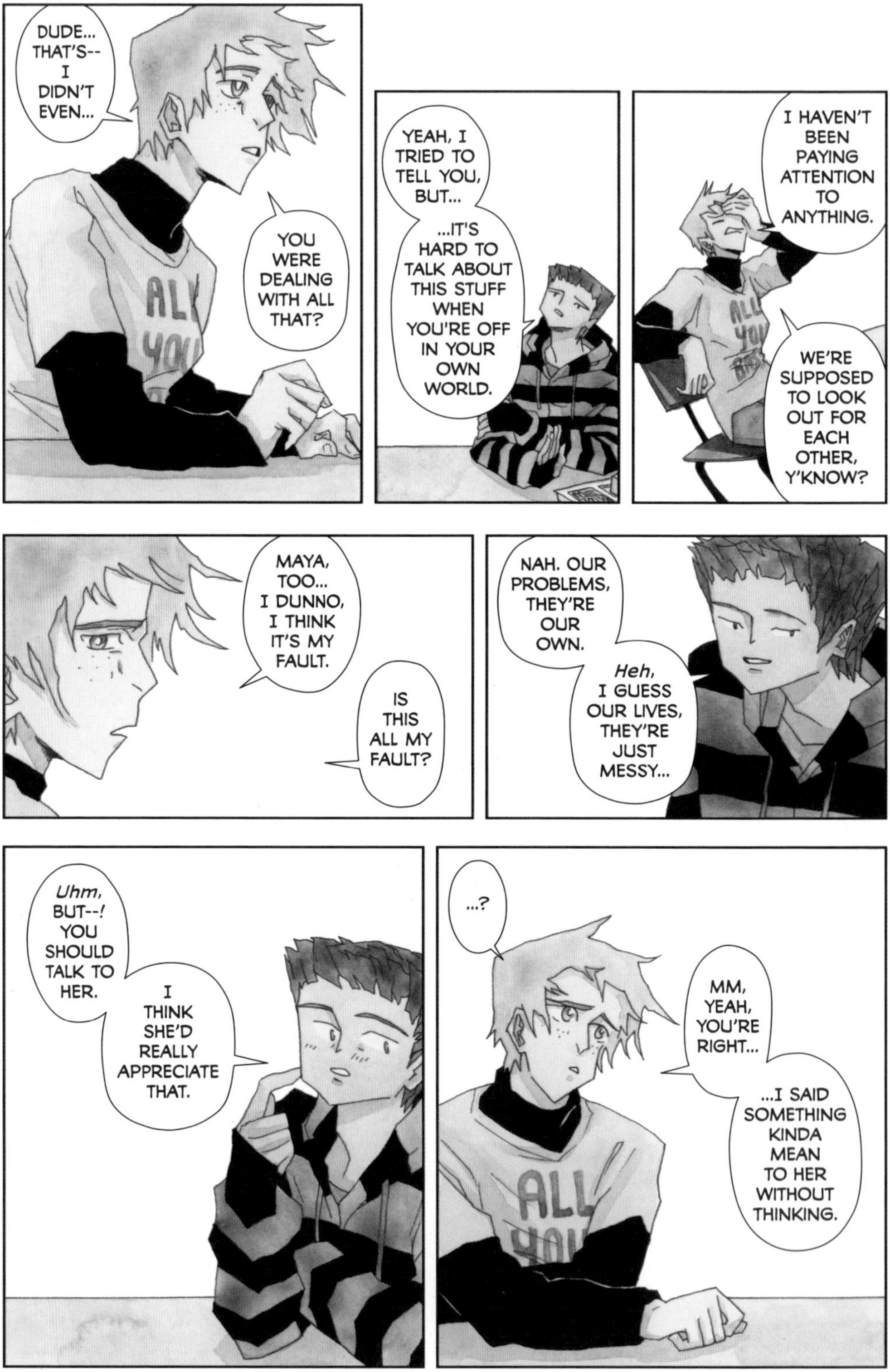
DUDE... THAT'S-- I DIDN'T EVEN...
YOU WERE DEALING WITH ALL THAT?
YEAH, I TRIED TO TELL YOU, BUT...
...IT'S HARD TO TALK ABOUT THIS STUFF WHEN YOU'RE OFF IN YOUR OWN WORLD.
I HAVEN'T BEEN PAYING ATTENTION TO ANYTHING.
WE'RE SUPPOSED TO LOOK OUT FOR EACH OTHER, Y'KNOW?
MAYA, TOO... I DUNNO, I THINK IT'S MY FAULT.
IS THIS ALL MY FAULT?
NAH. OUR PROBLEMS, THEY'RE OUR OWN.
Heh, I GUESS OUR LIVES, THEY'RE JUST MESSY...
Uhm, BUT--! YOU SHOULD TALK TO HER.
I THINK SHE'D REALLY APPRECIATE THAT.
...?
MM, YEAH, YOU'RE RIGHT...
...I SAID SOMETHING KINDA MEAN TO HER WITHOUT THINKING.

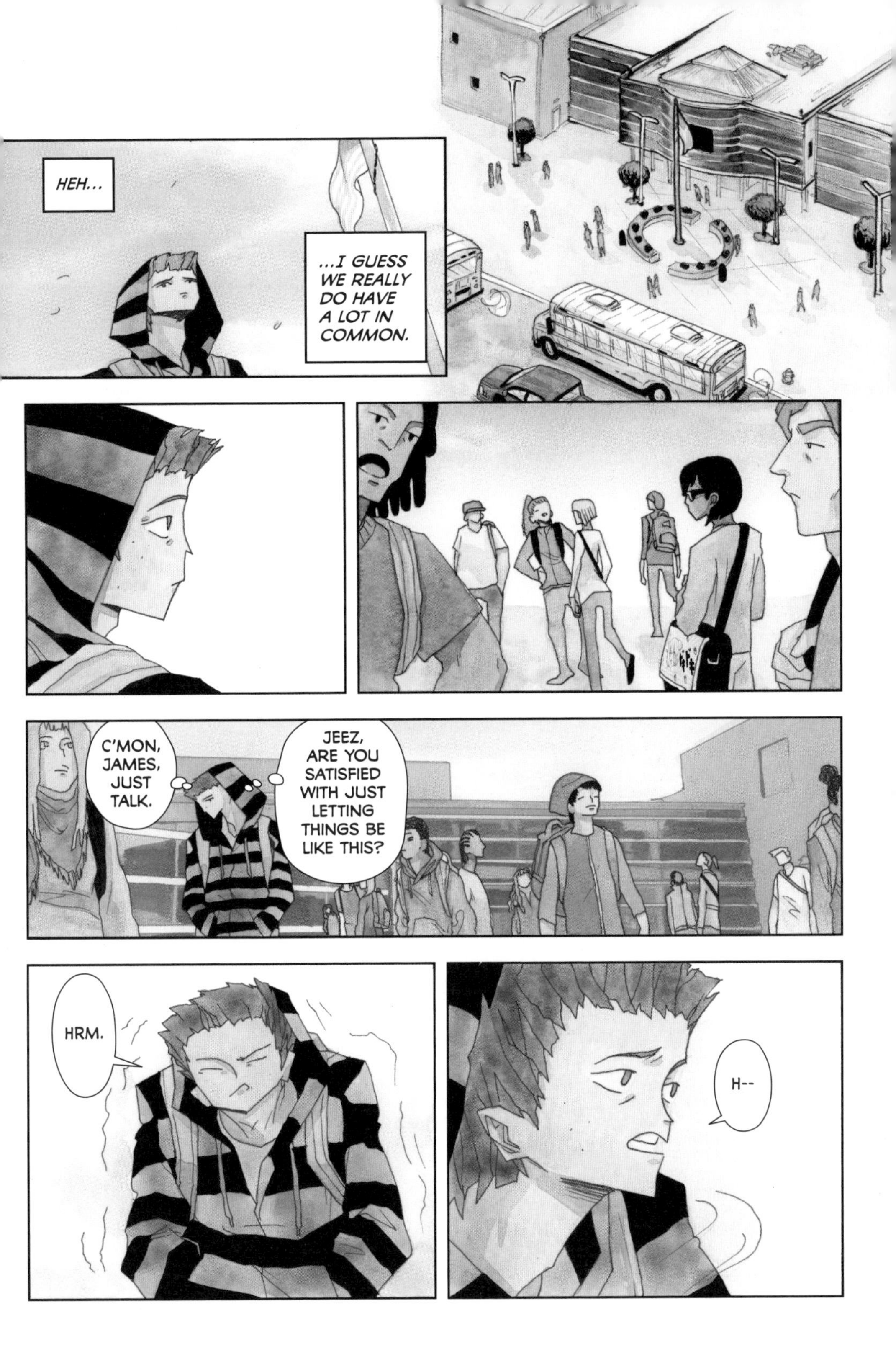
HEH...
...I GUESS WE REALLY DO HAVE A LOT IN COMMON.
C'MON, JAMES, JUST TALK.
JEEZ, ARE YOU SATISFIED WITH JUST LETTING THINGS BE LIKE THIS?
HRM.
H--

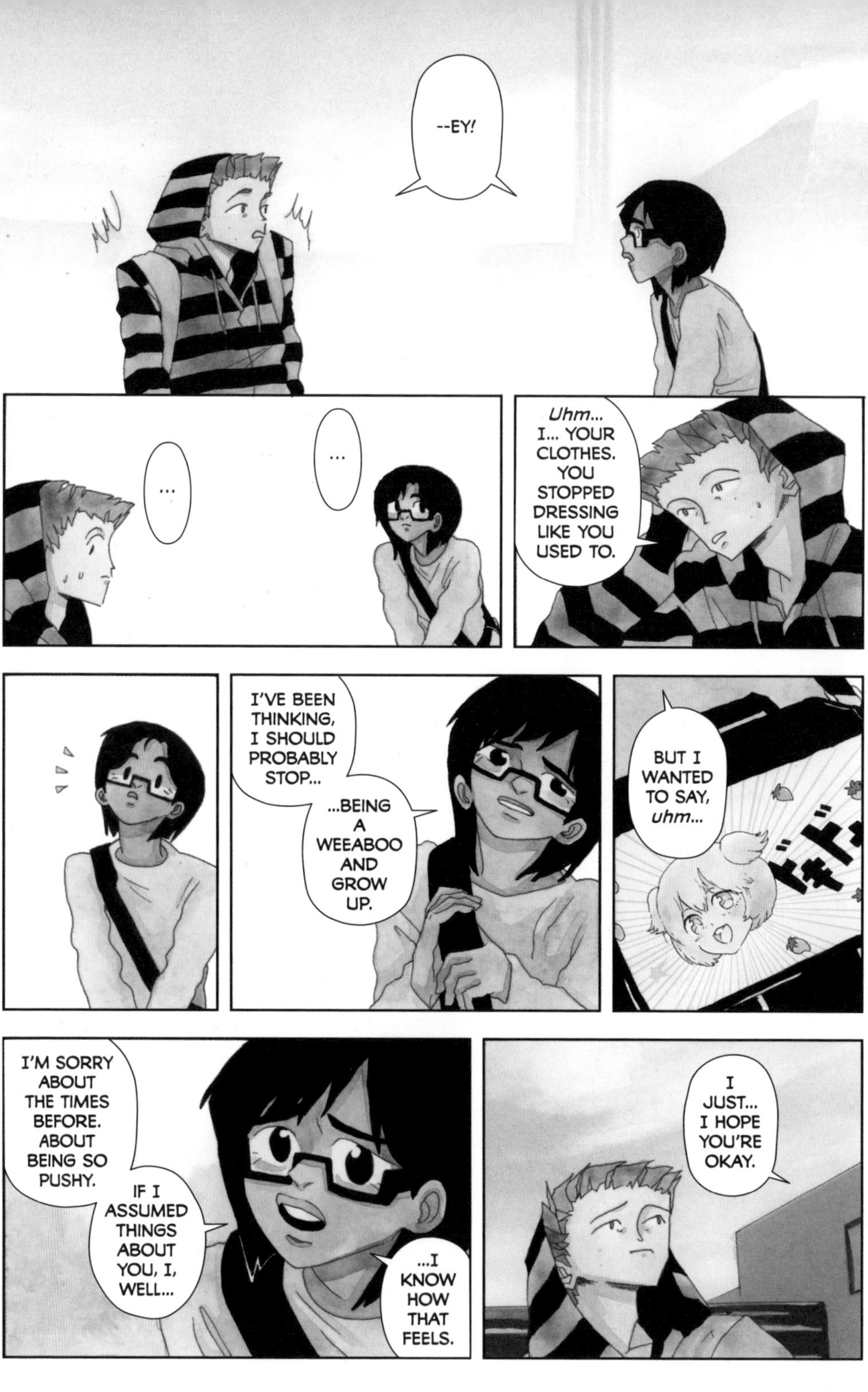
--EY!
...
...
Uhm... I... YOUR CLOTHES. YOU STOPPED DRESSING LIKE YOU USED TO.
I'VE BEEN THINKING, I SHOULD PROBABLY STOP...
...BEING A WEEABOO AND GROW UP.
BUT I WANTED TO SAY, *uhm*...
I'M SORRY ABOUT THE TIMES BEFORE. ABOUT BEING SO PUSHY.
IF I ASSUMED THINGS ABOUT YOU, I, WELL...
...I KNOW HOW THAT FEELS.
I JUST... I HOPE YOU'RE OKAY.

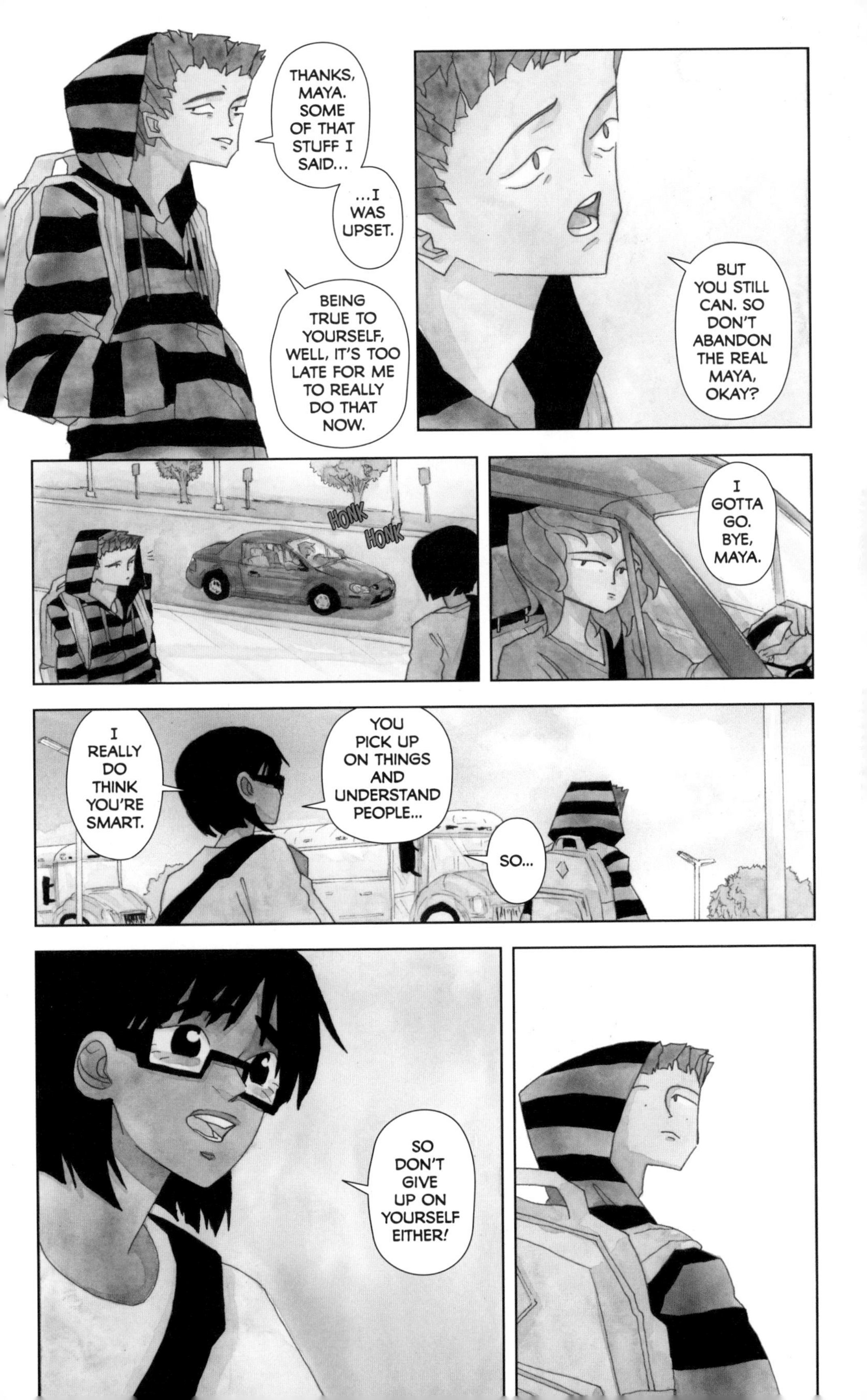
THANKS, MAYA. SOME OF THAT STUFF I SAID...
...I WAS UPSET.
BEING TRUE TO YOURSELF, WELL, IT'S TOO LATE FOR ME TO REALLY DO THAT NOW.
BUT YOU STILL CAN. SO DON'T ABANDON THE REAL MAYA, OKAY?
HONK
HONK
I GOTTA GO. BYE, MAYA.
I REALLY DO THINK YOU'RE SMART.
YOU PICK UP ON THINGS AND UNDERSTAND PEOPLE...
SO...
SO DON'T GIVE UP ON YOURSELF EITHER!

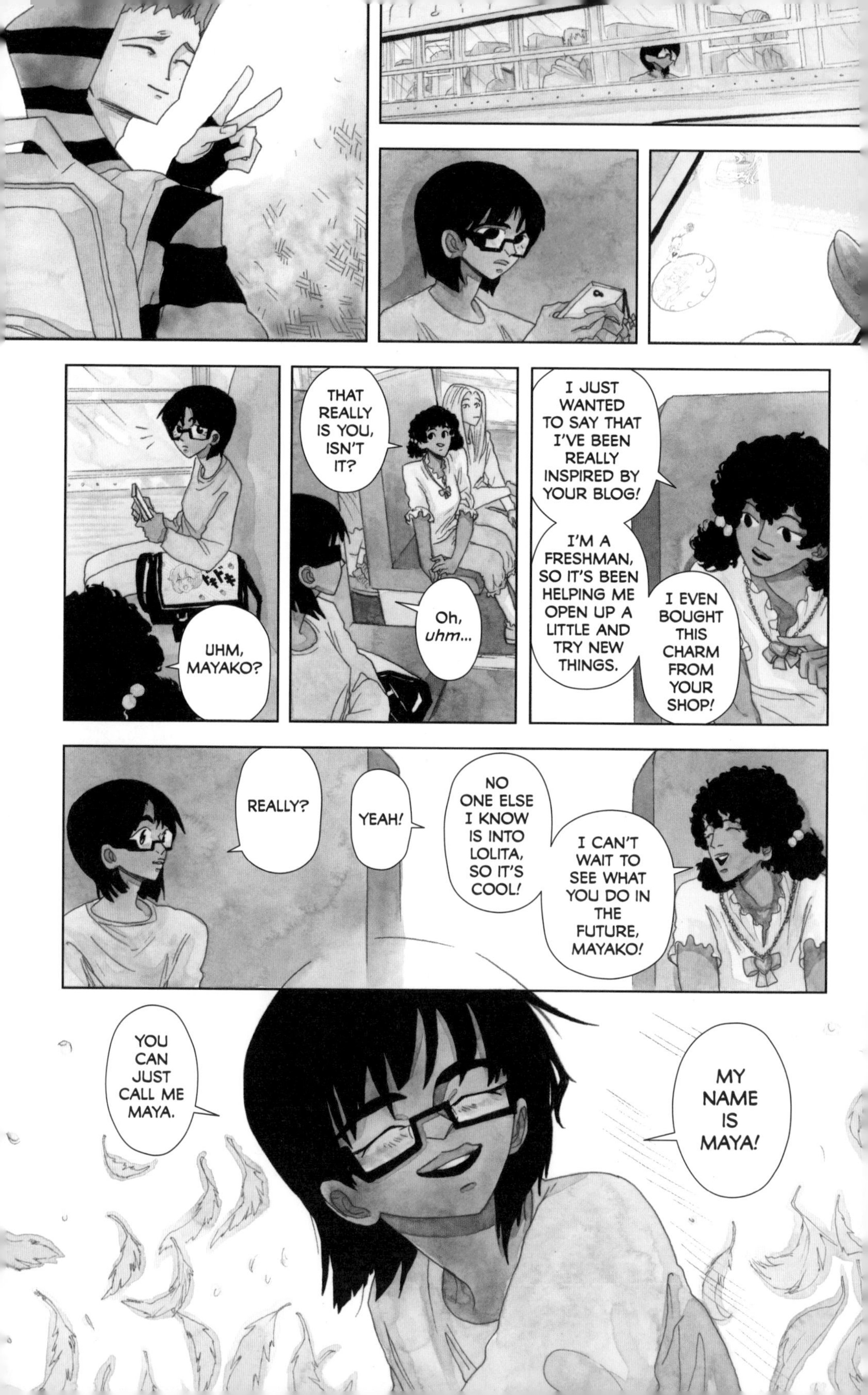
UHM, MAYAKO?
THAT REALLY IS YOU, ISN'T IT?
Oh, *uhm*...
I JUST WANTED TO SAY THAT I'VE BEEN REALLY INSPIRED BY YOUR BLOG!
I'M A FRESHMAN, SO IT'S BEEN HELPING ME OPEN UP A LITTLE AND TRY NEW THINGS.
I EVEN BOUGHT THIS CHARM FROM YOUR SHOP!
REALLY?
YEAH!
NO ONE ELSE I KNOW IS INTO LOLITA, SO IT'S COOL!
I CAN'T WAIT TO SEE WHAT YOU DO IN THE FUTURE, MAYAKO!
MY NAME IS MAYA!
YOU CAN JUST CALL ME MAYA.

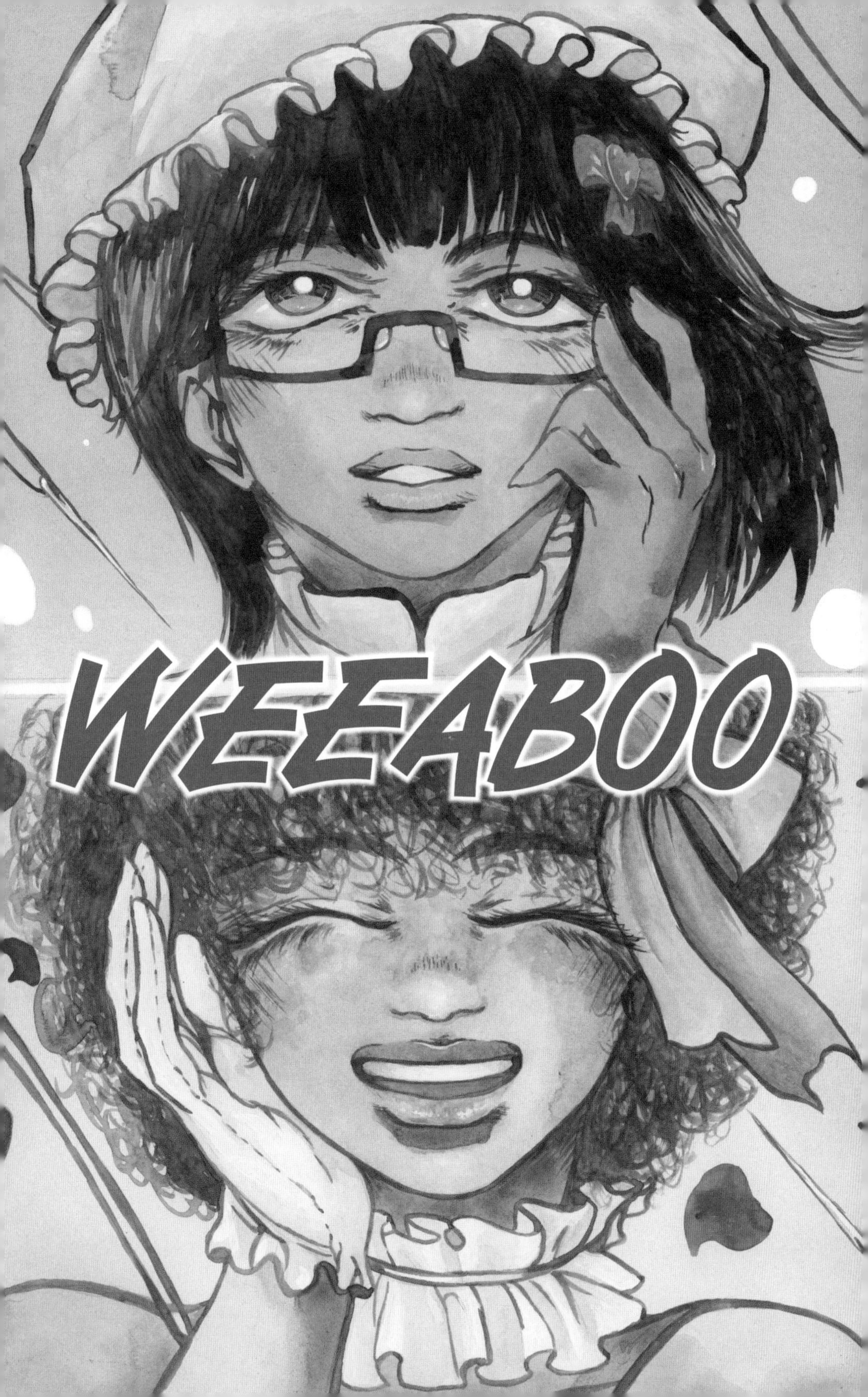
WEEABOO

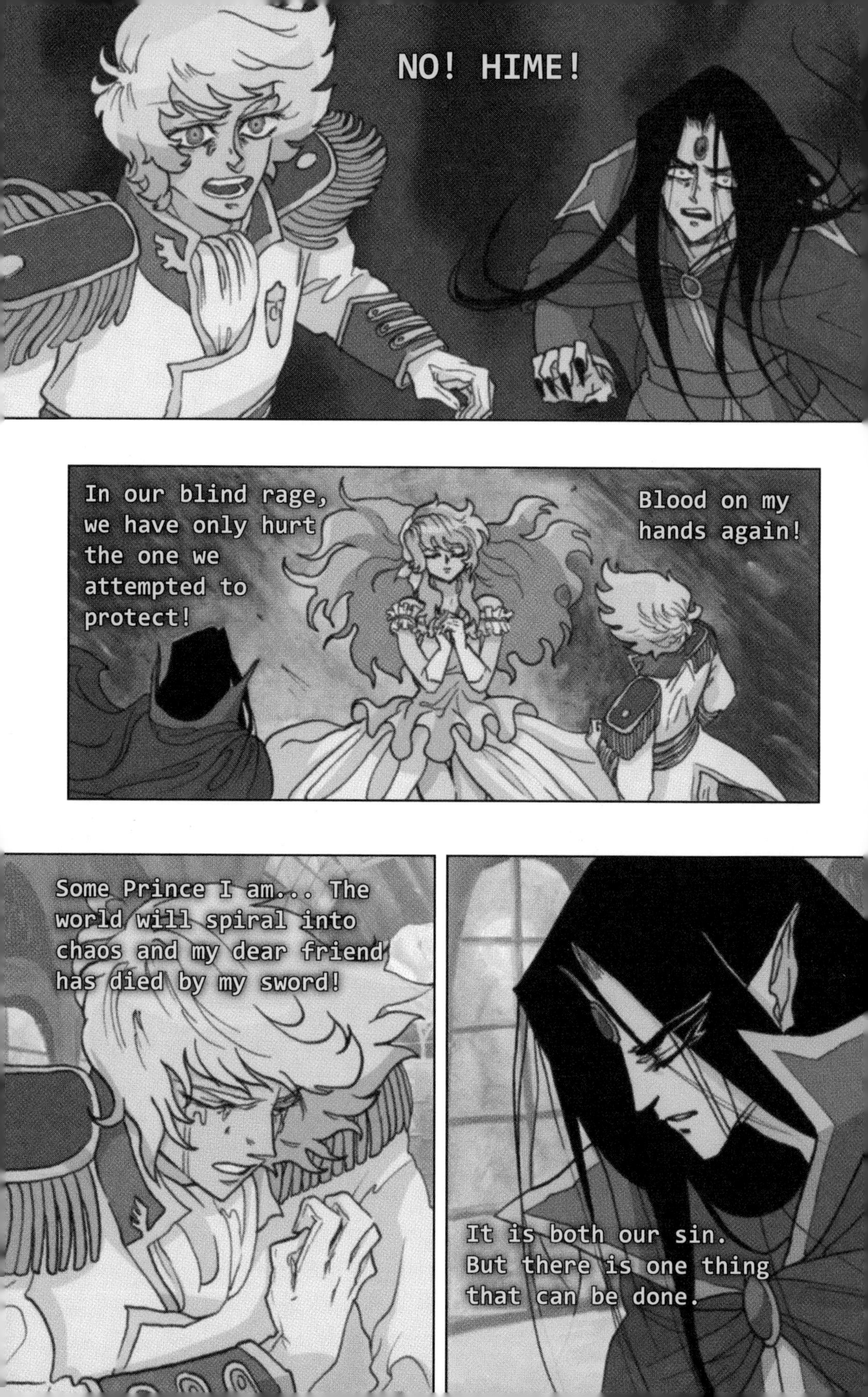
NO! HIME!
In our blind rage, we have only hurt the one we attempted to protect!
Blood on my hands again!
Some Prince I am... The world will spiral into chaos and my dear friend has died by my sword!
It is both our sin. But there is one thing that can be done.

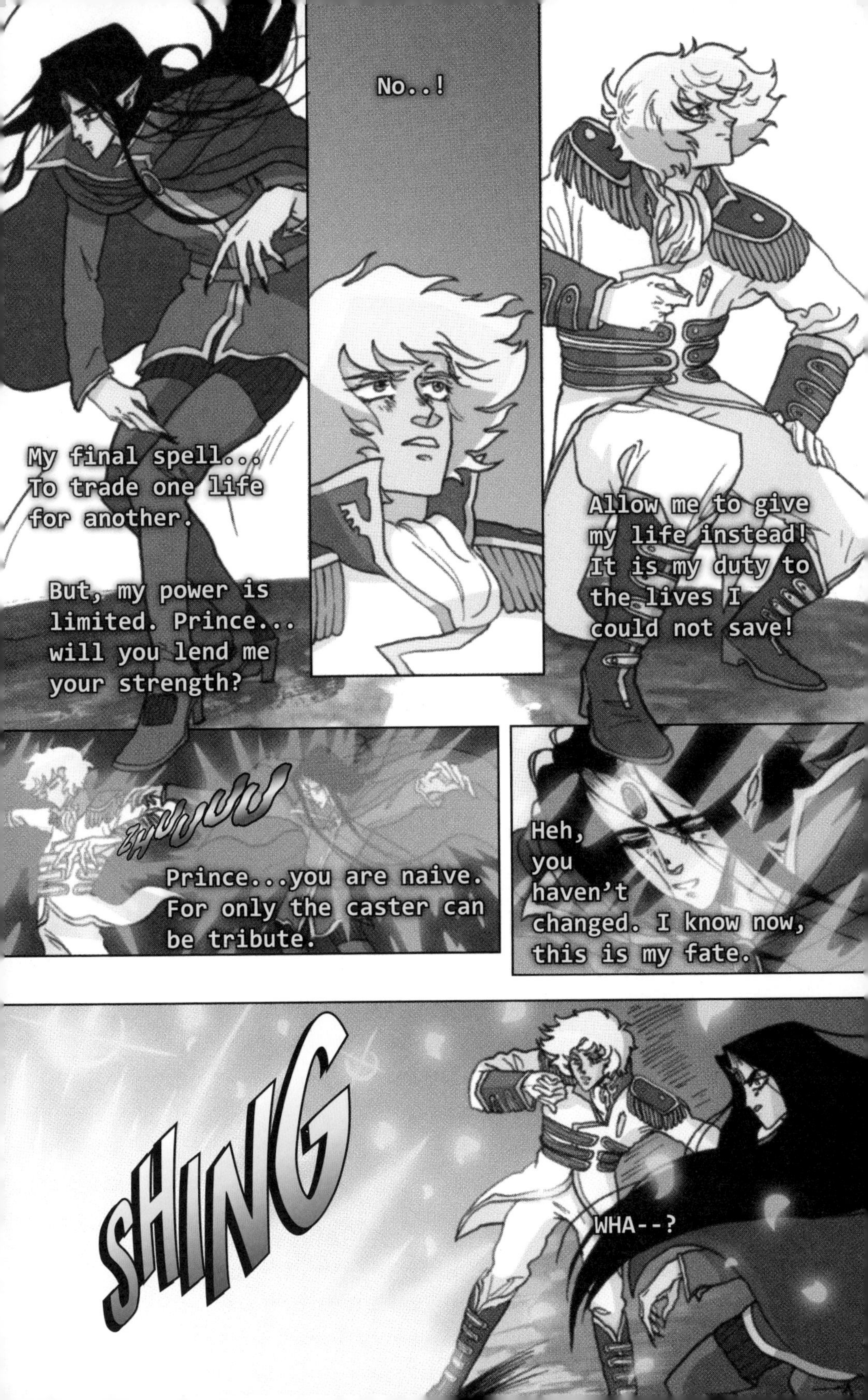
My final spell... To trade one life for another.
But, my power is limited. Prince... will you lend me your strength?
No..!
Allow me to give my life instead! It is my duty to the lives I could not save!
ZHUUUU
Prince...you are naive. For only the caster can be tribute.
Heh, you haven't changed. I know now, this is my fate.
SHING
WHA--?

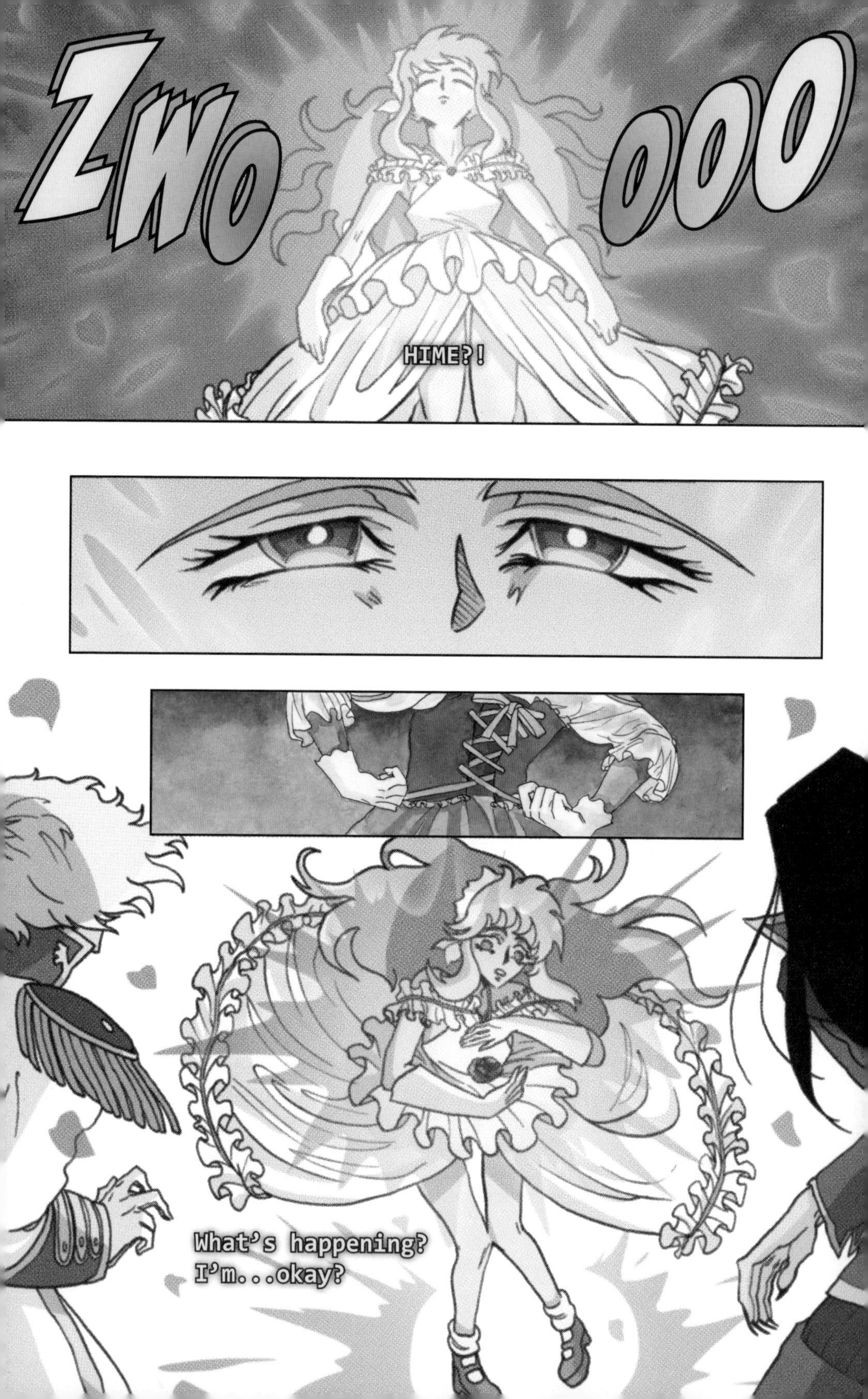
ZWOOOO
HIME?!
What's happening?
I'm...okay?

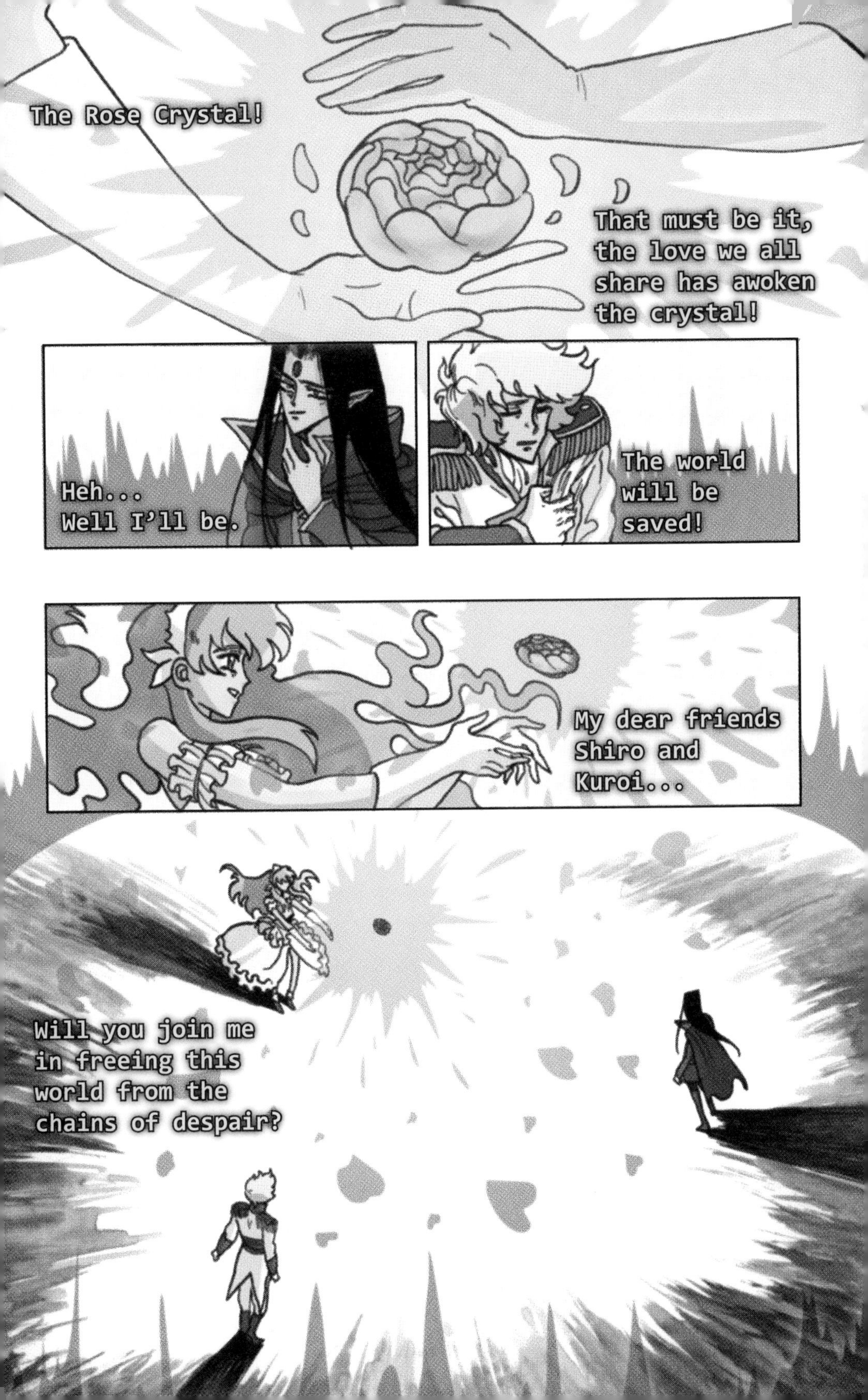
The Rose Crystal!
That must be it, the love we all share has awoken the crystal!
Heh... Well I'll be.
The world will be saved!
My dear friends Shiro and Kuroi...
Will you join me in freeing this world from the chains of despair?

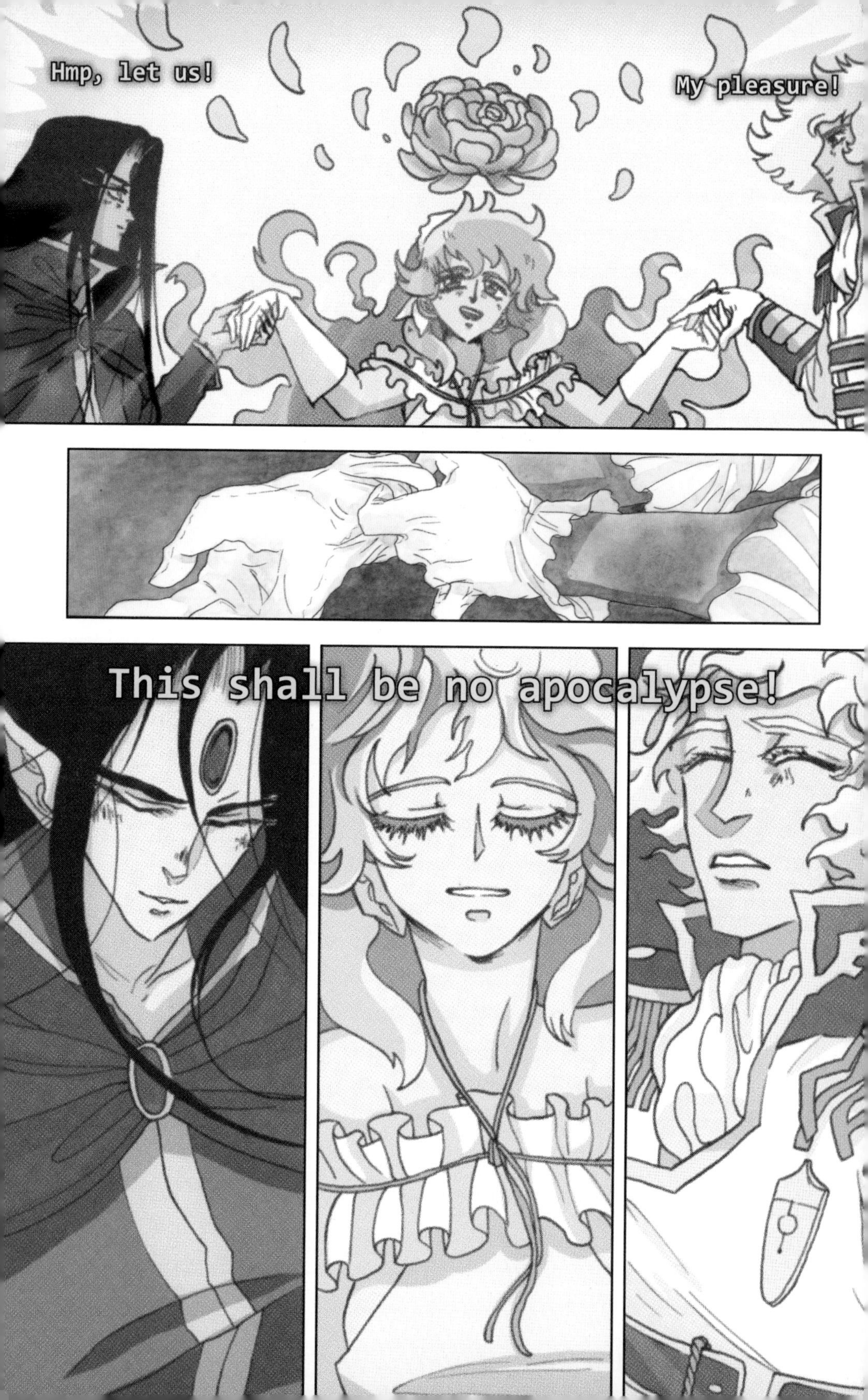
Hmp, let us!
My pleasure!
This shall be no apocalypse!

It's been an adventure, hasn't it? With the world finally at peace, we've all gone our separate ways.

Prince Shiro has returned to the palace, now with the weight of the world off his shoulders.

DAKA DAN

DAKA DAN

Now a respected scholar, Kuroi found a place where he truly belongs.

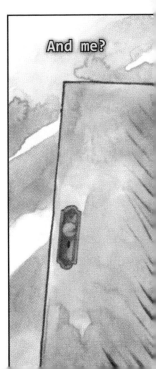

And me?

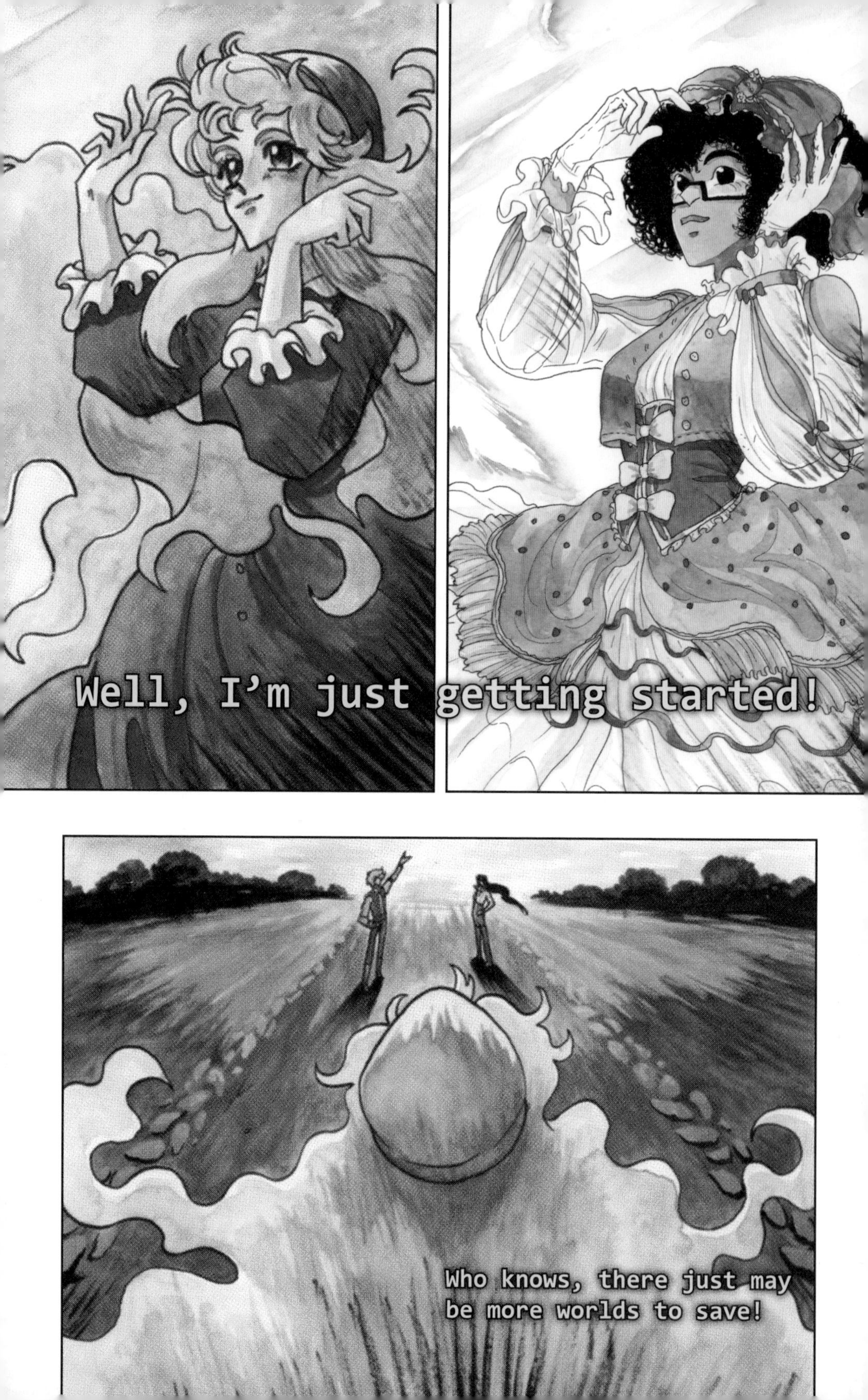

Well, I'm just getting started!
Who knows, there just may be more worlds to save!

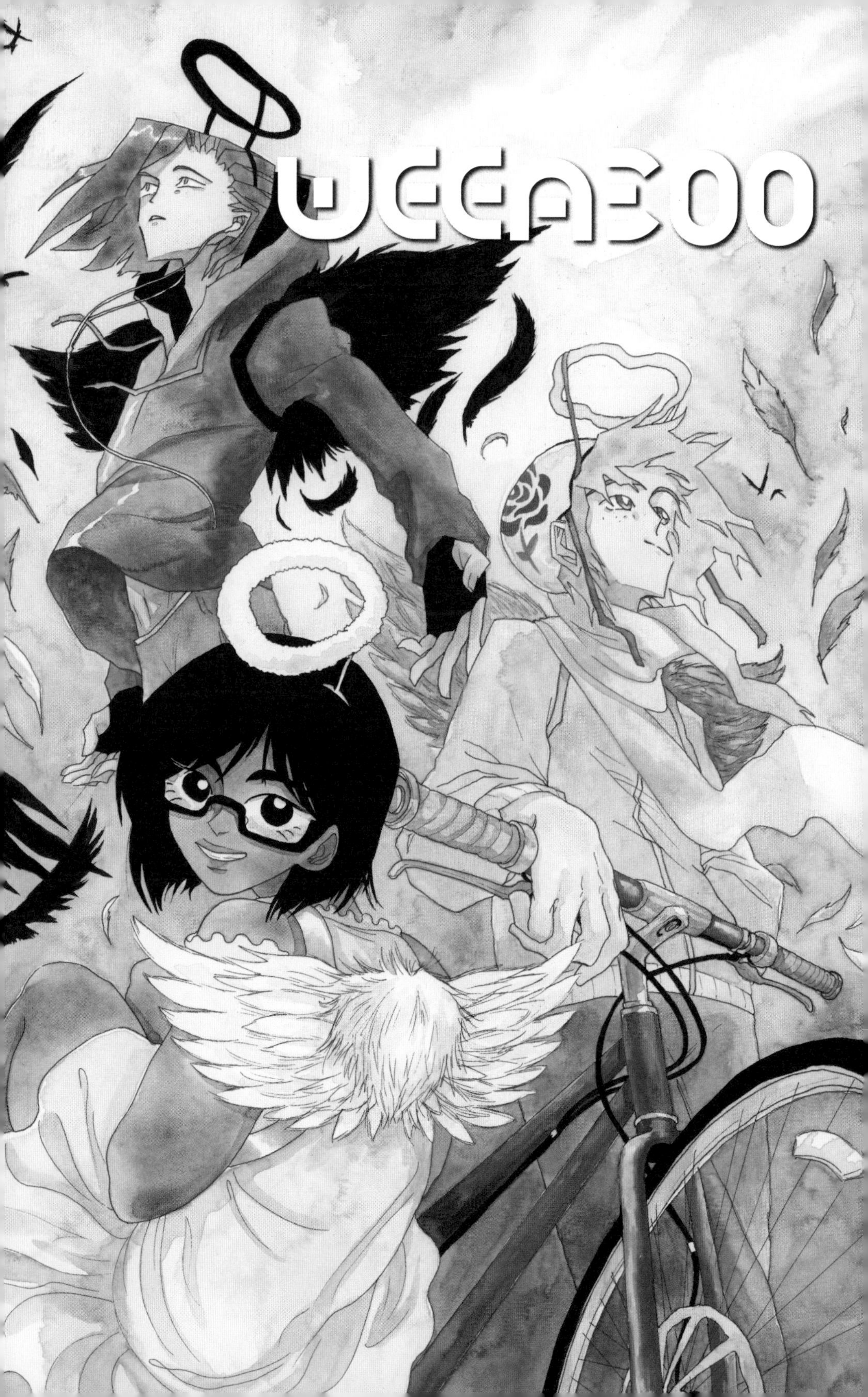
WEEABOO

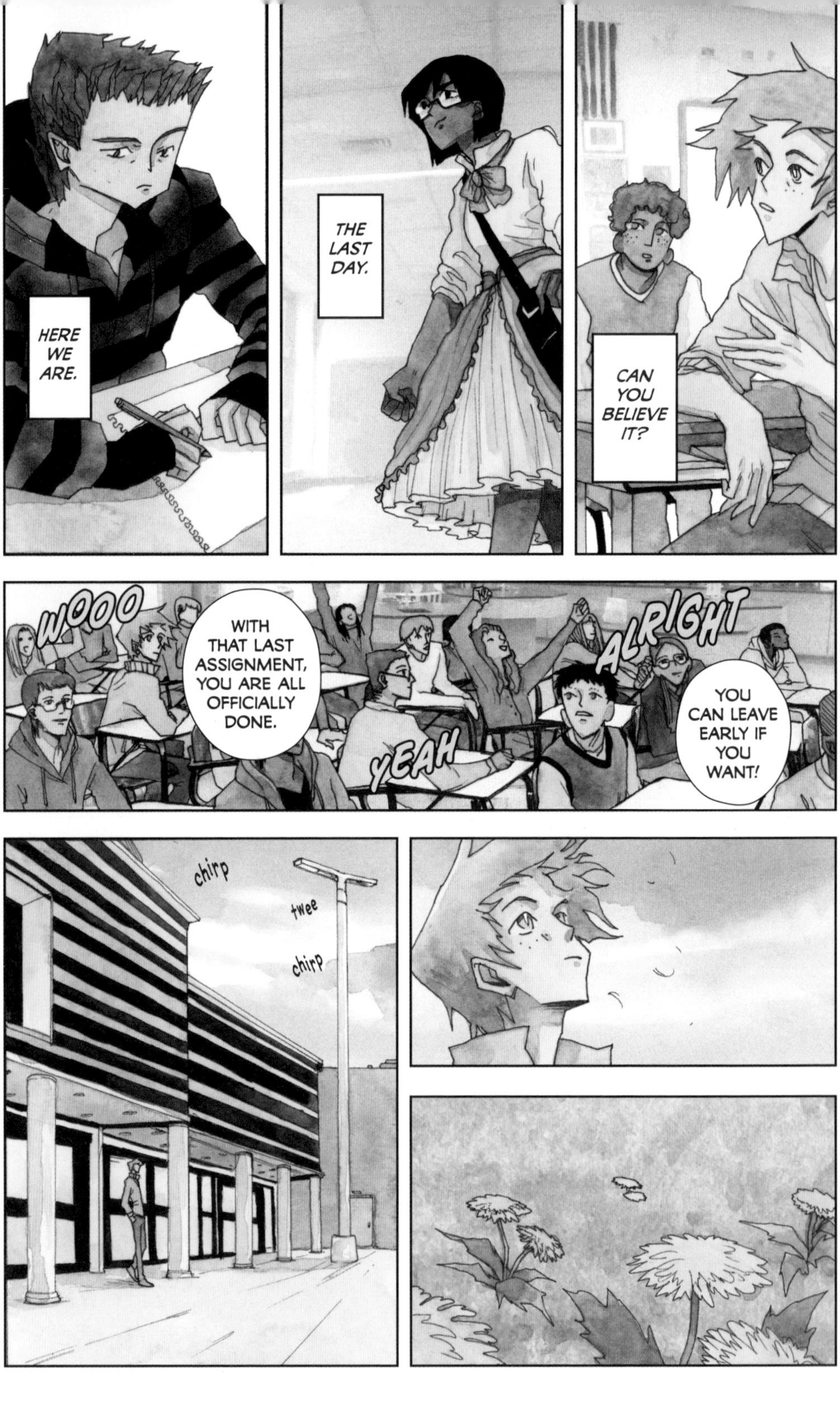
HERE WE ARE.
THE LAST DAY.
CAN YOU BELIEVE IT?
WOOO
WITH THAT LAST ASSIGNMENT, YOU ARE ALL OFFICIALLY DONE.
ALRIGHT
YEAH
YOU CAN LEAVE EARLY IF YOU WANT!
chirp
twee
chirp

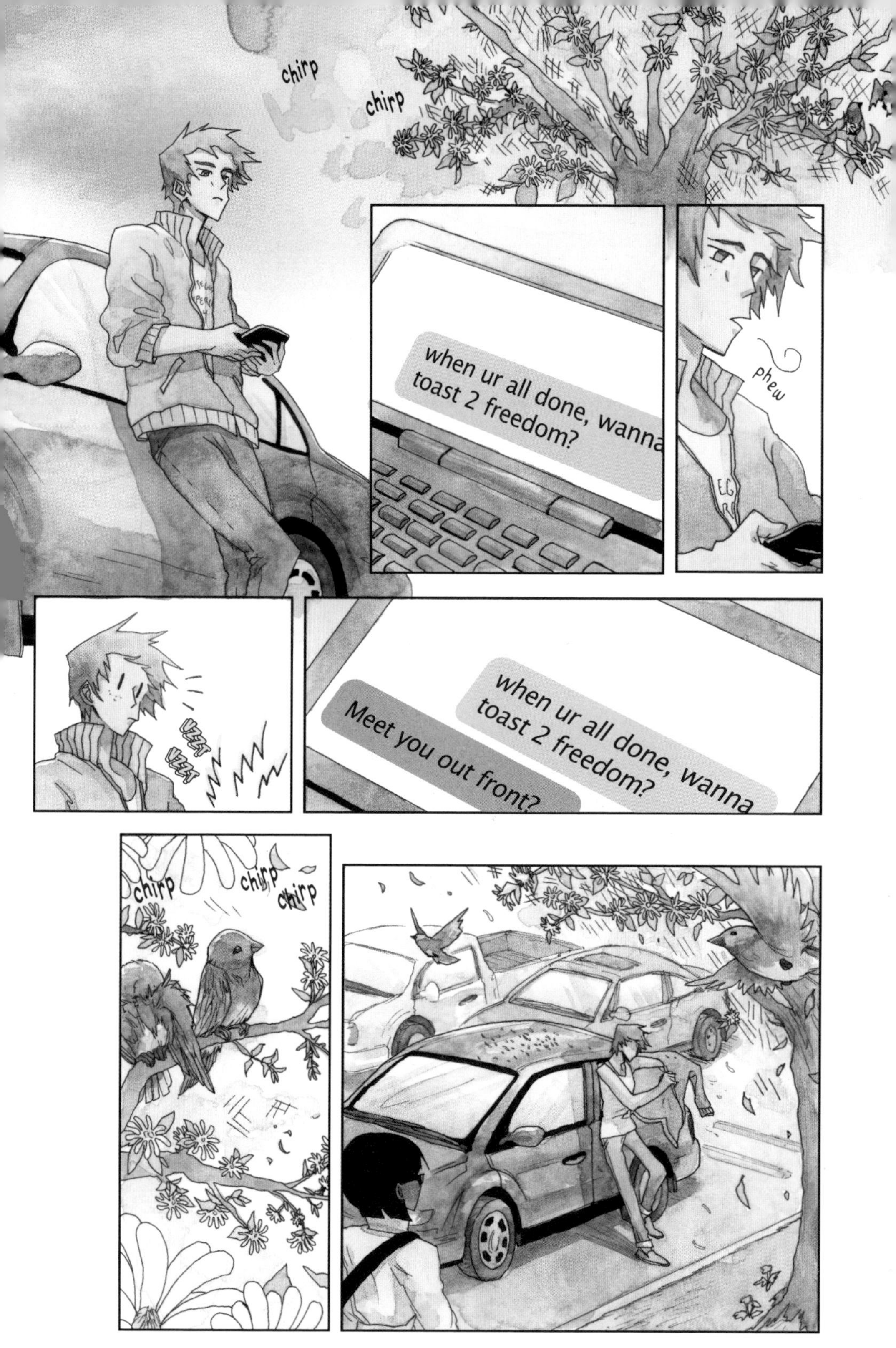
chirp
chirp
when ur all done, wanna toast 2 freedom?
phew
VZZT
VZZT
when ur all done, wanna toast 2 freedom?
Meet you out front?
chirp
chirp
chirp

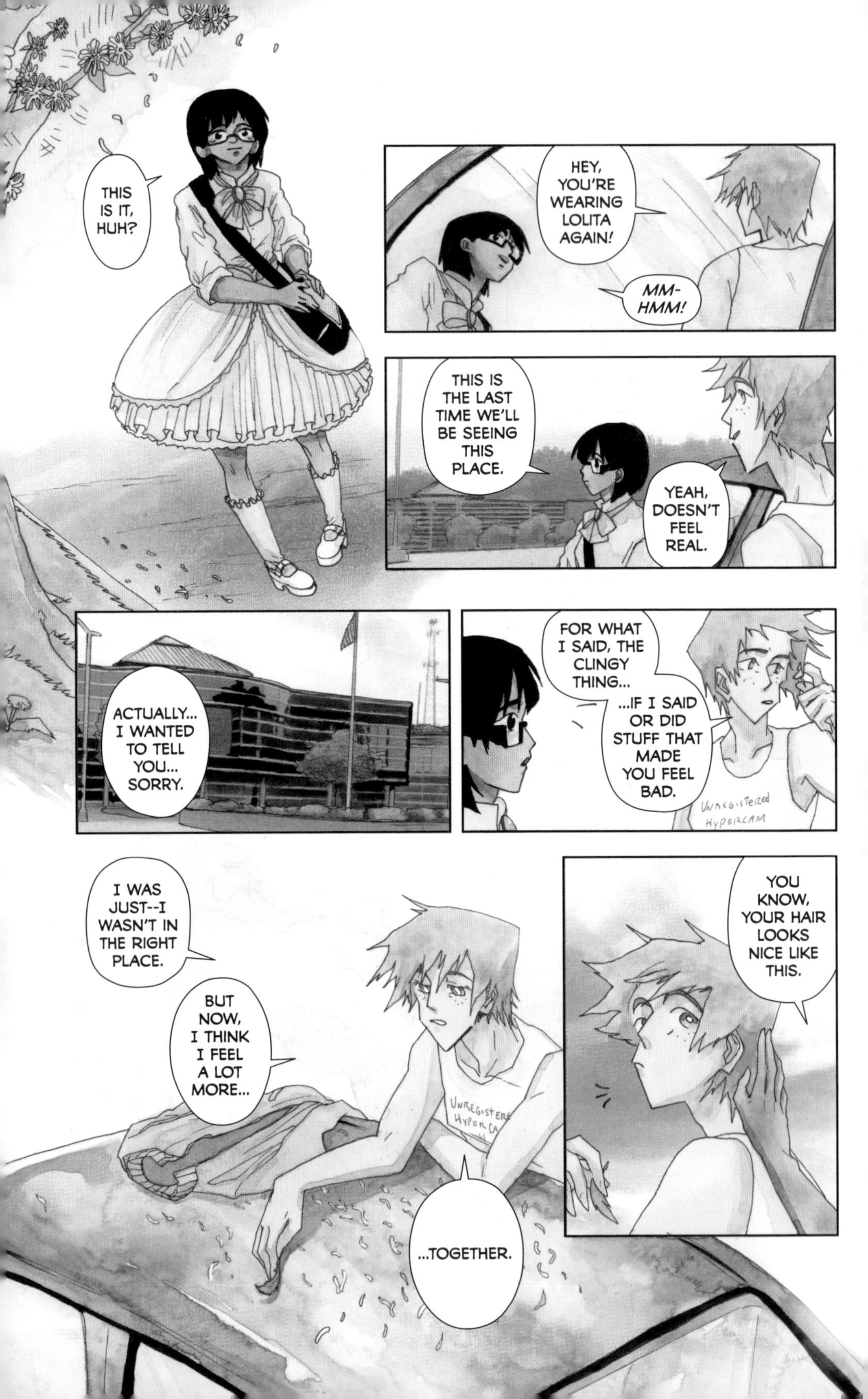
THIS IS IT, HUH?
HEY, YOU'RE WEARING LOLITA AGAIN!
MM-HMM!
THIS IS THE LAST TIME WE'LL BE SEEING THIS PLACE.
YEAH, DOESN'T FEEL REAL.
ACTUALLY... I WANTED TO TELL YOU... SORRY.
FOR WHAT I SAID, THE CLINGY THING...
...IF I SAID OR DID STUFF THAT MADE YOU FEEL BAD.
UNREGISTERED HYPERCAM
I WAS JUST--I WASN'T IN THE RIGHT PLACE.
BUT NOW, I THINK I FEEL A LOT MORE...
...TOGETHER.
YOU KNOW, YOUR HAIR LOOKS NICE LIKE THIS.

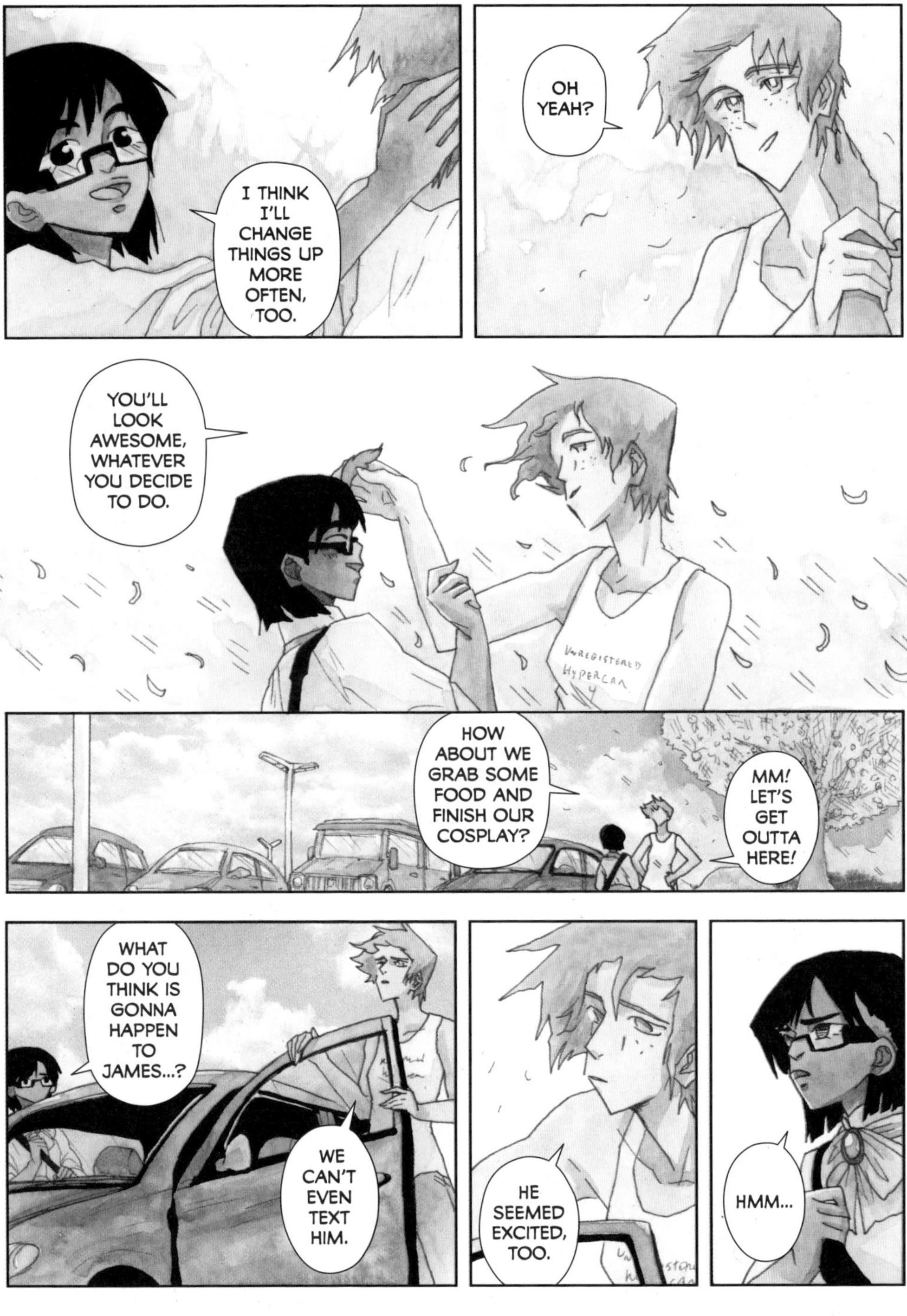
I THINK I'LL CHANGE THINGS UP MORE OFTEN, TOO.
OH YEAH?
YOU'LL LOOK AWESOME, WHATEVER YOU DECIDE TO DO.
UNREGISTERED HYPERCAR
HOW ABOUT WE GRAB SOME FOOD AND FINISH OUR COSPLAY?
MM! LET'S GET OUTTA HERE!
WHAT DO YOU THINK IS GONNA HAPPEN TO JAMES...?
WE CAN'T EVEN TEXT HIM.
HE SEEMED EXCITED, TOO.
HMM...

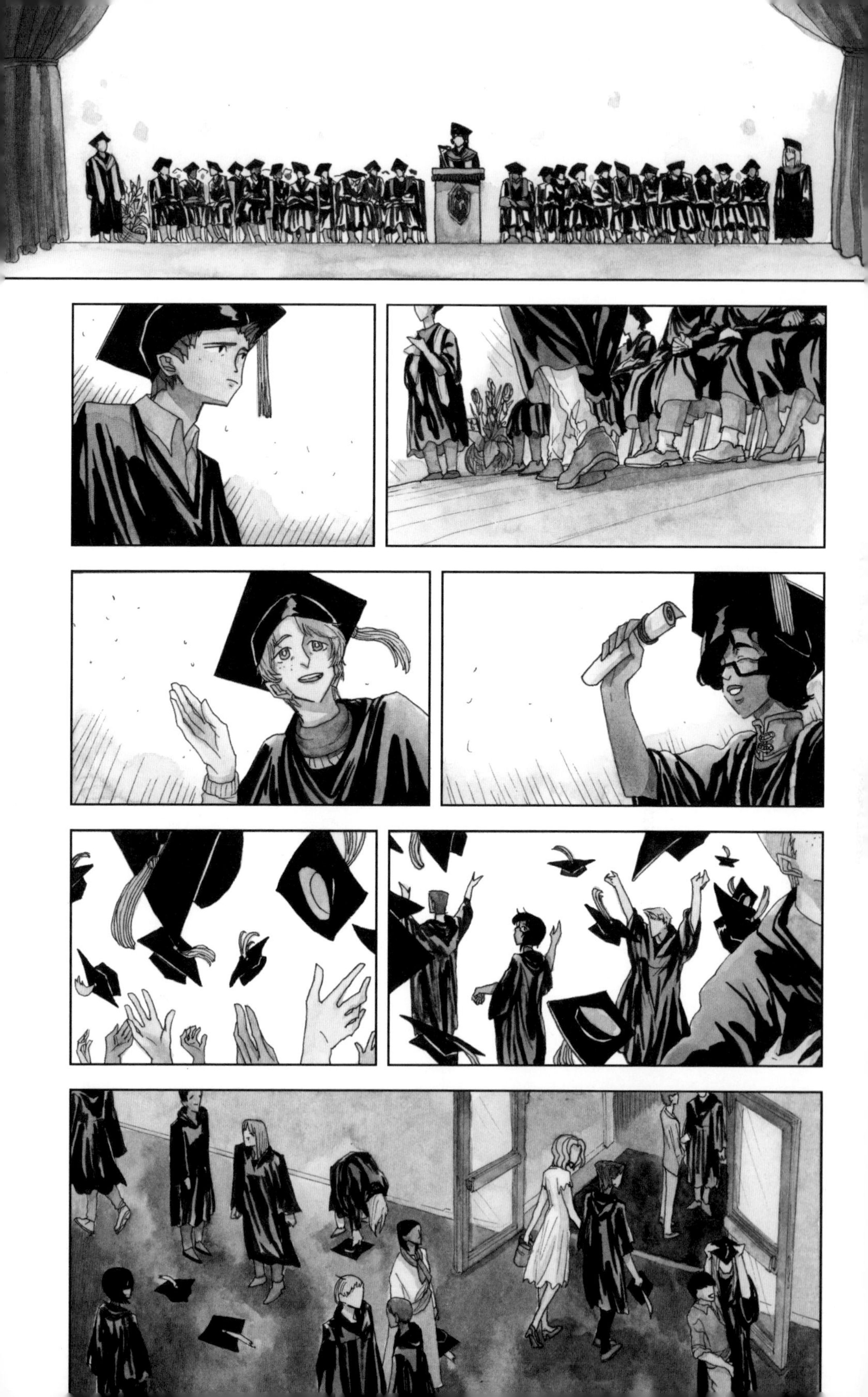

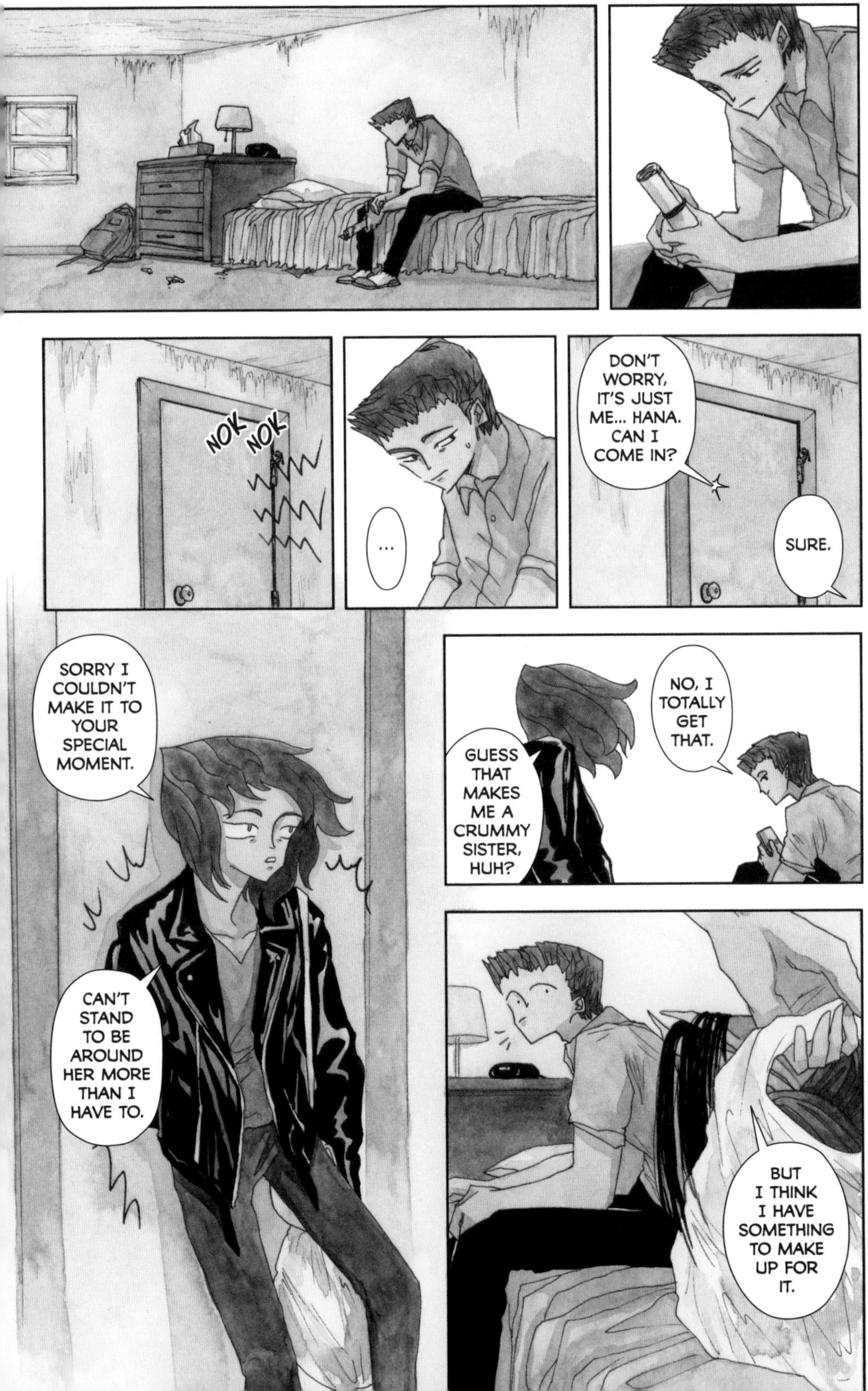
NOK NOK
...
DON'T WORRY, IT'S JUST ME... HANA. CAN I COME IN?
SURE.
SORRY I COULDN'T MAKE IT TO YOUR SPECIAL MOMENT.
CAN'T STAND TO BE AROUND HER MORE THAN I HAVE TO.
GUESS THAT MAKES ME A CRUMMY SISTER, HUH?
NO, I TOTALLY GET THAT.
BUT I THINK I HAVE SOMETHING TO MAKE UP FOR IT.

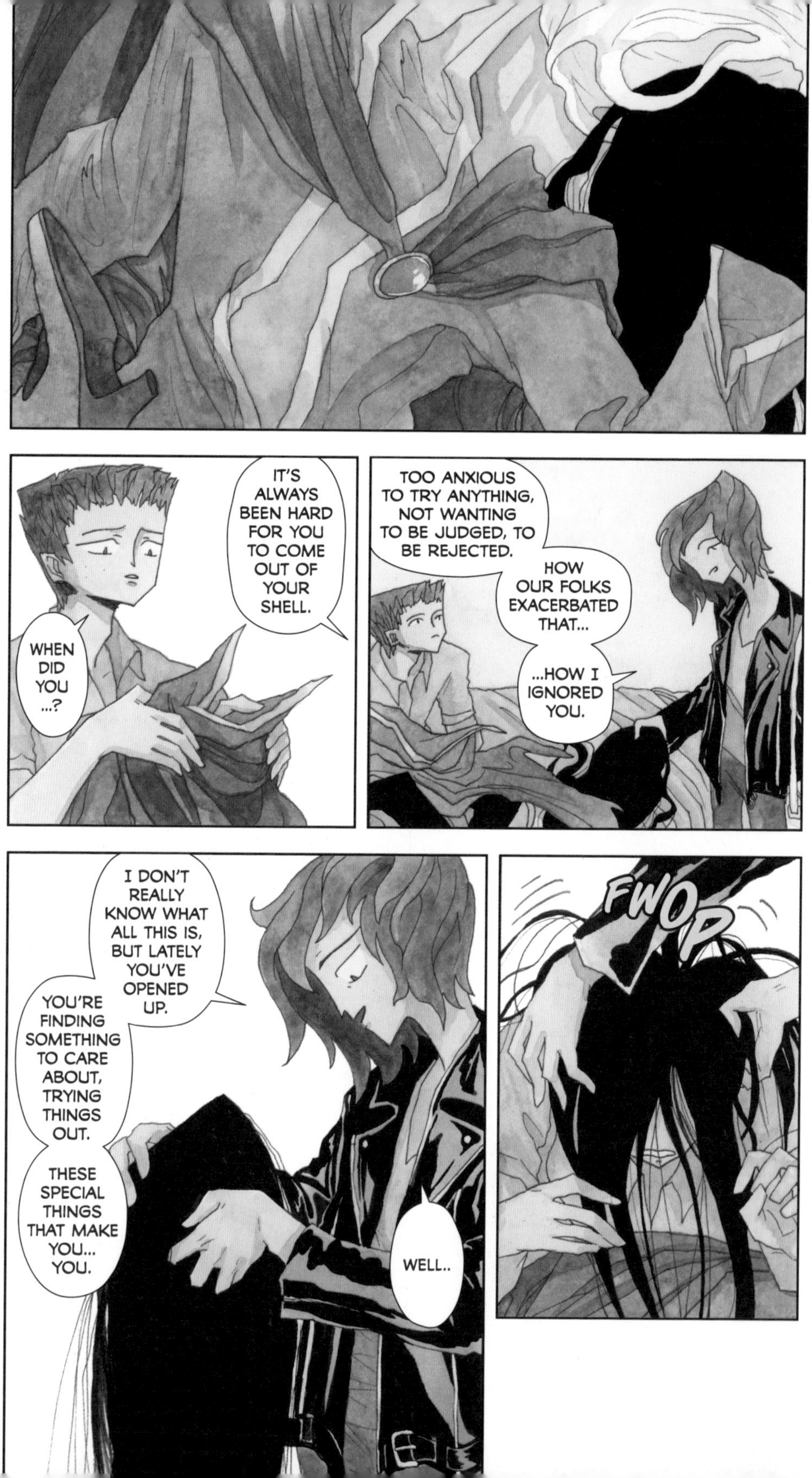
IT'S ALWAYS BEEN HARD FOR YOU TO COME OUT OF YOUR SHELL.
WHEN DID YOU ...?
TOO ANXIOUS TO TRY ANYTHING, NOT WANTING TO BE JUDGED, TO BE REJECTED.
HOW OUR FOLKS EXACERBATED THAT...
...HOW I IGNORED YOU.
I DON'T REALLY KNOW WHAT ALL THIS IS, BUT LATELY YOU'VE OPENED UP.
YOU'RE FINDING SOMETHING TO CARE ABOUT, TRYING THINGS OUT.
THESE SPECIAL THINGS THAT MAKE YOU... YOU.
WELL..
FWOP

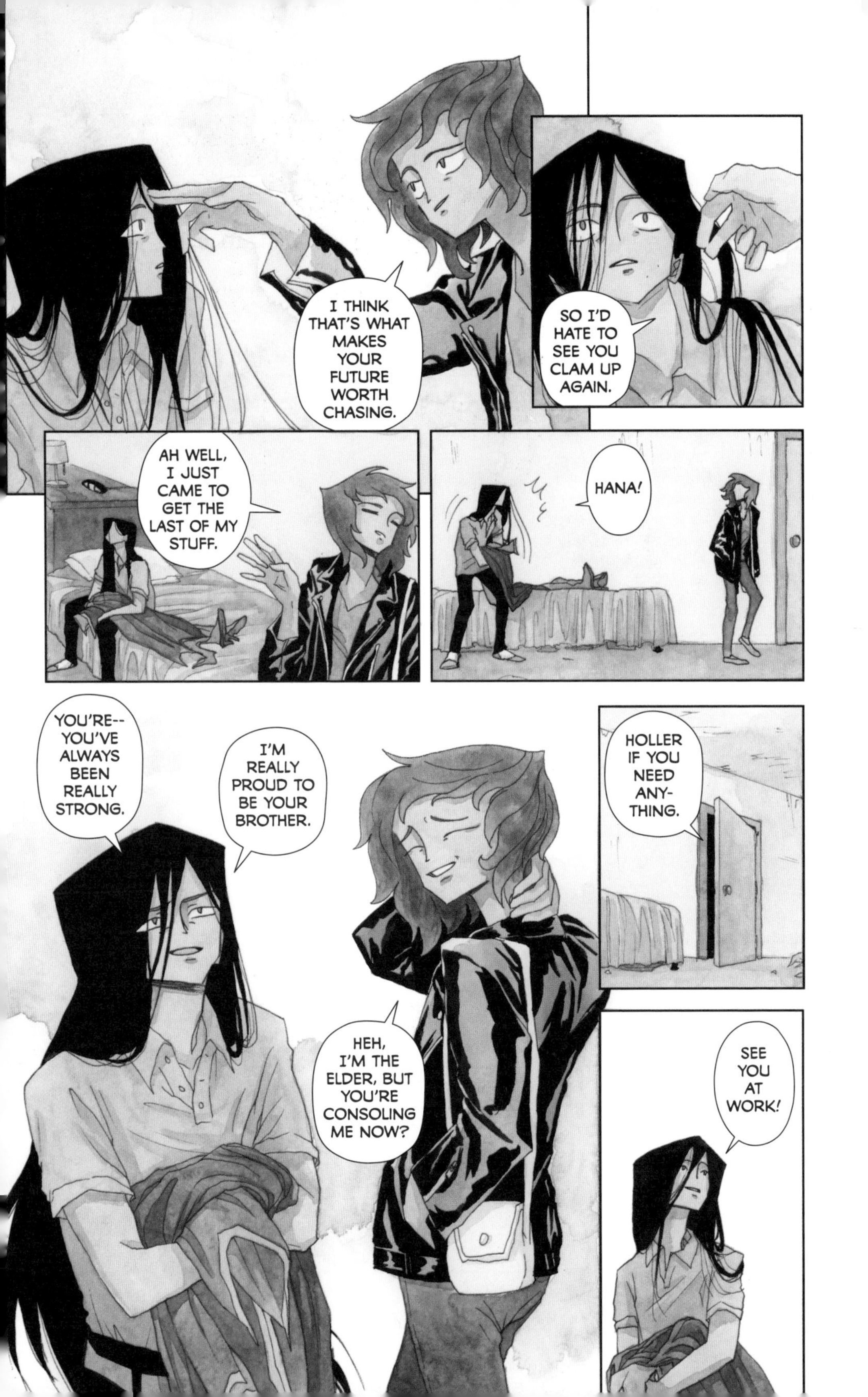
I THINK THAT'S WHAT MAKES YOUR FUTURE WORTH CHASING.
SO I'D HATE TO SEE YOU CLAM UP AGAIN.
AH WELL, I JUST CAME TO GET THE LAST OF MY STUFF.
HANA!
YOU'RE-- YOU'VE ALWAYS BEEN REALLY STRONG.
I'M REALLY PROUD TO BE YOUR BROTHER.
HEH, I'M THE ELDER, BUT YOU'RE CONSOLING ME NOW?
HOLLER IF YOU NEED ANY-THING.
SEE YOU AT WORK!

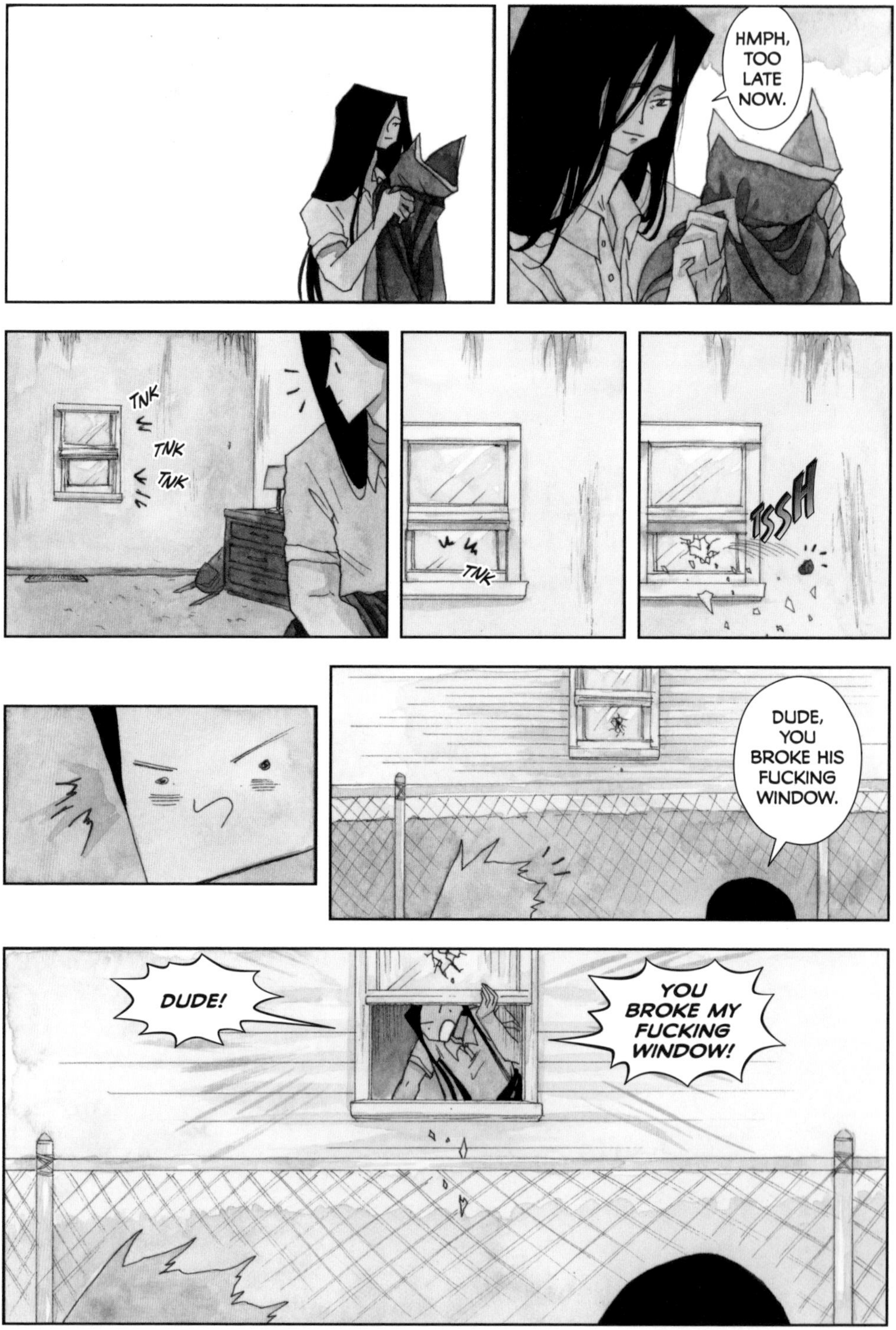
HMPH, TOO LATE NOW.
TNK
TNK
TNK
TNK
TSSH
DUDE, YOU BROKE HIS FUCKING WINDOW.
DUDE!
YOU BROKE MY FUCKING WINDOW!

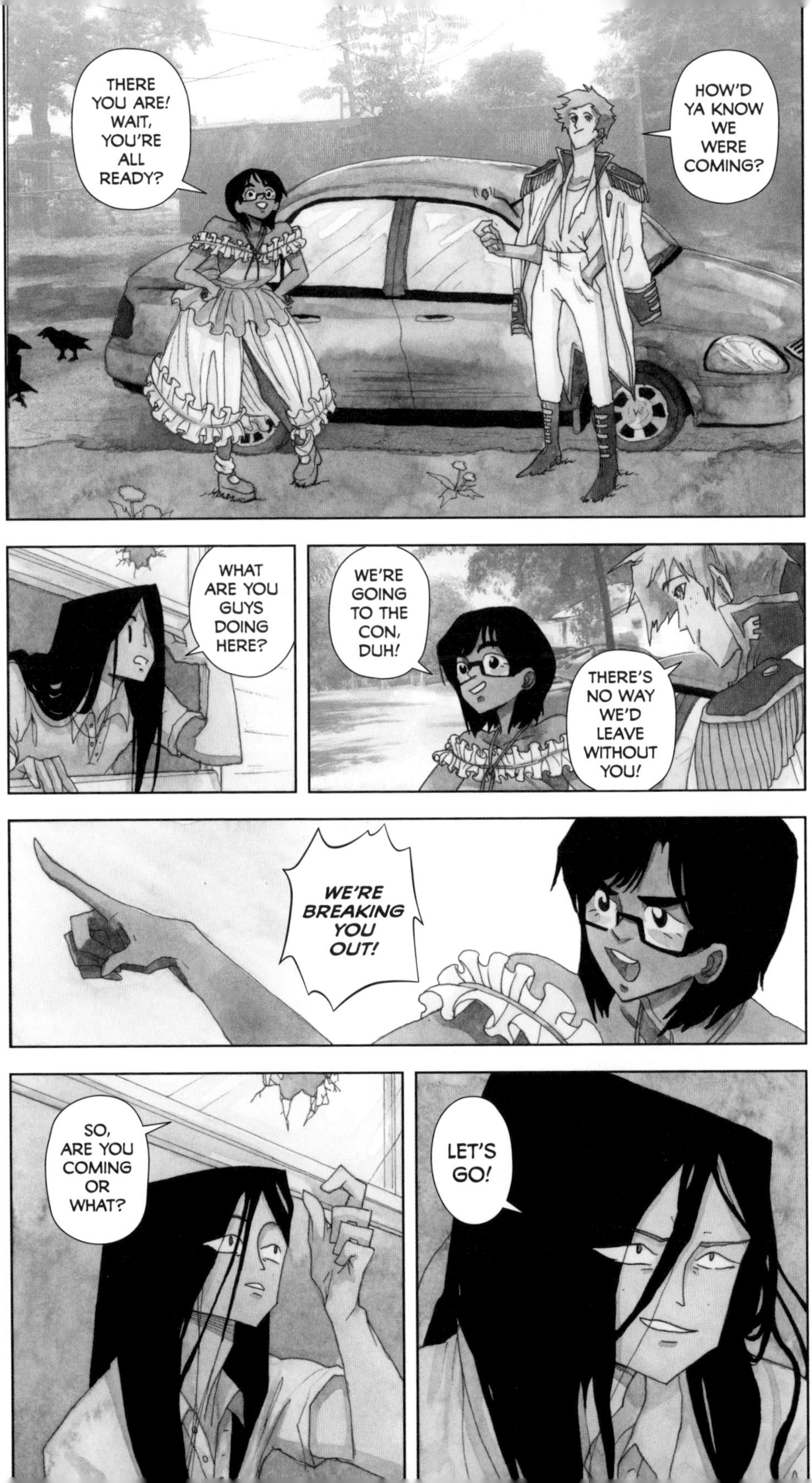
THERE YOU ARE! WAIT, YOU'RE ALL READY?
HOW'D YA KNOW WE WERE COMING?
WHAT ARE YOU GUYS DOING HERE?
WE'RE GOING TO THE CON, DUH!
THERE'S NO WAY WE'D LEAVE WITHOUT YOU!
WE'RE BREAKING YOU OUT!
SO, ARE YOU COMING OR WHAT?
LET'S GO!

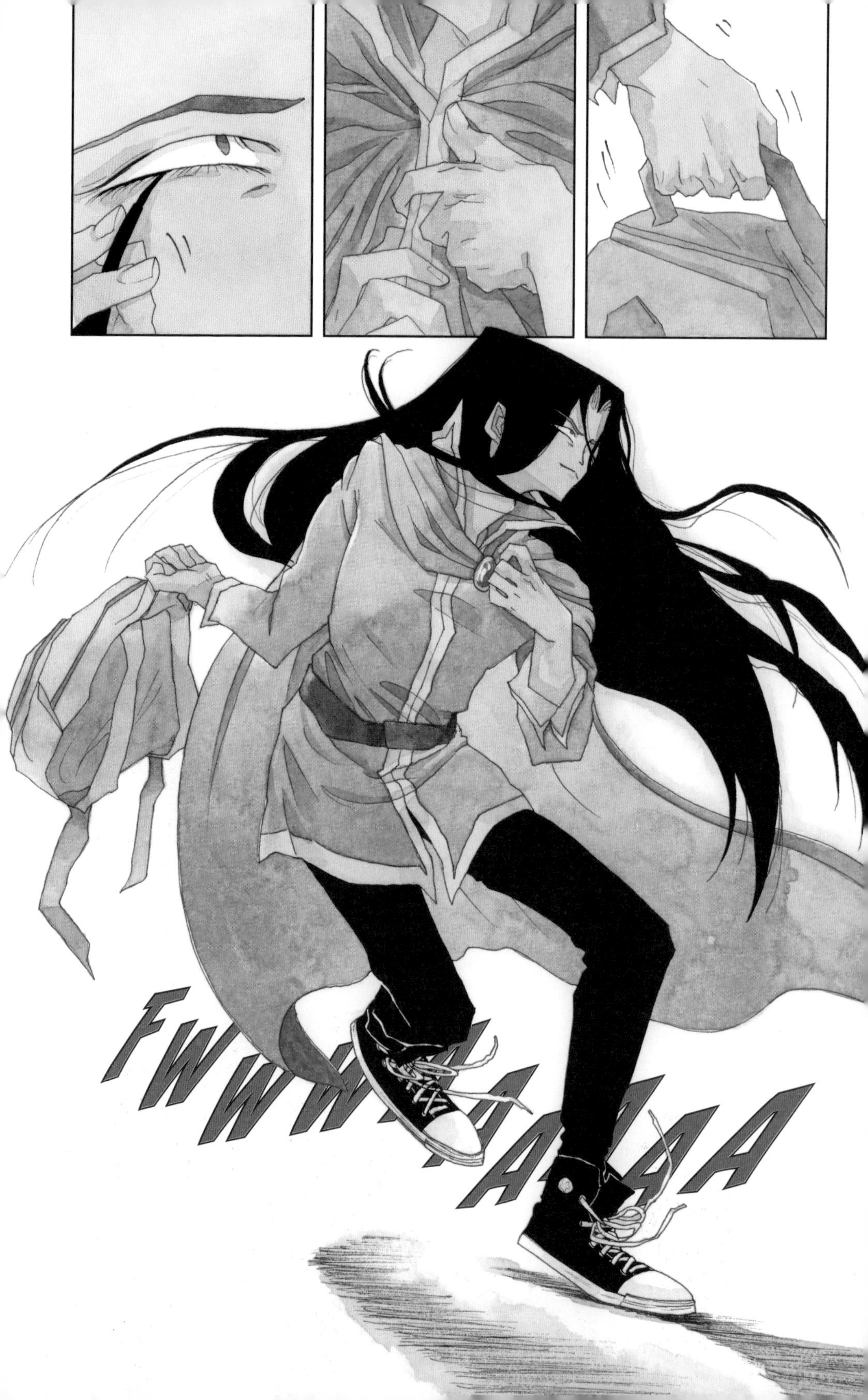
FWWHAAAA

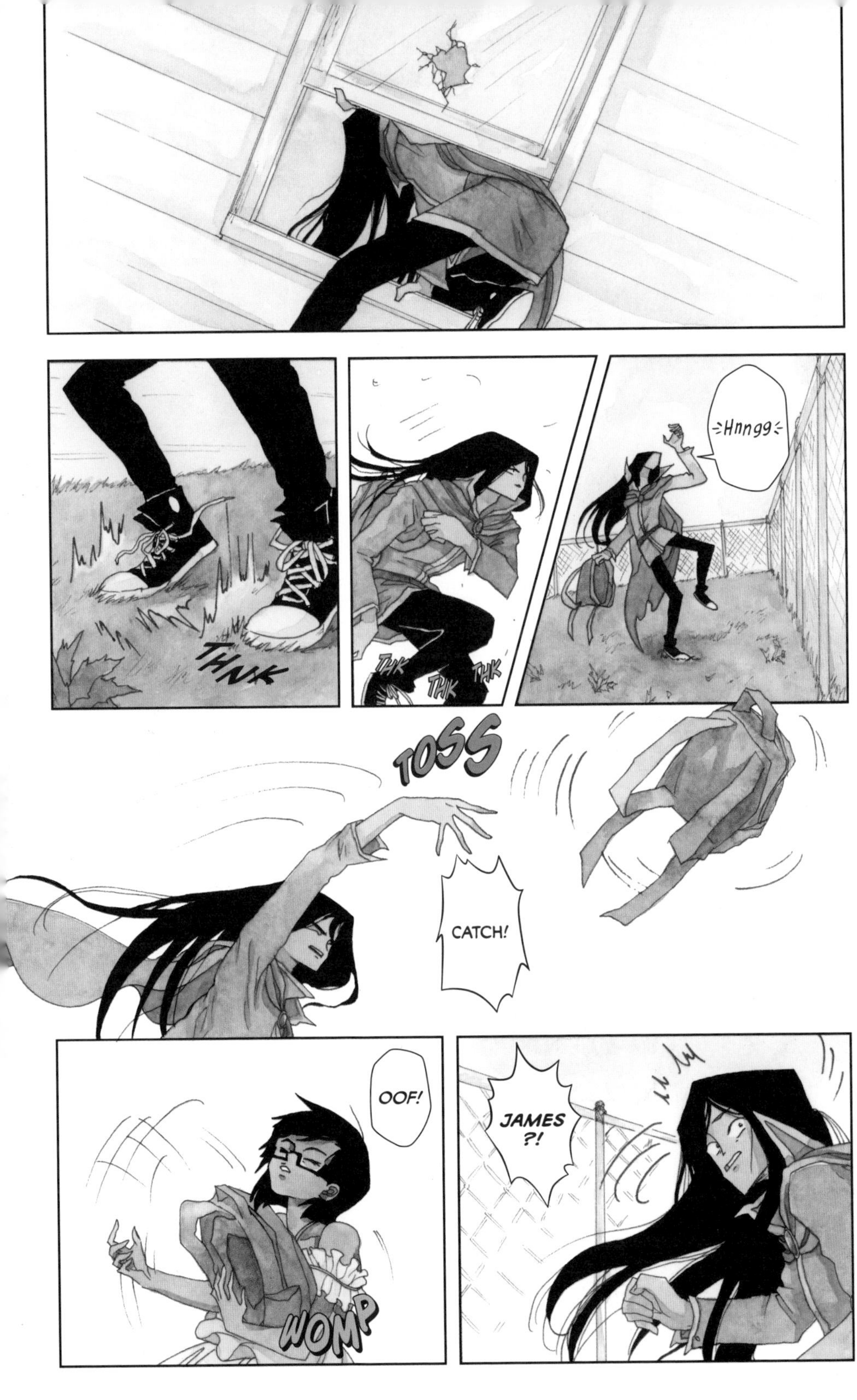
THNK
THK
THK
THK
Hnngg
TOSS
CATCH!
OOF!
WOMP
JAMES ?!

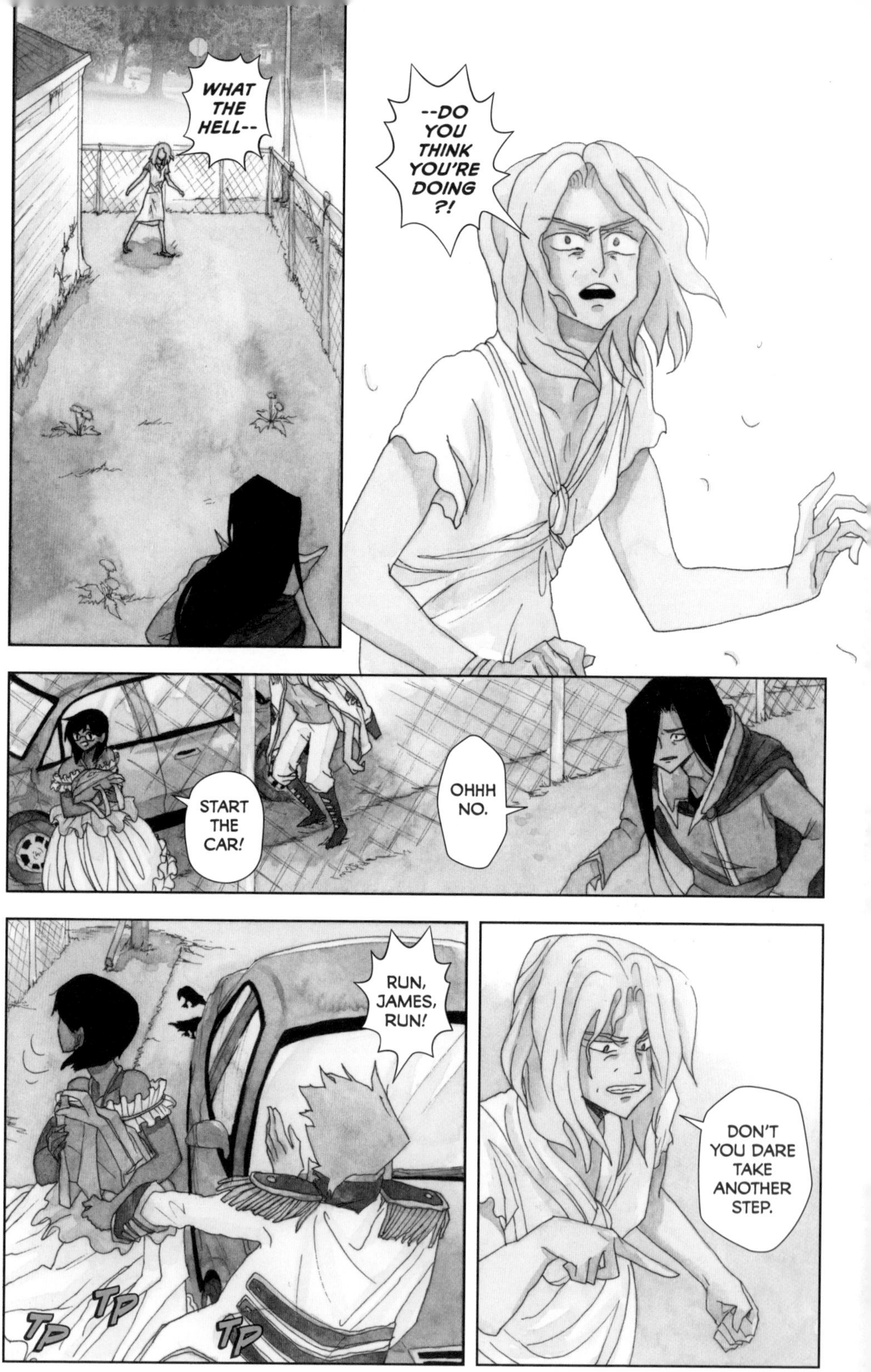
WHAT THE HELL--
--DO YOU THINK YOU'RE DOING ?!
START THE CAR!
OHHH NO.
RUN, JAMES, RUN!
TP
TP
TP
DON'T YOU DARE TAKE ANOTHER STEP.

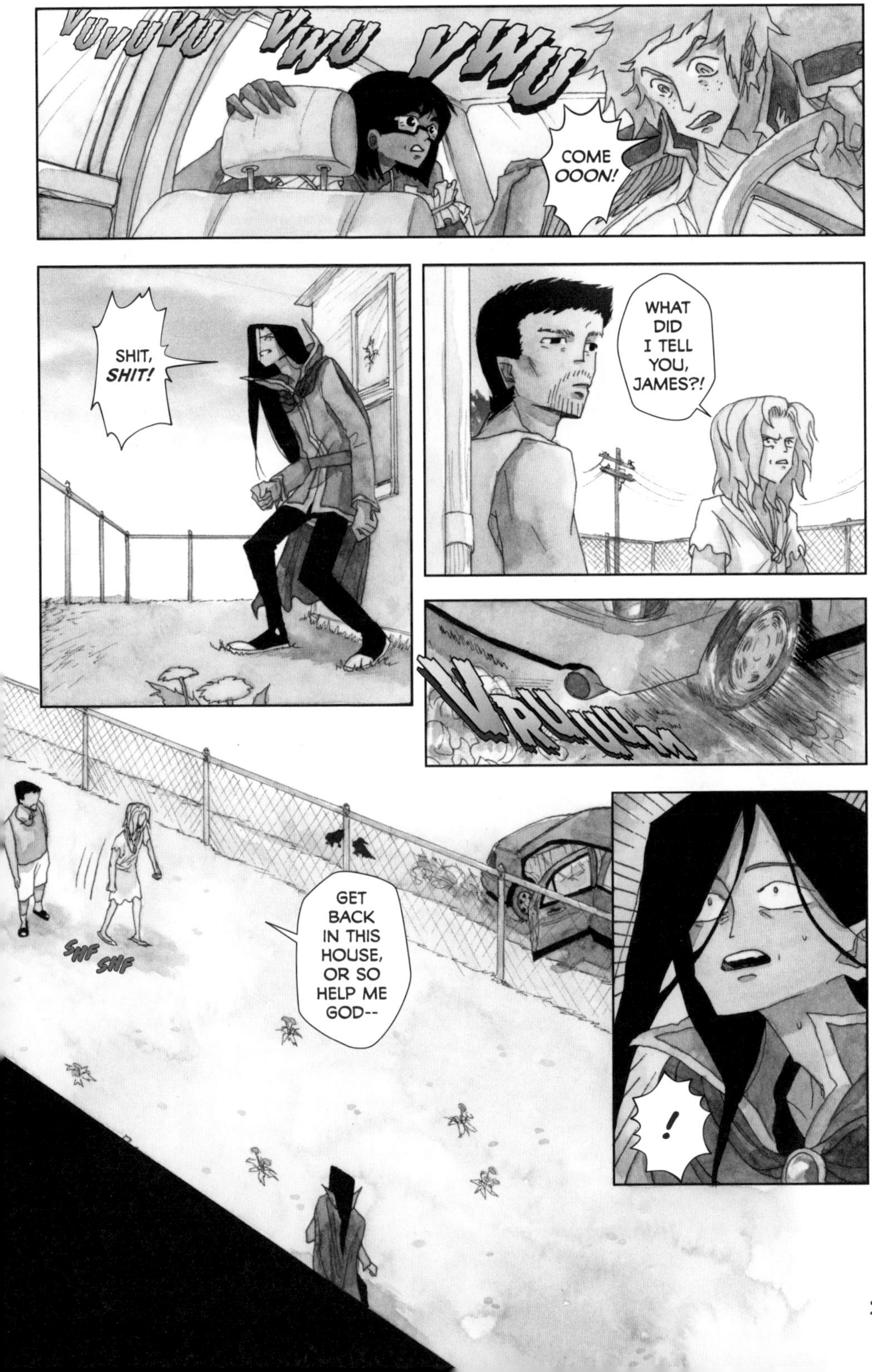
VUVUVU VWU VWU
COME OOON!
SHIT, SHIT!
WHAT DID I TELL YOU, JAMES?!
VRUUUM
SHF SHF
GET BACK IN THIS HOUSE, OR SO HELP ME GOD--
!

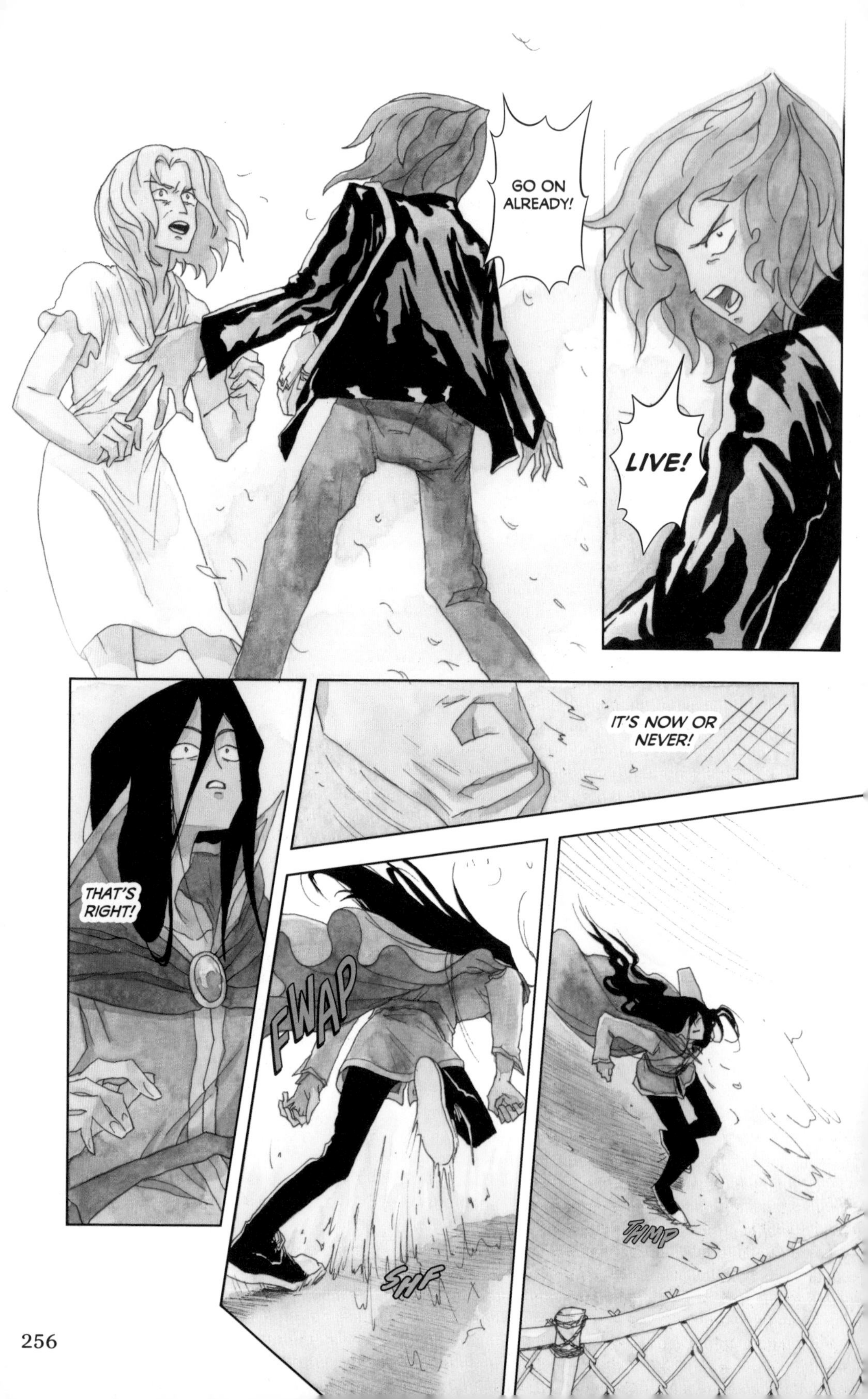
GO ON ALREADY!
LIVE!
THAT'S RIGHT!
IT'S NOW OR NEVER!
FWAP
SHF
THMP

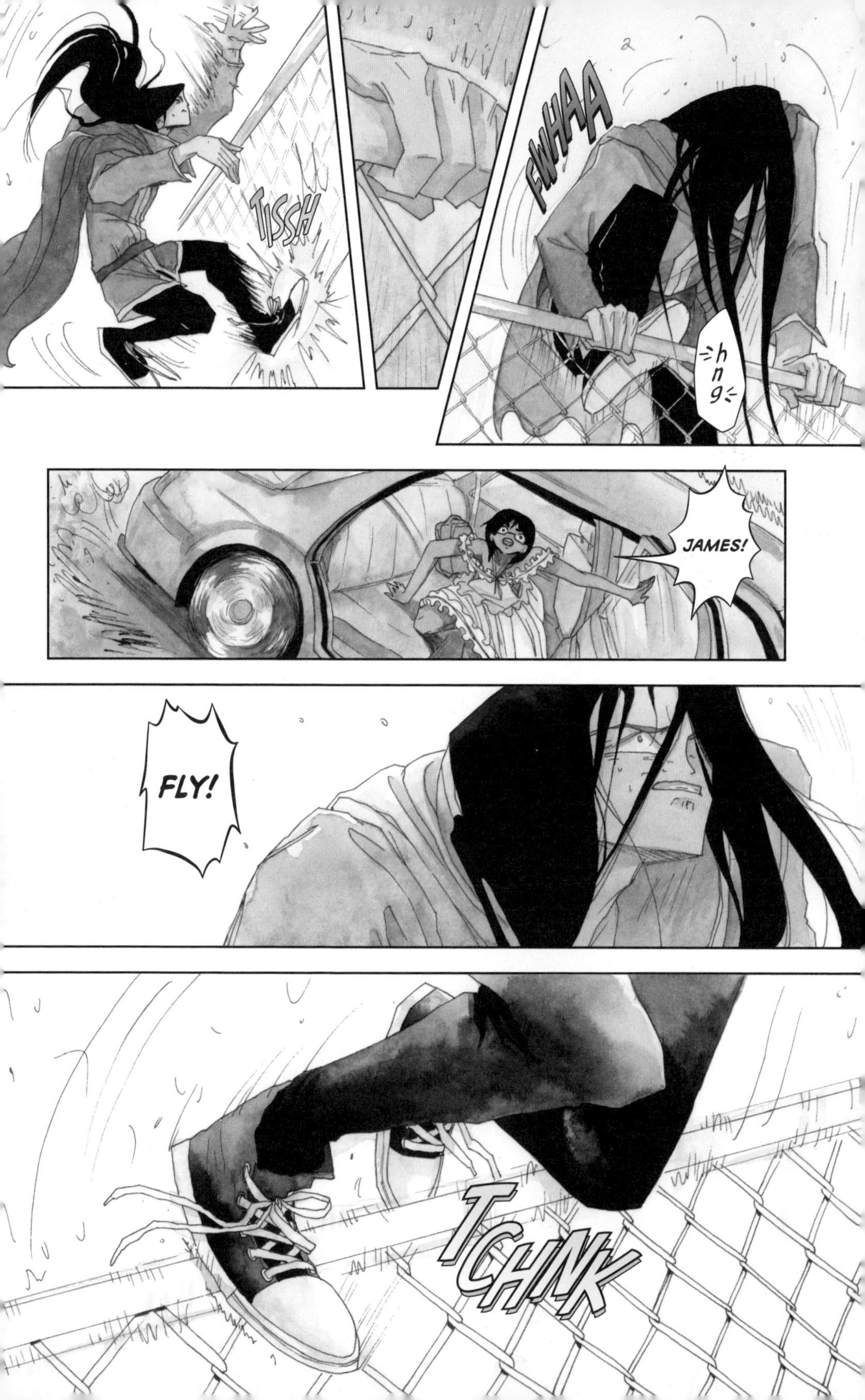
TISSH
FWHAA
hng
JAMES!
FLY!
TCHNK

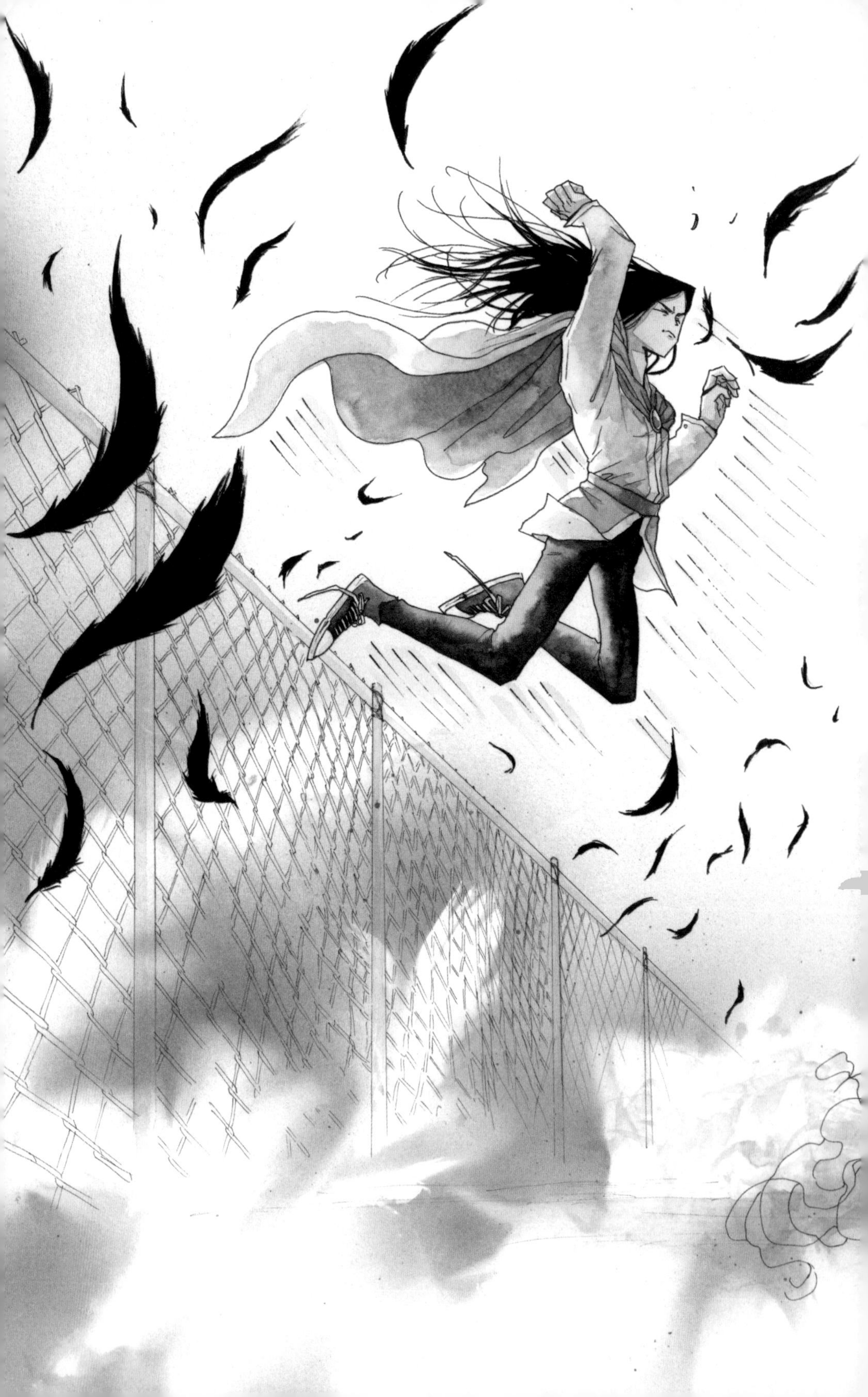

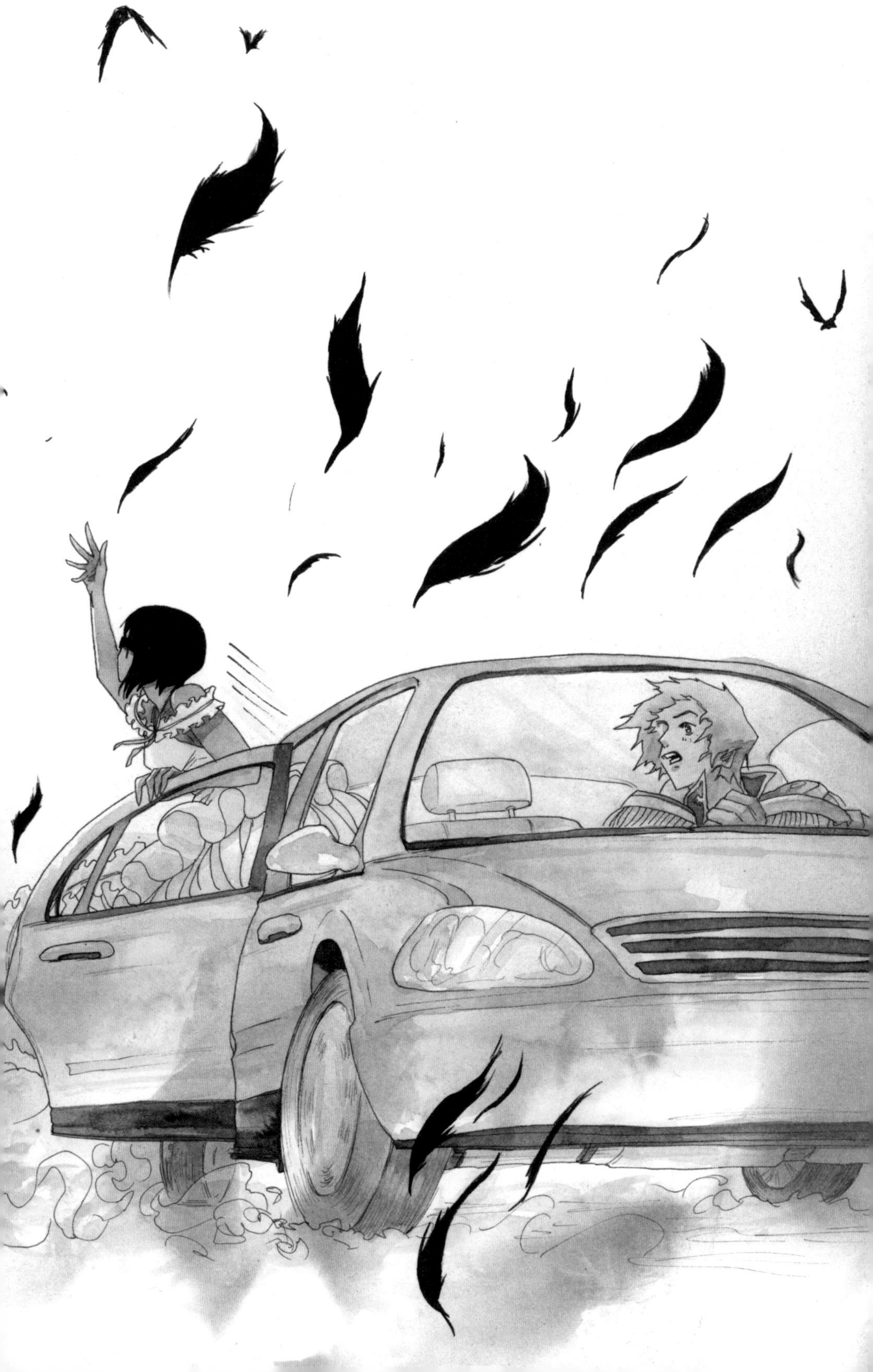

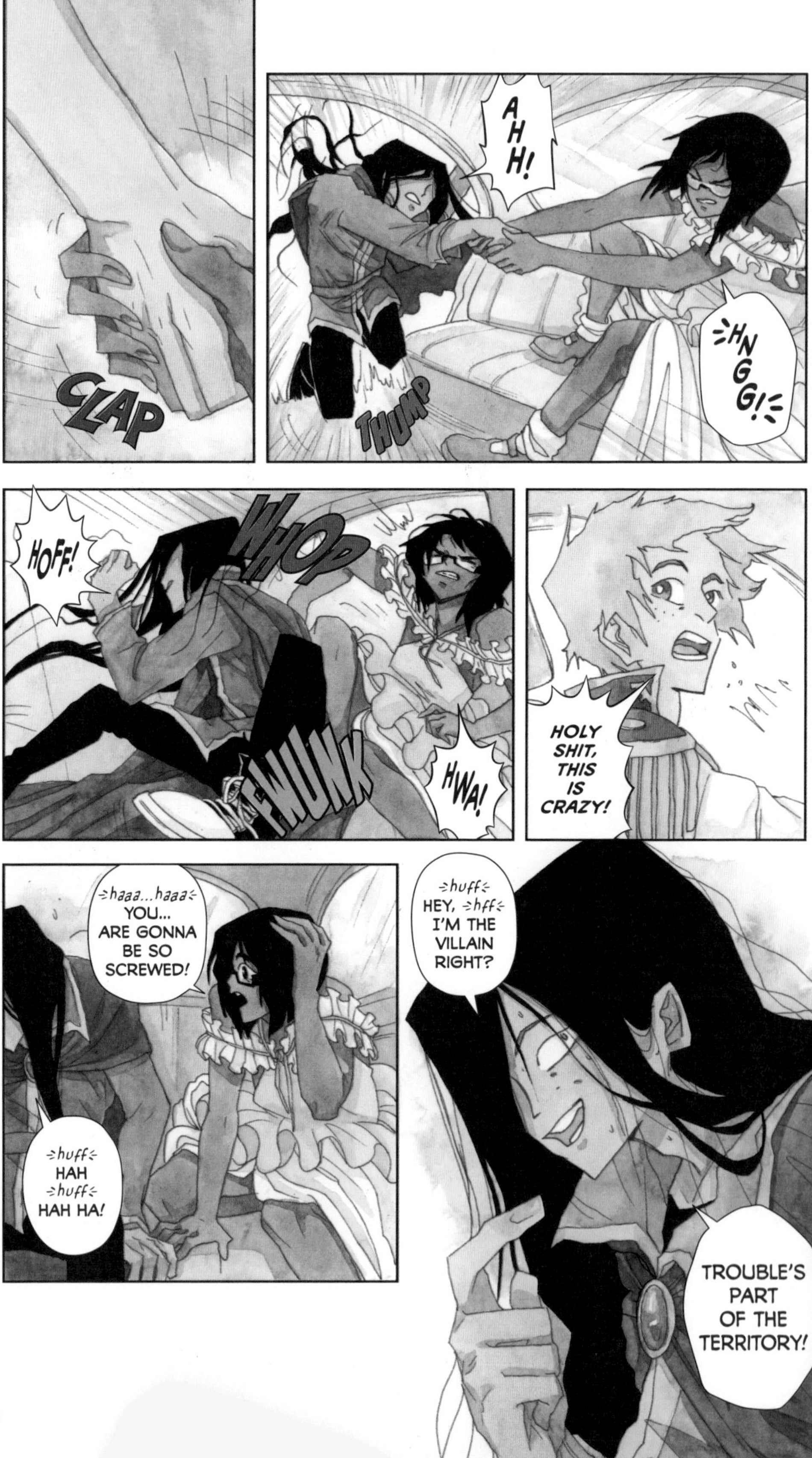
CLAP
AHH!
THUMP
HNGG!
HOFF!
WHOP
FWUNK
HWA!
HOLY SHIT, THIS IS CRAZY!
haaa...haaa YOU... ARE GONNA BE SO SCREWED!
huff HAH huff HAH HA!
huff HEY, hff I'M THE VILLAIN RIGHT?
TROUBLE'S PART OF THE TERRITORY!

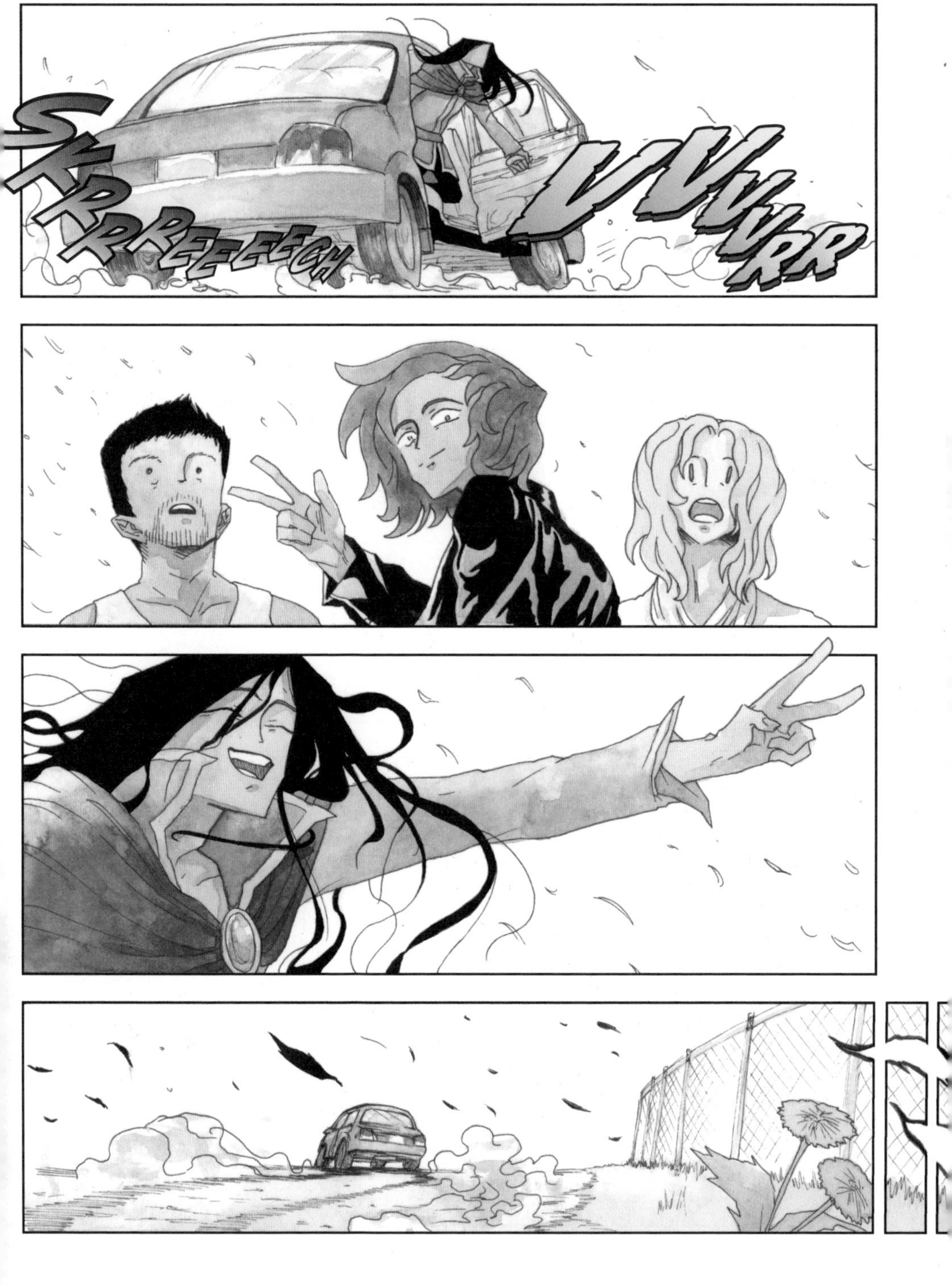
SKRRREEEECH
VVUURR

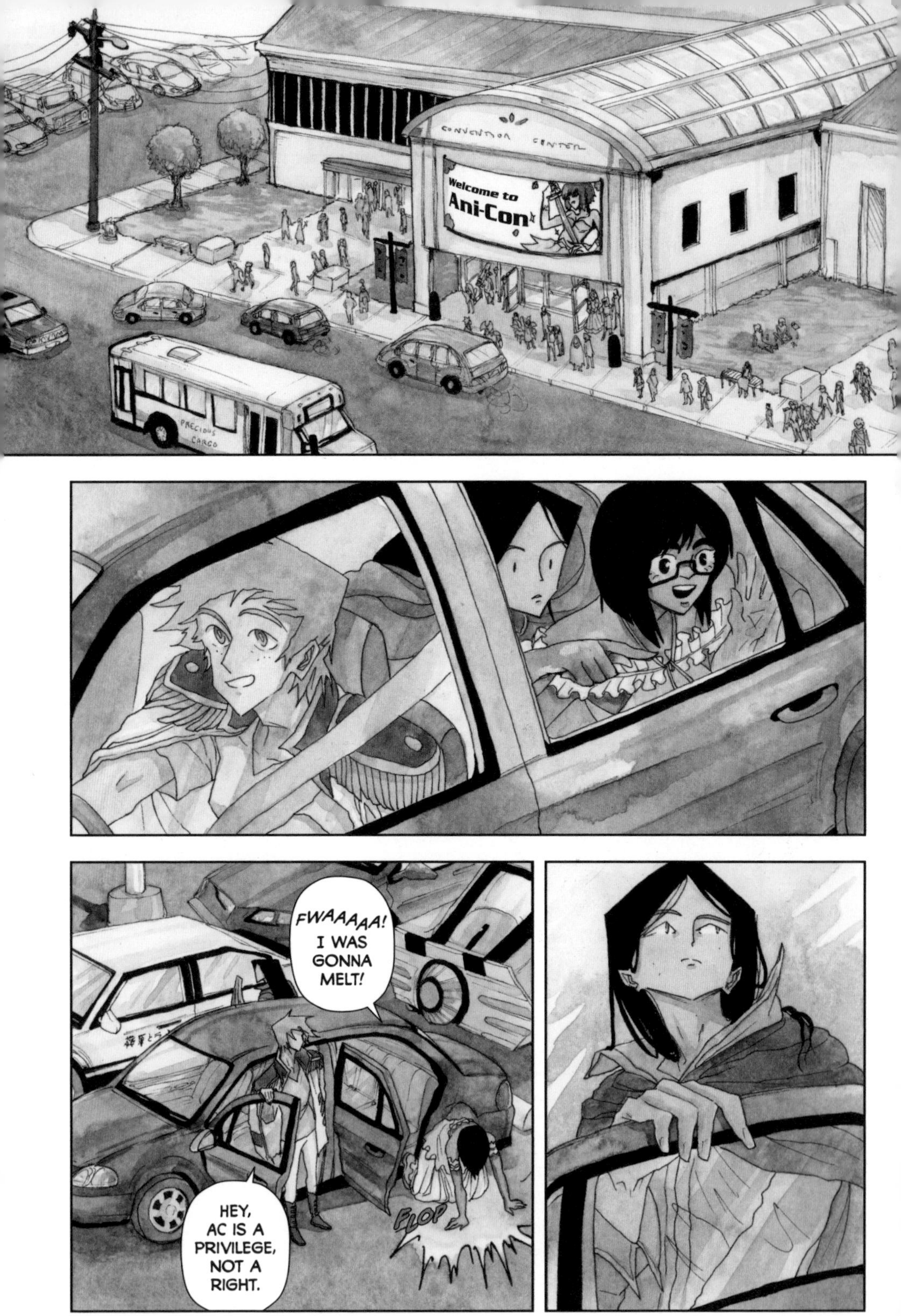
CONVENTION CENTER
Welcome to Ani-Con
PRECIOUS CARGO
FWAAAAA! I WAS GONNA MELT!
HEY, AC IS A PRIVILEGE, NOT A RIGHT.
FLOP

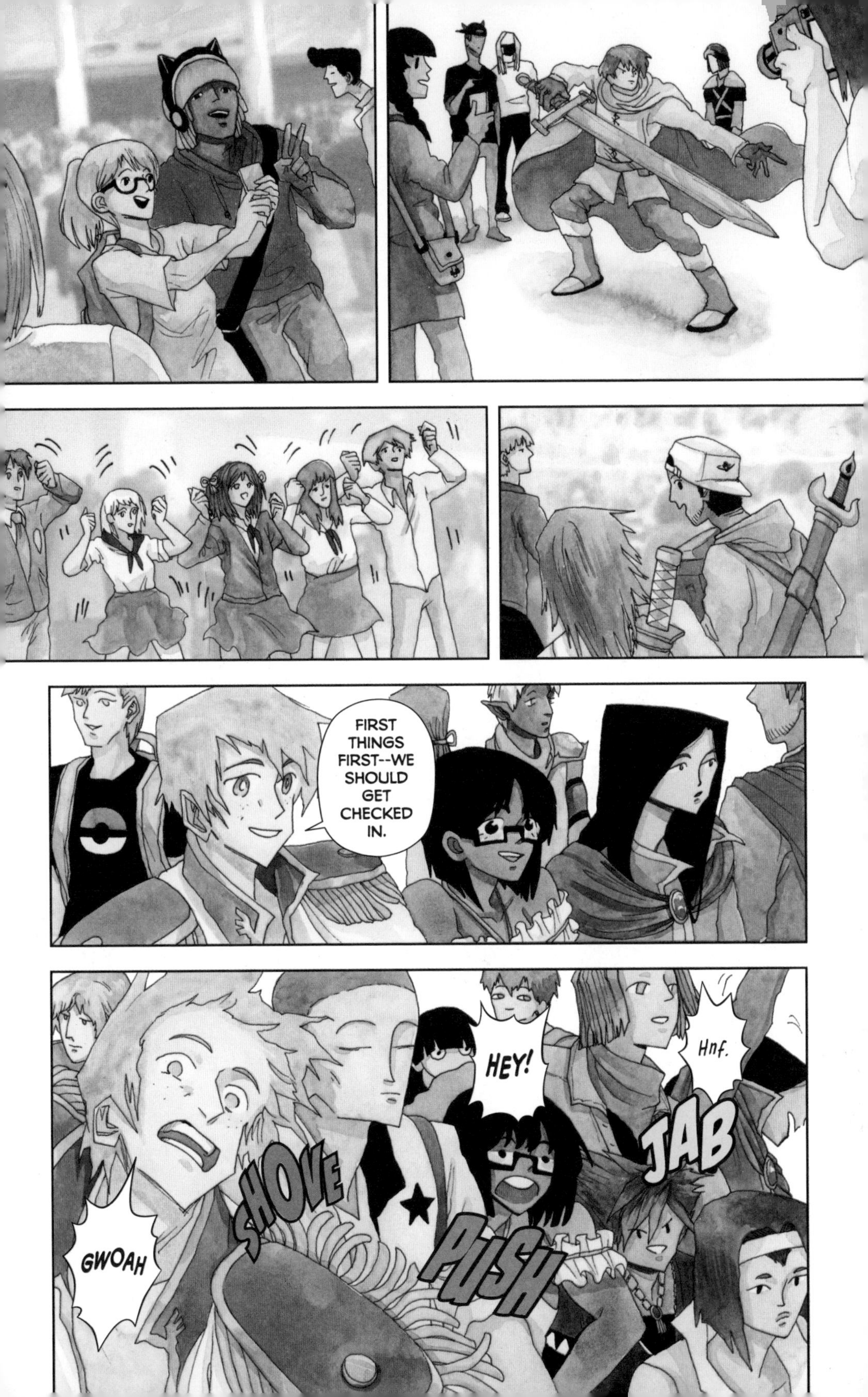
FIRST THINGS FIRST--WE SHOULD GET CHECKED IN.
HEY!
Hnf.
JAB
SHOVE
PUSH
GWOAH

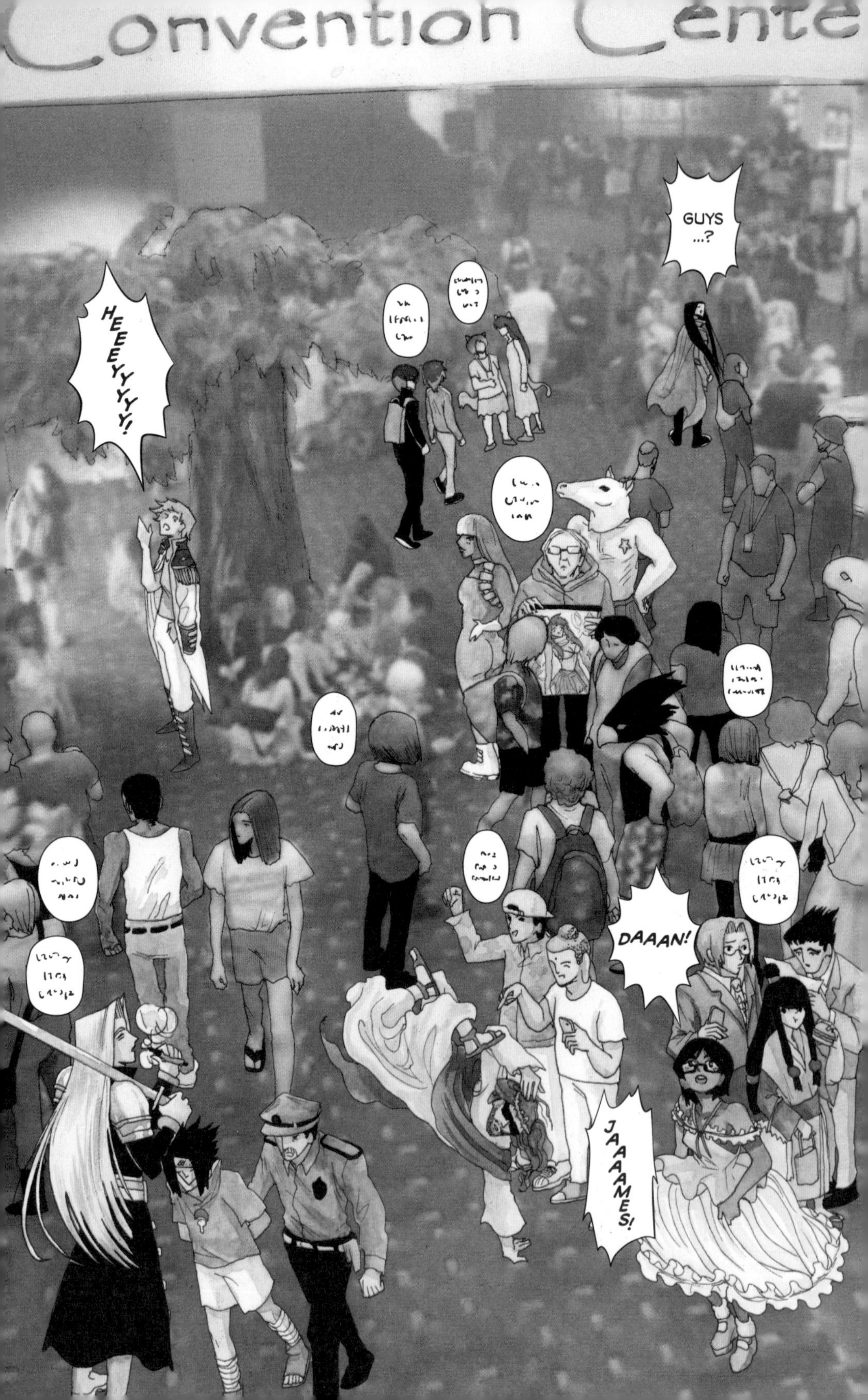
Convention Cente
HEEEYYYY!
GUYS ...?
DAAAN!
JAAAAMES!

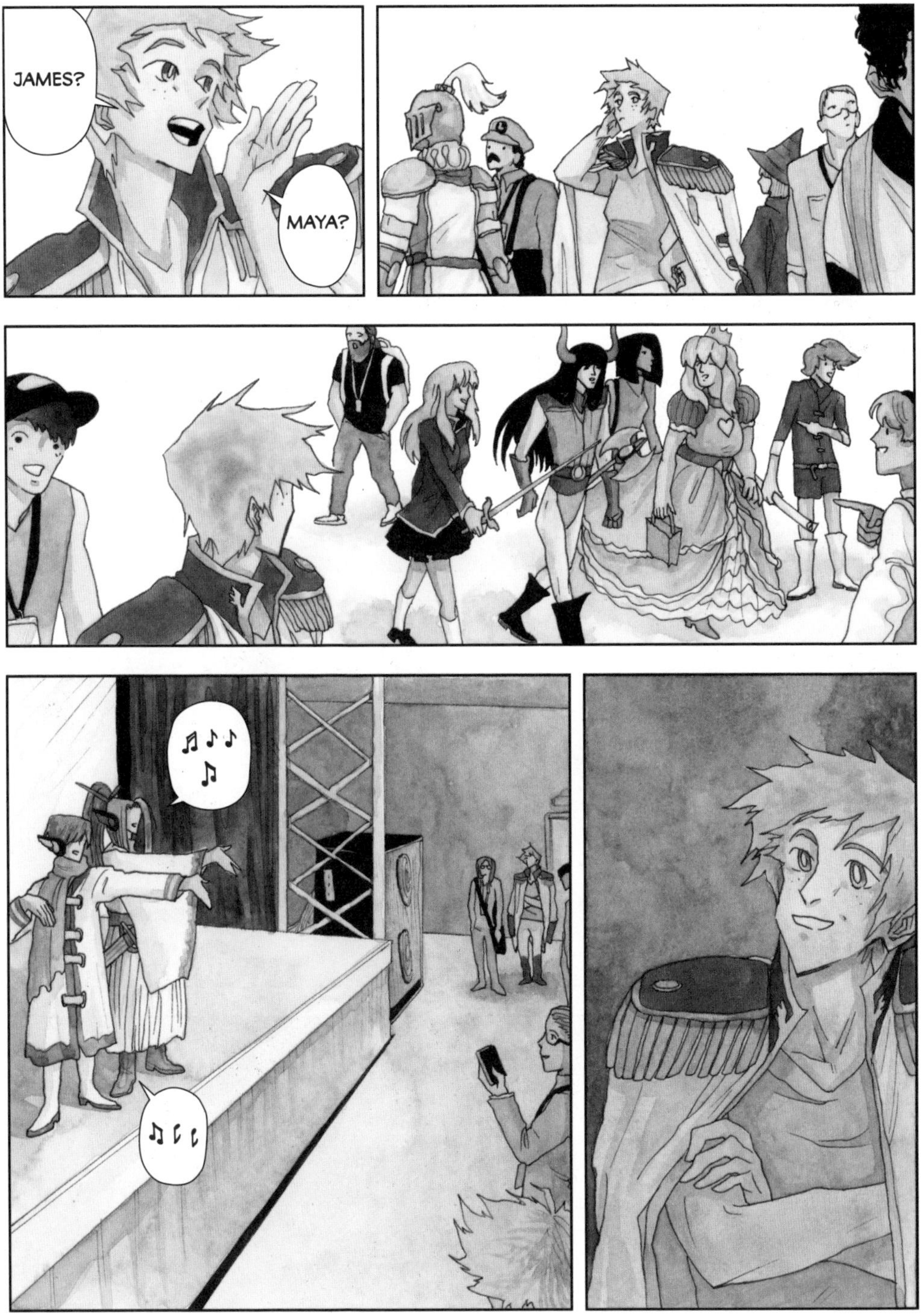
JAMES?
MAYA?
♫♪♪
♫
♫♪♪

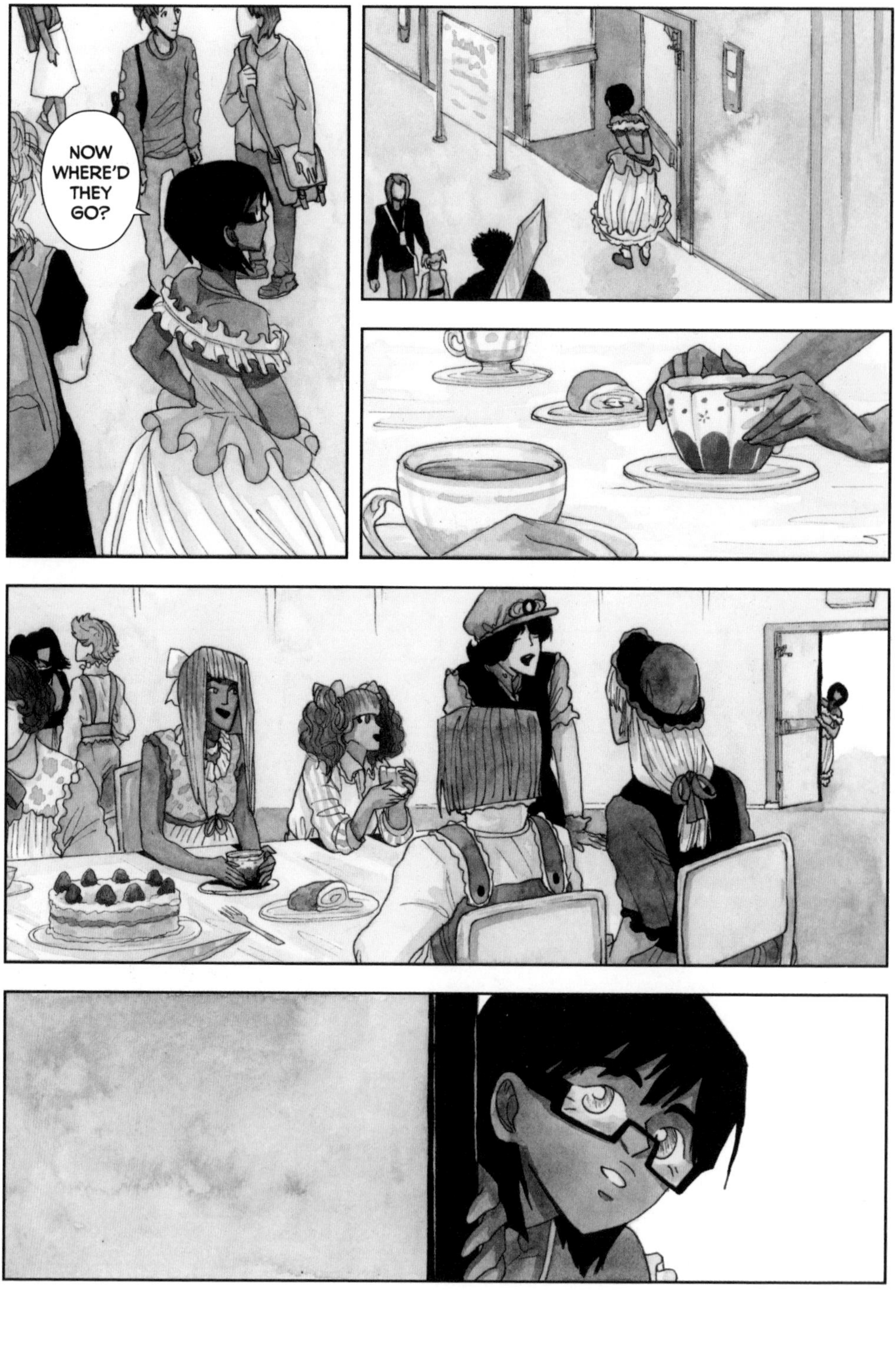
NOW WHERE'D THEY GO?

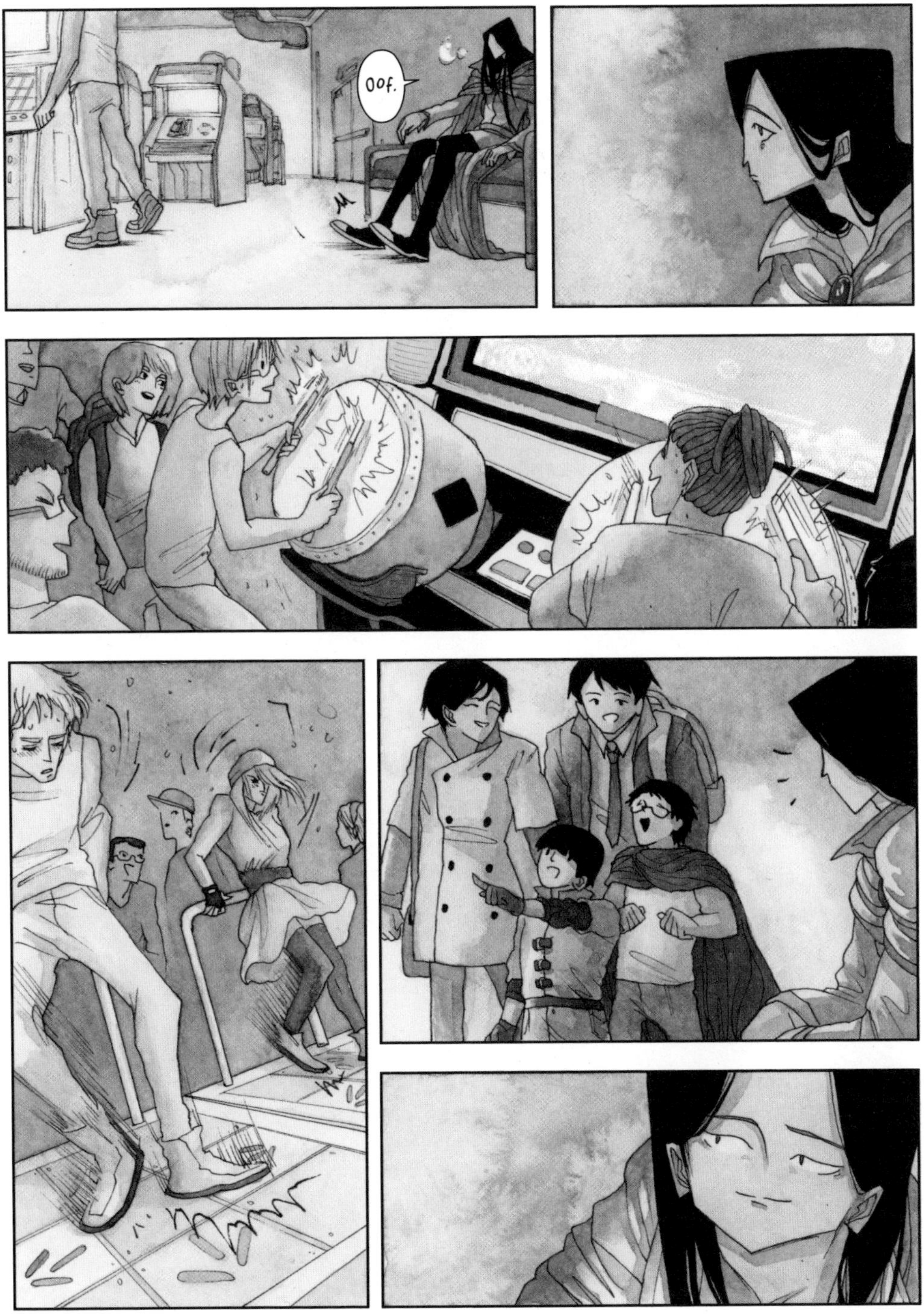
Oof.

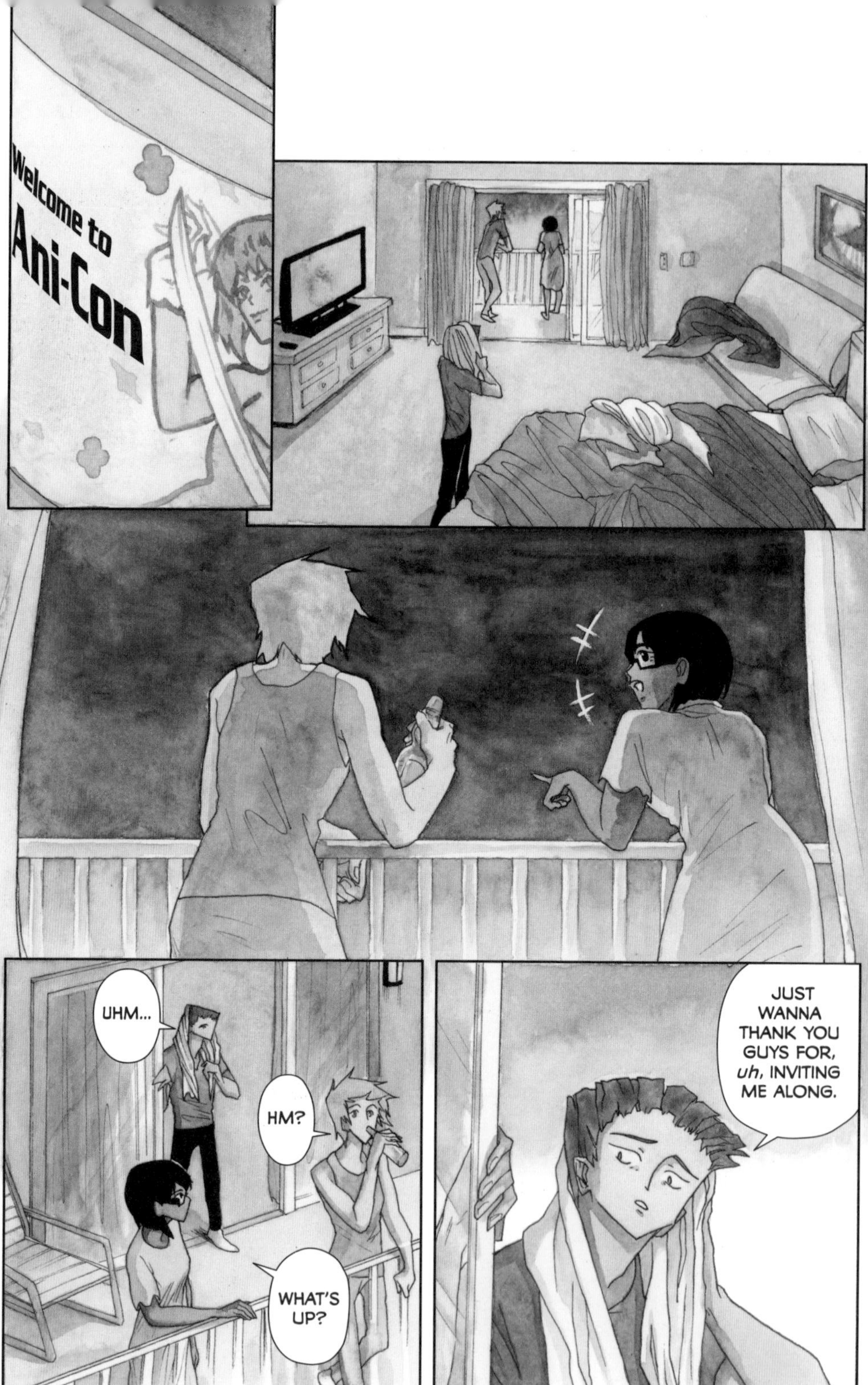
Welcome to
Ani-Con
UHM...
HM?
WHAT'S UP?
JUST WANNA THANK YOU GUYS FOR, *uh*, INVITING ME ALONG.

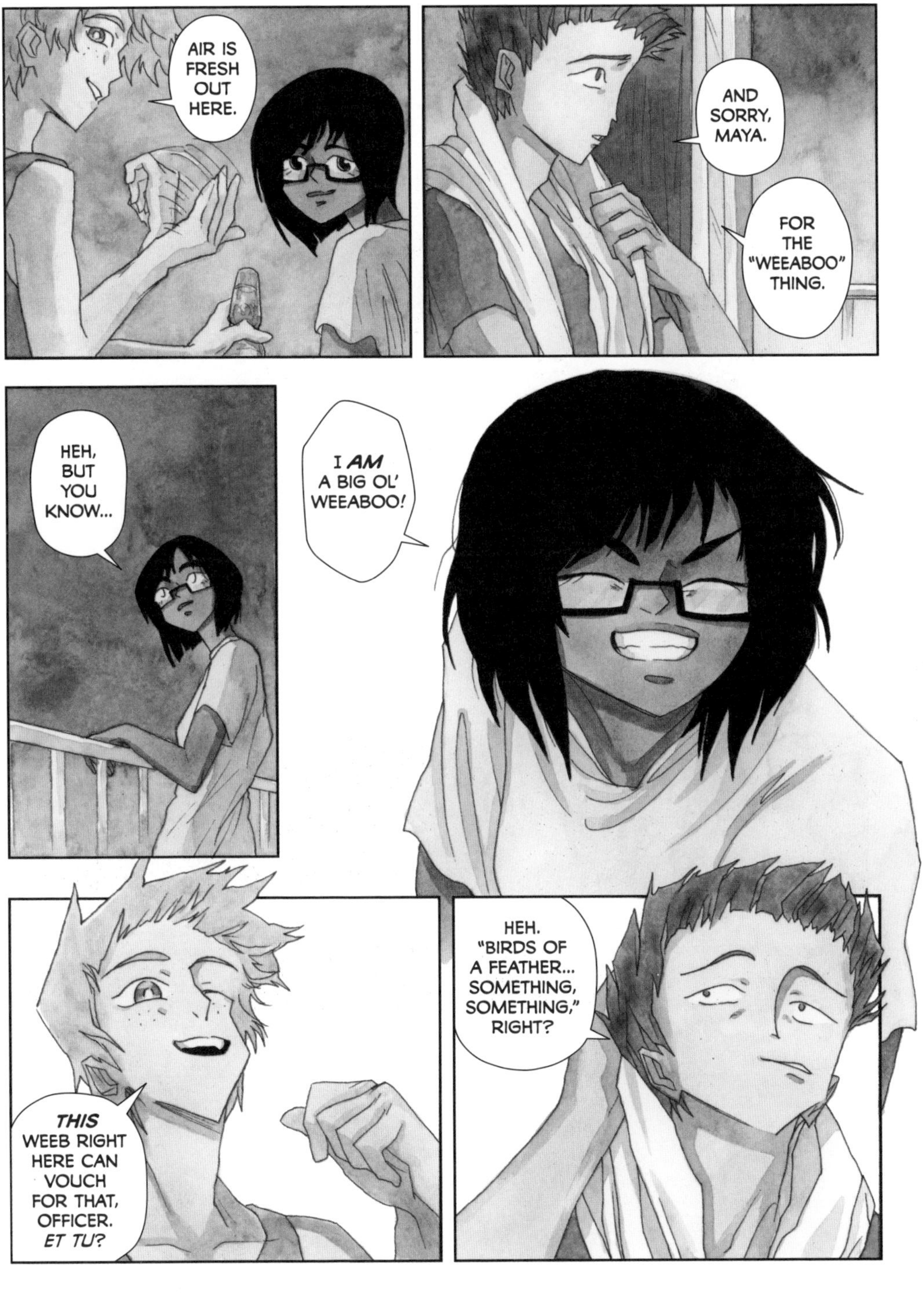
AIR IS FRESH OUT HERE.
AND SORRY, MAYA.
FOR THE "WEEABOO" THING.
HEH, BUT YOU KNOW...
I *AM* A BIG OL' WEEABOO!
THIS WEEB RIGHT HERE CAN VOUCH FOR THAT, OFFICER. *ET TU*?
HEH. "BIRDS OF A FEATHER... SOMETHING, SOMETHING," RIGHT?

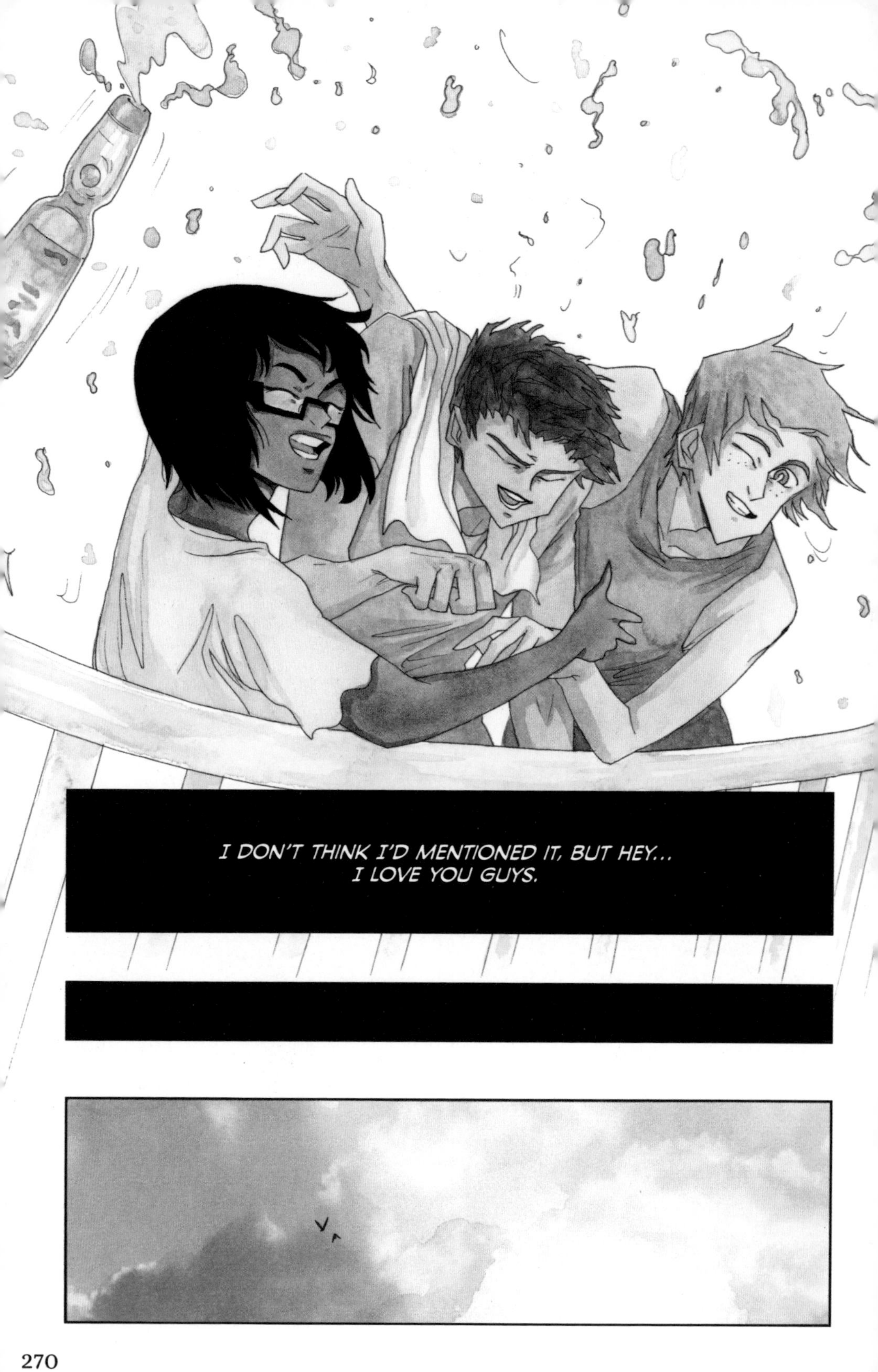
I DON'T THINK I'D MENTIONED IT, BUT HEY...
I LOVE YOU GUYS.

THINGS HAVE BEEN WEIRD
THIS LAST YEAR.
LEARNING ABOUT PEOPLE.
LEARNING ABOUT MYSELF.

FINDING OUT WHAT IT MEANS
TO LISTEN.
HOW IT FEELS TO BE LISTENED TO.
THOSE BEAUTIFUL, SELFISH ACTS
WE GIFT EACH OTHER.

IT'S NOT THE END OF THE WORLD.
MORE LIKE THE START...
OF ONE WHOLLY NEW.

 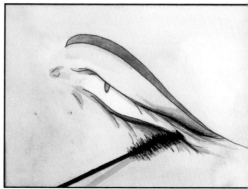

SO DON'T GIVE UP ON IT, OKAY?
YOU'VE STILL GOT A LONG WAY TO GO.

 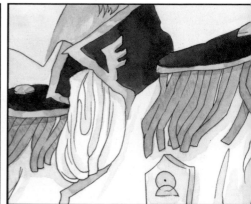

THERE WILL BE UPS.
AND THERE WILL BE DOWNS.

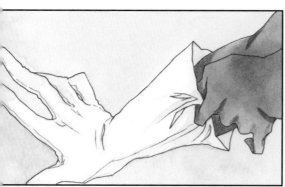 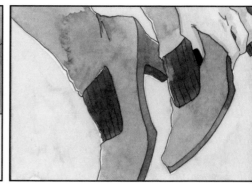

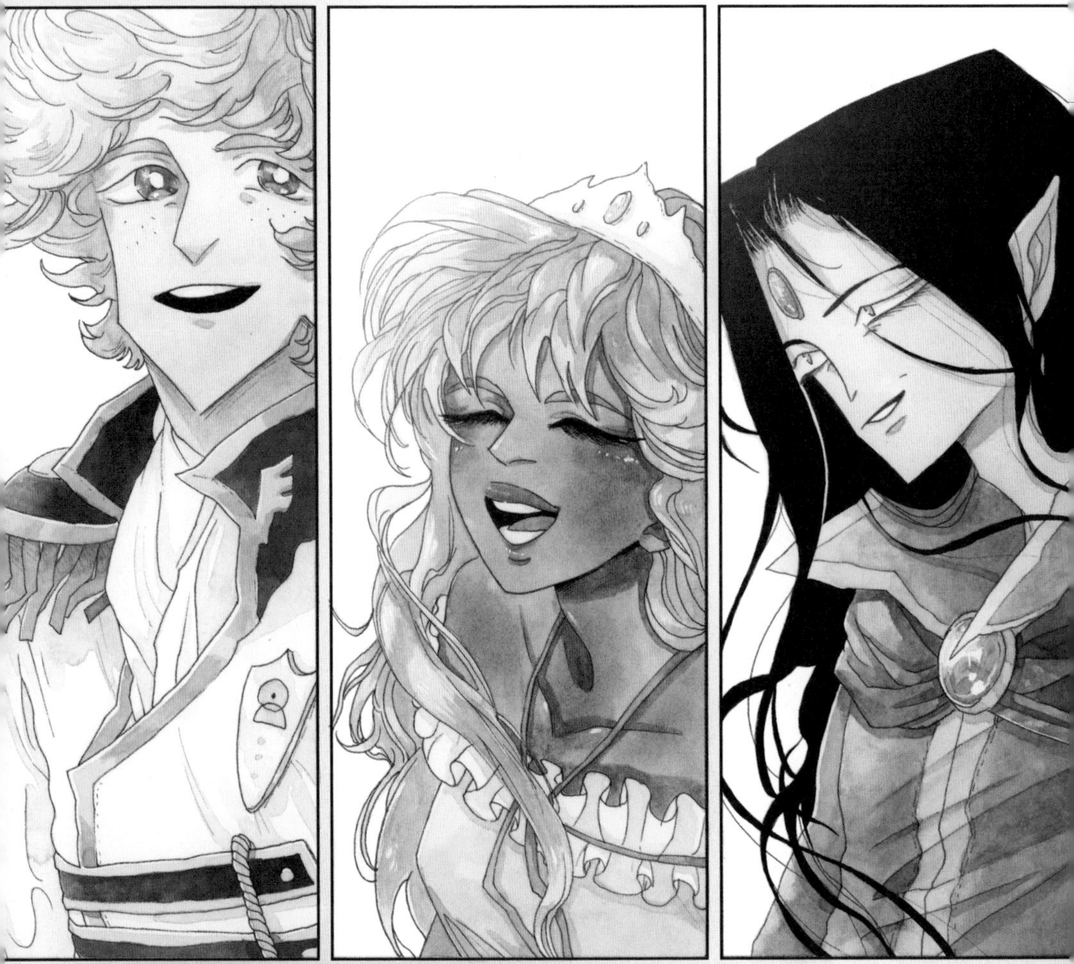

BUT I'LL BE THERE, HOLDING ONTO SOMETHING REAL.

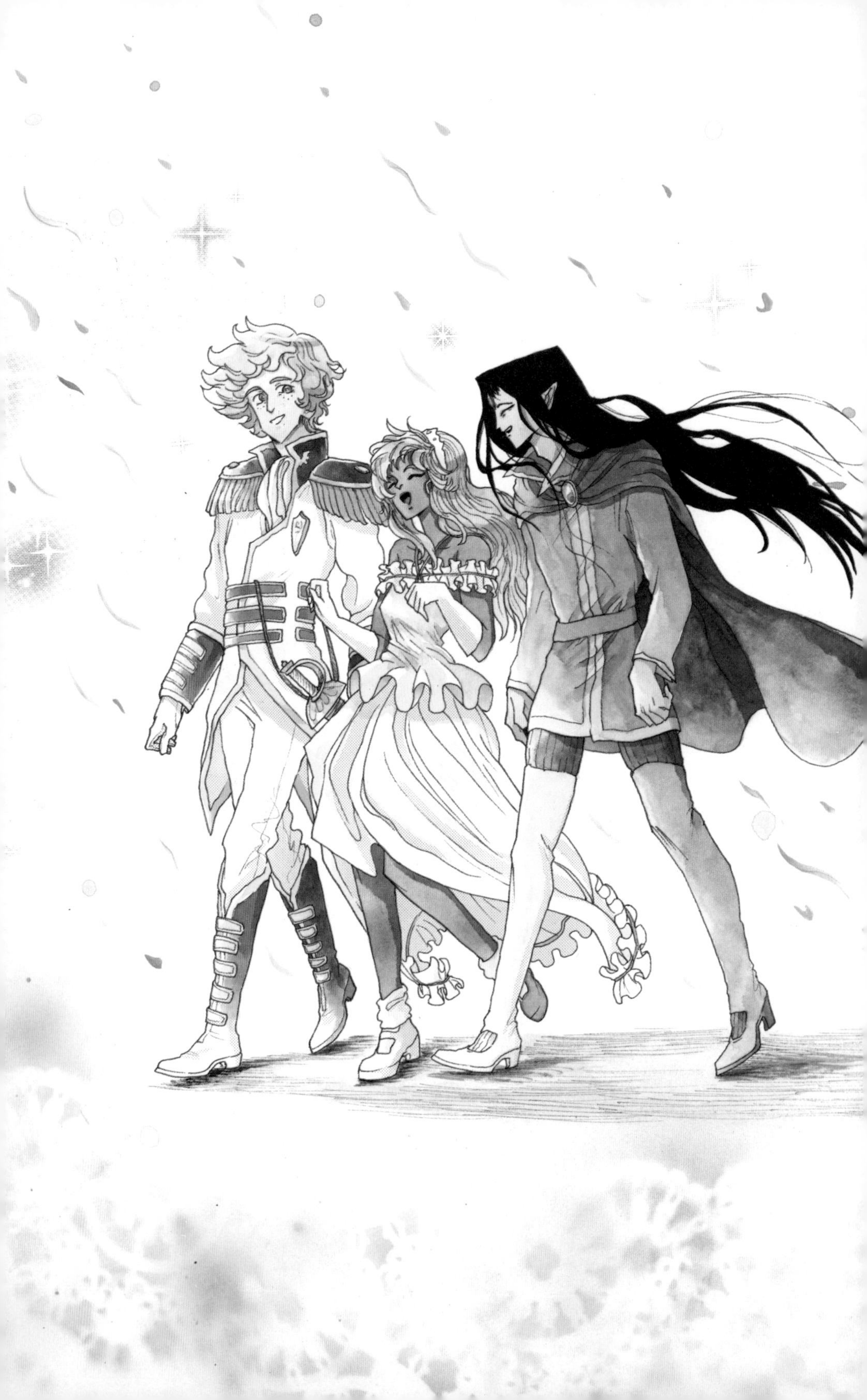

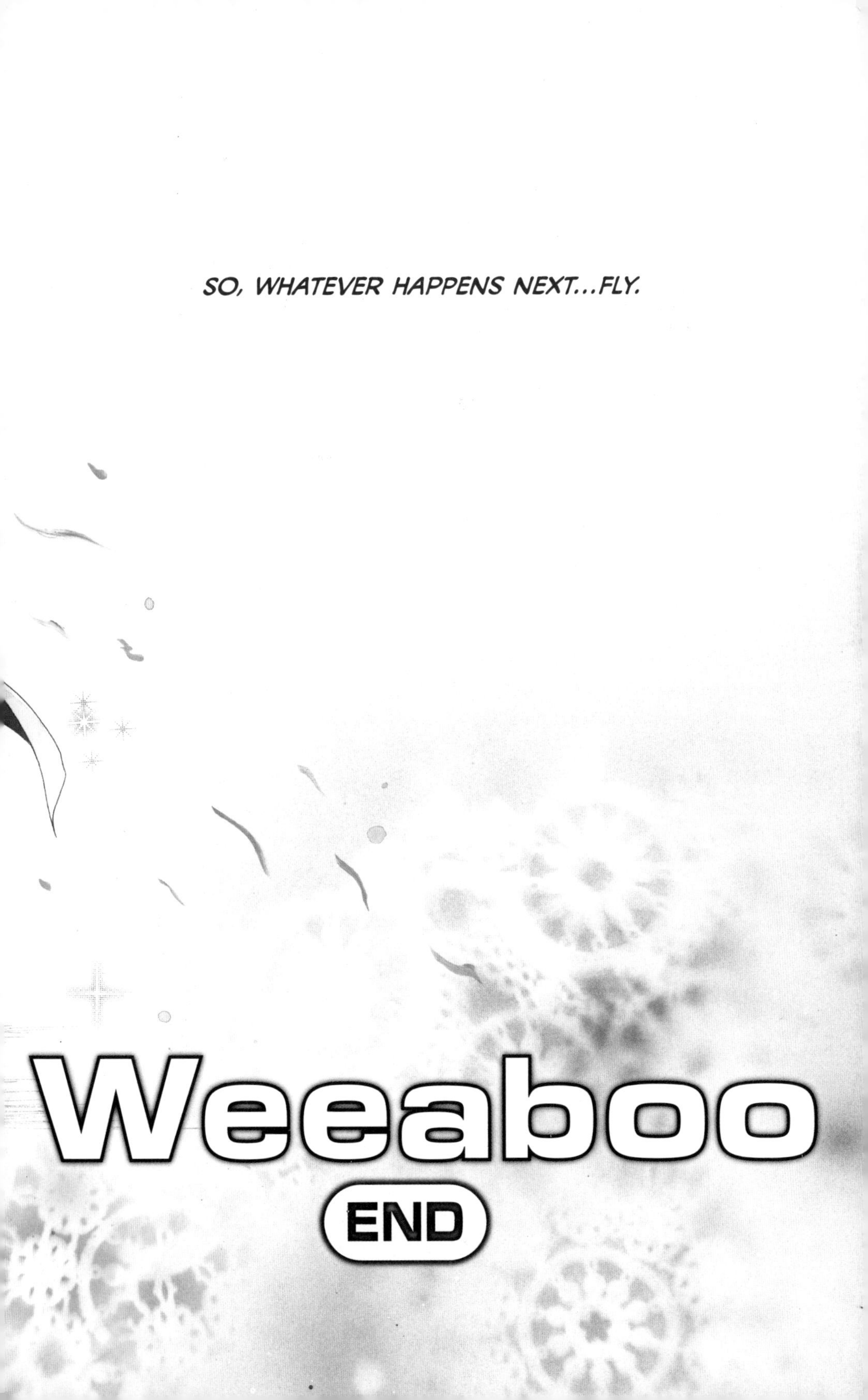
SO, WHATEVER HAPPENS NEXT...FLY.
Weeaboo
END

Mixed Media

A Process Breakdown of *Weeaboo*

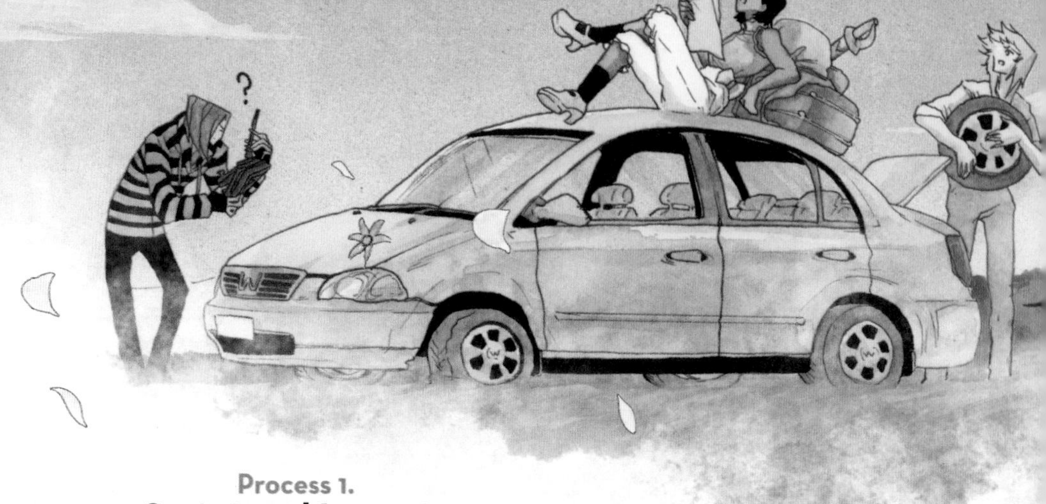

Process 1.

Script and Layouts

Where the story takes shape. Scripting is definitely the most challenging part for me because there are so many factors that go into making the narrative work. On the flipside, layouts are the most fun! It's really where I get to make the story come to life since visual storytelling is a lot more natural for me. The main focus of the layout step is acting, movement, page flow, and staging.

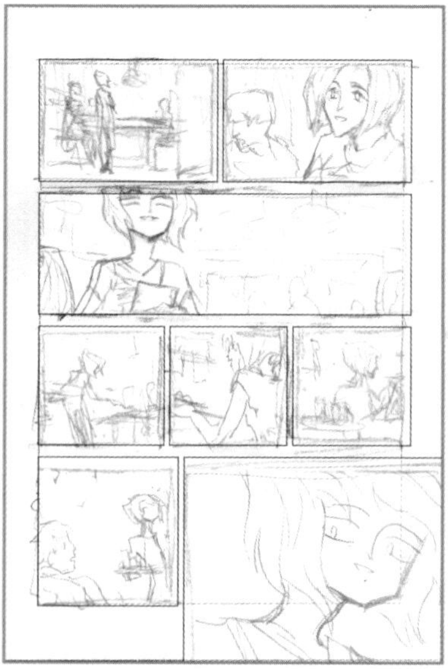

Process 2.

Pencils

A pretty simple step since my layouts do most of the heavy lifting. I print the drawing out at a much larger scale then trace over it on my light table. I'm just focusing on cleaning up the drawing and adding details.

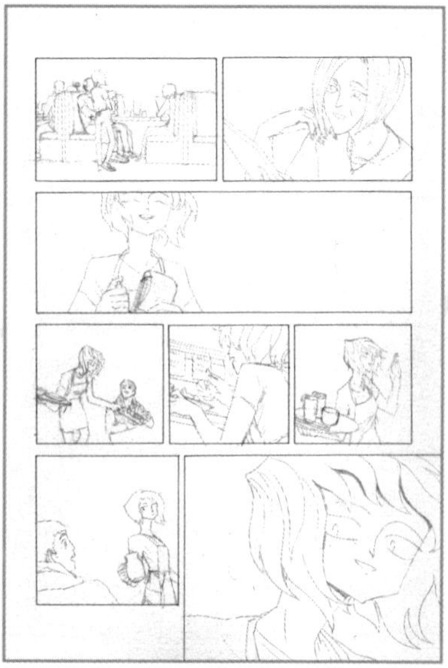

Process 3.
Inks and Watercolors

I use a variety of different materials for the coloring stage. Since it's more of a painterly style, I usually do the linework with waterproof ink, then move to watercolor washes. But I'll bounce around to different tools like gouache, colored ink, and airbrush to get different results.

Process 4.
Computer Compositing

The last step is where I'll collage the separate images and any digital effects. For specific backgrounds, I paint into real reference photographs and mix them into the art with Photoshop. Then I'll do some clean up and any digital effects to finalize the art for Susie to letter, bringing everything full circle back to the script!

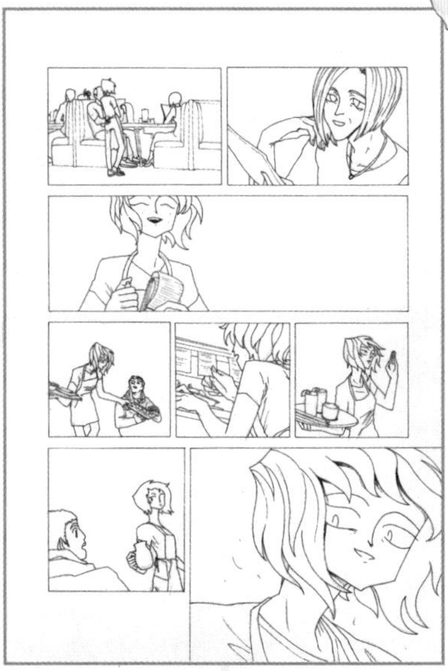

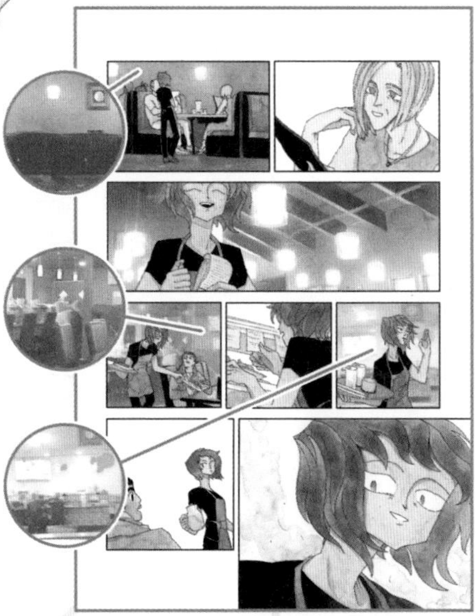

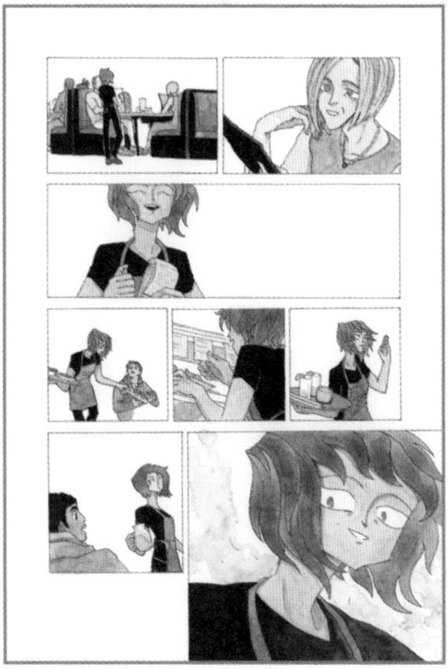

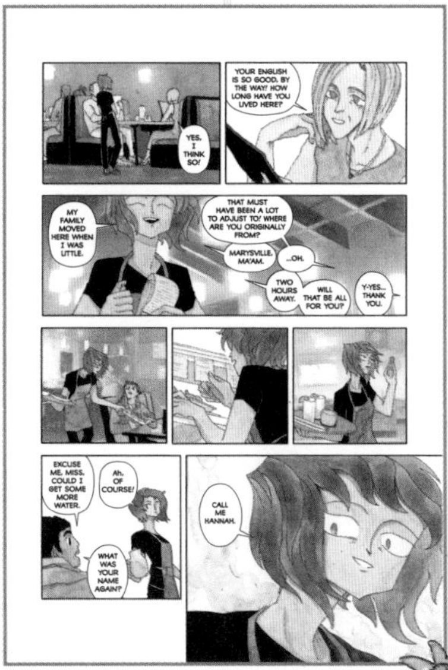

YES, I THINK SO!
YOUR ENGLISH IS SO GOOD, BY THE WAY! HOW LONG HAVE YOU LIVED HERE?
MY FAMILY MOVED HERE WHEN I WAS LITTLE.
THAT MUST HAVE BEEN A LOT TO ADJUST TO! WHERE ARE YOU ORIGINALLY FROM?
MARYSVILLE, MA'AM.
...OH.
TWO HOURS AWAY.
WILL THAT BE ALL FOR YOU?
Y-YES... THANK YOU.
EXCUSE ME, MISS. COULD I GET SOME MORE WATER.
Ah, OF COURSE!
WHAT WAS YOUR NAME AGAIN?
CALL ME HANNAH.

COVER &
CHARACTER
DESIGNS

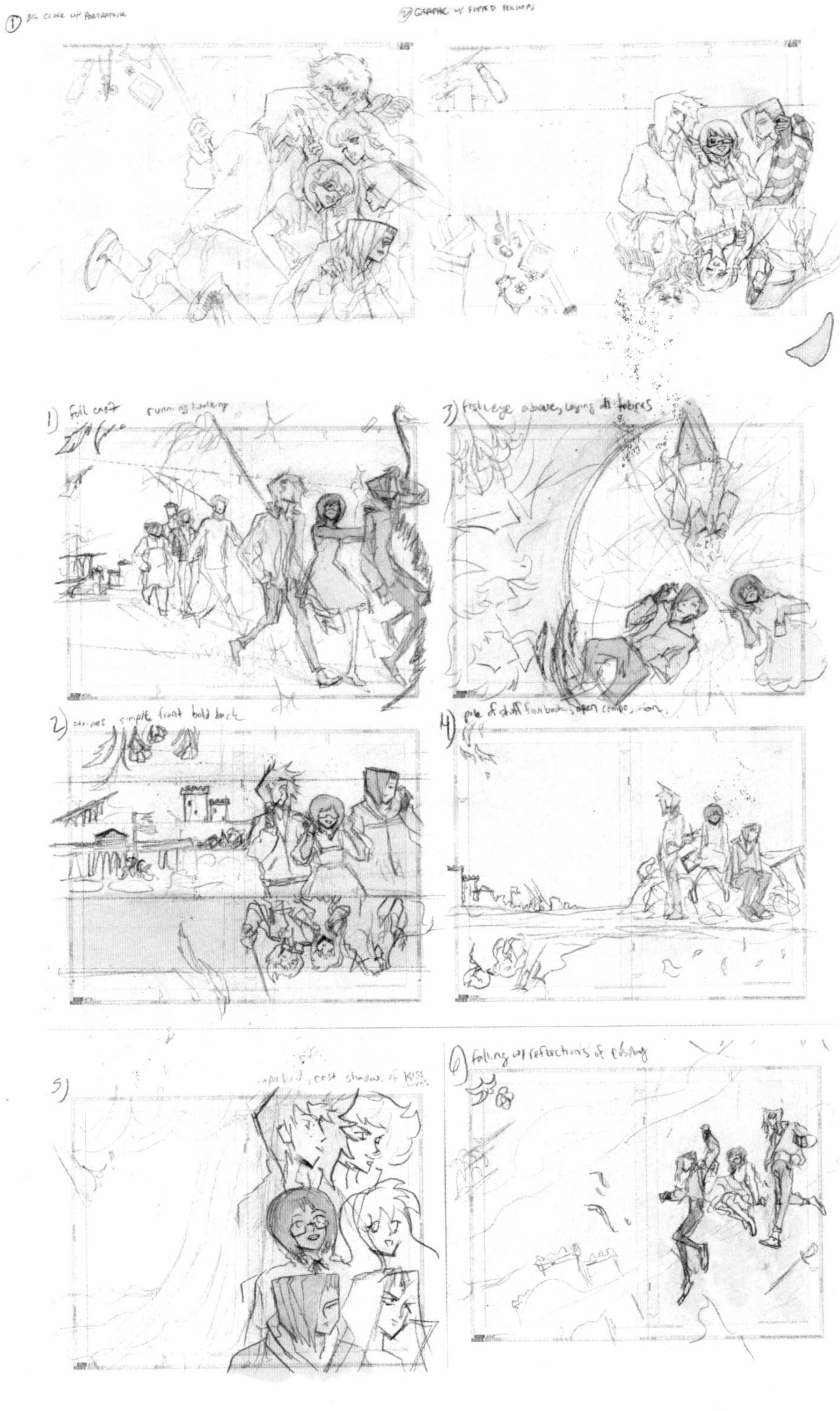

1 BIG CLOSE UP PORTRAITURE
2 GRAPHIC w/ FLIPPED PERSONAS
1) full cast running/walking
3) fisheye above, laying on fabrics
2) stripes simple front bold back
4) pile of stuff from book, open composition.
5) stacked, cast shadow of KISS
6) falling w/ reflections of cosplay

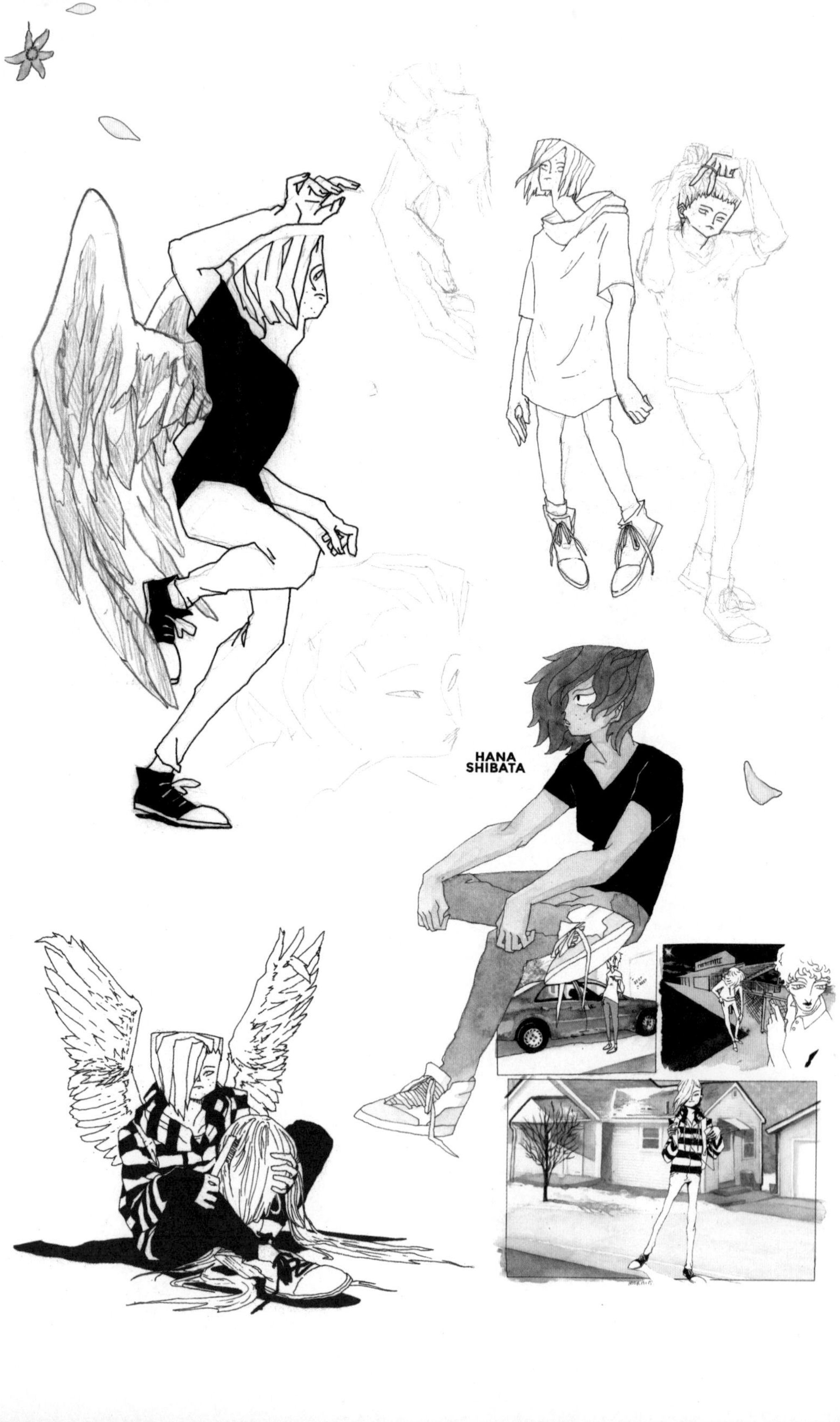
HANA
SHIBATA

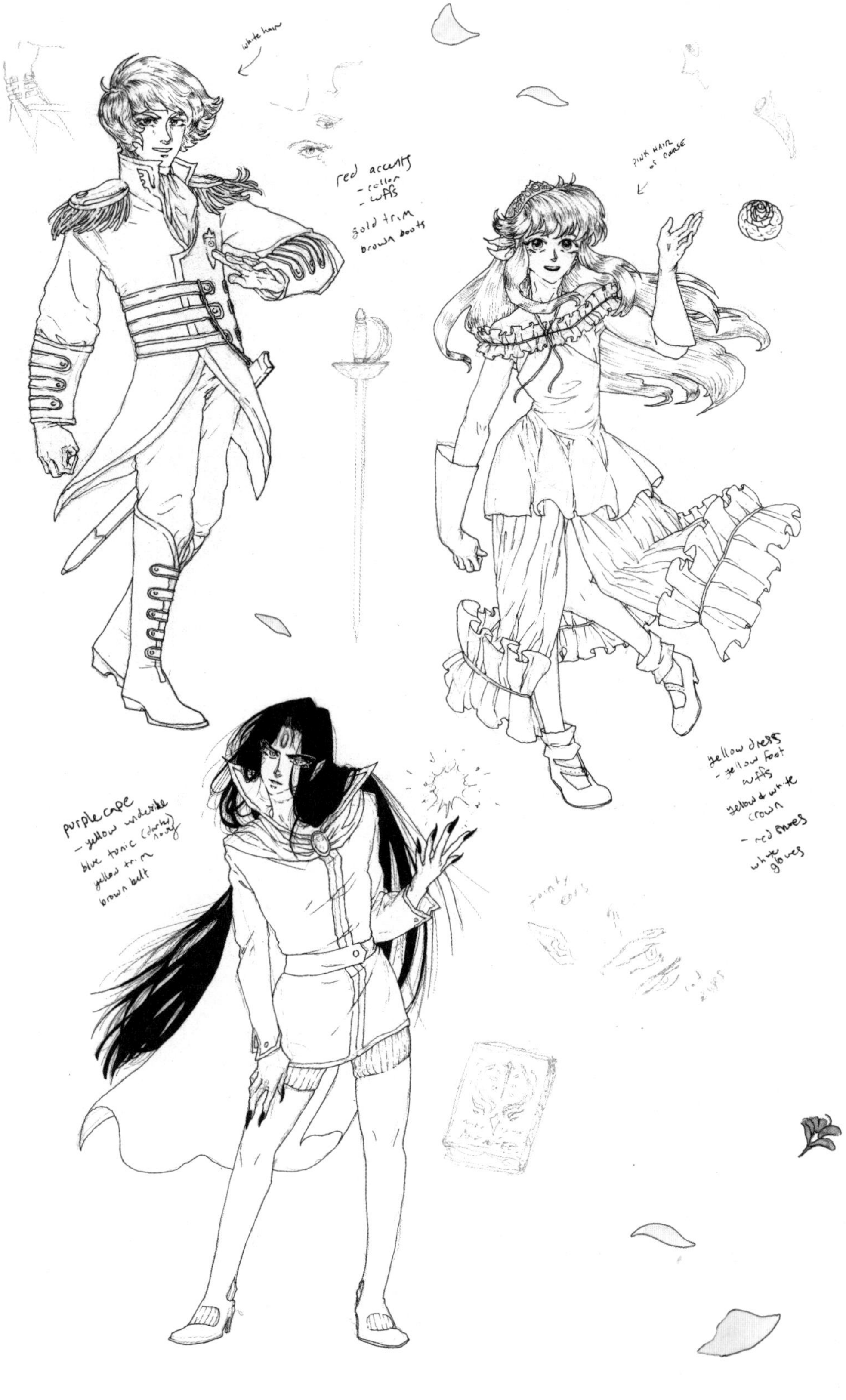
white hair
red accents
- collar
- cuffs
gold trim
brown boots
PINK HAIR of course
yellow dress
- yellow foot cuffs
yellow & white crown
- red shoes
white gloves
purple cape
- yellow underside
blue tunic (darker navy)
yellow trim
brown belt
pointy ears

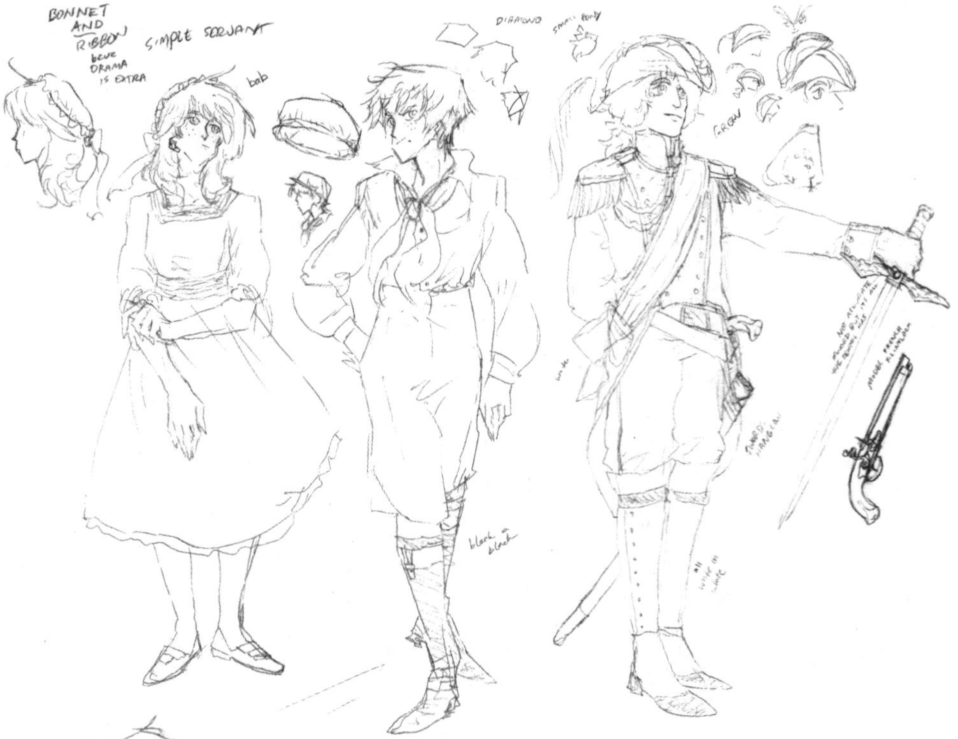
BONNET AND RIBBON
DRAMA IS EXTRA
SIMPLE SERVANT
bab
DIAMOND

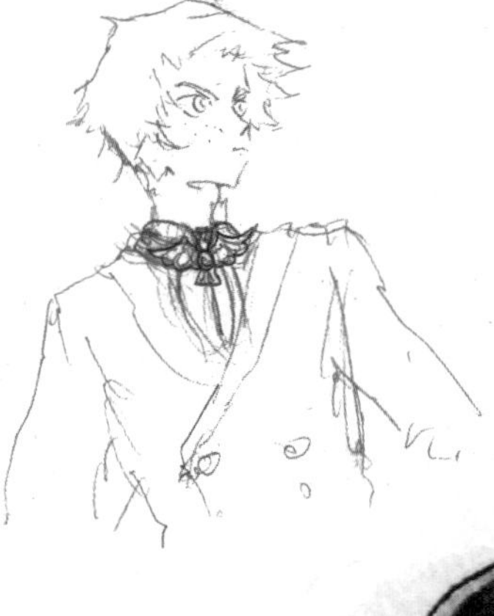

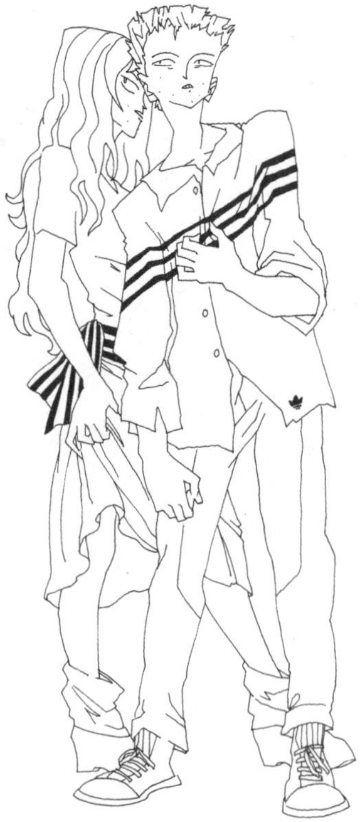

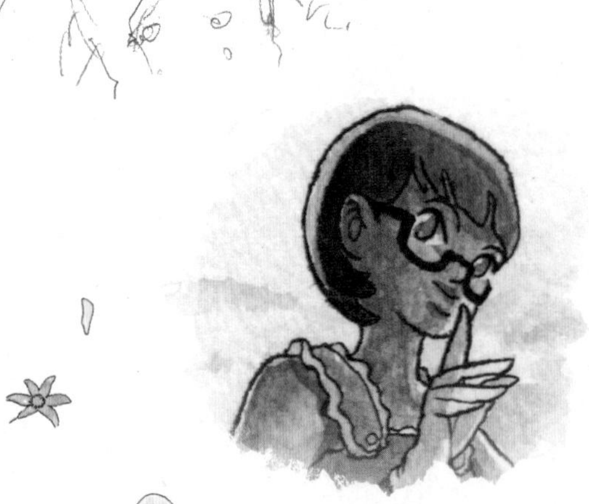

SPECIAL THANKS

LAURENN MCCUBBIN—
for your guidance and support
through my development
of this book

JUAN ARGIL, ASHLEY WARE
& CHRIS PASSABET—
for letting me bounce my ideas
off of you so many times

OLIVER ONO
& SHAE BEAGLE—
for telling me your story

MIKE LAUGHEAD—
for teaching me a thing or two

HELIOSCOPE—
for the space to develop
my voice

KELLY SUE & MATT—
for opening one more door

ERIC MYERS—
for helping get the perfect shot

TANNER SKELLY—
for those stupid, dumb
high school things

JANET LUNDEEN—
for your view of the sky

CHRISTOPHER BUTCHER
& DAVID BROTHERS—
for your feedback and inspiration

MY FAMILY—
for always supporting this
little weirdo

I'd also like to give homage to the books and shows that influenced the look and feel of this graphic novel, including *Classmates: Dou kyu sei* (Asumiko Nakamura), *Rose of Versailles* (Riyoko Ikeda), *Peepo Choo* (Felipe Smith), *A Silent Voice* (Yoshitoki Ōima), and *FLCL* (Gainax). Artists who inspired me overall throughout the creation of *Weeaboo* include Masaaki Yuasa, Moto Hagio, Hellen Jo, Koji Kumeta, Ron Wimberly, Inio Asano, and Taiyo Matsumoto.

Additional reading:
Manga in Theory and Practice by Hirohiko Araki
Takarazuka: Sexual Politics and Popular Culture in Modern Japan by Jennifer Robertson
The Comics Journal No. 269 / Shojo Manga Issue by Fantagraphics Books, Inc.

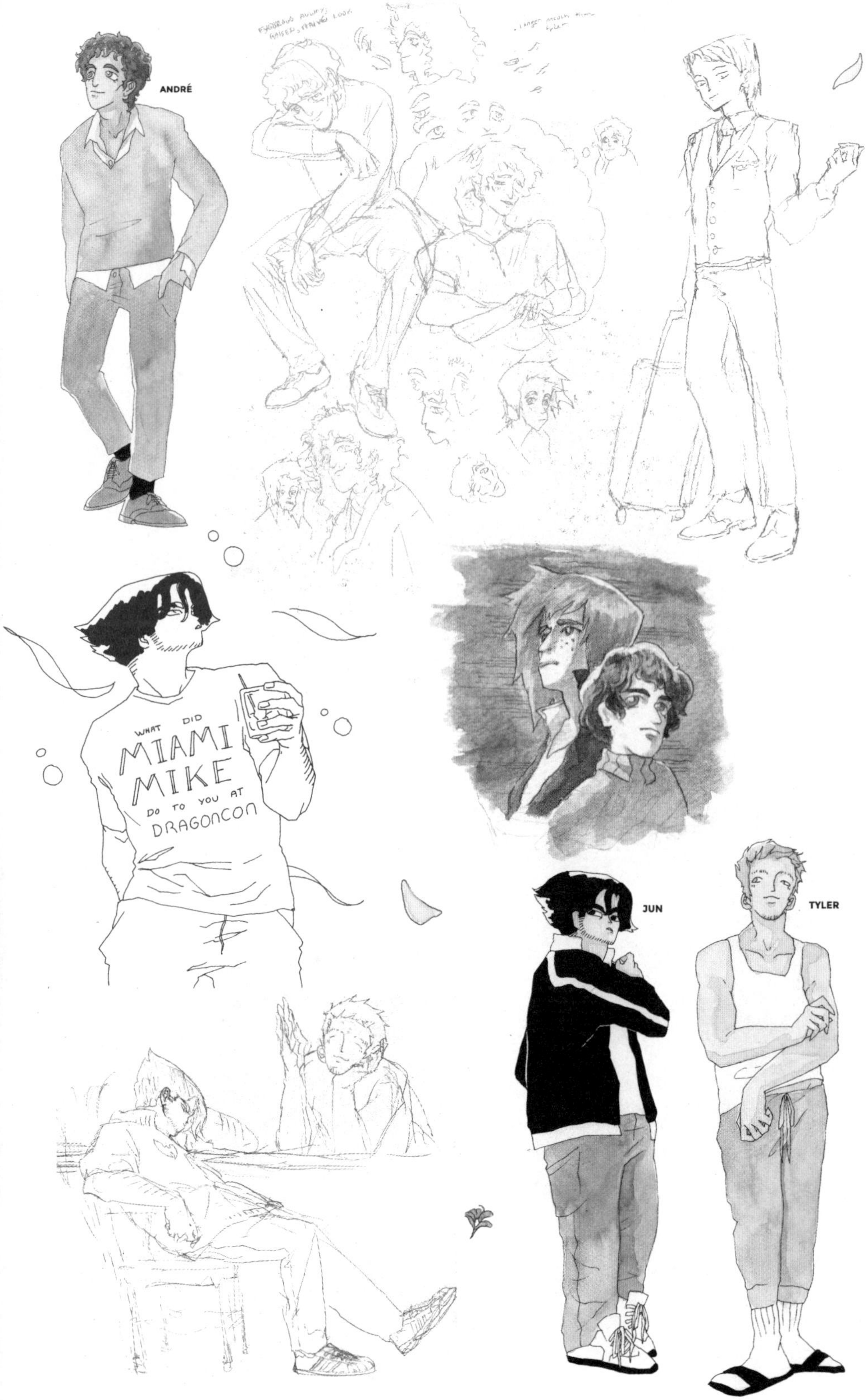
ANDRÉ
WHAT DID MIAMI MIKE DO TO YOU AT DRAGONCON
JUN
TYLER

ALISSA SALLAH

is a cartoonist (and cosplayer) from small-town Ohio.
She edits and contributes to the Bonfire Yearly Anthology
(*Stratos, Topia, Silk & Metal*), has been featured in the *Bitch
Planet* Triple Feature, the *Yakuza 6 Song of Life* artbook, and
was the colorist on the Image comic series *Sleepless*.
Her work can be found at alissasallah.com.

SUSIE LEE

graduated from the Academy of Art in San Francisco
with a BFA in Illustration. She started Studio Cutie when
she began lettering comics back in 1994 and has lettered
comics, with a specialty in manga, ever since. She lettered
such classics as *Oh! My Goddess*, *Gunsmith Cats*, and *Ghost
in the Shell*. Her studio has also translated and localized
dozens of comics, including various versions of *Trigun* and
Gantz. When not working on comics, she enjoys tai chi,
Pokéwalks, and pursuing various arts and craft projects.